The men who surrounded the Queen

Uncle Leopold, King of the Belgians. The first man to win the devotion that fatherless Victoria was so eager to give. He never let her forget about her handsome cousin, Prince Albert.

Lord Melbourne. Victoria's first prime minister, who made the teenage queen laugh and gave her self-confidence.

Prince Albert. The young queen proposed and he accepted and they lived happily ever after . . . almost!

John Brown. The queen's Scottish servant whose informal relationship with Her Majesty became a scandal.

Lord Palmerston. The prime minister whom *no* one could persuade the Queen to like.

Mr. Disraeli. The prime minister with whom, like Lord Melbourne, the Queen could gossip and joke.

Bertie, Prince of Wales, later Edward VII. The Queen's firstborn, whose unhappy childhood was compensated for by scandalous grown-up adventures that would have done justice to Victoria's notorious royal uncles.

VICTORIA VICTORIOUS

Jean Plaidy

FAWCETT CREST • NEW YORK

A Fawcett Crest Book
Published by Ballantine Books
Copyright © 1985 by Jean Plaidy

Library of Congress Catalog Card Number: 85-12193

ISBN 0-449-21251-3

This edition published by arrangement with G.P. Putnam's Sons, a division of the Putnam Publishing Group, Inc.

Manufactured in the United States of America

First Ballantine Books Edition: February 1988

'Send her victorious
Happy and glorious
Long to reign over us
God save the Queen.'

Contents

VICTORIA VICTORIOUS

In *Victoria Victorious*, the third in the *Queens of England* series, Queen Victoria shows herself as an innocent young girl growing into a great Queen. Her childhood was dominated by two strong women, the Duchess, her mother, and her governess, the Baroness Lehzen. The latter she loved with all the fierceness of a sentimental and emotional nature, but she soon felt the need to escape from Mama's influence and was embarrassed by the conflict between that forceful lady and the two uncles, George IV and William IV.

When Victoria became aware that she would almost certainly become Queen her first words were 'I will be good.' She meant that sincerely and adhered to that sentiment throughout her life. Essentially feminine she looked to strong men to guide her. The first of these was Uncle Leopold, the father figure, ambitious for his little niece—and himself, living close to the Court to be near her until the irresistible offer of a crown came his way.

Then came that early morning when she was called from her bed to hear that she was the Queen, no longer to be governed by Mama, free to make her own decisions and to sleep in a room by herself. Uncle Leopold had gone but there was Lord Melbourne, handsome, suave, worldly, witty, having emerged most romantically from scandals to become Prime Minister. The great affection between them was immediate and mutual but alas obvious so that there were those to refer to Her Majesty as Mrs. Melbourne. But Lord Melbourne had the gift of ignoring anything unpleasant; and he helped her through the difficult times of the Flora Hastings scandal and the Bedchamber Affair.

Then came Albert, the great love, who brought changes not only into her life but to her character, so that a serious young woman soon replaced the fun-loving young girl. There were storms at first, and the bearing of children—nine of them—was as she called it

'The Shadow Side of Marriage'. Her grief at his death was so shattering that she could not forget it and made sure no one else did. Long years of widowhood stretched ahead; but there were John Brown and Benjamin Disraeli to offer her masculine shoulders to lean on.

Victoria's long life spanned one of the most eventful eras in history and some of the most outstanding figures of all time were her subjects, among them Sir Robert Peel, Lord Palmerston, Disraeli, Gladstone and Florence Nightingale; the peace of those years was broken by such events as the Crimean War, the Indian Mutiny and the Boer War. England flourished and built up a great Empire with this serene little woman at its head, having survived assassination attempts, upheavals in Europe and the bearing of nine children. These children brought certain anxieties as well as comfort. Naughty Bertie had a tendency to become involved with women and the fast set; Vicky, her father's favourite, was to give birth to trouble-making Wilhelm; there was sweet Alice and her domestic tragedies; and dear Baby Beatrice whom she found it hard to relinquish to a husband—and the rest.

Devoted to her family, Victoria lived to see them scattered throughout the royal houses of Europe; and all the days of her life she remained candid, truthful, sentimental, and essentially human—a great Queen and a lovable woman.

Prologue

I was quite young when I started to keep a journal. Mama said it would be good for me. She would read it, and that made it like a lesson; then she and Baroness Lehzen could put their heads together and say: The child is too exuberant, too emotional, and lacking in dignity. She is too impulsive and there are too many storms. All true, of course; but during the time of what I called my captivity I was never free from them; and it continued from the day of my birth to that glorious moment on the 20th of June in the year 1837 when the Archbishop and the Lord Chamberlain came to the Palace of Kensington to tell me I was the Queen.

I do not remember ever being alone. I even had to sleep in Mama's room, and Lehzen used to sit with me until Mama came to bed so that I should not be left to myself. How significant it was that one of the first things that occurred to me on that memorable day was: Now I can be alone.

So in my journal I would write that which would win their approval and that was sometimes not in accordance with my true feelings. I have always found great pleasure in writing, in music and painting; and I truly believe that I could have excelled at any of these occupations if destiny had not had other plans for me.

When I was a child and beginning to be aware of the frustrations of being watched and forbidden to do so many things which I wanted to, I longed to have a secret diary in which I could write down the daily happenings, for one is apt to forget important details if one does not record them at the time. I wanted to write of my life in Kensington Palace, of Lehzen, Spath, of my beautiful lifelike dolls and my scandalous uncles; I wanted to write of sinister Sir John Conroy and his influence on Mama and his determination to ensnare me when I was too young and inexperienced to resist him; I wanted never to forget the shivers he sent down my spine, for I do believe he seemed to me as menacing as my wicked one-eyed Uncle Cumberland. I wanted to be quite frank about the growing change in my feelings towards Mama. Naturally one *must* love one's mother; it is a duty; but I used to wish I could stop my eyes from seeing so much and my mind from coming to such conclusions. But that is no way for anyone to act—certainly not one who may become a queen.

If I could have had my secret diary, I could have confided in it. I could have recorded the sudden changes in my feelings. I could have found a reason for those sudden outbursts which Mama referred to as the 'storms'. I might have come to a better understanding of myself as well as others.

But now, at this time, I am my own mistress, and in my lonely years when the one who was all the world to me has been taken away, I can indulge my whim. I like to spend long hours remembering the past, re-reading my journals and setting it down as I should have done had it been for my eyes alone. There are differences now from what I wrote then, and in the writing I seem to see myself more clearly, to know myself—and the task absorbs me. I recall days of childhood in Kensington Palace—the prison, as I called it. I like to think back to that time when I first realized that I was not as other children about me, that I was Victoria who was destined for a crown.

That destiny dominated my childhood; it was the reason for Mama's concern. How she longed for the crown to be mine—far more than I ever did—preferably before I was of age so that she could reign in my stead. How she hated poor old Uncle William because he refused to die! How she hated all my paternal uncles! She was protecting me from them, she would say. I must never forget how much I owed her. Poor Mama, she did not know that one cannot wholeheartedly love, however much one wants to, just because it is one's duty. There were times when Mama could become quite wearisome.

Now I can write for my eyes alone without consideration of what may be construed by my words, without the probing eyes of Mama or Lehzen finding in my simple observations characteristics which must be suppressed. Poor Mama! Dear Lehzen! They are beyond passing judgement on me now. And I am a lonely widow, with only memories of happier days left to me and the hope of finding comfort in the memory of time past.

The Wicked Uncles

If my cousin Charlotte had not died so tragically—and her baby with her—I should never have been born and there would never have been a Queen Victoria. I suppose there is a big element of chance in everybody's life, but I always thought this was especially so in mine. But for that sad event, over which the whole nation mourned, my father would have gone on living in respectable sin—if sin can ever be respectable—with Madame St. Laurent who had been his companion for twenty-five years; my mother would have stayed in Leiningen, though she might have married someone else, for although she was a widow with two children, she was only thirty-one years old and therefore of an age to bear more children. And I should never have been born.

It is hard to imagine a world without oneself, as I remarked to my governess, Baroness Lehzen, when she told me all this. She was a gossip and she liked to talk about the scandals which seemed perpetually to circulate about my family. She excused herself by pointing out that it was history, and because of what lay before me—although it was not certain at that time that I should come to the throne—it was something I should know.

It was unfortunate that my family—on my father's side—had a flair for creating scandal—although this made those conversations with Lehzen more interesting than if they had been models for virtue. Almost all the uncles behaved without the decorum expected of a royal family; there were even rumours about the aunts. Poor Grandpapa, who had been a faithful husband and kept strictly within the moral code—so different from his sons—had to be put under restraint because he was mad; and Grandmama Queen Charlotte, even though she had been equally virtuous, had never found favour with the people. So many queens in our history had failed to win approval because they could not produce an heir; Queen Charlotte

3

had overdone her duty in that respect and fifteen children had been born to her. 'Encumbrances,' 'A Drain on the Exchequer,' it was said. How difficult it was to please the people!

I was always interested in hearing of my cousin Princess Charlotte, which was natural since I owed my life to her death. Her father, who was the Prince Regent when I was born and became King George IV when I was about seven months old, had created more scandal than any of his brothers and one of the greatest scandals in that family of scandals was the relationship between Charlotte's parents.

Charlotte had married my mother's brother, Prince Leopold, and Louisa Lewis, who had lived at Claremont with Charlotte and Leopold, told me they had been true lovers. Charlotte had been a hoyden. 'There was no other word for it,' said Louisa, her lips twitching, implying that the frailties of Charlotte made her all the more lovable. That puzzled me considerably and I wondered why some people's faults made them endearing, when virtues did not always arouse the same kindly feelings.

Charlotte, however, this flouter of conventions, this wild untamed girl, had won the hearts of all about her, and chiefly that of Prince Leopold, her young husband, whose character and temperament were so different from her own.

'He was heart-broken when she died,' Louisa told me. 'Everyone was heart-broken.'

Discussing this later with Lehzen, I remarked that perhaps people loved her because she was dead, for I had noticed that when people died they did seem to become more lovable than when they were alive.

However, the story was that Charlotte was the hope of the nation for she was the Regent's only child, and heiress to the throne, for although his brothers had many children they were illegitimate. Therefore when the much-loved Charlotte died, and her baby with her, there was great consternation throughout the family, for without an heir the House of Hanover would come to an end. Much later I talked of this with Lehzen and she confirmed what Louisa had told me of Charlotte's popularity.

'Her death was unexpected,' she said. 'What was to be done? The Regent was married, though unhappily, and he refused to live with his wife, so there was no hope there. And what of the others? There was Frederick, Duke of York, the second son.' She shook her head. 'He was the Regent's favourite brother and a gentleman much respected, although there had been a scandal . . .'

'Of course there was a scandal,' I said. 'There is always a scandal.'

'Well, we will pass over that . . .'

'Oh no, Lehzen, we will *not* pass over that.'

When this conversation took place I was in my early teens and already developing a certain imperiousness—which was so deplored by my mother. But although I was bubbling over with affection for those I loved, and could be equally vehement in my dislikes, I was at this moment aware of my destiny, and I was determined to have obedience from those about me . . . even my dear old Lehzen . . . just as I had made up my mind that I would not be frustrated by my mother or the odious John Conroy. So I insisted that she tell me of the scandal attached to Uncle Frederick.

'It was a woman of course. It was often women with your uncles—almost always in fact. He was Commander in Chief of the Army and she was an adventuress, Mary Anne Clarke by name, born in Ball and Pin Alley, a little byway near Chancery Lane, so they say. She married first a compositor and his master fell in love with her and sent her to be educated. I do not know what happened to the first husband, but there was a second named Clarke. Well, a woman like that will have lovers by the score, and somehow she came to the notice of your Uncle Frederick.' Lehzen pursed her lips. 'It's her sort who make the money fly when they get a chance. You'd think they would respect it. But oh no, my lady Mary Anne was eating off the best plate. The Duke promised her a thousand pounds a year so that she could live in a style she thought suited to her talents, but money was always a problem in the family and when Mary Anne did not receive her money she looked round for means of adding to her income. She had the idea that she would accept bribes for the service of getting commissions for those who paid her.'

'And did my uncle assist her in this?'

'That's how it seemed. Charges were brought against him and there was a great scandal. She threatened to publish his letters . . .'

I nodded and remained silent. I knew from experience that if I spoke too often and betrayed too much interest, Lehzen would remember she was talking too freely and that would be an end—temporarily—to these interesting revelations.

'Then of course . . . his marriage. He was separated from the Princess Frederica almost as soon as he was married to her, and, as you know, the Duchess went to live at Oaklands Park with her dogs and other animals where she stayed till she died. So although

Frederick was the next in line, he was old and could not be expected to produce an heir . . .'

I loved this saga of the uncles. But because they were a scandal and a disgrace to the family, as my mother said, I found it hard to get information about them and had to prise what I did learn from Lehzen over a long period.

Next to Uncle Frederick came Uncle William. He was the Duke of Clarence, who was in time to become King William IV. He had always been a rather ridiculous figure. He was different from all the other uncles, for whatever else they were, they were highly cultivated, courtly, with exquisite manners. Not so Uncle William. He had been brought up differently and sent to sea at an early age; he prided himself on being a bluff sailor. He was garrulous and fond of making public speeches which were often diatribes against this and that, and sometimes quite incoherent. In his youth he must have been quite a romantic figure because he entered into a relationship with Dorothy Jordan, an actress, and by her had ten children. He had set up house in Bushey where he and Dorothy Jordan lived harmoniously albeit without benefit of clergy just as my father had with Madame St. Laurent. The uncles seemed to have a flair for that sort of relationship. But with the death of Charlotte he had to find a wife quickly, just as my father had. In the end he had treated Dorothy Jordan badly. She went to France and died there unhappily. Uncle William had made a fool of himself on several occasions by asking the hand in marriage of certain ladies—none of them royal—and being publicly refused, except by one, a certain Miss Wykeham, who did accept him; but when Charlotte died and the need for an heir was imperative, he had to abandon her and be married to Adelaide, the daughter of the Duke of Saxe-Meiningen. I grew to love her dearly.

Well, that was Uncle Clarence who was to conflict so bitterly with my mother. Next to Clarence came my father. I often wished that I did not have to rely on other people's picture of him. It is sad never to have seen one's own father. I loved to hear stories of him although, of course, they were not all flattering.

I knew he wished to marry Madame St. Laurent, and I came to believe that the Royal Marriage Act was responsible for a great deal of the immorality in my family, for this act forbade sons and daughters of the King who were under the age of twenty-five to marry without royal consent; and when they were past that age, they had to have the consent of Parliament. It was a cruel act in a way, but because of the nature of the Princes, I suppose it was necessary.

So my father knew he would never be allowed to marry Madame St. Laurent. I heard that she was not only beautiful but kind and wise. She had escaped from the revolution in France and must have been a very romantic figure.

The Regent had honoured her. He had always been lenient with his brothers' misdemeanours—and quite rightly so, because he had committed many himself. Poor Madame St. Laurent! I was sorry for her, but I suppose it is what women must expect if they enter into irregular relationships.

My father must marry. An heir was of the greatest importance if the family was to survive. Adelaide of Saxe-Meiningen and Victoria of Leiningen, widow of the ruler of that principality, were available. Which was for which did not seem to matter very much. I have often thought how different my life would have been if Adelaide had been my mother. But then I suppose *I* should have been different, so that is futile conjecture.

It was decided that my father, being more cultivated and princely in his manners than William, should have Victoria because she would have to be wooed, whereas Adelaide, no longer in the first flush of youth, and there having been a dearth of suitors for her hand, would be obliged to take what was given her. Victoria, on the other hand, as a widow once married for reasons of state, would have the right to choose her next husband.

So it was to be Victoria for Kent and Adelaide for Clarence.

And after Kent, Cumberland. From my earliest days I had thought of him as wicked Uncle Ernest. His appearance was enough to strike terror into the bravest child. This was largely because he had lost his left eye, and I was not sure what was more terrifying—the glimpse of that empty socket or the black mask he sometimes wore over it. But perhaps it was not so much Uncle Ernest's appearance as his reputation which struck those chords of alarm in my youthful heart.

But his reputation fitted his appearance and this was largely due to the fact that about nine years before my birth he had been involved in a very unsavoury case when his valet, a man called Sellis, was found in his bed with his throat cut. The Duke himself was wounded in the head, and this could have been fatal if the weapon which had struck him had not come into contact with his sword. There was no explanation of what happened but Sellis did have a beautiful wife and Ernest's reputation with regard to women was rather shady. The general belief was that Uncle Ernest had quarrelled with his valet over the latter's wife and had wounded himself in the affray. It was a most unpleasant case and never forgotten.

About three years before Charlotte's death he had married a woman whose reputation was as sinister as his own. This was his cousin Frederica, daughter of the Duke of Mecklenburg—so her aunt was Queen Charlotte of England—who had been married twice, once to Frederick of Prussia and once to Frederick of Solms-Braunfels, both of whom had died mysteriously.

So there was Uncle Ernest with Aunt Frederica, and suspicion of murder had been attached to them both; and it was not entirely due to my mother's hatred of them that I felt this repugnance.

Uncle Sussex was the sixth son and ninth child of King George and Queen Charlotte. He lived in Kensington Palace so I saw him now and then during my childhood. He was what is known as an eccentric; and his contribution to the family scandal was, as had come to be expected, through marriage. He was not promiscuous. As a matter of fact, that was not really a great sin of the uncles. Even George IV was faithful—more or less—to his women while they kept their positions. Uncle Sussex fell in love with Lady Augusta Murray when he was on the Continent and they were married there; and when they came to England they went through the ceremony once more. Alas, although it was a love match it was not approved of by the King and Parliament, so it was not recognized as a marriage. The happy pair did not mind that at first. But such considerations blight a marriage, I suppose. Sussex had always been a rebel. I remembered hearing that when he was very young he had been locked in his bedroom for wearing Admiral Keppel's colours at the time of an election—and the King was against Admiral Keppel. It may have been that there was such a strict rule in the household that the children were certain to rebel. Uncle Sussex went on rebelling all his life.

When King George was put away and his eldest son became Regent, Sussex was welcomed back to Court. He had made a second marriage to Lady Cecelia Buggins, the widow of Sir George Buggins, and that was when they were at Kensington Palace. Being eccentric, Sussex never considered what people thought of his actions, and as he was an intellectual he was looked on with suspicion by most members of the family—except the Regent, of course; but Sussex was in a way a good man and gave his support to benevolent causes. It was only his marriages which had brought him notoriety.

The last uncle was Uncle Adolphus, the Duke of Cambridge, and it seemed that the younger uncles were less wild. Uncle Adolphus was the seventh son and the tenth in the family; he had gone to Germany and distinguished himself in the army. When Clarence had been floundering round, looking for a wife, he had promised to keep an eye open for a suitable one for him and his questing eye had fallen on Princess Augusta, the daughter of the Landgrave of Hesse-Cassel. He had written to Clarence extolling her beauty. The letters grew more and more adulatory until it was obvious that Adolphus himself was in love with the lady. This was actually the case, for he married her himself. Yes, Cambridge was really the most ordinary of the uncles.

So there they were, my rather disreputable uncles, the princes of the House of Hanover, which must be kept going at all cost. So any eligible uncle must do his duty and build up the succession. Ambition, which had lain dormant when it seemed that healthy bouncing Charlotte would live and produce a batch of healthy sons, as her grandmother had done, had been fanned into a bright blaze. There was not one of the eligible dukes who did not aspire to producing the heir to the throne.

Clarence, Kent, Cumberland and Cambridge were on their marks, as it were. There was speculation throughout the family . . . and the country. Who was going to reach the coveted goal?

Poor Aunt Adelaide produced and lost her child, so Clarence had set off to a bad start. Both Cumberland and Cambridge produced sons—both christened George, a good name for a king; but they were the younger sons, and if Clarence failed and the Duchess of Kent was fruitful, the palm would go to the Kents.

How exciting it must have been! I could imagine poor blustering Uncle William urging on Aunt Adelaide; and Cumberland grinding his teeth and plotting Heaven knew what with his sinister wife whose reputation matched his own. Cambridge? Well, he would be gently hopeful, I supposed; but his chances were a little remote as it was hardly possible that the others would fail completely.

I heard of a strange thing which had happened to my father. It was remembered when I was born and he found that, instead of the longed for son, he had a daughter. He had been in the forest of Leiningen, before his marriage, when I think he must have been beset by doubts and anxiously considering the suffering he was about to inflict on Madame St. Laurent. He had been on his way to visit my mother, and put up for the night at an inn. While he was seated with a few members of his company, a gipsy came in, and selecting him from the group, asked if she might tell his fortune.

They laughed and feigned their disbelief in such arts as people do, while at the same time, they find them irresistible. The gipsy took his hand and told him he was going to marry shortly and that he would be the father of a great queen.

This amazed him, for if she had read his thoughts and was trying to give him what he wanted, it would have been a king.

He said: 'No. A king.'

But the gipsy shook her head. 'A queen,' she insisted.

He was much impressed. So much so that his mind was made up. He must recognize his duty to the family and the State; he must marry Victoria and make sure that Madame St. Laurent was well looked after.

There was no Salic law in England and the gipsy had said a great queen.

Well, that was the prophecy, and, as I believe first and foremost in honesty, I will say that it came as near true as any prophecy can.

The year 1819 dawned. It was the year of royal babies. In March the Clarences had a little girl who did not survive. The Cambridges had a boy. May saw two more babies. The Cumberlands' George was born on the 27th, but before that, on the 19th, I made my appearance.

My father was exultant. He was sure then that the gipsy's prophecy was coming true.

I liked to imagine my nursery. There was such rejoicing. It would have been pleasant to know what an important baby I was. But perhaps that would not have been good for me and I should have been even more wilful and petulant than I actually was in those early years. Louise Lehzen, who was to have charge of me, had brought her pupil, the Princess Feodore, my half-sister, over to England to live with us. It was from her and from Feodore—and I came to love both dearly—that I learned so much of those early days.

There I was, a healthy baby—'plump as a partridge', some said. 'Determined right at the start,' said Lehzen, with a twitch of her lips and a nod of her head, 'to have your own way.'

Feodore said that I was the most adorable baby that ever was. I daresay when she had her own she changed her mind about that! And I did wonder how many babies she had been acquainted with—but no matter. That she should think so was a sign of her love. Not only was there excitement in Kensington but in Saxe-Coburg too. The Coburg relations always stuck together and rejoiced in the advancement of the family; they were very different from my English relations who were always in conflict with each other.

My maternal grandmother, the Duchess of Saxe-Coburg-Saalfeld, referred to me as the May Blossom, which I thought rather charming when I heard it. 'The English like queens,' she added, 'and the niece—and also the first cousin—of the ever-lamented and beloved Charlotte will be most dear to them.' It was true that the English *had* liked queens ever since the reign of Elizabeth. How the people had revered that one! The greatest monarch ever to sit on the throne, some said—and a woman! Yes, after Elizabeth, the English must like queens.

There was a great deal of controversy about my name and that ended with a scene in the Cupola Room.

My uncle, the Regent, had taken a great dislike to my mother—so had Uncle William. Feodore told me that our mother said it was because she was young and healthy, and they, poor things, were decrepit old gentlemen who had no hope of getting healthy children. The Regent even hated the way my mother dressed. She loved feathers and rustling silks and lots of flounces, which the Regent said was Bad Taste. He was known throughout the kingdom, in spite of all his failings, as the arbiter of Good Taste. I have never known much about that, noticing that people are apt to believe that what they like is good taste and that all those who have different opinions have bad. However, that dislike was there and my mother—such a forceful lady—would always feel that there was something very wrong with those who criticized her.

There had, so Feodore told me, been a great deal of trouble about choosing my names. My father was so sure that I was going to be a queen that it was imperative that I should have a name suitable for one. After a great deal of thought it was decided that my first name should be Georgiana. There had been three Georges and likely to be a fourth, so that seemed the best choice. This was to be followed by Charlotte (after the Princess who had made this possible), Augusta Alexandrina (after the Tsar) and Victoria after my mother.

Etiquette, of course, demanded that the names be submitted to the Regent for his approval. My mother had argued, so said Feodore. 'Why all this fuss about a name?' One might have asked the same of her. Of course my name was important and I have no doubt that the Regent regarded me with suspicion. After all, when one holds a position, it is not the most pleasant thing in the world to view one's successor. There is a feeling of being edged towards the grave. All monarchs feel it at some time—and particularly when one is obese, overcome with gout and other ailments, desperately trying to appear young, and handsome as one has been in one's youth.

My parents knew that there would be trouble because on the very evening before the ceremony he sent a brief note saying that the name of Georgiana could not be placed before that of the Emperor of Russia; and he could not allow it to follow.

I am sorry that I cannot recall that scene from personal experience—although I was at the centre of it. The Cupola Room must have looked very grand with the golden font which had been brought from the Tower and the crimson velvet curtains which had come from the chapel in St. James's. I had three distinguished sponsors, the most important of these being Alexander the First, Tsar of Russia; the second was my Aunt Charlotte, the Queen of Württemberg (who had been the Princess Royal of England), and the third my maternal grandmother, the Duchess of Saxe-Coburg-Saalfeld. These illustrious sponsors were not present in person, of course, but were represented by my uncle, the Duke of York, and my aunts the Princess Augusta and the Duchess of Gloucester.

The Prince Regent at length arrived and from that moment there was trouble. I can imagine the animosity which must have flashed between him and my mother. There we were assembled in that splendid room before the golden font, my mother preparing for battle. Many times have I seen her in the mood she must have been in on that occasion.

The Archbishop held me in his arms waiting. He asked the Regent to announce my first name.

'Alexandrina,' he said, and then he paused.

The Archbishop was waiting.

'Charlotte,' whispered my father.

But the Regent shook his head reproachfully to show definite disapproval.

'Augusta?'

'Indeed not,' said the Regent. 'Let her be named after her mother. Alexandrina Victoria.'

So, to the fury of my mother and the consternation of my father, I, who was to have emerged from the Cupola Room enriched by so many grand names suited to a future queen, came out with only two.

The Regent had shown his disapproval of what he called my parents' presumption. He was not dead yet, and he clearly hoped that one of his other brothers would provide the heir to the throne, for his animosity towards my frilled and feathered mother—as I believe he called her—was great.

And there I was—'plump as a partridge'—full of lusty health and ready to start my life—a possible heir to the throne.

We were very poor. My father had many debts. Indeed, the hope of getting these settled was one of the reasons for his marriage—a secondary one, it is true, but none the less a reason. He was apparently disappointed in his hopes in that direction, and the need for economy was urgent.

As was to be expected, Uncle Leopold—*dear* Uncle Leopold— came to the rescue. Uncle Leopold, who was to mean so much to me, was my mother's brother—and he it was who had been the devoted husband of Princess Charlotte. He had won her affections so wholeheartedly and kept her in restraint so admirably that he had become a person of some standing in England, although he was no favourite of the Prince Regent and Uncle William. Uncle Leopold was abstemious, careful, so *right* in everything he did, and people of less moral rectitude are inclined to dislike such people, I suppose because they bring home to them too forcibly their own shortcomings. One of the accusations Uncle William brought against Uncle Leopold was that he did not drink wine at dinner. He was quite angry about it and on one occasion said severely: 'Sir, gentlemen do not drink water at my table.' Some might have been cowed but Uncle Leopold was quite unperturbed and went on drinking water.

However, Uncle Leopold had retained Claremont, where he had lived in such amity with Princess Charlotte, and because we were in such financial difficulties he lent us the house. So to Claremont we came.

When I grew older I came to love my visits to Claremont dearly. It was small as royal residences go, but Uncle Leopold told me once how delighted Charlotte had been when she had first come to it. She had said it was the perfect setting for married lovers for they could shut themselves away from the fashionable world and live there simply. I loved it, partly for itself, partly because it was Uncle Leopold's and I loved everything about him. Looking back over a great many years, I see that he was the first man to win that devotion which I was so eager to give. I think now that it was because I needed a man in my life to be all important to me, a father when I was a child, a husband later. He had to be there, because although I was most imperious, so certain of my destiny which was to rule, in a way I wanted to be ruled—and thus it ever was. How strange people are, and how little we know ourselves. But when one looks back in serenity tempered by sorrow and perhaps wisdom gleaned over the years, one sees so much which one missed before.

So to Claremont we went—Claremont with its thirteen steps to the entrance. I always counted them when I ran up eager to be greeted by Uncle Leopold. I loved the Corinthian pillars which held up the pediment; and it thrilled me to enter the large rooms on the ground floor. There were eight of them, I remembered. Uncle Leopold used to take me through them and talk of what he and Charlotte had done and said to each other; and we would mingle our tears, for Uncle Leopold cried easily, which I always felt showed deep sensitivity in a man.

I know my mother was very resentful about the incident at the christening. It seemed to her so shocking—Lehzen told me afterwards—that I should have only two names, and names which were not well known in England. Alexandrina was very foreign. They called me Drina in those days and it was only later that it was changed to Victoria.

There was a great deal of resentment from the uncles—Cumberland particularly—because he had a son and I came before him; and Uncle William, of course, for all his wife's efforts to bear children came to nothing. The tension had by no means ceased with the royal marriages. It had become like a race. Perhaps more than any the Regent resented it. It seemed as though they were all waiting eagerly for his departure.

When my father took me to a military review the Regent was furious. He demanded loudly: 'What is that infant doing here?'

I am sure my father smiled complacently. The possibility of my being the heir to the throne could not have escaped anybody—least of all the Regent.

I was vaccinated, which caused quite a stir. Some years before Dr. Edward Jenner had discovered that by injecting a person with cow pox he could prevent their catching smallpox. Many people were uncertain about this, but if it was considered good for a Princess they decided it was good enough for them. It was interesting, said Lehzen, how popular these injections became after I had set the fashion.

As we were so poor my parents thought it would be cheaper to live in Germany than in England and they were contemplating making the move. In the meantime it seemed a good idea to rent a house by the sea where not only could we save ourselves expense but profit from the sea breezes—so good for us all and particularly for Baby Drina.

On the way down to the coast we stopped at Salisbury where, on a bitterly cold day, my father went for a tour of the cathedral. He caught a cold and by the time we reached Sidmouth it had not improved.

An alarming incident occurred there which might have been the end of me. I was in my cradle when suddenly the glass of the window was shattered and an arrow sped into the room coming so close to me that it pierced the sleeve of my nightgown. By a miracle—Providence, they all said—I was not hurt, but if the arrow had pierced my body, as it might well have done, it would most certainly have killed me.

I could imagine the consternation which must have spread through the household. Some must have given thought to the uncles, particularly Cumberland and his wife, who had both been involved in mysterious deaths. But finally it was discovered that the arrow had been shot by a mischievous boy. He had meant no harm, he insisted; he had only been playing wars.

Everyone was so relieved that I was unharmed that after being sternly reprimanded, the boy was forgiven.

Meanwhile my father's cold was developing into something worse; in a week it had turned to pneumonia and he had taken to his bed. Uncle Leopold came hurrying down to Sidmouth with young Dr. Stockmar, in whom he had the utmost trust, but it soon became clear that my father could not survive.

It was a great shock to all for he had always been more healthy than any of his brothers.

What disturbed him more than anything was the prospect of leaving us. He had had such hopes of grooming me for the throne; and he was very worried as to what would happen to my mother with a young child—and in the position which I was—to care for.

Naturally he turned to Uncle Leopold.

It was from my mother that I heard of those anxious days. She was always dramatically vehement in her hatred of her husband's family, tearfully affectionate towards her own. In those days when I was very young I thought of my father's family as monsters and the Saxe-Coburg relations as angels.

'There we were,' my mother told me, 'in that little house in Sidmouth . . . your father dead. What was to become of us? We had so little . . . not even enough to travel back to Claremont. And Claremont, of course, was not our home. It had only been lent to

us by your dear Uncle Leopold. I was frantic. There was one matter
which gave me some relief. Your father had appointed me your
sole guardian, which shows what trust he had in me. Do you know,
his last words to me were ''Do not forget me.'' So you see he was
thinking of me until the last.'

I wept with her and wished as I always have done that he had
lived long enough for me to have known him.

'He was a great soldier,' she told me. 'He wanted you always to
remember that you are a soldier's child.'

'Oh I will, Mama,' I said. 'I will.'

'He was a great liberal too . . . and a friend of the reformer,
Robert Owen. He was talking about visiting him at New Lanark
just before his death. For him to die . . . he, who was so
strong . . . His hair was black and so was his beard. Mind you, he
did colour them a bit . . . but never mind. They looked fine and so
did he. So young, so full of vigour . . . and there he was . . . in
such a short time . . . dead.'

Mama loved drama and although at that time I wept with her I
did wonder afterwards whether she really did feel so strongly about
his death. She was one who liked to have her own way, although
she did bend a little to Sir John Conroy. I was told that Sir John
looked something like my father, so perhaps that was one of the
reasons why she thought so highly of him.

Mama went on to tell me how she was left bereft . . . no husband, very little money, in a strange land where she could scarcely
speak the language.

'I could hope for little help from your father's family,' she said
with that snort of contempt she often used when speaking of them.
'True, the miserly Parliament had granted me six thousand pounds
a year in the event of my widowhood. I daresay when they granted
me that—it was a year before you were born—they had thought
they would not have to pay it for a long time.'

'Mama,' I said. 'They did give you our home in Kensington
Palace.'

'A few miserable rooms!' she retorted. 'And there I was . . .
with so little and all your father's debts on my shoulders. I shall of
course do my very best to settle them . . . in time.'

That was very honourable of her, I thought. She was very good,
I was sure; but I did wish she was not so venomous towards my
father's family.

'I had thought there was only one thing for us,' she had gone on,
'and that was to go back to Germany, but your dear Uncle Leopold

was against that. He said, 'In view of her prospects the child must stay in England. She must speak English. She must *be* English. There must be no trace of anything else. The people here like their own kind.' And so I stayed here and dear Leopold . . . he gave up so much to stay with us! What I should have done without him I cannot imagine.'

'Dear *dear* Uncle Leopold,' I murmured.

'He is wonderful. You are fortunate indeed to have such an uncle and such a mother to care for you. True, you are fatherless, but you have had so much to make up for that.'

I replied fervently that I had, but I was thinking of Uncle Leopold rather than my mother, for I was just moving into that state when I was beginning to draw away from her.

'He is so careful of both you and your dear cousin Albert, who has the same reason to be grateful to him as you have. He is three months younger than you so you could say that you are of an age.'

'I am hoping one day I shall meet Albert.'

'I am sure your Uncle Leopold, who so likes to please you as well as instruct you, will arrange a meeting one day.'

'That will be wonderful.' I spoke with honest fervour, but I could not know then how wonderful it was going to prove to be.

Of course Uncle Leopold was right. And because we had not enough money to make the journey from Sidmouth, he paid for our transport to Kensington Palace and there we remained for some years to come.

It appeared that my father had appointed Sir John Conroy as one of the executors of his will and that seemed to me, as I grew older, not a very good choice. My mother did not share that opinion, but it was very repugnant to me that Sir John should actually live in our household.

My mother relied on him a great deal. She was always saying that she had few friends, but while she had Uncle Leopold and Sir John Conroy she felt ready to face the hostile country in which—on my account—she was forced to live.

There were some members of my father's family who tried to be friends. There were my two aunts, Princess Sophia and the Duchess of Gloucester. They were old then. Sophia had never married but long ago she had been at the centre of a scandal. A certain General Garth had fallen in love with her and she with him. The consequences were grave and Sophia had to be hustled out of the palace to give birth to a child. The voluminous skirts proved useful and her sisters helped to smuggle her to Weymouth where she was delivered of a boy. Sophia was unrepentant; she had loved the general and she loved her son, who still came to see her. The children of George III had been brought up so oddly that they all seemed to be involved in scandalous situations. My grandfather had refused to allow any of his girls to marry. He had loved them dearly . . . too dearly. Poor Grandpapa! He must have been mad for a long time before people realized it. Well, Sophia offered friendship to my mother and so did Aunt Mary of Gloucester, who had married Silly Billy Gloucester late in life.

Another one who would have been kind to her was Adelaide, at that time Duchess of Clarence; but my mother regarded the Clarences as the enemy and was very suspicious of Adelaide who, when she was Queen, I came to know as one of the kindest ladies it had ever been my good fortune to meet. But there was no overcoming Mama's prejudices. So she need not have been so entirely without friends as she liked to believe herself to be.

Nine days after my father's death, there occurred another one of the greatest importance.

Poor Grandpapa, blind and mad, passed away; and the Prince Regent became King George IV.

Looking back it is difficult to decide between what I remember and what was told me. There are certain things, though, which stand out very clearly in my mind and one was the visit to Windsor and my meeting with the King.

I was playing with the dolls and talking to Feodore about them. I adored my sister. She was very pretty and twelve years older than I, so she seemed very grown up. I was about seven at this time, so she must have been nineteen. I also had a half-brother, Charles, who was three years older than Feodore, but he was in Leiningen looking after his estates there, although he did come to England now and then. Feodore was with us all the time, and I do believe she loved to be with me as much as I did with her.

She was very interested in the dolls—almost as interested as Lehzen. Lehzen thought they were wonderful. It had been her idea that I should start the collection in the first place; and she and I made some of the costumes together.

Being Lehzen, who always had her eyes on education, she pointed out that the dolls represented historical characters. Of course we had Queen Elizabeth. 'The great Queen,' Lehzen called her; but when I learned more about her, I did not like her so very much. She seemed to have acted in a way which was not always good.

Aunt Adelaide, who always showed affection for me and would have liked to see me more often if Mama would have permitted it, gave me a beautiful doll. It was bigger than all the others and it had such splendid clothes that Lehzen said we should not attempt to dress it in any other way. So among my collection of historical dolls, it was just the Big Doll; and she always reminded me of kind Aunt Adelaide.

Feodore was saying that Queen Elizabeth's dress had a little rent in it. I knew this. I had torn it myself when I had thrown her down rather roughly. I had just heard that when she had died there had been three thousand dresses in her wardrobe, which was an excessive number. She had clearly been very vain and I was going to let her have a rent in her skirt for a while.

'She is the most beautiful of the dolls,' said Feodore. 'I am sure Lehzen will mend that tear very soon.'

'It won't hurt her to have a torn skirt for a while, the vain creature.'

Feodore laughed. 'I believe you do not like Queen Elizabeth very much,' she said.

At that moment Mama came in. She was quivering. Mama often seemed to quiver, either in rage or excitement. It was because of all the feathers she wore, and the pendants about her neck and in her ears, the frills on her bodices and the rustling of her skirts. It gave an impression of perpetual violent emotion.

She had something to tell us. Normally she would have sent for us and we should have had to go to her, not forgetting to curtsy respectfully. We must always show our respect for Mama, always remember what she had done for us, sacrificing herself all the time for our good.

But as this was a matter of great importance, she had dispensed with the usual formalities.

'At last,' she announced, 'that man has seen fit to invite us to Windsor.'

I knew at once that she was talking of my uncle, the King, for he lived at Windsor.

'I am of two minds as to whether I shall accept the invitation, but . . .' began Mama.

I knew she meant that she would accept the invitation and I happened to have gleaned that it was a source of irritation to her that we had not been invited before.

'I suppose, as after all he does *call* himself King . . .'

'Do not other people call him King?' I asked innocently. I was very direct and as Mama and Lehzen constantly told me, at this stage of my development I took what people said too literally. In any case, Mama had implied that it was only the King who called himself King.

'You must learn not to make foolish interjections,' said Mama, quivering more than before. 'The fact is we are going to Windsor. I shall insist that we are treated with due respect. Hold your head up. Have you been wearing your holly necklace?'

'Yes, Mama, but I think I can manage without it.'

'It does not appear to be so. *I* shall decide when you may dispense with it. Why are you not wearing it now?'

'Lehzen said that when I was playing with the dolls I could leave it off.'

She was referring to the sprig of holly attached to a cord which I had to wear round my neck to induce me to hold my head high, for when I did not my chin came into contact with the prickles. It was a form of torture which I greatly disliked, and whenever I could I would inveigle Lehzen into letting me go without it.

I could see that Mama's annoyance with me was really her dislike of the King; but at the same time she was pleased that he had invited us to Windsor.

She looked at her elder daughter and said: 'You shall accompany us, Feodore.'

'That will be lovely, won't it, Sissy?' I said.

Feodore hugged me. I sometimes felt that she wanted to protect me from Mama's severity.

'You will enjoy the visit,' she said.

'Yes, especially if you are there.'

Mama softened a little. She liked to see the affection between us two.

'Well then,' she went on. 'I shall make plans. Victoria, you must remember to behave perfectly so that there can be no criticism. The King is very insistent on good manners. It is the one virtue he himself has managed to retain. People will be watching you. Any little slip will be noticed, you can be sure. There will be malicious eyes on you and tongues to wag if you misbehave.'

I was already beginning to feel nervous. But Feodore pressed my hand reassuringly and I thought: She will be there, so it will be all right.

That this was a most important visit was obvious. Mama might express her contempt for all my paternal uncles—the King among them—but when all was said and done he *was* the King and we were all—even Mama—his subjects.

Lehzen tried to prepare me.

At Windsor Lodge, where I should be presented to the King, I should meet a lady in his company whom it would be quite important not to offend.

'A lady? Do you mean the Queen, Lehzen?'

'Well no . . . not the Queen, a lady. Lady Conyngham. She is a very great friend of the King.'

'I do know that the King and Queen don't like each other very much.'

Lehzen looked alarmed. 'You must never say anything about that.' There were times when she was afraid she had told me too much. I was beginning to recognize signs like that.

'You may be surprised when you see the King,' she went on. 'He is rather old.'

'Yes, Lehzen, I know. Mama has often said so.'

Lehzen looked even more alarmed. 'You must guard your tongue. It would be wise to speak only when the King speaks to you and then only answer what he asks.'

I was beginning to feel more and more nervous.

'Don't worry,' said Feodore. 'Say what is natural to you. I am sure that will be all right.'

Dear, comforting Feodore!

When we were riding in the carriage on the way to Windsor Lodge, Mama was giving instructions. 'I hope you have practised your curtsy. You must be grave. Do not laugh in that really vulgar way you seem to be developing . . . showing all your gums. Smile. Just lift the corners of your mouth . . . and remember that although he is the King, you are royal too.'

'Yes, Mama . . . Yes, Mama . . .'

I really was not listening. I was admiring the countryside and wondering what Uncle King would be like, and why there was all this pursing of the lips when Lady Conyngham and her family— who seemed to live at Windsor Lodge with the King—were mentioned. I would ask Lehzen. No, not Lehzen. She could be reticent at times. I would ask my other governess Baroness Spath . . . or Feodore. How wonderful to have such a dear sister who was so much older—grown up and yet not exactly a grown-up. Yes, I would ask Feodore.

My hand crept into hers and she pressed it reassuringly. I loved her so much and thought: we shall always be together.

We had arrived.

At length the great moment came and I was ushered into the presence of the King.

I saw a figure so huge that even the very large and ornate chair in which he sat seemed too small to hold him and he flowed over it as though someone had tried to pour him in and spilt some of him. The analogy made me want to giggle. I restrained myself severely and swept the most profound curtsy I had ever made in my life. It was effective, I am sure. It should have been. I had been practising it ever since I had known I was to meet him.

'So this is Victoria.' His voice was soft and really musical; and I loved music. 'Come here, my dear child.'

So I went and looked up into that huge face; his cravat came right up to his chins and his cheeks seemed to wobble. He had beautiful pink cheeks and his hair was a mass of luxuriant curls. I thought: Some parts of him are so beautiful.

He was watching me as intently as I was watching him.

Then he said: 'Give me your little paw.'

Paw! What a strange name to give a hand! It seemed very funny and I forgot Mama's instructions and laughed.

He took my hand in his, which was very large, white and sparkling with rings.

He laughed with me, so at least he was not annoyed.

'Such a pretty little paw,' he said. He turned to the lady who was standing close to his chair. She was very beautiful though rather fat—but not nearly so fat as the King. Perhaps it was her clothes which made her seem so splendid. He said: 'Lift her up, my dear. I want to see her closely.'

So I was set on his knee, which was soft and wobbly like a feather cushion. It was an odd sensation to be so close to his face. I was fascinated by the delicate pink of his cheeks and the curls of his hair, which looked as though they belonged to a young man, and yet the pouches under his eyes made him look like an old one.

He looked at me as though he found my appearance interesting and because of his lovely voice and his kindly looks I began to wonder why Mama hated him so much. He was not nearly so awe-inspiring as I had expected him to be. He seemed as though he wanted to please me as much as I wanted to please him.

He said how delighted he was that I had come to see him. 'It was good of you,' he added.

'I was told I must come,' I said.

Then I felt that was the wrong thing to have said because it sounded as though I didn't want to. I went on hurriedly: 'I was so excited. But there was a great deal to remember . . . so I hope I do not do anything wrong.'

He laughed. It was a very friendly laugh. He said: 'My dear little Victoria, I very much doubt that *anything* you did would be wrong in my eyes.'

'But I do *do* things which are wrong . . .'

'Perhaps we all do . . . now and then.'

'Even you, Uncle King?'

There! I had said it! Mama would be listening. Oh dear, there would be a lecture.

He was smiling still. 'Yes, even Uncle King.'

'Of course I should have said Your Majesty.'

'Do you know, I like Uncle King better.'

'Do you really . . . Uncle King?'

Then we both laughed again. I was so relieved and I quite liked sitting on his blubbery knee and watching his old-young face and wishing my hair curled as beautifully as his did, and thinking how different he was from what I had expected.

'You look rather pleased,' he said. 'I believe you are enjoying your visit and finding Uncle King not such an old ogre as you may have been led to believe.'

I hunched my shoulders and nodded, for that was exactly the truth.

He asked me questions and I told him about the dolls and how I was rather pleased that Queen Elizabeth's skirt was torn and had been for several days and Lehzen had not noticed it yet. 'She was so vain,' I said. 'She deserved it.'

He agreed.

Then he said he must give me a little memento of our meeting. I was not sure what that meant but guessed it was some sort of present, and so it proved to be for he said to the plump lady: 'Bring it, my dear.'

She brought a miniature of a very beautiful young man set in diamonds.

'It is lovely,' I cried. 'What a beautiful young man.'

'You don't recognize him?'

I looked puzzled. I lifted my eyes to his face. The plump lady was nodding and trying to tell me something. I did not understand.

'I daresay I have changed since that was done,' said the King sadly.

Then I knew. I looked closely and I did see a faint resemblance between the face in the picture and that of my benign young-old Uncle King.

I smiled. 'It is *you* . . . Uncle King. It was because it was so small and you are bigger now . . . I didn't see it at first.'

It was a little late, but he did not seem to mind so much after all.

He turned to the fat lady. 'Pin the miniature on her dress, my dear.' The fat lady, perfumed and silky, leaned over and smiling at me, obeyed.

'There! That will remind you of this day.'

'Oh, I should not have forgotten . . . not ever.'

'You are a very nice little girl,' he said. 'I have given you a present. What will you give me?'

I thought hard. One of the dolls? Queen Elizabeth perhaps . . . we could mend her skirt.

He said with a smile: 'A kiss would be very nice.'

That was easy. In spite of my disapproval of Queen Elizabeth I was glad I was not going to lose her. He put his face forward and I was so happy because the visit, which I had been dreading so much, had been so easy, and because he was kind and hadn't minded in the least being called Uncle King; and partly because he had been a little hurt because I had not recognized him as the beautiful young man in the picture, I put my arms round his neck and kissed him twice.

There was a brief silence. I had done something terrible. Mama would say I had behaved in a most vulgar way. Lehzen would be hurt because I had disgraced her. I had been warned, time after time, that should I be in the presence of the King, I was only to lift my lips and smile, and I was not to do that often. The King would be furious. He would say I had ignored his royalty. Oh dear, what had I done!

I drew away and then I saw his face. There were tears in his eyes. He seemed suddenly much nicer than the man in the picture. He put his arms round me and held me tightly against him. It was like lying on a featherbed.

He said: 'You are a dear little girl and you have given me great pleasure.'

Then he kissed me.

And in that moment I loved Uncle King.

When the audience was over and we went to our rooms in Cumberland Lodge which were made ready for us, I was still thinking about

Uncle King. Mama said nothing about my behaviour which was very strange. But she was thoughtful.

I longed to be alone with Feodore so that I could ask her why there was this odd silence. There was something else I wanted to ask Feodore. What had she thought of the King? When she had been presented to him, he had shown clearly that he liked her. Her chair had been placed next to his and he had engaged her in conversation for quite a long time. I had heard them laughing together. I think she quite liked him, too. In fact, it was difficult not to like him. He was so pleasant and charming to everyone, and if one did not look at him one could quite imagine someone as handsome as the young man in the miniature.

As Lehzen sat in my bedroom until Mama came to bed, I did not talk, but lay quietly thinking of the visit. I was still not asleep when Mama came up.

She came to my bed and looked down at me. 'Not asleep?' she asked. 'Why not?'

'I do not know why not,' I answered. 'It is just that I am not asleep.'

Mama said: 'It has been an exciting day. You were presented to the King.'

I thought: Now it is coming. I am going to hear what a disgrace I was to them all, how badly I had behaved, throwing my arms about the King's neck; and kissing him twice when only one kiss had been asked for was an offence to royalty. I might be sent to the Tower like poor Sir Walter Raleigh, one of the most splendid of the dolls.

'The King was in a good mood today,' said Mama.

I was going to say how much I liked him, but I did not think that was what Mama wanted to hear.

'You should be careful, Victoria.'

'Oh yes, Mama.'

'Remember your uncle is the King.'

'Oh, I won't forget.'

'Sometimes he hardly behaves like one.'

'I thought he was very nice, Mama. He has lovely hair and such pink cheeks . . . and yet he is very very old.'

'Things are not always what they seem. The hair is not his own. It is a wig and his cheeks are painted.'

I was astounded, and tried to imagine what he would look like without those lovely curls.

'They did look very nice,' I commented, still wanting to speak for him, 'and even if the curls were not his own, his kindness was.'

Mama ignored that. She said earnestly: 'If he were to make any suggestion to you, you must tell me at once.'

'What suggestion, Mama?'

'I think he liked you.'

'Oh yes, he did. He said I was a dear little girl. He didn't mind that I called him Uncle King. I think he liked it.'

'He would! If ever he should ask you if you would like to live at Windsor, you must tell me at once.'

To live at Windsor! To see the King often! To ride in the park . . . perhaps to be alone now and then . . . It did not seem such a terrible prospect.

'To live at Windsor . . .' I said excitedly.

'You must tell me at once. It may be that the King will want to take you away from me . . . from your home . . . and to keep you at Windsor.'

'Why, Mama?' I asked eagerly. 'Why?'

'Never mind why.'

What a constant cry that was! If one never knew why, one remained ignorant about so many things.

She kissed me. 'Now go to sleep.'

But I could not sleep. People cannot command sleep any more than they can make people never mind why.

That was only the beginning. It was very clear that the King was determined I should enjoy my visit to him and that it should be one which I would never forget. Feodore told me that he had asked her what I liked and she had said that I liked dancing and music. He had declared: 'Then dancing and music there shall be. At all costs we must please the little Victoria.'

Feodore told me that she thought he was charming also. He was *very* attentive to her. In fact I began to believe that he preferred her to sit close to him rather than me. Though I could not complain of his treatment of me. His eyes would light up when he saw me in a way I can only describe as tender, and he had that soft look in them which was near to tears but not quite, and his cheeks would wobble and his lips twitch as though he found me rather amusing.

There was an entertainment in the conservatory and I was seated next to him to watch. I could not help clapping my hands in appreciation of the magnificent movement of the dancers and when there was singing I sat there entranced. The King kept looking at me and smiling; and although Mama might disapprove of my obvious delight—once I jumped up and down in my seat—the King seemed very pleased about it; and when I looked at him uncertainly, he said: 'Yes, I quite agree. If I were as agile as you, my dear, I should do the same. They are worthy of such appreciation.'

It occurred to me that he made a point of remarking on everything I liked of which Mama would disapprove. Once I caught him looking at her and his expression was very different from that which came my way.

He likes *me*, I thought, but he does not like Mama.

He leaned towards me and said, 'I know you would like to ask the band to play something—a favourite of yours. Would you?'

'Oh yes,' I replied.

'What shall it be?'

I looked at him steadily—his pink cheeks and his lovely curls and his wrinkled, pouchy eyes—and I loved him because he was so kind to me and made me feel that I could be myself and not have to be the little girl Mama wished me to be.

I said: ' "God save the King." That is a very good song.'

He gave me that strange look again and said: 'Yes, I do indeed think you are a very nice little girl. Thank you. I will tell the band that you wish to make a request.'

Then he said loudly: 'The Princess Victoria is going to ask the band to play something of her choice. Now, my dear.'

I stood up and said very loudly and clearly: 'Please play "God Save the King".'

People clapped. Everyone was smiling. I heard someone whisper: 'She is a little diplomat already.' And I wondered what they meant.

And then the band was playing and everyone except the King stood up; and I felt very pleased and wondered whether Mama would say I had made the right choice.

The King evidently thought so for he suddenly took my hand and pressed it in a way to imply that we were very good friends indeed.

The next day there was a visit to the zoo which the King had established at Sandpit Gate.

It was a very exciting day and one of the reasons why it was so enjoyable was that Mama did not come. She had not been invited to join the party and I fancied that the King knew I should be glad to escape from her critical eyes. I was very perceptive in some ways and I had quickly gathered that although he liked me—and Feodore perhaps even more—he disliked Mama and he was of such a nature—as were all his brothers—to let her know it if the opportunity arose.

So it was a most exciting day looking at the strange animals—zebras, gazelles and such as I had never seen before.

When I was united with Mama I had to answer endless questions. Who had been there? What had been said? It went on and on but I was still living in that delightful memory of having had such a wonderful day without being watched all the time.

The day after that Mama and I, with Lehzen, were walking towards Virginia Water when we heard the sound of wheels on the road. Mama took my hand and drew me to the side of the road and we waited while a very splendid phaeton came towards us. I had never seen a carriage driven so fast, but as it approached it drew up.

Seated there, with my Aunt Mary, was the King.

He stopped and said it was a fine day. Then he looked at me and gave me that amused smile.

'Pop her in,' he said, and a postilion in silver and blue livery leaped down and put me into the phaeton between the King and Aunt Mary.

'Drive on,' cried the King; and we drove off leaving Mama and Lehzen standing on the side of the road, looking not only angry but rather frightened. I do believe Mama thought the King was kidnapping me. The King was laughing. I think he was rather pleased to see Mama's dismay.

I was a little disturbed but I quickly forgot it because it was so exhilarating driving along in the phaeton at a greater speed than I had ever known before.

'How do you like this?' cried the King, taking my hand in his.

'It is lovely,' I shouted. I suddenly realized that I could shout as much as I liked and I could do and say just what came into my head. In addition to this wonderful ride I was free of Mama's supervision.

The King talked to me all the time and Aunt Mary now and then said something, and she was smiling as though she liked me very much.

The King asked me questions and I told him I loved riding on my dear pony Rosy. She could really go very fast when she wanted to; but sometimes she had to be coaxed a little. I told him about the lessons I had to do and how I hated arithmetic and liked history because my governess, Baroness Lehzen, made that very interesting.

He listened with the utmost sympathy and I confided that what I liked best was dancing and singing.

He was not a bit like a king. When he talked of certain people he changed his face and way of talking. He was very good at imitating people and some of them I recognized.

I said: 'I had never thought that talking to a king could be like this.'

'Ah,' he said, 'many people speak ill of kings and it is harder for them than most people to win real affection. If they do one thing which pleases some, it displeases others . . . so there is no way of pleasing everybody all the time.'

I pondered this and said that if one were good, God would be pleased so everyone must be pleased too.

'Except the devil,' he suggested. 'He likes sinners, you know. So I am right, am I not?'

'But of course you are right because . . .'

'Because I am the King?'

'No . . .' I said judiciously, 'because you are *right.*'

Aunt Mary laughed and said we should go to Virginia Water as it was a lovely drive.

We went to the King's fishing temple where we left the phaeton and went into a barge. Several important people were there. The King presented me to them and they showed me a great deal of respect. One of them was the Duke of Wellington about whom Lehzen had told me a great deal. He was the hero of Waterloo who had played such an important part in our history. He was a very great man, but I did not like him very much. He was rather haughty and I believed was trying to remind everyone of his importance. I supposed that as Waterloo had happened nearly ten years before, he thought they were beginning to forget it and the memory must be constantly revived. He was not so very tall and rather thin, with a hooklike nose and eyes that seemed to look right through one—which made me rather uncomfortable. The King seemed to like him very much—at least to respect him. I supposed because of Waterloo.

There was music and the band played 'God Save the King' while I clasped my hands and looked up with affection at my uncle, who noticed this and gave me a very pleasant smile.

But all good things must come to an end and I was taken back to Cumberland Lodge where Mama was waiting for me.

What an interrogation there was! 'What did the King say?' 'And what did you reply to that?' 'And then?' 'And then . . . ?' With here and there Mama clicking her tongue. 'You shouldn't have said that. You should have said this . . . or this . . .'

'But, Mama,' I insisted, 'I think the King liked me to say what *I* meant.'

'He wanted to know exactly what was going on. He wanted to trap you.'

'Oh no, Mama. He just wanted me to laugh and enjoy it.'

She shook her head at me. 'You are very young, Victoria,' she said.

'But I am getting older. No one stays young forever.'

'You do not listen enough. You are too anxious to say what *you* think.'

'But, Mama, how can I say what anyone else thinks?'

She turned away and suddenly I felt sorry for her. It was odd to feel sorry for Mama when everyone in our household obeyed her . . . well perhaps not all. Perhaps not Sir John Conroy and it might well be that sometimes *she* obeyed *him*.

The time came when the visit to Windsor was at an end and we must return to Kensington. The King asked them to lift me onto his knee when he said goodbye. He told me how much he had enjoyed my visit and hoped I had too.

'Oh yes, indeed I have,' I said. 'It has been particularly wonderful because I had been afraid that it might not be.'

'Why were you afraid?'

'One is afraid of kings.'

'Because of what one has been led to expect?'

'Yes because of that.'

'And I was not such an ogre after all? In fact I think you and I liked each other rather well.'

'Well, I liked you, Uncle King, and I think you liked me too because you gave me such a wonderful time . . . besides the picture.'

He smiled and said: 'Tell me what you liked best of your stay.'

I hesitated for a moment and then I said: 'I liked so many things but I think the best was when you said ''Pop her in'' and we galloped off in the phaeton.'

'Did I say that?'

'Yes. ''Pop her in''.'

'It was not really kingly language, was it? But perhaps it was pardonable between an uncle and his niece . . . even though she is a princess and he a king. And that was what you liked best.'

I nodded.

'You are a dear little girl,' he said. 'I trust you will always have the sweet nature you have today, and that events . . . and those about you . . . will not succeed in changing you.'

Then I said goodbye and he kissed me again.

I was almost in tears at the thought of leaving him and he was very sad.

Mama wanted to know exactly what he had said and what I had replied. I told her and added: 'I think the King must be one of the nicest gentlemen in the world.'

That did not please her; but that visit to the King had changed me a little. I had the impression that it was sometimes better for me to say what I meant rather than what I was expected to say.

The King had thought so in any case.

But there was so much I did not understand. Mama was right when she said I was so young; and quite often I did feel as though I were floundering in the dark.

But I did know that the visit had made Mama very uneasy—not only about me, but about Feodore too.

Life seemed dull after the visit to Windsor. There were so many lessons and far too few holidays. If I complained Lehzen told me that it was my duty to acquire knowledge. A princess must not be an ignoramus.

'But there is so much to learn!' I cried.

'Of course there is,' retorted Lehzen. 'We all go on learning all our lives.'

'What a dreadful prospect!' I cried. At which she laughed and said that there was little to be compared with the joy of learning.

I wanted to dispute that and say that I knew of many more pleasant things, but Lehzen brought forth her favourite argument. 'You are too young to know. In time you will realize.'

And as I was young I could not really say this was not so. But I used to long to escape from the schoolroom. Then I would find Feodore and during the lovely summer days we would go into the gardens where I liked to water the plants. I had a very special watering can and I loved to watch the water spray out so prettily. I used to get my feet wet and Feodore would smuggle me in and Baroness Spath—whom I loved dearly because she was quite indiscreet and very kind—would put me into dry stockings, shoes and gown and there would be the added excitement because neither Mama nor Lehzen must know. That was imperative because if they did, the watering would be forbidden.

We often went into my Uncle Sussex's garden and I watered his plants. He had apartments like ours in the Palace and although he was a very odd gentleman—like most of the uncles—he was a very kind one. When I was little I had been frightened of him because when I had screamed on one occasion, someone had said: 'Be quiet or your Uncle Sussex will get you.' I suppose it was said because his apartments were near ours. And for a long time after that I regarded him with suspicion until I discovered him to be the last person who would complain, and in any case he would have been too absorbed in his books, his birds and his music to be aware of my tantrums. But then I had been scared of all the paternal uncles until I came to know them—with the exception of Uncle Cumberland who really did strike terror into me, and I believe not without cause.

However, there we were on those lovely summer days with the Baroness Spath—always so much less stern than Lehzen—in the gardens at Kensington—slipping into that of Uncle Sussex, Feodore with a book, I with the watering can, and Spath sitting on the grass beside Feodore watching me and now and then calling out a warning that I was pouring water onto my feet.

I was so happy smelling the lavender, listening to the hum of bees, hidden away from the windows of our apartments in the Palace.

Every time we were in Uncle Sussex's garden a young man would come to join us. He was Cousin Augustus, son of Uncle Sussex by his first marriage. Cousin Augustus was very handsome in his dragoon's uniform and he liked very much to sit beside Feodore and talk to her and Spath while I did the watering.

It was very pleasant for they laughed a good deal and old Spath sat there nodding and smiling as she did when she was pleased. Such happy afternoons they were and then suddenly they ended; and we were not to go into Uncle Sussex's garden again.

Spath was in disgrace; so was Feodore. I found her crying one day and I begged her to tell me what was wrong.

'Augustus and I had planned to marry,' she said.

'Oh, that will be lovely,' I cried. 'You would live so close and I could come and water your garden every day.'

Feodore shook her head. 'Mama is very angry. I am going to be sent away.'

'Oh no, Feddie . . . You mustn't go away!'

She nodded miserably and the sight of her tears set me weeping with her.

'Mama is blaming poor Spath. She may be sent away, too.'

Feodore, in her abject misery, was more communicative than she would otherwise have been.

'Augustus is not considered suitable.'

I was beginning to know something of these matters and I demanded: 'Why not? He is *my* cousin.'

'Well yes, but you see, although the Duke married Lady Augusta Murray, because she was not royal, the marriage was not considered to be a true one and therefore they say that dear Augustus is not legitimate. So I can't marry him.'

'It is so unfair,' I said. 'It would have been lovely.'

'I know, little sister. But they won't allow it.'

'Uncle Sussex wouldn't mind.'

'Oh no. He only cares about his books and his clocks, and his bullfinches and canaries. He wouldn't mind. But Mama says we have behaved disgracefully. Oh not you . . . you are not blamed. It is poor old Spath and I.'

I was right to be concerned. Very soon Feodore came to me, very quiet and sad, and told me that she was going to Germany to pay a visit to our grandmother.

I was desolate and could not be comforted. Poor old Spath went about hanging her head in shame; and Lehzen took up a very superior attitude towards her.

I hugged Spath when we were alone and said: 'Never mind. We were all very happy in the gardens. It wasn't your fault about Augustus not being right for Feodore. How were you to know? He is so handsome.'

At which Spath held me tightly and said that her greatest fear was that she should be taken away from me, which I thought very gratifying and which consoled me a little.

I overheard Spath and Lehzen talking together once and although I knew it was very wrong to listen to people when they did not know you were present, I couldn't help doing so because they were talking about Feodore. They talked in an odd sort of language when together. They would have preferred to speak in German but Mama had forbidden German to be spoken because *I* must speak English as my native tongue. There must be no trace of a German accent in my speech. That was very important. And although I learned German, it must be a secondary language. The English did not like royal people to speak English with a foreign accent. So dear Spath and Lehzen managed very well usually in English but when they were excited—particularly Spath—the odd German word or phrase would be thrown in.

Now they were talking about Feodore.

'There will be *die Berlobung* . . .' That was Spath.

'A betrothal,' corrected Lehzen sternly. 'I think that is certain. Her grandmother, the Duchess, will see to that.'

'Poor dear little Feodore . . . they were so happy.'

'You should have reported what was going on.'

'*Ach . . . wunderbar* . . . the two . . . so young . . . *Lieben* . . .'

'Baroness Spath, English please.'

'I forget. I am so unhappy. The Duchess blames me. I should have spoken. But they were so happy . . .'

'And you carried notes from one to the other! Oh, Baroness, you have behaved completely without discretion.'

'Sometimes . . . for love . . . it happens.'

'And Victoria was there!'

'Dear innocent child . . . so happy watering the plants.'

'And getting her feet wet.'

'I always made sure she changed her wet things.'

Spath began to whisper and I could not hear so well but I did gather that they were talking about my brother Charles.

Then I realized that I was eavesdropping, which was a very ill-mannered thing to do; and if I were caught I should be severely scolded, so I slipped away. I went to the dolls and explained to them that sometimes in the interest of knowledge it was necessary to listen to what was not intended for one's ears.

I thought Lady Jane Grey looked at me rather sadly as though she deplored my frailty. I shook her a little. Some people were too good.

Feodore would be leaving soon to stay with our grandmother in Saxe-Coburg. She was very sad, but looked just as pretty melancholy as she did happy. She talked a little more freely than normally. I suppose because she was going away. She was a little resentful towards Mama, for she believed that, but for Mama, she might have married the handsome Augustus. His father would not have minded; but there was every reason why Mama and our Uncle Leopold should object.

'Why are they so set against it?' I asked Feodore.

'It is all so stupid. It is because they don't accept him as legitimate. They don't accept the Duke's present wife either.'

'Mama doesn't like her, I know. She calls her that Buggins woman.'

'That's because she was the widow of Sir George Buggins before she married the Duke. The King would not have objected . . . nor would anyone except Mama and Uncle Leopold.'

'I am sure Uncle Leopold was thinking of your good . . . Mama too.'

'But they weren't thinking of my happiness. I love Augustus, Victoria.'

Then she wept and I wept with her. She held me close and said: 'There is something wrong with Charles.'

'What?'

'He is in love with Marie Klebelsberg.'

'Is she . . . unsuitable?'

'I'm afraid so.'

'Will they send Charles away?'

'They can't do that.'

'Will they forbid him to marry her?'

'I think Charles may not allow himself to be forbidden.'

'But he is Mama's son and if she says . . .'

'Well, there comes a time when people are old enough and in a position to have their own way.'

Those words seemed to me full of significance.

I nodded slowly.

I said: 'I hope Charles marries Marie Klebelsberg. Don't you think, Feodore, that people should marry for love?'

'Oh, I do indeed, little sister,' she said.

Then she held me more tightly and again we wept together.

When Feodore left I was desolate. Mama said I moped. Lehzen, putting it more kindly, said I pined. I told the dolls how very unhappy I was and that I could not bear to go into Uncle Sussex's garden again, even though I knew his flowers must be missing the benefits of my watering can.

Life seemed to be all lessons with the Reverend Davys presiding. There was Thomas Steward, who taught me penmanship as well as the hated arithmetic; I learned German from Mr. Barez and French from Monsieur Grandineau. I was quite good at languages and often enjoyed these lessons. I was beginning to learn Italian, which was quite enjoyable. Then there was music with Mr. Sale, who was the organist at St. Margaret's Westminster, drawing with Richard Westall, the academician, and dancing and deportment with Mademoiselle Bourdin. So, with all these excellent people making demands on my time, there was little left for anything else.

I was often not a very good pupil; the poor Reverend Davys sighed over me, I knew. I wanted to please them but it was so tiresome to do lessons all the time. Sometimes I gave way to fits of temper 'storms' as Mama called them. On one occasion, when Mr. Sale was in despair over my performance at the piano, he said: 'There is no royal road to music. Princesses must practise like everyone else.' I was so frustrated that I shut the lid of the piano with a bang and said: 'There! You see, there is no *must* about it.' Poor Mr. Sale! He was quite taken aback, but that did end the piano lesson for the day.

These people were all quite fond of me, I believe, in spite of my lack of application and my occasional storms. There were quite a number of times when my natural enthusiasms and feelings towards them made me go against Mama's instructions and let them know it. They thought those lapses, which Mama would have called vulgar, charming. So, in spite of everything, we got along very well together, and often when I made an effort to please them, they were so appreciative of that.

But with Feodore gone, I was really melancholy, and nothing . . . simply nothing . . . could lift the gloom.

On Wednesdays Uncle Leopold came to Kensington to visit us. These were the red-letter days. I would stand at the window with Lehzen beside me waiting for the sound of carriage wheels which would herald his arrival. I loved to watch him step down from his carriage. He was so handsome. 'I think Uncle Leopold must be the most distinguished man in the world,' I told Lehzen.

As soon as I was summoned I would rush down and throw myself into his arms. Mama would stand aside, not at all displeased that, on this occasion, I had allowed natural affection to triumph over dignity. Uncle Leopold did not mind either.

He would ask me if I loved him as much as ever and I would assure him fervently that I did.

I would sit on his knee and he would talk to me about being good and doing my duty and remembering that it was the only true way to satisfaction.

Mama said: 'We have had quite a few storms lately.'

'Storms?' echoed Uncle Leopold. 'Oh I do not like to hear that.'

'We are still sulky over the Sussex matter.'

Uncle Leopold looked very sad and that made me almost burst into tears.

'I watered the flowers,' I tried to explain. 'They did need it.'

Uncle Leopold sighed.

'There have been many storms because Feodore has gone,' said Mama.

'Dear me,' said Uncle Leopold. 'That is not like my princess.'

'Yes, Uncle Leopold,' I corrected. 'It is very like your princess.'

'To be stormy when she does not get what she thinks is her due,' supplied Mama.

'My dearest,' said Uncle Leopold, 'but it was very necessary for your sister to go away. She had behaved rather foolishly as you now know, and I am sure she will be happy with the new arrangements which are being made for her.'

'She was very happy with the arrangements she and Augustus were making.'

My mother exchanged a look with Uncle Leopold as though to say: 'You see.'

Uncle Leopold then began to ask me about my progress with my lessons, a less than happy subject, and after that he spoke to me so beautifully about the joys of endeavour, and as I sat on his knee watching his handsome face, my attention strayed from what he was saying and I was thinking how good he was and how lucky I was to have such an uncle.

Finally he said it was time I visited him at Claremont and asked if that were agreeable to me.

'It is the most agreeable thing in the world,' I told him, 'apart from Feodore's coming back.'

'I am disappointed that it is not the *most* agreeable event,' said Uncle Leopold, and I was ashamed because I knew that he always liked to be the first. But it was true that more than anything I wanted Feodore back, and I could not deny that.

He stayed with us for some time talking first to me and then I was sent back to Lehzen while he talked alone with Mama; and when he left I went down to wave him goodbye.

How I loved Claremont! I bounded up the steps to the front door, counting them as I went until I reached the triumphant thirteen. Uncle Leopold was waiting to take me in his arms. Lehzen kept a discreet distance. She would go back to Kensington afterwards so that I should be alone with Uncle Leopold. Louisa Lewis was there to greet me. She looked so happy to see me that I even forgot I had lost Feodore and prepared to enjoy every moment of my stay at Claremont.

'How delighted I am to have my dear little niece in my home,' said Uncle Leopold. 'You have brought me the greatest comfort I have known since the loss of my dearest Charlotte.'

So we were sad for a few moments—but rather agreeably so— while Uncle Leopold remembered Charlotte, which I fancied he rather enjoyed doing. This lovely house, surrounded by the beautiful Vale of Esher and which took its name from the Earl of Claremont who had built it, was really a shrine to Charlotte. I knew that I would hear her name constantly mentioned while I was here.

Louisa Lewis took me to my room.

'It's a great joy to have you here,' she told me. 'We will have some of our little gossips, shall we not?'

I agreed gleefully. Louisa was one of those gossipy people with whom it is such fun to talk. They are so pleasantly indiscreet.

In every room she kept mementos of Charlotte. Whoever said that Charlotte was dead, was wrong. Charlotte lived on at Claremont. She seemed to be there in every room. Uncle Leopold and Louisa Lewis had kept her alive.

Louisa talked of her constantly. I did not mind. I liked to hear about her. She had been one of those people who had the miraculous ability of turning her faults into virtues. 'Such a hoyden,' said Louisa, as though that was a wonderful thing to be. 'The dear Prince did what he could to cure her, but he gave up in despair . . . such loving despair.'

It was fascinating. I learned about the King's objection to Leopold and how he had wanted Charlotte to marry the Prince of Orange. 'But she would have Leopold.' Charlotte must have been cleverer than poor Feodore, I thought, and wondered how she had managed it. By being a hoyden? Of course she *was* the heiress to the throne. Perhaps that had had something to do with it.

'You should have seen her in her wedding dress . . . silver tissue . . . and the King had given her those jewels which pass to all the Queens of England. But her favourite was one diamond bracelet. Guess why? Because that was a gift from Prince Leopold . . . so it was most precious to her.'

I listened with tears in my eyes.

'She loved Claremont. To her it meant more than all the royal palaces. She insisted on living like an ordinary housewife. Oh, she would have her own way, Charlotte would. She even did some cooking . . . and she was so good to the poor of the neighbourhood. They loved her. She looked after Leopold, and he was very amused although he was always trying to remind her of her royal dignity.

Useless, of course. Charlotte did not care much for dignity. I remember how she used to comb his hair. Oh, they were so happy. It was such a joy to serve her and then . . . for her to go like that. She was so well, so delighted because she was to have a child . . . her baby. She didn't think so much of being a future king or queen. It was just to be her little baby. And then . . . it happened . . . so suddenly . . . I just went stone cold. Something died in me. I could not imagine going on without Charlotte to look after.'

Claremont was a house of mourning still and I wondered why I was so happy in it. But it was not a sad sort of mourning. I had the impression that they would be unhappy if it stopped—particularly Uncle Leopold.

We talked a great deal about Charlotte, how he had guided her, how he had changed her after their marriage. Before that she had been so uncontrollable. She had not had a good relationship with either of her parents. It had been difficult to imagine a child with more unfortunate parents. 'Oh, how grateful you should be, dearest, to have your Uncle Leopold always so concerned for your well being . . . and your Mama also. We shall care for you, dear child, as poor Charlotte was never cared for . . . until she became my wife, of course.'

'She must have been very happy then.'

Uncle Leopold smiled into the past. 'She worshipped me. My dear, dear Charlotte. My child, I hope you never know sorrow such as I did when she went.'

When I come to think of these talks with Uncle Leopold I realize how often they were concerned with melancholy. Life was very serious for Uncle Leopold. I was inclined to think that life could be rather merry. I loved dancing, singing and laughing—all of which, Mama said, when done to excess, were vulgar. Perhaps I was a little vulgar. No wonder Mama and Lehzen had to keep such a sharp watch on me. And yet I enjoyed these talks with Uncle Leopold. I loved to shed a tear with him over all his sorrows. He was a martyr to many illnesses and he liked to talk about them to me: the mysterious pains, the easy way in which he caught cold. After discovering that the King's luxurious curls were a wig I found myself studying Uncle Leopold's hair. He must have noticed this for he explained: 'I wear this thing just to keep my head warm.'

'Well,' I replied, 'that is a good reason for wearing it, for you do suffer from pains in the head, dear Uncle.'

I noticed, too, that he had high soles and heels on his shoes. I had thought at one time that this was to make him look taller, but I guessed now that it was to help some ailment in his feet.

During that visit Uncle Leopold mentioned quite casually that he had made a great sacrifice for my sake. I was quite alarmed and he went on: 'I have been offered the throne of Greece and I have declined it.'

'Do you mean you would have been a king?'

'Yes, I should have been a king. But what of that? The first thing that occurred to me was: I should be separated from little Victoria.'

'Oh, Uncle Leopold, did you give up a crown for me?'

'It was worth it, my love. At least, I believe it was worth it . . . if I can be proud of my dearest child.'

'Oh, you will be, Uncle. You will be.'

'I know it. Never forget, my dearest, how much I care for you.'

I swore I would not and I felt very happy because he had given up a crown for my sake.

Then he told me about my little cousin who had been born at a beautiful place called Rosenau exactly three months after I made my appearance into the world.

'This dear little boy, who is one of the most beautiful I ever saw, is my nephew . . . as you are my little niece. I often think how lucky I am to have two such little darlings to care for.'

'Do you care for him then, Uncle?'

'Indeed I do.'

I felt a little jealous of this intruder and wanted to ask if Uncle Leopold cared more for him than for me, but I guessed that would not be a good thing to ask, so I waited to hear more of this boy. I was glad he was younger than I. I felt that gave me an advantage.

'He has a little brother who is not quite a year older than he is.'

'I have a sister who is twelve years older than I.'

Uncle Leopold ignored that. He did not want to go back over Feodore's misfortunes. He wanted to talk about his little nephew.

'His name is Albert and his brother is Ernest.'

'They must be German.'

'Their father is the Duke of Saxe-Coburg-Gotha. They are two charming boys.'

'I should like to see them. They are my cousins, are they not?'

'They are indeed your cousins. I have heard from your grandmother that Albert is as quick as a weasel.'

'Yes, I suppose weasels are rather quick.'

Uncle Leopold smiled a little impatiently. 'He has big blue eyes and is very good-looking. He is very lively and good-natured.'

'He sounds very good,' I said uneasily.

'He is full of mischief.'

That sounded more likeable and I asked some questions about him.

'I believe you would be very good friends with your cousins,' went on Uncle Leopold. 'You see they have no mother now, and you have no father.'

'I see,' I said.

'It makes a bond between you.'

'Shall I meet them? Will they come here? I do not think Mama would want me to go to Germany.'

'You may very likely meet them one day.'

'Oh, I do hope so.'

'In fact,' said Uncle Leopold, smiling, 'I am going to make sure that you do.'

And after that he talked to me often about my cousins; and when I asked questions about them he seemed very pleased indeed.

Feodore returned to Kensington. She seemed different, no longer the broken-hearted Feodore who had left us. There was an air of serenity about her. Resignation, I supposed.

She was to be married very soon to Count Hohenlohe-Langenburg.

We were so delighted to see each other. I could not bear her to be out of my sight. I showed her all the dolls. There were one or two new ones. Mama had said that I should give up playing with dolls. She did not understand that my dolls were not ordinary dolls. They were real people to me. Lehzen wanted me to keep them. She loved them as much as I did. They were educational, she said, which was her verdict on anything that she liked.

'What changes have there been while I have been away?' Feodore wanted to know.

What changes could there be? Life went on in the same way at Kensington.

In spite of having been separated from Augustus, I believed Feodore enjoyed her stay in Germany for Mama was almost as strict with her as she was with me, and she too felt that she was in a prison. So I supposed the comparative freedom she would get with marriage was agreeable to her although her husband would not be Augustus but the Count of Hohenlohe-Langenburg.

What was he like? I asked when we were together with Lehzen sitting in the room sewing. We were never really alone.

'He is very kind.'

'And handsome?'

'Yes, he is handsome.'

'And do you love him?'

'I must love him for he is to be my husband.'

Feodore was talking like Mama or Lehzen. I realized with a little pang that she had changed. She had crossed the line and become a grown-up person and they invariably said not what they meant but what they thought it was right to say.

I was a little saddened and asked no more questions about the Count.

Feodore was to be married at Kensington Palace. It was a great occasion. I had a lovely white dress and Lehzen spent a lot of time curling my hair. The wedding was to take place in the Cupola Room where, Lehzen reminded me, I had been christened.

'Yes,' I said, 'and where there was a storm because the King wouldn't have me named Georgiana. Do you know, I think he wouldn't mind my being called after him now. He was so kind to me when we met.'

'And so you became Victoria. Well, that is quite a nice name.'

'I intend it to be a very good name,' I said. 'I really don't think Georgiana would have suited me. But perhaps that is because I have got used to Victoria now. After all, I used to be Drina. I am glad that changed.'

Lehzen shook her head and adjusted one of my curls.

'Well, you look very nice.'

'The King is going to give Feodore away,' I said. I giggled. 'I do believe he would prefer to keep her for himself.'

'You must not say such things.'

'Well, when we were at Windsor he did seem to like her.'

'I think he liked you too.'

'Oh yes, but Feodore more, and in a different way.'

'Those bright eyes see more than is there sometimes.'

'Dear Lehzen, how could they see what is not there?'

'Come along, my little wiseacre. Let us go and see how the bride is getting on.'

Feodore looked beautiful—not a bit afraid, as I feared she might. She looked more remote, it was true—not quite young any more, secretive perhaps, learning to hide her feelings. I wondered if I should ever be like that. I thought not.

She was wearing a beautiful diamond necklace, I noticed it immediately.

'It is a present from the King,' she told me.

'Oh, I knew he liked you! It's lovely. Feodore, I believe he would have liked to marry you.'

'Nonsense! He is an old man.'

'Old men like pretty young women sometimes.'

'How observant you are!'

'Lehzen says I see things which are not there. How could anyone?'

'Ordinary rules don't apply to Victoria.'

That made me laugh.

'Don't say that about the King to anyone,' she advised.

'Why not? *I* think it is true.'

'Dear little sister, you talk too frankly, you know.'

'You sound just like Mama.'

'Oh no . . . please not.'

Then we laughed again and it was like the old days again.

We went to the Cupola Room. Through the windows as we passed along I saw the crowds outside the Palace.

'They love a royal wedding,' said Lenzen.

The bells were ringing and everyone seemed very happy. The only regret was that Augustus was not the bridegroom. Well, I thought, one cannot expect everything—although of course the bridegroom *was* rather an important part of the ceremony.

I looked around for the King as I entered the Cupola Room. He was not there, but Uncle Clarence was. Mama hated Uncle Clarence just as much as she hated the King. I quite liked him. He was so jolly and I think he would have liked to be friendly with us, but Mama would not have it, of course. He always smiled very kindly at me and I was really fond of Aunt Adelaide. She kissed me and asked after the dolls and talked about them just as though they were real people, which made me like her even more. I told her the Big Doll fitted in very well. She was bigger than the others and her clothes were just as splendid, although they were merely a court lady's dress. 'I think she looks quite as grand as Queen Elizabeth,' I said.

'Oh dear,' said Aunt Adelaide. 'Queen Elizabeth will not like that!' which made me laugh. Aunt Adelaide joined in and Mama noticing, frowned. I was not supposed to be on terms of levity with Aunt Adelaide.

I realized then that there was a growing uneasiness in the room. Where was the King? He was supposed to be present to take an important part in the ceremony and they could not proceed without him.

Uncle Clarence said in a loud voice: 'The King is clearly not coming. No need to delay further. I'll take his rôle.'

My mother would have protested but I knew she was undecided whether to wait a little longer for the King and allow herself to be further humiliated, or to ask Uncle Clarence to carry on. It must have been galling to see her daughter given away by a duke when she had been expecting a king to do so.

But it did seem as though the King would not come, so Clarence went on to take his part, and I stepped into my place as bridesmaid.

And so my sister Feodore became the wife of Count Hohenlohe-Langenburg.

Mama had had the idea that I should go among the guests with a basket which contained little gifts for them; and everyone applauded when I presented them.

Then the bride and groom went to Claremont and we went back to our apartments in the Palace. How Mama raged against the King and all her husband's family. They were crude, ill-mannered; they were against a lonely widow. They did all they could to humiliate her and they hated to see her daughter marrying the Count; and they were jealous of her younger daughter who was in such good health.

The King would soon be dead and that pineapple-headed oaf would take his place. He was incapable of getting an heir . . . he was incapable of anything except stepping into the grave.

She was really angry and I heard her in the room where I sat with Lehzen and Spath. Spath was wide-eyed and seemed rather excited by it; but Lehzen was terrified that I should hear something which was not for my ears.

I heard Sir John Conroy's hated voice, calming her, soothing her, as he often did.

Spath was nodding as though she had secret thoughts, and Lehzen had that tight look about her mouth as she always did when Sir John was near. I was gratified that Lehzen felt the same about Sir John as I did.

A great deal was going on of which I knew nothing and only learned later, and piecing little bits of evidence together found out what it was all about.

Uncle Cumberland was suspect. People saw him as the ogre. He really wanted the throne for his son George—such a nice boy whom

I had met once or twice—and he did actually want me out of the way. Because my father had been older than he was, I came before George Cumberland, and that irritated his parents. They had such evil reputations that I am not sure now whether the rumours were circulated because of that, or whether they really were menacing my life.

When I was very young they had put it about that I was a weak child and not expected to live; and Mama had to take me for walks very publicly so that all the people were able to see for themselves how strong I was. Indeed I was quite plump and brimming over with good health. I still went for these walks with Mama or Lehzen —usually as far as Apsley House, and the people often stopped and cheered me.

Mama said later that the reason why I was never left alone was because of the forces round me and the need to protect me from them all the time. I was not so sure of that because I became aware that Mama wanted me to do exactly as she wished, so that I should be like a puppet she was controlling.

The Cumberlands were at the centre of more than one scandal— and not minor ones either. There was the one long ago concerning the Duke's valet; and at this time there was another when Lord Graves was found dead in bed with his throat cut, the evidence being that he had killed himself. And why had he done this? Because his wife was having a love affair with the Duke of Cumberland; and one must never forget that his Duchess also had a dubious past with two husbands who had died young.

Aunt Sophia, when she was very young, had had a child presumed to be by Colonel Garth. Now they were saying that the real father of Sophia's child was her brother, the Duke of Cumberland.

There was no end to the scandal which surrounded that family.

Aunt Adelaide used to call on my mother occasionally, and I always thought Mama behaved very regally towards her, although as the wife of the Duke of Clarence, who was older than my father would have been, Aunt Adelaide should have taken precedence. She might have been put out by this—most people, and certainly Mama, would have been—but she was not. I really think she liked to come to Kensington to see me, because she was always so kind to me, and I noticed a special look on her face when she talked to me. She always asked about my pony, Rosy, and the dolls, and what I was doing. She wanted me to go to visit her at Bushey; she told me something about the parties she gave. The two little Georges came—Cumberland and Cambridge. 'Such darling boys,' said

Aunt Adelaide. 'George Cambridge is with us now, because his mother and father are abroad. He and the other George are great friends. We have singing and dancing and games.' How I should have loved to go to Bushey!

But I was never allowed to. I asked Mama why and she grew very red in the face and muttered something about those dreadful FitzClarences.

Later I discovered they were the children and grand-children of Uncle William's liaison with the actress Dorothy Jordan and Aunt Adelaide had adopted them as her own family when she married Uncle William. More family scandal!

My chief companion at this time was Victoire Conroy whom I never liked because she was her father's daughter, and the older I grew the more resentful I became of his presence in our household. I felt sure I was right to be wary of him because both Lehzen and Spath disliked him too. They did not say much to me—at least Lehzen didn't—but Spath used to purse her lips and mutter '*Das Schwein.*'

Victoire was like her father; she was a little superior and seemed to forget I was a princess, or perhaps she felt that with such an important father, she was of as much consequence as I was.

Several times I asked Mama why I could not go to Aunt Adelaide's parties and meet gentle George Cambridge, who had the good fortune to live with Aunt Adelaide, and George Cumberland, who might not be as sinister as his parents.

But Mama was adamant. I simply could not go to Bushey because of what I heard her call 'The Bastidry'. 'And how Adelaide can behave as she does amazes me,' she added.

So I was left to my lessons, the company of Lehzen, my walks and my dolls.

One day when I was out walking with Lehzen, showing myself to the people, I saw a beautiful doll in a shop window. I stopped and said: 'Oh, Lehzen, isn't she lovely!'

Lehzen admitted that she was.

'I should love to have her,' I went on. 'I often think the Big Doll does not quite fit in with the others, and that one would be a companion for her.'

The doll was priced at six shillings.

'I will ask your Mama if you may have her,' said Lehzen.

Mama and Lehzen put their heads together to discuss what would be good for me and they came up with the idea that I must not think everything was mine for the asking. I might have the doll if I bought her myself and to do this I must save up my pocket money. In the meantime I could go into the shop and ask them to put the doll on one side until I could pay for it.

That seemed an excellent idea and I liked the thought of buying her myself. It gave me a feeling of independence. The man in the shop was eager to please. He said, certainly he would hold the doll until I had the money to pay for it.

'You won't let anyone else buy her, will you?' I asked anxiously.

His answer was to take a big ticket which he hung round the doll's neck. On it was printed in large letters SOLD.

I found it exciting to walk past his windows every day and look for the doll. There she was, sitting waiting for me, and with great glee I counted my money each morning. At last I had the six shillings and in great triumph went to collect my darling.

Exultantly I carried her out of the shop but as I was walking along beside Lehzen I saw a poor man sitting on a bench. It always distressed me to see people cold or hungry and I would remember them at night when I was in bed, and think how warm *I* was, how cosseted, and that made me uneasy because it was so unfair.

I was not allowed to speak to people, only to smile and wave my hand when they cheered me. But I did speak to this man. I said: 'Wait a moment.' And to Lehzen's horror I ran back to the shop and asked the man there to take back my beautiful doll and give me my six shillings. 'Put the sold ticket back,' I said, 'and when I have saved it I will come back for her, but now I want my six shillings back.'

He gave me the money and took the doll, putting the sold ticket round her neck.

'What is this?' called Lehzen breathlessly. But I was already off. I put the six shillings into the poor man's hand.

Lehzen was panting behind me. 'Princess,' she cried in shocked tones. She was almost in tears, but not angry.

She took my hand firmly. 'You are a good sweet child,' she said and I thought she was going to cry. 'I am proud of you.'

What Mama said when the incident was repeated to her, I did not know. I expected to be scolded. But nothing was said. And I saved up six shillings again and in due course the ticket SOLD was taken from the beautiful doll's neck and she joined my company much, I imagined, to the joy of the Big Doll.

Mama and I were spending a few days at Claremont. What a joy it was to be there! Uncle Leopold devoted so much time to me and I never wearied of listening to him. He talked of being good and the purpose of life, and how one was born to a certain destiny which it was one's bounden duty to fulfil.

He was so good himself that sometimes I felt he was too good for this life and I trembled at the thought, because that was what was said when people died.

But perhaps he was not quite so good, and he, too, may have had secrets in his life. I did not understand what happened at the time, but I was aware of something. That is so frustrating about being young. One is aware of what goes on and yet does not fully understand its significance. People are secretive and make faces at each other when they think you are not looking—Lehzen and Spath were always doing that—and then one began to ponder. What does that mean? And, there is something very secret—and when it is a secret it is often rather shocking.

This incident occurred in Claremont Park.

One early evening Mama and I were out riding and when I rode with her I always liked to ride a little ahead of her. This was permitted as long as I kept in sight.

Well, there I was in the park. There was a clearing among the trees and suddenly two women emerged. They stopped short when they saw me, but I rode up to them and said: 'Good evening. Who are you?'

The elder lady looked quite taken aback but the younger, who was very beautiful, was quite self-possessed. 'Good evening, Your Highness,' she said. 'I am Caroline Bauer, Dr. Stockmar's cousin.'

'Oh, Dr. Stockmar's cousin. My uncle is very attached to Dr. Stockmar.'

Mama had arrived. She was staring stonily at the two women. The elder blushed deeply; the younger held her head higher and looked defiant.

Mama said to me: 'Come along.' And without a word to the two women, she turned her horse.

I looked at them, bewildered and apologetic; but of course I had to follow Mama.

'How many times have I told you not to speak to strangers,' she demanded.

'But, Mama, they were not strangers. She was Dr. Stockmar's cousin.'

'I should like to know what she was doing in the park.'

'She was visiting her cousin, I expect.'

'Never do such a thing again.'

Of course I knew there was something special about Caroline Bauer. I would ask Lehzen, but she would probably not tell me. Spath might know.

I did discover a little myself because when we returned, Mama told me to go to my room, but before I could do so Uncle Leopold came into the hall.

'Did you enjoy your ride, my darling?' he asked.

'Oh yes, Uncle. I met Dr. Stockmar's cousin.'

Mama looked angrily at me, and even Uncle Leopold was a little abashed.

'Go to your room, Victoria,' said Mama.

And Uncle Leopold made no effort to detain me.

She went off with him into the drawing-room and I have to admit that I hesitated for a while before going up the stairs so I heard her say: 'It is terrible. Victoria met that woman.'

'I see no harm,' said Uncle Leopold.

'No harm! To have her here like that! Here . . . where you lived with Charlotte!'

'It has been many years since Charlotte died.'

The door was shut and I went upstairs.

What did it mean? And why had Mama been so angry because I had met that really rather pleasant young woman and her companion? It was all very mysterious. But I had discovered that Mama was not very pleased with Uncle Leopold and that was a very strange state of affairs.

Later I discovered that Caroline Bauer was Uncle Leopold's mistress. I was shocked a little because, although by then I knew something of the nature of men, I had always thought my dear Uncle Leopold would have been above that sort of thing.

Aunt Adelaide was very worried because people were saying that the Duke of Clarence was going mad. When there is madness in a family people are suspect, and they only have to act with a little eccentricity and they will be labelled crazy.

I knew that Uncle William was a little peculiar; he talked and talked, and very often about nothing; and then he would fly into rages; but I also heard that he was very kind to all his children. There were so many FitzClarences because the grandchildren were now coming along. The Bushey household where they lived with Uncle William and Aunt Adelaide was a very noisy one apparently. The little ones used to slide down the banisters and play all sorts of tricks on Uncle William, but he never minded and just laughed with them. There was a great deal which was rather nice about Uncle William. Oh, how I longed to go to Aunt Adelaide's parties at Bushey! I should not have minded in the least playing with the FitzClarences. I wondered what it felt like to slide down banisters; and couldn't help laughing to think of myself doing that in Kensington Palace.

Aunt Adelaide came to see Mama and they were closeted together. I could see Aunt Adelaide was worried.

Lehzen came to me afterwards and spoke to me very seriously. I had to be careful, she said. I must always have someone in attendance.

'But I always have to, Lehzen.'

I listened and questioned Späth and through her discovered that they were all worried about Uncle Cumberland. He lived with the King now at Windsor Lodge and the King was getting very old and feeble and relying on Cumberland for everything.

Mama said: 'It is Cumberland who is really ruling us all. The King is nothing now . . . nothing at all. And he is trying to get Clarence put away. We know what that means.'

She was talking to Sir John Conroy, not to me, of course, but I did happen to overhear.

Conroy said: 'He would stop at nothing.'

'He has proved that. He is a monster. My God, these brothers . . . they are mad, all of them.'

'Hush, dear lady,' said Conroy. He had seen me come into the room.

'Where is Lehzen?' Mama demanded of me.

'She is just here, Mama.'

Oh yes, they were very frightened about me; and it was because they thought something dreadful could happen to me. Mama did not care a rap if Uncle William should be put away. In fact I think she would have been rather pleased.

What she feared was that some attempt would be made on my life. I used to have bad dreams in which my one-eyed uncle figured. He would not be the first wicked uncle in history.

Mama said I was not to go up and down stairs without a companion. Did she think someone would creep up behind me and push me down?

Then suddenly the danger was removed.

The King died at Windsor.

Poor Uncle King! I was very sad remembering that drive to Virginia Water, and how he had said 'pop her in'. I am sure if Mama had been friendly with him, and I had visited him more often I should have loved him.

He had been ill for so long, and quite influenced, it was said, by the wicked Duke of Cumberland. He was half blind and at the end he would lie in bed all day with fires burning during the warm weather and drinking quantities of cherry brandy. When they cleared out his apartments they found that he had hoarded clothes over a long time, and his cupboards were full of pantaloons, coats and boots which must have been there for years. There were five hundred pocket books, all containing money. When they counted this money it came to ten thousand pounds. There were also locks of women's hair, women's gloves and many love letters.

Dear Uncle King! I wished I had known him when he was young and handsome and clever and charming. It was a pity that all I had seen was the fat be-wigged, rouged old man, who had somehow managed to charm me just the same.

If I was sad at the King's passing, Mama was not. She could not hide her pleasure.

'And now we have mad William on the throne,' she said, and added with a laugh: 'How long will he last, I wonder?'

It was strange to think of Uncle William as King. He was too friendly with everyone. He had no dignity, said Mama. He laughed at his grandchildren—who should never have been there—sliding down the banisters and playing tricks on him. And dear, plain Aunt Adelaide was the Queen.

I could not imagine any pair less like a royal couple.

I was seated in the schoolroom when Lehzen came in and said: 'It is time for our history lesson.'

I was rather pleased. History was one of the subjects which I liked.

Lehzen handed me *Howlett's Tables*, in which was the genealogical tree of the Kings and Queens of England. I noticed that an extra page had been pinned into the book.

I said: 'What is this? I have not seen it before.'

'No,' said Lehzen, faintly mysterious. 'You did not see it because it was not there. But now it is believed that it is necessary for you to see it.'

'Why?'

'Just study it, will you?'

My own name seemed to start out of the page. I saw clearly its

significance. Uncle William was King of England. He had no legitimate heirs—and next to him came Victoria.

I raised my eyes to Lehzen's face; she was looking at me with a
mixture of love and fear, tenderness and anxiety.

'It means,' I said slowly, 'that when Uncle William dies, I shall
be Queen.'

Lehzen nodded.

I felt dizzy. So many things seemed to be slipping into place.
All Mama's care; all Uncle Cumberland's threats; Mama's insis-
tence on my being given my proper dues. I was destined—very
likely—to be Queen of England.

I said shakily: 'I am nearer to the throne than I thought.'

'Yes, my dearest,' said Lehzen.

'I understand now why you have all been so anxious for me to
learn . . . even Latin. You told me that Latin is the foundation of
elegant expression. Oh, Lehzen, I understand now . . . I do. I do.'

I put my hand into hers and the tears ran down my cheeks.

'My little one,' said Lehzen, 'you will do well . . . very well.'

'Many boast of the splendours of such a position,' I said, 'but
there are difficulties too.' I raised my hand a little and added solemnly: 'I will be good.'

The Waiting Years

My discovery could not fail to make a difference. The possibility of being Queen was dazzling. I daresay I assumed new airs and graces. That was inevitable, although I tried to remind myself that although all the balls and banquets, riding through the streets in a splendid carriage and waving to the loyal people would be the greatest of pleasures, I must remember the responsibilities too. I recalled the poor man to whom I had given six shillings. He and many like him would be my subjects. I wanted to make them all happy, as well as to live in a pleasant state myself.

I became more restless. I hated the restrictions of life in the Palace. Uncle Cumberland was out of favour now. The new King, William, had denounced him and made it clear that he would not have him trying to guide him as he had their brother George. I was free now of that threat. Cumberland would not dare to harm one whose ascension to the throne was imminent. Uncle George's death had made a great difference.

I used to lie in my white-painted French bed with the chintz curtains and pretend to be asleep when Lehzen sat there waiting for Mama to come to bed, and tell myself that I was nothing more than a captive. They watched everything I did.

It was a great trial to be heir presumptive to the throne, to be guarded day and night and be only eleven years old. I felt there was so much I ought to know and there was no one except Lehzen and Spath in whom I could confide. I loved Spath very much, and Lehzen more than anyone else, but if I broached certain subjects, a barrier would always be drawn up and I could see in their eyes— even dear Spath's who was much more inclined to be indiscreet than Lehzen—that it was Not Good for the Child to Know . . . just yet. If Feodore had been there it would have been different. Oh, how I missed Feodore! But when people are absent for a long time they grow away from one; and I could read in dear Feodore's letters that she was becoming more and more accustomed to life with her Ernest, of whom she seemed to grow more and more fond, and was not only reconciled but was enjoying married life with its prospect of motherhood.

So surrounded as I was by people who were determined to protect me, and never let me be by myself, oddly enough I often felt alone.

I was very careful how I behaved, and tried not to show any difference in my conduct from what it had been before I knew of my possible future.

I smiled to remember how arrogant I had been when I was about six years old and I had already been aware that I belonged to the royal family. When little Lady Jane Ellice had been brought to play with me, I had adopted a superior attitude to her and told her she must not play with the toys which were mine. 'Though I may call you Jane,' I informed her, 'you must not call me Victoria, but Princess or Highness.' I still remember the blank look on little Jane's face, and how she turned away and started to play by herself.

There must be nothing like that now that I was older and wiser. But eleven is still not very old, less still a wise age.

Ever since I had met Dr. Stockmar's cousin in the grounds, Mama had not been quite so effusively fond of Uncle Leopold. I sensed this because, I suppose, at that time Uncle Leopold was the most important person in my life—with perhaps the exception of Lehzen.

I was a little uneasy and meant to ask Uncle Leopold why Mama was displeased with him because Dr. Stockmar's cousin was at Claremont, but before I had the opportunity a matter of great importance drove it from my mind.

I was paying one of my cherished visits to Claremont.

Uncle Leopold greeted me with great pleasure, and there was dear Louisa Lewis looking so happy because I had come. I was delighted to be there but I noticed immediately that Uncle Leopold was looking a little strained. I asked after his health and he told me he suffered cruelly from insomnia.

'Dear Uncle, you work too hard.'

'I could not be happy if I did not do my duty.'

'But I must insist that you rest more.'

'My dearest little Doctor Victoria, rest is not so easily come by. My rheumatism is particularly painful at night.'

'It is so wrong that you who are so good should suffer so.'

Uncle Leopold sighed. 'It is my fate, dear child, I fear.'

He looked at me sadly and I thought tenderly of all his ailments:

his built-up shoes which gave comfort to his feet; his wig to keep his head warm; and the feather boa he sometimes wore to keep the cold from his shoulders. Yet in spite of all these weaknesses Uncle Leopold did not look in the least like an invalid.

I should never forget that he had given up the crown of Greece to be with me. He had reminded me of it many times.

'How many men would give a great deal to be a king!' he had said. 'I happen to think that life would be more rewarding guiding one who is dearer to me than anyone else since my beloved Charlotte died.'

Dear Uncle Leopold, who had given me so much!

'My dear little Victoria,' he said. 'I want to talk to you . . . very seriously.'

I was surprised because it seemed to me that Uncle Leopold never talked in any other way than seriously.

'I have pondered long over this matter and have at last come to a conclusion. I am deeply concerned about the Belgian people who have severed their connection with Holland.'

'Is that a bad thing, Uncle?'

'It could be a very good thing. You see they need a ruler . . . a strong ruler. They need a king.'

'Perhaps they will have one.'

'Yes, my child, they are going to have one. You see him before you.'

I looked round sharply.

'No, my dearest. Here.'

'You, Uncle Leopold?'

'None other.'

'You are the King of the Belgians! But, Uncle . . .'

'They have offered me the crown. I have had sleepless nights thinking of the matter.'

'You often have sleepless nights, Uncle.'

'Yes . . . yes . . . but more since this proposition was made to me.'

I waited. I was beginning to feel very apprehensive.

'I know now where my duty lies. The saddest thing will be to say goodbye to my dear little niece.'

'So . . . you are going away?'

'I must, my child. All my inclinations are to stay here . . . to be near you . . . to guide you . . . as I have done all these years. But I know in my heart that my duty is to my Belgian subjects. So, my dearest Victoria, I am going away. Oh, we shall be in constant

contact. You write such interesting letters. They will sustain me i»
all my tasks. I shall watch for them . . . Indeed I shall watch ove
you . . . I shall never be far away from you . . . and I shall war»
to know all that goes on.'

Desolation swept over me and Uncle Leopold and I wept together.

I was going to lose him. There would be no more visits to Clare
mont. And if by some chance there were, how empty the place
would be without him.

I went back to the Palace and told Lehzen. She was dismayed
too.

Mama did not seem as unhappy as I thought she might be. O»
course she admired Uncle Leopold greatly and always discussed
important matters with him, but since the visit of Caroline Bauer
and her mother to Claremont, she had not been quite the same.

I overheard Lehzen and Spath discussing Uncle Leopold's departure.

Spath said in a voice of foreboding: 'This means that that ma»
will have more and more sway.'

Growing up made one knowledgeable so I knew she was referring to Sir John Conroy.

I was very melancholy. Life could become sad so unexpectedly.
First I had lost my beloved sister and now—devastating blow—my
dear, dear Uncle Leopold.

I was becoming more and more aware of Sir John Conroy.

Now that Uncle Leopold had gone Mama seemed constantly in
his company. My Aunt Sophia often came from her apartments in
the Palace to ours, and she, too, seemed to like him very much.
They were always laughing together and Mama seemed quite different when he was there; her expression softened and her voice
changed when she spoke to him.

When I mentioned this to Lehzen she said sharply: 'Nonsense!'

I wished that Feodore was there so that I could talk about it with
her.

I had always found it difficult to veil my feelings and while I was
perhaps overflowing with affection for those I liked and was—Mama
said—too demonstrative, when I disliked people I could not help
showing that either.

I must have shown that I did not like Sir John.

I knew that Lehzen and Spath also did not like him. He used to
look at them very sardonically, with a rather unpleasant expression

in his eyes. I heard him speak of them both quite disparagingly to Mama when I was present. He said Spath was a silly blundering old woman, and he sneered at Lehzen's plebeian habit of munching caraway seeds. What shocked me was that Mama laughed with him, which I thought was disloyal to dear Lehzen who had been such a good friend to us both.

Sir John was a man who had a very high opinion of himself. I found out quite a lot about him because since the departure of Uncle Leopold he seemed to be forcing himself on my attention. He had abandoned his career in the Army to enter my father's service. He was half Irish and had an estate in Ireland which brought him a small income. He was an adventurer really; and had a swaggering way with him and seemed very confident that people—particularly women—were going to find him irresistible. He might have had some cause for this because Mama did seem to like him very much, and so did Aunt Sophia and several women of the household. I did not dislike Lady Conroy, but she was so insignificant that one hardly noticed her. His daughter Victoire gave herself airs and was certainly not my favourite companion. I felt I had continually to remind the Conroys that *I* did not regard them as of any great importance.

Victoire in particular was constantly referring to her father as though he were the head of the household. 'My father says this . . .' 'My father says that . . .' And she behaved as though these pronouncements were law.

It was through her that I learned of the sneering remarks he made about my father's relations.

The King was mad, said Victoire to me; and she referred to Aunt Adelaide as 'Her Spotted Majesty' which was because Aunt Adelaide's skin was not very clear and there were sometimes blotches on it—a remark which must have come from her father because it was just the spiteful sort of thing he would say. She also told me that Aunt Adelaide wanted me to marry one of those horrid little Georges, and that her father was going to see that *that* never happened.

Victoire was always talking about the *Bâtards* who were trying to get all they could out of the King. She meant the FitzClarence children. She said it was disgraceful that they were allowed to come to Court, and her father had said that I should be forbidden to mingle with them.

It was infuriating to be told these things through Victoire and when I said this to Mama all she said was: 'Oh, she is only a child and *you* should control your temper.'

I mentioned it to Lehzen, too. She was very distressed and poor old Späth said: 'I don't know what things are coming to in this household. Now that the good King of the Belgians is no longer with us, things have changed for the worse.'

It was not only my relations whom Sir John sneered at. He made fun of me because he knew I did not like him.

'And how are the little dollies?' he would say, and there was a snigger in his voice as though he were implying what a child I was to be playing with dolls at my age. One could not explain to such a man that they were not ordinary dolls.

Then he would make fun of me. 'You are getting more and more like the Duke of Gloucester every day.'

The Duke of Gloucester, who had married my Aunt Mary, was the most unprepossessing of men, and he was commonly known as Silly Billy because he was not very bright.

He could have reduced me to tears if he had not made me so very angry.

But these were small irritations and I was to learn what real trouble this man could make.

One day when I was to present myself to Mama I went to her apartments. Späth was with me, but I ran on ahead.

When I entered the room Sir John Conroy was with Mama and they were talking together. I heard the words . . . 'A Regency . . . for the old man cannot live till she is of age . . .'

My mother was standing very close to Sir John and he was holding her hand.

I heard him say: 'What a beautiful Regent you will make!'

I gasped because I thought he was going to kiss her.

Mama saw me then. Späth had come in and was hovering behind me.

Mama's colour was very high and her earrings shook angrily. She seemed to quiver more than usual.

'Victoria,' she said in an angry voice, 'what are you doing here?'

'Mama, it is my time for coming to you.'

'Dear me! You should not walk about so stealthily.'

I was often accused of boisterousness. This was something new. I felt very uneasy.

'Well, now you are here . . .'

'I see the Princess is not unaccompanied,' said Sir John in his sneering voice.

My mother frowned. 'Oh . . . Spath . . .' The very way in which she said the poor Baroness's name was contemptuous. 'It's you. Well, you will not be needed.'

Poor Spath, scarlet with embarrassment, faded away and I was left with them. Mama seemed in an odd mood but Sir John was just the same as he always was, very composed, regarding me with that unpleasantly critical look as though I amused him because of some deficiency. I began to wonder whether I was getting too fat, as he was always hinting that I was.

When I saw Spath shortly afterwards she seemed in a state of shock. I wanted to hear what she thought of the incident, for I could not get it out of my mind.

'Spath,' I said. 'Did you think Mama was standing very close to Sir John Conroy?'

Spath looked at me with wide troubled eyes and as she did not reply I went on: 'It did occur to me that he was on the point of kissing her.'

Spath caught her breath and still continued to look at me in silence.

'I think perhaps,' I went on, 'Mama did not like our being there and seeing them er . . . like that, because she immediately began scolding me, which people do sometimes when they are doing something about which they feel uncomfortable.'

Spath took a few more seconds to recover.

'My dear Princess, you must say nothing of this . . . of course that was not the case. The Duchess was no doubt asking his advice . . . about some . . . er . . . document . . . some matter . . . and it was necessary for her to stand close to him to show it to him.'

'I saw no document,' I said. 'It was her hand he was holding . . . not a document.'

'Oh, you have been mistaken and I should say no more of this . . . not to anyone.'

I was very disturbed and that made me more alert. Poor Spath became so absent-minded that I knew she could not forget it either. I heard her whispering with Lehzen. I could not hear what was said but I knew from Lehzen's manner that she was giving Spath stern advice.

Aunt Sophia was having a little party in her rooms at Kensington Palace. There would be music and my two cousins George Cambridge and George Cumberland would be there, and so would Aunt Adelaide.

Aunt Adelaide, now Queen Adelaide, had come to ask Mama's permission for me to attend.

'Victoria sings so prettily,' said Aunt Adelaide. 'We do want her to come.'

Mama graciously said I might go.

Mama never treated Aunt Adelaide as though she were the Queen. Indeed seeing them together one would have thought that Mama was of superior rank. Some might have resented that; Aunt Adelaide did not. She was all for peace and for overcoming family quarrels and getting us all together. I often thought that if they had all been like her we should have been a happier family.

I practised singing with Mr. Sale all the morning; Lehzen had said other lessons might be set aside for once; and Mr. Sale said I was in good voice and was sure they would all enjoy my singing.

Lehzen helped me dress in my lovely white silk dress with the blue sash and white satin slippers.

'Lehzen,' I said, 'do I look too fat?'

'You look lovely.'

'But fat! Sir John said I was a plump little princess.'

'That man! If you are plump, my dearest, then it is good to be plump. They will all think how beautiful you are and when they hear you sing . . . well, they will be astounded.'

'Oh, Lehzen, you are the dearest person in the world.'

'Now, now. Stay calm. Remember you have to give a performance.'

What a pleasant afternoon! I did like my two cousins, they were both very attentive, and after my performance, which was very much applauded, Aunt Adelaide kissed me and said I sang like an angel. She also whispered how delighted she was that I had come and that the King wanted me to go and see him; and she was sure, if my Mama would allow it, there could be many happy gatherings like this with all the children.

I supposed that meant the little FitzClarences. I was sure Mama would not allow that; and it struck me as strange that a queen could love little children whereas a mere duchess thought herself too good for them.

I said: 'I should love to come and to see the King.'

She smiled as though we shared a secret and said she would do her best to arrange it.

When I arrived back in our apartments it was to find Lehzen distraught and Spath almost hysterical with grief.

'What has happened?' I cried.

Spath could not speak but Lehzen came to me and put her arms round me.

'The Baroness is to leave us,' she said.

'To leave us!'

'Yes, she is going to your sister. Feodore needs her now that she is a mother. The Duchess thinks that Feodore needs her more than you do.'

'But I can't lose Spath.'

Spath emerged from her grief to give me a loving look. I dashed to her: 'Oh dear, dear Spath . . . what does it mean? I will go to Mama . . . I will not have it. I am going to the Queen. I will not have it, Spath.'

Lehzen said quickly, 'You must not talk like that. It is unseemly to talk of seeing the Queen. Neither the King nor the Queen would like it. It is very wrong. Baroness Spath is going, and sad as that makes us, we must think of the joy your sister will have in welcoming her. She needs help with her babies.'

'I am sure Feodore could find someone to help her with the babies and she would not want me to lose dear Spath. I will go to Mama.'

'It is already settled. Your mother and . . . er . . . Sir John have decided.'

'That *odious man.*'

Neither Lehzen nor Spath contradicted me. They hated him as much as I did.

I embraced Spath and we clung together, mingling our tears. I knew, and she knew, that there was nothing we could do.

One day, I told myself, it will be different.

There was gloom in our apartments. Mama pursed her lips and when I spoke of Spath, said she was an interfering gossiping old woman and she was not really suitable to be in the household.

'But I love her,' I said defiantly.

'You must not be so vehement,' said Mama. 'You are a little vulgar in your expressions of affection for these people.'

'These people! We are talking about darling Spath.'

'Oh dear, we are going to have a storm, are we? Listen to me, Victoria. I have done everything possible to bring you up in a manner befitting your position. You know now that you have to be careful . . . far more careful than others. You have your destiny to fulfil. That is why I have devoted my life to bringing you up.'

It is always disconcerting to be the object of so much self-sacrifice and I could not deny that Mama had taken great pains to be with me all the time. Often I had wished she was less zealous; but that did not lessen the sacrifices she had made.

I could see I was no match for her so I continued to brood in silence.

Lehzen was worried. I know now that she was thinking: It is Späth today. It could be me tomorrow.

It was a good thing that I did not know that then. I should have been completely terrified if I had. The thought of losing Lehzen too would have been intolerable.

It was from Späth that I heard more of what had happened. I supposed that when she had her marching orders she felt justified in being indiscreet.

'What started it,' she told me, 'was due to that daughter of his.'

'Victoire?'

'Oh, I could do without those two . . . her and her sister Jane.'

She lapsed into German which I understood well enough. Victoire had come to her while she was sitting at her tatting just after I had left for Aunt Sophia's apartments.

Victoire had taunted her. She wanted to know why she, Victoire, had not been invited to sing at the party. Why should Victoria go and she not? It was not fair. Her father was important. He was the most important man in the country. Everybody knew it. He gave the orders.

'It was more than I could bear,' said Späth. "I shouted at her: "You ill-bred monster. You have no right here, you and your upstart father . . ." She called me an old German woman and said I was a silly old fool, I . . . and caraway-seed-eating Baroness Lehzen, who had only been made a baroness because she had to mingle with people of high rank where she could not very well be a mere *Fraulein*.'

'Victoire can be a horrid child,' I said.

'Well, my Princess, I could bear no more, so I went to the Duchess. I was not thinking very clearly. I was so enraged. I said, "That Conroy child has been rude to me . . ." And your mother shrugged it aside and said she was only a child. I then lost my calm.'

'Dear Späth,' I said, 'you never had much.'

'I said what I should not have said.'

'What, Späth? Tell me what.'

She shook her head and it took me a little time to prise it out of her.

'I said, "And that man, Duchess. The Princess Victoria has noticed . . . the friendship between you and him . . ." '

'You really said that, Spath?'

Spath nodded.

Oh, it was clear to me now, Mama was guilty. Those flirtatious looks which Sir John bestowed on her and on others too . . . Aunt Sophia for one . . . but more on Mama . . . had a meaning. I felt horribly disillusioned.

I tried to comfort poor Spath. I told her that she would love being with Feodore.

'Feodore is the most loving girl in the world. Dear Spath, she is better than I . . .'

'No one could mean more to me than my dear little Victoria.'

'Oh, Spath, you will love it! There won't be any storms . . . and you know how quickly they blow up. No storms and dear little babies. You know how you love them. And Feodore's will be especially lovely. Oh, you are going to love it. You're going to say it is all for the best. I have got away from the storms to these dear little babies.'

She shook her head. 'My darling child, I know you can be wilful . . . but then you can also be the most lovable little girl in the world, and I would rather serve you than any other.'

I wept with her and Lehzen came and found us together. She did not reprove us. She just sat with us, looking very sad. I had lost Feodore, Uncle Leopold and now Spath.

Fearfully I wondered: Who next?

My feelings towards Mama were changing rapidly. It was all because of Sir John Conroy. I disliked him more with every day which passed; and I blamed him for taking Spath away from me.

Instinctively I knew that he wanted to remove Lehzen in the same way. But that was something which I should never tolerate.

I began to see very clearly what was going on. Mama was one of those forceful women who want to rule everyone about her. How delighted she would have been if *she* had been destined to become Queen. In fact if ever I ascended the throne she wanted to be there, not beside me, but ruling in my place.

And with her would be that odious man. *They* would be King and Queen; they would rule the country as they now ruled the household.

Mama was always talking disparagingly about the King. What an old fool he was; he was doubtless going mad; anyone less like a king she had never known. He went among the people like a common man. Some might be able to behave so. Not bumble-headed William. He looked what he was, a foolish old man teetering on the edge of madness. He had even said on one occasion that he and his wife were quiet people. The Queen and he liked to sit by the fire, she tatting and he 'nodding a bit'. If he got bees in his bonnet he would forget all dignity and make speeches about them—incoherent, rambling, boring speeches. That was her opinion of him. She even spoke kindly of Aunt Adelaide in her condemnation of him. 'Poor thing, she has a lot to put up with. The best thing he can do is join his forefathers and leave the throne for those better able to manage it.'

That meant Victoria, of course, with Mama in control!

And in control she would be if I were not eighteen years old. When I reached that magic age I could tell Mama No! You will not do this and that, because it is my wish that you should not. What a day that would be!

Mama was so exuberant now that she talked to me more openly.

'There will be a Regency,' she said. 'That is if he dies before you are eighteen. You are not quite twelve yet. Six years. He can't last that long.'

I hated to hear her talk like that of poor Uncle William who had always been so pleasant to me; and I loved Aunt Adelaide who, I was sure, would be very unhappy if Uncle William died.

And I thought: A Regency! Mama as Regent! Oh no! Please God don't let Uncle William die until I am eighteen.

I thought I should never get over my sadness at losing Späth, but a greater catastrophe threatened. They were going to send Lehzen away.

I think they both realized that they would have to tread more warily over Lehzen. I had loved Späth but Lehzen was very special to me. She was, I had often said, the best friend I had ever had up to that time—and I meant it. If I faced any difficulties it had always been to Lehzen I had gone; and she had smoothed them out. She had been something of a disciplinarian, of course, but I think I needed that and I respected her for it. It gave me a sense of security. I could not really imagine my life without Lehzen, and as soon as I realized what was going on I became very determined to stop it.

I heard Aunt Adelaide say to Mama: 'But you couldn't. It would kill poor Lehzen. Victoria is her life.'

They stopped talking when I came in—but I knew.

They shall never do it, I said to myself firmly.

I was growing up. I was destined to be the Queen; they must realize that they had to go very carefully with me.

Mama said to me one day: 'Dear Feodore, she is so happy. Two little babies. What a joy. She needs a very good governess for them.'

I was alert. I said quickly: 'I am sure she and the Count will find an excellent governess.'

'There is one Feodore would rather have than any other.'

I waited. Now it was coming.

'Who is that?' I asked in a cold voice.

'Well, there is only one,' replied Mama with a little laugh. 'She is a very good governess, and now you are beginning to grow up, you need a different sort of tuition. Feodore would be delighted and so would dear Lehzen. She would be so good for the children.'

I said very firmly: 'Mama, *I* could not do without Lehzen.'

Sir John had come in and I knew that they had discussed this together, arranging it, and he had come to add his voice to my mother's; that enraged me.

My mother laughed. 'Oh, come, come. She was very useful to you when you were young, and I know how fond you are of her.'

'You do not know how fond I am of her, Mama,' I said. 'She is the best friend I ever had.'

'My dear child, you have many friends and you will have many more.'

'There will never be one like Lehzen,' I said.

Mama laughed again. 'Dear me, you are so vehement.'

'Yes, Mama,' I said. 'Vehement and determined.'

Sir John said with an unpleasant sneering laugh: 'Oh, here is the Queen herself.'

'I am not the Queen . . . yet, Sir John,' I retorted. 'But I will not allow you to send Lehzen away.'

'*You* will not allow it,' said Mama.

'That is what I said, Mama. *I* will not.'

'You are only a child.'

'I am old enough . . . and I am getting older every day.'

'A profound statement,' sneered Sir John, 'and one with which we must all agree.'

'If you attempt to send Lehzen away,' I told them, 'I shall go to the King and ask him to forbid it.'

'That pineapple-headed old bore,' said Mama contemptuously.

'The King, Mama, whom I respect more than some.' I looked

venomously at Sir John. 'I am his subject and so are you . . . both of you. It would be well for us all to remember that.'

They stared at me in amazement and I could see that Mama was trying to reduce me to the child I once was. But I had acquired a new dignity since seeing that table in the history book. I was going to be the Queen, and as heir to the throne these two took their importance through me. But for me what would they be? I was young, it was true; but this was a matter of vital importance to me. I was learning to rule.

I could see that I was making some impression for they were both startled, and yes, I was sure they were a little alarmed.

'Oh,' said Mama, 'I see we are in for a little storm.'

'Not a little storm, Mama,' I corrected her. 'A big one. Lehzen is not going to leave me.'

'You are arrogant . . . conceited . . .' spluttered Mama, her earrings shaking with the rage she felt.

'I am the heir to the throne,' I said. 'I may be Queen very soon, though I hope Uncle William will live for a long time yet. But for now I say this: Lehzen is staying with me. I know the King will forbid you to send her away, and whatever you say about him he is the King and it would be well for us all to remember that we are his subjects.'

With that I walked out of the room. I was trembling with fear.

They were absolutely startled by my firmness—and so was I. But they knew they were defeated; and there was no doubt of it because there was no more mention of Lehzen's leaving.

I had scored a victory, but that did not mean that I had changed anything very much. Mama was still in command and although she realized that I could be what she called stubborn on matters over which I felt deeply, I was still the child as far as she was concerned.

Aunt Adelaide, who was a mediator between my mother and the King, intimated that, now I was recognized as next in the succession, I should appear more in public. Mama agreed with this.

Aunt Adelaide was doing everything she could to bring about a reconciliation between the King and my mother; and I have to say that it was Mama's fault that it was without success. That the King disliked her there could be no doubt, but if she had not continually asserted what she called her rights and attempted to push me forward and to behave generally as though Uncle William was already as good as dead and I on the throne, I think there might have been, if not a friendship, a fairly reasonable compromise between them. But she would not.

I was not so much invited to Court as summoned to Aunt Adelaide's birthday party celebration. I wanted to go. I loved such occasions. I was quite intrigued by the two Georges and they were very attentive to me on the rare occasions when I had met them; and there was dancing, singing and playing games which I very much enjoyed. Aunt Adelaide did everything possible to make all the young people happy, so I could have been very amused if I had been allowed to be.

That occasion was a failure. I should have thought that after my victory over Lehzen I should have been able to shake off Mama's influence, but this was not so and there were times when I felt completely overawed.

I was very apprehensive when I considered the way in which Sir John and my mother had managed to get rid of poor Spath and the attempts they had made to do the same to Lehzen. I was really worried and sometimes I felt very young and inadequate.

On the occasion of Aunt Adelaide's birthday there was a certain formality, which even the King could not escape, although, as my mother said, never had a king behaved with less majesty. This was true in a way. The King would go about and talk to his most humble subjects and when after a visit his guests left he would go down to see them off and help them into their carriages and then stand waving them off—which no king had surely ever done before. He was a bluff sailor, and he was not going to change his ways just because he was a king.

Before we set out Mama continued to lecture me. 'The King will try to keep you down. You must be sure that you are in your rightful place. It would never do for the people to forget that you are the rightful heir to the throne. You must not be too effusive. You always are. You must not look as though you think it is a great honour to be presented to the King. It is as much an honour for *him* that *I* allow you to go. Do not smile on all and sundry. Show them you are serious . . . aware of your rank . . .'

And so it was that whenever the King looked my way I cast down my eyes because I was afraid that I should smile in too friendly a way, and yet if I did not smile it looked as though I were sulking.

I was glad when it was over.

But my demeanour was noticed. Aunt Adelaide looked bewildered and unhappy; and the King scowled.

I heard that he had been very angry and had said: 'That child would not look at me. I will not have it. She is getting like her mother.'

That amused my mother and she told me I had behaved with dignity. I was less pleased and very sorry that I had hurt the King and Aunt Adelaide.

My mother said I should travel a little to show myself to the people, and let them become acquainted with their Queen-to-be.

I loved the excitement of travel. I enjoyed seeing new places. Sir John Conroy and Mama planned the journeys, where we should stay and when we should meet the people. We were greeted with enthusiasm wherever we went and that was very pleasant. But it was always Mama who spoke to the crowds, who took the front seat. She brought me forward sometimes, and told them how she had devoted her life to me ever since I had been born.

There was one thing which worried me very much and that was that wherever we went, Sir John ordered the guns to fire the royal salute.

I said to Lehzen: 'I thought that was done only for sovereigns.'

Lehzen shook her head. She had not fully recovered from the scare we had had when we thought that Sir John and my mother might succeed in getting her sent away. She was more reticent than usual, but I knew she agreed with me and that it was not correct to insist on the royal salute.

I heard the King was very annoyed when he discovered what was happening. 'Guns popping here, there and everywhere,' he said. 'There's to be an end to this popping and pretty sharp.'

Sir John's reply was that as Victoria was heiress to the throne, the firing of the guns was in order. He was getting reckless, I believe. He thought the King's end was near; and he saw me on the throne with Mama as Regent and himself governing Mama.

How people love power! A little while ago my life seemed to be in danger because Cumberland wanted me out of the way and a clear run for himself; now Sir John was taking risks, for after all Uncle William was the King, and Sir John was causing him great offence. In fact he was always urging Mama to further reckless-ness—not that she needed much urging.

We were at Norris Castle in the Isle of Wight. The guns had been popping away in Portsmouth in my honour, when a summons came from my mother to attend the King's coronation.

'You,' said Mama, 'will walk immediately behind the King. As heir to the throne that is your place.'

But it seemed the King had other ideas. Further news came from Windsor. I was assigned a place behind the royal dukes.

'Never!' cried Mama.

'Certainly not!' echoed Sir John. 'We must have our little girl where she belongs.'

I talked it over with Lehzen. 'But what difference does it make where I am. I shall be there . . . and walking behind the uncles doesn't make me any less heir to the throne.'

Lehzen said it seemed of great importance to the Duchess that I should walk immediately behind the King.

'He will be very angry,' I said anxiously. 'He is already cross because I didn't smile at him when I last saw him. Oh, Lehzen, I wanted to. I like him and I love Aunt Adelaide. But . . . it is so difficult.'

'Life often is, my dear,' said Lehzen.

The wrangle went on. 'No,' said the King. 'Behind the royal dukes.'

I believed that he did not greatly care where I walked but he did dislike Mama so much that he would not give way to her.

'In her rightful place or not at all,' said Mama.

And so it was not at all.

I wept with frustration. I had wanted so much to go to the Coronation; and most of all I hated quarrels.

I watched the Coronation procession from Marlborough House.

Soon after the Coronation there was a great deal of controversy throughout the country because of the Reform Bill.

Lehzen was well informed and explained to me what it was all about.

'The trouble started,' she said, 'because there are what are called Rotten Boroughs, which means that there are under two thousand people there who are able to send a member to Parliament to represent them, while on the other hand there are others who have only one member for a very large population. And some people don't get a vote at all.'

'That seems very wrong,' I said.

'You are in agreement with a large number of people, it would seem,' said Lehzen.

There was so much personal intrigue in our apartments with the machinations of Conroy and his schemes with Mama, which were all about their own gains really, that not much attention was paid to what was going on in the country.

I knew it was very serious and I became quite worried when I heard that violent rioting had broken out all over the country.

When we went for our walks I saw placards on the walls: 'Give us Our Rights'.

Lehzen said: 'The people believe that once the Bill is passed all their dreams will come true.'

'Everybody will have Everything', I saw on another poster.

I did not see how that could be.

'When the people become obsessed by an idea they will make the wildest claims. They believe everything that is told them,' said Lehzen.

'I never would,' I asserted.

'Of course not. You have been well brought up. I have taught you to think for yourself . . . to face the truth, however unpleasant.'

'It will be unpleasant for the people if this Bill is passed and they find they have not everything.'

'They will learn,' said Lehzen. 'I heard one of the serving maids say that when the Bill was passed, her Fred would marry her and they would have a little house in the country.'

'Oh dear!' I sighed. 'How disappointed she will be!'

'And children believe that there will be no more school when the Bill is passed. It will be all picnics and strawberry jam.'

'Is that why they are rioting?'

'They are rioting because, although the Bill has been passed by the Commons, the Lords have thrown it out, and Lord Grey has asked the King to create new peers so that the Bill can be passed.'

'But I don't understand, Lehzen. If when something is refused and new people have to be brought in to pass it . . . why has it to be passed in the first place?'

'Ah, my dearest, you are getting into deep waters. The King has refused Grey's request so he has resigned and the King has no alternative but to call Wellington back to office. Wellington's windows at Apsley House have been smashed. They say Wellington is the most unpopular man in the country.'

'How long is it since he was the most *popular* after Waterloo?'

'There! You see how the pendulum swings. The most popular man one day, the most unpopular the next.'

'Like Palm Sunday and the Crucifixion.'

'Yes . . . like that.'

I thought a great deal about the Reform Bill. It was quite wrong that those few people should send one man to represent them in Parliament, and thousands of others only have one—and some no

chance to vote at all. Of course quite a lot of them were without
education and knew nothing of what they were voting for. They
could not write their names even . . . let alone vote. It all seemed
very complicated. But I did hate to hear of the riots. They always
frightened me because I had heard a great deal about the French
Revolution and in my lessons I had suffered with poor Marie Antoinette and King Louis XVI who had been so badly treated by the
mob and had even lost their heads in a most humiliating manner.

I was relieved when Wellington was able to form a Ministry and
Lord Grey was brought back. The new peers were created and the
Reform Bill was passed. Seats in Parliament were to be more fairly
distributed in accordance with the number of people in the boroughs.

Peace settled over the country.

But when I thought of how Wellington had lost the admiration
and love of the people, I was depressed by their fickleness, for
whatever were his personal views about reform, he had saved the
country from Napoleon at Waterloo. The thought of angry mobs
throwing stones at Apsley House made me very sad.

I was becoming more and more aware of the responsibilities I
should have to face if that destiny which my mother was determined
should be mine—and indeed was mine by right of birth—should
ever come to pass.

The Coronation of King William did not curb my mother's inclination to show me to the people and to receive the honours due to
my rank. In August we left Kensington for Wales. Before we went
Mama presented me with a Journal in which she said I was to write
every day. That was when I first discovered the joy of writing down
my thoughts, but, of course, I was fully aware that every word I
wrote would be read by Mama. Therefore I was most cautious. I
could not set down my enthusiasms—except of course for such
things as the countryside and what would please her; I could not
record my deep dislike and suspicion of Sir John. I couldn't help
laughing to imagine what the outcome would be if I did! So although I dutifully wrote in my Journal every day, I did not, of
course, mention my secret thoughts. And Mama was very pleased
because it must have seemed to her that I was much more innocent
than I actually was—and therefore, I supposed, more malleable.

After leaving London we went to Birmingham, Wolverhampton
and Shrewsbury, and over the Menai Bridge. We rented a house
for a month in Beaumaris; and I presented the prizes at the Eis-

teddfod. While we were there there was an outbreak of cholera and it was hastily decided that we move on.

We visited so many places that I am afraid, looking back, I confuse one with another; but I do remember staying at Chatsworth and visiting some cotton mills at Belper.

And I remember Oxford because Sir John Conroy was actually made a Doctor of Civil Law there and received the Freedom of the City which irritated me considerably—but not so much as my visit to the Bodleian Library where some gentleman very proudly produced Queen Elizabeth's Latin Exercise Book. I glanced at it and saw at once that her grasp of the language quite outdid mine. There were gasps of amazement that one so young could have been so proficient.

'And she was only thirteen years old!' demanded Mama, looking sternly at me, for that was my age.

'That is all she was, Your Grace, when she used that exercise book. It is one of our most treasured possessions.'

'*She* was a very clever girl.'

'I doubt there has ever been one to excel her,' said the old man.

Queen Elizabeth! I seemed to be haunted by her, for there had been a time when some Member of Parliament had suggested that I change my name to Elizabeth. They had wanted me to be Elizabeth II. That, they said, would be a good omen, in view of the outstanding abilities of the first Elizabeth, and the benefits which had come to the country throughout her glorious reign.

Yes that and Sir John's complacency over his advancement, which I should have stopped had I been able, spoilt Oxford for me.

Mama was always to the fore on these occasions, speaking to the people as though she were the Queen. I wondered what the King would have said if he could see her, and I had no doubt that there would be some to carry reports of her unseemly conduct to him.

So it was rather pleasant to go back to Kensington.

I had passed into a new phase. They were all realizing that now I was in my teens I was no longer a child.

Mama had introduced a new lady into her household. This was Lady Flora, a daughter of the Marquess of Hastings. Mama said she would be a friend for me, but as she was about twelve years older than I was, and she and Lehzen took an instant dislike to each other, our friendship did not progress very fast. I was beginning to feel that I wanted to choose my own friends.

There were many visitors to Kensington Palace now. I think that was because I was growing up; and although Mama was very anxious to keep me segregated from the royal family, she welcomed distinguished people at the Palace. I remember how awestruck I was to be presented to Sir Robert Peel—a man of whom Lehzen had talked a great deal. He was very pleasant. Lord Palmerston came with him. *He* talked to me earnestly as though I were quite grown up and at the same time gave me the impression that he thought I was pretty; and I had to admit that I was quite amused and rather delighted by that.

I was sure I was going to like meeting important people.

I even softened a little towards Sir John. Mama liked dogs and he gave her the sweetest little King Charles spaniel I ever saw. I loved him on the spot and was sure he felt the same about me. He came to me at once and lifted his beautiful eyes to my face.

I cried: 'He is lovely! Whose is he?'

Mama said: 'He is mine. His name is Dash. Sir John has just given him to me.'

Even that could not alter my feeling for Dash. I even looked forward to going to my mother's rooms so that I could see him. Mama had two birds—a most delightful parakeet and a canary who used to come out of his cage and fly about the room. One could never be sure when he would descend on one's head. But it was little Dash whom I loved.

One day Mama said to me: 'I think Dash is really *your* dog.'

'He is a darling.'

'I think you two liked each other on sight. Sir John says I should give him to you.'

'Did he?' I cried, flushing with pleasure.

Sir John came into the room. I always had the feeling that they discussed together what they were going to say to me. It was rather like a play with one of them waiting in the wings for their cue.

'I know how you love him,' said Sir John, giving me one of his odious smiles.

But of course I loved Dash, and I did want him for my very own.

'I do love him,' I said.

'Well then . . . he is yours.'

I took him up in my arms. He knew, the little darling, for he started to lick my face.

'No, Dashie,' I said gleefully; and he barked happily.

'Oh, thank you, Mama,' I said.

'I am sure you are very grateful to Sir John for such a gift.'

'Thank you, Sir John,' I said, a little grudgingly, I'm afraid. 'May I take Dash now?'

'But of course,' said Mama smiling graciously. 'I will have his basket sent along to you.'

So I went, so happy to have Dash. But I did not like Sir John any more for all that.

I was very happy. Dash made such a difference. I bathed him; I tied a ribbon round his neck, and told him over and over again that he was mine now.

Dash was not the only great pleasure I had that year. My music master thought that as I had shown such an interest in singing, and was something of a performer myself, I might be taken to the opera.

Oh, the joy of hearing beautiful music exquisitely sung! I was in transports of delight. I wrote about it in the Journal Mama had given me more naturally than I had written of anything before. Here was something which gave me profound pleasure. Mama was quite pleased by my enthusiasm for once. She said that if I behaved with decorum she saw no reason why there should not be frequent visits to the opera.

I was amazed to hear from Uncle Leopold that he intended to be married. He wrote me long letters about it. It was so many years since Charlotte had died and he had mostly spent them mourning for her. Now he had decided that he would be lonely no longer.

Of course I wanted to hear all about her for I did not believe anyone could be worthy of Uncle Leopold.

He wrote back:

'My dearest Love,
    'You have told me you wish to have a description of your new Aunt. She is extremely gentle and amiable and her actions are always guided by principles. She is at all times ready and disposed to sacrifice her comfort and inclinations to see others happy. She values goodness, merit and virtue much more than beauty, riches and amusement . . .
    'Now to her appearance. She is about Feodore's height; her hair is very fair, light blue eyes and a very gentle expression . . .
    'You will see by these descriptions that though my good little wife is not the tallest of queens, she is a great prize which I highly value and cherish.'

I was so delighted for Uncle Leopold. For in addition to all her beauty and virtue, Louise of Orlèans was very highly born, being the daughter of Louis Philippe, King of France. It seemed that Leopold's marriage must be perfect.

I hoped it would not prevent his writing to me as frequently as he had in the past, and when I expressed this fear to him he assured me that it would not. He stressed that my welfare was as dear to his heart as it had ever been, and if I were faced with any problems I must write to him and he would give all his thoughts to solving them. I was his dearest love, his darling child. Nothing could change that.

It was a great comfort to think of Uncle Leopold—though across the sea—always ready to listen to me as he had done when I was close at hand.

My fourteenth birthday was approaching. I really was growing up; but I was still four years from the magical eighteen.

I was so happy when Aunt Adelaide said she would give a ball for me. It was to be a juvenile ball for young people all around my age.

Mama could hardly insist that I decline the invitation to my own ball, and if she had attempted to I should have raised a storm. Fortunately I did not have to.

I awoke early on the morning and felt irritated because I could see Mama's bed and the hump in it which showed me she was still there. Really, it was ridiculous. A girl of fourteen to have to sleep in her mother's bedroom! Uncle Cumberland could not possibly harm me now. What did she imagine he would do? Send in his servants to smother me like the Princes in the Tower?

It was a lovely morning. I could see Dash at the foot of my bed. Spring is so beautiful and I could hear the birds singing in the gardens, and I knew the trees would be sprouting with green buds and the colours of the spring flowers would be so fresh and lovely. May was a good month in which to be born.

And today was the day of the juvenile ball.

The present-giving was a very happy part of a day like this. Mama was very good with presents. She did give the most delightful ones. There was a bag she had worked herself, a bracelet of topaz and turquoise, handkerchiefs and books; and from Lehzen there was an exquisite china basket and a dainty figure in china too. They were lovely. The only jarring note was the presence of the Conroys who behaved as though they were members of the family. All the five Conroy children were there—Victoire, Jane and the three boys. They gave me a watch chain between them. From the

odious Sir John there was something which I could not help loving
in spite of its donor. It was a beautiful painting of Dash—so lifelike
that it seemed as though he was going to dart out of the frame into
my arms.

I could not help exclaiming with delight. Mama looked very
pleased and the moment was spoilt because I detected one of those
glances passing between her and Sir John—those intimate secret
looks which I hated.

Sir John went with us to St. James's although he had not been
invited. He certainly did behave like a member of the family.

I was determined to show Uncle William how sorry I was for the
uneasy atmosphere between our two households, and make him
understand that it was not of my making. So I was delighted when
the Queen took me into his closet to greet him. Aunt Adelaide must
have guessed my thoughts. She was such a dear understanding lady,
and so eager that everyone should be happy and forget this bickering.

I was wearing the earrings which the King had given me and
when I approached him I put my arms round his neck and kissed
him.

I said: 'I am so glad to see you like this . . . privately, dear
Uncle William. It is so much easier to say Thank You for my lovely
earrings.'

He was warm and loving immediately. He did not mean to quarrel with me—only with Mama. He was really quite a cosy old
gentleman and very sentimental. I saw the tears in his eyes which
was quite affecting.

'So you liked them, eh?' he said.

'They are lovely.'

'And your Aunt Adelaide's brooch? What about that?'

'Lovely too. I am lucky to have such a kind uncle and aunt.'

He patted my arm. 'Good girl,' he said. 'Nice girl. You're right,
Adelaide. She's too good for that lot, eh?'

I could see that the thought of my mother and Sir John made him
angry. Adelaide said quickly: 'This is going to be a very happy
evening. It was a good idea, don't you think, a juvenile ball?'

I said it was the nicest possible idea and Aunt Adelaide always
had nice ideas.

That pleased Uncle William because he liked to hear the Queen
praised.

'You are to open the ball with your cousin George.'

I knew she meant George Cambridge. The King and Queen were

very fond of him, perhaps because he lived with them while his parents were out of the country. I had heard Mama say that they looked upon him as the son they couldn't get and that they had plans for him.

I knew what *that* meant . . . plans for marrying *me*. They wanted him to be Prince Consort. I did not think he could be King.

Mama said smugly: 'They will have a nasty shock.'

In any case I was too happy to worry on that night about remote possibilities; and I prepared to enjoy the dance with George Cambridge.

I liked him very well. He was a charming boy and danced with grace. He told me I did too and he said it was a pity I did not come often to Aunt Adelaide's gatherings for the young. He also said I was pretty, which I liked to hear as often as possible because I had certain doubts about the matter myself. I was too plump for one thing. So it was always pleasant to hear compliments.

He told me that poor George Cumberland was going blind and his parents were very worried about him. I was very concerned for George Cumberland and saddened for a while. I could think of nothing worse than losing one's sight.

It was a pity Madame Bourdin had to be seated there watching every one of my steps to see if they were correct. It made it seem like a lesson; and dancing with George Cambridge I could have felt differently were it not for the presence of my dancing mistress.

The Queen brought several other partners for me and I had the impression that they all felt greatly honoured to dance with me—which made me very amused and happy. She also took me in to supper and I sat between her and the King. I did not look in Mama's direction but I knew she was louring because the King behaved as though she were not there and she thought she should be beside me taking all the honours as she did during our tours.

Toasts were drunk and there were quite a number to me, and the King lifted his glass and looked at me with a smile of affection which I returned. Aunt Adelaide was beaming on the other side of me and I thought how happy we could all be without these family troubles.

When we were driving back to Kensington Palace I knew that Mama was displeased. She said to Sir John: 'It is easy to see what they are planning. And they are going to be disappointed.'

I knew she was referring to George Cambridge opening the ball with me. But I was too happy to care.

When I awoke next morning, I wrote in my Journal: 'I was dancing at midnight. I was so amused.'

It was a few days later when Mama told me that some cousins would be visiting us from Germany.

'You will find *them* charming boys,' said Mama, meaning that they would be far more pleasant than George Cambridge. 'Your Uncle Leopold is delighted that they are coming and he says that you should get to know your German cousins.'

'I shall like that, Mama. It is always so interesting to meet cousins.'

'These are your Württemberg cousins. Your Uncle Leopold says that one day you must meet Ernest and Albert of Saxe-Coburg. I do believe they are his special favourites. '

'If they are Uncle Leopold's favourites, I daresay they will be mine.'

Mama smiled, for once pleased with me.

In due course the Württemberg cousins arrived—Ernest and Alexander. I was delighted with them. I liked the way in which they bowed over my hand and clicked their heels as they did so. So German! I thought. So enchanting! They were both tall and handsome and I found it hard to make up my mind which one I liked the better.

When the King and Queen heard that the Württemberg cousins were at Kensington, they decided to give a ball for them. I was very excited.

'You will love it,' I told the cousins. 'Aunt Adelaide gives such wonderful balls.'

Mama grumbled and Sir John went to her apartments, I guessed to discuss the invitation. I was in a state of terror lest she find some excuse for refusing it, which I was sure she wanted to do if she dared.

I could not understand why she should be so anxious to keep our Württemberg relations to ourselves as I was quite proud of them.

Mama went about all that day and the next with tight lips and I thought she was on the point of saying I was to refuse the invitation to the ball, but she did not; and I was greatly relieved when it was time to leave and we set out in the carriage for St. James's. I was determined to enjoy it. To dance would be delightful. There would be George Cambridge as well as the Württembergs—and they would all want to dance with *me*. I should dance till midnight. Nothing could be more exciting than that.

When we arrived, the King, with the Queen beside him, received our guests, and I was kept at their side so that the guests could greet me with them. Mama tried to stand beside me but the King signed to Sir John to move on with her.

I saw Mama's face flush and her earrings quiver; and my heart sank. However we were safely here and nothing could be done about that now.

My feet were twitching with their longing to dance, but the King said to me very kindly: 'I do not see as much of you as I should wish. The Queen wants to arrange some parties for you. There are people you should meet. There's your cousin—young George. He is here all the time. How do you like him, eh?'

I said I liked my cousin George very much.

He went on to tell me what a fine boy he was. 'Just about the same age as you. Good for people of an age to be together.'

I said I was sure it was. The Queen smiled encouragingly at me and said she would be happy to arrange some balls for me because she knew I liked dancing so much—and singing too. I had such a pretty singing voice. We ought to have concerts. She would invite people . . . good singers. She had heard how much I liked the opera.

I spoke of my enthusiasm and they both smiled at me in the most kindly manner.

Then the Queen said: 'I know Victoria is longing to dance. Are you not, my dear?'

'Let her dance with George,' said the King. 'I like to see them dance together.'

Aunt Adelaide took my hand. 'There is George. We will go to him.'

As we moved away Mama swept down on us. I knew by her face that something awful was going to happen.

'I have come to inform Your Majesty that I am leaving with my party. Come, Victoria.'

'But, Mama,' I cried indignantly, 'the dancing is only just starting.'

'Come along,' she replied sternly.

'But the dance is for your guests,' protested Aunt Adelaide.

'My guests are exhausted.'

'They . . . they look very well,' began Aunt Adelaide.

'They have been to a review in the Park this afternoon.'

'But they appear to be . . .'

'Absolutely exhausted. Your Majesty must understand that I cannot allow my guests to overtire themselves.'

'The King will be most annoyed. The ball was expressly in their honour.'

Poor Aunt Adelaide! I was almost as sorry for her as I was for myself. I was furious. I so wanted to dance. But Aunt Adelaide was terribly worried because she was afraid of a scene between the King and my mother. Fortunately he had not noticed what was going on, but I could imagine his fury when he did discover.

Aunt Adelaide was trying to smooth everything over, trying to look as though this were not an unprecedented affront to royal dignity, which it was.

'The Princes must come and stay for a few days at Windsor,' she said.

'Their time is already accounted for,' said Mama coldly.

I saw the Queen flinch, but she said nothing and Mama gripped my hand firmly.

I sat silent, ashamed and angry, as the carriage took us back to Kensington.

The memory of that evening lingered on even through the exciting days which followed. I was more and more enchanted by the cousins, particularly as, when I appeared to pay more attention to one than the other, the other was a little jealous.

There was a wonderful occasion when we went to hear the great Paganini play the violin. He played some variations most wonderfully and I was glad to notice that dear Lehzen, who was with us, enjoyed it thoroughly. Unfortunately Sir John Conroy also accompanied us, but even he could not spoil such a marvellous experience.

Then Mama suggested that as the cousins must see something of the countryside, we should take them for a trip, and we might go to the Isle of Wight. That would have been perfection, but Mama would insist that the royal standard should fly over Norris Castle, and the guns were firing the royal salute, which reminded me of Uncle William and that terribly embarrassing time at the ball.

There was, however, one thing to be grateful for. Sir John and his family did not stay with us at Norris Castle. This was because he owned a small house on the island called Osborne Lodge. It was close to the Castle and, of course, we visited the Conroys there. I thought how pleasant it was—or would have been if they had not been there; and indeed, I preferred it to Norris Castle. It was a blessing—though a small one—that when we were at this castle he was not under the same roof.

What happy days they were! I walked and rode with the cousins and took Dash down to the sea. The little darling loved everything as long as I was there to share it. The cousins played with him and he was quite fond of them. I was sure he preferred Alexander— because I did—although Ernest was very charming. Then there were the occasions when I was presented to the people and they cheered me and the guns fired; and I could see how impressed my cousins were because of my importance and popularity.

Mama watched me closely and told me that I must not become arrogant just because the guns were fired and the royal standard flown: 'They are for the crown, not you, my child.'

I pointed out then that they must be for Uncle William.

At which she said: 'Don't be so trying, Victoria.'

But I liked the truth and could become very obstinate even though I knew it would result in Mama's getting annoyed. She and I were growing farther and farther away from each other. I was seeing her too clearly. I wondered how fond she was of *me*; and whether it was the crown for which she had such overwhelming affection. She always stood forward and in front of me on ceremonial occasions, as though she were the heir to the throne and the one the people wanted to see even though they shouted my name and 'God bless the little Princess.' Of course she liked to hear that because it meant that I was more popular than the King; but all the time she wanted them to cheer *her*. And the fact was that they did not really like her.

They liked me because I was the heir to the throne, destined to be Queen; I was young and innocent and smiled at them, and looked as though I was pleased. Mama always looked haughty, as though they were far beneath her—and naturally they did not like that.

There was one embarrassing incident when I was to open a pier. Mama suddenly decided that I was becoming conceited and must be taught a lesson. I should not open the pier, she said. She would.

I was astounded. It made me very ashamed to have to be present at such times, for there was great consternation when Mama announced to the Mayor and his councillors that I should not be opening the pier and that she would do it instead.

They were so dismayed, they did not know what to say. Then the Mayor stammered that the crowds had come to see the little Princess.

'They may see her,' said Mama, 'but I shall open the pier. Pray proceed with the ceremony.'

Mama was not always very wise. She did not seem to be aware that the people were greatly displeased and they liked her even less after that than they had before.

To make matters worse she, being aware of their disappointment, told them that we could not stay to the luncheon which was to follow the ceremony. We had an engagement elsewhere.

I could imagine the preparations which had gone into the luncheon and the expectations of the people.

Oh yes, Mama could not only be overbearing but foolish; and her behaviour spoilt many days which should have been blissful.

I did not write then of my feelings in my Journal. How could I for Mama to see? I often thought as I wrote laboriously—best handwriting—how much more relieved I should feel if I could only set down what I felt when it was happening. How much better I should have known myself if I could. But I had to remember that Mama and Lehzen read every word I wrote, and that had been Mama's intention when she gave me the Journal. So I wrote an exercise, and only allowed my real feelings true range for enthusiasm over the opera and my pleasure in my cousins' visit—all of which were subjects which would not irritate Mama.

To crown my embarrassment when we returned to Norris Castle there was a letter awaiting Mama from Earl Grey which stated that standards and royal salutes must only be employed when the King or Queen were in residence.

Still smarting from the reception the people had given her at the opening of the pier, Mama was furious.

How sad it was to say goodbye to the cousins. I was almost in tears. So were they.

'Please, please, come and see us again soon,' I begged.

They said they would not be happy until they did.

Mama smiled benignly to see the affection between us, and for once she and I shared the feeling of sorrow because they were leaving us.

They were so amiable, good-tempered and interested in everything.

I wrote in my Journal: 'We shall miss them at breakfast, at luncheon, at dinner, riding, sailing, driving, walking—in fact everywhere.'

* * *

I looked forward to Uncle Leopold's letters and was delighted when he wrote to say that as soon as possible, he was going to bring his new wife Louise to England to meet his favourite child.

So that was something to look forward to.

I was so happy when he wrote to say he was expecting to become a father.

'That,' I said to Lehzen, 'is just what he needs. It will make him happy. He mourned so long for Princess Charlotte.'

'Oh,' said Lehzen, 'I think he revelled in his mourning now and then.'

I did not quite understand, but she would say no more. Was Lehzen a little jealous of my affection for Uncle Leopold? I am afraid that my vanity overcame my better nature when it was a question of people's being jealous, as had been the case with my cousins. It was so comforting to know that I was important to them.

But all the same I did not quite like any criticism of one who seemed so perfect to me as Uncle Leopold.

My fifteenth birthday was approaching and I was hoping that Aunt Adelaide would give another ball for me. I had so enjoyed the one on my fourteenth birthday, and surely Mama could not spoil it this time. In three years time I should reach the all-important age of eighteen.

Mama was getting more and more contentious; each day she said something detrimental about Uncle William because he refused to die; and there were only three years left. Any little rumour about his illness sent her into transports of delight. It seemed to me very wrong to wish another person dead with such vehemence. It was like murder . . . in a way.

Shortly before my birthday I had sad news from Uncle Leopold. His baby was dead.

Dear Uncle Leopold, how sad he must be! He wrote to me at length about his sorrow. He was desolate. Life was cruel to him. He and Louise were staggering under the blow.

I tried to comfort him, repeating many of those homilies he had delivered to me over the years, and he wrote back saying my letter brought him consolation.

Aunt Adelaide had not forgotten my birthday. She visited Mama and when I was present she reminded us of the coming birthday.

'We must have another juvenile ball,' she said. 'I know how much you enjoyed the one we gave on your fourteenth birthday. The King and I were saying we must do it again. I shall never forget the sight of you opening the ball with your cousin George.'

I saw Mama bridle and feared the worst.

'Dear Adelaide,' she said, 'it is kind of you, but you have forgotten that I am in mourning for my brother's child.'

The Queen looked startled. 'Oh . . . I had forgotten . . .'

'*I* do not forget such a bereavement in my family.'

'Perhaps,' said the Queen seeing my crestfallen looks, 'Victoria might come. It is her birthday and there should be some celebration.'

Mama raised her eyebrows in that haughty way she had, and her earrings trembled. 'I cannot see how Victoria could fail to be in mourning too. Leopold is her uncle . . . her very *favourite* uncle.'

The Queen looked as near annoyance as I had ever seen her. There was a look of resignation on her face. 'Very well,' she said; and soon after that she left.

'How insensitive!' said Mama. 'Some people have no family feeling.'

'I think she only wanted to please me.'

'She might have known that it is not the time for dancing and that if you have any fine feelings at all, it is the very last thing you would want to do.'

I was silent—sullen perhaps. I did not see what good I could do to Uncle Leopold's baby by staying at home on my birthday.

I think Aunt Adelaide had been very put out, but being herself she did not want to spoil my birthday any more than it had been already.

The next day she wrote to my mother and said that she was sorry there would be no ball, but she would call at Kensington Palace on the morning of my birthday to convey her good wishes and those of the King.

Then Mama did an outrageous thing which made me more ashamed than I had been over the birthday.

She sent a note to the Queen saying that as she was in mourning—and the Princess with her—she was unable to receive visitors.

I was shocked. I could not help talking to Lehzen.

'How dare Mama tell the Queen she is not receiving! Receiving! She talks like a queen herself. Oh, Lehzen, I am *so* ashamed.'

Lehzen shook her head but did not leap to the defence of my mother. I supposed she was remembering that Mama had allowed Sir John to attempt to dismiss her.

But the birthday was not quite so mournful as I had feared it might be, for on it I received a letter from Feodore; and its contents delighted me. She was coming to see us.

Feodore was now a happy mother of four children. There were Charles and Eliza, little Hermann and now another baby named Victor. Although we had corresponded regularly, it was six years since I had seen my dear sister and the prospect of actually talking to her again was so exciting that it made my birthday a happy one.

I would notice the change in her, Feodore warned. Well, I expected she would notice a change in me! I tried to remember what I had been like at nine. I could picture my beautiful Feodore as she had been on her wedding day . . . perfectly. She was always pretty—prettier than I ever would be, I supposed.

Even Mama was delighted at the prospect of seeing Feodore. She bustled about giving orders and preparing for their arrival. She kept talking about the dear little babies and for once seemed to have forgotten her obsession with Uncle William's long delayed death and her own importance in the country.

It was a lovely June day when they arrived. Such excitement there was! Lehzen, chewing away at her caraway seeds, was in a state of bemused delight. And there was Feodore, getting out of the carriage with her husband, Ernest, and the children.

I dashed forward but Mama laid a hand on my shoulder and she herself went forward to kiss Feodore.

Then it was my turn.

'Darling, darling Vicky!'

'Dearest, dearest Feodore!'

'Oh, how you have grown!'

So had she. She was no longer the sylph-like girl who had left England; she was quite plump, but beautiful as ever, and all my love for her came flooding back and I was so happy to see her.

Oh, the joy of that reunion! I put an arm through Feodore's; and Mama had her arm round her. Mama looked really happy. She did love Feodore even though she was not destined for a crown. She loved the babies too. Even Mama seemed different while Feodore was there. I quite liked the Count Hohenlohe-Langenburg and I adored the children. They called me Aunt Victoria. It felt very strange to be an aunt but I loved it.

'We will have such talks,' I said; and Feodore squeezed my hand. When they had all rested awhile it was decided that Feodore and I should go for a drive with Lehzen in the Park and that was the greatest delight to me.

Lehzen was laughing all the time and we chatted away about those days when we were all together, and the things we used to do. Feodore told us about the babies and I believed she had forgotten all about Augustus and how he used to talk to her while I watered the flowers—which was a very good thing, because what everybody had wanted for her had turned out to be right.

A programme had been arranged for Feodore's stay and we were to visit Windsor. I guessed Mama would have liked to have refused but the invitation was extended to Feodore and Ernest and they accepted graciously, so there was little Mama could do.

On that first day we were to go to the opera. Feodore said she was so tired and Mama, looking at her tenderly said: 'Well, my darling, you must go to bed. It has been a long day for you and I do not want you to be exhausted.'

I cried impulsively: 'Feodore, go to bed and I will sit with you and we will talk until you go to sleep.'

'No,' said Mama firmly. 'You must go to the opera. It will be expected.'

So I went although I should have loved to stay with Feodore. But I have to admit I did enjoy the opera. Giulia Grisi was singing and I thought her voice quite divine; and it was Rossini's *L'Assiedo di Corrinto*. Moreover the opera was followed by *Les Sylphides* in which Taglioni danced. So I was in a state of bliss.

To have seen Feodore, Grisi and Taglioni in one day made it one of the most thrilling of my life so far.

I awoke next morning with the glorious feeling of anticipation and the first thing I said to myself was: Feodore is here.

What joy there was during those days! I contrived—rarely—to be alone with Feodore for then we would talk easily and naturally. But, of course, either Mama or Lehzen was usually there. I loved the children. They were so affectionate and so amusing.

We went to Windsor where Feodore was received most kindly by the King and Aunt Adelaide, although I must admit the King rather pointedly ignored Mama, and my happiness was tinged with apprehension while we were there because I was terrified that a storm would blow up between them and I pictured Mama marshalling us all out at short notice.

But Feodore's visit did seem to soften even her and I believed she did want Feodore to enjoy it. Feodore was of a gentle, peace-loving nature; she accepted life more readily than I did. Perhaps Mama was right and I had been affected by the knowledge that I might step one day into a very exalted position. It may be that that gives one a determination not to be subdued.

The best way to be alone with Feodore was to go riding, and this we did frequently. There were others with us of course but with

little manoeuvring we could sometimes escape from them. One day
we did this and as we walked our horses through a narrow lane I
said to her: 'I believe we have escaped.'

Feodore looked at me quickly and said: 'Do you sometimes feel
you would like to escape?'

'I should like to be alone sometimes.'

Feodore smiled. 'I understand. Do you sometimes feel like a
prisoner?'

'Yes, I think I do. You see there is always someone there. I even
have to sleep in Mama's bedroom. One of the things I want most
is a room of my own where I can go sometimes . . . and be alone.'

'I understand.'

'When you were there . . . did you feel like that?'

'Mama was determined to take care of us but sometimes she
seemed like a jailer. But you will soon be eighteen, Victoria, and
then . . .'

'Then I shall be free.'

'You will be the Queen. Does that frighten you a little?'

'It makes me very serious.'

'You will be good, I know.'

'I shall try. And I shall be free.'

'I think,' she said, 'that you will know how to have your way.
It is not long now. You will marry, as I did.'

'That meant freedom for you.'

'One is never really free. There are always obligations.'

'Yes, but free to be alone sometimes.'

She said suddenly: 'What did you think of the cousins?'

'They were charming.'

'We have several cousins. I wonder what you will think of the
Saxe-Coburgs. I find them the most charming of all.'

'Uncle Leopold has written to me about Ernest and Albert. He
thinks I shall enjoy meeting them very much. I believe they will
visit us one day.'

'I feel sure they will.'

'What are they like, Feodore?'

'Very handsome. Uncle Leopold watches over them with great
care.'

'As he does over me.'

'He has a great family feeling.'

'Tell me about the cousins. What do they look like?'

'They are tall and good-looking. My favourite of the two is Ernest.'

'Oh, why? Uncle Leopold writes most glowingly of Albert.'

'They are both admirable. Ernest is so honest and good-humoured.'

'Is not Albert honest and good-humoured?'

'Oh yes, but Albert is more clever, sharper. What I mean is Ernest is more . . . innocent.'

'I do long to meet them.'

'They must miss their mother.'

'Why?'

Feodore looked at me sharply. 'I suppose you haven't heard the scandal?'

'You mean about the cousins?'

'Well not exactly about them. It is their parents.'

'Do tell me.'

Feodore hesitated and I wailed: 'Oh, Feodore, don't be like the rest of them. Don't have secrets from me. They are always implying that I am too young for this and that. Don't be like that, dear Sissy.'

Feodore said: 'Well, I suppose you will know one day. Their mother was Luise of Saxe-Gotha, and when she married Duke Ernest of Saxe-Coburg it should have been a happy match. But something went wrong. After the birth of her eldest son, Ernest, there was trouble between her and the Duke. He was not as faithful as he might have been; she was lonely and there were people at Court to flatter and amuse her. There was scandal about her, and soon after Albert was born at Rosenau. It is a beautiful yellow stone castle surrounded by trees—oak, beech, elm and ash . . . You can look out from the windows to the Thuringian Forest. There Albert was born on a lovely August day.'

'I know. It was three months after I was born.'

'Yes. You are almost of an age. He was a particularly beautiful child from the moment he was born. Some babies are very ugly . . . and they grow prettier every day. That was not so with Albert. He was born beautiful . . . His father was at that time the Duke, *his* father having died. Luise loved her child—even more, they said, than she had loved her first-born, Ernest. He was like an angel, she said, with his blue eyes, well-shaped nose and dimples. He was only about three years old when the trouble, which had been brewing for some time, burst out into an open scandal.'

'What scandal?'

'Luise, left alone by her husband, had made certain friendships; one was with a certain Leutnant von Hanstein. She had a great enemy at her husband's Court in Maximilian von Szymborski who was determined to destroy her. This he succeeded in doing by fomenting scandals and rumours and blowing them up out of all proportion to reality; and in time the Duke was so convinced that his wife was unfaithful that he decided to divorce her.'

'Divorce!' I cried. 'How terrible! Oh, poor little Albert and Ernest.'

'Yes. The children loved their mother dearly but she was taken from them. There was great sorrow in the household. But the people loved Luise. They thought she had been wronged and they called for von Szymborski's blood. He had great difficulty in getting out of the country alive. But there was a divorce. Albert was seven years old at the time. Luise married von Hanstein, but when she was only thirty years old she died.'

'What a sad story! What happened to Albert and Ernest?'

'They were left to the care of their grandmothers . . . and Uncle Leopold. They were greatly loved but they must have missed their mother.'

'I am sure they did. She seemed so gentle and so falsely accused. I long more than ever to meet my Saxe-Coburg cousins.'

'The Duke was married again to Mary of Württemberg, but I don't think that was a very happy marriage either.'

'He should not have been led astray by that wicked von Szymborski. How strange it is. Albert had no mother and I had no father. It seems as though there is a special bond between us . . .'

I rode on thoughtfully. I could not keep Cousin Albert out of my mind.

It was too much to expect life to go on smoothly with Mama and the King under one roof. Every day when I rose I used to pray that nothing would go wrong, that Mama would continue in the more mellow mood which Feodore's presence seemed to have brought about. Now, I thought, she is acting more like a mother than a would-be regent.

The King arranged that we should go to the races, and what fun it was to be in the royal box and watch the dear horses vying with each other. I jumped up in joy and urged them on until Mama laid a restraining hand on my shoulders, and I saw the King was amused and rather liked it that I seemed to forget my dignity for a moment.

Aunt Adelaide was smiling. She said: 'We must do this again.'

But trouble came as I feared it would.

It was one evening before dinner. Mama seemed suddenly to

remember how important she was and to fear that the relaxation of the last few days may have given the impression that she was ready to be relegated to obscurity.

We were waiting to go in to dinner. The King was getting impatient, no doubt wondering why the Queen did not give the sign for us to leave for the dining-room.

Aunt Adelaide was nervously trying to continue talking so that people did not notice the time. But the King suddenly shouted: 'Are we waiting for that woman?'

Everyone knew who 'that woman' was; and I felt myself growing very hot.

'She is a nuisance,' went on the King. 'We will go in without her.'

Then Mama appeared, looking quite splendid in bows and feathers and swinging jewellery. I was beginning to think that she was often a little overdressed.

Aunt Adelaide said smoothly as though nothing had happened: 'Shall we go in to dinner now?'

She was the most tactful woman I had ever known. She hated scenes and with a husband like Uncle William she had plenty of practice in avoiding them.

We went in and I sat between the King and the Queen, and although he was pleasant enough to me, I kept intercepting the glares he sent in my mother's direction.

It was a small incident really but it did spoil the complete perfection of Feodore's visit.

Alas, it was time for Feodore to go. We parted in tears. She said she would come again and I must go to her. It was doubly hard to have to part from the dear little children. That was the worst of these visits from relatives. When they were over, one was so very sad.

Writing in my Journal solaced me a little, and this time I could set down exactly what I felt.

'How sad at breakfast not to see the door open and Feodore come in smiling leading her little girl; and not to get the accustomed kiss from her. At one we lunched and I missed dear Feodore here again terribly. I miss her so much today. At three we drove with Lehzen. How dull the drive seemed without dear Feodore. We dined at seven and after that Aunt Sophia came. We passed a dull, sad evening . . .'

How sad that those who loved each other so dearly must be apart.

* * *

My sixteenth birthday was approaching. I was very conscious of the fact that in two years I should be eighteen. I mentioned it in Mama's hearing and she looked very startled. She did not want me to grow up and was constantly telling me that I must be less selfish, less conceited; I always wanted my own way and could be stubborn about getting it. I knew now what she meant. She wanted Uncle William dead *now* so that she could be Regent.

I wrote in my Journal: 'Today is my sixteenth birthday. How very old that sounds! But I feel that the two years to come till I attain my eighteenth are the most important of any.'

And of course Mama read my Journal.

She invited some of my favourite artists to the Palace to give a concert for my birthday, dear, beautiful, talented Grisi among them. It was a most wonderful birthday present, and I felt the old affection for Mama welling up in me because she had taken such trouble to please me.

Then I saw the complacent looks Sir John Conroy exchanged with her, and the thought entered my mind that since I was getting older they were trying to placate me a little.

However the concert was wonderful and I could not have had a birthday present I liked better.

After the birthday, Mama, who had been complaining about the lack of space which was allowed to us in the Palace, decided that as there were plenty of rooms available she would appropriate more to our use.

She selected seventeen. They were very grand.

'And why not?' she said to Sir John. 'They are to accommodate the heiress to the throne. I suppose we shall have to ask that old buffer's permission.'

They laughed, but later they were very annoyed because the King refused his permission for them to have the rooms.

'Well, Lehzen,' I said, 'we did really have quite enough, and there are so many of the family to live here.'

Lehzen said nothing but I believed she agreed with me.

My confirmation took place in the Chapel Royal at St. James's and many members of the family were present. I wore a white lace dress and a bonnet trimmed with roses; and as usual I was in an agony of suspense as to what Mama would do to offend the King. She had talked very seriously to me beforehand about being good and friendly to those about me, but not too friendly, and to curb that rather common habit of smiling on everyone and gushing—yes, positively gushing—over those for whom I believed I had some affection.

'Mama,' I said, 'I always *know* when I have affection for some-one, which is rather different from believing it.'

She ignored that and went on to say that she had cared for me since my birth (which was true enough) and she was the only one I could trust and if I obeyed her in *everything*, I could not stray from the right path. I was a little unappreciative of Sir John Conroy, which grieved her. I must show more friendliness towards him.

I set my lips firmly. I would show no friendliness when I did not feel it, however much Mama insisted, and even though I was being prepared for confirmation.

There was trouble from the start. The King said my mother's retinue was far too large and some of them would have to go. He incensed her by ordering Sir John to leave the chapel.

I was very upset, but the King took my hand and pressed it kindly, which implied that he was not in the least angry with me. Of course my mother was beside me and I stood between her and the King at the rail of the altar.

I had to remove my bonnet which Mama took; and after the confirmation ceremony the Archbishop began to lecture me about the stern duties which lay ahead. It seemed to me that I was going to have a very miserable time and if that was what it meant to be a queen I would rather remain as I was. I could not imagine why people were so eager to get the crown. According to the Archbishop it brought nothing but strict duty and overpowering responsibilities.

While he was talking the King at my side started shifting his feet impatiently; and I guessed that he was on the point of commanding the Archbishop to put an end to his homily. Fortunately the Arch-bishop understood what the King meant and brought his lecture to an end.

When we retired to the closet the King said: 'Well, that's done.' Then he leaned towards me and said: 'Don't want to take too much notice of all that *stuff*. Priests!' He shook his head in disdain. 'I've got a present for you. You're a nice girl and you want to enjoy life.'

I said: 'Oh, Uncle William, you are a *kind* man.'

His present to me was a set of emerald jewellery and the Queen gave me a tiara of emeralds to match. I thanked them warmly and Aunt Adelaide embraced me.

'It was all very serious, wasn't it?' she said. 'You must not be upset by it. Things usually work out very well, and I am sure they will for you.'

Dear Aunt Adelaide and kind Uncle William! I did wish more

than ever that we could be friendly with them and that I did not have to hide my affection for them from Mama.

On the way home Mama said I had been a little forward with the King and Queen. It was only right that they should give me valuable jewellery. After all the jewellery belonged to the crown . . . and that would soon be mine.

She brightened a little because she said *he*—meaning the King—had looked strained and he seemed to have some difficulty in walking.

I said: 'I don't want to think of his death. I don't want to be Queen.'

Mama laughed. 'You shouldn't let the Archbishop's sermon upset you. I daresay he thought you were young and a little frivolous—which indeed you are—and needed a warning. You should thank God that you have a mother to look after you and guide you—a mother who has always made you the centre of her life.'

'Yes, Mama,' I replied, supposing that was true; but how I wished that she had made something else the centre of her life and left me a little more on the edge.

When we returned she gave me a bracelet containing a lock of her hair.

'Something to remind you of me . . . always,' she said.

Great joy awaited me. There was a letter from Uncle Leopold who was very soon setting out for England with his wife. His great delight in coming to England would be to see his dearest child.

My excitement was so great that Lehzen feared I would be ill. Mama had arranged that we should go to Ramsgate and Uncle Leopold could stay with us there. It was an ideal way of keeping clear of those nuisances at Windsor who, she was sure, would try to interfere if we stayed at Kensington.

So to Ramsgate we came.

There was more wonderful news. Feodore had given birth to another child—a little girl—and they were both doing well.

'We have pondered over names,' wrote Feodore, 'and we have decided that this little girl must be named after her dearest aunt. So Victoria is to be her name; but because I could not have two Victorias so close to me—I should be muddled and wonder which one was which—she will be Adelaide first and Victoria second. I thought the Queen would be pleased. She was so good to us when we were at Windsor. So the baby is to be Adelaide Victoria Mary Louisa, Constance.'

I laughed with Lehzen. 'How strange to think of this little one
. . . my niece. And Charles has a child too. He could do as he
wished. You see he did marry Marie Klebelsberg and is happy with
her. Poor Feodore, who wanted Augustus . . . although she does
seem happy now so perhaps it was all for the best. But I think dear
Feodore would make herself happy doing what people want her to
rather than what she wants herself. I don't think I should ever be
like that.'

'You have a will of your own,' said Lehzen, with a grudging
sort of admiration.

I made presents for the little newcomer, but my thoughts were
really with the coming of Uncle Leopold and my new aunt whom
I was longing to see.

I hoped all would be well in Ramsgate and there would be nothing to irritate Mama. She loved Uncle Leopold and she knew that
his aspirations regarding me were the same as her own, so there
should be no reason for conflict. However, she was rather disgruntled because she could not fly the royal standard over the house we
took in Ramsgate; and of course there were no more 'poppings' as
Uncle William called the royal salute—and that gave her cause for
complaint.

It was decided that we should go to the Albion Hotel to await
the arrival of the ship which would bring Uncle Leopold to us, as
we should be able to watch it come in from there; and as we rode
from our house to the hotel I was gratified to see how the people of
Ramsgate had decorated the streets; and as we passed through they
called out: 'Long live the little Princess!' or 'Welcome Victoria.'
Mama sat in the carriage waving regally, but they had only silence
for her, and went on shouting my name as though to make it clear
that the cheers were not for her.

Lehzen and Lady Conroy with Flora Hastings came with us.
Lady Conroy might not have been there she was so insignificant;
and as Flora Hastings and Lehzen disliked each other, I rather
wished Mama had brought someone other than Flora.

However what did it matter? The ship bringing Uncle Leopold
was coming nearer.

And there he was, looking slightly older than when I last saw
him, for it was four years and two months.

He was coming towards me and I flew into his arms. Mama
smiled, not at all displeased. Uncle Leopold was delighted and so
were the crowds. They liked exuberant displays of affection.

Uncle Leopold took my face in his hands and said how I had grown and this was one of the happiest moments of his life.

I told him how wonderful it was for me to be with this dearest of uncles.

He presented his bride and I was so happy because I liked her immediately. She was slim and pretty with lovely fair hair and blue eyes. Her bonnet was blue to match them; and she looked so elegant in her light brown silk dress.

'Oh, you are just as Uncle said you were!' I cried.

'You must love each other,' commanded Uncle Leopold, 'because that is what I wish.'

'I shall, I shall,' I said in what Mama would call my impetuous way. 'I do already.'

And I did, for I knew at once that we were going to be friends.

Uncle Leopold contrived that he and I should have some long talks together . . . just the two of us. He talked to me as seriously as the Archbishop had, but how different it was coming from Uncle Leopold! He made me very much aware of the responsibilities I should have to face in the future, but reminded me again and again that he would always be there and all I had to do was write to him. He would be my guide and comforter, as he had always been. I was growing up fast, I was no longer a child. There would be many things I had to consider. He had heard rumours which deeply disturbed him. The King had ideas for me to marry my cousin George Cambridge. He did not think that a very good idea. Some of my relatives on my father's side were a very odd group. Quite unlike those on my mother's who were serious, right-minded and good-living.

I told him I thought both Georges were very good boys, and George Cumberland was quite unlike his father and mother. In fact he was very charming indeed and it was so sad that he was going blind.

'There can be no cure for him,' I said. 'It is a great grief to his parents, and although I know they are not good people, they do love him.'

'My dearest child,' said Uncle Leopold, 'you are apt to allow your emotions to take charge, you know. Of course you are very sorry for George Cumberland. It is indeed a great affliction. It may in a measure be retribution for the sins of his father. There have been the most unpleasant rumours about that gentleman.'

'To make George blind because of his father's wickedness! Oh, I think that is most unfair.'

'Dearest child, it is not for us to question the ways of God. But enough of these cousins. They may be pleasant boys but they cannot compare with your German cousins. What did you think of Ernest and Alexander?'

'They were delightful.'

'Far more interesting than your Cumberlands and Cambridges, I'll swear.'

'Well, they were different . . . and most amusing.'

'You thought them delightful, I know, but you have not yet met your Saxe-Coburg cousins.'

'You mean Ernest and Albert.'

'The most delightful boys I ever knew in my life.'

'I have heard of them.'

'If you liked your cousins Alexander and Ernest . . .'

'Oh, I did, Uncle. I did.'

'How much more will you be enchanted by these two.'

'When am I going to meet them?'

'Soon, my dearest, very soon.'

'I long to see them . . . particularly Albert.'

'Well, Albert is indeed a wonderful boy. I look upon him as my own. He is as close to me as you are, my dearest. If I may be a little indiscreet . . .'

'Oh do, Uncle, please do.'

I thought he was going to tell me about the scandal regarding Albert's mother of which I had wanted to speak to him, though some caution had made me hold back, for I felt it might well be that Feodore should not have told me and if I mentioned it she would be reprimanded for her indiscretion.

Evidently I was right because Uncle Leopold made no reference to it. All he said was: 'It is wrong of me to have a favourite in this case, but it is difficult to prevent it. I will tell you this, Victoria, but don't mention it: Albert is my very favourite of all your cousins.'

'Then I am sure he will be mine.'

'I hope so, dear child. I fervently hope so.'

Then he talked at length about Albert. How he loved to ride through the forest on his English ponies; how he collected plants and geological specimens.

'He is more of a student than a sportsman. He once said to me that he could not understand why people made such a business of shooting. Which shows very fine feelings, do you not agree?'

I said I did. 'Is he very clever?' I asked.

'He is very studious.'

'He would probably think I was rather frivolous.'

'Your mother tells me that you are a little . . . and apt to let your emotions rule your head. Well, my darling, I am of the opinion that that is not always a bad thing. You are overflowing with affection, and when you love you do so wholeheartedly. I am sure Albert would admire that in you. He finds it less easy to express his emotions. You could help him to be more demonstrative. He could help you to be more restrained.'

I liked the thought of helping Albert.

'He is so good-tempered. It is only that which is unjust or dishonest which makes him angry. I remember once watching them play at Rosenau. There were a party of them and some were to defend the castle. Albert was with those who were trying to capture it. One of the boys found a way in through the back, but Albert would not take it. He said it was not becoming in a Saxon knight to do anything underhand and that the enemy should be attacked from the front.'

'How noble!'

'Albert *is* noble. You will find him the most honourable, noble and handsome knight that ever was.'

'I long to meet him.'

'You shall . . . very soon, I think.'

'Will you arrange it, Uncle Leopold?'

'I shall. He will come to see you with my blessing and my urgent wish that you shall each realize the other's virtues—and all you have to offer one another.'

'I hope he will come soon.'

Uncle Leopold drew me to him and kissed me tenderly. 'Understand always, dearest child, your welfare is the most important thing on earth to me—yours and that of dear Albert.'

'I feel I love him already,' I said.

'I have no doubt you will love him very dearly.'

Then Uncle Leopold began to talk of other matters, explaining how necessary it was for me to have humility, which was one of the greatest Christian virtues. Fate had set me in a difficult position. Great responsibilities loomed ahead. I told him that I knew this, and the Archbishop had made it very clear to me when I had been confirmed.

'Always be on guard against hypocrisy. It is the besetting sin of our times. I am sorry to say, my dear love, with all my affection for old England, the very state of its society and politics renders

many in that country humbugs and deceivers. The appearance of
the thing is generally considered more than the reality. Defend
yourself against this system. Let your dear character always be true
and loyal. Always be prudent and cautious . . . but at the same
time be sterling and true.'

Oh, how wonderful it was to listen to his eloquence! Although
there were a great many dos and don'ts and one often seemed to
cancel out the other. I must say what I meant and yet I must be
careful. I must listen to the hypocrites and be true to myself and
yet at the same time be prudent, which must mean disguising my
true feelings, and how could one be truthful if one did that?

It seemed to me that I was going to find it difficult to do the right
thing because it was all rather contradictory, and I consoled myself
with the thought that Uncle Leopold—although a strip of water
would separate us—would be there if I needed him. And I should
shortly meet this Cousin Albert who seemed to combine all the
virtues which could be found in one person—with none of the vices.

I had some pleasant times with Aunt Louise too. She turned out
to be just a little frivolous when Uncle Leopold was not present.
That made a delightful intimacy between us. I told her how elegant
she always looked and how I loved her clothes. We talked about
clothes at great length and she told me what colours would be best
for me. She took me to her apartments and showed me some of her
gowns. She said they were a little old for me, but I tried them on
and paraded in front of the mirror. She put her head on one side
watching me and she said French fashions became me. In fact they
became everybody because they were the best in the world. I had
to agree with her, and I really did look rather nice in some of her
gowns. She was small but slimmer than I; and she had the prettiest
figure while I was a little fat.

I said: 'My clothes are always little-girl clothes. I do wish I had
something grown-up to wear.'

'You will,' she said. 'After all you are no longer a little girl.'

In a rush of confidence I said: 'I think Mama wants to keep me
a little girl as long as possible. She is very much afraid that I shall
soon be eighteen.'

I stopped hastily. I was being indiscreet. I must remember all
the injunctions Uncle Leopold had given me. But it did seem that
every day my resentment against Mama was growing.

Then came the sad day when Uncle Leopold and Aunt Louise
must leave us.

I flung myself into Uncle Leopold's arms and sobbed: 'Don't go.'

He stroked my hair and said how it grieved him to leave me.

'But I have a country to govern, my little one.'

I clung to Aunt Louise. 'I am going to miss you so. It's going to be so *dull* without you.'

Uncle Leopold put his lips to my ear and whispered: 'Soon I shall send Cousin Albert to comfort you.'

That did comfort me a little, but I was very sad as I watched the ship, flying the flag of Belgium, sailing away.

How many years would it be, I wondered, before I saw Uncle Leopold again?

It was shortly after that when I became desperately ill. Ramsgate will always remind me of those dark days which came almost immediately after Uncle Leopold and Aunt Louise had departed.

I was only vaguely aware of the figures round my bed. Dear Lehzen, of course, was there, and so was Mama. They thought I was going to die. Poor Mama, she must have been in despair for all her hopes rested in me, and I could imagine the excitement in the hearts of the Duke and Duchess of Cumberland. My death would be as much a boon to them as Uncle William's would be to Mama. To come near to death oneself makes one realize how wrong it is to desire other people's departure from this life so that one's own may become more comfortable in it.

I remember Lehzen's cutting off most of my hair.

'It is for the best, my darling,' she murmured and her voice shook with emotion for the tresses she had so lovingly curled.

There came a day when the crisis came and after that had passed they believed I would live.

I loved them all then—Lehzen, of course, my dearest and most faithful friend, and Mama, who looked so pale and wan without her frills and feathers, so anxiously had she been watching over me.

I was amazed at my weakness. I could scarcely sit up without help.

'She needs the greatest care,' said Lehzen; and she was going to supply that care, and not even Mama was going to come near me if Lehzen thought it best for me to be left alone. But Mama and Lehzen were together in this. Their great aim was to have me well.

How tired I felt! I just wanted to sleep and sleep. So I slept through the days and nights, and whenever I opened my eyes Lehzen would be there seated by my bed, and if she were not it would be Mama.

They brought nourishing things for me to eat. 'Do try to eat, my darling, for Mama's sake,' or 'Lehzen will be so worried if you don't.' So I tried to eat to please them.

'Rest,' they said. 'You are getting better every day.'

I believed them, but I felt so terribly weak.

I noticed that neither Lehzen nor my mother would bring a mirror to me. That was why I guessed they did not want me to see myself. So one day I insisted; and as I was growing agitated Lehzen brought me a looking-glass. I could hardly believe that it was myself who looked back at me. That pale little face instead of the plump, blooming one which had been mine! My eyes looked enormous and my hair . . . I put up my hand in despair.

'It will grow again when you are well,' said Lehzen.

'What has happened to me?' I cried.

'You had typhoid fever, dearest. But you have recovered and your hair will be as lovely as ever and so will you be . . . quite soon. Young people recover from these upsets very quickly.'

'But I am sixteen, Lehzen. That is not really a young person.'

'It is still young. You are going to be well in next to no time. I shall see to that.'

'You have been here all the time?'

'Day and night, my dearest, and when I cannot be here your Mama is.'

'That is comforting. And tell me the truth, Lehzen, will my hair grow again?'

'I swear it,' said Lehzen, putting some caraway seeds into her mouth as she always did when she was emotional.

'Oh, dearest Lehzen, how glad I am that you are here to look after me. *You* are the dearest friend I ever had.'

She nodded, kissed me and bade me rest. 'The more rest you have, the more good food you eat, the sooner you will be better.'

I trusted Lehzen. I would soon be well.

A rather unpleasant incident took place one evening which I could not think of for a long time after without experiencing shivers down my spine.

It was just beginning to get dark, when I was awakened suddenly by a sense of evil. I saw the darkening room and felt the heaviness of my limbs to which I had become accustomed. I could not understand what had awakened me. I saw the familiar objects of the room begin to take shape. Lehzen was sitting by the fire; her needle-work had fallen from her hands and she was asleep.

Someone was in the room, coming stealthily towards the bed.

To my horror I saw that it was the man whom I had come to think of as a sinister enemy—Sir John Conroy—and he was tiptoe-ing silently towards me.

I started up. 'What do you want here . . . in my room?' I de-manded.

He put his finger to his lips and glanced at Lehzen.

I went on: 'I have been ill. I do not have visitors.'

'This is different. This is only your old friend.'

'No,' I said firmly.

He was right beside my bed now, and he laid a hand on mine which was outside the bedclothes. I withdrew it sharply.

'A quick word,' he whispered. 'Nothing more. I just want you to give me your promise.'

'What promise?'

'Your solemn promise . . . that's all. Give it to me and I will go.'

'Do you think I would promise you something without knowing what it is?'

'Your mother has agreed that it is best for you to do this.'

'I want to know what.'

'It is all very simple.' He was still whispering and poor Lehzen, tired out from looking after me, slumbered on. He glanced towards her and smiled. Then he went on: 'You are going to need a private secretary when you are Queen. I have been with you for years. I know you well. I respect you so much. The post should be mine. Just give me your solemn promise. That is all I want. Give that to me and I will go and tell your Mama that you have agreed. She will be so delighted.'

'No,' I said firmly. 'No. No.'

'You are very weak at the moment. We can talk more of this when you are fully recovered . . . Just for now your promise . . . your solemn promise will do. You are naturally honourable and would never go back on a solemn promise. That is all I ask. We can talk together . . . your mother, you and I . . . when you are well—and that will not be long now.'

'I will give no promise.'

'The matter is urgent.'

'Why?'

'You must be ready when the time comes.'

'I am ready.'

'You are young . . . young and pretty. You like to dance and sing and play. It is only right that you should. So you need a secretary to take on all the disagreeable work. I have a paper here. Your signature is all that is needed.'

'No,' I repeated. 'No.'

This conversation had been conducted in whispers, but now I spoke loudly. I said: 'Go now. I am not well enough to be disturbed like this.'

That woke Lehzen. She jumped to her feet in alarm.

'What?' she stammered. 'Why . . . ?'

'Do not disturb yourself, Baroness,' said Sir John suavely. 'The Princess and I have been transacting a little business.'

'The Princess is not well.'

'This was nothing to harm her. Just a little light conversation.'

'The Princess does not receive visitors.'

'Oh come, I am a member of the household. And I have the Duchess's permission to call on the Princess.'

Lehzen was splendid as I knew she always would be.

'I will not have you disturbing the Princess. Please leave at once.'

'My dear Baroness, you exceed your authority.'

'It is my duty to protect my Princess from upsets of *any* sort. She wishes you to leave at once.'

He turned to me appealingly and I cried: 'Yes, I do. Go away. I will give you no promise. Leave me alone.'

'Oh come, come,' he said placatingly. 'We don't want a storm, do we?'

'If I want a storm I will have one,' I retorted, 'and I shall not appoint you as my private secretary now . . . or ever. Please go.'

Lehzen went to the door and held it open. He lifted his shoulders and bowed to us, smiling that sneering smile which I hated so much.

He went out and Lehzen firmly shut the door.

She came to the bed and took me in her arms, holding me tightly against her.

'I hate that man,' I said.

'He is a monster. It is a pity . . .'

'Yes, Lehzen, say it. It is a pity he is here. How dared he! To come into my room like that and try to get a promise from me when I was feeling too weak to resist. That was what he wanted, and he thought I would be too ill to fight him. It is clear to me.'

Lehzen stroked my hair.

'You must not be upset, my pet. It is bad for you. And I was asleep when he came in! I cannot forgive myself.'

'Dear Lehzen, you were worn out with caring for me.'

'To think I was asleep!'

'I dealt with him. Lehzen, they . . . he is getting worried. It is because I am past sixteen, and there are less than two more years to go when Mama might be Regent and before I am Queen. Who knows, she may hope to be Regent even then.'

Lehzen did not say anything. She was too upset. She kept calling me her baby; and I had a feeling that she, like my mother, did not want me to grow up.

It took me quite a long time to recover from my illness. Lehzen used to brush my hair every night and she always said it was growing and would soon be as thick as it used to be, but whether that was true or whether she was comforting me I was not sure. But I did begin to feel stronger and more like my old self.

I think many people had believed that I would not get over my illness. It was certain that the Duke of Cumberland did. How he longed to be King himself with poor blind George to follow him. Sly and ruthless as he was, he did act rather incautiously. Very often instead of furthering his schemes, he ruined them.

I did hear a disquieting story. During my illness he had been often with the King. I remembered how he had been in attendance on the late George IV right up to the time of his death and what anxiety there had been when Mama had thought he was trying to get Uncle George to insist that I go to Windsor, where Mama was sure Cumberland would try to get rid of me. Now that I was ill he was currying favour with William.

That was not easy. Uncle William might be called a bumbling old fool, but he was not without a certain shrewdness and he could not be so easily duped.

The story was that during a banquet when the monarch's health was being drunk, Cumberland raised his glass and said: 'The King's heir. God bless *him*.'

There was silence round the table for Cumberland was behaving as though I were as good as dead—in which case he would be the next.

Uncle William was furious. He went very red in the face and standing up he lifted his glass and cried very loudly: 'The King's heir. God bless *her*!'

Dear Uncle William!

Mama laughed heartily over that. I heard her talking to the odious one about it.

'That has finished him! He was a little too sure of himself this time.'

It seemed that she was right. Cumberland disappeared from Court and I begán to get better.

What a joy it was to return to Kensington. There, a surprise awaited me, for I found that we had better apartments than before. We had seventeen rooms in all and that was a great improvement.

'Only what is due to the dignity of a queen,' said Mama.

I wanted to remind her that I was not yet that, but refrained from doing so. She was so excited because Uncle Leopold had written to tell her that two cousins, with their father, were coming to England; and she was always delighted to see her relatives.

This was her brother Ferdinand and his two sons, Ferdinand and Augustus. I was a little disappointed, for when I had first heard that cousins were coming I had thought of Ernest and Albert. However the prospect of a visit from cousins was always interesting and I shared Mama's happy anticipation.

In due course they arrived, and they were all charming, particularly Ferdinand, the elder cousin. He was on his way to Portugal to be married; and that made him seem a very romantic figure.

It was a repetition of that other cousinly visit; we rode, walked, danced and sang together. They were able to bring us news of Uncle Leopold and Aunt Louise; and I was very happy for them because they now had a little son who was named Leopold after his father. I had been in transports of joy when I had heard of the child's safe arrival. Dear Aunt Louise must have been particularly joyful as she had been disappointed once before.

When Uncle William and Aunt Adelaide invited the cousins to Windsor I was in a fever of apprehension lest there should be tension between the King and Mama.

He did ignore her and made a point of my sitting between him and George Cambridge at dinner there; but perhaps due to Aunt Adelaide's tact, we managed to avoid a real upset and Mama and the King satisfied themselves with black looks.

I was glad when the visit was over, which was such a pity, for I did love Windsor and the King was always so kind to me. We danced often and that was a great pleasure. I had too little dancing. Mama said I should not dance with anyone who was not royal, which meant that there were very few people with whom I could dance. But the cousins loved dancing, and would often whirl me round the drawing-room—which was of course permissible.

I was very sorry when they left and kept telling myself how fortunate I was to have such delightful cousins.

That was like a prelude. It was not long after the departure of those cousins when Mama summoned me to her apartments. She was waving a letter in her hand and I knew that it was good news.

My heart began to beat more quickly. Could it really be . . . at last?

'Your Uncle Ernest is coming.'

Uncle Ernest! He was the one who had been so harsh with his wife Luise—Albert's mother.

'And,' went on Mama, 'he is bringing with him his two sons— your cousins Ernest and Albert.'

'Oh, Mama!'

'I thought you would be pleased. Uncle Leopold is delighted that they are coming. He says he very much hopes that you and Albert will like each other. He is, as a matter of fact, certain that you will. He says he knows you both so very well and he regards you as his beloved children.'

'Oh, Mama, that is wonderful!'

'They will be here in May.'

'For my birthday?'

Mama nodded.

I said: 'My seventeenth birthday!' Mama looked a little less pleased, but I took every opportunity of reminding her how old I was getting.

Excitedly I discussed the visit with Lehzen. I would get out my drawing books to show them. I wondered if Albert . . . the cousins . . . liked drawing. I wondered if they sang. Did they like dancing?

'They would have been taught these accomplishments as a part of their education,' said Lehzen.

'Yes, Lehzen, but there is a difference between being taught and liking.'

Lehzen patted my shoulder and smiled at me.

Inevitably trouble began to show itself. I had not realized before how anxious people were for me to marry a husband who should be chosen for me by them. Being in my position meant that there were differing opinions in the family and it was a foregone conclusion that the one chosen for me by my mother would not be the King's elect.

The King very much wanted me to marry George Cambridge.

There was no doubt that George was a very charming boy; he had been more or less brought up by Aunt Adelaide when his parents were abroad, and she and the King looked upon him as the son they had not had. They considered him ideal for me. But on the other hand Uncle Leopold and my mother had chosen Albert. It was natural for me to lean towards Uncle Leopold's choice. I had adored him, looked up to him. Of course the dearest friend I had ever had was Lehzen, but that was different. I did not idolize her; I merely loved her. Besides, Uncle Leopold's being a man made him seem more grand, more important; and I felt, at that time, that if Albert was his choice, he must be mine too. The fact was that I had fallen in love with Albert's image before I met him. I was determined to love Albert, because, since Uncle Leopold thought he was the most charming and the most suitable young man in the world, he must be.

The King was very well aware of Uncle Leopold's intentions— just as Uncle Leopold was of the King's. I had heard the King refer to Uncle Leopold as 'that water-drinking nincompoop, always thinking he is ill,' prancing about in built-up shoes in his feather boa'. Uncle Leopold's opinion of the King was equally unflattering.

I was horrified though when the King tried to prevent my uncle and cousins coming to England. But the Prime Minister apparently said this could not be done, for there was no political reason why their visit should be banned. Then Uncle William looked round for the best ways of discomfiting them and he decided to invite the Prince of Orange and his sons to come to England, and their visit should coincide with that of my uncle and cousins. The Prince of Orange had long been an enemy of Uncle Leopold's.

It seemed that, as usual, someone was going to do something to spoil the visit.

Uncle Leopold was incensed.

He wrote to me:

'My dearest child, I am really *astonished* at the conduct of your old Uncle, the King. This invitation of the Prince of Orange and his sons, this forcing him upon others, is very extraordinary . . .

'Not later than yesterday I got a half official communication from England, insinuating that it would be *highly* desirable if the visit of *your* relations *should not take place this year*. The relations of the King and the Queen, therefore, to the God-knows-what degree, are to come in shoals and rule the land, when *your relations* are to be *forbidden* the country, and that when, as you know, the whole of your relations have ever been very dutiful and kind to the King. Really and truly I never saw or heard anything like it, and I really hope it will *a little rouse your spirit*; now that slavery is even abolished in the British Colonies, I do not comprehend *why* your lot alone should be to be kept, a little white slavey in England for the pleasure of the Court, who never bought you, as I am not aware of their having gone to any expense on that head, or the King's even having *spent a sixpence for your existence.* I expect that my visit to England will be prohibited by an Order in Council . . .

'I have not the least doubt that the King, in his passion for the Oranges, will be *excessively rude to your relations*'; this, however, will not signify much; they are *your guests*, not *his* . . .'

How angry he was! And how disappointed I was that this great occasion should be tarnished by this perpetual family bickering.

But nothing could really spoil that encounter.

Albert! What can I say of that first meeting? It is so sad to recall it now and remember him as he stood before me—tall, handsome—more handsome than anyone I had ever seen—*quite* beautiful—those large clear blue eyes, so earnest, so serious. I chide myself now because there was a time when his seriousness irked me a little. How could I ever have been irked by anything about my beloved Albert?

I was greeted first by Uncle Ernest, who smiled so warmly and affectionately; then Albert's brother, that other Ernest, who was tall and handsome, but not quite so tall, nor quite so handsome as Albert; and he was very thin, far too thin. Albert was a little . . . just a little stouter—and that was just right.

Mama was so kind and gracious. How charming she could be when she allowed her love to overcome her need always to have her position recognized! There was a wonderful family feeling about this encounter. Mama knew Uncle Leopold's wishes about Albert and me and she was in wholehearted agreement with them. So this was the happiest occasion I had ever known because it was my first meeting with my beloved Albert.

It is hard to recall it in detail, and it is too sad now that he has gone and there are only memories left. But I remember our going into the drawing-room where Uncle Ernest gave Mama a beautiful lory, knowing how fond she was of birds; and Albert told her that it would not bite even if she put her finger into its mouth.

'The colours are so lovely!' I cried. 'I shall paint your lory, Mama.'

'Victoria is very pleased with her little sketches,' said Mama; and dear Albert said he would like to see them; so I sat on the sofa, between my two cousins, and showed them my sketch books.

Ernest said flatteringly: 'They are wonderful. You are a great artist.'

Albert commented that they were really quite good, which was, after all, honest.

Then we talked about music and I discovered that they both loved it, and that they played the piano and sang. How wonderful to sing duets with Albert!

Mama clapped her hands and said how well our voices went together.

My seventeenth birthday came. Another year and I should be eighteen—the magic age. Seventeen seemed almost there. I wrote in my Journal:

'Today I completed my seventeenth year. I am an old person indeed.'

The days were so short. Every morning I woke up, I thought: The cousins are here. Dear Ernest and dear, dear Albert.

I wonder sometimes whether I should have been quite so taken with Albert had it not been that Uncle Leopold had imprinted such a picture of his perfections in my mind.

Perhaps I eulogize, looking back, and imagine I felt more strongly than I did. I had been deeply impressed by all the cousins. Should I have been as ready to fall in love with any one of them as I was with Albert? And was I in love with Albert at this stage, or did the overwhelming love for him which came later, make me believe I had been?

We were not so much alike in those days although afterwards we grew to think alike, to admire the same things and strive for the same ends.

I was at that time frivolous and pleasure-loving. How I enjoyed dancing! And it was my great delight to stay up late indulging in light entertainment. I was impetuous, loving people almost as soon as I set eyes on them, and showing my feelings. I could dislike people too. There was nothing restrained about me and my dear Albert was all restraint.

Then he did not care about dancing when to me it was the most enjoyable of entertainments, and he grew very sleepy at night. I was never sleepy when something was going on and I wanted to take it all in.

No, we were not very much alike. It was only later that we grew together. So it may well be that I did not appreciate him at the time as much as I later thought I did.

We were invited to Windsor. The King could hardly ignore them, even though he had not wanted them to come. I was in a fever of apprehension during the visit, but it went off fairly smoothly. I noticed that Albert was yawning during one of the King's levees and I was afraid that others would see it too. I could imagine the King's comment. Not that he could talk. He often nodded off and everyone knew it for when he opened his eyes he would often say something quite irrelevant to what was happening.

Albert was aloof, reticent by nature; I was the reverse. He was witty and very thoughtful; he was cleverer than his brother; and when I looked at Albert I wondered why I had ever thought Ernest handsome.

So it was a wonderful and memorable visit, and when it came to an end I was desolate. I could not bear it. The days had been so full and exciting.

Albert said goodbye regretfully, but quietly. I on the other hand could not stop my tears from falling.

'Dear Albert . . . dear Ernest . . . you *must* come again.'

Mama wept too and said how delightful it had been to have her dear relations with her.

'There must be more meetings,' she said.

I had written a letter for Uncle Ernest to take to Uncle Leopold and in it I told him of my pleasure in meeting Albert.

'I must thank you, my beloved Uncle, for the prospect of *great* happiness you have contributed to give me in the person of dear Albert. Allow me then, my dearest Uncle, to tell you how delighted I am with him, and how much I like him in every way. He possesses every quality that could be desired to render me perfectly happy. He is so sensible, so kind, so good, and so amiable too. He has besides the most pleasing and delightful appearance you can possibly see.

'I have only now to beg you, dearest Uncle, to take care of the health of one, now so *dear* to me, and to take him under your *special* protection . . .'

I was desolate for weeks after they had left and my only comfort was in remembering little scenes from the visit and some of the wise comments of my dear Albert.

He told me, long afterwards, that when he saw Uncle Leopold after that visit, and our uncle asked him what he thought of me, his only comment had been: 'She is very amiable.'

I laughed when he told me and compared his comment with all the fulsome compliments I had paid him.

But, as I said at that time, Albert and I were very different from each other.

Dash comforted me during those days after the cousins' departure. The dear little thing seemed to understand. When I sat remembering, he would leap onto my lap and nestle up to me as though to say, The cousins have gone, but you still have me.

'Yes, darling Dashy,' I said, 'I have you.' And then I remembered how funnily Albert had played with him, for the two had taken to each other immediately, and that made me sad again.

Now that I was soon to be eighteen I felt a new independence. My dislike for Sir John Conroy had increased. I should never forgive him for coming into my bedroom when I was ill and trying to extract a promise from me in the hope that I was too weak to refuse. It seemed a dastardly act—and typical of him. Mama was as close to him as ever, and I began to think of them as 'the plotters'. Mama was so furious because Uncle William lived on, and she was becoming so dictatorial to me, and told me several times a day how much she had done for me. I said, very coldly, on one occasion: 'No, Mama. You did it for yourself.' And I swept out of the room and left her.

I think that shocked her, for she was silent, and there was a long conference with Sir John.

I was changing. I was beginning to feel that there were two factions in our household, and my mother and I were opposing each other. Sometimes I felt I had only one real friend in the household; and that was my dear Lehzen.

My half-brother, Charles, Prince of Leiningen, was with us at this time. He had two adorable little boys and I loved playing with them; but I believed that Charles was on my mother's side and planned with her and Sir John to make me subservient to her will, which was for her to be Regent, even after I was of age, and to make Sir John Conroy my private secretary. I knew what that would mean. They would make the rules and I should be expected to obey them.

No! It was not going to be like that at all.

For a long time Aunt Sophia, who was a constant caller at our apartments as she was also living in the Palace where visiting could then be easy and unceremonious, was somewhat enamoured of Sir John. I knew that she was a spy for him. What was it about that man that women found so irresistible when he was to me quite odious? I was always careful what I said in Aunt Sophia's presence.

Another sly creature was Flora Hastings whom I had never liked since she was so rude to Lehzen, sneering at her German ways and her love of caraway seeds—as though that mattered, weighed up besides loving and selfless devotion, which was very different from what I found in some quarters!

Looking back, I can see that I actively disliked Mama at this time.

I wished to dissociate myself from her. I did not want the King and Queen to think that I approved of her behaviour towards them. I am afraid my mother was not a very wise woman. She was very uneasy about the growing change in me but she did not attempt to alter her ways by practising a little diplomacy. She could so easily have won me back, for she was after all my mother, and I felt a strong sense of duty towards her. I wanted to love her and tried hard to—but it was just that she would not let me. She must have known that I was acutely embarrassed by her assumption of royalty, but she continued in exactly the same way. I think in her heart she could not accept the fact that I was no longer a child.

I was deeply distressed when Aunt Adelaide invited us to Windsor on the thirteenth of August.

Mama said: 'Here is an invitation to celebrate Adelaide's birthday.'

'Oh, that will be fun,' I cried.

'Not for us,' said Mama, in the role of haughty Regent which she loved to play. 'We shall not be there.'

'But, Mama . . .'

Mama held up a hand and I saw Sir John's eyes on me . . . mocking . . . because he knew that I wanted to go to Windsor and even if I did not enjoy going I would believe we should do so on such an occasion.

'Adelaide'—Mama rarely referred to her as the Queen—'forgets it is *my* birthday a few days later and I do not intend to celebrate *that* at Windsor.'

'Your Grace will wish to go to Claremont to celebrate your birthday, I expect,' said the odious one.

'You are right, Sir John,' said Mama. 'That is what I intend to do. So I shall decline this woman's invitation. I suppose she thinks her birthday is so much more important than mine.'

'Oh no, she wouldn't think that at all, Mama,' I began.

But Mama just smiled at me. 'My darling, you don't understand these things.' She turned to Sir John and just as though I were not there said: 'I shall send a note at once.'

I went back to Lehzen, fuming with rage. How dared they? Why had I allowed it? Why did I not say, I am the heir to the throne. I could be Queen at any moment now . . . but I hope not. I want Uncle William to go on living. I don't want to be Queen . . . not until it is too late for you to interfere.

Oh yes, there was beginning to be war between Mama and me.

The King's birthday was on the twenty-first, not long after the Queen's, and of course that was a time when I must be present because it was a State occasion. No doubt Mama would like to give a regal refusal, but even she could not do that.

So we travelled down to Windsor.

The King had been to Westminster to prorogue Parliament and before returning to Windsor he decided to call in at Kensington Palace because he would know we were not in our apartments. Whether he had some inkling as to what had happened about our apartments I did not know. All I was aware of was that Mama had asked for more rooms and they had been refused. I naturally thought, when I came back to Kensington after my illness, that he had relented and given the required permission. I was to learn otherwise. I felt sure that he must have had some suspicion of what had happened and no doubt Mama's impolite rejection of the invitation to celebrate the Queen's birthday had particularly incensed him.

The fact was that he called at the Palace to inspect our apartments and was filled with rage when he discovered that, in spite of the fact that he had refused Mama permission to take the extra rooms, she had deliberately disobeyed him.

We were in the drawing-room when he returned and he came straight there. His eyes were bulging and his face was crimson. There was no doubt of his anger.

I approached him and curtsied and he softened slightly, but as I kissed him and he returned my kiss I could sense that he was quivering with rage; and I knew that it was against Mama. Even so I was unprepared.

Mama was close behind me. She always resented my being greeted before her. The King did not ignore her. He bowed almost imperceptibly and his eyes blazed at her.

He then said in a voice which could be distinctly heard all over the drawing-room: 'A great liberty has been taken with one of my palaces. I have just left Kensington Palace where, against my express command, apartments have been taken. I cannot understand such conduct. Nor will I endure it. It is quite disrespectful towards the King.'

Mama stood there, pale, but with her head held high, regarding the King haughtily. I was so ashamed, I could have wept. I should have known. How dared she! And I had so enjoyed those lovely rooms at the Palace. If I had known that we had no right to them I should have hated them. I should have forced her to vacate them. Yes, that was what I should have done. I should not have allowed Mama to behave as she had. I should let her know that her importance came through her relationship to me.

I wanted to leave Windsor. I could not look at all these people. I saw in their faces that amused excitement which people have when there is trouble for others. I wanted to run away and hide.

The Queen said: 'The King is very tired. It has been a long day for him and the journey from Westminster to Windsor can be exhausting.'

She went out with him. Mama and I followed them. I could not bear to look at Mama. I was seething with anger against her and I knew I should show it.

Part of me did not care. And yet I held myself in check. Perhaps the time was not yet ripe. But it was coming.

Worse was to follow.

I spent a restless night though Mama, in the same room, seemed to sleep peacefully. I could not understand how she could reconcile herself to such behaviour. If anyone had flouted her authority or attempted to rob her of one iota of the dignity she thought due to her, she would have been incensed; yet she continually defied the King, which was actually defying the Crown.

When I was eighteen, when I took on responsibility, she must never be allowed to dictate to me.

I was longing to leave Windsor for I grew so apprehensive when Mama and the King were under the same roof, and I had rarely seen him so angry as he had been on the previous day. I thought he was going to have a fit—and if he had it would have been Mama's fault.

Perhaps tomorrow we could leave.

So it was with great trepidation that I went down to dinner that night. My fears were on a firm foundation although the King was charming to me; but I noticed Aunt Adelaide was watching him in that uneasy way she had when she feared there might be trouble. The King behaved as though Mama were not present, looking right through her as though she were invisible; but when he turned to me he was very friendly and kept patting my hand. He said my eighteenth birthday would be in the coming May . . . another nine months. Then I should be of age. He stressed that once or twice, and although he did not look at Mama, I think he wanted her to hear it.

There were a hundred guests because it was his birthday, and it was naturally a very grand occasion. When the meal was over the Queen proposed the King's health, and he got up to reply.

We were all relaxed and even the Queen seemed to be lulled into a sense of security. The evening was almost over and it had passed without any unpleasantness.

And then it happened.

The King rose to reply to the toast. We all expected him to ramble on as he invariably did at such times, but soon we were all roused from our complacency.

'Thank you all for your wishes for my continued health,' he said. 'I trust to God that my life may be spared for nine months longer, after which period, in the event of my death, no Regency will take place.' He looked at me. 'I should then have the satisfaction of leaving the royal authority to the personal exercise of that young lady . . .' He pointed a finger at me and I shrank into my seat. I dared not look at Mama. '. . . the heiress presumptive to the throne, and not in the hands of a person now near to me who is surrounded by evil advisers and herself incompetent to act with propriety in the station in which she would be placed. I have been insulted—grossly and continually—by that person, and I am determined to endure no longer a course of behaviour so disrespectful to me. Among many other things I have particularly to complain of the manner in which that young lady has been kept away from my Court; she has been repeatedly kept from my Drawing-Rooms, at which she ought to have been present, but I am fully resolved that this shall not happen again. I would have her know that I am the King, and I am determined to make my authority respected, and for the future I shall insist and command that the Princess on all occasions appear at my Court, as it is her duty to do.'

As I listened I felt the tears gushing to my eyes. He was more than angry; he had been deeply wounded; and he was a kind old gentleman although I knew he could not be considered a good king; he was more like a bluff country squire. He blundered and rumbled on and was often incoherent, but he was kind and meant well, and what more can one ask of people than that?

Mine were tears of humiliation. I was ashamed of Mama, who sat there as though stunned, for once speechless and bewildered as though, in spite of the King's outburst only the night before, she could not believe her ears.

The Queen as usual came to the rescue. As the King sat down she rose; and that was the signal for the ladies to follow her from the dining-room.

When we were in the drawing-room Mama's fury burst out.

'I . . . I have never been so insulted in my life,' she cried. 'We are leaving at once. I shall order the carriage immediately.'

'No, Mama,' I protested. 'We cannot do that. Please, Mama, listen to me.'

Mama was too distraught to notice the firmness of my tone.

The Queen said gently: 'You cannot leave tonight. It is too late. Wait until the morning.'

I suppose Mama realized how impossible it would be to leave at that hour for Claremont, so tightening her lips and clenching her fists, she agreed to stay for the night.

'But not a moment longer,' she cried. 'The first thing in the morning we leave. To be so insulted . . . in front of all those people . . .'

I felt a coldness enter my heart. It was true she had been chastised publicly. But, Mama, I thought, you deserved it. You deserved every bit of it.

After that the rift between myself and my mother was apparent to everyone. I could not sympathize with her. I could not forgive her for taking possession of those rooms at the Palace when the King had refused them to her. They were his rooms; it was his Palace; and to take them was, in a way, stealing.

Mama would not learn lessons and there was another unfortunate incident.

The King had appointed his daughter by Dorothy Jordan, who

had become Lady de l'Isle and Dudley, custodian of Kensington Palace, which meant that she had apartments there.

Mama was outraged. The Palace should be for the convenience of members of the royal family, she said, and she did not count an actress's bastards in that category. But the King evidently did . . . I had always heard that he was very fond of the FitzClarences and that from the moment she came to England Aunt Adelaide had treated them all as her step-children.

I did not care for them—not because of their birth, but because I found some of them decidedly arrogant. This did not apply to Lady de l'Isle and Dudley, however, whom I quite liked. She was heavily pregnant when she came and while she was at the Palace she was confined. Mama was furious at all the fuss. The King sent his doctors, and the condition of Lady de l'Isle and Dudley was said to be very grave.

Mama had arranged a dinner party and I said to her: 'Mama, you must cancel the party. We cannot have it while the King's daughter is in this condition so near us.'

Mama cried angrily: 'What has the King's bastard to do with me? Why should I not receive my guests because of that creature?'

'Mama,' I said, 'she lives here. They are all very anxious about her.'

Mama shrugged her shoulders and went on with her preparations. The party took place and while it was in progress Lady de l'Isle and Dudley died.

I was horrified for I hated to be associated with such conduct. I went to Lehzen. She agreed with me, of course. It seemed to me that she was the only one in the household to whom I could reveal my feelings.

After that I became more aloof. I found it increasingly difficult to cloak my attitude and a definite coldness crept into my relationship with Mama.

My brother Charles tried to reason with me, and I made it clear to him that he was interfering in matters which were no concern of his. I was sorry for I did not want to be on bad terms with my family, but Charles heard only Mama's side and he tried to tell me that I was incapable of acting without her.

'No,' I said firmly, 'I shall be incapable of acting with her.'

I needed Sir John Conroy to be my secretary, he said. I had no idea what burdens of state would be mine. How could a young girl without experience rule on her own?

I said: 'I shall have my ministers to help me.'

They were the people I wanted. Not Mama. Not Sir John Conroy. Not my brother Charles.

Charles left soon after and went to see Uncle Leopold.

As a result of that visit Baron Stockmar arrived.

I knew that he had been very close to Albert; he had also been with Uncle Leopold at the time of Charlotte's death. He was three years older than Uncle Leopold and very wise, so I had always heard from my uncle and, of course, I believed every word he said. Uncle Leopold had brought him to England as his physician when he had married Charlotte, and as my uncle himself was plagued by many ailments, he had great need of Dr. Christian Friedrich Stockmar. He had had such confidence in Stockmar that he had sent him to assist in Albert's upbringing, which clearly showed his regard for him.

I greeted Baron Stockmar warmly, so did my mother. He was close to Uncle Leopold and that made me pleased to see him; but I soon realized that he too had my mother's side of the story, and he began by urging me to take Sir John Conroy as my secretary.

I was most emphatic about that. I had grown very much stronger in the last few months. It may have been because of Mama's activities which made me see her in an increasingly unflattering light; or it may simply have been that I was growing up.

My brother Charles joined with Stockmar in trying to weaken my resolve. I was young, so young, they kept reiterating until I could have boxed their ears. I was so inexperienced, they said.

I pointed out that they, being new to the country, were more lacking in experience of it than I.

They were amazed; but I made it perfectly clear that I would not be forced into making decisions which I might regret afterwards.

Later Lord Liverpool came to Kensington. He saw Sir John who, I knew, was fighting desperately for his political position. If I had had any say in that it would have been defunct long ago. I guessed he was telling Lord Liverpool that I was unfit to rule, that I needed guidance, that I was young for my years. For he had said these things and often implied them to me.

I managed to see Lord Liverpool alone.

He said: 'Since you will not have Sir John Conroy for your private secretary, in the event of your becoming Queen, would you put yourself in the hands of the Prime Minister?'

I had seen Lord Melbourne once or twice and he had made a very favourable impression on me. I replied at once that I considered that would be most suitable. Perhaps Sir John Conroy could

take the post of Keeper of the Privy Purse? suggested Lord Liverpool.

'No,' I said. 'Never. Sir John Conroy will have no post in my
household.'

I begged Lord Liverpool to try to understand the position into
which I had been forced.

He looked at me very steadily and then he said: 'I understand.'

I felt much better because I believed that if I could rid myself of
my *bête noir*, John Conroy, and could escape from my mother's
rule and take the advice of a man of the world like the Prime Minister—who after all was in charge of the country's affairs—I could
face the tasks ahead of me with some confidence.

The King was as good as his word in insisting on my attending his
next Drawing-Room. My mother must have been shaken by that
outburst of his, and although she laughed at him and called him an
old buffoon, she did realize that when the summons came, it must
be obeyed.

She seemed impervious to his insults and declared that he injured
himself more than he did her—with which I did not agree. But I
had for some time given up agreeing with my mother.

My eighteenth birthday was a short time ahead. Somehow I believed that when I reached that age a great deal of the petty irritation
which I had to endure would pass away.

My mother talked of the King as though he were dying. Indeed,
I knew he was getting more and more feeble; she was very resentful
towards fate, which was allowing me to creep slowly up to my
eighteenth birthday while the King still lived. Sometimes it seemed
like a race between me and Uncle William. Would he die before I
was eighteen? He saw it in that way, too, and I was sure he was
determined not to die until I had come of age. He hated my mother
as strongly as she hated him—more so perhaps, because he knew
she was longing for him to die.

I was dismayed to find the Queen absent. Nothing went smoothly
when she was not there. The King told me she was unwell and he
had insisted on her resting.

I showed my concern and that pleased him. He said: 'She will
be about again soon. She does too much, you know.'

'I know how we all miss her when she is absent,' I said.

He nodded and at that moment caught sight of Sir John Conroy,
whom my mother had insisted should come in our party.

The King called to the Lord Chamberlain, and Lord Conyngham came hastily to his side.

The King pointed to Sir John. He said: 'I won't have that fellow in my drawing-room. Throw him out.'

Conyngham looked bewildered. The King growled: 'You heard me. Out! Out! I'll not have him here.'

Anyone but Sir John would have been overcome with shame. I had never seen anyone before turned out of the King's Drawing-Room.

Sir John smiled insolently at Lord Conyngham and there was a nonchalant smile on his face as he was escorted out of the room.

I was pleased. At least the King shared my opinion, even if others were trying to convince me of the advisability of making him a member of my household.

I was getting letters full of advice from Uncle Leopold. Not that there was anything unusual about that. He had always advised me and he was getting more and more concerned. I wondered what Mama was writing to him and what my brother Charles had said to him when he went over to Belgium in such haste.

The eighteenth birthday was approaching fast. They all knew that once I reached it, I would no longer be the child whom they had taken such pains to direct in the way they wanted her to go.

Uncle Leopold was very happy that year because Aunt Louise had given birth to another son and for a while his letters were full of that happy event. I rejoiced with him and secretly would rather hear news of the babies than quite so many injunctions to do this or not do that—which sometimes seemed contradictory to me.

The new baby was named Philippe and Uncle Leopold told me that little Leopold was very interested in his brother, but not at all impressed by his appearance. After putting his head on one side and regarding the newly born infant for some moments he said: *'Pas beau frère.'*

'He now thinks better of him,' wrote Uncle Leopold, 'but he makes an odd little face when he sees him. Later on they will have titles and I think young Leopold will be the Duke of Brabant and Philippe Count of Flanders.'

I smiled to think of those two children with such grand titles; and how happy I was because Uncle Leopold had found happiness at last, after all he had suffered in his marriage to Charlotte.

Now, all too rarely, he wrote of his family. There were constant injunctions on how I was to choose my household, how I was to act with my ministers . . . when the time came. I was beginning to be apprehensive and hoping that the time would not come just yet.

Uncle Leopold wrote: 'My object is that you should be no one's *tool.*'

That phrase stayed with me for long after I had read his letter; and a rather disloyal thought came into my mind. No one's tool . . . No. Not even yours, dear Uncle.

A few days before my birthday Lord Conyngham called at the Palace. A message was sent to me asking me to go to the drawing-room. When I arrived there I knew something important had happened. Mama looked very angry and Sir John was certainly put out.

Lord Conyngham bowed to me and said: 'I have a letter from His Majesty who has commanded me to put it into no hands but yours.'

'Thank you,' I said, taking the letter.

Mama would have taken it from me and I guessed that she and Sir John had tried to get their hands on it before I arrived; but Lord Conyngham had had express orders from the King to give it to no one but me.

I felt very important.

Mama said: 'Well, open it, my love.'

I was aware of Sir John's snake-like eyes upon me and I replied: 'I will open it in my sitting-room.'

I was very confident of myself. Only a few more days to go before I reached my eighteenth birthday. It would be too late now for Mama to interfere with me. Her hopes of becoming Regent of England were over. It was time for her to realize I was grown up and would brook no interference.

I walked out of the room and when I opened the letter I read that the King was offering me ten thousand pounds a year and an establishment of my own—apart from that of my mother.

My joy was intense. I felt like a person who has been in prison and at last sees freedom ahead.

But of course I could not escape so easily. Mama and Sir John discovered what was in the letter and together they drew up a draft for me to sign. When I read it I refused to sign for it stated that while I gratefully accepted the ten thousand pounds, I begged to remain as I was because of my youth and inexperience. The draft set out, too, that my income should not be 'Mother-free'

I said I should like to consult one of the ministers—Lord Melbourne, for instance.

They went on and on. Mama would not stop telling me all she had done for me. I had misjudged my strength. I had so recently emerged from my captivity. I was still unsure of myself and needed advice. I thought of Uncle Leopold but I knew he would say 'Sign'; for he it was who had said I needed to be with my mother for a while yet.

I thought: If I sign this, it is only for a few days. When I am eighteen, I shall do as I please.

I signed, to stop my mother's constant haranguing and to escape from the evil looks of that man.

As soon as I had left them I repented of what I had done, and I wrote a statement to the King in which I said that the draft was not my own.

I knew he would understand, and he apparently did.

At last the great day came. My eighteenth birthday. I was of age.

While I lay in bed contemplating what this meant, I heard the sound of singing below my window. It was George Rodwell, who was the Musical Director at Covent Garden, and I learned later that he had composed the song he was singing expressly for me on my eighteenth birthday.

I guessed that Mama had arranged this as a special treat, and instead of gratitude for such thoughtfulness in giving me the sort of pleasure I liked best, a notion came into my head that she was very worried and was trying hard to placate me.

The King had sent me a grand piano—one of the finest I had ever seen. I rushed to it and began to play while Mama looked on scowling. I knew she would have liked to send it back. But she could not. It was mine—and I was eighteen years old.

There was to be a grand ball in the evening at St. James's to celebrate my birthday—another gift from the King and the Queen. How wonderful! Mama *must* not spoil this. I wanted to tell the King how happy his gift had made me and that I should never forget to be grateful to him every time I played my beautiful piano.

It seemed that everyone was aware of the importance of the day. A deputation came from the city of London to congratulate me. Mama was at my side when I received it.

How she irritated me! She would never learn. I had been thinking she must realize now that she could no longer treat me as a child; but when I was about to reply to the deputation and thank them most sincerely for their good wishes and all the trouble they had taken to come to the Palace, Mama pushed me aside and talked to them herself. It was clear to me that I was not yet prepared to show my intentions. She still overawed me as she had when I was a child. So I was silent while she told them that I owed everything to her upbringing, a woman who had been left without a husband, how she had sacrificed herself for me, how she had never failed in her duty.

They were dismayed and disappointed because they had wanted to speak to me and they did not really like Mama; they did not like her fussy clothes, nor her accent. Why she, who had been so insistent that I should have no trace of a German accent, could not see that they resented hers, I could not imagine.

I found I was frowning at Mama with cold dislike.

Later in the day we rode through the streets.

'We must show ourselves,' said Mama.

And I wanted to reply: 'No, Mama, *I* must show *myself.* It does not matter whether you accompany me or not.'

But there she was, regally inclining her head while the people shouted my name. I smiled at them and waved; and it was heart-warming to see how they loved me.

But Mama still seemed to think that all the cheers were for her.

Then it was time to get ready for the ball at St. James's. As always on these occasions I felt twinges of apprehension wondering what trouble would arise between the King and Mama.

How I loved a ball! I wanted to dance and dance all night. Nothing else could have given such a happy finale to a great occasion. And Mama would spoil it all—if she possibly could.

But she did not that time, which was due to no lack of venom on her part. It just turned out that neither the King nor the Queen were able to attend.

It was a wonderful ball. Dancing, I forgot all the irritations and fears of the past year. I opened the ball with the Duke of Norfolk's grandson who was an excellent dancer and executed his steps with perfection. I felt as though I were dancing on air.

And that was just a beginning.

I danced all the time and I was so happy as we rode home through the streets and there were still people out to cheer me.

Eighteen years old! The milestone passed!

How exuberantly I wrote in my journal next day about the crowd in the streets who had stood about just to see me ride by.

'I was very much amused,' I wrote.

* * *

I stayed in my sitting-room. I hardly spoke to Mama; and when she came to bed at night I pretended to be asleep.

She and Sir John were very apprehensive.

Mama wrote notes to me. I think she believed she could impress me more by writing than by speaking because when she spoke she became so angry. There were tirades of wrath, to which I appeared to shut my ears. I would sit stolidly while she raved, and then make an excuse to go.

She and Sir John must have felt me slipping out of their grasp and that was very worrying to them both—particularly perhaps to Sir John. Mama would always be mother of the Queen and have some standing because of that, even though she did fail in her grandiose schemes for becoming Regent, whereas Sir John was in danger of losing his career.

'You are still very young,' wrote Mama, 'and all your success so far has been due to your mother's reputation . . .'

No, Mama, I thought. If I have had any success that has been mine in spite of my mother.

'Do not be too sanguine about your own talents and understanding . . .'

No, Mama, I am not. I am just determined not to be the puppet of you and your friend, Sir John . . .

We were now well into June and the news from Windsor was grave. The King was very weak.

On that never to be forgotten Tuesday morning of the twentieth of June in the year 1837 I was awakened from my sleep to find Mama standing beside my bed.

'Wake up, Victoria,' she said, 'the Archbishop of Canterbury and Lord Conyngham are here with the King's physician. They are waiting to see you.'

'Why, Mama? What time is it?'

'Six o'clock,' she said. 'But never mind the time. They are waiting to see you.'

I knew what this meant and an awesome feeling swept over me. I rose and put on my dressing-gown and slippers.

'Come,' said Mama, and she led me into the sitting-room.

At the door, I paused and looked at her.

'I shall go in alone, Mama,' I said.

She stared at me.

But I knew then what position I held. I could feel the crown on my head. I had no need to do what she told me now.

'Alone,' I repeated firmly.

She looked stunned but she did not attempt to detain me.

The three men knelt down as I approached, and I knew what that meant. I held out my hand for them to kiss as naturally as though I had rehearsed it.

They called me Your Majesty and I felt a great surge of emotion. There were tears in my eyes and in theirs. I suppose I looked so young and defenceless with my hair streaming down my back and wearing only my dressing-gown and slippers.

The Archbishop told me that the King had died happy and had directed his mind to religion and was prepared for his death.

I turned to Lord Conyngham and asked after the Queen for I knew how she loved him.

I said: 'Please take my condolences to the Queen.'

Lord Conyngham replied: 'I will do as Your Majesty commands without delay.'

Then I left them and went into my bedroom to dress.

I was eighteen years old. I was a queen. Oddly enough the first thought that occurred to me was: Now I can be alone.

The Crowned Queen

I put on a black dress and went down to breakfast. Everything was different. Now I was a queen. There was one thought which kept hammering in my brain. I must be good. I must be wise. I must do my duty. I must put aside all frivolous desire for pleasure. I must serve my country.

There was Uncle Leopold to tell me what to do as he had been telling me all my life; but of course he was the king of another country and it was not really suitable for the King of the Belgians to have a hand in the ruling of England. I knew that in future I was going to have to be wary, even of Uncle Leopold, for as a good king—and I was sure he was that—he would have to put the interests of his country first.

Yes, I had to walk very carefully.

While I was breakfasting Baron Stockmar came down to talk to me. He was wise but of course he was Uncle Leopold's man. Everything had changed since I had become Queen.

I talked to him about Uncle William and my pity for Queen Adelaide, for I understood how deep her grief must be.

I left him after breakfast and went to my sitting-room to write letters—one to Uncle Leopold, another to Feodore.

How strange it was to sign oneself *Victoria R*.

While I was writing, a letter arrived from the Prime Minister in which he said he would wait on me before nine o'clock.

I was very pleased that Lord Melbourne was Prime Minister. I had met him once or twice and been most impressed by his handsome appearance, his courtly manners and his amusing way of talking.

Lehzen was with me when the letter came and I said to her: 'I shall see him *quite alone* as I intend to see all my ministers in future.'

Lehzen nodded. She understood. But she was a little uneasy, fearful that the crown was going to change me.

'It will change me,' I told her. 'But nothing will ever change my love for you, dear Lehzen. You will find the Queen can be as affectionate as the Princess ever was.'

At which we wept, and she told me that I was the meaning of life to her, which was very affecting.

Lord Melbourne came as arranged. What a charming man! He bowed and kissed my hand and his beautiful blue-grey eyes filled with tears as he surveyed me which made me feel very warm towards him. I knew he was thinking of my youth and all the burdens which would descend on my shoulders.

He was most respectful and made me feel quite at ease, for although I knew he was so affected by my youth, at the same time he conveyed his faith in my ability to perform the tasks which lay ahead of me.

'Lord Melbourne,' I said, 'it has long been my intention to retain your ministry at the head of affairs.'

'I am overwhelmed with gratitude, M'am,' he replied.

'I know it could not be in better hands.'

'Your Majesty is gracious.' He went on: 'It is my duty to bring you the Declaration which Your Majesty will read to the Council. Would you just glance through it and see if it has your approval?'

'You wrote it, Lord Melbourne?'

'I confess to the deed,' he said with a slight lifting of his lips which I thought rather amusing and which made me smile.

'I am sure it is just as it should be,' I said.

'I must leave Your Majesty to consider it. The Council meeting, which can be held here in the Palace, should take place at eleven-thirty. I will call again about eleven in case there is anything with which you do not agree. I must not encroach upon Your Majesty's time now. You will want to study the Declaration. It will be my great pleasure to call again in case Your Majesty wishes to make use of me.'

'You are very kind, Lord Melbourne.'

He replied: 'Your Majesty is too gracious to your humble servant.'

And he said it in an ironical way, which I thought so amusing. I knew that my meetings with my Prime Minister were not going to be the dreary sessions one might expect. They would be light-hearted, even though we were carrying out the most serious business.

I knew from the first day that I was lucky to have Lord Melbourne for my Prime Minister—a good, honest, clever man, who was at the same time such an attractive one.

When he had gone I read through the Declaration and composed my thoughts. It was very important that I behave with the right degree of dignity and modesty before the Council.

I thought Lord Melbourne's Declaration beautifully worded and as he would be present I should draw a certain confidence from him. The way in which he had looked at me gave me belief in myself. He was a very *feeling* man. I had seen in his eyes that he was very much aware of my youth and felt protective towards me, and yet at the same time he would never forget for one instant that I was the Queen. That was a very comforting thought. Once again I rejoiced that he was the Prime Minister. It might so easily have been someone else—the Duke of Wellington or Sir Robert Peel—very honourable men, of course, but without the charm of Lord Melbourne; and a queen did rely so much on her prime minister.

He came again at eleven and asked me if there was anything I wished to say to him before the Council meeting began.

'I hope I shall not disappoint them,' I said, for I felt I could talk like that with Lord Melbourne.

'Disappoint them, M'am! Why, you will enchant them. I'll tell you something. A queen is more appealing than a king. And a beautiful, young queen . . . well, none could be so effective. Have no qualms. Your youth . . . your sex . . . they are an advantage.'

'Do you really think so?'

'I do indeed.'

'But perhaps they are not all like you, Lord Melbourne.'

'I trust not, Your Majesty. I should not like to be among the common herd.'

That made me laugh and I felt considerably relaxed. He had made me feel that it was not such an ordeal after all.

'I was just wondering how I should be before them all.'

'Be yourself, M'am. No one else could be more delightful.'

Oh, what a comfort he was! I should be thinking of him all the time I was facing them.

The Council was held in the Red Salon at Kensington Palace. Mama would have loved to accompany me but she was beginning to understand that everything had changed since this morning.

I went in alone. At the door of the Salon my two uncles, Cumberland and Sussex, were waiting with Lord Melbourne. Cumberland looked as repulsive as ever. What a contrast to handsome Lord Melbourne, who gave me such an enchanting smile, with a twinkle in his eyes—while he showed the utmost respect—as though there were a conspiracy between us.

I was led to the seat and sat down. I remained seated while I read the Declaration, I am glad to say without faltering.

A good deal of formality followed. There were a great many Privy Councillors who had to be sworn in. I received the homage of my uncles and my hand was kissed and allegiance sworn by important men like Lord Palmerston, Wellington and Sir Robert Peel.

I was not nervous and I sensed that all—except Lord Melbourne—were surprised at my confident manner. I think they had been expecting a nervous young girl.

I went back to my room where there were audiences with Lord Melbourne, Lord John Russell, Lord Albemarle, who was my Master of Horse, and the Archbishop of Canterbury.

Then the ordeal was over.

Lord Melbourne whispered to me: 'You were superb. A queen . . . every inch.'

What a charming way he had of expressing himself!

I wanted to tell him that what might have been an ordeal had been an invigorating experience, and it was due to him and the confidence he had inspired in me.

I felt excited at the prospects of more meetings with him. The country is in very good hands, I thought.

I spent several hours writing letters. I must convey my condolences to Queen Adelaide, who had always been so kind to me. Dear Aunt! How lost and lonely she must be feeling now. She would be thinking of me too—no doubt remembering incidents from my childhood. When she had given me the Big Doll would be one of the pleasantest of memories. There would be many—all due to Mama—which would be less so.

That reminded me.

When Lehzen came in, I said to her: 'Lehzen, my bed is to be removed from my mother's room. In future I shall sleep alone.'

'I shall give orders that it is to be done at once,' said Lehzen.

I thought a great deal about Lehzen. She would have a position in the household now.

She came back to me and told me that the bed had been taken away from my mother's room. 'The Duchess is most upset,' she added.

'Alas,' I replied, 'I fear this will not be the only thing which upsets her.'

Lehzen shook her head.

I said: 'Lehzen, what is your position going to be?'

'I pray to God it will be as it ever was.'

'Lehzen, I don't need a governess any more.'

She looked alarmed, and I threw my arms around her. 'But I shall always need you,' I went on.

She wept a little. Dear Lehzen! Her greatest fear in life was that she should be separated from me.

She said: 'I think it would be better, my dearest, if I took no position but just remained beside you . . . always . . . the one who loves you . . . and none could love you more.'

'Dear, dear Lehzen, you will always be my friend. You shall have the title of Lady Attendant upon the Queen. What do you think of that?'

'Is there such a post?'

'There could be if I made one. But I don't see why you should not be the first. I will ask Lord Melbourne.'

'The Prime Minister! He would not want to concern himself with me!'

'Oh, he would, Lehzen. He is the most understanding man. He is so kind . . . so anxious to help.'

'You form your judgements too hastily. You always did.'

'Well, they are sometimes wise judgements. I hated Sir John Conroy from the moment I saw him and I loved you. Was I right, Lehzen? And how dare you criticize the Queen!'

We hugged each other, and Dash woke up, got out of his basket and leaped into my arms.

'Dear Dashy! He doesn't want to be left out.'

I felt very happy and confident in the future. I would have dear Lehzen as my closest friend; I had darling Dash; and now . . . Lord Melbourne.

He called again, which delighted me. The first thing he said was how impressed they all had been by the manner in which I conducted the Council.

'Believe me, M'am, they were all overwhelmed with admiration.'

'I think Sir John Conroy has given the impression that I am a frivolous girl.'

Lord Melbourne did not deny this.

'I am dismissing him from my household,' I told him.

'That does not surprise me. He will, however, remain in the Duchess's. It is a matter which you and I will discuss at greater length some time . . . very soon . . . with Your Majesty's permission, of course.'

'Yes. That would please me,' I said.

'We will deal with Master Conroy . . . Your Majesty and I.'

I laughed. How good it was to have such a man beside me!

'I was telling Your Majesty how successful the Council was. I heard it said that Your Majesty's hand was remarkably smooth and sweet.'

'Did they really say that?'

Lord Melbourne placed his hand on his heart and raised his eyes to Heaven.

'I swear it, M'am.'

I laughed and he laughed with me. He had such a wonderful gift for making everything *amusing*.

After he had left I decided that I would not keep Sir John Conroy in my household a day longer. I had the Prime Minister's approval for my actions. So I sent a note telling him that I should no longer need him to serve me.

I wondered what his reaction would be. I imagined his going to my mother, and their moaning together over the cruel fate which had allowed me to come of age and ascend the throne and so destroy their grandiose schemes for ruling the country together.

I was so glad to be free of them that I felt a twinge of pity for them—but not much. And in any case I had too many other matters with which to concern myself.

I said I would take my dinner upstairs . . . and alone.

How I enjoyed that! I felt I could look back over the events of the day with satisfaction.

I had not seen Mama all day and I was a little uncomfortable when the time came to say goodnight to her.

She looked different—subdued even. I felt a little sorry to see her so unlike her old self, but I forced myself to remember all the trouble she had made, and reminded myself that the only way I could make her happy was by giving way to her, which would have meant to allow her to run the country's affairs.

No. I had to be firm. She was vain in the extreme; she was quite unfit, as the last King had said, to take any part in affairs. She did not understand the people and had done much to antagonize them during the years of waiting.

No, Mama, I thought, this has to be an end to your ambitions.

I kissed her and said a cool goodnight. She looked stricken but she knew there was no turning back. Mama would no longer dare advise me as to what I must do.

I turned and left her and went to my bedroom—my own bedroom with my bed in it—and no other.

For the first time I should sleep alone.

I lay in bed thinking over my first day as Queen of England.

The very next day Lord Melbourne called upon me.

'There is this matter of our friend Sir John Conroy to discuss with Your Majesty,' he said.

The very manner in which he said 'our friend' implied that Sir John was far from that; and that Lord Melbourne disliked him as much as I did.

'Oh yes. It is a matter which I should like to get settled as soon as possible.'

'The man is a mountebank.'

How clever of Lord Melbourne to have discovered that so quickly! Sir John had deceived so many—chiefly Mama; but also Aunt Sophia, and people like Flora Hastings had been ready to work for him.

'When I was leaving the Council yesterday,' went on Lord Melbourne, 'I was approached by Baron Stockmar who said he wished to speak to me urgently about Sir John Conroy.'

'So soon?' I asked.

'There is a man who knows when the battle is lost. Your Majesty was indeed a formidable enemy . . . fighting the forces of evil, I must say, and never wavering.'

How well he understood!

'Baron Stockmar told me that Sir John has given his terms.'

'Terms?' I cried.

'Oh yes. A sort of treaty. But he does not seem to realize he is the defeated. He is making the most exorbitant demands. He wants three thousand pounds a year, the Grand Cross of the

Bath, a peerage and a seat on the Privy Council. I can tell Your Majesty that when I saw what was written in the paper, I dropped it in my disbelief.'

'I am not surprised.'

'Indeed not, M'am.'

'It is outrageous. I shall say No.'

'Quite so, M'am. There is a point. Unless we come to some compromise, he may still remain in the Duchess's service. Your Majesty can dismiss him from yours, which you have so rightly done. But the Duchess's service is another matter.'

'But we shall not give way to his demands.'

'It is a delicate matter, M'am.'

'Delicate? But I want to be rid of him.'

'And so do we all. We have taken the measure of Master Conroy and wish him . . . out. Let us wait a while, Your Majesty. Let him simmer in his uncertainty.'

'I should like to know that he was out and that I should never have to see him again.'

'There is no need for you to see him. Indeed, I fancy he will be ashamed to look Your Majesty in the face. At least, he should be. But will he be? He is a slippery customer.'

'I should like to be rid of him once and for all.'

'Ah. ''. . . 'Tis a consummation devoutly to be wished.'' But let us be diplomatic, M'am. Let us leave it alone for a while. That can do no harm.'

'And meanwhile he will stay with my mother.'

'That is a matter for the Duchess to decide.'

'But if I wish . . .'

He looked at me, his head on one side, and there was a very tender expression in his beautiful eyes. He said: 'Your Majesty's wish is law to her Prime Minister. Believe me, M'am, if I could wave a wand and grant your wishes, that is what I would do. But this . . . it is a difficult matter and when one is faced with a tricky situation, it is always better not to take hasty action.'

'I will take your advice, Lord Melbourne.'

He took my hand and kissed it.

And although I was a little sorry not to make a clean cut and get rid of Sir John without preamble, I was sure that Lord Melbourne knew best.

* * *

I was seeing Lord Melbourne every day and my regard for him grew rapidly.

I no longer looked for Uncle Leopold's letters with quite the same eagerness. I did not need advice from him now that I had someone near at hand.

I wondered whether he sensed this. If I did not write to him so regularly and so fully, he must understand that I had my new duties and that my position had changed considerably.

He wrote to me:

> 'My beloved Child, Your new dignities will not change or increase my old affection for you; may Heaven assist you, and may I have the happiness of being able to be of use to you, and to contribute to those successes in your new career for which I am so anxious . . .
>
> 'I have been most happy to learn that the swearing in of the Council passed so well . . . The translation in the papers says, *'J'ai été elevée en Angleterre.'* I should advise you to say as often as possible that you are born in England. George III gloried in this, and as none of your cousins are born in England it is your interest *de faire reporter cela fortement.* You never can say too much in praise of your country and its inhabitants. Two nations in Europe are really most ridiculous in their ex-aggerated praises of themselves; these are the English and the French. Your being national is highly important, and as you happen to be born in England, and never to have left it a moment, it would be odd enough if people tried to make out to the contrary . . .'

I felt faintly irritated by Uncle Leopold's criticism of the English. But, after all, I told myself, he is not an Englishman, and foreigners are inclined to regard us with certain dislike . . . as perhaps we regard them. Lord Melbourne seemed to me to be the perfect English gentleman; and it is hard to find a more agreeable type of man.

How lucky I had been in Lord Melbourne!

I had heard that he was a man who had had what is referred to as 'a past'. He had been involved in two divorce cases, and had had a tempestuous marriage. His only son had died. And yet he was full of good humour and always appeared to me to find life comical and amusing.

I longed to hear all about him but of course I could not ask him personally.

There were means of finding out.

I had appointed Harriet Leveson-Gower, Duchess of Sutherland, Mistress of the Robes. She was a very beautiful woman and I had always been drawn to beautiful people. She loved clothes and gossip, although she was involved in all kinds of good works. In fact she was a very interesting companion; and best of all she loved to talk and seemed to know a great deal about everyone at Court.

I found it easy to slip into conversation with her about Lord Melbourne.

She agreed that he was indeed a fascinating man. 'And what is most amazing,' she went on, 'is that he could have gone through all that scandal and yet become Prime Minister.'

I did not get the whole story all at once and I could not make Lord Melbourne the topic of conversation every time I was alone with Harriet, but I always tried to bring the talk round to him and after a few weeks I had acquired most of the facts.

His name was William Lamb, and he had inherited the title on the death of his elder brother. Even his birth was romantic. His mother had been the beautiful Elizabeth Milbanke, whose father was a Yorkshire baronet. Her family was more noble than that of the Lambs, for Lord Melbourne's father was only the first viscount. The Lambs had been lawyers who had built up a great fortune and were comparative newcomers to the peerage.

Lady Melbourne was fond of admiration. One of her lovers was said to be the Earl of Egremont.

'Lord Melbourne bears a striking resemblance to the Earl,'' Harriet told me, 'and I heard that he, as a boy, spent a great deal of time at Petworth, where the Earl made a great fuss of him. As his brother did not accompany him, it seemed rather significant that William was singled out. So perhaps the story is true.'

'How very shocking!' I said delightedly.

'But romantic,' added Harriet, and secretly I agreed with her. Everything about Lord Melbourne seemed romantic.

'He must have been very handsome when he was young,' went on Harriet.

'He is still very handsome,' I replied firmly.

'Indeed yes. Men like that are attractive from the cradle to the grave. What is so fascinating about him is that he does not seem to *care* . . . I mean he is never striving for anything. He just takes everything that comes as his right, as it were. He seems unhurried. I don't mean about people. His manners are beautiful. I mean about what happens to him. He is always so unruffled, so unperturbed.'

'I think that is because he is so much a man of the world,' I said.

She agreed.

'He *is* a man of the world. He goes everywhere. He was very friendly with George IV . . . especially when he was Regent. He was at Carlton House, Holland House and of course the Bessboroughs' place at Roehampton. That was where he met Lady Caroline Ponsonby—Lord Bessborough's youngest daughter. They say she was very attractive. They called her Ariel . . . Sprite and the Fairy Queen.'

'She must have been lovely,' I said, 'and I daresay you are going to tell me that he fell in love with her.'

'Unfortunately for him . . . he did.'

'Why unfortunately?'

'At first her family did not think he was worthy of her.'

'Lord Melbourne . . . not worthy!' I cried indignantly.

'He wasn't Lord Melbourne then, only plain William Lamb. But then his brother died and Lord Melbourne was the heir, of course, and they changed their minds. At first the married pair were happy, and then she became . . . wild.'

'Wild? In what way?'

'Doing unconventional things.'

'Poor Lord Melbourne!'

'They said he endured it by developing that aloofness, that indifference. It was his only way of coping with that strange wife of his. And there was a child . . . a little boy who was never quite like other boys.'

'You mean he was mentally deficient?'

'Yes, I mean that.'

'My poor, poor Lord Melbourne. How wonderful he is! He is so merry . . . always.'

'But do you find him a little cynical?'

'I would say that he is laughing at the world . . . finding it amusing. He is very clever, I am sure of that.'

'He just shuts himself away with his books.'

'He is so well read.'

'Oh yes, he is certainly that.'

'And what happened about Lady Melbourne?'

'The great scandal was due to Lord Byron.'

'The poet?'

'Yes. She conceived a passion for him, and of course Your Majesty will have heard of his reputation.'

'Most scandalous.'

'She pursued him. He was very cruel to women. He took them up and discarded them. He took up Caroline Lamb, after she had made a shameful exhibition of herself, chasing him everywhere. He lived for a while at Melbourne Hall . . . about nine months, rumour has it. But of course he tired of her as he did of all women, and then, in the normal way, he discarded her.'

'And what happened then?'

'She was wild with jealousy and that meant that she behaved more outrageously than ever. She wrote a novel. I found an old copy and read it. It was called *Glenarvon*. The heroine, Lady Avondale, was of course Caroline herself. Lord Avondale was Lord Melbourne and the wicked Glenarvon was Byron. It had a big circulation. The whole of society was reading it. Poor Lord Melbourne separated from her, and then went back to her, and they lived in the same home but led separate lives, I believe.'

'How could Lord Melbourne endure such a life?' I asked.

'I have heard it said that his nature helped him. He cultivated that quality of aloofness which he has now. He was able to get outside events and view them from the edge. He did not allow himself to get involved. He devoted himself to his books. They say that he never fails to read every publication even now. It was his books which were so important to him. They enabled him to shut himself away from everyday life. He was just indifferent. Of course that maddened Caroline. She would have liked him to be frantically jealous of all her love affairs; but he would not be. He just smiled at them and let them pass over his head. Perhaps that is the only way to survive in such a situation.'

'He is a wonderful man. And what happened to her? She died, I know.'

'The end came when Byron died. She discovered this by accident and it was a terrible shock to her. She became really mad then and had to be shut away. She went down to Brocket, one of the Melbourne residences, and she died there.'

'That must have been a happy release for poor Lord Melbourne.'

'Indeed it must have been. He was already a Member of Parliament and he became Chief Secretary for Ireland in Canning's government. He went to Ireland and there he got caught up in another scandal. There was a certain Lady Brandon there with whom he became friendly and Lord Brandon accused him of improper intimacy with his wife, and sued him.'

'I daresay he was just being friendly with her. He is a very friendly man.'

'The Lord Chief Justice who tried the case pointed out to the jury that nobody could give a word of proof against Lord Melbourne who firmly denied the accusation, as did Lady Brandon. The case was dismissed.'

'I am sure that was the right verdict.'

'Then later there was the case of Caroline Norton.'

'I have heard of her. Was she not the playwright Sheridan's granddaughter?'

'She was. A very attractive woman, Your Majesty, and married to a rather insignificant man who was several years older than she was. He was a Member of Parliament but when the Reform Bill was passed and several boroughs were absorbed into others, he lost his seat. Caroline Norton asked Lord Melbourne's help to find a post for her husband. Lord Melbourne did help to find him something.'

'He is always so kind.'

'There was a friendship between Lord Melbourne and Caroline Norton, for she was a very intelligent woman and liked good conversation. She quarrelled with her husband and he said he would divorce her and cite Lord Melbourne as co-respondent.'

'So that was the second divorce case in which he was involved.'

'There was a great deal of noise about that as you can imagine, he being Prime Minister; and of course the Tories thought this would be of great use to them and they decided to make the best use of it they could. The Norton servants gave evidence, and it was proved that they had been bribed, and many of them were far from reputable characters. The verdict in due course, much to the chagrin of the Tories, was in Lord Melbourne's favour.'

'I am sure it was the right one.'

'Your uncle, the King, was delighted, but he did say that Melbourne was lucky to have got away with it, and his friends induced him to be more careful in future. He *was* really very lucky both in the Brandon and Norton cases. He did offer to resign.'

'He would, of course. He would feel it was the honourable thing to do.'

'The Duke of Wellington would not accept his resignation. I believe he was of the opinion that Lord Melbourne was too good a politician to have his career ruined because of what might have been a run of bad fortune.'

'How right he was!' I shivered. Suppose Lord Melbourne *had* resigned. Someone else would have been Prime Minister. I could not imagine that there could be anyone who would please me as Lord Melbourne did. I was indeed glad that he had not resigned.

'And that son of his?'

'He died.'

'Oh dear. What terrible sadness he has had in his life!'

'In a way he was lucky. Lady Caroline would have been no wife for a Prime Minister. Imagine the scandal she would have created. He is better without her. As for his son . . . he would have been a grief to him. Imagine a man as erudite as Lord Melbourne with a son who could not read.'

'Oh yes, indeed. But he has had a sad, sad life.'

'He is really very resilient.'

'He is a wonderful man, and, of course, there are always those who are ready to pull down those who tower above them.'

'Your Majesty is right, but his lordship did get involved on these occasions, and he does seem a little unfortunate with the women with whom he became involved.'

'I have always found his conduct just what it should have been. I am sure he has been the prey of unscrupulous people.'

The Duchess looked at me intently and said: 'I see that Lord Melbourne has made a favourable impression on Your Majesty.'

'I find him honest and straightforward; and I am sure he will not fail to be truthful to me.'

I was glad I knew something of his past. A man who had

come through so much would naturally be very worldly and sophisticated. I admired him more than ever. I liked that easy nonchalance; and most of all, I think, I liked his manner, which was so delightfully protective. He gave me courage, which was what I needed at that time; he made me feel that I was entirely capable of performing my duty, and I was confident that, with such a man to guide me, I could not fail.

After I had learned about Lord Melbourne's adventurous past I felt closer to him than ever. I had the greatest admiration for a man who could go through so much and appear unscathed by it. It was the right attitude to life, I decided. I must try to emulate it.

I told him once how I never ceased to be grateful that I had come to the throne when he was Prime Minister. 'For,' I added, 'it could so easily have been someone else.'

'You would have found whoever was there was just as able to advise Your Majesty.'

'This is the first time I have had to disagree with you, Lord Melbourne.'

'It is true, Your Majesty.'

'Lord Melbourne, I must ask you not to contradict the Queen.'

Then we burst into laughter. He stood up and bowed very solemnly. 'A thousand pardons, M'am,' he said. 'You are right, and to be honest, in my heart, I am in complete agreement with you.'

There was nothing solemn about him. He made everything a matter for amusement. He was so consoling.

I told him about my dear friend Harriet, of whom I grew fonder every day.

'Your Majesty is of a most affectionate nature.'

'Anyone would be fond of Harriet. She is so handsome . . . so tall. I do wish I were not so short. Everyone else seems to grow . . . except me. I always have to look up to people.'

'No, M'am, it is everyone who must look up to you.'

'I mean in inches.'

'We have so many instances in public life of people who are less than average height in stature rising to great heights in achievement. Think of Lord Nelson. He was a little man. Napoleon . . .'

'I would not wish to be as *he* was.'

He put his hand inside his jacket and struck a Napoleonic pose which made me laugh.

'I think there is very little danger of that happening, M'am,' he said. 'Oh, there are instances everywhere. Personally I think giantesses and Amazons a most unappealing brand of female.'

'You make me feel better, Lord Melbourne, as always.'

'Shall I tell you a secret?'

'Oh yes, please do.'

'You remember the first Council meeting when you came in looking so young . . . so tiny . . . so regal . . . ? There was not a dry eye in the place. You conquered all by your . . . slightness. You looked so young, so appealing that there was not a man there who would not have died for you. I doubt they would have felt the same emotion if confronted by a monumental figure of a Queen.'

He looked at me with tears in his eyes and I thought, Yes, he is right. They did like me. I could sense their feeling for me. So perhaps it is not so bad to be small.

'Of course,' I went on, 'I *am* a little plump.'

'We do not want a skeleton to rule us, M'am.'

And I was laughing again.

'It is because the Duchess is so beautiful . . .' I tried to explain. 'I love to look at her face. She is so animated . . . almost always. She has a delicate nose, so beautifully shaped. Mine is rather big. You must admit it.'

'I will only admit to its being exactly the right shape and size to fit. In fact, did you know that people with little noses rarely achieve greatness?'

'Is that so?'

'Undeniable.'

I laughed and said: 'This is a strange conversation for a queen to have with her prime minister. We ought to be talking of serious matters. Harriet is very serious.'

'She seems to possess all the virtues.'

'She is very good, quite noble. She is worried about the poor. She is on committees about slavery and chimney sweeps and children working in the mines. She says the government should *do* something about it. She talks very earnestly and sometimes she makes me weep. When I think of little ones dragging trolleys through underground passages . . . little children bent double . . . They are so young . . . little more than babies.'

'It is better for them to do that than to starve.'

'Harriet thinks something should be done for them. Could it be looked into? Harriet says it is the Government's problem.'

'I don't think these children would be happy if their livelihood was taken away from them. It is better to leave these things alone.'

'It worries me. I think of it at night.'

'Your thoughts should not be disturbed by such matters. The Duchess of Sutherland is a very worthy lady—oh, so tall with the most *squeeny* nose . . . but that does not necessarily mean that she is the fount of all wisdom. As I told you, smaller people with larger noses can have a greater share of that desirable commodity.'

So I was laughing with him again and he made me forget about those little children down the mines. After all, I told myself, it *is* better to work than to starve.

I did have one disagreement with Lord Melbourne and I think I rather surprised him by my firmness.

There was to be a review of the troops in Hyde Park and to my horror Mama suggested that I should ride in a carriage. I believe she had suggested this because if I did so she could ride with me. I imagined her sitting there haughtily acknowledging the cheers of the crowd, which were meant for me.

I laughed at the idea.

'Of course not,' I said. 'Monarchs review troops on horseback. The idea of reviewing troops in a carriage!'

Mama pointed out that I had not ridden since my attack of typhoid fever and I was unfit to do so.

It was true that I had not ridden since then, and that I had taken a long time to recover, but to ride in a carriage . . . Never!

I told Lord Melbourne about it and to my dismay he said: 'I agree with the Duchess. Your Majesty must not review the troops on horseback.'

'How can troops be reviewed from a carriage?'

'Quite easily. Everyone will understand.'

'Understand what? That I am unfit to ride a horse . . . that I am afraid?'

'It would be too much of a risk, M'am. You would have to ride with Wellington.'

'And why should I not?'

'It must be a carriage. Parliament will insist.'

'Can they do that?'

He nodded gravely.

'Well then,' I said, 'if there is to be no horse, there will be no review.'

He looked at me in astonishment. It was the first time I had seen him at a loss for words.

I did not believe for one moment that the review would be cancelled; but it was. They were all—including Lord Melbourne—afraid that because it was some time since I had ridden, I should be unable to stand the strain.

Of course I realized that his attitude was due to his care of me and it did not make any difference to our relationship. But I think he was a little taken aback by my resolution to have my own way.

Kensington Palace was not a suitable home for the sovereign and about two weeks after my accession, I decided to make Buckingham Palace my London residence. The rooms pleased me. They were high, pleasant and cheerful. It was great fun inspecting it. I decided that the Picture Gallery and the Bow Room should be properly ventilated, and that sinks must be put in the chambermaids' bedrooms. This could be done while I was at Windsor where I should be going shortly. I was delighted that Dash loved the gardens, and we enjoyed romping together on the grass all by ourselves.

There was one thing I did not like so much about the Palace. It was vast, and my bedroom seemed a long way from that of Lehzen. My mother, of course, had her own separate apartments, and I had made sure that they were some way from mine. Sometimes I would wake in the night and listen to the silence. Then I would hear a creaking board and fancy the little noises I heard were footsteps. I had never been nervous in Kensington. How could I have been? I was never alone, with Lehzen sitting with me until Mama came to bed. But now that I had the satisfaction of being alone, I found the nights eerie.

I was talking to Lord Melbourne one day. He came every morning to discuss State matters—and of course we liked to talk of other things as well. Nothing could have been less like a queen talking to her prime minister. I even used to bring Dash in with me. I was delighted that when Lord Melbourne spoke in his charming musical voice, Dash immediately responded. In no time he was licking the Prime Minister's hand.

'That is wonderful!' I cried. 'He is not so friendly with everyone, I can tell you.'

'He knows I am a friend of yours. But dogs always like me.'

'They know who is good and kind to them.'

'Good and kind in an animal world often means the supplying of food; but I do believe dogs have a special sense.'

'Oh, so do I.'

'This little fellow would protect you with his life.'

'Yes, that is what I feel when I wake up in the night and see him asleep in his basket. I feel very comforted.'

Then because I could talk to him as easily as I could to Lehzen, I told him that, in the night when I awoke, I felt a little shivery. 'It is so quiet there . . . so vast . . . I feel . . . rather alone.'

He was deeply concerned.

'You see,' I explained, 'all my life I wanted to sleep alone, and I never did until I became Queen. Always I slept in Mama's room and Lehzen was there until Mama came up. I was never left alone for a moment and I thought, As soon as I become Queen, the first thing I shall do is sleep alone. On the very first day I had my bed removed from Mama's room. But when we went to Buckingham Palace I found that I was uneasy. When I am in bed alone I hear creaks in the corridors . . . sometimes they sound like footsteps, and I think of all the kings and queens who have been murdered in their beds.'

'Oh, but you are quite safe.'

'So thought they . . . and they were not. I think of the little Princes in the Tower and their wicked Uncle Richard having them murdered.'

'There is a theory that he did not do it.'

'Well, if he did not, who did?'

'It was, some say, Henry the Seventh. Horace Walpole started it a number of years ago.'

'I had not heard it.'

'We must discuss the evidence one day.'

'But that does not alter the fact that they disappeared mysteriously. Then there was Edward the Second, Richard the Second and what about Henry the Sixth and the Duke of Clarence. I believe he was pushed into a butt of Malmsey.'

'What dramatic lives your ancestors lived! But I suppose that is inevitable, taking into consideration the times.'

It occurred to me that kings were not the only ones who had

dramatic lives. My dear Lord Melbourne had had his share of drama.

He went on: 'But we cannot allow your fears to continue. We must make sure that you sleep soundly. You have your beloved Lehzen near at hand, I believe.'

'She seems very far away at Buckingham Palace.'

'I know what we will do. We will have a hole made in a wall and a communicating door to the next room made—and the next room shall be Lehzen's chamber.'

'I do not want *not* to be alone.'

'Of course not. To be alone! It is an achievement. You cannot go back to the watchdogs. That work must be put in hand right away and then I feel sure that instead of brooding on the gory ends of your ancestors, you will be lulled to gentle sleep.'

'Oh, Lord Melbourne,' I said, 'you are so good. You have an answer for everything.'

And in the shortest possible time the work was done and I began to feel very comfortable at night, and to be entirely pleased that I had made the move to Buckingham Palace.

I wanted to give an entertainment there—a sort of house-warming; but it seemed out of the question because we were in mourning for the death of Uncle William. But Lord Melbourne, who was so *advanced*, said that he thought mourning was an old-fashioned custom which should have gone out long ago, and he suggested that there should be one day when the Court could go out of mourning. It was to be a concert which, he said, could not be called a riotous entertainment, but really very serious and in keeping with a mourning period.

'What an excellent idea!' I cried; and I started to plan.

I engaged my favourite artiste who was, of course, Madame Grisi. Madame Albertazzi, Signor Lablache and Signor Tamburini joined her, and I was in an ecstasy of delight listening to their wonderful voices. It was a great success.

It had been an excellent idea to stop the mourning for a day, I told Lord Melbourne. I was sure Uncle William would have approved of that; he had always been one who liked to enjoy life and he would be the last to want people to be miserable because he was dead. Lord Melbourne agreed with me.

A few days later I went on my first official engagement after coming to the throne. It was to open a new gate in Hyde Park in the Bayswater Road, which I christened Victoria. I enjoyed it. I did like seeing the people, but as I remarked afterwards to

Lord Melbourne, I hoped they would not get tired of seeing me.

'There seems to be no sign of that, M'am,' he said.

'Not yet. But they have not seen much of me. I am young, you see, and I may be Queen for a very long time.'

'I pray that may be so,' he said fervently; and I saw the tears in his beautiful eyes. Again I thought how fortunate I was to have him as my Prime Minister.

I said to him: 'Later on, when there is less talk of mourning, I should like to give a small dance once a week. Not a big ball . . . just a little dance for friends. You know I love to dance.'

'We all love doing that which we do well,' he commented, which was a lovely compliment; and he thought that a weekly dance was a good idea.

'Perhaps we could have a band in the Palace to play for us before dinner and during it.'

'Another excellent idea!' declared Lord Melbourne. 'I can see you are going to give the Court a more cultural standing.'

'You do think that is a good idea . . . really?'

'I think all your ideas are good.'

'What of riding on horseback to review the troops?'

'There have to be exceptions to all rules. It is a law of nature.'

'I believe you were really worried about my falling off.'

'It is long since you rode, and reviewing troops can be a long and tedious business.'

'I am going to ride every day when we get to Windsor, and I will show you that I am as good a horsewoman as I ever was.'

'I am sure you will be.'

'In August we shall go to Windsor.'

'Your Majesty knows that there is to be an election.'

I was alarmed. 'You will still be the Prime Minister.'

'If we are returned to power, yes.'

'And if not?'

'Doubtless my place will be taken by Sir Robert Peel.'

'Oh *no*!'

'He is a very worthy gentleman . . . highly thought of.'

'I could not bear it if you were taken away from me.'

'Then we will do our best to get a majority.'

'I hate those Tories!'

'Some of them are very estimable gentlemen. It is not their fault exactly if their views do not coincide with ours.'

'Of course you will be returned.'

He raised his eyebrows and a terrible misgiving came to me. I knew there had been a great deal of murmuring because the ladies of my household were the wives and daughters of Whigs. Sir Robert Peel did not like it. He thought I should have a mixture of Whig and Tory.

As a matter of fact so did Uncle Leopold. He had written to me telling me to select the ladies of my household with the greatest care, making sure not to let politics come into it. But Lord Melbourne and I had drawn up the list and had had the most amusing things to say about it; and all the ladies were of Whig persuasion naturally because Lord Melbourne was one and therefore so was I. Of course I did not listen to Uncle Leopold as much as I used to. He was after all a foreigner—which seems an odd thing to say about one so close to me—but Lord Melbourne was on the spot and he naturally was far more conversant with English politics than Uncle Leopold could possibly be.

It was my duty to go in state to dissolve Parliament, for according to law there must be a new election on the death of a sovereign. Had it not been for my fear that an election might rob me of Lord Melbourne, I could have enjoyed the occasion. I did feel very exhilarated by such state duties. They were so dignified and I do believe that I performed them well; and in those days there was scarcely a breath of criticism. I really was the beloved little Queen.

I set out in a crimson mantle lined with ermine over a dress of white satin embroidered with gold with a stomacher of diamonds; my tiara was of diamonds, and I looked scintillating.

There were gasps of admiration from the crowds and when I read the speech I felt overwhelmed with pride to be the sovereign of such a country.

When it was over Lord Melbourne came to me; he was very emotional.

'You were splendid,' he said. And later he told me that Fanny Kemble, the actress, who was present, said my voice was exquisite; and she had never heard a more musical rendering of the English language.

I was pleased and I knew that it was not false flattery. I had had to study speech assiduously, for Mama had been intent on eliminating any trace of a German accent, and I had practised enunciation and perfect pronunciation very thoroughly. Moreover, my voice was one of my assets—both in singing and in speaking; and if I had not been the Queen I might have made some progress as a singer.

But the triumph was tarnished by the persistent fear that the coming election might rob me of my Prime Minister.

A great deal of election fever followed. Harriet talked of it constantly. She showed me an article in the *Quarterly Review* by a Tory named Croker who called attention to the fact that I was surrounded by the female relations of the Whig leaders; and Sir Robert Peel was making speeches in which he declared that I was ruled by Lord Melbourne, the head of one political party—a matter which must be rectified.

There were headlines in certain periodicals such as: 'Release the Queen from Whig tyranny.'

Whig tyranny! How dared they! My relationship with the Prime Minister was one of understanding and trust.

A verse was shown to me. It was one which was being circulated throughout the country.

> ' "The Queen is with us," Whigs insulting say;
> "For when she found us in she let us stay,"
> It may be so, but give me leave to doubt
> How long she'll keep you when she finds you out.'

The Tories were growing in favour, and life, which I should have enjoyed so much because I saw that I could throw myself entirely into my new role and enjoy it to the full, was spoilt by this terrible fear. I tried to imagine Sir Robert Peel visiting me every day—his stiff manners, his serious face . . . I should not find it nearly so easy to understand politics as I did when they were so amusingly explained by Lord Melbourne. There would be none of those pleasant little chats. I should not be able to take Dash with me. I was sure the little darling would not want to lick the hand of Sir Robert Peel.

'Oh, please God, let the Whigs stay in power,' I prayed.

There was a great deal of talk about Uncle Cumberland, who on the death of Uncle William had become King of Hanover. That crown did not come to me because in Hanover the Salic Law prevailed and that meant that a woman could not inherit. Uncle Cumberland was something of a tyrant and as soon as he arrived in Hanover he had overturned the constitutional government and made himself a sort of dictator. The Whigs reacted to the Tory campaign by stressing the danger of the Duke of Cumberland's returning to make trouble in England; they were determined to keep him out at all costs. That wicked man wanted to bring the Salic Law into England so that he could add our crown to that of Hanover. There were cartoons showing us side by side—Uncle Cumberland and myself. I looked beautiful, young, with a dewy innocence—like an angel really—and my uncle was portrayed like a monster with his gaping eye socket quite repulsive. It was called 'The Contrast'.

And the Whigs insisted that they were the only ones who could make the crown safe for me.

I shall never forget the day when the results were declared.

Lord Melbourne came at once to see me. I rushed to him and looked into his face. I could not read the truth there. He was always so impassive.

'Please tell me what has happened,' I begged.

He said slowly: 'The Tories have gained many seats.'

'No!' I cried.

'Thirty-seven,' he said. 'But we have just beaten them. You see before you one who is still your Prime Minister.'

He took my hands and kissed them. I lifted my face to his and saw the tears in his eyes.

Late in August we went to Windsor. I missed Buckingham Palace. The country seemed rather gloomy. There were a great many rooks at Windsor and I found their constant cawing not only monotonous but a little depressing.

I loved London—the streets and the people. Of course one could ride very happily in the Park at Windsor and it was perhaps the most splendid of all the royal homes; but for the first few days I was homesick for London.

Then Lord Melbourne came down. He arrived on a magnificent horse and he and I went riding. The forest was so beautiful and Lord Melbourne so witty, that I was much amused.

There was a letter from Uncle Leopold. He was proposing visiting me and he would soon arrive at Windsor. This threw me into a flutter of excitement. It would be wonderful to see this favourite uncle again. I talked of him most enthusiastically to Lord Melbourne who listened most attentively.

And then Windsor became like a home. In the morning I was

with Lord Melbourne—who was having a short stay at the Castle—and we went through the state papers which he made so easy to understand, and I was so happy because he was still in power, although he did warn me that the ministry had a very tiny majority, and that was not a healthy state for a government to be in.

'Oh, we shall defeat those silly old Tories,' I said.

'Not so easy, M'am,' he said. 'Not so easy.'

'Surely everyone must prefer *you* to Sir Robert?'

'Everyone has not Your Majesty's discernment,' he replied; and how we laughed together.

There were several children in the household. I remember chiefly the little Conynghams because they had such beautiful black eyelashes and the little one called me Tween, which I found very amusing. If I could I would play games with the children. It was fun running through the long corridors; and I indulged in battledore and shuttlecock with my ladies.

I was reading every day and found Coxe's *Life of Sir Robert Walpole* a little heavy going; but I did enjoy some of Sir Walter Scott's novels, also Fennimore Cooper's and Bulwer Lytton's.

I used to discuss them afterwards with Lord Melbourne who, of course, seemed to have read everything and could discuss these books with grace and erudition. I thought of what Harriet had told me about his giving his life to his books when he had found Lady Caroline intolerable.

I often reflected on the sadness of his life and it made me all the more fond of him.

We dined at half-past seven to the strains of the band which I had had installed, and the soft music made such an agreeable background. After dinner I usually played cards or chess or draughts and so passed many pleasant evenings. When the period of mourning for Uncle William was over there would be regular dancing and more music, but quiet table games were considered to be more suitable at this time.

Mama had her own separate table where she played whist with some of her attendants. It was the only thing which could keep her awake. Sometimes she would try to catch my eye and look at me appealingly, at others angrily. I was very sorry to be on those terms with her but it was the only way, for if I softened just a little towards her she would have tried to dominate me and browbeat me into taking Sir John Conroy back. He was still in her household. Nothing had been done yet and he refused to move until his demands were granted. I had spoken to Lord Melbourne about him once or twice but he had always said: 'The time is not quite ripe. Leave it alone a little longer.'

So conditions with Mama remained very uneasy.

How wonderful it was to see dear Uncle Leopold! I was enfolded in his arms. Then he held me back to look at me and murmur: 'My Queen . . . My little Queen.'

He kissed me again and again. And after that I was embracing Aunt Louise.

There was so much to talk about. How were the little ones? Had they seen Feodore? What were the children's latest sayings? Did young Leopold still think his little brother was *pas beau frère*?

We walked together in the gardens. I liked to see Uncle Leopold in conversation with Lord Melbourne . . . the two for whom I had such regard must like each other, and when I realized that they did, I was very happy.

When we rode out or walked together, Uncle Leopold contrived to be alone with me and then he spoke of my cousin Albert.

'Do you remember how much you liked him when you met?'

'Oh yes. I liked all the cousins.'

'But I think you had a special feeling for Albert.'

'Yes, I do believe he was my favourite of them all.'

'He is a splendid young man.'

'I thought he would be.'

'He would like to see you again.'

'He must visit us. What of his brother Ernest?'

'They are both in excellent health.'

'I am glad. I thought Albert seemed a little delicate.'

'Delicate?' cried Uncle Leopold.

'He was very tired sometimes and he did not like staying up late. *I* love staying up late. I think it is a shame to cut the night short.'

'Oh, Albert was growing. People get tired then.'

'Do they? I do not remember getting tired. But then I have not grown so much as Albert.'

'I thought you and he matched so well together.'

'Oh,' I said, 'you are thinking of marriage.'

'Haven't you thought of it?'

'There has been so much to do. No, I had not thought of it, Uncle.'

'I believe you did once . . . when Albert was here.'

'I was young and romantic then. Now I have state duties. There has been little time to think . . . of other matters.'

Uncle Leopold laughed. 'You have so recently come to the throne. You will learn that royal people have other duties besides officiating at ceremonies and signing papers.'

I thought he was a little displeased with me and I sought to mollify him.

'You are right, Uncle, of course,' I said. 'I hope Albert will pay us another visit.'

'Oh he will. He will.'

Then he talked of other things, of the possibility of there being another election soon, the near balance of the parties making it difficult to conduct government. I told him how relieved I was that the Whigs had retained power because I could get along so easily with Lord Melbourne; and the thought of his being replaced did not please me at all, and that I was taking singing lessons with dear old Lablache and that these took place twice a week.

'It is such a pleasant relaxation from all the business I do. Lablache is so delighted that I have called him in. He would like me to sing more in French but actually I prefer to sing in Italian which seems to suit the music so much more. Dear Uncle, you and I must sing some duets. I have learned some of your favourites . . . just for the joy of singing with you.'

He was so delighted and we did sing together. Uncle Leopold said I had the sweetest voice and asked me to compliment Lablache on the excellence of his tuition.

In the evenings I played chess with Aunt Louise who—I suppose because she played with Uncle Leopold—was very good at the game.

On one occasion when we played, several of the gentlemen who were clearly eager for me to beat her, hovered over the table. There were Lord Melbourne, Lord Palmerston and Lord Conyngham and they were all telling me how to move and very often the advice was contradictory. I do not think there is anything so disturbing—particularly in chess—as to be looked at while one is pondering the moves and to be given advice. Very naturally I lost to Aunt Louise.

I turned to my advisers and said: 'The Queen of the Belgians has triumphed over my Council.'

They all thought this rather amusing, but I did feel I could have given a better account of myself if I had been left alone.

Uncle Leopold and Aunt Louise stayed at Windsor for three weeks. I urged them to stay longer but Uncle Leopold pointed out that he had a kingdom to govern.

Before he went he said: 'Albert often thinks of you. You will meet soon, I hope.'

I assured him that I should be delighted to see Albert again Then they had gone; and how I missed them!

I sat down and wrote to Uncle Leopold at once:

'My dearest and most beloved Uncle,
    'One line to express to you, *imperfectly*, my thanks for all your *very* great kindness to me, and my *great, great* grief at your departure. God knows *how sad, how forlorn* I feel. *How* I shall miss you, my dearest dear Uncle! *every every where.* How I shall miss your conversation! How I shall miss your *protection* out riding. Oh, I feel *very very* sad, and cannot speak of you both without crying.
    'Farewell, my beloved Uncle and father! May Heaven bless and protect you, and do not forget your most affectionate, devoted, attached Niece and Child. Victoria R.'

How glad I was that Lord Melbourne and Lord Palmerston were staying at Windsor. They did help—both of them—and particularly my dear Lord Melbourne—to alleviate my grief.

I had the great pleasure when I was at Windsor of reviewing the troops. I wore something very like the Windsor uniform—and the garter ribbon; and I had a lovely little mare at Windsor called Barbara. She was very frisky and Lord Melbourne insisted that I did not take her to the review but went on steady old Leopold, which was really very wise of him for one needs a patient steed for such a ceremony, which lasts two and a half hours.

'There,' I said to Lord Melbourne afterwards, 'I have shown you that I can review my troops on a horse and let me tell you, Prime Minister, that I shall never do so from a carriage . . . until I am very very old.'

'You did splendidly, M'am,' said Lord Melbourne. Then he turned away to hide his emotion. 'Forgive me,' he said.

My dear Lord Melbourne! I grew fonder of him every day.

I was very sorry when we had to leave Windsor, for although I had been there only six weeks I had grown to love the place. Time passes so quickly when one is happy and the summer of this wonderful year had been the happiest I had ever spent. The people loved me; there were compliments every time I appeared in public; I had spent three weeks with my beloved uncle; and Lord Melbourne had retained the premiership, by the skin of his teeth, as some said, but nevertheless he had held on. The election had been the only thing which had marred perfection, but as Lord Melbourne said, continual perfection might be a little dull, and it was as well to have the odd cloud to make one appreciate the beauty of the summer sky.

But all was well and the glorious year continued.

Alas, we must leave Windsor for I had to be in London for the opening of Parliament.

On the way home we were to call in at Brighton and of course we stayed at that really rather odd palace which my eccentric Uncle George had created.

This was not so pleasant because Lord Melbourne and Lord Palmerston had returned to London and the Chinese-looking structure with its low rooms did not appeal to me. One could get only the smallest glimpse of the sea from the strange place and it was all rather dull.

I wrote to Lord Melbourne and told him of my impressions of the place and stressed how sorry I was that he was not there.

He wrote back so charmingly—as he always did—and thanked me gracefully for my description of my coming to Brighton.

'Lord Melbourne entirely partakes in the wish Your Majesty has been graciously pleased to express that he had been there to witness the scene; but Your Majesty will at once perceive that it is better that he was not, as in that case Lord Melbourne would have been accused of an attempt to take a political advantage of the general enthusiasm and to mix himself and the government with Your Majesty's personal popularity . . .'

I supposed he was right. But how tiresome people were! Why could they not accept Lord Melbourne as their Prime Minister and be grateful for him. I was sure there could not be a better.

It was November when I rode into London. The people

cheered wildly welcoming me back; and I was so pleased once more to be in dear Buckingham Palace.

Before the opening of Parliament I was to attend the Lord Mayor's Banquet at Guildhall.

At this time Mama showed me clearly that she did not really understand the state of affairs between us.

She wrote a note to me asking me to allow Sir John Conroy to attend the banquet.

I was astonished. Did she not know of the demands Sir John was making? Blackmail, Lord Melbourne called it. I heartily wished that the matter could have been settled and that Sir John would be banished from the Palace, but negotiations still hung fire.

'The Queen,' wrote Mama, 'should forget what displeased the Princess.'

I showed the note to Lord Melbourne. 'I do so dislike that man,' I said. 'I shall never forget how offensive he was to me when he thought he had me in his power.'

'And now,' said Lord Melbourne, 'he is in your power.'

'But he is still here. Mama says that my attitude towards him is causing talk.'

'The attitude of people in high places always causes talk.'

'She says my obstinacy in this matter is hurting me more than it is Sir John.'

'Are you hurt?'

'No, I am not. He deserves everything that comes to him. He is the most odious of men.'

'Then ignore him . . . until that time when we shall come to our decision.'

'What shall I say?'

'Nothing. Ignore your mother's letter. Leave it alone.'

'I do wish we could finish with him.'

'We will . . . in time. At the moment . . . let it go. Say nothing. That is the best way.'

I sighed. I did so wish it could be settled and I need never think of Sir John Conroy again.

Another letter came from Mama.

'Really, dearest Angel, we have had too much of this affair. I have the greatest regard for Sir John. I cannot forget what he has done for me and for you, although he has had the misfortune to displease you . . .'

That is it, Mama, I thought. *I* cannot forget how much he

has displeased me. And your relationship with him has shocked me deeply.

Never, never would I forget opening the door and seeing them together and the dire incident that had been for poor Spath.

But I forgot the bitterness when I rode through the streets of London on my way to the Guildhall. The crowd was dense—so many people had come to see their Queen ride by and to express their loyalty to her. What a moving sight! I smiled and waved and there were tears in my eyes. They knew this and loved me for showing my emotion. And as I was sitting down they couldn't see how short I was, although Lord Melbourne was quite right. Many small people had done very well indeed and one should not be bothered by one's height.

There were fifty-eight carriages, and at Temple Bar I was received by the Lord Mayor, Sir John Cowan, with the sheriffs and members of the Corporation of London. It was really a splendid occasion and I had to confess that I was beginning to love such ceremonies, with myself the centre of attraction and the people showing so vociferously that they loved me.

But there was an angry note from Mama. She had not been given the right place at the dinner. Those who should not have been had been set above her. She must see me. It was cruel of me to shut myself away from my own mother. She was writing to me not as the Queen but as a daughter.

I did see her and it was like being a child again in Kensington Palace. Mama showed clearly that she had forgotten that I was now the Queen. She was quivering with indignation. My treatment of her, my treatment of Sir John Conroy was monstrous. I was ungrateful. I had forgotten all she had done for me. It poured out of her, all that I had heard so many times before, how she had given up everything for me, how my welfare had been her one concern.

Before I entered the room I had been inclined to believe that I was a little harsh. I had made up my mind that I must see more of her. After all, she *was* my mother. But when I saw her like that, the old resentments came back, and my heart was hardened.

I remained cool and calm and she went on: 'You have been so gracious to the Dowager Queen. You have visited her; you have told her that now she is settling in Marlborough House to take any pieces of furniture from Windsor which she may like to have. Oh, you can't do enough for spotty old Adelaide. It is very different with your poor mother.'

I said: 'The Dowager Queen was always good to me. I have always been fond of her. She is very sad now, for she loved the King and she has lost him. I want to make her as happy as I can.'

'You always turned to her. And you were against me . . . your own mother. Adelaide tried to turn you from me.'

'She never did.'

'All those invitations to balls . . . so that she could get you to marry George Cambridge.'

'She thought I should live a normal childhood, that I should have some pleasure and be with other children. She knew that I was more or less a prisoner in Kensington.'

'I never heard such nonsense. And the bastards . . . the FitzClarences . . . You have taken good care of them too.'

I said: 'They have never done me any harm. Aunt Adelaide treats them like her own children.'

'Then more fool her! All these you go out of your way to favour, and your poor mother, who looked after you, who gave her life to you . . .'

I said coldly: 'Mama, you saw that I was fed and clothed, but your goal was to become Regent through me. That was why I was so important to you . . . not for my sake . . . but for your own. Always you pushed me aside—ridiculously often at ceremonies when people had come to see me. They called my name and you took it as homage to you. It never was. Nor to me either. It was to the Crown. Let us be fair. Let us be honest. I am now the Queen. I will not have Sir John Conroy in my household, and I will not be told by you what I must do. You have your apartments here, and I must ask you to keep to them unless you are invited otherwise.'

I turned and went out of the room, leaving her deflated and bewildered.

She could not now remain unconvinced that I was determined. I was of age. I was the Queen, and she must perforce obey me.

Ten days later I opened Parliament.

During the first session of that Parliament the Civil List came under discussion and to my joy I was voted £385,000 a year— £60,000 of which was for my privy purse. This was £10,000 more than had been allotted to my Uncle William and was most gratifying. I was now rich, but Lehzen had brought me up to be provident and I had learned that however much one had, if one were extravagant, that could not be enough. I should not be as my father had been and hoped that when *I* died I would not leave behind a mountain of debts as he had done. Certain debts of his were still outstanding and the first thing I should do was settle them out of my privy purse.

As a Queen I should have great expenses but I had been careful ever since the days when I had saved up six shillings to buy the beautiful doll which I coveted.

Mama had received a further £8,000 a year.

'Which,' Lord Melbourne told me, 'has been granted solely for your sake.'

'Oh, how good the government is to me!' I cried.

'Well,' admitted Lord Melbourne, 'there was some opposition. There are some very mean fellows about. And do you know, I believe our odious friend Conroy did all he could to stop your getting such a large amount.'

'Oh,' I said, 'he is a fiend.'

'The transition has taken place merely by removing the letter r. How easily it is done.'

I thought that was very amusing and typical of Lord Melbourne.

It was soon after that that Lord Melbourne attempted to get rid of Conroy.

'That man continues to importune and is a thorn in our flesh,' he said. 'I think the best thing we can do is settle the matter.'

'Nothing would please me more,' I said.

'Well,' went on Lord Melbourne, 'let us give him his pension of three thousand pounds a year and a baronetcy. That will shut him up.'

'Is that not giving in to his demands?' I asked.

'Sometimes it is better to make a compromise with the enemy. It saves a lot of trouble. We do not want this man creating trouble, do we?'

'It seems to me a little . . . weak.'

'Sometimes one has to appear weak to be strong.'

That sounded very profound and at length I agreed, although I hated to see our enemy get what he had demanded.

But that was not the end of the matter. Instead of being

grateful that most of his demands had been met, Conroy stuck
out for a peerage.

'It is too bad,' I said. 'Why should this man benefit from his
evil deeds?'

'We have much with which to concern ourselves. Let us get
rid of him. I'll offer him an Irish peerage when one becomes
available. That might get him out of the country.'

'I should like to see him go.'

'Then so be it. An Irish peerage . . . if I am Prime Minister
. . . when one falls vacant. That should satisfy our rapacious
gentleman.'

Lord Melbourne was smiling to himself and the thought occurred to me that he could be thinking that if and when an Irish
peerage was available he, Lord Melbourne, might not be in a
position to bestow it; and that worried me so much that it drove
all thought of John Conroy out of my mind.

Christmas came. We spent it at Buckingham Palace and then
left for Windsor. The days sped by and that glorious year was
coming to a close. It had been the most exciting and happy
year of my life.

I had not realized before how very irksome it had been to be
kept under such close restraint, and in my mind Kensington
Palace would always be remembered as a prison by me. Perhaps that was why I was so enchanted by Buckingham Palace
and Windsor.

I was soon to be nineteen—no longer very young. I knew
that I should have to consider marriage . . . but not yet. I
thought of Albert who was clearly meant for me. Uncle Leopold was very anxious for our union; and of course Uncle Leopold was right. I remembered how charming Albert had been—
quite handsome, but really rather serious. He was not merry
like Lord Melbourne, who seemed to make a joke of everything. With Lord Melbourne one was constantly convulsed by
laughter. I knew there were people who said I laughed too
loudly and I opened my mouth as I did so, and that it was
rather vulgar; but Lord Melbourne said it was the way to laugh.
What was the good of restrained laughter; it made a mockery
of the entire practice of laughing.

He was so comforting; he always made me feel that my
faults were virtues. I could discuss anything with him; and I
could feel sure of a reply which would be amusing and comforting at the same time.

Lehzen said I should guard my temper. It rose quickly and subsided very soon. But I should control it.

I asked Lord Melbourne if he thought I was hot-tempered.

'Perhaps a little choleric,' he replied.

'Choleric! I am passionate. I feel deeply . . . for the moment, and then I am good-tempered again, and sorry that I have been in the wrong. My Uncle George the Fourth was like that.'

'Let us be thankful that you are not going to be like him in other ways.'

He liked to talk about my relatives. He told me stories of them vividly and amusingly. I had never really known that Uncle Sussex went to find a bride for Uncle William and fell in love with her himself, until Lord Melbourne told me. I did not know the rather sad story of Maria Fitzherbert and how it was said that my uncle loved her till the end of his days and regretted not giving up the crown for her.

He told these stories so wittily that although I thought some of them a little sad, he soon had me laughing.

What a wonderful year, which had brought me the friendship of Lord Melbourne!

I always felt sad when he did not come to see me. He had so many engagements. I could not stop myself asking where he was going and I used to say how sorry I was he was not dining with me.

He once told me that the Whigs were having a rough passage. It was devilish trying to make a ministry work on such a trivial majority. 'It may be,' he said, 'that we cannot hang on much longer.'

'But you must. I, the Queen, command you.'

'Alas, M'am, these matters are decided by the electorate . . . and since the passing of the Reform Bill we have all sorts and conditions deciding our affairs.'

But I refused to have these wonderful days spoilt by such gloomy predictions.

I wanted everything to stay as it was during that wonderful year.

It was the 24th May of the year 1838—my nineteenth birthday had arrived . . . my first birthday as Queen, and of course it must be very specially celebrated.

Mama threw a damper on the day by presenting me with a copy of *King Lear*. I had never greatly cared for that play and

I realized that she was calling attention to ungrateful daughters. How characteristic of Mama!

But I was too happy to care very much.

The Coronation was fixed for the 28th June and the festivities for that were to start before the great day so they coincided with my birthday.

There was a wonderful state ball. People clamoured for invitations. Lord Melbourne went through the lists of guests with me and he said that it was quite pushing and degrading for some of them to *ask* to be invited.

It was so amusing sitting with him and ticking those who were suitable and crossing off those who were not.

How I enjoyed that ball! I danced whenever I could—quadrilles and cotillions; but I could not of course try the waltz, because that would have meant dancing with someone's arm about my waist which would have been quite improper. It would have to be a king or someone as royal as myself. It was irritating to have to sit with my aunts and watch others dance the most delightful waltz.

Lord Melbourne was not present and that made me very anxious because I knew there was only one thing which would have kept him away. He was ill.

I was very relieved next morning to have a note from him begging me to excuse his absence. He had been indisposed but was a little better that morning.

I immediately wrote to him, begging him to take care of himself. I told him the ball had been a great success apart from one thing—his absence; and my anxiety would only cease when he called on me in person and I could satisfy myself that he had fully recovered.

I was relieved when he did call on me and was his old amusing self.

There were so many preparations for the coming Coronation.

I confessed to Lord Melbourne that I was a little nervous.

'Oh, you will like it very well when you are there,' he assured me. 'There is great excitement throughout the capital. The whole of the country wants to see its little Queen crowned.'

'I hope everything goes well.'

'We shall see that everything goes well,' he replied firmly.

And I knew that *he* would.

It was wonderful to see Feodore again for she came over, with my brother Charles, for the ceremony. There was so much to talk about with my sister. I had heard about the children and it seemed to me that she was very happy; she was different from what I was—more amenable, which was admirable. Feodore would do what was decided to be right for her without complaint. I admired her very much, and it was a great pleasure for me to be with her again. I did not feel so warmly towards my brother because of the way he had tried to interfere over Sir John—and he had always been a friend of that man, which meant there must be certain vital matters about which we must be in disagreement.

The presence of my brother and sister meant that I saw more of Mama than I had been doing recently. She was a little wary of me but she made an attempt to behave as though there had been no upset between us—and I did my best.

I was not able to spend a great deal of time with Feodore for there was so much business to be done, including the preparations for the Coronation and for most of the entire morning I was with Lord Melbourne going through state papers and having a little light amusing conversation in between.

Parliament had voted me £200,000 for the Coronation, which was indeed generous as Uncle William had only been given £50,000 for his. I was sure I owed this generosity to my dear prime minister.

There would be a royal procession to the Abbey and this had not happened during the coronation of the two previous monarchs.

'The last time there was a procession,' said Lord Melbourne, 'was in 1761 for your grandfather George the Third.'

'Why are we going back to it then?' I asked.

'This is the coronation to surpass all coronations. We have a pretty young girl as our sovereign, and I can assure Your Majesty that there is nothing the people like better than a pretty young queen. Naturally they want to see her.'

'You are making me feel less and less nervous,' I told him; and so he was.

I took great comfort that he would be there in the Abbey while I underwent this awesome ordeal.

The great day arrived. I had had little sleep the night before. All through the previous days people had been crowding into London. They were camping in the streets and later I heard that there were four hundred thousand of them.

At four o'clock in the morning, I was awakened by the guns

in the Park. I could hear the people shouting to each other; and then bands started to play.

At seven Lehzen was at my bedside.

In spite of a lack of sleep I felt exhilarated and ready. I went to my windows and looked out. There were crowds in the Park and bands were playing and there were red-coated soldiers everywhere.

Lehzen was fussing round with breakfast.

'Now you must eat, my darling. I am not having you starting off on an empty stomach.'

To please her I ate a little, but I was really too excited to think of food.

Feodore came into my dressing-room. She hugged me and was very emotional.

'Dearest sister,' she said, 'it has come at last . . . the day we were all waiting for all these years. What a future is yours! I wish you every happiness and joy.'

'Wish for me to do what is right, Feodore,' I said.

'I know you will.'

I said: 'I shall do what I *think* right, but will that be what truly is?'

'I believe this will be a glorious reign,' said Feodore and she was too overcome to say more.

Dear sister! How I wished that we could have been together over the years as we had been when I was little. So many thoughts enter one's head at such a time. I remembered her in Uncle Sussex's garden and how happy she had been; and that had been the end of our close association. They had stopped her making the marriage she wanted to; but she seemed happy enough.

Marriage! That was something I did not want to think of yet. I had my coronation before me.

It was ten o'clock when I left Buckingham Palace. We passed down Constitution Hill along Piccadilly and down St. James's Street to Trafalgar Square. The crowds were denser than ever here. I supposed many of them wanted to see the square which had so recently been made a memorial for Lord Nelson. Our progress was slow. The people wanted to see me. They pressed forward on every side. Many of my German relations were there and they had gone on in advance. Most countries had their representative. The French had sent Marshal Soult. Lord Melbourne told me about his reception afterwards most amusingly. He said: 'The people cheered him madly as though they were so delighted to see him, which was strange as he had recently been one of our enemies.' Perhaps it was because of his magnificent uniform or more likely they were cheering him for giving us a chance to beat the French at Waterloo. However, Soult had a good welcome from the crowd, but when I appeared the tumult was at its height. I smiled and waved, and wiped the tears from my eyes because I was so touched by my dear people's loyalty.

'Long live little Victoria!' they cried. 'God bless our little Queen!'

I thought then that Lord Melbourne was right and it was not such a disadvantage to be small. People seemed to like one for it. It made them feel protective. I was deeply touched.

We passed through Parliament Street to the Abbey, and by that time it was eleven-thirty.

I went into the robing room and put on my mantle. My eight train bearers were waiting for me, looking so beautiful, all dressed alike in white satin and silver tissue trimmed with silver corn-ears and small pink roses.

The ceremony began and I became a little concerned because I did not know what was expected of me. I whispered to the Bishop of Durham, asking him what I must do, but he could not tell me because he did not know. It was very confusing. When I told Lord Melbourne afterwards he said it was remarkably *maladroit*.

As soon as the anthem started I was glad to retire to St. Edward's Chapel where I took off my crimson robe and kirtle and put on a little gown of linen, and over that I wore a supertunic of gold. My diamond circlet, which I had worn on my head, was taken off and I went bareheaded into the Abbey.

I was led to St. Edward's chair and Lord Conyngham came forward with the Dalmatic Robe which he proceeded to wrap round me.

The Crown was put on my head and at that moment I looked up and saw Lord Melbourne. What a comfort to see him! He was watching me intently with such a dear fatherly expression on his good handsome face. He gave me that half smile of his which was so tender and meant he was proud of me and yet at the same time he found the ceremony, in spite of its solemnity, rather amusing. I thought: What fun it will be talking of this afterwards!

The drums and trumpets, the shouting . . . it was all so impressive. Mama burst into tears, rather noisily, to call attention to herself; but few looked her way. They were all intent on watching me. I could only pray that I should be worthy of the trust all these people were placing in me.

There I sat, with the crown on my head, accepting the homage of the Bishops and the Peers.

Poor old Lord Rolle, who was eighty-two years old and whose limbs were so stiff that he could scarcely walk, tried to ascend the few steps to my chair. He slipped and rolled down to the bottom of the steps.

I was most alarmed; but he got up immediately and attempted to ascend the steps again. But I would not allow that. I went down to meet him.

There was a gasp all around. I realized it was a most unconventional thing to do. Lord Rolle looked at me disbelievingly. And how the people loved it! As for Lord Rolle, as he swore his homage he looked at me as though I were an angel. It seemed a fuss to make of an ordinary action.

Lord Melbourne said afterwards: 'You acted just as I knew you would.'

'It was not a very *queenly* thing to do,' I murmured.

'It was a spontaneous act of kindness, and that is to be applauded in queens and serfs. You did the right thing. People talk of it. They love you for it more than they do for your charm and grace.'

Most of all I cherished the moment when Lord Melbourne came to do his homage. It is a touching ceremony at all times when they laid their hands on the crown and then kissed my hand. Lord Melbourne pressed my hand warmly and raised his face to mine, half laughing, half serious; he was telling me that I was doing very well indeed. There were tears in his eyes—as there often were when he looked at me; I loved to see them because they assured me of the depth and nature of his affection for me.

I raised my eyes to the gallery just above the royal box where dear Lehzen was sitting. She smiled at me with a look of infinite pride and I returned that smile, hoping I conveyed to her my gratitude for all the love and devotion she had given me during my life.

With her was dear old Spath who had come over with Feodore. I had had little chance to speak to her but I must do so before she left England. Dear Spath, did she think sadly of the old days? I should never forget how she was sent away. She was happy now, of course, for Feodore would see to that; and she had loved Feodore—in fact she had been her governess before she came to me. She would love Feodore's children. Oh yes, she must be happy now; but there would be sad memories, and I do not think I shall ever forget the tragedy on her dear face when she knew she was to be banished. So I do not suppose she would forget either.

The ceremony went on and finally I was in my purple velvet kirtle and mantle, and carrying the regalia, with all my ladies and the peers, I walked into St. Edward's Chapel.

'Anything less like a chapel I never saw,' whispered Lord Melbourne, for on the altar sandwiches and bottles of wine had been laid out.

'A new use for an altar,' murmured Lord Melbourne, and I tried not to laugh. It would have been laughter of relief as well as amusement, for I had passed through quite an ordeal. The Archbishop came in and he should have given me the orb, but he did not.

'Nobody except Your Majesty seemed to know what to do,' said Lord Melbourne afterwards.

'I did not either,' I confessed.

'Ah but you knew by instinct.'

Standing there by the altar he helped himself to a glass of wine. 'I need some fortification,' he whispered.

Then came the walk through the Abbey—I with my crown on my head, the orb in my left hand, the sceptre in my right. I felt *loaded*, for it was certainly uncomfortable to carry so much and keep the crown on my head.

As I walked through the Abbey the cheers rang out to the rafters, and I walked slowly, as though, I told Melbourne, I was performing a balancing feat. He said no one would have believed it. I looked as though I had been carrying a crown, sceptre and orb all my life, I carried them so expertly.

There was one more error—a painful one for me—when the Archbishop rammed the ring on the wrong finger for which it was far too small. I almost called out with pain and afterwards we had great difficulty in getting it off.

I could not help being relieved when I was seated in my carriage, crown balanced on my head, sceptre and orb in my hands and we rode back through the crowds to Buckingham Palace.

The cheers were deafening and the loyal greetings heart-warming. It was half-past four when we left the Abbey and I was not inside the Palace until after six.

Lehzen was there with dear old Spath.

They helped me change and I told Spath how pleased I was to see her.

Lehzen said: 'I was so proud of you. You looked . . . perfect. The people thought so too. And now you are exhausted.'

'Indeed I am not,' I said. 'I just feel exalted. Wasn't the singing magnificent.'

'It was you who were magnificent,' said loyal Lehzen; and she and Spath looked at each other and wept.

I said: 'This is not an occasion for tears. It is the proudest day of my life and I shall never forget it.'

Dash rushed up, fearful that he was being forgotten. He leaped into my arms and started to lick my face.

'A little respect please, dear Dashy,' I said. 'Your mistress is now a crowned Queen.'

But he wasn't going to let that make any difference.

'It is time for your bath, you naughty old dog,' I said. 'You have been in the pond and then rolling in the grass.'

I then turned up my sleeves and gave Dash his bath.

Lehzen said: '*That* is a strange thing to do after a coronation.'

We dined at eight that night. My uncles, my sister and brother were with us; and I was delighted that Lord Melbourne was one of the party.

At the table I sat next to Uncle Ernest and Lord Melbourne was on the other side of me as though to protect me from Uncle Ernest of the unsavoury reputation. But I must say that he had behaved impeccably at the coronation, and none would have guessed that he had had plans to take my throne.

Lord Melbourne asked me if I were tired.

I said: 'Not in the least. And you, Lord Melbourne?'

'No. I am wide awake. I must admit that the Sword of State which I had to carry was very heavy. I wondered how you were getting on with the sceptre and the orb.'

'It was the crown which weighed me down.'

'Symbolic,' he said. 'The duties of the crown are sometimes arduous.'

'Unless one has a good prime minister to lighten the load.'
He pressed my hand.

'You did well,' he said. 'Excellently. The robes suited you, particularly the Dalmatic.' He then remarked about Soult's reception and said that the English were a very kind people where their enemies were concerned, so kind that they had gone out of their way to give a special acclaim to Soult just in case he might have thought they were being cool to him, which any other nation would have been.

Lord Melbourne talked in his witty way about the peculiarities of the English, which I found most amusing.

He was beside me during the whole evening. Again and again he told me how beautifully I had done . . . 'Every part of it,' he said.

'I wished that I had known what was going on all the time,' I said. 'There were occasions when I was quite in the dark. I should have been told. Some of those churchmen did not know any more than I did.'

'It is a thing you cannot give a person advice on,' said Lord Melbourne. 'It must be left to a person. And you did it all perfectly . . . with such taste.'

'Well, I should be satisfied with that . . . coming from such a dear friend.'

He looked at me very tenderly and said it was wonderful that I was not exhausted.

'Tonight,' he added, 'I think you must be more tired than you think you are.'

'I had hardly any sleep the night before. There was such a noise in the streets and the guns woke me at four.'

'There is nothing more that keeps people awake than any consciousness of a great event's going to take place—and being agitated. You should retire and get some sleep with the satisfaction of knowing that all went off splendidly and that it was all due to you.'

I would, I told him; but before he left we went onto the balcony and watched the fireworks in Green Park.

Then I went to bed and that was the end of the most exciting, the proudest, and the most important day in my life up to that time.

I was now the crowned Queen of England.

Flora Hastings and the Bedchamber Plot

I suppose it was inevitable that, after having lived in that state of euphoria bordering on ecstasy, there must be a reversal. Life is like that. It gives and then, when one is lulled into security, it takes away.

After the Coronation, life began to look less rosy, and at the core of all the discord was the odious Sir John Conroy. He was still in the Palace. It seemed ridiculous to me that I, the Queen, could not choose those I would have under my own roof.

Lord Melbourne's reply was: 'It is kings and queens, M'am, who have less freedom than others to have their chosen friends around them.'

He admitted that Sir John was a big problem. 'He is there in the Duchess's household. If she dismissed him, then we should be happy. But she will not, and he will not go unless we agree to *all* his monstrous demands. Therefore leave him alone. He will depart in time, but we cannot have him go in triumph.'

So we left him alone, but he refused to leave *us* alone.

There were growing in the Palace two factions: one for me, one for Mama. I did not like it at all, although some of those concerned found it exciting. It suited Mama's sense of drama, and as, since my accession, she had been relegated to a very minor position, it seemed as though, if she could not rule me, she wanted to make things as difficult for me as she could.

There was always a great deal of conflict between her attendants and mine. Lehzen was closer to me than ever.

I said to her: '*You* are more like my mother.' And once or twice I called her Mother. 'I am going to give you another name,' I said. 'What about Daisy? I always liked daisies.'

Lehzen laughed, well pleased. She was very happy during those days. She was—with Lord Melbourne, of course—my greatest confidant.

When I read through my journal, Lord Melbourne's name occurred very frequently and I thought it was more endearing to write of him as Lord M. When I told him this, he was amused and said he liked it.

'It is economical, which is a good trait. Even queens must not be too extravagant.'

To add to my uneasiness Lord Melbourne hinted that he was finding it more and more difficult to perform his duties with that small majority.

'Those damned Tories,' he said, 'they baulk us at every turn.'

I did not really approve of strong language, but coming from Lord Melbourne it did not seem offensive, merely dashing—and it made me laugh.

'I wish Mama could have a household somewhere else,' I said. 'Somewhere outside the Palace.'

He pondered this and said I must remember that I was an unmarried lady, and as such could scarcely live alone.

'Alone! Here! With dear Lehzen and all my ladies. You call that alone?'

'It is thought to be wise for unmarried ladies to have a duenna. That is the custom of the times, and whatever contempt we have in secret for customs outwardly, it is often easier to conform to them. So . . . until the day you take a husband, the Duchess should remain.'

That was another matter which depressed me slightly. I did not really want to marry. I had so recently become Queen; the people adored me; I had just spent the most wonderful year of my life; I did not want change of any sort.

But it came nonetheless.

My spirits drooped a little. Instead of leaping out of my bed in the mornings I would lie there thinking of what would happen that day, and it did not seem as exciting as it once had. I was putting on a little weight. There were so many dinners to attend, and of course I had to eat. I was discovering that if one were a queen people watched everything one did and commented on it. Not only that, they exaggerated; and this was brought home to me when I heard that people in the streets were saying that I was getting fat.

I was outraged. More so because it was true that I was putting on a little weight.

'It is good for you, my darling,' consoled Lehzen, 'you need nourishment.'

Lord Melbourne was less comforting. 'You must take more exercise,' he advised.

'I do ride and I do not greatly care for walking.'

'Sometimes it is necessary to do what we do not greatly care for.'

'Walking . . . in the cold wind! I really do dislike it. My hands get so cold, and so do my feet.'

'You should walk faster. That would keep your feet warm and you should wear gloves.'

'My hands get so red in the cold. That is why I wear my rings to hide the redness—and then I cannot get my gloves on because of the rings.'

'An absence of rings could mean a presence of gloves. Wouldn't that be wiser?'

I sensed a lack of sympathy in Lord Melbourne and I had a feeling that he was a little critical of my increasing weight.

But that was unfair. He was as good and kind as ever. He was really worried, that was what it was. He greatly feared that a situation would arise when he could no longer continue in government. Then I should have another prime minister—which Heaven forbid.

It may be that fear was at the root of my discontent. I became fractious and my temper would flare up at the least provocation. Lehzen begged me to guard against it.

I was not quite so fond of the Duchess of Sutherland whom hitherto I had liked so much; and it was because she looked so elegant always and had so much to say which was witty and amusing. It seemed to me that she contrived to sit near Lord Melbourne in order to say it: and she quite monopolized him.

He had important Whig friends and was constantly in demand. There were many dinners which he attended, and to which I could not go.

When I complained to him he would always brush the matter aside with that nonchalance which was so much a part of his character; and I always had the impression that he did not find our absences from each other so hard to bear as I did.

He was constantly at Holland House and had a great admiration for Lady Holland. Of course, people like Lady Holland and the Duchess of Sutherland were women of the world and would be able to converse with Lord Melbourne in a manner more suited to him than I was. Once I asked him about this and he said that he thought the conversations he had with me were very suitable for a queen and her prime minister.

'But I am much more fond of you than Lady Holland could ever be,' I cried.

He looked at me with that wonderful gentle expression, with the tears gathering in his eyes and nodded; so that for a time I was happy again. And when I persisted and asked if Lady Holland attracted him more than I did, he said very calmly and sweetly: 'Oh no . . .'

But the real trouble came from Mama. The ladies of her household were continually making mischief with those of mine; and just as Lehzen was the most important of those in my household, Mama's special favourite was Flora Hastings.

I had never liked Lady Flora. Lehzen hated her; and with good reason. She never lost an opportunity of plaguing poor Lehzen, and was constantly making references to German habits and laughing about her fancy for caraway seeds.

Lady Flora was not young. I think she must have been about thirty-two years of age. She was unmarried and not unattractive to look at. It was just her manner which was unappealing. She was rather elegant and quite vivacious; she wrote poetry and people said she had a way with words, which often means a venomous tongue. She could really make people cringe when she attacked them verbally. She was rather like Sir John Conroy in this; in fact she was a great friend of his, and I had heard it whispered—although I must admit among her enemies—that there was more than friendship between her and that odious man.

Lord Melbourne did not like Flora Hastings either. She belonged to a family of staunch Tories and, being a Whig, Lord Melbourne regarded the entire Hastings clan as enemies. He said Lady Flora was typical of them and he was not surprised that Lehzen disliked her.

He did not like Mama much either; and if it had not been for the fact that she was my mother and he had such perfect manners, he would have said a great deal more than he did. There were occasions, however, when he was goaded into making observations about her. I loved to talk to him about how I had been treated during my childhood, of how I had been pushed aside again and again and how it had embarrassed me.

'The Duchess's real feeling was not for you but for power,' said Lord Melbourne. 'I fear she was not really strong-minded or she should have understood the futility of her actions; nor had she as much real affection for you as she feigned to have.'

How right he was!

One day when I was talking with Lord Melbourne in the closet where we discussed state matters and had those delightful personal conversations, Mama came in without warning. She had a conspiratorial look on her face—almost as though she thought she was going to surprise us in a most unpleasant way.

I was really quite angry.

I said: 'I am engaged in business with the Prime Minister. I think it would be better if you made an appointment when you wish to see the Queen.'

Mama looked stunned but she made no attempt to argue; she just disappeared.

Lord Melbourne was looking at me, half amused, half admiringly.

'The Duchess should know that when her daughter refers to herself as the Queen she is going to be very firm indeed.'

And after that what I thought of as the war between our two factions seemed to become more fierce.

The ladies of the households became quite spiteful with each other; and Lehzen and I used to talk sometimes indignantly, sometimes laughingly, of the little battles that went on.

All the same I would rather not have had it so.

Meanwhile Sir John Conroy stayed on and I suspected that he set a great many rumours in progress, such as the fact that I was getting fat. There was another more pernicious one which I did not hear much about until later. This was that my friendship with Lord Melbourne was very close indeed—closer than the relationship between the Queen and her Prime Minister should be.

It was just after Christmas of that year 1839. That lovely morning when Lord Conyngham had come to me and told me I was Queen seemed more than eighteen months away. So much had happened since then. There was one matter which I had tried not to think too much about, but it would keep forcing itself into my mind. This was my changing attitude to Uncle Leopold. All my life until I became Queen, he had been the one I had looked up to perhaps more than any other. He had been the father I had never known. I had sought his advice on every occasion. I had strived to please him. I had believed everything he had told me. He had been more of a god than a man as far as I was concerned.

Now that had changed.

Ever since I had ascended the throne I had begun to detect something in Uncle Leopold's letters which made me very uneasy. It was quite insidious at first, but as time passed it became more and more obvious. Uncle Leopold wanted to manage the affairs of Europe and I was in a very powerful position. He had always exerted a great influence over me, so naturally he thought to *use* me now.

There was one sentence in one of his letters which seemed of special significance. 'Before you decide anything important, I should be glad if you would consult me; this would also have the advantage of giving you time . . .'

I wrote back assuring him of my love and devotion, which I certainly felt, for I was not the sort of person who could dissimulate. Pretence was quite alien to my nature. In fact one of my faults was in betraying my feelings too openly. So I still did feel a great affection for Uncle Leopold and I never *never* could forget all he had been to me in my childhood; but the young Princess Victoria sheltered in her palace prison was not the Queen of England, and it was her task—with the help of her own government—to manage the affairs of her country.

Uncle Leopold wanted everything done in a way which would be advantageous to him.

There came the time when he was manoeuvring with France and Holland for the rights of Belgium, and he wanted England to come down in his favour. He needed English support and he could not understand why England remained neutral. A little persuasion from me might save Belgium, he wrote.

'All I want from your kind Majesty is that you will occasionally express to your ministers—and particularly to good Lord Melbourne—that as is compatible with the interests of your dominions, you do *not* wish your Government should take the lead in such measures which might in a short time bring in the destruction of this country as well as that of your Uncle and his family . . .'

I was very upset when I read this letter. I showed it to Lord Melbourne who read it and nodded his head. 'Leave it to me,' he said; and of course that meant: Leave it alone.

I waited for a whole week before replying and then I assured Uncle Leopold that he was very wrong if he thought my feelings for him could change. But at the same time I skimmed over the subject of foreign politics. All I said was that I understood and sympathized with his difficulties and he could be sure that Lord Melbourne and Lord Palmerston were very anxious for his prosperity and that of Belgium.

I had to make it clear to Uncle Leopold that he could not command me. I loved him dearly but I could not allow my affection to interfere with my country's foreign policy.

All this was distressing and added to my feelings of unrest.

It was in the middle of January when Lehzen came to me in a twitter of excitement. She said: 'I have something really rather interesting to tell you.'

'Well, what is it?' I asked.

'It's . . . Scotty . . .' Scotty was a name which had been given to Flora Hastings by her enemies—I supposed because of her origins.

'Oh dear, what fresh mischief has she been up to?'

'Your Majesty may well ask. I think this is going to be rather amusing and not a little shocking. You know that she has for a long time been very friendly with that man? The Duchess has been quite jealous at times and so has the Princess Sophia.'

'It is past my understanding why these women think so highly of him.'

'He is supposed to be good-looking and they like his slimy way of talking.'

'I cannot understand how anyone could. But what is this about Flora Hastings?'

'You know Conroy went to her mother's house with her for Christmas.'

'Yes, in Scotland. Loudon Castle, wasn't it? I suppose he was a member of the house party.'

'She came back in the post-chaise with Conroy. The two of them would have been . . . alone.'

'She would have liked that. It must have given them one or two intimate moments.'

'So it seems,' said Lehzen.

'Oh come on. What are you trying to tell me. Really, Daisy, you can be most perverse at times.'

'I don't know whether I should tell you.'

'You know you are longing to tell me. I command you to get on with it.'

'Well, she arrived back after her most delightful post-chaise journey and complained of feeling ill; and there was a distinct change in her appearance.'

'What on earth do you mean?'

'She was a little larger below the waist than it is good for an unmarried lady to be.'

'Oh, no. I can't believe it. Not Lady Flora.'

'Even Lady Flora has her foolish moments. She went to see Dr. Clark. She complained of pains and there was this significant protuberance.'

'What was it?'

Lehzen looked at me and raised her eyebrows.

'Oh no! It couldn't be.'

Lehzen shrugged. 'Dr. Clark gave her rhubarb and ipecacuanha pills and she said they relieved her and the swelling had gone down. But that did not seem to be the case. Such swellings do not disappear until the appointed time. And now the truth has come out as such truths must. Dr. Clark told one of the ladies that Lady Flora Hastings is pregnant.'

'What a scandal! What will Mama do?'

'The Duchess is in a difficult position. If Sir John is responsible for Lady Flora's condition, the Duchess will have to do something about that.'

Lehzen laughed, already enjoying Mama's discomfiture.

I said: 'Should not Mama be told at once?'

'Lady Tavistock does not feel that she can approach the Duchess who, as Your Majesty knows, might well refuse to see one of your ladies.'

'Perhaps I should tell her. But then in view of how difficult everything is between us that would not be easy. Perhaps Lord Melbourne's advice should be asked.'

'Lady Tavistock should tell him,' insisted Lehzen. 'It would be somewhat indelicate for Your Majesty to do so.'

I wanted to say that I could discuss anything with Lord Melbourne; but I thought it best to let Lady Tavistock approach him first; and this she did.

I could hardly wait to see Lord Melbourne. He was amused by the *contretemps*. He thought it would raise quite a little noise.

'I cannot understand why these women like him so much,' I said. 'There is Mama, Aunt Sophia and now Flora Hastings.'

'He is an amazing fellow to keep three ladies in good humour all at once.'

'Oh, he is capable of every misdemeanour there is.'

'It seems that he might be capable of a good many.'

I was horrified that there could be such behaviour in the Palace. There was no doubt in my mind that Flora Hastings was pregnant and it did seem clear that the cause of her predicament was that demon incarnate, that monster whose very name I could not bring myself to utter.

Lady Flora went about looking pale and ill and very bitter, yet defiant. She had heard the talk and professed to be horrified by it. She was a virgin, she proclaimed; and it was not possible that she could be pregnant.

'There is only one thing to do in such circumstances,' said Lord Melbourne. 'That is wait and see.'

I sent for Dr. Clark and talked to him about the case. Lehzen was present because she felt it would be improper for me to talk of such things with him alone.

'Have you told her outright that she is with child?' I asked.

He said he had not.

'Then all she complains of at the moment is gossip. Perhaps you should tell her that her symptoms suggest pregnancy.'

Lehzen said: 'Why not ask her if she is secretly married? She will know what you mean then; and if she says she is not, tell her she ought to be.'

'That would be a way of putting it,' I said.

Dr. Clark said it was difficult to make an accurate diagnosis without a proper examination and he had only seen the protuberance over Lady Flora's skirts.

'There should be a thorough examination,' said Lehzen, 'and until that has been made and Lady Flora proved to be innocent, she should not be allowed to appear at Court.'

I thought that seemed reasonable and gave Dr. Clark permission to confront Lady Flora, which he did. She was very distressed, insisted on her innocence and said she would indeed not submit to an examination which naturally she would find distressing and humiliating.

I sent Lady Portman to Mama to tell her what was happening. Lady Portman came back and said the Duchess was stricken with horror and she did not believe that Lady Flora was pregnant. She thought it was a wicked plot of which there were many in the Palace.

On no account, she insisted, should one of her ladies be submitted to such a test; and that must be an end to the matter.

Mama was as foolish as ever. As if there could be an end until the matter was solved.

Lady Flora realized the position because she was a very astute person; and after a few days of consideration, hearing that Sir

Charles Clark was in the Palace and that he was a specialist in such matters, she said she would submit herself to the examination.

It was a pity that these events were not confined in the Palace walls. Unfortunately gossip has a way of seeping out and there was talk everywhere about the scandal and how the Queen was playing a big part in the war against immorality in the Palace.

Everyone seemed to know that the examination was to take place. I could imagine the salacious expression on their faces. They loved all scandal but nothing could delight them more than one of this nature. They were prepared to damn Lady Flora as a scarlet woman or applaud her as a saint. It all depended on the result of the examination.

We were all stunned by the verdict which was that Lady Flora was a virgin.

As soon as Lady Portman told me the news I came to the conclusion that I had behaved in a foolish way. I should have kept aloof from the proceedings and should never have allowed myself to take sides. Everyone knew of the feud between my mother's household and mine and when one of my mother's retinue attracted so much attention, it appeared that I had put myself at the head of those who had denounced her.

What could I do? I must immediately see Lady Flora and express my deepest sympathy and offer my regret for what had happened. I sent a message to her asking her to come to me that evening that I might speak to her in person. I received a message from Lady Flora to the effect that she was suffering from exhaustion and bad headache; and while she appreciated the honour done to her, begged me to allow her to postpone her visit until she had had time to recover from her ordeal.

Lord Melbourne came to see me.

He was surprised at the verdict and inclined not to believe it.

'But they have given Lady Flora a certificate which she insisted on, and it states that she is a virgin.'

'Sometimes these matters can be rather complex.'

He did not discuss it in detail, which would have been indelicate and Lord Melbourne would never be that; but I did hear afterwards from Lady Tavistock that there had been cases where someone believed to be a virgin had given birth; and there was a certain enlargement of the womb as there would have been if Lady Flora were pregnant.

'The matter must rest there,' said Lord Melbourne.

But that was not to be permitted, for Lady Flora lost no time in writing to her brother, the Marquess of Hastings, who, although he was on a sick bed, dashed up to London.

He was a young man who was determined to make trouble and Mama was not one to miss an opportunity like this. The enemy—that was myself and my household—had committed a tactical error. Interest in the Hastings scandal was growing, Lady Flora Hastings was the heroine; and as in all melodramas there must be a villain. I was selected for that role. Although I had had little to do with the matter, just as the captain is responsible for his ship, so was I for the Court.

The people were murmuring against me and my cruelty to the sainted Lady Flora; I quickly noticed the absence of those cheers in the street, and I heard an occasional hiss.

'What about Lady Flora?' I heard someone in the crowd shout. It was most distressing.

I began to feel ill. I could not sleep at night and lost my appetite.

Lord Hastings determined not to let his sister's cause be forgotten. Lord Melbourne told me he had come bursting in upon him demanding 'this and that'. He said he wanted a complete vindication of his sister's honour.

'He has had that,' I insisted. 'The doctors have said . . .'

'That is not enough. He is consulting the law and threatens to take action.'

'Against whom?'

Lord Melbourne put his head on one side and smiled dolefully at me.

'I assured him of our innocence,' went on Lord M, 'and the only way I could mollify him was bustling him off to consult the Duke of Wellington.'

'Why should he think he could help?'

'Your Majesty, people think that the man who beat Napoleon at Waterloo could settle all difficulties with the same success. I saw Wellington afterwards. He told me that Hastings was in a state, and that the best way he could serve all concerned was to Hush It Up. A sentiment with which I am in entire agreement.'

It was several days before Lady Flora came to see me.

Poor woman, she was clearly ill. She knelt before me but I took her hands and made her rise.

'My dear Lady Flora,' I said, 'I am truly sorry that this has come to pass.' I spoke with feeling for it was indeed true. 'I wish it could all be forgotten. The Duchess is most distressed.'

'The Duchess has always been so tender to me . . . so loving . . . so kind.'

Lady Flora's voice broke and I kissed her again.

'I thank Your Majesty,' she said, 'and I will try to forget . . . for the sake of the Duchess.'

I do believe that Flora Hastings would have let the matter drop but, of course, there were those about her who had no intention of allowing this to happen.

Gossip continued, fostered, I suspected, by Conroy, who saw a chance of having his revenge on me.

If only we had met his demands—anything to have got rid of him! Letters were appearing in the Press, and they were all in praise of Lady Flora and against me.

One day Lord Melbourne came to me and said that he had had a letter from Lord Hastings demanding the dismissal of Sir James Clark from the Palace.

'This man is determined to make the matter public,' said Lord M.

'That must not be,' I replied.

'It shall not be, M'am, if I can help it.'

There was gossip about Lehzen. 'The German woman', they called her. There were stories of how she had wormed her way into my affections and had ousted my mother. She, they said, was responsible for the terrible ordeal which Lady Flora had undergone. I was becoming more and more distressed. It was all so unfair and so untrue. I was very worried.

I would not have believed that this domestic matter could have been so blown up as to become an attack on me. I was sure that Sir John Conroy was at the bottom of it and that it was he who sent the snippets of gossip to the Press. The story was taken-up by foreigners, exaggerated and embroidered.

Lady Flora had written a letter to her uncle, Hamilton Fitzgerald, and when this was published in the *Examiner*, there was no longer any hope of hushing up the matter. The whole world was talking of it. In this letter Lady Flora had set out the sequence of events as they had happened. She praised the Duchess for having treated her with sympathy and affection and there were veiled criticisms of me. She implied that I should have dismissed Sir James Clark and those who had spread the gossip about her. She said Clark was the tool of certain women and he alone should not be sacrificed for the sake of others who were more guilty.

Lord Melbourne made a public statement to the effect that I had taken the first opportunity to express my regret and sympathy to Lady Flora; but the Tory Press, headed by the *Morning Post*, was determined to make a battle of it.

The Whigs were limping along in government. The ladies of my bedchamber—who were regarded as the instigators of the plot against Flora Hastings—were all from Whig families. It was unhealthy, it was said, that the Queen should be led by that party just because its chief minister happened to be her very special friend.

As if that were not enough, a greater catastrophe loomed.

I knew there was trouble in the House of Commons. This all came about because of what was happening in far-away Jamaica. The abolition of slavery in British colonies had become law as long ago as 1833, and because the slaves in Jamaica had been freed, the planters were now in rebellion and demanding to have them back.

Lord Melbourne, who always believed in delaying unpleasant matters, along with his party, wanted to suspend the law for a while until some agreement could be come to. Sir Robert Peel and his Tories were against this, and when the motion was put before the House, it was passed with such a small majority that Lord Melbourne decided that it was quite impossible to continue in government.

I shall never forget the day he came to me. There was a great sadness about him.

'Your Majesty,' he said, 'you know that for some time it has been difficult for your government to carry on its business in the House because we have such a small majority, and to govern for long in such circumstances is certain to become an impossibility. The Cabinet had decided to stand by this Bill regarding the slaves in Jamaica, but Sir Robert Peel is opposing us in the matter and if he should persist and a majority in the House of Commons agreed with him, it would be impossible for Your Majesty's government to remain in office.'

'No,' I said. 'No. I will not allow it.'

He looked at me, half smiling. He did not say as much but he was reminding me by the tenderness of his looks that it was not a matter for me to decide.

He did not remain long. He knew I was too upset and that there was nothing he could say to comfort me.

Lehzen found me sitting in my chair staring ahead of me.

She knelt down and put her arms round me.

'I am afraid,' I said, 'that dreadful Robert Peel is going to force Lord Melbourne to resign.'

'Oh no, my love, not that!'

'Lord Melbourne has been to see me . . . to warn me.' Then I burst into tears. 'I will not have it, Lehzen. I am the Queen, am I not?'

'There!' she soothed me. 'It hasn't happened yet. Lord Melbourne won't let it happen. He is clever, that one.'

I tried to believe her. But I could not. Life had changed. Who would have believed that a short time ago I could have been so happy!

The horrible business of Lady Flora was still in everyone's mind. They were still writing about it in the papers; the people in the streets regarded me with dislike.

This I could bear—but not the separation from Lord Melbourne.

It had happened. The government had resigned. He came to see me looking doleful and I knew that was due to the disruption of our relationship which had been such a happy one. But for that reason he would not greatly care about resigning the premiership. I think he found managing the country's affairs something of a burden. I knew he would have liked to retire, to be alone, to have more time for reading; he liked good talk and of course he was welcome in the greatest Whig houses throughout the country, where, I heard, the conversation was scintillating and he was always at the centre of it.

No, it was the severance of our close relationship which would be so painful to us both.

I could not be dignified and royal—not in the face of such misery. 'Why all this bother about Jamaica! Those wretched Tory dogs! They are just seizing on it to make trouble.'

Lord Melbourne's wry smile suggested that he agreed with me.

'Do not blame Jamaica,' he said. 'If it were not there the dogs would find another bone of contention. We happen to think we are right in this matter and they think that they are. Sir Robert Peel is a very fine gentleman. I think you might come to like him very well.'

'I hate him! He behaves like a dancing master and when he smiles it is like looking at the silver fittings on a coffin.'

'Have you been gossiping with Charles Greville?'

'His conversation is very lively.'

'The description of Sir Robert is his, I believe. But for all that he is a very able man—dancing and coffins notwithstanding—and he will do his best to serve Your Majesty well. Your Majesty, being of sound good sense in spite of your youth, and having a clear determination to do your duty to the state to which God has called you, will understand this change must be. Alas, I fear the time has arrived when you will be obliged to work with a new government. I believe you will make a great success of it . . . I shall be nearby and I shall watch you with pride.'

'You will not go away entirely? You will come and dine? I could not bear it if you did not.'

'Your Majesty is gracious to me, and has given me more affection than I deserve.'

'What nonsense! You deserve it all . . . and more. You are my dearest good friend. You always were and always will be my very own Lord M. You know my feelings for you.'

'I know that you wish me well . . . Your Majesty has ever been gracious to me; and I trust you will show the same amiability towards Sir Robert, for I assure you he is a very good man.'

'He has one great fault,' I said, 'and for that I can never forgive him.'

Lord Melbourne looked at me sadly and I went on: 'He is not Lord Melbourne.'

And with that I ran from the room for I could not restrain my tears.

And so I came face to face with Sir Robert Peel.

I had tried to prevail on the Duke of Wellington to form a ministry, but he would not do so. He was, after all, nearly seventy years of age and I had to agree that that was rather old to take on the burdens of state.

Sir Robert Peel, however, was willing and ambitious. I saw him in the Yellow Closet; I was not going to take him to the Blue Closet, the scene of so many happy meetings with Lord Melbourne.

How I disliked him as he stood there—awkward, graceless, lacking in breeding. How different from my dear Lord M! He was proud and reserved—and very unsure of himself. I rejoiced in that. Let him remain so. He fidgeted, twitching from one leg to the other and I felt like giggling when I thought of Charles Greville's description of the dancing master. The silver fittings on the coffin were only visible when he smiled—and that was rarely.

I found myself looking at his feet. He pointed his toes as though he were about to dance. Oh yes, it was a very apt description!

I began by stressing the unfortunate happenings in Parliament which had made it difficult for Lord Melbourne to continue in office and for that reason I was asking him to form a ministry.

He hemmed and hawed and said he would do so. He seemed to think it was necessary for him to make speeches and talked all round the subject. How dreadfully different from the frank, open, *natural*, most kind and warm manner of dear Lord M!

The more I saw of Robert Peel, the more I was reminded of Lord M by the very contrast of the two men.

He mentioned one or two names to me of those who would hold posts in his ministry. I listened to him vaguely, wondering all the time how I could get rid of him and bring back Lord Melbourne. The Earl of Aberdeen, he was saying. He was one of those who had said that Lord Melbourne ruled the country and that I was wax in his hands, so I was not inclined to favour him; Lord Lyndhurst; he had openly sided with my mother and Sir John Conroy. Sir James Graham; I knew nothing against him, but on the one or two occasions when I had seen him I had thought he resembled Conroy, which was enough to make me dislike him. I felt I was going to loathe Peel's ministers as heartily as I did him.

Oh, it was a sad and sorry business!

I was glad when the dancing master bowed himself out. I thought he was going to fall over the furniture as he did so and was disappointed when he did not.

The next day he called again and we took up the interview where we left off. I remained seated, haughtily watching his gyrations on the carpet. He was really very uneasy. Perhaps I should have been more gracious to him, but I could not forget that he was depriving me of my dear Lord M—and delighting in it.

'Your Majesty,' he said at length, 'there is the matter of your household.'

'What of my household?' I asked.

'Your ladies, M'am.'

'What of my ladies?'

He coughed slightly, nervously, and pointed his toe and lifted his foot for all the world as though he were about to perform in the minuet. He went on: 'M'am, they are all members of Whig families. In view of the . . . er . . . alterations in circumstances, it would be advisable if changes were made. Your Majesty will understand . . .'

'But I do not understand,' I said firmly. 'And I do not wish to have my household disrupted.'

'Your Majesty does not intend to retain all your ladies?'

'All,' I said firmly.

'The Mistress of the Robes . . . the Ladies of the Bedchamber . . .'

I looked at the wretched man and repeated firmly: 'All.'

'These ladies, M'am, are all married to Whig opponents of the government.'

'I never talk politics with my ladies. I believe some of them have Tory relations, which might be a comfort to you.'

'It is the ladies who hold important posts who must be changed.'

'This sort of thing has never been done before.'

'You are a Queen Regnant, M'am, and that makes a difference.'

'I shall maintain my rights.'

He looked so miserable and helpless that I was almost sorry for him, but I continued to regard him haughtily and he said he thought he should discuss the matter with the Duke of Wellington.

'Pray do so,' I said, showing my pleasure in his dismissal.

But when he had gone I was so overwrought that I sat down and wrote to Lord Melbourne.

'The Queen feels Lord Melbourne will understand her wretchedness among enemies of those she most relied on and most esteemed, but what is worst of all is being deprived of seeing Lord Melbourne as she used to.'

In a short time he replied to me urging me to the necessity of making the best of everything. He stressed the worthiness of Sir Robert Peel and pointed out that I should not condemn him because his outward appearance did not please me. As for the ladies of my household, he did say that I should stand out for what I desired because that was a matter for my personal concern; and he added that if Sir Robert found himself unable to concede the point, I should not refuse to reconsider it.

I was disappointed. I was not going to submit to tyranny. The dancing master must remember that I was the Queen.

I wrote back to Lord Melbourne: 'I will never consent to give up my ladies. I think you would have been pleased to see my great composure and firmness. The Queen of England will not submit to trickery. Keep yourself in readiness.'

My spirits were lifted. I saw this matter of the Bedchamber Ladies as a way out of this tragic situation. If I would not give way and Peel would not either, we should have reached an impasse and he would not be able to form a government.

I was not surprised to receive another visit from the Duke of Wellington.

'I heard there is a difficulty, M'am,' he said.

'Peel began it, not I,' I retorted.

He looked at me intently. I wondered if he were comparing me with Napoleon. He would find the little Queen as formidable a foe as the little Corporal. My will was going to prove stronger than Napoleon's military genius; it would stand more firmly than French artillery.

'Why is Sir Robert so adamant?' I asked. 'Is he so weak that even ladies have to share his opinion?'

That seemed to decide him. He was defeated.

I immediately wrote to Lord Melbourne to acquaint him with the interview.

'Lord Melbourne must not think the Queen rash in her conduct. She felt this was an attempt to see if she could be led like a child.'

I was not really surprised when Sir Robert asked for another audience. I granted it willingly.

He came quickly to the point on this occasion. 'If Your Majesty insists on retaining all your ladies I could not form a government.'

I was cool, hiding my exultation. I bowed my head in acceptance of his decision.

I was delighted to have a letter from Lord Melbourne telling me that he had shown the Whig Cabinet my letters and his advice to me was to break off all negotiations with Sir Robert Peel.

This I most willingly did and to my great joy recalled Lord Melbourne.

He came at once and stood before me, tears in his dear eyes. He laughed and said my conduct had been most unconstitutional.

'Is that important if it achieves the desirable result?'

'Desirable for whom? Sir Robert Peel?'

We laughed together and I am sure I showed my gums and laughed too loudly on that occasion; but I did not care. I was so happy. And I reflected sagely that if I had not known such despair, I could never have been quite so joyous.

Afterwards we talked about it in the old cosy fashion. Lord Melbourne reminded me that I had not taken his advice, but when the whole story was laid before his Cabinet they declared that it would be impossible to abandon such a Queen and such a woman. So, hampered as they were by that feeble majority, they decided to come back and attempt to carry on.

It was a great victory.

That evening there was a grand ball. I danced into the early hours of the morning. I was very joyous—happier than I had been since the miserable Flora Hastings affair had started.

The visit of the Tsarevitch Alexander, Hereditary Grand Duke of Russia, helped me to forget the upset of what was being called the Bedchamber Plot. There was, as was to be expected with the Tories putting their case, a real scandal about this. It was a little different from that of Flora Hastings because I had some supporters this time. There were pro-Peel and pro-Queen factions. Of course I had flouted the Duke of Wellington's advice, and that was a bold thing to have done.

However, I was always delighted to have visitors from other countries, because it meant a round of entertainments, including balls which I loved.

I found the Russian Duke a very charming man. He was good-looking and dignified, and I began to think that he liked me as much as I liked him. I was reminded of the visits of the German cousins before I had come to the throne. What fun they had been! And how I had enjoyed them and how desolate I had been when they went away. That brought my thoughts back to Albert a little guiltily. I had liked him so much when we had met and had been reconciled then to the possibility of marriage. I had, in fact, almost welcomed it. But how differently I felt now! It must have been because in those days, when I thought of myself as Mama's prisoner, I was so glad of any excitement, any change . . . and marriage would have been that. But being the Queen was quite another matter. There was so much happening in my daily existence and even the minor irritations like the Flora Hastings affair and that of the bedchamber women occupied my mind to such an extent that I did not want to think of marriage.

But now there was this charming young man, and I did find his society amusing.

He was very Russian, which meant that at times he could assume a very melancholy countenance, and then he would be very merry and light-hearted; which made one a little unsure of how one was going to find him. But that made him interesting.

He danced divinely. He taught me the mazurka—a lovely dance which I had never seen before. It was amusing for the Grand Duke was so agile that when one was required to run round, one had to be very quick to follow him. Then, when we were close together, he whisked me round in a valse.

Another dance he taught me was the *Grossvater* which was a country dance performed a great deal in Germany. The men had to jump over a pocket handkerchief which was very tricky and often resulted in a fall for some of them. I laughed and laughed. I used to stay up dancing until after two in the morning; then I would be unable to sleep for very excitement, lying in my bed, remembering how the Grand Duke leaped and some of the dancers had fallen over. It was very amusing and I was growing more and more fond of the Grand Duke.

I could not help writing of him to Uncle Leopold who wrote back rather coldly, begging me not to be rash. I knew he was thinking of Albert.

Lord Melbourne was a little critical too.

I told him it was good for me to have a little excitement. There had been much to plague me lately.

'Excitement is not very desirable if one is to suffer for it afterwards,' was Lord Melbourne's comment.

But I continued to dance the new dances and to stay up until after midnight. I threw myself into a frenzy of excitement. I felt I was half-way to falling in love with the Russian Grand Duke.

I needed the excitement for underneath it I was still uneasy. I had passed out of that mood of enchantment. I had learned that life could suddenly take an unexpected turn to disaster. Flora Hastings still went about the Palace. Ladies, meeting her in the corridors, said she made them shiver; she was like a ghost from another world; and she looked at them with staring, accusing eyes. She looked, as they said, 'like death'; and those who had been most active in stirring up gossip about her, were really afraid of her.

She hung over me like a dark shadow. There were still reverberations in the Press about the case, and the Hastings family were most dissatisfied; and as they were Tories they would not let the case be forgotten.

In the House of Lords, Lord Brougham was constantly attacking Lord Melbourne and his Cabinet and making sly allusions to me and my fondness for the Prime Minister. The wicked hypocrites insisted on their loyalty to the *Crown* while they made their subtle attacks upon the *Queen*.

The matter of the Bedchamber Ladies was not allowed to pass into oblivion. It was a very tense situation.

The Duke of Wellington came to see me about Sir John Conroy.

'I have long been working to put an end to his case, M'am,' he said, 'and I am of the opinion that it would be well for all concerned

if he were out of the country, and I believe I am working towards
a settlement with him.'

I was so relieved. I had a notion that once I was rid of that man
my troubles would be over.

'We shall be obliged to pay him a pension of three thousand
pounds a year and offer him a peerage. Lord Melbourne will make
the arrangements and this peerage will have to be an Irish one.'

'If he has an Irish peerage that will mean he can come to Court.
I never want him in my Court. I shall never forget all the mischief
he has caused me.'

'Quite so, M'am,' said the Duke. 'But it seems likely that the
Irish peerage could be long delayed, and it may be that when one
does come, there may be a prime minister other than Lord Melbourne, in which case that prime minister would not feel it incum-
bent upon him to agree to terms made by a former prime minister.'

More abhorrent to me even than Conroy's having a peerage was
the thought of there being a prime minister other than Lord Melbourne.

However, the Duke prevailed on me to agree to these suggestions, which I did think might have been completed earlier and in
that case we might have avoided all the horrible complications of
the Hastings affair; I was sure there would not have been so much
talk about the bedchamber ladies if Sir John Conroy had not been
at hand to foment trouble.

So I agreed, and Lord Melbourne and I celebrated the occasion
of Sir John Conroy's departure.

'Although,' said Lord M dolefully, 'we have yet to see whether
he will leave us entirely in peace. Still, it is good to have him
removed from Court.'

But even though he was removed, the effect of his evil remained.
Lady Flora continued to move about the Palace like a grey ghost.
She appeared in public too. There were those who encouraged her
in this, and wherever she was seen there were cheers for her, and
her frequent appearances helped to keep the story alive.

Lord Melbourne continued to say darkly that we must wait and
see. I am not sure whether he believed she really would produce an
infant in time or implied it to comfort me. If only she would! What
a difference that would have made! Public opinion would have
swung round and we, who had been called the villains, would be
proved to have been maligned.

But Lady Flora continued in her ghostly appearances and she
looked so wan that she inspired pity in everyone who saw her.

There was one distressing incident at Ascot which I shall never forget. It was humiliating. I rode up the course as was the custom with Lord Melbourne, and as I did so I distinctly heard a hissing. Then came those terrible words. I could not believe my ears. 'Mrs. Melbourne!'

The implication filled me with horror. How could people say such wicked things! As though my relationship with my Prime Minister was not entirely honourable.

Lord Melbourne was quite unperturbed. He had always said one should not attach importance to insults. They were like the weather. Everyone forgot how it had rained when the sun came out.

But this was something I could not easily forget.

I heard later that it was the Duchess of Montrose and Lady Sarah Ingestre—both ladies—no I will not call them *ladies*—in my mother's service, and active in the feud against me—ardent Tories, both of them.

But this was an indication of the state of affairs. The seeds sown by that arch-conspirator Conroy were beginning to ripen, and the continued sickness of Flora Hastings did not help matters.

One day I noticed that it was some time since I had seen her.

'Perhaps,' said Lord Melbourne significantly, 'the time has come when she is in need of a little retirement.'

I really came to believe that one day I should hear that Flora Hastings had been delivered of a child. Perhaps it was wrong of me to long for this; but I did feel so much depended on it.

I found that on every occasion when Lord Melbourne and I were together, the name of Lady Flora crept into the conversation.

I sent a kind message to her—rather against my will—but I thought it politic to do so. I expressed my sympathy for her suffering and asked her to visit me. She thanked me for my concern but regretted she was not well enough to come to me.

There was no alternative. I must go to her. So, putting aside the disinclination and even repulsion I felt, I went to visit her.

I was astonished when I saw her. She was lying on a couch and obviously could not rise to greet me. I did not think that anyone could be so thin and still be alive. She was like a skeleton; but at the same time her body was swollen in one part and I thought she must be pregnant.

I asked solicitously how she was and she replied that she was feeling comfortable.

She added: 'I am very grateful to Your Majesty for your kindness and I am glad to see you looking so well.'

I replied: 'When you are better we will meet . . . and talk.'

She smiled gently and shook her head. 'I shall not see Your Majesty again,' she said.

I felt a shiver run through me, for indeed she looked like a woman close to death.

In a terrible state of uneasiness I left her.

Two days later a note came from Mama. She advised me that I should postpone the dinner party I was giving that evening because Lady Flora had taken a turn for the worse and she felt it would be rather unseemly if I were merrily entertaining guests while Lady Flora was so ill.

I remembered that occasion at Kensington Palace when King William's daughter was dying and my mother had gone on with *her* dinner party. She had been condemned for that. I must not provoke more criticism, so I gave the order that the party was to be cancelled. I decided that my only guest that evening should be Lord Melbourne.

He was a little more grave than usual. In fact he had been so since the affair of the bedchamber ladies, and I realized that although he had come back as a result of it, it could only be temporarily, unless there was an election and his party came back with a big majority.

I was not naive enough to believe that would be easy—desirable though it was.

We were a little solemn that evening and even Lord Melbourne had given up the belief that Lady Flora would produce a child who would vindicate us all and bring back my popularity.

Shortly after two o'clock the next morning, Lady Flora died.

Nothing could be more disastrous. Lady Flora Hastings caused us more concern dead even than she had alive.

It seemed as though the whole country went into mourning for her. To make matters worse there was an autopsy over which five doctors presided and the verdict was damning . . . to me. Flora had had a tumour on her liver which had pressed on her stomach and enlarged it.

The Press took up the matter. Lord Hastings kept them supplied with a continual flow of information. Everywhere all over the country the martyrdom of Flora Hastings was discussed, together with the heartlessness of the Queen.

She had died, announced one paper, not of a deadly tumour on the liver but of a broken heart.

Pamphlets were sold in the streets. 'A case of Murder at Buckingham Palace.' 'A voice from the Grave of Flora Hastings to Her Gracious Majesty the Queen.' The *Morning Post* was openly critical of my behaviour in the affair and Lord Brougham continued to thunder against me in the Lords.

Even Lord Melbourne was downcast, but he tried to put on a brave face.

'Ignore it,' he said. 'Think of how the people behaved to your ancestors. Your grandfather, your uncles . . . none of them escaped.'

'But the people loved me,' I wailed.

'The people are fickle. This will blow over. They will love you again.'

'It seems as though they will never forget.'

'The mob is fickle. They hate today and love tomorrow.'

'I should never have allowed myself to listen to scandal about her.'

'A queen must look to the morals of her Court.'

'Yes, but she was not immoral. There was never a child. She was truly a virgin. She was ill and we maligned her. I shall never forget her lying on that couch. She looked dead already. She knew she was going to die. She said: "I shall never see you again". I do not think I shall know peace of mind again.'

'Your Majesty is very young. In a short while this will be forgotten, I promise you. It will pass. But meanwhile there is her funeral. A tricky matter. It is a pity she died in the Palace.'

'She is to be buried in Scotland. They are taking her body to the family home.'

'It is a pity she did not die there. That would have saved a lot of trouble.'

'I shall have to go to the funeral.'

Lord Melbourne was silent for a few moments. Then he said: 'I do not think that would be wise.'

'But what will the people say if I am not there?'

'I am concerned with what they will say . . . and even *do* if you are there.'

'You think they would harm me?'

'It is not so very uncommon for the common people to show their annoyance with sovereigns.'

I covered my face with my hands.

'Look upon it as experience,' soothed Lord Melbourne.

'Do you think that if I had not listened to gossip . . . if I had been on her side . . .'

'Well then, there would have been no complaint. You would have been on the side of the angels.'

'How I wish I had been!'

'I think,' he said, 'that you should send your carriage. But on no account should you go yourself. I would not allow that.'

I was about to protest but there was a note of firmness in his voice—yes, and even fear. This matter was of even greater importance than I had thought and the people who will cry 'Hosanna' one week will be calling 'Crucify Him' the next.

Lord Melbourne said: 'They are taking her body to Loudon by barge and unfortunately the cortège will have to leave the Palace. Peel's policemen will be guarding it all along the route. The plans are for them to set out at six A.M., and I think I shall give orders that they start two hours early. Even so, there will doubtless be a crowd waiting, for I am sure some of them will have been there all night to get a good view.'

I thought how careful he was, and how fortunate I was to have him with me. And then the horrible doubt came back to me. For how long?

It was a wretched day when Flora's coffin was taken back to her family home.

Crowds had turned out to see it pass through the streets to the waiting barge. I could imagine the scene, the people weeping for her and murmuring angry threats against me; the ballad singers waving their scandal sheets. I could not bear it and my thoughts went back to my coronation—not so very long ago—when they had shown me such love and devotion.

I was horrified and deeply wounded to learn that someone had thrown a stone at my carriage.

Lord Melbourne tried to comfort me. 'It was only one stone. The people were only half-heartedly against you. They just wanted to blame someone and they like having scapegoats in high places. She is gone. That will be an end of the matter. This time next year people will be saying, "Who was Flora Hastings?" '

I should have liked to believe him.

The Wedding

I was very melancholy after that. Lord Melbourne did his best to cheer me up.

He asked me one day what I thought about marriage.

'Marriage? Oh, I have not thought of marriage for a very long time.'

'When did you last think of it?'

'Years ago. You know Uncle Leopold always wanted me to marry my Cousin Albert.'

'I did know,' said Lord Melbourne. 'He made it abundantly clear. But it is you who will have to make the match. What do you think?'

'I have no wish to marry . . . yet.'

'Have you not? You are now twenty years of age. It is a marriageable age . . . particularly for a queen.'

'I feel it should be set aside for a while.' I burst out laughing. 'I have been your pupil for so long that I think as you do. Do *you* not always say "leave it alone." '

'Advice, I believe, which has more than once proved effective.'

'Indeed it has. Well, now I will keep to it. What do you think of Prince Albert?'

'He is a German.'

'Did you find him a little . . . solemn?'

'Many Germans are.'

'He was always tired in the evenings and never wanted to dance.'

'And Your Majesty is indefatigable and loves to dance.'

'I do not think that Uncle Leopold should choose my husband for me.'

'With that,' said Lord Melbourne, 'I am in complete agreement. But the matter should be given some thought. We have to consider the Cumberland threat.'

'But I am young yet and although the people like me less after the Flora Hastings affair, they still do not want Cumberland.'

'Royalty has to look far ahead. It might be well for you to think a little seriously about marriage.'

'Uncle Leopold believes there is an understanding between me and my Cousin Albert. When he visited me in Kensington Palace before I was Queen he made a very good impression.'

Lord Melbourne nodded.

'That was some time ago.'

'People change,' I said.

'Some become queens, and that is a great transition.'

I laughed, then I was thoughtful. 'If people could forget they don't like me so much,' I said, 'and if we could hold off the Tories . . . if we could go on like this . . . I would ask nothing better.'

'If is a very important word and life rarely remains static.'

'You are thinking I should marry.'

'I think you should give the matter some consideration.'

I did; and that brought Uncle Leopold into my thoughts. In spite of the fact that a barrier had grown up between us, I was still very fond of him. I was faithful by nature and I would never forget all that he had meant to me in my childhood. He had been a substitute for the father who had died before I knew him. Once I had thought him the most wonderful being in the world. I did not forget such friendships. It was only because he had wished to interfere in English politics that I had had to withdraw from him a little. My affection remained the same.

I knew so well that he had set his heart on my marrying Albert. He loved Albert as he loved me. We had been his children at the time when he had had none of his own. His greatest dream was to bring us together. A marriage to me would be very advantageous for Albert. After all, he was but the younger son of a German duke. Marriage to the Queen of England would be a very good match for him. And for me? I believe Uncle Leopold considered Albert to be wise and good and that he would be a help to me. He had the welfare of us both at heart.

But I was unsure of myself. I had grown up a good deal since the days when I had first met Albert and been overwhelmed by him. Uncle Leopold had talked so much of his virtues that when he had arrived he had seemed wrapped in an aura of beauty and goodness. I had been very young and impressionable . . . perhaps I still was . . . but under the worldly guidance of Lord Melbourne I had grown up a little.

Stockmar had left us some time before this because Uncle Leopold had wanted him to devote all his time to Albert. Uncle Leopold had doubtless seen that Stockmar could do little to guide me when I had taken so wholeheartedly to Lord Melbourne and listened only to him.

I thought I should write frankly to Uncle Leopold, so I did, explaining that for the time being I was quite content with things as they were, and the country did not seem over anxious for me to marry. I thought it would be wiser for Ernest and Albert *not* to pay a visit to England . . . just yet. What were Albert's thoughts about the matter? He did realize, did he not, that there was no binding engagement. It would be well for him to understand this. I heard such glowing reports of Albert, and I was sure I should like him, but that might be as a friend, a cousin, or a brother. I could not know until I met him again and I did not want anything to be *expected* from such a meeting. It made the situation rather delicate, particularly if Albert did not have a clear understanding of it. I thought there was no urgent need to come to a decision for two or three years . . . at the earliest.

I felt relieved when I had sent off that letter. It would give Uncle Leopold a clear picture of how I felt.

I was thrown into a whirl of excitement by the visit of yet another uncle. This was Uncle Ferdinand, Mama's brother, with his two sons, Augustus and Leopold and his daughter Victoire. With them came another cousin, Alexander Mensdorff-Pouilly, son of Mama's sister, Princess Sophia, and a French nobleman who had escaped from the French Revolution. I found Alexander quite fascinating; his manners were so perfect and he was more restrained than the other cousins who were noisy and liked playing rough games, which I had to admit I enjoyed. But there was something romantic about Alexander. He was a little in awe of me and although I assured him that he must not be, I did like that in him. I told Lord Melbourne that it showed a modesty which was most becoming.

'He is not entirely German,' said Lord M. 'Therefore he lacks Teutonic arrogance.'

'Lord M,' I said, 'I do not think you like the Germans.'

'Oh,' he replied airily, 'it is a mistake to generalize. There might be some very pleasant Germans . . . but perhaps not so many pleasant people as one would find in other nations.'

'In England, I suppose,' I said ironically. 'Gentlemen like Sir John Conroy or Sir Robert Peel.'

'You slander the right honourable gentleman to speak of him in the same breath with that other . . .'

'Reptile,' I finished. 'But you must admit that he is at least not a German.'

I laughed with him and continued to enjoy the company of the visitors. I was joining in their games, laughing as loudly as they did and I was on the most familiar terms with them, but Alexander remained the one I liked because he was more serious and I think a little in love with me.

As usual these visits were all too brief. I went down to Woolwich to see them off and actually went on board the ship which was to take them away. There were so many sighs and regrets, so many promises to come again. Then I stood waving while the ship sailed away and the band played *God Save the Queen*.

At our next meeting I detected a certain relief in Lord Melbourne's face and I said: 'I believe you are glad the cousins have gone. Confess. You did not like them.'

I was rather pleased because I thought the reason he did not like them was because they had taken my attention from him; also to watch them riding and leaping, running and performing the dances of their country had made him feel old and tired.

'Children must play games,' he said.

'So they seemed childish to you?'

'They are perhaps a little young for their years.'

'I enjoyed the romps.'

He smiled a little sadly and that made me thoughtful.

I looked afresh upon this man whom I loved so dearly. He was very handsome with those wonderful blue-grey eyes which were fringed with dark lashes, such expressive eyes, which so often had filled with tears, indicating his tenderness for me. And I thought of all the talk of marriage and the uneasiness of the political situation, and the horrible fear that he might be thrown out of office which would mean that we should see little of each other, for a Tory minister would never allow the Queen to be on friendly terms with the Leader of the Opposition. I pondered on this and thought how unpredictable life could be and it was foolish to imagine one could go on in the same way for ever.

I said on impulse: 'Lord Melbourne, I want you to have a portrait painted. I shall hang it in my sitting-room and then I shall always be able to look at you even when you are absent.'

He was deeply touched and with tears in his eyes said that although sitting for a portrait was not his idea of the best way of passing time, he would gladly endure the ordeal if it was my wish.

'Oh, it will not be so bad,' I told him. 'I will come and watch the work in progress.'

'That will be a great inducement.'

'I daresay Dashy would like to come, too. You know how fond he is of you.'

'Then I shall be assured of good company.'

I was not going to let the matter be forgotten and engaged Sir William Charles Ross to paint the portrait which I insisted should be done at the Palace.

I enjoyed the sittings far more than Lord Melbourne did. I could sense that he was somewhat restive. I sat with him and Dashy came and watched the progress with an interest which amused us all and sent me into gusts of laughter.

It was the best way of forgetting all that unpleasantness through which I had recently passed, and living in the moment, which was so amusing.

When the portrait was finished, I was not altogether pleased with it. It was like Lord Melbourne, but not nearly as good-looking as the original.

When I mentioned this to Lord Melbourne he said: 'Oh Ross always likes to make his sitters look worse than they are. He thinks it is such fun.'

'I do not,' I said. 'I like to see people as they are.'

'An artist will talk about seeing through an artist's eyes.'

'Well, if an artist cannot see what is there, his eyes need attending to.'

'Your Majesty is as ever the Mistress of Logic.'

I hung up the picture, and even if it was not entirely true to life, at least it was pleasant; and I did feel it would be comforting to have it there . . . for ever.

Uncle Leopold must have been rather disturbed by my letter for I had one from him which said that he intended to pay me a short visit. When he said short he meant very brief indeed.

He intended to leave Ostend overnight and I was to be in Brighton where he could join me for a few hours, talk to me and then return.

The idea of travelling to Brighton did not appeal to me. Moreover I distrusted this idea of a few hours. I thought I might be pressed into making some agreement which I did not wish for. If anything was suggested I wanted time to talk it over with Lord Melbourne.

So I wrote back and said I could not be in Brighton for I had so many duties in London. He knew what a trying time I had passed through recently for he was fully aware of what was going on in England.

He must make it a proper visit. Let him come to Windsor. I should be so delighted to entertain him there.

I think he was a little put out because in the past I had immediately fallen in with his suggestions.

However, I guess he was very disturbed by what I had said about Albert; and he agreed to make arrangements for a visit to Windsor.

I was as excited as ever at the prospect of seeing him. I had forgotten those little differences we had had. What were they in a lifetime of devotion! Of course Uncle Leopold must act in a way which would be advantageous to Belgium. Of course he must rally as many friends as he could. It was only natural that he should ask for my help if I could give it.

When he, with Aunt Louise, arrived, I was waiting to greet them. I ran into Uncle Leopold's arms and he embraced me warmly.

'Still the same dear child,' he said.

'I am twenty now, Uncle Leopold.'

'Yes . . . yes . . . growing up.'

And there was Aunt Louise, looking much older, not the light-hearted young woman I had known when she was first married to Uncle Leopold.

I spent a great deal of time with him for he was with us for only a few days. There was, he said, so much to talk about; and the theme of his conversation was Albert.

He was surprised, he said, at my attitude to marriage.

I replied that I thought my attitude to marriage was quite normal.

'I mean your own marriage. You seem to avoid all thought of it.'

'Oh no, Uncle. It is just that I am young as yet and there seems no immediate need for it.'

'My dear child, as you have said, you are twenty years of age. That could be quite mature. You are certainly ready for marriage. A monarch has duties towards the State. You have to give the country heirs. Do you realize that your uncle, the Duke of Cumberland, the King of Hanover, is waiting to pounce.'

'He has always been the bogeyman. I used to be terrified of him when I was young. I thought he was a horrible one-eyed monster, a Cyclops.'

'Nor were you far wrong. He is just waiting now, as he always has been, to seize the crown.'

'Oh, Uncle, I am not going to die yet. I am years younger than he is.'

'Don't talk of dying, dear child. Just be reasonable. Think of the future . . . what is expected of you. You enjoyed the visits of your Coburg cousins.'

'Oh yes. They were such fun . . . all of them. I thought Alexander was charming.'

'I remember how much you enjoyed the visit of your cousins, Albert and Ernest.'

'Yes. That was long ago. But I do remember.'

'I have had the most excellent reports of Albert from Stockmar. He says he is a young man in a million.'

'Stockmar would not say that if he did not believe it.'

'Indeed not. I have the highest hopes for Albert.'

'Yes. I know you always did.'

'You and he . . . my niece, my nephew . . . my dearest children, both of you. You remember those days when I was a widower . . . mourning Charlotte and the loss of our child. You were my comfort, you and Albert. Planning for you, spending my days trying to discover what would assure the happiness of you both . . .'

'I do remember, Uncle. You were so good to me . . . to Albert too.'

'It was always my dearest wish that you two should come together.'

'Yes, Uncle, I know.'

'I think I should be completely happy if I could see you and Albert married.'

'It may come to pass . . . in time.'

'I am not sure that Albert is prepared to wait . . . indefinitely. I think you should make up your mind soon.'

'Not prepared to wait! But there has been no agreement . . . no engagement.'

'That is true. But it is known that you and he . . .'

'But why is it known? I have never given my word.'

'Albert cannot be humiliated.'

'I certainly do not wish to humiliate him. But marriage is a serious matter. One wants to consider.'

'You *must* consider. It is unwise for you to go on living as you do. I know, of course, that you and your mother are not on the best of terms, and that grieves me . . . It grieves me deeply. You are living here in separate households. There was that unsavoury matter of the girl who died.'

'Yes, but at least we have rid ourselves of Conroy.'

'I did hear of that. It was most unfortunate. And there is another matter. You seem to be on terms of very special friendship with your Prime Minister.'

'My Prime Minister is a wonderful man.'

'I have no doubt of his excellence, but does that mean that he should be on . . . er . . . such terms with the Queen?'

'He is a great friend as well as adviser.'

'My dearest child, you are so good, so honest, so honourable, that it does not occur to you that there are people in the world who are less so. Royalty cannot afford . . . scandal. It can be the end of them. In view of everything . . . you must consider marriage.'

'I have considered and have decided that it is for the future.'

'That will not do. You need marriage soon. You need the good, sober companionship of one who can stand beside you and assist you, someone to share the burden which has been put on these dear young shoulders. I will arrange for Ernest and Albert to pay you a visit. I think when you see this unusually talented young man you will be in entire agreement with me.'

I could not bear to see Uncle Leopold so disturbed and I cried: 'Oh, I hope so, Uncle. I do indeed.'

Their visit was coming to an end. I had had little time with Aunt Louise. Poor Aunt Louise, so different now! She was still elegant— that was innate—but she did not seem to have the same joy in her clothes. I think her life with Uncle Leopold must have been very serious.

My acquaintance with Lord M had made me see people differently. I loved Uncle Leopold dearly, of course, but he was so serious; and he had somehow drained all the merriment out of Aunt Louise. One could not laugh with them as one could with Lord Melbourne. There were none of those dry cynical comments which amused me so. I could not laugh . . . vulgarly . . . with Uncle Leopold. I always had to remember to keep my mouth shut when I did so. It was almost as bad as having the prickly holly under one's chin; but there should be nothing tormenting about laughing. Uncle Leopold was so good really, whereas my dear Lord M was just a little wicked. Those divorce cases and then Lady Caroline Lamb, his wife, being so mad and all that scandal about Lord Byron. It was not Lord Melbourne's fault; but the dear man did seem to have become caught up in so many scandals. And that had an effect on him and made him easy to get along with. It made him fascinating, too.

Was I faintly critical of Uncle Leopold? Although I had soothed him and listened patiently to his eulogies on my cousin Albert, was I beginning to build up that obstinacy—which Lord M knew existed and did not hesitate to call attention to? Now, was it a sort of resistance to Albert?

In any case, when Uncle Leopold and Aunt Louise were about to leave I felt the old desolation at the prospect of parting and I told them, with absolute sincerity, that I should miss them sadly.

I said a tearful goodbye on their last day for they were leaving early in the morning, but when morning came, I woke early, got out of bed and went to their apartment where they were having an early breakfast.

They looked very sad in the light of the candles and I told them I was too because they were leaving. Their visit had been far too brief.

Uncle Leopold agreed that it had been and assured me once again of his love and continual concern for me.

'I want to see you happy, dearest child, before I depart this life,' he said.

'I *am* happy, Uncle,' I replied. 'If only we can keep the Tories out and all these horrible things which have been happening are forgotten, I can be quite happy.'

'I want to see you fulfilled. I want to see you looked up to. I want to see you doing your duty to the State.'

That meant he wanted me to marry Albert.

And in that tender moment of parting I thought: Oh, Uncle, I will try to like him. I really will.

We embraced again and parted.

I went to my room and watched their carriage carry them away to the ship which would take them across the water.

There came that memorable October day—the tenth to be precise.

I awoke to find Lehzen standing by my bed.

'Good morning, Daisy,' I said. 'I feel a little sick.'

'It was the pork last night,' said Lehzen. 'And you do gobble so, you know.'

'You sound like Mama. You will be telling me soon that I show my gums when I laugh.'

'Are you feeling very sick?'

'No, only a little. Nothing that a walk in the park will not put right.'

'There is something else. Some of the windows were broken last night. It looks as though someone took it into his head to throw a stone or two.'

'How dreadful!'

'Are you going to get up?'

'Yes, I must.'

After breakfast I expected Lord Melbourne to come to see me but instead he sent a message. He, too, felt sick and thought it was due to the pork.

'It should have been all right,' said Lehzen. 'There was an R in the month.'

'I shall go out now,' I told her. 'All I need is fresh air.'

'Wrap up well,' advised Lehzen. 'The wind is fresh.'

As I walked in the park I was thinking of what Uncle Leopold had said during his visit. Indeed, I had thought of little else since his departure; and the more I thought of it the more determined I became not to be forced into marriage.

Lord Melbourne agreed with me. What an understanding man he was! He was not overfond of Germans and was always stressing their failings.

Dear Uncle Leopold, I thought. I do love you as much as ever, but you must not interfere.

In the distance I saw a page. He was running towards the Palace.

'What is it?' I called out. Then I saw that he was carrying a letter.

'Your Majesty,' he panted. 'I was to deliver this to you immediately.'

I took it and saw that it was from Uncle Leopold.

I tore it open and read:

'Your cousins, Ernest and Albert, will be with you this evening.'

I could not believe it. This very evening!

My heart was pounding as I went back to the Palace.

Lord Melbourne said it was short notice, particularly for people who were suffering from a surfeit of pork. We must forget our discomfort and prepare ourselves for the arrival of the august gentlemen.

'They will be exhausted when they get here, no doubt,' went on Lord M. 'There is quite a gale blowing across the Channel. I don't envy them the trip.'

All preparations had been made. I had dressed for the evening and was waiting with great impatience for the arrival of the cousins.

Then I heard the sound of carriage wheels in the courtyard and was waiting at the top of the stairs to receive them.

And they came; Ernest and Albert. And when my eyes fell on Albert, whom I recognized at once as the more distinguished of the two, my heart leaped and I knew in that first moment that nothing could ever be the same again.

They were coming towards me, these two young men. I am afraid I did not notice much about Ernest. My attention was all for Albert.

He was tall and very pale. Lord Melbourne had been right; it had been an atrocious crossing and I heard later that poor Albert had been very sick. He was in dark travelling clothes which in a way accentuated his pallor and his beautiful blue eyes more than colourful garments could have done. His nose was perfectly shaped, and his mouth pretty with delicate moustachios and very very slight whiskers. What a handsome figure he had! Very broad shoulders and a small waist. His hair was about the same colour as mine, so he was fair. Ernest was dark and had very fine eyes, but really my attention was all for Albert.

He stood before me. I raised my eyes to that beautiful face and a great exultation possessed me.

This, I thought, is being in love.

Oh the joy of that visit . . . *discovering* Albert!

I could not sleep that night. I lay in bed thinking of him. Oh dear Uncle Leopold, to have my happiness so much at heart. Of course he was right. Albert was perfect. And I was so happy.

There was so much to talk about. Albert loved music. We would sing together. Duets were so pleasurable. Dash—dear, discriminating Dashy—selected Albert for his special attention and Albert played with him *enchantingly*. Everything Albert did was done with such grace. He had brought his greyhound with him. Its name was Eos.

He said: 'We could not be parted.'

Oh, what feeling! How I understood his love for Eos. It was exactly like that which I had for dear Dash.

I was looking forward to the next day and could hardly sleep at all. I got up early and wrote a letter to Uncle Leopold. I owed him that for sending me this most superb of cousins.

'Ernest is grown quite handsome,' I wrote. 'Albert's beauty is

more striking and he is so amiable and unaffected . . . in short he
is very fascinating . . .'

I could have gone on writing of Albert's perfections but I forced
myself to stop.

I smiled as I sealed the letter. Uncle Leopold would be very
pleased indeed.

That day we went riding. It was so exciting. I knew that I looked
my best in the saddle. Then people could not see how short I was.
I rode well and my riding clothes, I believe, became me more than
any other except ball gowns and suchlike. I loved my horses and
they reciprocated my affection, so we got on well together.

I rode between the two princes, but I was hardly aware of Ernest,
although he was very charming, of course. Lord Melbourne was of
the party, and on this occasion, instead of riding beside me, he was
a little way behind.

Soon I would talk to him alone. I would discuss with him my
opinion of Albert . . . of both princes . . . but just for a while I
wanted to keep my thoughts to myself. I was bemused and yet
certain. There would never be anyone quite so perfect as Albert. I
had no doubt of it. Uncle Leopold was so clever; he had known
who would be just the right one for me.

Albert and his brother spoke English well. Clever Uncle Leopold
had insisted on their being proficient in that language. Of course
they had German accents but that did not prevent their being understood perfectly.

We talked of many things during that ride but chiefly of music.
Albert had composed a little. How clever of him! It was just what
I would have expected. And I was longing to hear some of his very
own music. He also spoke most lovingly of Rosenau, the place
where he had been born, and which had been the home he loved
best, which showed genuine sentiment and sensitivity.

He made me long to see it.

I returned to the castle more in love than ever. There I had my
first talk, after the arrival of the cousins, with Lord Melbourne.

I said: 'I want to tell you what I think of my cousins.'

Lord Melbourne smiled at me very tenderly. 'I can make a good
guess,' he said. 'Your Majesty was never one to conceal her feelings.'

'Do you think Albert is handsome?'

'Undoubtedly. Very handsome. And his brother has fine dark
eyes.'

'Albert's are blue.'

'That is absolutely true.'

'And he is much more handsome than his brother. At least *I* think so.'

'I did note Your Majesty's opinion. I think Ernest is a very clever young man from what I have been able to observe so far.'

'Oh, but not as clever as Albert.'

'I should think Ernest possibly has the better brain.'

I turned on him angrily and saw the glint in his eyes. He was teasing me, of course. But he really should not do so on such a serious matter.

'I see that Your Majesty has changed her mind a little regarding marriage,' he said.

I smiled at him. 'Yes, dear Lord M, I have.'

He nodded. 'That was my inference. I daresay you will not wish to delay the marriage.'

'I see no reason for delay. Do you?'

'None whatever. As Your Majesty has made up her mind and is so well satisfied, the sooner the marriage takes place the better. I take it the Prince will be of the same mind as ourselves.'

I was silent and Lord Melbourne went on: 'Oh, is he not yet aware of his happy fate?'

'It presents a certain difficulty. Albert would never act rashly, nor would he disregard etiquette.'

'But of course Your Majesty does not always follow it . . . if I may be so bold as to say so.'

'You have never hesitated to say what you mean, my dear Lord M. That is why our association has been of such value to me.'

He bowed his head slightly. 'You will agree that there will have to be a proposal.'

'I see you understand the difficulty.'

'Indeed I do, and I am sure Your Majesty will overcome it. Then we shall have a royal wedding. That is just what is needed now. The people will love it.'

'*They* are not exactly in love with me just now.'

'All the world is in love with a bride . . . particularly a royal one. Let us have a wedding and you will see.'

'I no longer feel the same about the people. I shall never forget how cruel they were to me . . . and they threw a stone at my carriage.'

'They will throw kisses and cheers on your wedding day.'

'Are you sure?'

'Absolutely.'

I smiled at him lovingly. What a comfort he was! But he was looking a little tired and I had not realized how *old* he looked. Of course he *was* old.

I suppose I was comparing him with Albert and his radiant youth and beauty.

Dear Lord M! I should always love him and cherish the memory of those years when we had been together. But already I was moving away from him. I should have another with whom I would discuss my difficulties, another who would share my personal burdens as well as those of state.

How wonderful it was to be in love! And what a change it was going to make.

I had made up my mind. There was one thing to do. Albert dared not ask me to marry him because I was a queen and he was only a prince of a minor dukedom . . . and not even his father's eldest son. *I* must propose to *him*.

It was the twelfth of October. Another memorable day. We had been out hunting and when we came back to the castle I asked him to come into the Blue Closet. He came in expectantly. He must have guessed what was going to happen.

I said to him: 'Albert, I think you must be aware of the reason for my asking you to come. It would make me very happy if you would consent to what I wish, and I believe you do . . . and that is for us to marry.'

Dear Albert! His joy was intense; and there was relief in it too. Uncle Leopold had been right when he had said Albert was uncertain of me.

Well, he need be so no longer.

Albert forgot his English then and I was glad. He told me in German how happy he was, and that above all things he wanted to spend his life with me.

We embraced with the utmost tenderness.

I had never been so happy in the whole of my life, and when we left the Blue Closet, I was betrothed to Albert.

What glorious days they were! We rode together, walked, sang and danced. Our voices blended perfectly and I loved to sing those songs—all with such beautiful sentiments—which Albert had composed himself. I could see that we were going to be very happy together. We discussed the wedding which could not take place immediately, but we thought it might do so early in the New Year.

Albert had to return with his brother to Saxe-Coburg, and because of the importance of a marriage like ours there was a great deal to be settled before the actual ceremony.

Albert was, of course, more restrained than I; but I felt no inclination to pretend that I felt anything but love for this supreme being. I would come up behind him when he was sitting and kiss the top of his head; and when we parted call him back for one more kiss. My love seemed to be overflowing and I saw no reason for stemming it.

Lehzen thought I was too effusive. Poor Lehzen! Was she a little jealous? I often caught a half-smiling look in Lord Melbourne's eyes, and I knew he was a little amused by my exuberance.

Well, I was as I was, and it was not in my nature to hide my feelings.

I think Albert, at times, was faintly embarrassed—when we were with others—at my displays of affection. Dear Albert, he was a little bemused by his good fortune, I think. I was three months older than he was and a queen. My rank must have been the reason why I behaved naturally and did not have to worry so much about what people were thinking of me. My uncles had done what they liked and what was natural to them; that was why some of them had been called eccentric. I was not exactly that. I merely betrayed my feelings—and I could see no wrong in doing that.

There came the sad day when Albert had to say goodbye.

'It will not be for long,' I assured him. 'Then we shall be together for the rest of our lives.'

The days seemed flat without him; but there was so much to do for the wedding.

Lord Melbourne said he would draw up a Declaration for me to read to the Privy Council, so that they could all be told formally of my intentions.

It was rather comforting to be sitting with Lord Melbourne in the Blue Closet, which would never be the same again because within its walls I had proposed to Albert.

I could not resist telling Lord Melbourne about it and how it had been a rather embarrassing thing to do. 'But poor Albert would never have proposed to me. Someone had to do it.'

'I told you you would, did I not?'

'Oh yes, you did. There may be other occasions when similar situations arise. Albert will have to remember that I am the Queen.'

Lord Melbourne gave me one of those wry side glances and

said: 'I am sure Albert will remember that because he will not be allowed to forget.'

'There are times, Lord M,' I said, 'when I feel you do not have enough appreciation for Albert.'

Lord Melbourne was silent and I stamped my foot and insisted: 'Am I right, Lord Melbourne?'

'Dare I tell Your Majesty that I think he is very young and perhaps inexperienced.'

'Everyone is inexperienced at first. Albert will support me with all his might. He is so good.'

'Oh yes, he is indeed a very virtuous young man.'

'And we shall have you at hand, my dearest Lord M.'

Then he gave me that sad look which meant that he was thinking of the Tories.

'Dear Lord M,' I said, 'I am afraid I have been absentminded, a little gruffish, lately.'

He smiled at me sweetly. 'It is natural,' he said.

'I have a little miniature which Ross did of Albert. I am having it put into a bracelet which I shall wear always.'

'I hope it is a good likeness.'

'It does not do him justice. I remember what you said about Ross's liking to make people worse because it was such fun. I don't think it is fun at all. I think it is rather silly. But nobody could have painted a picture of Albert which would have been half good enough.'

He regarded me with his head on one side and with that tenderness which always moved me. Dear Lord Melbourne! Although I loved Albert, there would always be a place in my heart for my Prime Minister.

How delighted I was to read Uncle Leopold's letter! His joy shone out of every line.

    'My dearest Victoria,

     'Nothing could have given me greater pleasure than your dear letter. I had, when I saw your decision, almost the feeling of Zacharias—''Now lettest Thou Thy servant depart in peace.''

     'You will find in Albert just the very qualities and dispositions which are indispensable for your happiness and will suit your own character, temper and mode of life . . . Albert's position will be a difficult one but much, I may say, will depend on your affection for him.

'Lord Melbourne has shown himself the amiable and excellent man I always took him for. Another man in his position, instead of *your* happiness might have merely looked to his own personal views and imaginary interests. Not so our good friend; he saw what was best *for you*, and I feel it deeply to his praise . . .'

I was so delighted with the letter, and as it was so complimentary to Lord Melbourne, I showed it to him. He had always been a little suspicious of Uncle Leopold, so I thought it a good idea to let him see that my uncle at least had a very good opinion of him.

Lord Melbourne's comment was: 'Simeon, I believe . . . not Zacharias.'

'What?' I demanded.

'Lord now lettest Thou Thy servant . . .'

I smiled at him. That was so like him.

'I am so pleased,' I said, 'that my dear Uncle Leopold has got what he wanted.'

'What pleased me,' said Lord M, 'is that Your Gracious Majesty has got what *she* wants.'

He then went on to talk about letting people know that I had decided to marry.

I dressed myself in one of my plainest gowns. I did not want to look in the least frivolous. I wore my bracelet to which had been attached the miniature of Albert. Then I was ready for the ordeal.

They all looked up at me. I imagined they saw the picture on my wrist. They would be aware that I was holding Lord Melbourne's Declaration and that would tell them the reason why I had come.

Anything Lord Melbourne wrote was always gracefully worded in elegant prose, and so was this. It was a pleasure to read his composition. I told them that I had decided to marry and whom, and that the marriage would be celebrated very shortly.

When I had read the Declaration I walked out of the Council Chamber.

Lord Melbourne came to see me a little later. He was mildly disturbed. I had never seen him more than mildly so even during the Flora Hastings trouble, so I guessed that something rather important had happened.

'It is my fault,' he said. 'I did not think it necessary to say that

Prince Albert is a Protestant. The Press are making a merry to-do about this. They are saying he is a Catholic, and that it will not be tolerated for a ruler of this country to marry outside the Reformed Faith.'

'But Albert *is* of the Reformed Faith. How could they possibly think he is a Catholic?'

'Your Uncle Leopold has made a point of marrying his relations all over Europe, and some of those advantageous marriages have been with Catholics. They are suggesting that as no mention was made of the Reformed Faith, Albert may be one of those who has collapsed into Catholicism.'

'That can easily be put right.'

'True. But it shows the temper of the people who are determined to make our way difficult.'

'Why are people so unkind?'

'In the case of the Press they want to sell papers so they are hunting for all sorts of spectacular titbits. In the case of the Tories, they want to put obstacles in our way. They want to raise issues which we have to defend and they are hoping that there will come a time when they will defeat us and make it imperative for us to go to the country.'

I shivered.

'Please, Lord Melbourne, let them know that Albert is a firm adherent of the Reformed Faith.'

'With all speed,' said Lord Melbourne.

I should have been prepared for more trouble.

Although it was easy to prove that Albert was not, and never had been, a Catholic—he was a Lutheran in fact and most certainly therefore of the Reformed Faith—there were other objections. I really believe there are some people who hate to contemplate the happiness of others.

One would have thought that my Uncle Cumberland, now that he was King of Hanover, would have been content to give up all thought of plaguing me. I was no longer a newcomer to the throne; I was the anointed Queen of England—but he was one who never gave up hope.

Naturally I had decided that Albert should be beside me at all ceremonies, and that meant he would take precedence over everyone else at Court, and that he would come before my uncles in order of importance. The Dukes of Cambridge and Sussex understood this and accepted it as natural; but of course Cumberland had to object. He was not only a duke, he was a king; he was the son of my grandfather George III, and but for the ill fortune which had brought my father into the world before him, he would now be on the throne of England. That fact had rankled throughout his life, and he now began to stir up trouble. He referred slightingly to Albert as a Paper Highness; and he persuaded Cambridge and Sussex to fall in with him.

I was furious and especially so when I heard that the Tories were standing with the dukes. How I loathed Sir Robert Peel—the horrid hypocrite, always pretending to be so good and stirring up trouble for me. When the Duke of Wellington supported him, I was really disgusted and declared that I never wanted to see that old man again.

I had suffered from their insensitivity before, but I had never felt so enraged against them as I did now when their venom was directed at Albert.

Uncle Leopold, having attained his heart's desire, was now writing telling me what must be done. Albert should have a peerage, he said.

When I showed his letter to Lord Melbourne he retorted: 'Parliament would never agree to that. They would be afraid that if he were in the Lords he would attempt to rule the country. They do not forget that he is a German.'

I knew they did not forget. They referred to him in the Press as the German Princeling.

I said to Lord Melbourne: 'They seem to think that no one is any good unless they are English.'

'A common trait among nations,' he commented.

'They are saying that there have been too many Germans in the royal family.'

'There have been a large number since the coming of George the First.'

'What would people have? Stuarts? I cannot remember that they were so good for the country. One of them brought about a civil war. Is that what they want?'

'Nations never want what they have, and look back nostalgically to those days which seem rosy because they are too far back to be seen clearly.'

'I do wish they would be reasonable.'

'That is what we must all try to be.'

'Albert is worthy of the highest rank. I shall defy them all by making him King Consort.'

Lord Melbourne looked at me with that half tender, half exasperated look which I knew so well.

'That could never be,' he said quietly. 'Parliament cannot confer kingship.'

'And why not?' I retorted. 'Since Albert will be the husband of the Queen, does not that make him a king?'

'No, M'am, it does not. He is a prince and cannot be anything else. If you allow Parliament to make kings, you could not be surprised if now and then they decided to *un*make them.'

'The French did. And what of Charles the First?'

'Your Majesty cannot be thinking of revolutions and civil wars. We want none of those here. There is no question regarding this matter. Prince Albert cannot be King Consort.'

'He cannot have a peerage! He cannot be a king! Then what can he be?'

'What he will be, M'am, is the Queen's husband.'

I talked about his allowance. Lord Melbourne said that it was customary to give the monarch's consort £50,000 a year, and he would ask the Parliament to agree to this. I was a little mollified because I knew that Albert was by no means rich. He had only £2,500 a year, so £50,000 would be wealth to him.

I longed to write and tell him that he was going to be rich. I was so certain that there would be no impediment, that I almost did. Lord Melbourne had reminded me that £50,000 had been awarded to Queen Anne's husband, George of Denmark, and to William of Orange, consort of Queen Mary, although William of Orange was, of course, a king in his own right.

It did not occur to me that Albert should fail to receive the same.

Lord Melbourne came to me in a subdued mood.

'I regret to tell Your Majesty that Parliament refuses the grant of £50,000. They will agree only to £30,000.'

I was outraged. 'This is monstrous,' I cried.

'Alas, the government was beaten by one hundred and four votes.'

'£30,000 when that oaf, Queen Anne's husband, was given £50,000! How can they be so stupid? What good was that man to the country? And dear, clever Albert . . .' I was so angry. I turned to Lord Melbourne: 'How could you allow it? You should have stopped it. You are the Prime Minister.'

'Your Majesty will know that it is not in the Prime Minister's power to go against the majority.'

'We must insist.'

Lord Melbourne just shook his head.

'Is it so very much more?' I demanded.

'£20,000 to be precise.'

'I know that!' I shouted. 'It is nothing . . . nothing . . . compared with the money in the country. It is done to insult Albert . . . and me. How can I tell him?'

'I do believe,' said Lord Melbourne, 'that Prince Albert, if he knew the circumstances, would be the first to understand.'

'What circumstances?'

'The state of the country. We are not very prosperous at this time. There is a great deal of unemployment. The Chartists are making a nuisance of themselves and they have their supporters. It would not do to bestow large sums of money on . . . forgive me, Your Majesty, but that is how people would see it—impoverished foreigners, while our own people are in need.'

I stared at him. I knew there had been troubles, but Lord Melbourne had always made light of them. The Duchess of Sutherland was always trying to interest me in what Lord Melbourne called 'causes'. 'They give the idle something to do and feel good about,' he had said. I had been interested in Lord Shaftesbury, who had made great efforts to improve conditions in the mines and had brought to light the terrible fate of chimney sweeps. But when I had talked to Lord Melbourne about this he had said that Shaftesbury had been quite cruel to his own children and that charity should begin at home. Lord Melbourne had mentioned these matters lightly, and then he had been quite amusing about some aspects, and I had not thought very seriously about them.

Now it seemed different. It was brought home to me. I remembered the poor man to whom I had given the money I had saved for the big doll. I just hated to see beggars in the streets and always wanted to give to them. I could not bear the thought of little boys going up chimneys and children in the mines.

That sobered me considerably and made me forget my anger about the refusal of the Tories to give Albert his £50,000.

'Yes,' I said slowly, 'I do see that.'

I wondered what poor Albert was thinking because he would now know what was going on. I feared he might experience some humiliation, which was the last thing I wanted. I was sure he would understand about his allowance. He would be the first to realize the needs of the people.

He accepted these insults stoically and wrote to me about his household. It was at this time that I began to realize what strict moral standards Albert had. I believe, in his heart, he did not approve of Lord Melbourne who had been cited twice as the lover of married women and had had a stormy marriage. He would have heard about the Byron scandal; and like so many very good people who could not bear a breath of scandal, felt that all those concerned in such cases were tainted, even though they might be innocent parties. *I* did not feel like that; but then I was not so very *good*.

Albert thought that his household could be composed of both Whigs and Tories. He thought it was wrong to have one party predominant. This was a faint criticism of my household which was entirely Whig. He always wanted members of his household to be completely moral.

When I put this before Lord Melbourne, he smiled wryly but was very firm.

'There could not be two households made up of different political leanings,' he said. 'Your Majesty has seen the disaster brought about by this sort of thing under your own roof—yours and your mother's.'

I agreed with that.

'Well then,' he said, 'there should be one household, and I do not think Your Majesty would wish to people that with Tories.'

'I would not endure them in my household.'

'You are the Queen. It is your decision. The Prince should have his own private secretary but he and I can share one for the time being. George Anson is a very worthy fellow.'

'It is good of you to offer to share him with the Prince. I will write to Albert at once.'

Albert's reaction was immediate. He did not think it was a good idea for him to share the Prime Minister's secretary. There was another matter. He believed that George Anson was up half the night dancing. That seemed to Albert a very frivolous occupation for the holder of such an important post.

I was resentful. *I* liked to stay up half the night dancing, and I had a responsible post. Sometimes I felt that Albert forgot I was the Queen of England. He would have to learn that I knew far more of my country than he possibly could; and it was no use talking about being fair to both political parties and allowing the hated Tories into the Palace. He did not know how odious they could be.

Uncle Leopold wrote. He was disgusted because Albert had not been given a peerage and because Parliament had seen fit to insult him by giving him only £30,000 a year when the custom had been to give £50,000 to consorts of reigning queens.

I was getting a little irritated, even with Albert. He did not understand. Uncle Leopold did not understand.

I wrote to Albert explaining to him that his suggestion about his gentlemen simply would not do. He must rely on me to see that gentlemen of the highest standing and good character would be appointed. I added that I had received a rather disgruntled letter from Uncle Leopold. He was annoyed because I did not take his advice. 'Dear Uncle,' I wrote, 'he is inclined to believe that he should be in command everywhere.'

I wanted to tell Albert—gently—that although I loved him dearly and respected him in every way, I was the Queen; and even he, dear, good, clever creature that he was, must not forget that.

I discovered that Albert, for all his outward gentleness, had a strong will. He was very disturbed regarding my comments about the household. He thought that he might get together certain noble, right thinking, moral, non-political German gentlemen who could accompany him to England. I would understand, he was sure, how lonely a man could feel in a strange land.

Lord Melbourne was horrified. 'A household of Germans! Never! The people would not endure it. Better Tories than that. Your Majesty knows how people distrust foreigners.'

Lord Melbourne looked at me with his head on one side as though to remind me that he had always pointed out the difficulties of a foreign marriage. Perhaps he thought George Cambridge would have been more suitable—an English cousin rather than a German one. Moreover Lord Melbourne had always expressed a certain dislike of Germans.

I told him severely that nationality did not come into the matter. I was not marrying Albert because he was a German but because I loved him.

The situation was growing tense. If Albert had been with me I felt we could have talked over these matters and come to an understanding. It was so difficult in writing. Words on paper looked so definite . . . so irrevocable. And the posts took so long that if one wrote when one was heated, by the time the letter was received one's mood would have changed considerably.

How I longed to see him and thrash out these difficulties in person.

Albert blankly refused to share the Prime Minister's secretary, and Lord Melbourne said that he would give him up and he should serve Albert only. Albert grudgingly agreed to this, so that was one little hurdle over which we had come.

But there were more. This time between Albert and myself, which was more distressing because there was no one to blame.

I did try to console myself that it was because Albert was inexperienced of customs and manners in England. He had been brought up very strictly and of course he was *naturally* good. I doubted there had been many storms in his childhood. He would always have been very conscious of his duty, and I was sure he had never strayed from the path of virtue.

The trouble with good people is that they expect such a lot from others whose natures are not so inclined towards goodness.

The first was an upset over the honeymoon. I had had such a delightful letter from Albert telling me how much he was longing to come to England and was so looking forward to our honeymoon. This should be spent at Windsor—*dear* Windsor—where we had enjoyed such a happy time, and where I had asked him to marry me. The wedding ceremony would be tiring. Dear Albert was often tired. It was because he rose early in the mornings, but then he liked to retire early. I remembered how weary he looked after some of the balls and how he could not prevent himself from yawning. 'So,' wrote Albert, 'we shall go to Windsor for a whole week where we shall be by ourselves. I shall insist on that.'

Of course, I was delighted that he should want to be alone with me, but dear Albert, he did not understand. The Queen had many duties. Of course he could not realize what the governing of a country like mine involved. How could he? He was but the Prince of Saxe-Coburg—and not the ruling prince either. There was a great deal Albert did not understand, but he would learn, of course; and being Albert he would learn quickly. One of these things was that one did not *insist* to the Queen.

'You forget, dearest love,' I wrote, 'that I am the Sovereign and state business can wait for nothing. Parliament is sitting so I could not be away from London for more than a day or so.'

When I sent off that letter I worried a little. There had been so much conflict after that joyous period when we had declared our love for each other. I wished I could see him. I wanted to know how he was feeling about all these hitches. Letters could sound so chilling sometimes. Had I been arrogant? I could not help it. I had to remind him that it was the Queen whom he was to marry.

I sent him the list of the bridesmaids. I wanted him to agree on every aspect, even this one, so I was amazed when he sent his disapproval of my choice.

He instanced two bridesmaids who should be struck off the list.

They were the daughters of Lady Radnor and Lady Jersey. The bridesmaids might be innocent young women, but their mothers had been involved in scandal, Albert pointed out. Lady Jersey had been notorious. Her ill fame had been known throughout Europe. Albert thought that none of our bridesmaids should be touched by scandal.

When I showed the letter to Lord Melbourne he was amazed, then he began to laugh.

'What does the Prince wish us to do? Check the annals of the past? God help us! What should we find? And what of the bridegroom's antecedents? I ask. His father was a notorious libertine and do not forget that he divorced his wife—the sainted Albert's own mother—for immorality. This, Your Majesty, is going a little too far.'

Much as I loved Albert, I agreed with Lord Melbourne. Albert was being a little illogical on this occasion. If we put his ideas into practice, Lord Melbourne would not be my Prime Minister. And what of my father who had lived so long with Madame St. Laurent without benefit of clergy?

No, Albert was taking his goodness too far; and I must write and tell him that the list of bridesmaids could not be changed.

Lord Melbourne sometimes regarded me with a certain sadness. I knew what was in his mind. Our relationship would necessarily change after my marriage. It would be another who was my constant companion, imbuing me with his ideas.

Was I easily led? Perhaps I was when I loved. And did I love too easily, too wholeheartedly? Perhaps there was that in me which looked for male domination. Uncle Leopold . . . Lord Melbourne . . . I had loved Uncle Leopold almost fanatically until Lord Melbourne appeared and showed me the flaws in him. And now Albert would be the man in my life.

But with none of these had I ever forgotten the all-important fact: I was the Queen.

In spite of these irritations the wedding day was fixed for the 10th February.

We were dogged by ill luck. I had been quite unwell and it appeared that I might have the measles which, fortunately, turned out to be not the case. I did not want to be a spotted bride. Lord Melbourne had a cold which left him with a cough. Mama, of course, could not be expected to let us live in peace. She did not want to move after the wedding, and she was also involved in heated discussions over precedence. It was the old pattern.

Albert's valet had come on in advance with his greyhound Eos. I had had another little dog given to me—a lovely Scotch terrier which I named Laddie. I was delighted to add him to my little family of dogs of which Dash would always be the favourite, although I loved them all. Lord Melbourne said I had too many dogs, for although they liked him, I fancy he did not like them very much.

I was getting many messages of good will and several presents too; and each morning when I awoke I reminded myself that I was one day nearer my wedding.

The Channel was particularly rough. 'Poor Prince Albert will doubtless be getting a buffeting,' said Lord Melbourne with the faintest hint of satisfaction; but he added: 'I am sure he will bear it with fortitude.'

Everything seemed to be in a state of confusion. I was so excited I could not sleep or eat. I had a terrible fear that something would go wrong.

Lehzen scolded me and said I must calm myself. Poor Lehzen, she was not quite herself. I think she resented anyone's coming into my life, and of course there could never be anyone as important as Albert.

Again and again I assured her that I should never change towards her; but I think she did not entirely believe me.

She went down to Windsor to make sure everything would be in order for our honeymoon—three days, not the week Albert had said he would insist on.

Mama had been difficult about Albert's and my staying under the same roof before the marriage. I protested. Where else could Albert stay? And did Mama expect him to be married on the day he arrived?

Mama insisted that it was 'unseemly', and to my dismay when I raised the point with Lord Melbourne, he said he thought it would be wiser if Albert stayed somewhere else.

My temper flared up. 'It seems to me,' I said, 'that everyone is trying to put as many obstacles in the way of my marriage as possible.'

Lord Melbourne patiently explained that he was really trying to remove difficulties and it was an English custom for prospective brides not to sleep under the same roof as their grooms before the marriage.

'Then I think it is the most ridiculous custom and Albert shall sleep at the Palace.'

'As you say, M'am,' said Lord Melbourne with an amused little smile. And since I had made my wishes clear, Mama had to agree.

So Albert came to Buckingham Palace. I was sure if there was anything wrong about it, Albert would be the first to know.

What a joy it was to see his dear face! Every silly little doubt I had ever had that this was the right thing to do, disappeared at once. He looked pale—the sea crossing had been atrocious. Albert was so unlucky with the sea. But nothing could mar his beauty and when I looked into his dear blue eyes, I knew how fortunate I was.

He came on a Saturday and the wedding was to take place on the following Monday. Those two days were very happy for me. We sang duets together, and we rehearsed the wedding ceremony; and the hours flew by.

I went to bed on that Sunday night too excited to sleep. It was the last night I should sleep alone. I remembered how much store I had set by that when I had been Mama's prisoner. That seemed years ago, but it was scarcely three.

At such times one is apt to go back in one's mind and think over the past . . . all the little incidents of childhood; the happy times, the stormy times. It is natural. It is the end of the old life.

When I awoke on that glorious morning of the 10th February, I could hear the rain teeming down. How unfortunate! The sun should have been shining. There is a saying 'Happy the bride whom the sun shines on.' Well, perhaps it would shine after all. In any case how could I fail to be happy with Albert?

The first thing I did was to write to him.

'Dearest,

'How are you today? And have you slept well? I have rested very well and feel very comfortable today. What weather! I believe, however, the rain will cease. Send one word when you, my dearly loved bridegroom, will be ready.'

'Thy ever faithful, Victoria R.'

There were crowds gathering in the streets. The crimson carpet was being laid out for us to walk on to the carriage. Very soon the moment would come.

I heard the shouts as Albert set out accompanied by his father and brother. I could imagine how splendid he would look in the uniform of a British Field Marshal with the ribbon of Garter—which

I had bestowed on him—across his breast. His father and brother would be in green uniforms—a contrast to the glory of Albert.

I heard the shouts and applause go up and I was thrilled because they were for Albert. I had been afraid that people might have been ungracious to him; but, of course, as soon as they saw him they must admire him.

Then it was my turn.

Mama was to be in the carriage with me. I had been against it but I did realize that on such an occasion we must waive our differences and consider what would look right in the eyes of the people.

When they saw me cheers rang out. Flags were waving and I heard the sound of trumpets. I was aware of the crowds, some on the railings and on the surrounding trees, so determined were they to get a good view.

I felt immensely gratified. The ghost of Flora Hastings had passed into oblivion—or almost—and the affair of the Bedchamber Women was forgotten. I was the Queen and this was my wedding day.

I heard gasps of admiration as I stepped out in my voluminous white satin gown trimmed with Honiton lace. I lightly touched the sapphire brooch—a present from Albert and therefore doubly valuable in my eyes. My diamond necklace sparkled about my neck and there was a wreath of orange blossom in my hair.

I sat beside Mama and we went through streets lined with people who shouted and cheered as we passed. I noticed that Mama was much less pushing than she used to be. I think she must have learned a few lessons over the past three years; moreover the odious Sir John was no longer there to guide her actions.

I was vividly reminded of my coronation when I had believed that to be a queen was the most wonderful achievement on Earth; and that if one were good, there would be no difficulties at all. What an innocent I had been! And still was, perhaps, to some extent. On solemn occasions like this one could feel so young . . . so inexperienced.

I was not yet twenty-one years of age—but three months older than my dear bridegroom. There was so much I should have to teach him about England and the duties of a queen, for he had shown himself—for example when he had thought we could take a long honeymoon—that wise and good as he undoubtedly was, he did not fully understand the duties and responsibilities of being a queen of England.

It was very impressive in the Abbey and I was deeply moved by the ceremony; and I shall never forget the moment when Albert put the ring on my finger. That sealed our relationship. We should be together now for the rest of our lives. So we were married.

Albert and I clasped hands and looked at each other in wonderment. Everything is going to be perfect for ever more, I thought! How could it fail to be with this divine being.

I caught sight of Aunt Adelaide. How she had aged since Uncle William's death! But she looked rather splendid in a gown of purple silk and velvet trimmed with ermine. Emotionally I turned to her, remembering all the kindnesses of the past—the big doll, how she had understood about the dolls as Mama never had, the occasions when she had tried to arrange for me to go to children's balls and parties, because she knew how much I loved them, and how Mama had prevented my going. Aunt Adelaide had always been gracious to Mama in spite of the rudeness she had received, and it was all because she had wanted to help *me*. Dear Aunt Adelaide! It was distressing to see her looking so old and tired. I embraced her warmly. She clung to me a little, and whispered that she hoped I should have a very happy life.

There was Mama, standing there, waiting to be embraced and told how much I appreciated all she had done for me. I had many faults possibly but hypocrisy was not one of them. No, Mama, I thought, the past cannot be wiped away just because it is convenient to do so.

She approached me holding out her arms. I took her hand and shook it. I knew by the almost imperceptible gasp of those who were watching that my gesture had been observed.

Then I left the Abbey with Albert beside me for the drive back to the Palace, through the cheering crowds—and the gloomy weather did not matter in the least.

The banquet which awaited us seemed to go on and on, but at last came the moment when I could go to my room and be divested of my wedding garments. There I put on a gown of white silk trimmed with swansdown; and I had a bonnet which was so big that I seemed to recede right into it, which was not such a bad thing, for I had to ride through the streets; and when one is feeling emotional one does not want to be seen too clearly.

I came down and there among those who had come to wave us farewell, I picked out the tall figure of Lord Melbourne.

I went to him and as he bowed, taking my hand and kissing it, all my love and tenderness for this dear man surged up in me.

I said: 'Lord Melbourne, you will always be there.'

'As long as you need me,' he said, 'and while it is possible.'

I nodded.

'You will come to Windsor and dine with us.'

'During the three days honeymoon?' I saw his lips lift at the corners in the way I knew so well.

'Yes,' I said.

He bowed.

I went on rather shakily: 'That is a splendid coat you are wearing, Lord Melbourne.'

'I am delighted with Your Majesty's approval. It seems to me to be built like a seventy-four gun ship.'

He made me laugh as he ever could. But I could see there were tears in his eyes.

I must not stay too long talking to him so I moved on. As I did so I heard him murmur: 'God bless you, M'am.'

And there was Albert beside me.

The carriage was waiting to take us to Windsor and our honeymoon.

Lovers' Quarrels

What happy days they were! I could not believe in my good fortune. Here I was married to the most perfect, divine being. Albert's beauty delighted me. I could not take my eyes from him. Marriage was wonderful during those two days at Windsor.

We rode together; we played duets on two pianos; we walked with the dogs, and just as Eos showed his appreciation of me, little Dashy, Ismay and Laddie gambolled round Albert as though he were an old friend.

It was so wonderful that rather grand Eos had no objection to my little ones, and I was sure Dashy thought he was a great joke. How I laughed—no doubt showing my gums—and Albert laughed too, though more discreetly.

We loved with excitement and tenderness and I had never been so contented in my life.

Albert loved Windsor. Up to that time, although I had changed my first impressions, the feeling that it was a little gloomy with all those ominous sounding rooks cawing away, had remained. The forest was dark and full of mystery; there were legends concerning it . . . some of them rather sinister.

It had been Buckingham Palace which I had really loved—the dear, comfortable place with the big light rooms which had been my first home when I had escaped from the captivity at Kensington Palace. Moreover it was London. I could see the Park from my windows, which was all the greenery I wanted; and the streets and crowds of people were close by. There was an excitement about London which had always appealed to me.

But Albert was quite different. He did not like the town and he loved the country. He knew the names of trees and flowers and liked to give me lessons about them. I was not very interested but I made a show of being so for his sake.

He said how pleasant it was to escape from all the functions, to be able to retire at a reasonable hour and to awake to the freshness of the early morning. He thought staying up half the night dancing was a rather foolish way of going on. The night was meant for sleeping.

'But, Albert,' I cried, 'I love to dance and it always seems more exciting after midnight.'

'Then,' he replied, 'you cannot feel fresh for the morning. One does one's best work in the early morning.'

I said: 'I shall make you change your mind. I should love to dance with you, Albert, until two in the morning.'

He looked so alarmed that it began to dawn on me that my tastes and those of Albert differed a little.

Lehzen was at Windsor and there was a slight change in her attitude. I realized that she did not like Albert very much, and he did not greatly like her, I feared.

Lehzen fussed. She had always fussed. I imagined she wanted Albert to know how devoted she had always been to me, and in the days when I had had such bitter quarrels with my mother, she, Lehzen, had been the one I turned to for comfort and consultation—with Lord Melbourne, of course.

'It is not a good thing for sons and daughters to quarrel with their parents,' said Albert.

'What is not good often happens. And if you know how Mama could be, you would understand.'

'One must have indulgence in such cases.'

I leaped up and kissed him. 'You are so good, Albert,' I said. 'I do not believe you would quarrel with *your* mother whatever the provocation.'

Albert looked sad and I guessed I had been a little tactless to mention his mother who had been accused of adultery and divorced.

There was a great deal that Albert did not understand about me; but I had no qualms during those days of the honeymoon.

People came down to Windsor, Lord Melbourne among them. How pleased I was to see him!

He told me that it was obvious that I liked married life; and he was delighted for me.

My mother was to leave Buckingham Palace. Lord Melbourne had hoped that the King of Hanover would allow her to have his apartments at St. James's Palace.

'He never occupies them,' said Lord Melbourne, 'so it would be no hardship. His Majesty, however, is adamant and refuses.'

'Oh dear,' I sighed. 'I fear there will be trouble if Mama stays at Buckingham Palace. I fancy Albert is inclined to believe I have been a little harsh with her.'

'Then he cannot understand the position.'

'No. But I have tried to tell him.'

'I suggest that you rent Ingestre House in Belgrave Square for the Duchess. I gather it is available and the rent is £2,000 a year. Perhaps later a more suitable residence could be found for her, but I think Your Majesty would wish the move to be made soon. Therefore, shall I go ahead with the arrangements for Ingestre House?'

'Oh, please do. I could not bear her to make trouble between Albert and me.'

Dear Lord Melbourne! How good and understanding he had always been to me!

We returned to London and I prepared to be ecstatically happy. How I loved riding and walking with Albert and those cosy evenings when we played duets together. Ernest was often with us; there was a great bond between the two brothers, though Ernest was very different from Albert—much less serious. I laughed a good deal with Ernest. I danced now and then. Albert was a superb dancer, but he always wanted to leave early. I should have liked to dance much more; but I always agreed to retire early when Albert wished it.

Looking back I see quite clearly how different we were and how so much that went wrong was my fault. Albert was *too* perfect. I remember Lord Melbourne's saying once that the saintly people are more difficult to get along with than the sinners because the saints are always attempting to make others as good as they believe themselves to be, whereas sinners have no grudge against the saints, and are quite happy to let them go their way as long as they may pursue the paths of pleasure themselves. He added: 'I have always thought that there is a lot of truth in the old saying: "There is a little good in the worst of us, and a little bad in the best of us; and it ill behoves the best of us to criticise the rest of us".'

I thought that was very funny—and true—and it made me laugh out loud. When I laughed loudly Albert always looked across the room at me—not exactly critically—indulgently, perhaps, as one would look at a child who commits some fault which is rather charming but must, nevertheless, be corrected.

We had been brought up differently, I supposed. Albert had been adored by his grandmothers, but he had lived to a strict Lutheran pattern. He was serious by nature. He was talented, and wanted to use those talents. He was the last man on Earth who should have been chosen for the part of consort to a queen.

'Early to bed, early to rise, makes a man wise,' had been one of his maxims. He could not understand why I liked to sit up half the night. There was so much about me that he could not understand; my devotion to Lord Melbourne, and for another thing, my absorbing love for Lehzen.

He was horrified when he heard me call her Daisy.

'That cannot be her name,' he said.

'Actually it is Louise.'

'Then why do you call her Daisy?'

'I wanted a special name for her. She is very special in my life. For so long she was my dearest friend. We used to have wonderful times together and when I was unhappy she could always comfort me. There were times when Mama could be very hard to live with. Do you know she used to make me wear a necklace of holly under my chin!'

'I am sure she believed that everything she did was for your good.'

'Oh no, for *her* good.'

Albert was silent. He thought that speaking disrespectfully of one's parents was almost as wicked as speaking disrespectfully of God.

He thought that Lehzen had too much authority in the household. I daresay he noticed that stubborn look which came into my face when her name was mentioned. Lehzen, too, made sly references to him.

She reminded me of the fun I used to have dancing.

'I remember how pleased you were when you danced till three o'clock in the morning.'

'Oh yes, I remember, Daisy. I did love it, didn't I?'

'I liked to see you so excited, so pretty you looked going off in your ball gown. You're doing a lot of reading now, my precious. You mustn't tire your eyes.'

'Albert is very interested in books.'

'You should get out into the fresh air.'

'Albert is a great believer in fresh air.'

'We don't want to grow into a sobersides. That wouldn't be my precious angel.'

'It will be, Lehzen. Whatever I am I shall always be your precious angel.'

Then she hugged me and demanded to be assured that nothing . . . simply nothing would change the love between us two.

Vehemently I told her that this was the case.

Then Albert mentioned my relationship with Lord Melbourne. 'Perhaps it is a little too familiar,' he said.

'My blessed angel, of course it is familiar. Lord Melbourne and I are old familiars. He has been my Prime Minister ever since I came to the throne.'

'The relationship seems to be closer than one would expect between the Queen and her Prime Minister.'

'Lord Melbourne is no ordinary prime minister and, dearest Albert, I am no ordinary queen.'

I showed my gums and laughed. Albert's smile was very faint.

'You are too demonstrative, my love.'

'Why should I not be? Why shouldn't one show people when one likes them?'

'Perhaps not quite so excessively.'

'Lord Melbourne has always been my greatest friend. I have always had the greatest regard for him and I see no reason why I should hide that. I lie in terror that his place will be taken by that horrid Peel man.'

'Do you mean Sir Robert Peel?'

'I do indeed. He behaves like a dancing master and looks as though he is going to break into the minuet at any moment.' I laughed, remembering the antics of the man.

'I have been talking to Anson about him. He seems to have a high opinion of Sir Robert.'

'Oh but, Albert, Robert Peel is our enemy. He voted against your income. He tried to force his wretched Tories into my household. He is doing all he can to oust Lord M from office.'

'Naturally he would do that as he is at the head of the Opposition. I believe Sir Robert has done a great deal for England. The Police Force, instituted by him, is the envy of many another country. Not only that—I have come to the conclusion that he has the good of the country at heart. He is happily married and lives a good moral life, which is more than can be said for all politicians.'

'Dear Albert, you have recently come here. *I* do not like Sir Robert Peel, and I hope and pray Lord Melbourne succeeds in keeping him out.'

'The fact that you do not like him does not mean that he is not a good politician.'

I yawned. 'Albert dearest, I do want to sing that lovely song of yours. And I heard you and Ernest playing Haydn this morning. I should love to hear that again.'

Albert gave me one of those looks which came my way quite often—the one of exasperated tenderness.

Oh yes, we were very different. Albert would change I was sure. It did not occur to me that *I* might change. I was after all the Queen.

He was even faintly critical of Lord Melbourne. He admitted that his manners were gracious and courtly, but he thought he was a little suave. He did not care for what he had heard of Lord Melbourne's past. He had discovered that he had been involved in scandals.

'Oh, it was not Lord Melbourne's fault,' I explained. 'It just happened.'

'It seems rather strange that it should have happened so frequently.'

'Life is like that. Lord Melbourne is a very distinguished man. People would be attracted by him and that could make trouble for him. He has been so helpful about you, Albert. He has done everything for us. He tried so hard to get that money for you. I may tell you that Sir Robert Peel was one of your most bitter opponents.'

That rather sad far-away look came into Albert's eyes. He looked so spiritual and beautiful that I just kissed him and I said: 'Come on. We will go and find Ernest.'

We could not expect Albert's family to stay with us indefinitely, and the day came for his father to leave.

He and Albert parted with protestations of affection and determination to see each other often and soon. I said there would always be a welcome for him in England. He kissed my hand and was most charming.

But when he had gone Albert broke down and wept.

I was horrified to see him so desolate. I tried to comfort him but he would not be comforted.

'You do not know what it is like to say goodbye to a father,' he told me.

'I do know,' I replied. 'But, dearest Albert, *we* are together. I am your wife. I will comfort you.'

But he just looked melancholy and I felt a little irritated. Of course he loved his father and it was most feeling of him to care so much. It was right for people to love their fathers and Albert would always do what was right. But he had his life with me now and that should alleviate any sorrow he felt at the parting.

It seemed to me that I was not enough for him. We had been

married only a few weeks. Surely he should not feel quite so desolate . . . A strange little doubt crept into my mind then. I was passionately in love with Albert; but was he so deeply involved with me as I was with him?

At first I had thought that the people were absolutely delighted with my marriage. They had cheered themselves hoarse at the wedding; but they seemed to get tired of approving very quickly and were looking for trouble. Sometimes I thought people did not like to see others happy.

Trouble was more exciting and they must have it.

I was very distressed when I heard that the Duchess of Cambridge refused to stand up when Albert's health was being drunk at one of the Dowager Queen's dinners. People commented on it. It was typical of the family; they were always afraid that someone was going to take precedence over them, and I expected they were angry because I had not married their son George.

There were cartoons in the press, some depicting Albert as a cowed husband who had to do what his wife told him to; others showed him as a scheming creature congratulating himself on having replaced his miserable £2,500 a year for £30,000.

The Coburgs were represented as ambitious grasping men who were worming their way into all the royal houses of Europe.

I wanted it stopped and naturally I brought up the matter with Lord Melbourne.

'We pride ourselves on a free press,' he said, shaking his head. 'The people will allow no interference with that.'

'But it is so cruel,' I protested, 'and so untrue.'

'Alas,' replied Lord Melbourne, 'people in high places must expect to be shot at.'

'But why?'

'Because they are easy targets. The people want to hear these things. They do not buy papers to hear that everything is just as it should be. They would find that very dull.'

'It is a very sad commentary on life.'

'Life is often sad,' said Lord Melbourne. 'Forget it. They will stop in time.'

Someone had even made a parody of the national anthem and I had heard it sung in the streets. I knew it off by heart.

> 'God save sweet Vic, mine queen
> Long live mine little Queen

God save de Queen
Albert's victorious
The Coburgs are glorious
All so notorious
God save de Queen.

Ah, Melbourne, soon arise
To get me de supplies
My means are small
Confound Peel's politics
Frustrate de Tory tricks
At dem now go like bricks
God damn dem all.

The greatest gifts in store
On me be pleased to pour
And let me reign.
Mine Vic has vowed today
To honour and obey
And I will have de sway
Albert de King.'

I was afraid Albert would hear it—that wicked slander and the way in which they attempted to poke fun at his accent.

Nothing it seemed could be kept long from Albert. He was so quick to notice everything. Already he had pointed out things in the household which he thought were not as efficient as they might have been.

'My dearest Albert,' I said, 'you must not be hurt by these stupid people.'

'I see,' said Albert, 'that they do not like me. At one moment I am an ineffectual fool who must take his orders from his wife; at another I am a scheming adventurer.'

'If they but knew how good you are! Oh, Albert, in time they will. We must be patient.'

He looked at me very steadily and said: 'Oh yes, we must be patient.'

And I had an idea that he was talking more to himself than to me.

Albert said to me one day: 'Do you not find it rather dull . . . these evenings?'

'Why no, Albert,' I replied. 'I love the evenings when we are together, don't you?'

He said: 'I think we could invite more interesting people to Court.'

'But the people we see *are* the Court.'

'At Rosenau we would have writers, scientists, artists . . . people like that.'

'Oh, I do not like such people. They talk of things of which I know nothing.'

'You could learn and find them very interesting, I am sure.'

'Of course Rosenau was only a little Court. I think this is rather different.'

'Your uncle, King George the Fourth, I believe, entertained people of culture.'

'Oh, he was considered very raffish. The people did not like him, you know.'

'He must have had some very interesting gatherings.'

'I thought you were happy.'

He took my hand tenderly and kissed it. 'My little one, you are charming. It is just that I miss certain interests.'

'Oh, my dear Albert, you must not *miss* anything.'

'You see, you have your work, your talks with your Prime Minister, your papers to study. I . . . I am just here. I would like to help you.'

'Oh, how good of you! But you see, I have to discuss matters of state which only the Queen can do. There are so many papers to sign. To be the Queen is not only opening things like Parliament and balls. It is not only showing oneself wearing the crown.'

'I want you to know that I am here to help you.'

'Dear Albert!'

It occurred to me then that he had not enough to do. At Rosenau, he was always busy and Albert was not a man who would look for amusement all the time. He was very serious.

Lord Melbourne came and left behind a batch of papers for my signature. I had an idea. I called to Albert.

'Dearest,' I said, 'I have work here. Would you help me?'

His dear face lit up with joy.

'With the greatest of pleasure,' he said.

'That is wonderful. Come into the closet.'

He sat beside me.

'What are these papers?' he asked, and picked them up.

Gently I took them from him.

'They are merely for my signature.'

'Oh yes. I gathered that. You are giving your seal to certain documents, but what are the content of these papers?'

'I have discussed it all with Lord Melbourne. All I have to do is sign them.'

I gave him the blotting-paper.

'There, my dearest. I will sign and you shall do the blotting.'

I penned my signature and handed the papers to Albert. I could not understand his expression but I imagined there was a hint of frustration in it, and that he was holding his real feelings very much in check.

I was beginning to feel unwell. I was sick in the mornings. Lehzen watched me with knowing eyes.

'Can it be?' she said. 'So soon?'

The frightening possibility had occurred to me. I was pregnant. I believe I was never really a motherly person and the thought of child-bearing did not bring me much joy. I thought more of the ordeal before me than the outcome. I liked children when they were of an age to talk and be amusing, but little babies had never really appealed to me.

Of course I had considered the possibility. When one is a queen there are hints that it is one's important duty to bear children. But it was a matter which I had shelved because I did not really want to think of it—not yet, at any rate.

I would never forget Louisa Lewis at Claremont who had made such a shrine there for Princess Charlotte; she had kept her room just as it had been when Charlotte was alive; and during those days I had spent at Claremont I had heard so much of Charlotte that she was a living person to me. She had been so merry, so much in love—and with a Coburg prince just as I was, dear Uncle Leopold himself—and then she had died in childbed.

So many people died in such circumstances. There were people at Court . . . people I had known. They had been young and healthy and then they had died.

It was rather frightening.

'We shall have to take care of you now,' said Lehzen. 'What does the Prince say?'

'I haven't told him yet.'

'I am the first to know,' said Lehzen with a smile of satisfaction.

'Yes, Lehzen. You are the first.'

'When shall you tell the Prince?'

'As soon as I see him.'

'Men don't really understand these things.'

'I suppose it is natural that women should understand them more. Yes . . . as soon as I see him I shall tell him. We don't have any secrets from each other. Uncle Leopold wrote to me before my wedding and he said, "Tell each other everything. And if there is a quarrel settle it before nightfall. Never go to sleep with strife between you." That is good advice, do you not agree, Lehzen?'

Lehzen said: 'You must keep your hands and feet warm. You know how cold they get.'

'Not in the summer, my dear old Daisy.'

I knew she was going to start fussing again; and I had quite liked that.

When I told Albert he was really joyous. He could scarcely believe it had happened so soon. 'When?' he asked.

'I don't know. By the end of the year. Perhaps the child will be a December baby.'

He took my hands and kissed them. Then he looked at me in amazement.

'You don't look very pleased about it,' he said.

'I believe that having a baby is not exactly a pleasurable experience.'

'Oh, but think of the joy to come, a little one . . . our own child . . . yours and mine.'

'Our child,' I said a little tartly, 'but I shall be the one who has to bear it.' I was a little irritated for he seemed to have forgotten the danger to me.

'My dear little wife,' he said, kissing me, 'thousands of women are having babies all over the world at this moment. You are not going to tell me that the Queen is afraid of doing what others do so naturally?'

I said rather shortly, trying to suppress a spurt of temper, 'Lehzen, for all her rejoicing, was really very worried about me. I could see that she was, though naturally she tried not to show me.'

'So you have already told her?'

'Yes, of course.'

'Who else?'

'No one else . . . so far.'

'So she must be the first to know!'

'She happened to be there.'

'It would seem that Lehzen is always there.'

'Of course she is. She has always been and I hope she always will be.'

'We grow out of old servants.'

'Lehzen is not a servant. You will have to realize that, Albert.'

'I shall *have* to?'

'Yes, you will have to.'

He looked at me with that pained expression which was beginning to irritate me. It meant that he was holding in his temper, choosing his words with care—an accomplishment which was beyond me.

He said: 'We shall have to make an announcement.'

'It is too early.'

'I do not think so. I believe the people will wish to know. The child will be the heir to the throne.'

'I must first ask Lord Melbourne.'

'My wish does not count then?'

'Oh, Albert, how can you say that!'

'Because Lehzen must be told first and Lord Melbourne must decide when we make the announcement. I see clearly that my wishes are of small account.'

Normally I would have flung my arms round his neck and told him that his wishes were of the greatest importance to me, but I felt sick and I knew that for the next months I should have much discomfort to bear.

I said coolly: 'You forget my position, Albert. I am after all the Queen.'

'I know it well,' said Albert in a pained voice. 'Please do not think that I am likely to forget.'

'Then that is well,' I said; and with that I got up and left him.

When I told Lord Melbourne he was deeply moved. I saw the tears in his eyes and I thought what a dear friend he was.

He said: 'May God bless Your Majesty and the little one.'

I was able to tell him of my fears and he was most understanding.

'Very natural,' he said. 'But you will have the best attention, and I am sure dear old Lehzen will do the required amount of cosseting; and your blooming health will carry you triumphantly through.'

It was just what I wanted to hear.

'No more galloping through Windsor Forest,' he said admonishingly, 'and only the less vigorous of the dances.'

'Albert says I am too fond of food. Perhaps I should eat less.'

'Ah, there are two mouths to feed now. The Hanoverians were always great eaters. They needed food. They liked it. And they believed they should enjoy the pleasures of life—and to them food was one.'

I was laughing with him. It did me much good to listen to him.

'Do you think we should make an announcement?'

Lord Melbourne shook his head. 'Much better to let the news leak out . . . and it will. The people will like that better. Is she? Is she not? It arouses their interest more than a bald statement.'

'Do you think they will be pleased?'

'Delighted. There is nothing they like more than babies. Weddings, coronations . . . yes. But babies . . . they are the top. And they go on being babies for a long time. ''Ah,'' say the people. ''How charming. Our dear Queen is just like us!'' '

'*You* do not like babies very much, Lord Melbourne.'

'Not in the first stages, but I shall like this baby. It will be a royal baby, a Highness, and *your* baby, M'am.'

I felt so much more at ease talking to Lord Melbourne than I had to Albert.

Albert was very sorry to have upset me and was very kind next time I saw him. I told him that Lord Melbourne thought the news should leak out, and although he would have preferred an announcement, he did not mention the matter again.

We were very happy, and as everyone else was so pleased about the baby, I tried to forget the terrifying ordeal ahead of me and to rejoice with them.

I had noticed that Ernest was not looking well. I mentioned this to Albert and he looked rather embarrassed.

I could see that he was turning over something in his mind and I said: 'Is anything wrong with Ernest?'

Albert looked sad and said: 'Yes, there is something wrong . . . very wrong.'

'You must tell me.'

'I have been wrestling with myself, trying to make excuses for not telling you.'

'You remember we said we would not have any secrets from one another.'

He nodded.

'We vowed to each other,' I persisted.

'I know. But this is most distasteful and I want to protect you from all that is unpleasant.'

'Distasteful? Ernest? What is it?'

'He has an illness.'

'Poor Ernest.'

'Brought on by his own folly.'

I immediately thought he had carelessly caught cold, but that did not seem a matter to make such a fuss about.

'It is a punishment God gives to those who sin. He . . . er . . . has had intimate relations with a woman who has given him a very shameful disease.'

'Ernest has!'

'You seem surprised. I was not . . . entirely. I knew of his habits.'

'Poor Ernest!'

'It is his just deserts.'

'I suppose he did not realize . . .'

'That he was going to get the disease? Of course he did not. He thought he could sin with impunity.'

'Poor Ernest! Is he very ill?'

'No. I thank God that it is only a mild attack. He will soon recover. He is responding to treatment.'

'Oh, I am so glad.'

'It should be a lesson to him.'

'A rather hard one.'

'Hard ones are often the most effective. I have told him many times that he should marry.'

'Oh yes, poor Ernest, he should.'

'If he would only settle down and give up this wild life.'

'It is hard to believe two brothers could be so different,' I said.

Albert looked gratified and pressed my hand.

'He will see our happiness and perhaps that will make him feel inclined to marry.'

'I think he has studied us. He talks glowingly of our Cousin Ferdinand's happiness with Queen Donna Maria. He has stayed with them in Portugal, you know.'

'I remember Maria. She came here when I was about ten years old. My Uncle George gave a ball for her to which I was invited because she was exactly my age. And it was one of those to which Mama allowed me to go. I remember she was very beautiful but she fell down at the ball and hurt herself. She cried and had to be taken to her apartments.'

'She has turned out to be a very good wife to Ferdinand. He is her *king* Consort. Ernest said she received no one until Ferdinand had seen them. It is a most felicitous match. I am sure it did a great deal to make Ernest realize how happy a marriage can be.'

'Portugal is not a very important country, of course,' I reminded him. 'I daresay things are arranged differently there.'

'A very happy marriage,' repeated Albert. 'Ferdinand is a very lucky man.'

I turned the conversation back to Ernest. Was he to know that I had been told of his illness? . . . Albert looked pained. 'I am sure he would be very upset if he thought you had. Though I hate deception . . .'

'Leave it to me. I will say nothing unless Ernest mentions it to me.'

'He would never do that,' said Albert, deeply shocked.

I did not suppose that he would; and although I was horrified at the awful fate which had overtaken Ernest, I was thinking more of Albert's comments about Ferdinand and Queen Donna Maria.

In spite of Albert's original reluctance to have George Anson as his secretary, a friendship was growing up between them. George Anson was one of those intellectual types whom Albert wanted to introduce into the Court to enliven our evenings; and as Anson had developed a deep respect for Albert—which was understandable—they spent a great deal of time together. Baron Stockmar was often with them and they formed a triumvirate, discussing the affairs of the country, for Albert had a great interest in politics. I was amazed to discover—gradually—how much Albert knew of them, and he had a good notion of how the country was being governed.

We were having tea one day—I always enjoyed these sessions for we took it without fuss—just like an ordinary husband and wife, which I thought was pleasant and very cosy.

On these occasions I liked the servants to leave us. I poured the tea myself, and so much enjoyed making sure that Albert was looked after.

Albert would sit there, amused, humouring me, smiling that very beautiful, pleasant smile of his, and I would be admiring him and thinking how handsome he was. It was irritating that in the papers they referred to him as 'pretty', and hinted that he was not the English ideal, which was far more manly.

Of course he was manly! It was merely that he had magnificent blue eyes and a beautiful trim figure. People were jealous, of course.

I don't know how the conversation turned to my ministers. I had wanted Albert to help me choose some material for a ball gown.

Albert had exquisite taste—a little quieter than mine—but I liked to hear his opinion and was pleased to take up his suggestions.

'There seems to be a lack of morality among many of your ministers,' he was saying. 'Lord Palmerston has quite an unsavoury reputation.'

'Oh,' I said laughing, 'Lord Melbourne tells me they call him Cupid, because he brings love to so many ladies.'

Albert looked hurt.

I said apologetically: 'I thought it rather suited him.'

'It does not say a great deal for his character.'

'Oh, he is a very astute man. Lord Melbourne thinks highly of him.'

'I do not think Lord Melbourne would be over-concerned about a fellow minister's morals.'

'Lord Melbourne is a very understanding man.'

I knew this subject of morals was a dangerous one because under Lord Melbourne's tuition I had begun to acquire a leniency towards those whose behaviour was not exactly exemplary. 'We are all human,' Lord M would say. 'Some more human than others.' I remembered giggling at that.

'Even the Duke of Wellington is not blameless,' went on Albert.

'You are thinking of Mrs. Arbuthnot.'

'I regret to say I am.'

'Would you like some more tea, Albert?'

He handed me his cup.

'I was therefore,' continued Albert, 'delighted to discover that there is one Member of Parliament at least—and one in a high place—who is absolutely beyond reproach.'

'Oh?' I replied, rather flippantly perhaps, 'who is this saint? Not my dear Lord M.'

'Most certainly not. I was referring to Sir Robert Peel.'

I felt my anger rising. I knew I had always been hot-tempered, but since my pregnancy and all the minor discomforts it had brought with it, I did find it more difficult to keep myself in check.

'My dear Albert,' I said, speaking like the Queen rather than his dear little wife, 'I do not wish to hear of the perfections of Peel. I loathe the man. I hope his party *never* comes to power. For I do not wish ever to see him again.'

'From what is happening in the country it is more than likely that he will soon be your prime minister.'

'Heaven forbid.'

'It is foolish, my love, not to face facts.'

'The fact at the moment is that I have a very good government presided over by a man whom I respect. I ask no more than that.'

'My dearest, it is not a matter of what *you* ask. There must soon be an election, and the tottering government will have to retire. These happy little *têtes-à-têtes* with Lord Melbourne will have to cease and you will be receiving Sir Robert Peel in his place.'

'You are spoiling this tea-time.'

'Dear little wife, please look at the facts. You must, you know. Try to forget your prejudice against Sir Robert. He is a fine man.'

'He is ill-bred.'

'Forgive me, my dear, but that is nonsense. He was educated at Harrow and Oxford. He made a success of his office as Secretary of State for Ireland.'

I began to laugh. 'Do you know, Albert,' I said, 'that the Irish called him Orange Peel. That was because he was anti-Catholic. Lord Melbourne told me.' I began to laugh because I thought it was really rather a clever nickname. But Albert was not amused.

'Peel is a man to watch. I have a high regard for him,' he said.

'Albert, you do not know him. He is so gauche. When he came to see me he behaved like a dancing master, and someone said that when he smiled it was like looking at the silver fittings in a coffin.' I was laughing again.

'Cheap abuse,' said Albert. 'I noticed none of these things.'

'You have met him?'

'I had the pleasure of making his acquaintance.'

I was astounded. My fury could not be controlled. Albert had gone behind my back! He had sought an introduction to the enemy. I picked up my cup of tea which stood before me and threw it into Albert's face.

Then I gasped . . . astonished at myself.

Albert did not seem to be so very taken aback. He stood up and I saw the liquid trickling down his chin and onto his coat.

One of the servants had appeared. Albert turned to the man and said: 'What do you think of that?' Then he bowed to me and said: 'I must go and change my coat.'

I sat staring after him. I felt so foolish, so wretched and so ashamed.

Oh, but I was angry. How dared he make disparaging remarks about my dear Prime Minister and go out of his way to praise the enemy. How dared he meet Sir Robert Peel! He was only the Queen's husband. He seemed to forget that.

Naturally I was angry. But to throw a cup of tea over him! That was scarcely behaviour worthy of a queen! How calm he was! What a contrast to my fury! Apart from the first look of surprise he had made only a brief comment and then gone to change his coat.

Contrition swept over me. How dreadful of me! How could I have lost my temper to such an extent and above all, with my dearest Albert!

I could never be happy again until I had his forgiveness. My anger was lost in remorse.

I remembered what Uncle Leopold had said. One must never let these differences persist. They must be settled before they made a deep rift. How could I have been so foolish? I loved Albert. It was my wretched temper. Even Lehzen, who could see no wrong in me, told me that I should curb it, and Lord Melbourne said—with a twinkle in his eyes—that I was choleric.

I went immediately to Albert's dressing-room.

I was about to open the door when I restrained myself and knocked.

'Who is there?' asked Albert.

'It is I. Victoria.'

'Come in.'

He was standing by the window. He turned slowly. I saw that he had changed his coat.

'Oh Albert,' I cried and ran into his arms.

I looked up at him. There was that gentle smile on his beautiful face. How I loved him in that moment. I had treated him shamefully and he was not angry.

'Oh, Albert,' I repeated. 'How could I?'

He stroked my hair.

'You do forgive me then?'

He was smiling. 'I think,' he said, 'that you are truly sorry.'

'I did not think . . .'

'My dear little one, it is often so with you.'

'Yes it is. I am impulsive. I am hot-tempered. In fact, I am not a very nice person.'

He kissed me gently. 'That is not true,' he said. 'You are a very nice person, but you have your tempers.'

'They arise and explode before I can stop them. I must try to be different.'

He said: 'We will together master that little demon.'

I laughed. It was all so easy.

'So it is forgiven?'

'Forgiven and forgotten,' he said.

'Oh, Albert,' I cried. 'You are so *good*. You are far too good for me.'

Albert smiled happily, and I was rather glad of the teacup incident because it showed me how much I loved him—as if I did not know!—and, better still, how much he loved me.

I could not resist telling Lord Melbourne of the incident when we were alone. Instead of being shocked, he laughed.

'You find it amusing?'

'I confess I do.'

I saw the corners of his mouth twitching and I could not help laughing with him.

'I hope the Prince was not wearing the Order of the Garter or even the Order of the Bath.'

'Lord M, it was a homely tea party *à deux*.'

'Very homely and fortunately *à deux*.'

'It was really very shocking of me.'

'Just a little example of royal choler, of which no doubt there have been some already and will be a few more.'

'I intend to control myself.'

'Good intentions are always admirable, although some say the road to hell is paved with them.'

'Lord M,' I said, 'there are occasions when you are irrepressible.'

'Forgive me. Put it down to the stimulation I receive in Your Majesty's company.'

'There are times,' I said, 'when I think Albert is too good, and that makes me feel rather worse than I am.'

'Your Majesty is unfair to yourself.'

'Do you really think I am?'

'A little temper now and then is not such a bad thing. It relieves the feelings and adds a little spice to living.'

'But Albert is good in all ways. You know about his brother Ernest?'

Lord Melbourne nodded. 'The entire Court is aware of the Prince's predicament.'

'How different from my dear Albert! Do you know, Lord M, he is not in the least interested in other women—his only wish is to dance with me.'

'He has one other wish, I think; and that is for the ball to be over at the earliest possible moment.'

I laughed. 'He gets very tired at balls. He thinks they are a waste of time and keep people up, making them not as fresh as they should be in the morning.'

'He certainly puts us all to shame.'

'That is what I feel. And when I compare him with other men . . .'

'They suffer in comparison. I would say *that* is a very happy state of affairs. Do not worry about his lack of interest in women. It often happens that when men are not interested in the opposite sex in their youth, they make up for it in middle age.'

I stared at him and then I saw that he was teasing again.

'Actually,' I said, 'I would not like Albert to be anything but what he is. Albert is an angel.'

'Even angels like to have some occupation.'

'What do you mean?'

Lord Melbourne looked at me quizzically. I know now, even more than I did then, what a good friend he was to me. He was so worldly-wise that he understood the position between me and Albert better than I did myself. He knew that Albert was restive, that he had been thrust into a position which would have been trying to all but the most spineless of men—the Queen's consort, the Queen's lapdog. It was a position which gave him no power at all to be himself.

Lord Melbourne's mood had changed. He was serious.

He said: 'The Prince is a very able man. Perhaps he would be pleased if you talked to him more.'

'I talk to him all the time.'

'I mean about affairs . . . the country's business. I think you might find that he could give you valuable help. At the moment he has too little to do. That can be very irksome to an energetic man.'

'I thought of that, so I have asked him to help me when I sign documents. He always blots them for me.'

Lord Melbourne smiled. 'I think his abilities could be put to better use.'

'I still feel angry that he should have met and talked with that odious Peel.'

'It is not a bad thing that he should become acquainted with politicians.'

'That man!' I felt my anger rising again.

'Your Majesty will forgive me. You have taken a hearty dislike to Sir Robert Peel. I feel sure that if you knew him you would change your mind. The manner in which he points his toes does not prevent him from being a very able statesman.'

'Lord Melbourne, I do not wish to speak of Sir Robert Peel.'

He bowed his head. Then he said: 'Think about it. I am sure you will find the Prince very happy to talk over affairs with you.'

Dear Lord Melbourne! How far-sighted he was!

'Now, M'am, there is a little favour I would ask of you. I should be happy if you would receive an old friend of mine.'

'My dear Lord M, any friend of yours is welcome at Court. Who is this friend?'

'It is Mrs. Caroline Norton.'

I was quite excited. This was the lady who had appeared in a scandal involving Lord Melbourne.

'She was much maligned,' said Lord M.

'My dear friend, I shall be delighted to receive her.'

Lord Melbourne kissed my hand.

I was indeed interested to meet Mrs. Norton. I found her very attractive with magnificent dark eyes which seemed to glow with an inner radiance; her features were set in a classical mould and her skin was smooth and dark. She talked rather much but she was very interesting and I was sure very clever for she was a poet of some renown. I was delighted to talk to her because of her past and I wondered how much Lord Melbourne had cared for her.

Afterwards Lord Melbourne told me that Mrs. Norton had found me gracious and very attractive, delightful, warm-hearted and essentially good.

'And I agree wholeheartedly with Mrs. Norton's diagnosis,' said Lord Melbourne. 'Your Majesty's gracious kindness is an example to us all.'

'That makes me feel very happy because I am constantly comparing myself with Albert and I often feel very uneasy confronted by such saintliness.'

'Oh, there is goodness and goodness,' said Lord Melbourne, 'and sometimes the least obvious is the best.'

My reception of Caroline Norton resulted in another little storm with Albert.

'Was it necessary,' he asked, 'to receive that woman?'

'You mean Mrs. Caroline Norton? Yes, indeed it was necessary—as well as pleasant—because she is a very old acquaintance of one of my very dearest friends.'

'I should have thought he would have been eager to put all that behind him.'

'Lord Melbourne would never put an old friend behind him. I believe him to be a very faithful man.'

'He cannot wish that unfortunate episode to be remembered.'

'I don't think it concerns him in the least. He has never attempted to hide his past.'

'I believe the lady's husband brought a case against Lord Melbourne for seducing his wife.'

'That is true. The husband was supported by the Tories who— vile creatures—saw an opportunity of creating a scandal against the Whigs. The case was decided in favour of Lord Melbourne and Mrs. Norton; and the husband was proved to be a very poor creature indeed.'

'Even so, people who have been involved in unsavoury cases do the country no good.'

'But if they are innocent?'

'They cannot be completely innocent. Otherwise they would not have been involved.'

'I do not agree with that. I think innocent people can be caught up in these matters. Do you know that Mrs. Norton is the grand-daughter of Sheridan, the playwright. She is a gifted poet, an artist and a musician. I thought they were the kind of people you wanted to introduce into the Court.'

'Not if their morals make them unworthy.'

'Oh, Albert, you ask too much.'

'I only ask that they live respectably.'

'How can you expect everyone to be like you?'

'I expect a certain morality.'

'*I* believe in forgiveness.'

'Forgiveness, yes. But such incidents cannot be forgotten. If they are, we shall have people thinking that they can indulge in them and be forgiven and forgetfulness will follow as a matter of course. But it seems that my opinions are of no moment.'

'That is unfair!'

'It is a fact. What do I do? I am called on when it pleases you to want a little light amusement. I am shut out while you have those long and I gather often hilarious conferences with your Prime Minister, whose reputation is not of the highest and who is allowed to bring those connected with his shady past into the Court to be received most graciously by the Queen.'

I stood up, my temper rising.

'Albert,' I said, 'I will not have anyone—not even you—speak like that of Lord Melbourne.'

In spite of my temper—and perhaps when it was at its height—I could be very cold, very regal, and because I was so short and that was such a disadvantage, I became more royal than I should have had I been a few inches taller.

Albert stood up, bowed and murmured: 'Your Majesty will excuse me.'

And before I could protest he had reached the door. 'Albert,' I called. 'Come back. I am in the middle of a conversation.'

There was no answer; he had gone.

I was very angry. First, because of what he had said about Lord Melbourne, and secondly because he had walked out while I was talking to him and ignored my command for him to return.

I loved Albert. But he must remember that I was the Queen. It is very hard to be involved in a relationship like ours and for the female in the partnership to be the one who is predominant. I realized that few men would care for such a position, for it is a trait of the masculine character that most men can only be content when they are the dominant one. Albert was essentially masculine. They could jeer at what the Press called his pretty looks, but he was every inch a man.

Still he must accept the fact that *I* was the Queen.

My anger seething, I went to his dressing-room.

'Albert,' I called. 'I want to speak to you.'

There was no answer. Albert was refusing to obey me. What was he proposing to do? Was he dressing to go riding or walking . . . without me?

I saw the key was in the lock outside the door. I went to it and with a vicious gesture turned it. There! Now he was locked in.

I sat down to wait. Soon he must plead to come out; and then I would make him talk. I would tell him that he must not walk away when I was speaking to him. He must not think he could treat me as though I were an ordinary German wife. I was the Queen of England.

I waited. Nothing happened.

The time was ticking away. Ten minutes passed. Fifteen minutes. It was too much. My fury disappeared almost as quickly as it came and it was leaving me wretched. I began to see that I had been hasty. I did not agree with Albert about Caroline Norton, but I should, all the same, respect his opinion. I was lax. I belonged to a family which had never really had a high regard for morals. The uncles were notoriously scandalous. My grandfather had been a good man, but as they said, he was mad.

Albert was very good and very sane. I must learn to control my anger. I must listen to Albert. I felt miserable. I wanted to be forgiven.

Albert was right. Of course Albert was right. I could wait no longer. I turned the key.

'Albert,' I said.

'Come in,' he replied calmly.

I went in and gasped. He was not in the least upset. He was seated at the window sketching.

'What are you doing?' I asked.

He held up the sketch. 'It struck me that it was a rather delightful scene from the window,' he said.

I looked at it. So all the time I had been sitting out there—angry, waiting—he had been sketching!

He was looking at me with that tender exasperation which I knew so well.

'Do you like it?' he asked.

'It's very good.'

'I was going to give it to you when it was finished—a reminder of the day you locked me in my dressing-room.'

'Oh, Albert,' I cried, almost in tears, 'how good you are! How calm! How wonderful! '

'*Liebchen* . . .' He always lapsed into German when he was most tender, 'do not be sad. It is all over.'

'I lost my temper.'

'Well? Is that so unusual?'

'I should not, Albert. I know I should not. But it overflows.'

'You have so much feeling . . . so much love . . . so much hate.'

'I have much love for you, Albert.'

'I know, little one,' he said.

'Then why do I do this?'

'Because you are . . . Victoria.'

'I am so sorry, Albert. Do forgive me.'

'You are my dear little wife.'

'Oh, Albert, then all is well.'

So we kissed and another little storm had blown over. But of course in the perfect married life there would have been no storms.

Ernest had recovered from his indisposition and had now left us.

Albert took a very painful farewell of his brother and was very sad at the parting.

Ernest was a self-evident libertine and yet that had not diminished Albert's love for him; the same thing applied to his father; and Albert's grief at parting from them had been so great that it had angered me.

It seemed to me that the Coburgs, my mother's relations, were every bit as immoral as my father's. I was on the point of taking this up with Albert since he had been so very censorious about Lord Melbourne, but I restrained myself—admirably I thought—for I guessed it would provoke another storm.

Albert was very melancholy in the days following his brother's departure and he spent a good deal of time with Anson and Stockmar. They went out together and I wondered whether Albert was renewing his acquaintance with Sir Robert Peel.

I knew that he was studying politics and history—particularly that of England. He told me he found it quite fascinating and he was almost wistful about it.

Albert was being very careful in what he said. I was sure he hated those storms as much as I did. My twenty-first birthday was approaching and I was now two months pregnant. I felt slightly less discomfort in some ways but I was beginning to feel very tired. What I had always thought was being borne out. Child-bearing was a very unattractive—though necessary, I admitted—part of marriage.

My spirits were always lifted by my conferences with Lord Melbourne, and when I found state matters a trifle boring he would always switch to gossip. He usually had some anecdote to bring out for my amusement . . . either some present scandal or one from the past. I always said I learned more of my ancestors from Lord Melbourne's stories than I did from the history books.

There were still ribald cartoons about us and sly hints in the Press.

'Don't look at them,' was Lord Melbourne's advice.

I refused to receive the Cambridges at Court as the Duchess had not stood up when Albert's toast was drunk; and one day Albert was at a function given by Queen Adelaide. I did not go. I was feeling very tired and uncomfortable and Lehzen had said it could be dangerous to exert myself. I gave in to her persuasions and as we had agreed to go, Albert reluctantly went alone.

He would have been delighted to have stayed with me, which was gratifying. We might have had one of our quiet evenings, singing duets, playing the piano, indulging in a game of chess which Albert invariably contrived to win. A quiet evening at home, early to bed, and then rising fresh in the morning. That was what he wanted.

Albert had a great tendency to go to sleep during banquets. He said it was because of the trivial conversation which generally prevailed and produced a soporific effect.

'You must not let people see it,' I said. But of course they did. We could not sneeze in public without its being noted and probably construed as our having one foot in the grave.

At this particular banquet when the meal was over Albert left. He had thought it a good opportunity to get away and had forgotten that after dinner speeches followed.

When the Duke of Cambridge rose to speak he said that he had noted the Prince had left.

'Can we blame him?' he asked. 'Naturally he is anxious to get home to spend the night with a fine girl.'

This was cheered and reported and enlarged on.

Albert was furious. 'The coarseness is unforgivable,' he said.

'The Cambridges are annoyed because I did not marry their son George. That is what they wanted. Uncle William and Aunt Adelaide wanted it too. That is why they say such things.'

Albert said it was crass, obscene.

Lord Melbourne chuckled about it and said it was a fine compliment to me.

I saw Lord Melbourne's point and laughed with him. But Albert was really angry. He said it set the public imagining . . . obscenely.

I had not thought of that. It was amazing how much more the good saw in these things.

It was my twenty-first birthday. How much had happened since this time last year. A wife and a mother-to-be.

I had always loved birthdays and there was to be a ball to celebrate the occasion. What would a birthday be like without a ball! . . . Albert would have liked to spend the day quietly in the country. I had had to remind him that that was not possible for a person in my position, even if I had wanted to—which I most certainly did not!

Presents were fun. Albert's was a bronze inkstand—a very fine one. Albert liked presents to be useful.

He had talked to me again about Mama. He did not like this discord between us, and was very anxious that it should cease. It is unnatural, he said. Again and again I told him of what I had endured during my childhood; he would smile gently, but I had the impression that he thought I was not quite innocent of blame.

How different from Lehzen, who saw only my side! But then she had been there. She had seen it happening.

But I loved Albert more dearly than ever. He was so beautiful and so good. I loved singing and playing duets with him, but I wished he enjoyed dancing. He danced well and gracefully, as he did everything, but he was always watching the clock and waiting for the moment when he could slip away. He had no desire to dance with anyone else. How gratifying! How touching! And how different from so many men! I thought of his brother Ernest and shuddered. How fortunate I was to have Albert. But I did wish he enjoyed dancing.

Lord Melbourne was quite sentimental when he congratulated me on my birthday.

'I feel so old,' I said.

'Never mind,' said Lord M, 'when you are forty you will feel much younger.'

That made me laugh. But Lord M insisted that it was true.

I had taken his advice and was discussing state affairs with Albert. This made me realize that I did not know a great deal about them. I had always taken Lord Melbourne's view, and I did find some of them rather boring.

How different Albert was! He said there were many things which I should be aware of. Trade was on the decline; the bad harvests in the last four years had raised prices and there were riots in some of the big towns. The Duke of Wellington had told Albert that, outside war, he had never known a town ravaged as Birmingham had been recently and by its own people. These things could not be brushed aside, as Lord Melbourne believed they could. They must be faced up to; something must be done. There was trouble abroad. The West Indian colonies were in revolt; Canada and Ireland were a problem; the Chinese were causing trouble.

Albert was very serious about these matters, and I almost wished I had not agreed that he should learn something of them.

He was meeting a great many people and I was sure he had renewed his acquaintance with Sir Robert Peel. He interested himself in causes. He had become President of the Society for the Abolition of Slavery and the Civilization of Africa; and soon after my birthday he was going to address the Society in that rôle.

He practised his speech with the care he bestowed on everything he undertook. I knew he was very nervous; and I was not surprised at that when I considered those wicked cartoons and paragraphs about him in the Press.

So I was delighted when his speech was well received and he was warmly applauded. I knew people would in time realize his worth, but the waiting for that to dawn was irksome, and he had so many enemies.

I shall never forget that day in June. It began ordinarily enough. It was our custom at six o'clock in the evening to take a drive in our little carriage drawn by four horses. We set out as usual, just Albert and myself with two postilions.

We had not gone very far—it could not have been more than a hundred and fifty paces from the Palace—when a shot rang out. It was so loud that I was quite stunned.

I looked round sharply and saw a man, small and most disagreeable looking, leaning against the railings and in his hand he was holding something which was pointed straight at us. I realized that it was a pistol for the man was very close—so near that I could see his face clearly. There was purpose in it— and that was to kill me.

Then I heard another shot. It was like a nightmare. Crowds of people everywhere. Someone shouted: 'Get him. Kill him.'

Albert was very calm. He put his arm round me, holding me tightly. 'Drive on,' he shouted to the postilion and we went on at a sharp trot.

'Are you all right?' asked Albert.

I nodded. I said: 'He was trying to kill me, Albert.'

'To kill us,' corrected Albert.

'But why? What have we done to him?'

'People blame their rulers for the state of the country. Dear *liebchen*, I feared for you. Are you sure . . . the little one . . . ?'

'The little one seems unaware,' I said.

'My dear brave little Victoria.'

It was strange really. I had not felt any great fear when I looked into that pistol. I often thought afterwards that rulers are given a special quality. Instinctively they know they may face death at any time. Although the people cheer and wish them long life, there can always be some in the crowd who are eager to make that life shorter.

When we came back to the Palace, there were crowds waiting for us. They cheered me wildly.

I had faced death and so won back their esteem.

* * *

Lord Melbourne called. He was most disturbed.

'Your Majesty,' he murmured, looking at me as he so often did with tears in his eyes.

I smiled at him and answered: 'I am still here, Lord Melbourne.'

'Thank God,' he said fervently. 'I must tell you we have the miscreant. It was quite easy to pick him up. He just stood there waiting to be taken.'

'What sort of man?'

'Vermin,' said Lord Melbourne contemptuously. 'A little revolutionary. He was immediately seized by a certain Mr. Millais who was there with his son.'

I always remembered that later, because the son, John Millais, became a great artist.

'He is eighteen years old.'

'So young to want to murder.'

'Oh, it is often the young who get what they think of as high-minded ideals. He is undersized, feeble in mind and body . . . a little rat of the gutters. His garret was full of papers of a revolutionary nature. He fancied himself as a Danton or Robespierre. My God, when I think of what might have happened . . . Your Majesty . . .'

He was far more upset than I and I felt I had to comfort him. 'I am still here, my dear friend,' I said.

'It could have happened so easily. The bullets went over your heads and buried themselves in the wall.' He shivered. 'And in Your Majesty's condition . . .'

'I think it was over before I realized what was happening. But I do hate it when people want to kill me.'

'It is not you they wish to kill but the system . . . law and order . . . all that makes our country great.'

I nodded. 'Albert was magnificent.'

'Yes. The Prince showed great calm. The best thing you could have done was to drive on and behave as though nothing had happened, and that is what he realized. It is what the people like.'

'The people were most loyal.'

'Oh yes indeed. There is nothing like a near assassination to bring out the people's affection. Had that villain succeeded in his vile task—praise God that he did not—you would have become sainted martyrs. As you escaped, you are merely the beloved Queen and her consort. A better proposition really, for although you are of slightly less value living than dead, it is better to be alive than holy.'

That was Lord Melbourne's way of making light of something which touched him deeply; and I felt very tender towards him.

He was right. We were wildly cheered at the opera, and the people sang the national anthem—the right version—with great enthusiasm.

'Long live the Queen.'

I was as popular as I had been before the Flora Hastings scandal. So some good came out of the incident.

I felt a little concerned about that young man. I talked of him with Albert.

'You see, Albert,' I pointed out, 'he believed he was right. He was really mad.'

Albert was astonished that I could speak for him; but Albert, being so good himself, could not understand the failings of others as easily as I, being less virtuous, did.

The young man, whose name was Edward Oxford, was committed to Newgate on a charge of high treason which warranted the death penalty. But it was judged that he was mad and he was sent to an asylum.

I felt a little relieved about this. I never wanted harsh punishment for such people and perhaps I preferred to think of him as mad, for in that case the man could have been said to have acted without reason—and I did not like to think that anyone hated me enough to want to kill me.

Lord Melbourne came to see me soon afterwards and said that he wished to speak to me on a rather delicate matter. After the shooting incident several members of the government had raised the question of a Regency.

'You mean in the event of my death?' I said.

Lord Melbourne looked unhappy.

'My dear Lord Melbourne,' I said, 'this is perfectly reasonable. I might so easily have been killed the other day. I am to have a child. I do not forget what happened to my cousin, the Princess Charlotte.'

'Your Majesty is very wise. I think I shall get agreement for the Prince to be named Regent in the event of such tragic circumstances of which it is too painful to speak, coming to pass.'

'You mean . . . Albert would be Regent?'

'That is so.'

I was delighted. It would give him so much pleasure to be chosen; and I was beginning to realize how left out he felt and what a difficult rôle he had been thrust into.

'I don't expect much opposition from the other side of the House,' went on Lord Melbourne. 'Peel will most certainly give his support.'

'Indeed he will,' I said with a trace of irony. 'They are very good friends.'

'It is well that it should be so,' replied Lord Melbourne.

I stopped him because I did not want to hear about the uncertain state of the government and the possibility of Peel's soon being Prime Minister. It was too depressing.

I said I should be pleased if Parliament agreed that Albert should be appointed Regent in the event of my death.

As Lord Melbourne had predicted, the motion was passed easily through the House; there was a murmuring from Sussex which was to be expected. That side of the family was annoyed that I had, as they said, 'brought in the Coburgs'. Lehzen did not like it either. She was very depressed.

'Silly Daisy,' I said, 'because they make preparations for my death that does not mean I am going to die!'

She was very worried these days. She had changed since my marriage. Dear Daisy, she would not accept the fact that a person grows up. One's children—and she looked on me as her child—cannot remain dependent all their lives. Poor Lehzen, how she fought against the passing of time!

Albert, of course, deplored my relationship with her. I gave her the affection which, he believed, should have been my mother's. As a matter of fact I had seen more of my mother since my marriage than I had for some time before. I think it was in Albert's mind to bring about a reconciliation. Lehzen knew this and resented it because she realized that my mother would never forgive her for the part she was sure she had played in our estrangement, and she had always been jealous of my devotion to Lehzen.

So poor Lehzen was very uneasy. She told me that the Prince was critical of her. He pried into household matters. *She* had always run the household. I supposed it ran smoothly enough. I never heard of anything going wrong. But of course Albert's Teutonic thoroughness demanded perfection.

And now Lord Melbourne, whom Lehzen had possibly looked upon as an ally in the camp against my mother, was becoming one of Albert's admirers and making him a possible Regent—which was the last straw.

She could no longer hide her animosity to Albert.

It was a very difficult position for me to be in when the two people I loved most dearly were antagonistic towards each other. In a way I was flattered because their animosity grew out of their love for me. Lehzen was certainly jealous of Albert. I don't know whether he was jealous of her or not, but he did resent her influence on me.

Albert was finding fault with matters in the household. Two people were employed, he said, where one would have served adequately. He discovered that one of the windows in the kitchens had been broken for some weeks and nothing had been done about repairing it.

'Oh, that is Lehzen's affair,' I said thoughtlessly.

'But it seems that Lehzen does not make it her affair.'

'A broken window in a big palace, Albert,' I said. 'What a fuss about a little matter.'

'A broken window is an invitation to intruders. I do not call that a little matter. I have your safety to consider.'

'Oh, Albert, how kind you are! I'll speak to Lehzen about the window.'

Lehzen was incensed. 'I never before heard of a prince strolling round looking for broken windows.'

'I don't think he looked, Lehzen. He just saw.'

She pursed her lips and thrust some caraway seeds into her mouth—a sign of being disturbed.

She told me that people did not like the idea of Albert's appointment.

'Oh, the people like or dislike according to their mood.'

'I'm afraid to open a paper these days.'

'Oh, Daisy, that's not true.'

I knew that she kept certain cartoons—those in which Albert figured. Now she flung open a drawer and took out some paper cuttings.

I took them from her. The top one was captioned 'The Regent'. It was a caricature of Albert—recognizable though not a bit like him—standing before a mirror trying on a crown.

I laughed. 'That is just the sort of thing they would do.'

'They don't like it, you know.'

'Daisy, he is not the Regent. He would only be . . . if anything happened to me.'

'I can't bear to think of it.'

I was staring at another cartoon. Albert had a pistol in his hand

and was aiming it at the crown—presumably meant to be me. At least they had not put me there in person. The caption said: '*Ach, mein* dear, I shall see if I can hit you.'

'Oh,' I cried, 'that is wicked.'

Lehzen looked at me, nodding.

I tore the paper in half and threw it from me.

'It is what the people are thinking,' said Lehzen.

'It is not,' I contradicted. 'It is what those wicked people do to sell their papers.'

'Oh, *Kindchen* . . . '

'Daisy, dearest Daisy, you must not be so jealous. I have lots of loving in me, enough for you both.'

But I was apprehensive because they appeared to dislike each other so much; and I had a notion that there would be no peace while they were both under the same roof. Albert was my husband and we were bound together for life; but how could I bear to lose Lehzen?

Albert was getting more and more involved in the affairs of the country. Often if I found something tedious I would pass it over to him. He was very disturbed about the unrest. There was a great deal of unemployment; there was trouble in Afghanistan; there were disputes with China. We were not on the best of terms with France. Louis Napoleon had made an attempt to return and had landed at Boulogne in a British steamer; but there were more serious troubles in the East.

Albert talked of this a great deal. England with Prussia, Austria and Russia were trying to force Mehemet Ali to leave North Syria. France stood against this and at one time it looked as though France would side with Mehemet Ali against the allies.

'Fortunately,' said Albert, 'this has been avoided. We did not want war with France.'

Albert became quite animated about these matters and discussed them at length with Lord Melbourne and Lord Palmerston.

They both said he had a good grasp of affairs.

In August I had to attend the Prorogation of Parliament, and I told Lord Melbourne that it was absurd that Albert could not come with me.

'He may be present,' said Lord Melbourne, 'but it would not be considered right for him to ride in the royal coach.'

'What nonsense,' I said. 'Albert knows a great deal about what is going on. He is a great help to me. It seems ridiculous.'

'So much in life does,' said Lord Melbourne sympathetically.

Albert was really quite hurt about it. No matter what he did, he said, he was still treated as though he were of no account.

I was at luncheon a few days later when a letter came from Lord Melbourne. Albert watched me while I opened it, read it, and turned pink with pleasure.

'Oh, dear Lord M,' I cried. 'He works so hard to make me happy. Listen to this, Albert. Lord Melbourne has found out that Prince George of Denmark once accompanied Queen Anne to the Prorogation in the royal carriage—so that makes a precedent. He says that as it was done once he sees no reason why it should not be done again. He thinks, dearest Albert, that you should ride with me to the Prorogation.'

It was wonderful to see the pleasure dawn in that dear face.

Lehzen was less pleased. I thought how different she was from dear Lord M who did everything he could to make Albert comfortable in our relationship and so make me—and him—happy.

Lehzen's devotion could be a little tiresome at times.

So Albert rode with me in the carriage and I was so pleased to hear the cheers.

I read my speech perfectly because I was so delighted.

What a happy day that was!

Old Aunt Augusta was dying. I had always been very sorry for her. Her lot had been even harder than that of the other sisters. At least Aunt Sophia had had her brief love affair from which a son had resulted, and I supposed that even a scandal was better than nothing happening at all. Aunt Augusta might have been quite clever if her father had allowed her to be. She could paint well and was quite a musician. She had actually composed in her youth, but her efforts had been scoffed at. Music was not a profession for ladies, said her father. Men like Handel did it so much better. Poor Aunt Augusta— always so gentle and loving—she had had no life outside waiting on her mother, filling snuff boxes and looking after dogs. And now she was dying.

She had always been fond of me and looked forward to my visits, so I went often.

It was no great surprise to us when she died.

Albert said I had tired myself visiting her. He was so concerned for me that he was going to take me to Claremont where we could live quietly, for a while.

'No late nights,' he said. 'Early to bed and in the freshness of the morning we will walk out under the trees and you will tell me how much more beautiful they seem to you now that you know a little—a very little—about them. You were so very ignorant of such things, my dear, before I took you in hand.'

'I was ignorant of so much,' I muttered.

And he was pleased. That was the remark of a meek little wife who had forgotten for a while that she was a queen.

There were so many memories at Claremont. I could imagine I was right back in my childhood when I used to come here to see Uncle Leopold. How he had loved the place where he had lived with Charlotte! He was happily married now to dear Aunt Louise and he had his children of whom he was so proud. I wondered if he ever thought of Charlotte now and the child she had lost.

They were lazy days, walking a little, the dogs barking round us, a little music and chess in the evening, or perhaps Albert reading aloud to me.

'It is so good for you,' said Albert.

It was wonderful to be together alone . . . or almost. I thought a lot about Louisa Lewis, now dead. I hoped she was with Charlotte and her baby. How Louisa had adored Charlotte! She had loved me too. But Charlotte had been her very special one. I could only be a second.

I used to go to Charlotte's bedroom—that one which Louisa had kept as a sacred shrine, just as it had been when Charlotte had slept . . . and died . . . there.

Dear Charlotte, bouncing her merry way through life. 'Right up to the last,' Louisa had said. 'You would never have dreamed . . .'

I could not get Charlotte out of my mind. I was becoming fanciful. It was due to my condition, I supposed. I imagined Charlotte was there, watching me, her merry eyes suddenly sad.

How similar our positions were! So much hung on her getting an heir . . . as it did with me. She had merely been heiress to the throne. I was the Queen. But old Uncle George had scarcely been in the best of health even then and the heir to the throne was most important. And she had died . . . her baby with her.

Child-bearing was so hazardous.

A terrible fear came to me. I thought: It is going to be the same with me. History is going to repeat itself.

I became obsessed with the idea. I would have my baby at Claremont. I would die . . . as Charlotte had died.

I considered having Charlotte's bedroom, Charlotte's death chamber, redecorated . . . made in readiness for me.

I cannot think what came over me. I was usually so full of life, so eager to enjoy it. I had everything to live for. Why did I have those morbid thoughts? Sheer panic, I supposed.

Where such ideas would have led me, I do not know, but for the good sense of Albert.

One day when I sat in Charlotte's room I heard a noise outside. I whispered: 'Charlotte . . .'

The door handle turned slowly. It is an indication of the state I was in that I expected to see her there.

It was Albert who came in.

'My love, you look startled. What are you doing here?'

'Oh, Albert.' I ran into his outstretched arms.

'What ails you? Why are you sitting here alone?'

'I was thinking of Charlotte. She died in this room.'

He was looking at me in horror.

'She was well before . . .' I went on. 'They were all surprised. It is a terrible ordeal. Albert, I am frightened.'

He comforted me and quickly led me out of the room.

He said: 'You will not go there alone again. If you want to go there, I shall go with you.'

I don't know why I found such relief in those words. I felt it meant that whatever happened, we would be together.

He took me into our bright sunny bedroom.

'There is nothing to fear,' he said.

I shook my head. 'Child-bearing is dangerous,' I said. 'People die.'

'Not you. Not the Queen.'

I laughed. 'Oh, Albert, I can be a little arrogant sometimes.'

He did not deny it, but stroked my cheeks.

'All will be well,' he said. 'There is nothing to fear. You will be well . . . I shall be here beside you.'

'Oh yes, Albert.'

'And always shall be. Do you not know that I am always right?'

I smiled. 'Yes, Albert,' I said.

'Then I will tell you something. Tomorrow we are leaving Clare-mont.'

'Yes, Albert,' I said again and felt floods of relief coming over me. Albert was looking after me. All would be well.

The birth was due in December but in November, three weeks before the appointed time, my pains began. Fortunately the doctors, the midwife, Mrs. Lilly, with the nurse, were in the Palace in readiness. Sir James Clark was one of them. Poor Sir James, he had never quite recovered from the Flora Hastings scandal. There were two others with him—Dr. Locock and Dr. Blagdon. Albert, who felt that a German doctor must be more efficient than English ones, had insisted that Dr. Stockmar hold himself in readiness in case he should be needed.

I had dreaded the ordeal—and not without reason. I suffered acutely for twelve hours and never never again did I want to go through such an ordeal. All the time I was conscious that waiting in the room next to the lying in chamber were several members of the government, including Lord Melbourne, Lord Palmerston and the Archbishop of Canterbury. I felt that was most undignified. At least it helped me in some way to resist my impulse to scream aloud in my agony.

Everything must come to an end and I thanked God when that did and I could lie back, quite exhausted and listen to the crying of the child.

Albert was beside me.

'A perfect child,' he said.

'A prince?'

'No, *Liebchen*, a little girl.'

'Oh.'

'It is wonderful,' said Albert. 'This little girl could be the Queen of England.'

They put the child in my arms. I am afraid I was not maternal and my first thought was: What an ugly little creature! for she resembled nothing so much as a little frog.

Albert did not think so. He kept saying she was perfect.

What a comfort he was!

Mrs. Lilly was bustling about, taking a proprietorial attitude about the child as though she had produced it; and when I was rested I received one or two people, including Lord Melbourne. He looked at me, with tears in his eyes, and said, 'God bless you, M'am . . . you and the child.'

I found that very moving.

Mama came. She was so different from what she had been in the old days. She was so anxious to be part of the family. I began to think I had been rather hard on her. She adored Albert; she thought he was quite wonderful, and this endeared her to me. Of course, Albert had been responsible for bringing her back into the household so naturally she thought a great deal of him. He was, also, of her family and they understood each other, for Mama had never reconciled herself to the English any more than they had to her. I suppose she felt that Albert was like one of her very own family. In any case, I was pleased to see amity between them; and I was not averse to forgetting the enmity of the past. Besides, my being on better terms with Mama pleased Albert.

Albert wanted the child named Victoria—after me; and as that was also Mama's name, she could believe the little girl was named after her.

I wanted to add Adelaide, after my very good friend the Queen Dowager who loved all children—particularly so because, poor lady, she had none of her own. I knew that would delight her and show her that I remembered her kindnesses to me during my childhood. So it was Victoria Adelaide and to that we added Mary Louisa.

I recovered quickly. The baby changed every day, losing that frog-like look and becoming more like a human being. We engaged a wet nurse—a very pleasant creature, a Mrs. Southey who was the sister-in-law of the well-known poet. I made a point of seeing the child twice a day to make sure that all was well with her.

I had many congratulations from all sides but one from Uncle Leopold irritated me a little.

'I can well understand that you feel astonished at finding yourself within a year of your marriage, a very respectable mother of a nice little girl, but let us thank Heaven that it is so.'

Thank Heaven! I thought. Have you any notion, Uncle Leopold what a woman has to go through to produce a child?

'. . . I flatter myself, therefore, that you will be a delighted and delightful Maman *au milieu d'une belle et nombreuse famille* . . .'

I felt incensed and took up my pen at once.

'I think, dearest Uncle, that you cannot really wish me to be the mother *d'une nombreuse famille*. Men never think . . . at least seldom think . . . what a hard task it is for us women to go through very often.'

How far I had grown from Uncle Leopold since the adoring days of childhood!

Lehzen, of course, was delighted with the baby. She was critical of Mrs. Lilly and Mrs. Southey. But then she naturally would be. She would have liked to drive them out of the nursery and to have taken sole charge of the baby.

On those occasions when the baby was brought to me Albert would be there.

He marvelled at the child and agreed with me that her looks improved every day.

'Little Victoria,' he murmured.

'It is what you call me sometimes.'

'It is rather a big name for such a little person.'

'She is like a little kitten.'

'Little Pussy,' said Albert; and then we took to calling her Pussy. It seemed to suit her better than Victoria, which had, since my accession, acquired rather a royal ring. So Pussy—or Pussette—she became; and as the days passed my affection for the child grew and I looked forward to our meetings—particularly if Albert was there. It was such a happy family picture—myself, my husband and our baby.

I noticed that Dash was a little jealous of the baby. He would stand watching me while I was with her; and then he would give a little bark as though to say: 'Remember Dash.'

But he was not nearly so lively as he used to be.

'He is getting old,' said Albert. 'Never mind. You have the others.'

'There is only one Dash,' I reminded him.

A few weeks after the baby was born something very strange happened, which was to have a great effect on Lehzen, and therefore on me.

It happened in the night—at about one-thirty in the morning, actually—when the household had retired.

Mrs. Lilly, the nurse, was startled out of her sleep by the sound of a door opening. She sprang up and called: 'Who's there?'

There was no answer. She went out into the corridor and saw the door of my dressing-room being slowly opened from the inside. Then it shut abruptly. Mrs. Lilly had the presence of mind to run to the door and lock it on the outside. Then she summoned one of the pages who was on night duty.

By this time Lehzen had come out.

'What is all this about? What are you doing? You will awaken the Queen.'

'There is someone in there,' said Mrs. Lilly. 'I saw, with my own eyes, the door opening.'

Lehzen cried: 'It's the Queen's dressing-room. Someone is trying to murder the Queen.'

She told me all this afterwards. Her one thought had been for me, and after that wicked man had shot at me she feared the worst.

Lehzen went in, so she told me, boldly, with the page who was shivering with fright thinking, quite naturally, that he might encounter an assassin. And there cowering behind a sofa was a small boy.

By this time Albert and I were awake and Albert took over with his usual efficiency.

We remembered the boy. His name was Jones and a few years before he had broken into the Palace.

'I like it here,' he said. 'It's nice. I can't help it. I have to come in. I don't mean no harm to no one. I love the Queen. I heard the little baby cry. I don't mean no harm.'

Albert said: 'Take the boy away. I will see him in the morning. Search the rooms.'

'There was no one with me,' said the boy. 'I climbed the wall. I come in on my own.'

Albert was magnificent on such occasions. Calm, quiet and very authoritative.

We went back to our bedroom.

I was laughing. 'Such a scare . . . about nothing. That boy came in before. Jones. That's right. The papers called him In-I-Go Jones.'

Albert said: 'It is not a matter for laughter. It was a harmless boy. But it might not have been a boy and it might not have been harmless. This is a matter which requires attention.'

The papers had the story, of course. It was served up in various forms—embellished and garnished to suit public taste and made a good story. In-I-Go Jones was the young hero of the day. He said he had been under a sofa and had heard Albert and me talking together.

'I am now going to consider this matter of Palace security very carefully,' said Albert; and as in everything he did, he set about the task with thoroughness. He went through the household asking questions and uncovered quite a lot of discrepancies. The extravagance was great; a number of servants entertained their friends lavishly at Palace expense; jobs were created for friends; but worst of all, security was lax; windows and locks were proved to be faulty.

Albert said: 'That shall all be put in order, and I fancy we shall find greater efficiency, with a possibly decreased budget.'

Of course, there was murmuring in the kitchens and talk of German interference.

The Press heard of it. 'The German invasion' they called it.

It was so disheartening. Everything Albert did was for the best—and he was never given any credit for it.

But the one who was most angry was Lehzen. Albert had come into her domain with his criticism and suggestions for improvements. She was tight-lipped and angry.

'I never heard anything like princes going into kitchens,' she said. 'It's people like that who are not used to being in royal circles.'

I defended Albert, of course. 'It is for the good of us all. He is thinking of our safety . . . my safety, Daisy.'

'Do you think I don't concern myself with your safety? If that had been a real assassin instead of that young boy, I would have thrown myself between you and him without a second thought.'

'I know you would. But Albert wants to prevent people getting into the Palace.'

'It was all right before he came.'

'But this boy broke into the Palace. How?'

'Boys can climb up anywhere.'

'If boys can do so, others can. Albert is right. There should be more security. People get lax when there is no supervision.'

'I have supervised . . .'

I looked at her sadly. I was more worried than she could guess, because I could see clearly that this conflict between her and Albert would not end here.

The day would come when I should have to choose between Lehzen and Albert; and there could only be one choice I could make.

Dear, dear Lehzen, companion of my childhood, the one I had sworn to love forever . . . But that had been before Albert came into my life.

Little In-I-Go Jones had made an amusing story for the Press; he had had his little adventure; but what he had done had gone deeper than that.

Christmas was almost upon us.

'We shall spend it at Windsor,' said Albert.

We should celebrate it in the German fashion, with Christmas trees and presents on the table. Mama had brought that fashion with her so it was not new to me.

Albert was very happy. He had instituted new rules into the Palace. He had scored several triumphs over Lehzen which she had perforce been reluctantly obliged to accept. There was an armed neutrality between them which I had decided I would not think about while we were at Windsor for the Christmas holiday.

Albert and I left in the carriage with the rest of the household travelling behind us. Immediately following was the baby with the nurses and Lehzen travelling with them. She was already regarding little Pussy as hers, much to the chagrin of Mrs. Lilly, who was a very forthright lady. Mrs. Southey was comfortable and unquarrelsome; she accepted with equanimity all that was asked of her—which I suppose was the right attitude for a wet nurse.

Mama was coming to Windsor to join us. Lehzen did not like that either. She knew that in the conflict with Albert, Mama would be her bitter foe. Albert wielded great influence with me and Mama was no longer the enemy. Moreover I was beginning to feel quite conscience-stricken by the way in which I had behaved, for Albert was convincing me that I had not been without fault.

Albert wanted a quiet Christmas, carrying out all the old German customs, which I had to agree was very pleasant; walking, riding, singing, a quiet game of chess, early to bed, rising at six, when it was dark, being ready to go into the forest to watch the dawn and stroll among the beautiful trees whose names I now knew—and much else that was growing also.

I was quite happy to do all this, for I was still easily tired after my ordeal. And I had to admit that if it was quiet, it was pleasant.

And then something happened to spoil it.

One morning when I went to Dash's basket to see why he did not come to me, I found him lying still.

'Dash! Dashy!' I cried.

He did not move and then I knew.

I sat there, the tears flowing. Albert came and found me.

He lifted me up and held me tenderly in his arms. He said: 'He was getting old, you know.'

I nodded.

'He was stiff with rheumatism. He could not run as he used to. That must have been a trial for him. He had to go, *Liebchen*. It happens.'

What a comfort Albert was. He said we would bury him with honours for he had been a good friend to me and I had loved him dearly. He used to enjoy going up to Adelaide Cottage and we decided he should be buried there.

I had a marble stone made for him and on it were engraved the words Albert and I had chosen for him:

Here lies
DASH
The favourite spaniel of Her Majesty Queen Victoria
In his tenth year
His attachment was without selfishness
His playfulness without malice
His fidelity without deceit
READER
If you would be loved and regretted
Profit by the example of
DASH

Whenever I was at Windsor I would walk to his grave and remember.

While we were at Windsor I wrote to Lord Melbourne. I was a natural writer and so wrote many letters; and I often picked up my pen and wrote to my friends when the mood took me—and Lord Melbourne of course was a very special friend who received his fair share of my letters.

I reproached him for not joining us at Windsor. I wished he had. Albert was less eager for his company. Although Albert enjoyed good conversation, he liked it to be serious, and Lord Melbourne's was hardly that. Albert had urged me again to invite what he called more interesting people to our dinners. He said conversation was often dull. It was never dull with Lord M but my dear Prime Minister's rather cynical approach to life did not appeal to Albert, and although Lord Melbourne had been a very good friend to Albert—and Albert realized this—he did not enjoy his company as I did.

Lord M wrote that the uncertainty of events kept him in London. He reminded me that I should have to return for the Opening of Parliament and he was sorry to take me away from the joys of domesticity at Windsor. He was giving a great deal of thought to a speech from the throne in view of the difficult situation. Moreover, there was the baby's christening to be considered.

I wrote back that I was reluctant to leave Windsor. I was growing more and more fond of the place because Albert loved it so much. The forest reminded him of his own dear Rosenau; and he had made me see so much more of the delights of nature than I ever had before. There was one reason why my return to London would be very agreeable. I should have the pleasure of seeing Lord Melbourne.

When I did see him I sensed at once that there was a certain gravity in his manner. Things, he said, were not good. The Exchequer was in a weak state; and I guessed that he was worried about the imminent fall of the government. I knew, of course, that this had to come. Conversations with Albert had taught me that a government cannot go on tottering for ever. It must collapse sooner or later. A very depressing thought. Albert was not in the least depressed by the prospect. I knew that he thought Sir Robert Peel was a politician of greater worth than Lord Melbourne. It was a matter we did not discuss because we both knew that the outcome might end in a storm which neither of us wanted.

I opened Parliament in late January and it was decided that the christening should take place on the anniversary of our wedding day.

Uncle Leopold promised to attend. I was delighted at the prospect of seeing him but I was without that wild joy with which I used to anticipate his visits in my childhood. I hoped he would not lecture me on the duty of producing more children or my behaviour with Albert. He would probably advise Albert, too. I often wondered what account Stockmar gave to him, and how much he knew of our domestic trials.

We had snow which turned to ice, and there was a strong wind buffeting the walls of the Palace. Albert enjoyed it. He loved the gardens at Buckingham Palace. They were quite extensive—forty acres actually—and in some parts of them it was like the country. Albert and I would walk under the trees and he would give me his little botany lessons which I tried hard to concentrate on to please him.

He was delighted when the pond froze so that he could go skating. He told me how he and Ernest had skated at Rosenau. Rosenau seemed perfection. The weather was always right and there always seemed to be harmony between the brothers—in spite of the differences in their characters. I began to suspect that events seen from a distance gained a certain enchantment which bemused even such a calm and reasonable person as Albert.

However, he went to skate. I would have joined him in this but he forbade it . . . oh, in such a tender way, because, he said, I was not yet recovered from Pussette's birth, so I contented myself with watching. Wrapped up in furs my ladies and I would go out and admire Albert as he moved across the ice so beautifully. He was very graceful. I knew the English did not like his looks. They said he did not look as an Englishman should look; with those beautiful blue eyes and dark lashes and clear-cut features he was almost like a woman. They liked men to be men, they said. What they meant was that they liked them to be Englishmen and not Germans. They commented on his figure—his small waist and well-shaped legs. Not entirely manly, they said.

A terrible thing happened that morning. I have never forgotten it. I might so easily have lost him then. I remember still those moments when I saw him disappear beneath the ice.

I had just been thinking that it was a little warmer, but that the ice might have thawed did not enter my head until it happened.

'Albert!' I screamed; and in the space of a few seconds I lived through nightmares. I pictured them bringing him out of the lake. I saw his body on a stretcher, stiff and cold. Albert, my beloved, lost to me forever.

Then I saw Albert's head above the hole in the ice and I ran. There was no time to do anything else. I had to save him.

I stepped cautiously onto the ice. Albert saw me. He called: 'Go back. The ice is too thin. It's dangerous.'

But I did not heed him. I was not going to stand by and wait for people to come and rescue Albert.

I moved towards him. The ice was holding and my determination to save him was stronger than my fear or my weakness. I was there.

I stretched out a hand.

'Go back,' cried Albert.

But I continued to hold out my hand. He grasped it and to my infinite joy, by clinging to me he was able to scramble out of the water.

'Oh, Albert,' I cried, sobbing with relief. But I was practical immediately. He was shivering with cold in his wet garments. 'Come quickly into the Palace,' I said.

Divested of his sodden clothes, wrapped in warm blankets, sipping hot punch, Albert smiled at me tenderly.

'My brave *Liebchen*,' he said.

'Oh, Albert, if I should lose you I should want to *die*,' I said; and I meant it.

I enjoyed the christening. It was wonderful to see dear Uncle Leopold, and it was amazing how little my resentments seemed to matter when I was face to face with him. He was one of the sponsors. Albert's father was also one, but as he was unable to attend, the Duke of Wellington stood proxy for him. Mama, Queen Adelaide, the Duchess of Gloucester and the Duke of Sussex were the other sponsors.

Pussy behaved with unusual decorum and did not cry at all. She seemed quite interested in the gloriously apparelled people who surrounded her. She was really becoming quite pretty. A fact which delighted me. I could not have borne it if she had retained the frog-like features of her birth.

Lord Melbourne attended the ceremony. He looked at me very sentimentally and I was touched with uneasiness for I knew things were going very badly for the government.

'The baby behaved impeccably,' he said. 'I can see she is going to take after her mother.'

I laughed.

'She might have shown some displeasure,' he went on. 'Think what an effect that would have had on the proceedings.'

He could always bring a light touch into everything even when he was disturbed.

I arranged that Lord Melbourne should sit beside me at the dinner party which followed the christening; and we talked a great deal about old times and he was his usual witty self.

I could not help thinking how sad I should be if I should have to accept another in his place.

It was soon after that when I made a truly alarming discovery. I was pregnant once more.

My first impulse was fury; then the fear came. Oh, no, I could not go through all that again . . . and so soon. I was only just getting over Pussy's birth, and here I was starting it all over again.

I loved Albert, and in spite of one or two storms, my marriage was a happy one, but this side of it could never please me. It was the shadow side of marriage.

Albert was delighted at the prospect of another child and I resented his pleasure.

'You, Albert, do not have to go through all the tiresome painful ordeals.'

Albert said that it was God's will, and that children had to be born as they were.

'Then I wish that He had given men a bigger share in it,' I retorted.

Albert was shocked by what he considered blasphemy; but I meant it.

When I told Lehzen she was horrified. 'But it is *far* too soon. My precious one, you have only just recovered. Oh, this is too bad . . . this is thoughtlessness. This is putting too big a burden on my little one.'

She took a delight in blaming Albert; and such was my mood at the time that I let her go on.

I said: 'I hated it. All those people in the next room, waiting . . . Oh, I know it is the custom in the case of a royal birth . . .'

'It's inhuman,' said Lehzen.

'I shall not allow it again.'

'And why should you?' asked Lehzen.

'I cannot bear it, Daisy,' I cried. 'Not again. So soon.'

'There, my precious,' she soothed. But much as she felt for me she could not hide the fact that she was pleased because she believed I felt some resentment against Albert.

I was always so very disturbed to see this animosity between those two whom I loved.

That was a sad year for me. During the months which followed I went through all the discomforts of pregnancy; but more than that, change was forced upon me and I had to face the fact that I was going to be deprived of one who was very important to me: my dear Lord M.

There was a conflict of loyalties. I had my ties with my foreign relations always in mind; and these were in constant opposition to the good of my country. Lord Palmerston was an arrogant man; I knew he was shrewd and very clever; he would have no interference in foreign affairs outside the government which meant that my wishes were of no importance to him.

The trouble was the growing breach between France and England; and of course Uncle Leopold had strong ties with France, Aunt Louise being the daughter of Louis Philippe.

It was due to that old nuisance, Mehemet Ali. Palmerston wanted to crush him and so put an end to French domination in Egypt. Lord John Russell did not agree with Palmerston, which meant there was a division within the government itself. Lord Melbourne, in his usual way, wanted to let it alone and I begged him to override Palmerston and seek a peaceful settlement with France. But Palmerston was not the man to be overridden. He ordered the British fleet to take action and so forced Mehemet Ali to go back to his allegiance to the Sultan.

Palmerston was triumphant when he succeeded in this for it turned out that his calculations had been correct, and Louis Philippe was disinclined to take the offensive on behalf of his Egyptian ally. Instead he joined with the other states involved, who pledged themselves to maintain Turkey and Egypt in *status quo*.

Palmerston's bold—and successful—action was regarded with dismay by Uncle Leopold and the French, and a great coldness blew up between England and that country. Albert sided with Leopold and the French; and he made me see that I should take their side.

Meanwhile the government was growing weaker. The triumph abroad meant little to the people; it was home affairs which were of the utmost importance to them.

The blow came in May—the month of my twenty-second birthday.

The government's budget, which leaned towards free trade and reduced the tax on sugar, was defeated by a majority of thirty-six. Sir Robert Peel immediately called for a vote of no confidence in the government and he won. It was true by only one vote. But that was enough.

Albert was very grave. 'This will mean an election,' he said.

'I pray the Whigs will succeed,' I replied fervently.

'I think, my love, that is most unlikely.'

'Oh, Albert, I cannot bear to think of those terrible Tories in power.'

'My dearest, Sir Robert Peel is one of the finest statesmen in the country—I might say the finest.'

I hated those sly references to Lord Melbourne and I felt my anger rising.

'I cannot endure the man,' I said shortly.

'I think if you give him a chance you will change your mind. When he came to see you he was aware of your animosity and that must have made him a little nervous. I think if you would set aside your dislike, you would get to know him very well.'

'How can one set aside one's dislikes!'

'By taking an unjaundiced view, by looking at the man as he is and not merely as the opponent of one whom you want to keep in office.'

'My dear Albert, you have no idea what I have suffered through that man. He wanted to turn out my bedchamber women. I cannot go through all that again . . . at this time . . . in my condition.'

Albert soothed me. 'Come and sit down, *Liebchen*. I want to talk to you and I want you to listen carefully and promise not to be angry.'

'Angry . . . with you!'

He nodded. 'I want you to know that everything I have done is for your good . . . to make you happy . . . to make life easy for you during these months which I know are trying for you.'

I lay against him. I loved to hear him talk like that.

'I know, dearest Albert, that you are so good to me. I have a hot temper. I am impulsive . . . and not always appreciative. But I do know . . . yes, I do, that you love me and that this love between us is the best thing that ever happened to me.'

'I believe that, too. My dear one, we have to face facts. There is going to be an election and the Tories are going to win.'

'How can you be so sure of that? I could not bear it.'

'It is almost a certainty. For a long time the government has been on the verge of collapse. It has come now.'

'Then the new Prime Minister will be Sir Robert Peel.'

Albert nodded.

'Albert, I cannot bear it. The trouble I had last time . . . I managed to get rid of them.'

'You managed postponement, but can you again? My dearest, you know that it is inevitable and it is for the country—not the Queen—to choose its government; and the country will choose the Tories.'

'To happen now . . . when I am in this state. It is too bad! There will be trouble about the household . . . just as there was before.'

'No,' said Albert.

'What do you mean?'

'I have arranged that there shall be no trouble.'

'Peel gave up last time because he could not remove my bed-chamber ladies.'

Albert hesitated, took a deep breath and said: 'I have made arrangements about that.'

'About my ladies?'

'My dearest, be calm. Remember, I think only of you. You must not excite yourself now. What has to be must be accepted.'

'If he brings in his Tory women, how foolish will I look? Being forced to obey my Prime Minister.'

'I have worked it so that this will not be the case.'

'But the ladies will have to go.'

'Yes . . . they will go, but they will resign . . . now.'

'They never would.'

'Yes, they will. The Duchess of Sutherland, the Duchess of Bed-
ford and Lady Normanby will resign . . . before the election.'

I could not help but feel relieved. I dreaded another confrontation
with Sir Robert Peel. I knew that he would not accept my entirely
Whig household; and I knew, also, that I could not, without great
humiliation, dismiss my Whig ladies and accept those with Tory
leanings. I had dreaded the conflict . . . But if they resigned, that
would be another matter.

'Albert, you have arranged this!'

'Thinking solely of you, my dearest. I understand perfectly your
feelings and how, after what you had gone through before, you
could not be subjected to the humiliation of accepting now what
you would not previously. So . . . I have arranged this. The ladies
are willing. They understand perfectly. They will resign, and when
the government is formed, it will be a matter for you to discuss
your new household with the Prime Minister. You could not, in all
reasonableness, have an entirely Whig household as before. But
you might have a sprinkling of Whig ladies.'

'You arranged all this! Oh . . . Albert!'

He said: 'I was not going to have you disturbed. I would not
have done this, but just now it is of particular importance.'

I was so grateful for all his care. I did not want to think of a
change of government. I would lose my intimate relationship with
Lord Melbourne, but now I had Albert that would make a difference. It was not the same as it had been. Everything was different
with Albert beside me.

'Oh, dear, dear Albert, what should I do without you!'

He said modestly: 'I did not bring this about on my own. I cannot
take full credit. It was after many discussions with others . . . Anson, Stockmar . . . Lord Melbourne himself saw the wisdom of it.'

'He did not mention it to me.'

'We all thought it was wiser that you should not be upset until it
was a *fait accompli*. The ladies are now ready to resign. They will
do so before the result of the election is known. Sir Robert will be
most understanding . . . as he has been all along; he would not add
to your discomfort.'

'Do you mean that *he* knows of this?'

Albert hesitated for a second or so. 'We thought it necessary to
take him into our confidence. He is a most understanding . . . a
most shrewd man. Believe me, he wants to make this transition as
comfortable for you as he possibly can.'

I lay against Albert. I could sense his relief and how apprehensive he had been about telling me.

But he was right, of course. I realized that. I loved Lord Melbourne; he was my dear friend; I wanted his government to stay in power so that he could continue to be my adviser. But, of course, it must be the people who decided who should govern them.

I had to reconcile myself to change.

I could . . . with Albert beside me. And once more I thanked God for giving me such a husband.

When Lord Melbourne came to me I felt very emotional.

I said: 'Albert has talked to me. He has told me that you knew what he was doing.'

'I do not feel so badly about leaving you,' replied Lord M, 'as I know you have such a worthy man beside you.'

'This is too sad for me to contemplate.'

'Change has to come and we have been warding this off for a very long time.'

'That man . . . that dancing master . . . in place of you!'

'Of course, Your Majesty is not in need of a dancing master, but, M'am, you are in need of good ministers, and I do assure you that Peel is one of the best.'

'That is what Albert says.'

'Albert is wise.'

'You will come to dine with us . . . often.'

He bowed.

'I shall write to you . . . long letters telling you just what I feel.'

'Your Majesty is gracious to me . . . as ever.'

'Oh, dear Lord M, it is so cruel that this should happen when I am . . . when I am . . .'

'I grieve for that, M'am.'

'And all because of your wretched enemy making all that fuss about sugar.'

'He is only my enemy in the House, M'am. Outside we are quite good friends. I firmly believe that when you get to know him, you will find that he is your very good friend.'

I tried to forget that I might be on the point of losing my Prime Minister; I tried to forget that growing discomfort culminating in a painful ordeal lay before me.

I thought of Albert's devotion and how he had worked so hard to save me from unpleasantness.

Yes, it was not a very happy year.

* * *

Albert was to be given an honorary degree at Oxford. I was to go with him to receive it and I was looking forward to the journey. I loved travelling and it was particularly enjoyable when honour was being done to Albert.

There was one of those little differences between us which might have blown up into a quarrel, but somehow we managed to avoid it.

Albert suggested that Lehzen should not accompany us.

'Not come!' I cried. 'But, Albert, Lehzen always comes with me. I have never been separated from her.'

'That was before your marriage.'

'Well, that makes no difference.'

Albert thought it did, and I was about to accuse him of being unfair to Lehzen when he said: 'Pussy cannot come with us. She is too young for the journey. Is not Lehzen in charge of the nurseries?'

'Yes, she is.'

'Then how can she leave Pussy?'

I saw this was a way of avoiding a great deal of unpleasantness. I was growing very uneasy about the conflict between Albert and Lehzen and in my condition I did not want to be involved in quarrels.

I was so happy because Albert had arranged the difficult matter of the bedchamber ladies and I just wanted to be peaceful. I grew exhausted very quickly and my temper was more uncertain than ever. I did not want to provoke it. I was a little like Lord Melbourne who always wanted to leave it alone.

'I shall hate being without you, Daisy,' I said, 'but you cannot leave Pussy. She needs you more than I do.'

It worked. Lehzen hated the thought of my going to Oxford without her, but on the other hand she loved to be thought indispensable in the nurseries. Albert had been very wise to bring up that point.

She wavered. 'I have never been away from you,' she said. 'You were always my baby. I can't think why *you* have to be dragged to Oxford.'

'I shan't be dragged, Daisy. I shall go in the carriage and I assure you I shall be well looked after.'

'In your state . . .'

'It is another five months before the baby is due. Surely I haven't got to live like a recluse until that time. I shall be all right.' I was going to say that Albert would look after me, but that would, of course, not help matters at all.

So Albert and I went to Oxford where Albert received his honorary degree, with the Duke of Wellington as Chancellor of the University presiding.

When we left Oxford we stayed at several houses on the way back—spending two nights at Chatsworth with the Devonshires and then going on to the Bedfords at Woburn and to Panshanger where we were entertained by Lord Cowper, Lord Melbourne's nephew.

'All Whig houses,' said Albert. 'Is that wise?'

'They are my friends,' I retorted. 'The country may choose the government but I will choose my friends.'

After Panshanger we took luncheon with the dear man himself at his country home of Brocket Hall. What a pleasure it was to be entertained by Lord Melbourne. He was so delighted to have us there.

'What an honour for me to entertain Your Majesty,' he said. 'I, who have had so much royal hospitality.'

'Dear Lord M,' I said. 'I hope in spite of everything, things will remain as they are.'

They did not. The election was in progress at the time and the result was a devastating defeat for the Whigs and a very large Tory majority.

It was a very sad meeting.

I held out my hand and he kissed it, then lifted his eyes to my face. He was trying to look his nonchalant self but he was not managing it very well; and I loved him the more for his inability to do so.

'It had to be,' he said. 'It has been coming for a long while. It is a decisive victory for them. Three hundred and sixty-eight against our two hundred and ninety-two. There is no doubt that the country wants a new government. But for Your Majesty it would have happened before.'

'At least I kept you with me a little longer.'

'Your Majesty's determination was fierce.'

'As fierce as my choleric temper?'

'That is certainly fierce, but it evaporates rather speedily and your determination persists.'

'Oh, my dear Lord M, how I shall miss you!'

'May I give you one piece of advice?'

'Of course. I hope you will never cease to give me advice.'

'Send for Peel at once. Be patient with him. I am sure you will soon be on excellent terms with him.'

'He will remember that incident of the bedchamber ladies. He must hate me as much as I hate him.'

'He is a loyal subject. He respects Your Majesty. Believe me, he understands the position. He wants affairs to run smoothly and will strive to win your confidence.'

'He makes me uneasy with his dancing steps.'

'It is only because you make him uneasy. Do not forget that you are the Queen.'

'I do not forget.'

'Be magnanimous. Give Peel a chance. That is all you need to do. He will give you excellent service for he is a dedicated man.'

'It is strange to hear you speak like this about your most bitter opponent.'

'Your Majesty, our enmity ceases to exist outside politics. We have different ideas as to how the country's affairs should be run. That does not mean that he is a villain . . . just because he does not agree with me. There are, in fact, many occasions when I see his point quite clearly. There are many sides to every question.'

'Oh, Lord Melbourne, you are a very clever man . . . so astute . . . so polished. How I shall miss you!'

I was almost in tears and so was he.

'You have the Prince,' he reminded me. 'I rejoice in the Prince. He will be beside you. He will help you. Listen to his advice for he is wise. When you married you made the best possible choice.'

'I know.'

'It comforts me greatly to know that you will have such a helper . . . right at your side . . . so close to you.'

'He should be the King.'

Lord Melbourne raised his eyebrows and smiled at me.

'Don't forget what I told you. Governments should never attempt to make kings. If they did they would soon be trying their hands at unmaking them. It is better as it stands. You have the Prince. Let us rejoice in that.'

'You will come to visit me. We shall write.'

'Your Majesty is so good to an old man.'

'As good as you were, I hope, to an inexperienced girl.'

He was too emotional to speak . . . and so was I.

This was the last time I should see Lord Melbourne as my Prime Minister.

When he left I went to the room where I did my drawing and I inspected several of my favourites—ones which he had admired.

I sent them to him.

His reply touched me deeply.

He would treasure them and they would remind him of my kindness and regard which he would cherish beyond measure.

It was a very very sad time.

It made it harder to bear that following on that scene with Lord Melbourne I had to receive Sir Robert Peel.

Albert talked to me before the meeting, extolling the virtues of the man, and telling me how eager he was for our relationship to run smoothly.

It was not quite such an ordeal as I had feared. Sir Robert was less ill-at-ease than he had been on our previous meeting two years before. He was very respectful and obviously eager to please. Perhaps, I thought, I had misjudged him. He was not Lord Melbourne, of course. He never would be. There was only one Lord Melbourne. But he was not disagreeable.

He showed me a list of the people he proposed for the Cabinet and wanted to know if they had my approval.

'I should need time to study them, Sir Robert,' I said.

'But of course, M'am.'

I noticed he did not fidget so much and there was none of that irritating pointing of toes.

All the same I was pleased when he went; and I was delighted to have come through our first meeting without too much annoyance.

I was unable to attend the prorogation in October. In fact I was not appearing in public as my confinement was getting very near. I was longing for it to be over. And then, I thought, there must be a long rest from this tiresome business.

Albert was so kind. He understood how I hated to have all those people so close, just waiting for the moment when the baby was born. He said that they should not be told until right at the last moment, and that would avoid their being close at hand during the wretched preliminary period.

I was greatly comforted by that; and although the entire business of child-bearing was loathsome to me, for I hated that a queen should be made to feel like an animal, on this occasion it was not quite so humiliating because of the greater privacy.

I was so relieved when it was over; and this time there was very special rejoicing. I had produced the longed-for boy.

The whole country was delighted. What store they set on boys! They had not felt the same about poor Pussy.

He was a lusty child, with large dark blue eyes, a rather big nose, but with a very pretty mouth. I was more accustomed to babies now and their original ugliness did not repel me quite so much because I knew it would change.

Albert was overjoyed about the new baby. He kept talking about Our Boy or The Boy.

I said: 'I hope he will grow up just like you, Albert.'

Albert modestly did not reply, but I am sure he hoped the same.

'And,' I said, 'he shall be called Albert.'

Of course there was opposition to that. This boy was the heir to the throne and there had never been a King Albert of England. There had been Edwards—six of them—and the English always liked their kings to have the same names. I never forgot that some people had wanted me to be Elizabeth when it was known that I would almost certainly come to the throne. I had refused that very firmly.

Edward was therefore a favourite choice for the Boy.

'It is only right that he should be Albert,' I insisted. 'Pussy is named Victoria after me; therefore the Boy should be Albert after his father . . . even if he had to be Edward as well.'

Christmas had come and we went to Windsor. The Boy was just over a month old. Pussy, of course, was now becoming quite a person. She was not exactly enamoured of her little brother.

Albert had instituted German customs and several fir trees were sent to us from Germany. These we decorated with brightly coloured baubles and candles. Beside the trees were tables where presents were laid out. Pussy was enchanted by the trees and looked at them with wondering eyes.

Poor Lehzen had caught the jaundice and looked very odd—and very ill, for her skin was quite yellow. I wanted her to rest but she refused to. She insisted that she was needed in the nursery.

There was a ball on New Year's Eve. Even Albert could not retire early at such a time and had to stay up to see the passing of the old year. We stood together while the trumpets sounded to usher in the New Year; my hand was in his.

'A happy year, my darling,' said Albert.

'For us both,' I said fervently.

And I hoped it would be happier than the last.

The christening of the Boy took place in St. George's Chapel. For political reasons it had been thought advisable to invite Frederick William, King of Prussia, to be the chief sponsor. The others were the Duke of Cambridge, Princess Sophia, and three members of the Saxe-Coburg family.

The King of Prussia stayed with us for about two weeks and was most affable and very interested in everything English. I found him pleasant.

There was the usual outcry, this time because the Boy was given the title of Duke of Saxony. He was the Prince of Wales, it was said, and people did not want to be reminded that he had a German father.

Albert was indignant, but he was accustomed to such comments now and more able to shrug them aside.

Albert thought he and I should be alone for a short while and he suggested a brief visit to Claremont. 'Alone,' said Albert. 'After all, you have to recover from the Boy's birth.'

So Lehzen and the nurses went back to Buckingham Palace and Albert and I had a blissful time at Claremont.

The weather was cold and there was snow. How we revelled in it! We skated a little and Albert made a snowman twelve feet high. It was good to see him so unusually playful.

But all too soon we must return to London. And there trouble awaited us.

We had talked constantly about the children. Pussy had given us some anxiety during the last autumn; she had grown a little thin and rather listless. But she had seemed much better during Christmas.

'She is so pretty now,' I said. 'That white and blue dress which Mama gave her is most becoming.'

'Your mother is very fond of the child. How glad I am to see you settling your differences. They should never have existed. Nor would they if . . .'

I looked at him appealingly as though to say, Please, Albert, don't spoil these idyllic days at Claremont. Please do not say that Lehzen ruined my character, indulged me, did not check my temper with the result that it is now uncontrollable . . . or I shall lose that temper and everything will be spoiled.

Albert understood although I had not spoken, and he did not want to spoil the holiday either.

He said instead: 'She is getting too old for Pussy now. She should be called by her proper name.'

'Then I shall not know whether you are speaking to her or to me.'

'She shall be Vicky.'

'Vicky! Very well. I don't suppose we shall be able to drop Pussy or Pussette right away. I hope she is all right. I do worry about her. Though she did seem better at Christmas. How she loved those candles in the trees!'

'She is adorable,' said Albert.

When we arrived back at the Palace the first thing we did was go to the nurseries. The Boy was asleep, the picture of health. Not so our daughter.

We gazed at her in consternation. Then Albert snatched her up. 'The child is ill,' he said. 'How thin she is! She is being starved.'

The nurse—Mrs. Roberts, I think her name was—glared at Albert. I was afraid the nurses took their cues from Lehzen who must have impressed on them that Albert was of no account, particularly in the nursery.

The nurse said: 'We carry out the doctor's instructions here in the nursery.'

Albert put the child back into her bed and strode out of the nursery. I followed him.

In our room he said: 'This is malicious. It seems to me that there is a conspiracy to keep me out of the nursery.'

I was very worried about the child; I hated these upsets and I knew that this was really another conflict between Albert and Lehzen. I lost my temper.

I cried: 'Do you mean that *I* am keeping you out of the nursery?'

'I am sure those who have your support wish to do so.'

How he hated Lehzen! How could he? How I should have loved to see those two good friends; but they hated each other and were constantly letting me know it.

My temper flared. 'I suppose *you* would like to keep *me* out of the nursery. *You* would like to be in charge. Then you could as good as murder the child.'

Albert stared at me as well he might. He looked bewildered. 'Murder our child,' he murmured. 'What are you saying . . . ?' He stood very still, his lips compressed as though he were fighting hard to retain his composure.

Then I heard him murmur: 'I must have patience.' And he strode from the room.

I was hurt; I was angry with myself, but more with him. He made no attempt to get along with Lehzen. He had hated her from the first day of our marriage, and was determined to do battle with her.

I knew Lehzen. *He* did not know her. I knew she would give her life for me and the child. Yet Albert was suggesting that Lehzen was responsible for Vicky's illness.

I could not restrain my anger. I went to him.

He was standing by the window looking out.

'So you are now avoiding me,' I said. 'You walk out when I am talking to you.'

'Considering your uncontrollable temper there is little else one can do.'

'Our child is ill,' I said. 'Can you think of nothing to do about that except to abuse those who serve her loyally?'

'It is because I fear they are not serving her wisely that I am concerned.'

'You have upset them in the nursery.'

'Mein Gott!' he cried. 'They need to be upset. They are incompetent fools. I am expected to stand by and see my daughter neglected just because some old fool has to be placated.'

'Please do not call Daisy an old fool.'

'I shall call her what I please. It is through her that we have this trouble. She is unfitted for the care of children.'

'She was my nurse, my governess, and my dearest friend.'

'And . . . we see the result. Ungovernable furies which should have been checked in childhood.'

'Albert, you should be careful what you are saying.'

'I shall say what I please. There is an attempt to shut me from the nursery. I am denied the care of my child. I am shown every day that I am of no importance in this household.'

'Albert, I am the Queen.'

'Of that all must be aware. As for myself I am constantly reminded of the fact.'

'Albert, that is not true.'

'It is apparent to all. You should listen to the truth and stop treating as gospel what is said by that crazy, common, stupid intriguer who is obsessed by her lust for power, and regards herself as a demi-god; and anyone who refuses to acknowledge her as such, as a criminal.'

'Oh, how dare you! I wish . . . I wish I had never married.'

'Has it occurred to you that that is something on which we might

both agree? Baroness Lehzen . . . Dr. Clark . . . My daughter is
in the hands of this incompetent pair. One only has to look at her
to see the result. Dr. Clark has poisoned her with his camomile; he
has starved her by giving her nothing but asses' milk and chicken
broth. We have seen his skills before . . . in the case of Flora
Hastings. If this Court had been managed in an efficient manner
that man would have been dismissed long ago. I suppose he is a
friend of the worthy Baroness who can do no wrong. Oh, I know
you are the Queen—it is a fact which is driven home to me every
day—and that I am brought in merely to provide heirs to the throne
and do as I am told. Take the child away from me. I have no rights.
If she dies it will be on your conscience.'

I had never heard Albert make such a long and bitter speech and
I had never felt so desperately unhappy in the whole of my life.

And as I stood there, he turned abruptly and left me.

I wept stormily, angrily. How dared he say such things! Yet he felt
them, and I could see that they were in a measure true. I could not
think what to do. I wanted him to come back. Let us shout at each
other. Let the storms of abuse flow. What I could not endure was
silence.

I passed a wretched night. The next morning Albert went to open
the new Stock Exchange. I sat in the Palace brooding.

I could bear it no longer. We must talk calmly, reasonably. The
child's health was important and it was necessary for her parents to
look after her jointly.

I wrote a letter to Albert in which I said that we had been over
hasty and we had based our assumptions on evil rumours. There
were always those who maligned others. I had already forgiven him
the cruel things he had said to me; and I thought he should come
to me and we should talk together.

I knew that Albert confided a great deal in Stockmar. We both
did. Uncle Leopold had sent him to be an adviser to us both, and
from our childhoods Uncle Leopold had been our guardian. I
guessed that, upset as he was, Albert would go to Stockmar and
tell him his side of the story.

As a result Stockmar came to me and said he wished to have a
very serious talk. He had heard, through Albert, of the disagreement between us. He said: 'I find these continual quarrels very
disconcerting. For some time now I have been toying with the idea
of returning to Coburg. My family is there. I should like to be with

them. And when I see how things go here, I feel I can make no progress with the task your uncle has set me.'

'You would not leave us!' I cried.

'It is in my mind. I can see that you are unaware of the great blessings which have been bestowed on you. There could be so much happiness . . . so much that is good, but . . .'

'Albert should not provoke me. I know I am hot-tempered and when my temper is aroused, I say things I do not mean. I hate these scenes. Albert should remember that it is not long since my son was born. One suffers not only before but after a birth. Men do not understand . . .'

'There are reasons other than physical weakness behind those outbursts. There are too many conflicts in the household.'

'What do you mean?'

Stockmar had never treated me as the Queen; he had always been frank and open, and implied that if he could not speak his mind he would not speak at all, but return to his family in Coburg.

He said, looking at me very shrewdly: 'Let us face the truth. There will always be these scenes while Baroness Lehzen remains in your household.'

I stared at him in horror.

He went on: 'It is a fact. There is not room in one household for the Prince and Baroness Lehzen.'

'I love them both . . .'

Stockmar shrugged his shoulders. 'The time has come for you to decide which is the more important to you.'

'Albert is my husband.'

'Exactly. He will always be with you. But you cannot hope for a happy marriage while the Baroness remains.'

'She is my dearest friend . . . She has been with me all my life.'

I was thinking: I could not live without Albert. I love Albert, yes, but I love Lehzen, too.

'That is all I can say,' said Stockmar. 'While she is here there will be trouble and although at this time there is great affection between you and the Prince, constant disagreements, violent quarrels, will kill love in time. I know the Baroness is devoted to you, but she loves you too possessively. She dislikes the Prince because she is jealous of anyone who takes you from her. I repeat, the Baroness should go, if you are to live in harmony with your husband and family.'

'No,' I said. *'No.'*

Stockmar lifted his shoulders. 'Then there is nothing more I can say.'

'I could not do it. How could I tell her? It would break her heart.'

'If she stays she will break yours . . . and Albert's.'

'I cannot see why people can't be nice to each other. It is a big palace. Why is there not room for us all?'

'It is not a matter of area,' said Stockmar.

He looked at me hopelessly and I could see he was preparing to take his leave.

'Wait a moment,' I said.

'Yes, Your Majesty?'

'Isn't there some way out . . . something we could do?'

I knew that I was telling him that at all costs I must keep Albert. Stockmar realized this and I fancied I saw something of triumph in his eyes.

'The Baroness has a sister in Coburg,' he said. 'The sister has children. The Baroness is very fond of children. She could go to her sister . . . adequately pensioned. She could have a very comfortable life.'

'How could I tell her? Oh no, no. I could not.'

'A holiday . . . at first. It could grow into a long holiday.'

I was silent.

I knew that he was right. I loved Lehzen. It would be heartbreaking to say goodbye to her. But Albert was my husband. My allegiance was to him; more than that he was what I wanted. If Lehzen were not there—much as I should miss her—there would be an absence of that tension which was so worrying to me. I should be at peace and happy.

Stockmar was going on: 'The Baroness has been ill recently. She has not yet recovered from her attack of jaundice. She needs rest, freedom from responsibility. A holiday should be suggested for her, just a holiday . . . at first . . . a holiday which should grow into a very long holiday.'

I nodded, slowly, wretchedly.

Stockmar was smiling. He said: 'Your Majesty shows great wisdom.'

I had known it would have to come. They could not exist peacefully under the same roof. This had been inevitable ever since Lehzen had been confronted by him. Their dislike was mutual. They were enemies through their love of me.

I had to accept that, and I wondered how I was going to tell Lehzen.

How delighted Albert must be! He had achieved what he had always wanted. He was going to be rid of Lehzen at last.

I would have to know that she was comfortable; she would have to be most adequately provided for. She had often talked to me about her sister and the children. Oh, it would be a terrible wrench but she would be happy in time.

Albert would come to me in delight. He would tell me how happy he was because I had come to this decision. It was for him, he knew, and he would be gratified. He must not go on thinking that he was of no importance in the Palace. I must show him that he was of the utmost importance to me.

I waited but he did not come.

Where was he? Stockmar had said he would go to him at once. Then as I was making such a sacrifice why did he not come at once and thank me?

The minutes ticked by and at last I could bear the waiting no longer.

I went to his sitting-room.

To my surprise he was sitting in an armchair, a book in his hands. Reading . . . at a time like this! I felt myself growing angry again.

He looked up at me and smiled.

'Why did you not come to see me?' I demanded.

'You were not in a very good mood when we last met,' he replied.

'I did not think you were in a very good one either. Albert, put that book down when I speak to you.'

'Is that a royal command?' asked Albert a trifle coldly.

Oh dear, I thought. This is not going as I expected it would. How can he behave so, after all I have done?

'When I come in I expect you to pay attention to me.'

He said: 'A thousand pardons.' He stood up and bowed.

'Oh not like that,' I said. 'Just talk to me.' He was still holding the book.

'Put it down,' I cried.

'If you ask me, instead of command me, I shall do so.'

'It seems that you would like me to request you to speak to me.'

'Perhaps that would be a courteous thing to do.'

The temper was rising. 'Perhaps you would like me to curtsy, beg permission to speak and walk out backwards.'

Albert stood up, and taking his book with him, walked into the bedroom. He shut the door.

I was now furious. I had come ready for reconciliation. I had agreed—much against my will—that Lehzen should take a holiday. And my reward was this. Another quarrel. I would not have it.

'Open that door,' I shouted.

Albert was standing on the other side of it. I was aware of him.

'Who is there?' he asked.

'You know. It is the Queen. Open it at once.'

Nothing happened. I was so miserable. I could have burst into tears. It was only my anger which kept me from doing so.

I knocked again.

'Who is there?' repeated Albert.

'What game is this? You know who is here.'

'Tell me,' he said.

'The Queen!' I shouted.

Nothing happened. What did he mean by shutting me out? I had agreed to their terms . . . his and Stockmar's. I had rashly promised that my dearest Lehzen should go for a long holiday; and now he was behaving like this . . . showing me, I supposed, that he was master in his own house.

That was all very well, but I was the Queen.

I cried angrily, my voice shaken with emotion: 'Will you open this door?'

'Who is there?' he asked again.

'The Queen,' I said, stifling my emotion.

I felt wretched, frustrated. I wanted to see him. I wanted him to open the door, put his arms round me and tell me that there would be an end to silly quarrels which hurt us both so much. I wanted to say I agree to Lehzen's going. I'll agree to anything, but we must be together because our love is really of the utmost importance.

I could not check the sob which rose in my throat. I think Albert must have heard it for he said in a very gentle voice: 'Who is there?'

Then I understood. It was not the Queen he wanted to hold in his arms; it was Victoria, his wife.

I cried: 'Albert, this is Victoria . . . your wife.'

The door was flung open. He was standing there.

I ran to him; he picked me up and held me fast.

I was so happy to be with him. I said I was hasty tempered, a shrew. He replied that he should never have uttered the words he did. We both agreed that it was out of our love for each other that these quarrels arose. We must guard against them. We must stop them. They were spoiling our bliss. We were so fortunate. Little Vicky should have the best attention. We would call in more doctors. There was Stockmar for one.

I knew Lehzen would protest. She let her jealousy of Albert overshadow all other feelings.

But we had to make Vicky strong and we had to preserve our marriage.

Of course I had Lehzen to face. I put it off and it was Albert who spoke to her first. Perhaps that was unfortunate. She would be suspicious of anything that came from him.

She came to me bristling, her rage apparent.

She said: 'The Prince has spoken to me.'

I knew what was coming.

'He is trying to take you away from me.'

'Oh no . . . Daisy.'

'Yes, he is. He has suggested that I go to Coburg for a long holiday.'

'I have been so concerned for your health. You work too hard.'

'I cannot work too hard for those I love.'

'I know . . . I know. How is the child?'

'She is all right. There is nothing wrong with her.'

'She does seem pale, thin and a little listless, too. She used to be so full of vitality.'

'It's people that are trying to make trouble.'

'Daisy dear, the Prince and I have decided that you need a nice long holiday in Coburg. There is your sister. You know how interested you are in her children. You will go . . . and have a really good rest.'

She was looking at me disbelievingly. I met her gaze steadily. She knew me well. She knew that I was telling her she would have to go and that the last nursery scene must be the final one. She could not believe that the ties which held me to her were not stronger than those which bound me to my husband.

I could not say to her what I should have liked to. Dear Lehzen, I shall never forget what we have been to each other. I love you. I am grateful for all the loving care you gave me over so many years. I cherish happy memories of the times we have had together. But I have a husband now . . . and my husband and my children must come first.

I could not say it; but she knew what was in my mind. She knew of my wretchedness because we must part; but she also knew that

I had come to terms with my new life. I had to accept her departure as I had that of my dear Lord Melbourne; and since the coming of Albert they had ceased to be of paramount importance in my life.

Poor Lehzen! How tragic she looked. I could not bear it. I put my arms round her and cried quietly, while she held me to her. She wept too, but there was resignation in our tears.

Lehzen could not go immediately, of course. After such a long stay in the household there were many preparations to be made. She had written to her sister and there was a ready welcome awaiting her in Coburg.

We did not talk about her departure very much. It was too painful for us both, but I knew she was sorting out her things and deciding what must be taken with her.

To our great joy, Vicky's health started to improve. Albert saw a great deal of her. I think he had a special feeling for Vicky. In fact I now know that he did, for that was borne out through the years. She was such an enchanting creature, and showed signs of brightness already, which delighted Albert.

The Boy was young yet, but we fancied he was not as forward as Vicky had been at his age. But all that mattered at this time was their good health.

My relations with Albert had become closer. I began to see things through his eyes. I realized my own shortcomings. I had been so long governed by that ill temper which would flare up so suddenly, and while it was with me I was capable of saying the most outrageous things.

'We must conquer it,' said Albert. 'I promise you we shall.'

'It is rather formidable,' I admitted.

'It is a dragon to be slain,' said Albert. And he looked like St. George himself setting out to slay it. 'It must be slain,' he said, 'before it slays us.'

How right he was! How right he always was! Even about Lehzen. I loved her dearly and always would. Loyalty and fidelity were two virtues I did possess. Of course I was arrogant at times. Perhaps I had had queenship thrust upon me at too early an age. I was, as everyone knew, hot-tempered, impulsive, apt to act first and think after . . . but at least I was loving, and when I loved I was faithful.

But in spite of my love for Lehzen, I knew that she was interfering, possessive, jealous, determined to capture the first place in my heart and to hold on to it. And it was true that she hated all those who came between me and herself. She was incapable of organizing anything. The affairs of the household were in disarray, and there was inefficiency everywhere. The boy Jones had betrayed the lack of security. Albert had seen these things before the rest of us, and Albert was right.

There was a letter from his brother Ernest, now, so he said, fully recovered from his malady. That was well for he was about to be married. The bride was to be Princess Alexandrina of Baden.

I was a little dubious about the wisdom of Ernest's marrying, knowing what I did of his reputation and the terrible consequences his ill deeds had brought upon him; but Albert was elated, he had very deep family feeling, and he believed that marriage would be the saving of his brother.

There was an invitation for us to go to Saxe-Coburg for the wedding. I could not leave. The state of the country was such as to keep me at home; and there was no hiding the true facts nowadays. Sir Robert Peel was different from Lord Melbourne. He did not think one should 'leave it alone', but that I should know everything that was happening, however unpleasant it might be.

Although I could not go, there was no reason why Albert should not. I hated to let him go, but it was his brother, and he naturally wished to be present at his wedding, particularly as it might be the saving of him.

Albert was torn between two desires, to see his home again—and how he loved it; he was always talking about the forests with their pine trees and old legends—and his wish to stay with me. He chose the latter, and I was immensely gratified although the thought did enter my mind that he might have chosen to stay because although Lehzen would eventually depart, she was still in the Palace. He might have wondered what I should have been cajoled into if he were not there.

However, I was delighted when he resisted the temptation to visit his old home and stayed with me.

I wrote to Uncle Leopold telling him what a great delight our marriage was to both me and Albert; and I had a very pleasant letter from Princess Alexandrina which suggested to me that she was a very gentle, sensible and religious young woman.

'That,' said Albert, 'is what Ernest needs.'

I had the idea that as Albert could not bring himself to go to Coburg for the wedding, the newly married couple should come to us.

'Let us invite them to spend their honeymoon at Claremont since you are not going to Coburg,' I said.

Albert thought this was an excellent suggestion and he wrote such a charming letter to Ernest which was full of good advice. Although Ernest was the elder, Albert's being so much more serious and sensible, he looked upon himself as his brother's protector.

I looked over his shoulder as he wrote.

'Do not leave your wife at home while you go after your own pleasures,' he wrote. 'If you always wish to have everything in the latest fashion and go to the races and hunt, you will not have enough. Here, people ruin themselves with such things. What does it bring?'

Dear Albert! He was so concerned. And it seemed ironical that he should have a brother so different from himself.

But he loved him nonetheless in spite of his inadequacies, and used to tell me with emotion how they had hunted together and walked with their dogs through the forest and skated in the rivers and lakes. In spite of their unsettled home life and the scandals attaching to their mother, they had a happy childhood . . . perhaps partly because of their affection for each other.

Ernest and his bride were delighted at the prospect of coming to England and accepted the invitation.

They came to us in July and I found my new sister-in-law amiable, charming and sensible.

Ernest was much as I remembered him—merry and courteous, but of course I knew he was something of a philanderer, and as he was so different from Albert I could not approve of him, and I did not believe he could make a quick change from a rake to a good husband as Albert had hopes that he would; but then he was his brother and he was surprisingly lenient with him.

But before their visit we had lived through some stirring times.

I shall never forget Felix Mendelssohn's visit to Buckingham Palace. Both Albert and I were delighted. I had always admired Mendelssohn's music and I told him so at once. Albert joined with me and Mendelssohn charmed me by asking Albert if he would play something for him.

'I shall be able to boast that the Prince played for me when I return to Germany,' he said.

'Yes, do play,' I cried. 'The Prince is a musician, I do assure you.'

Albert said: 'Victoria!' reproachfully, but he was not displeased. And to Mendelssohn: 'You must forgive the Queen's enthusiasm. It is due to affection rather than critical judgement.'

But when Albert played a chorale by Herz, Mendelssohn was

enraptured, and said the performance would have done credit to a professional musician.

'Please sing for us, Mr. Mendelssohn,' I begged; and he sang his chorus from *St. Paul*, in which Albert and I joined.

I clapped my hands when it was over and asked the musician if he had written any more songs.

'The Queen is very fond of your songs,' said Albert to Mendelssohn, and to me: 'Why do you not sing one for him?'

I hesitated and was at last persuaded; and we went to my sitting-room where I had my piano.

Mama came in. How different she was nowadays! I wondered how much of her arrogance had been due to that odious John Conroy. I was thankful that he was now out of the way. Albert was so pleased because we were on better terms.

I sang the *Pilger's Spruch* and *Lass Mich Nur*. Mendelssohn went into raptures over my singing, which I think was moderately genuine—quite a lot of praise for the Queen, but some for the singer, too.

It was a very happy and informal meeting; and when the sheets of Mendelssohn's music were caught in a gust of wind and scattered all over the floor, I ran about collecting them; and I think he was astonished that a queen could act as naturally as I did.

That was a pleasant interlude—not only because we were delighted to have a famous composer, but because he was the sort of person Albert enjoyed talking to, and I, hitherto, had been wary of inviting to the Palace—although, of course, I was more at home with musicians than writers, because I knew something of music and felt by no means at a loss in conversation.

Soon after my birthday—my twenty-third—a very unpleasant episode took place.

While we were driving in the Mall Albert saw a dark, ill-favoured man close to the carriage. When he was within about two or three paces from us he brought out a pistol and held it towards us. There was a shout. I saw the man run, but before he could be caught he was lost in the crowd.

When we returned to the Palace there was great consternation. It had been a narrow escape. The villain had got away. It was considered to be dangerous for he might very well try again.

Lehzen was in a state of nerves. She wrung her hands and said I must not go out again. It was too dangerous. She went about muttering that she wished she could lay her hands on the villain.

I said: 'I do not propose to stay in forever.'

I talked about it to Albert when we were alone.

'We have to go out,' I said. 'So let us go . . . well protected. It may be that he will make another attempt. They will be on the alert for him and catch him.'

Unknown to Mama and Lehzen we set out with two equerries guarding us, one on either side of the carriage.

Rather surprisingly the man appeared again with the pistol and this time the police were waiting for him. He was seized, but not before he had fired.

I was glad that he had been caught. Otherwise we should have been expecting to see him every time we rode out.

It always depressed me to know that there were people who wanted to kill me; but I always felt calm at the time of danger, which surprised me as well as others. I cannot explain this, but my grandfather appeared to have it for on the occasion when he came within inches of being killed he presented an exterior of almost indifference.

Sir Robert Peel came at once to the Palace. He was deeply distressed.

'The man is named John Francis, Your Majesty. He is in his early twenties . . . and a joiner.'

'Is he mad?' I asked.

'He doesn't appear to be, M'am.'

'Sir Robert, I cannot bear to think he will die because of this.'

'His object was to kill Your Majesty.'

'All the same . . . I do not like it. I always think these people are mad and can't be blamed for that. It is an illness in a way.'

'Your Majesty is magnanimous.'

'I should like his life to be spared. I do not want anyone to die because of me.'

'One has to make an example of these people,' said Albert. 'Otherwise we shall have others trying out the same sort of thing just to gain notoriety.'

Sir Robert said: 'Mercy towards this man could only be a matter for the Government to decide. It is not a royal prerogative, but I will put Your Majesty's wishes before Parliament.'

He did; and as I had stated my wishes so firmly, instead of being hanged, John Francis was to be transported for the term of his natural life.

It seemed that Albert was right.

He had said I was sentimental over Francis and such leniency as had been shown might encourage others to imitate him. I had disagreed with this and had retorted that I was glad that I did not have the death of John Francis on my conscience. Albert was exasperated but in a tender way and that discussion did not end in a display of temper on my part. I found I quite enjoyed having these little disagreements with Albert, so that we could put our points of view and discuss them; but now that Lehzen's future was settled, although she was still with us making her preparations to depart, they were usually pleasant little *têtes-à-têtes*, with Albert usually gently persuading me to take his opinion.

He said now that if John Francis had had his just deserts we should never have heard of John William Bean.

He came into our lives one day when Albert and I were driving to chapel in St. James's. A boy—a poor deformed creature, not more than four feet high, with a humped back, dashed out of the crowd to our carriage. He was carrying a pistol which he pointed at us.

Two other boys dashed after him; one of them seized the hunchback and brought him to the ground, the other took the pistol.

'Mischievous children playing games,' said Albert as we drove on. 'You see, my love, it is unwise to let sinners go unpunished. People think they can treat us with impunity.'

I pointed out that John Francis had not gone unpunished; he had been sent to Australia for life. That was a punishment surely—perhaps as harsh as death. I was glad I did not have his *blood* on *my* hands.

Albert shook his head as though he considered my reasoning illogical.

When we returned to the Palace we heard that the police, thinking it was a game being played, had reprimanded the boy while complimenting the other two—they were brothers named Dassett—on their prompt action.

But the matter was not to be as easily dismissed as that. One of the Dassett boys had kept the pistol and on examination, although it was packed with paper and tobacco, it was also found to contain gunpowder. Had it been fired, it could have been highly dangerous.

This brought the matter into another light. The police, ashamed of having allowed a possible assassin to escape, set about a hunt for the hunchback, and because of his physical appearance, he was not hard to trace. They discovered him quickly. He was not a child; it was his deformity which had made him seem so. He worked in a chemist's shop. Very shortly he was arrested. He was of the same leaning as John Francis.

'These people,' said Albert, 'are revolutionaries in the making. They are the kind which abounded in France at the end of last century.'

What I remembered chiefly about that incident was the manner in which Sir Robert Peel—who was in Oxford at the time—came with all speed to the Palace.

When I heard he had arrived I guessed it was because of the Bean case and asked that he be brought to me immediately.

I shall never forget the sight of his face when he came in. He was clearly distraught.

'I came as soon as I heard, Your Majesty,' he said in a shaking voice.

'It was good of you, Sir Robert,' I replied. 'But you see we are safe and sound.'

He looked at me and I saw the tears well into his eyes. 'Your Majesty,' he muttered, 'pray excuse me.'

He turned and stumbled away.

I was deeply touched. The dear man was so concerned for my safety that he, whom I had always thought so cold, so aloof—although he and Albert had now convinced me that he was a fine politician—was moved to tears in his relief at my safety.

Bean was sentenced to eighteen months imprisonment.

But what was so significant about this matter was that my feelings towards Sir Robert Peel changed. I could trust him as I had trusted Lord Melbourne. He had become a dear friend. I had to agree that he was a more efficient politician—as I was now beginning to see more and more clearly—than that brilliant raconteur, that man of immense charm and social grace, my dear Lord Melbourne.

Sir Robert never prevaricated; he always wanted to get things done. He came to the Palace to discuss his concern about the two attempts on my life which were particularly disturbing because they had followed so quickly upon each other.

'I do believe,' said Sir Robert, 'that Bean's was not really a serious attempt on Your Majesty's life. He is simple-minded, looking for notoriety, no doubt. He is a poor thing. But we cannot allow people who feel so inclined to think they may amuse themselves by making even mock attempts on Your Majesty's life. I propose to bring in a new Bill immediately. Attempts on the Sovereign's life will be punished by seven years' transportation, or imprisonment for three years, added to which the accused will be publicly whipped.'

'Why do you think there are these attempts?' I asked.

Sir Robert was thoughtful. 'Of one thing I am certain. It is not criticism of Your Majesty. You have shown yourself caring for your people, graciously friendly on those occasions when you make public appearances and your family life is exemplary.'

I thought of those wild storms and the angry words which passed between Albert and me; and I made up my mind that there should be no more such scenes, but I was becoming more and more convinced that I was to blame for them.

'No. It is not Your Majesty who arouses this discontent in the minds of unstable people. It is the state of affairs in the country.'

I knew he was referring among other dangers to the Chartists with their People's Charter. Albert had talked to me a great deal about this. In the days when Lord Melbourne had been my mentor he would have shrugged them aside. 'Tiresome people who had nothing to do but make trouble.' But discussions with Albert had taught me that they were demanding electoral reform and voting by ballot. They were rioting in various parts of the country, and riots always sent a shiver of alarm down people's spines because the French Revolution was not so very far behind us, and we all knew what happened to that unfortunate country. Those of us in high places were particularly apprehensive for we would never forget what had happened to our counterparts in France.

There was always trouble abroad. Wales was in revolt with the people calling themselves Rebecca and her daughters; Cobden was making a nuisance of himself and causing concern to Sir Robert over the Corn Laws; and in Scotland there was some controversy over the Established Church.

All these things added up to unrest and when there was hardship in a country people expressed their dissatisfaction by turning against their rulers.

Albert had made me aware of all these things, and as a queen I should be aware. I was so grateful to Albert. He not only kept me informed; he was improving my mind by reading history to me. It was wonderful to sit beside him. I loved being read to, and what would have seemed incredibly dull to study by myself, became interesting when Albert read it.

I was changing. I was growing up; and when I thought of how I had behaved to Sir Robert, calling him the dancing master, failing

to recognize his worth, I was quite ashamed. My eyes were opened.
Albert had opened them.

The Bill for the protection of the Sovereign's Life went through
Parliament with the greatest ease. They had all been impressed,
said Lord Melbourne when he came to see me, by the courage I
had shown. He looked at me with that loving expression, now a
little sad; but he was genuinely delighted because I had at last
discovered the worth of Sir Robert Peel, and I felt that was very
noble of him. After all Sir Robert was his political enemy; and
there had been a very special relationship between Lord Melbourne
and myself. Yet he was so anxious for *my* well-being that he was
glad that I was appreciating Sir Robert and Albert.

What a good friend he had always been!

I almost fell into a trap over the Cambridges, and it was really Lord
Melbourne who helped to extricate me from what might have been
a dangerous situation. Sir Robert was very clever with political
matters, but I think my dear Lord Melbourne understood more about
people and how they would act in certain circumstances, and why.
Lord Melbourne had been an inveterate gossip; and when I looked
back over our relationship it had been more—or at least equally—
concerned with the private lives of the people who surrounded us
than it had with politics.

I had been on uneasy terms with the Cambridges ever since the
Duchess had refused to stand up for the toast when Albert's name
had been proposed. Of course they would never forgive me for not
marrying their son George.

I must confess to a certain pleasure when I heard that Lady Augusta Somerset was pregnant and that George was responsible.

I discussed the matter with Albert. He was always upset by immorality and particularly so when it touched the family. The Cambridges had been consistently hostile to him and he said that it was
a chance for me to show my disapproval and that I would not allow
them to continue to insult us.

'You have been so lenient with the people around you,' said
Albert with a mixture of tenderness and censure. 'You have accepted people who have been at the centre of scandal—your own
Prime Minister, who was at one time your constant companion, for
instance, was not untainted by scandal.'

A short while ago that would have been the beginning of a storm,
but although I felt my anger rising as it always did at criticism of
those of whom I was particularly fond, I said calmly: 'People are

sometimes involved in scandal when they are innocent. I never believed they should be blamed. Your father and brother have scarcely been blameless in that respect, but in my eyes that only makes you seem the more virtuous because of your defence of them.'

Albert did not pursue the matter. He was very sensitive about the misdeeds of his family.

However he did think some action should be taken about the Cambridges and in this case I was only too eager to agree.

'Invite the Duchess to a Drawing-Room, and tell her that you cannot receive Lady Augusta.'

'And George?'

Albert admitted that was difficult, George being a prominent member of the royal family, and in line for the throne.

The Duchess was soon asking for an audience which I gave her and I must admit that I looked forward to the encounter with some relish.

'I must know the reason for Your Majesty's ban on my lady-in-waiting,' she said.

'Dear Duchess,' I replied. 'I should have thought the reason was obvious.'

'It is not to me, Your Majesty.'

'Ask your son or your lady-in-waiting. They should know. The Prince and I are aware of the lady's condition, and we will not accept immorality at Court. We shall not receive those who err in a certain way—and if members of the royal family are concerned, so much the worse. But we will stamp out laxity.'

'I can assure Your Majesty that you have been misinformed . . . as you were on another occasion.'

Any reference to Flora Hastings always unnerved me. It was not only the trouble it had brought me. It was the thought of that poor girl dying of a terrible disease and all the time being accused of immorality.

The Duchess left in a state of great indignation. As she departed she said she could not allow this matter to rest there.

I was very disturbed, particularly when I discovered that there was no truth in the rumour.

Lord Melbourne, who even now he was no longer Prime Minister, was still living a very social life, was very much aware of what was going on in people's private lives.

I was delighted when he asked if he could see me privately.

'Dear Lord Melbourne,' I welcomed him. 'This is like old times.'

'I am happy to know that Your Majesty realizes the good points of your present Prime Minister.'

'I was very young and inexperienced. I am sorry I spoke of him as I did. He is a very dear man . . . so feeling, really—although he cannot always show it.'

'No longer the dancing master?' said Lord M, who could never resist a joke.

'He has given up that profession,' I replied with a laugh.

'And the silver ornaments on the coffin?'

'I don't notice them. I do know that he is a dear, good, clever man, and that he is determined to do what is best for the country and for me . . . and even though you and he might not agree on the first, you would, I am sure, on the second.'

'That is true. And what I came to talk to Your Majesty about is this affair of the Cambridges. Your Majesty cannot afford another Hastings scandal just now.'

'Oh no . . . no!' I cried.

'It would not be so easy to extricate yourself now as it was then . . . and even then it was a difficult time, was it not?'

I nodded. 'I shall never never forget how the people turned against me so quickly.'

'It is the way of the mob. The Duchess of Cambridge is incensed. She is involving the Press. You must take the utmost care, for this could explode into another scandal. You will know there are riots in various parts of the country. There is unemployment. Peel will have kept you informed about this.'

I nodded.

'He would. It is nothing much. These things happen.'

I looked at his dear face and I thought, Sir Robert doesn't think it's nothing much. Sir Robert says these things must not happen if we can help it.

There was a great difference in the two men but they were united in their care for me.

'There is one thing which should be done without delay,' went on Lord M. 'An apology must be sent to the Duchess.'

'An apology! From me!'

'Let it come from the Prince. He seems to be the target for their enmity. But it must be done swiftly before this blows up into something very like the Hastings affair. Moreover, that will be revived if this goes much farther. That would be unwise and very difficult for Your Majesty.'

'I will tell Albert. '

'He will not wish to humiliate himself naturally, but Your Majesty will impress on him that having had experience of what a scandal like this could turn out to be, you are aware of the danger to your standing with the people—and you are sure this must be done.'

'I do understand. You are my very dear friend and I will talk to Albert immediately.'

As Lord Melbourne had said, Albert was very reluctant to apologize; but I did manage to impress on him the importance of this. I recalled the terrible days when I had suffered so much from the Flora Hastings matter and that even now I occasionally had nightmares about it.

'There were placards in the streets, Albert,' I said. 'On them was ''Murder at Buckingham Palace''. I shall never, *never* forget; and it must not happen again.'

At last Albert was prevailed upon and he made an apology to the Duchess. It was ungraciously given and curtly received. The matter was allowed to drop, but the Cambridges continued to show their enmity to Albert; and they made it clear that they did not consider his rank as high as their own.

But at least—thanks to Lord Melbourne, who in such matters was far more knowledgeable than Sir Robert Peel—we had passed safely through danger.

September was almost upon us.

It was the time, said Albert, for a little holiday. He had revised the nursery and there had been no protests from Lehzen. September was the month she was due to leave. Albert had sent off all the nurses who had worked with Lehzen and had replaced them.

Vicky, to our delight, was now thriving and becoming very amusing. Albert was enchanted by her and I was glad to see that she had a very special feeling for him, calling to him whenever he came into the nursery, running to him and catching hold of his legs. He would lift her in his arms, and I even saw her riding on his back while he pretended to be a grisly bear or a fierce tiger, rousing her to shrieks of terrified delight.

What a happy scene that was! The Boy was growing well, but of course was younger and therefore not so interesting.

I should be glad to have a holiday. It was really rather a strain to be with Lehzen and to know that she would soon be gone.

She was sad, in a resigned sort of way. She made no criticism of Albert now, and it really did seem as though she were looking forward without too much sorrow to her new life, but that quiet melancholy air did distress me.

I was sure her sister would be glad to have her and the children would love her. I remembered so vividly how it used to be between us and how she had thrown herself wholeheartedly into all my childish pleasures.

So it would be delightful to get away for a few short days of holiday alone with Albert.

I thought we should go to Claremont as we often did at these times, but Albert had other ideas.

'I have always wanted to go to Scotland,' he said.

'Scotland! It seems so far away.'

'After all,' said Albert, 'it is part of your kingdom. You should put in an appearance now and then. The people expect it.'

So we made plans to visit Scotland.

How glad I was that we did!

It was late August when we left Windsor at five o'clock in the morning and we reached London in three quarters of an hour and were at Woolwich before seven. People had heard that we should be there and quite a crowd had gathered to see us get into the barge. The Duke of Cambridge, Lord Jersey, as Master of Horse, Lord Haddington, First Lord of the Admiralty, Lord Bloomfield, Colonel Commandant of the Royal Regiment of Artillery, and Sir George Cockburn, Senior Naval Lord, were present as it seemed quite a state occasion. Unfortunately it was raining and we had to go straight to the sitting-room. Then we set off, the Trinity House steamer and packet forming our squadron; we were followed by several little pleasure steamboats, their occupants eager to catch a glimpse of us.

It was three days later before we caught sight of the Scottish coast. The Scots gave us a wonderful welcome with bonfires all along the shore.

It was the first of September before we reached our destination, and when we arrived we could not see Edinburgh, because it was shrouded in dim fog. It was a great pleasure to be greeted at the pier by the Duke of Buccleuch and Sir Robert Peel, the latter having made the journey to Scotland to be there on our arrival.

I was enchanted by Edinburgh—quite beautiful and unlike any other city—everything of stone and no bricks at all—and the main street steep, and the castle on the rock right in the middle of the city.

I loved Scotland—partly because Albert was so delighted with

it. I thought the people attractive. Quite a number of the girls had
long red hair which they wore flowing down their backs. I thought
it enchanting. I ate porridge, which I found very good, and I tried
another of their Scottish dishes called Finnan Haddies.

What happy days they were, discovering Scotland. I was fascinated by the most unusual dress of the people—the kilts and the
tartans; and I soon grew accustomed to the sound of bagpipes. I
thought them most romantic.

We travelled extensively and were warmly welcomed everywhere. I was sorry the holiday was coming to an end but I longed
to see the children. I did miss them and although I had heard from
Lady Lyttelton, who had now been appointed royal governess, that
they were well and happy I thought about them a great deal.

I believe Albert was more than a little sorry when it was time to
sail southwards. He stood on deck watching the coastline of Scotland fade away.

His comment was: 'An enchanting country. We must visit the
Highlands again soon.'

And I agreed most enthusiastically.

I was very sad for the time had come when Lehzen was to leave
us.

Albert watched me anxiously. I was sure that, right up to the last
minute, he was afraid I would find some excuse for her to stay. I
was tempted to do so. One cannot easily dismiss more than twenty
years of devotion; but I knew in my heart that it was a choice
between Lehzen and Albert—and it had to be Albert.

Moreover, since it had been agreed that Lehzen would depart,
Albert and I had been so much happier together. There had been
scarcely any disagreement. We were growing closer. During the
holiday in Scotland everything had been perfect.

My life lay with Albert.

Lehzen knew this and that was why she was going. But the
sadness was like a heavy cloud which hung over the household.

Our last day together! We were both aware of it and the slightest
thing would have set me crying and I should have been clinging to
her telling her she must not go. Lehzen herself was wonderful. She
knew it was better for me to turn to Albert. He was a fellow German
and she understood him. I believe she would have admired him if
she had not been so jealous of him. Lehzen loved me truly . . . just
as Lord Melbourne did. And love is selfless. I had learned that.

When I said goodbye to her she said: 'This is the last time. I shall not see you in the morning before I go. Partings are so sad. There is no need to prolong the unhappiness. My dearest one, take care of yourself. You will write to me and I shall write to you. I shall follow your life in all you do. I know you will be happy because you will make those around you happy. You are a dear good girl, and I am proud of you.'

She held me in her arms for the last time; and I went to my bedroom and wept.

In the morning she left.

There was no doubt of Albert's pleasure; but he did understand my feelings and was most kind and sympathetic.

Then I stopped to brood for I discovered that I was once more pregnant.

Rumblings of Revolt

In April of the following year my little daughter was born. This was a much easier pregnancy and birth than the others, and I wondered whether one became accustomed to that. That was a happy thought because I seemed to be the sort of woman who would be excessively fertile. In three years I had managed to have as many children.

She was to be Alice Maud, and as she had been born on the Duchess of Gloucester's birthday, she was to be Mary also—after her.

Everything had gone so much more smoothly after Lehzen's departure. Albert had had a thorough examination of the household and had made some astounding economies. I knew that lots of the servants did not like it for life must have been very easy for them under Lehzen's rule. They grumbled among themselves, I knew. Poor Albert, he was very unpopular with them; but that is often the reward of doing what is right.

For Alice's christening we had to invite Uncle Ernest, although I did so with the utmost reluctance. He was still the bogeyman of my childhood, and I could never feel perfectly at ease when he was in the country. He seemed to be in a state of constant resentment because he had not inherited the crown of England. *I* did not grudge *him* that of Hanover. So why could he not be content now that he was a king? There was conflict between us now because he was claiming Princess Charlotte's jewels. I wore them often for I really had very few of my own—for a queen; and I saw no reason why he should have them, so I refused to give them up. But I thought he might feel a little reconciled if he were asked to act as sponsor for the baby.

My dear sister Feodore was to be another and the apprehension at the prospect of seeing Uncle Ernest was forgotten in the joyous one of having Feodore with me. Albert's brother, Ernest, and Aunt Sophia were to be the other two.

Feodore and I hugged each other; we kissed and studied our faces, entwining our arms as I took her to her room where I sat on the bed and we talked and talked.

'You . . . my little sister . . . a mother of three!' she said. 'I cannot believe it. I shall never forget the sight of you with your dolls. Live dolls are different, are they not?'

How easy it was to talk to darling Feodore. I was able to tell her of the anguish over Lehzen. She listened and what was so wonderful, she understood.

'I know Lehzen well,' she said. 'A wonderful woman . . . but possessive, and it was only natural that she and Albert should resent each other. Your life, dearest sister, is with Albert . . . him and the children. It is your family which matters most.'

She loved the new baby who was plump and contented.

'She is a wonderful baby,' I said. 'Quieter than the other two. I think she will be a great comfort to me.'

'Vicky is very bright.'

'Indeed, yes. Albert is so pleased with her. I wish Bertie was different. I think he is going to be rather lazy. He just mumbles to himself, shouts and runs all over the place.'

Feodore laughed. 'Bertie is adorable. He is a normal boy. They are the best sort to have.'

'There speaks the wise mother.'

I looked at her lovingly. That lovely willowy figure she had had was no more, for she had grown rather plump; but Feodore would always be beautiful because of her lovely expression. Her face was illuminated by an inner goodness.

She was in complete contrast to Uncle Ernest who radiated malevolence.

He arrived late and after the christening ceremony was over. I wondered whether he did it on purpose. He looked even more evil if less physically able to carry out any wicked intentions. He was rather bent and bald and obviously hard of hearing. Alice behaved perfectly during the ceremony; and everyone said what a lovely child she was.

I had some uneasy moments afterwards in the nursery when Uncle Ernest asked to see the children, which I thought rather an odd request, coming from him, for I was sure he was not really interested in them.

Vicky came running up with her usual lack of self-consciousness. 'Where is your eye?' she demanded.

'Lost in action,' replied Uncle Ernest shortly.

'Did someone take it?'

'Yes,' he said.

'Why?'

Albert came forward and laid a restraining hand on Vicky's shoulder. I saw him smile; he thought anything Vicky did was very clever and amusing.

The King of Hanover had turned away. 'And where is the boy?' he said.

Bertie came forward. He said nothing and I was aware of Albert's frown. Bertie was such a disappointment to him, which was largely due to Vicky's brightness; they made such a contrast. I was always reminding Albert that Bertie was a year younger than Vicky.

I felt a tremor of alarm when Uncle Ernest picked up Bertie and held him at eye level, studying him intently with his one eye. I imagined he would be thinking that this young boy would in all probability be King of England, a title for which Uncle Ernest had lusted all his life.

I glanced at Albert and saw that his thoughts were the same as mine. I felt that everyone in the nursery was waiting for something to happen. It was a most uneasy moment.

Bertie, however, was unperturbed. He stared at the King's empty eye socket with the utmost fascination.

'Looks a healthy little fellow,' said Uncle Ernest.

'He is,' I told him. 'He takes after his father.'

'Can't see it,' said Uncle Ernest. 'More like our side.'

Vicky was looking up at him in a rather impatient way because Bertie was getting more attention than she was, which was most unusual.

'I'm not just Vicky,' she said. 'I am the Princess Royal.'

But Uncle Ernest continued to look at Bertie, and it seemed a long time before he set him down.

I talked to Albert about the incident when we were alone.

'He really alarmed me,' he said, 'when he took Bertie up and displayed such an interest in him. He quite ignored Vicky and was not in the least interested in the baby—although he had asked to see the nurseries.'

Albert thought that the only reason he could have been more interested in Bertie than in Vicky was because the boy was heir to the throne, for if he had a general interest in the children, Vicky would surely have been the target for his attention.

It was very sad having to say goodbye to Feodore, but the visit had necessarily to be brief, for Feodore had many duties in her own home.

'We must meet again soon,' I said.

'Why should you not come to us?' asked Feodore. 'How I should love to show you my children.'

'We might well do that,' I replied. 'We did go to Scotland recently . . . Albert and I without the children. It was one of the happiest times of my life.'

'Then there is hope,' said Feodore.

People remembered Uncle Ernest's reputation and the rumours he had set in progress about me when I was a child; and we had one or two letters telling of a plot to kidnap the children. Sir Robert Peel took these letters seriously, although they did appear to have been written by mad people. We even had some letters from people who went so far as to say that they proposed to kidnap the children.

All this came out of Uncle Ernest's visit. I wished that I had not invited him to the christening.

We were all a little shaken and very watchful. Albert made the rounds of the nurseries each night himself, for he would trust no one else.

'Remember the boy Jones who paid us a visit,' he said. 'He was innocent. Some might not be.'

How glad I was to have Albert to take care of such things.

Mama, whose main interest in life now was the children, was in a state of great anxiety about them. She told Albert of the agonies she had suffered during my childhood when she had feared that wicked Cumberland—as he was then—was plotting to have me poisoned; and how she had watched over me day and night.

'You and Lehzen never left me alone,' I said.

'Oh yes . . . Lehzen was trustworthy in that respect.'

Mama smiled complacently. Lehzen's influence was now removed and there was dear Albert. Mama doted on Albert. I supposed that was understandable. It was through him that we had become reconciled.

About a week after the christening, Princess Augusta of Cambridge was married to the Grand Duke of Mecklenburg-Strelitz; and there again Uncle Ernest showed he had not lost one bit of his ambition. At the altar steps he tried to step in front of Albert, but Albert would not allow that. He forced himself in front of his right-

ful position and Uncle Ernest almost fell off the altar steps. I smiled
to myself. It was what he deserved. And I was ready for him when
the time came to sign the register and he manoeuvred himself into
a position beside me so that when I had signed he could snatch the
pen from me and sign next. In that case his signature would be
above that of Albert. But I was too quick for him. I was not going
to allow him to sign before Albert. Nor did I want a scene. There
were several people standing at the table and in spite of the fact
that I was in a dress with a train which was by no means light, I
slipped round to the other side of the table, so that I was immediately beside Albert. I took the pen, signed my name, and quickly
handed it to Albert before Uncle Ernest could get round the table
and snatch the pen from him.

How Albert and I laughed about it afterwards! I was very relieved
when Uncle Ernest left.

A very pleasant time followed. I was often in the nursery, discovering quite maternal instincts which I had not known I possessed.
But I do not think I was a very motherly woman. The little babies
did not greatly interest me; it was only when they talked and were
amusing and looked pretty that I wanted to spend a lot of time with
them. Alice was a dear baby though. Such a good child! She was
so fat that we called her Fatima. She had a contented smile and
would lie gurgling and laughing to herself in her cradle. The nurses
loved her.

Lady Lyttelton said that Alice adored Bertie and laughed with
pleasure every time he came near her. He was very gentle with her,
she added, and loved her dearly. I fancied that Bertie was Lady
Lyttelton's favourite because she was always making excuses for
his backwardness.

I had mentioned this to Albert and his comment was: 'I hope that
she does not spoil the child. We must watch that.'

I hoped so too, for Lady Lyttelton was so good with the children
and they were all extremely fond of her.

Sir Robert Peel was rather anxious about our relationship with
France and he thought we ought to try for a *rapprochement*.

Our new yacht the *Victoria and Albert* was now ready, and as
the country's affairs were quieter than they had been for some time,
Sir Robert thought it would be a good idea if we took a trip to
France to stay with Louis Philippe. I thought it was an excellent
proposition; it would mean another holiday with Albert all to my-

self, for he was getting so involved in politics that I did not see so much of him as I should have liked.

After the Prorogation of Parliament we set out in the yacht. First we cruised round the Devon coast and then crossed to France. The King of France came by barge to meet the yacht, and the shore was lined with people who displayed banners and shouted *Vive la Reine*, which was very gratifying.

There was a delightful surprise waiting for me. Aunt Louise, Uncle Leopold's wife, who was also the daughter of Louis Philippe, had joined her father's Court in order to help to entertain us.

What a joyous reunion that was and how we laughed together and recalled those times when she had shown me her beautiful clothes and how I had tried them on and she had advised me about styles and colours.

I always grew sentimental looking back on the old days. Albert said I saw them through a rosy glow. He didn't really believe I could have been so happy with that old dragon Lehzen always with me. There were some things which even Albert did not know.

We were with the King for five days; he took us about the country and there was a *fête champêtre*. Then we saw some plays which I loved—particularly the comedies at which I laughed heartily.

After we said goodbye to the King of France we took the Prince de Joinville to sea with us and we called at Brighton and stayed at the Pavilion, which amazed the Prince. He had never seen a palace like it, he said. I did not tell him that neither had we!

Then we went back to stay with Uncle Leopold for a short visit, Aunt Louise having left France and joined her husband so that she would be there ready to entertain us in Uncle Leopold's palace as she had in her father's.

Uncle Leopold was overjoyed to see us.

'My dear children!' he cried. 'My two favourites! I am so glad I brought you together. What happiness that has given us all.'

Aunt Louise introduced us to her children. Albert was rather taken with Charlotte—perhaps because she was about the same age as his beloved Vicky.

So on that occasion Aunt Louise and I talked of children instead of fashions; and I was so happy to be with those dear people again.

All too soon it was over and we were back at Windsor.

Sir Robert said the visit had been a very useful one.

A pleasant way of doing one's duty, I thought.

* * *

A very sad thing happened soon after our trip to France. Lord Melbourne had a stroke. I was desolate when I heard the news and immediately wrote to him in terms of the utmost affection.

Fortunately it was only a slight one; but I wanted to hear frequently of his progress and for him to know that I was thinking of him. I wrote that I should never forget what he had done for me when I was young. He would always be my very dear friend.

I was delighted when he wrote that, apart from one or two small inconveniences, he was almost himself; and I wrote back at once and told him he must come and see me as soon as he was well enough to come up from Brocket.

When he did come, I was rather saddened, though he was as ebullient as ever, and soon his pithy remarks had me laughing almost as much as they had in the old days. I noticed with great sadness that he dragged one foot a little and that an arm seemed slightly impaired. I asked if he was taking care of himself and he said the best tonic he had—or could ever have—was seeing me so well, so happy with my husband and growing family—a wife, a mother and a great Queen.

Then he looked at me with that expression I remembered so well; the half-tender amused look, with tears in his eyes; and he was once more my own dear Lord M.

Poor Lord Melbourne! Out of the office he had so much enjoyed; growing old was a great trial, for all that he made such an effort to deny it.

I thought of him often. I wrote to him frequently. I told him I should never forget our friendship—nor must I.

In the New Year we heard that Albert's father had died. We had known he had been ill for some time so it was not entirely unexpected.

Poor Albert was desolate. He wept bitterly and talked to me of his great sorrow.

I did remember that Duke Ernest had not been such a good father as he might have been. Although he had self-righteously divorced Albert's mother, his own morals were by no means of the highest. She may have had one lapse and was branded for that, whereas her husband had been completely promiscuous; and his second marriage had not been a success either. Moreover he had pestered Albert to get me to settle an income on him which would have put me in a very awkward position had I done so; then he had been furious because we had not called Bertie after him.

No, I could not in my secret heart agree that Albert's father had been such a good man; but Albert seemed to have forgotten his sins now he was dead and so earnestly and so movingly did he talk of his father's virtues to me that I began to believe in them too.

'I shall have to go to the funeral,' said Albert.

'I must come with you,' I replied.

But that was not possible. Sir Robert said it would not do for me to be out of the country at this time.

'It will be the first time we have been separated,' I said. 'The thought to me is terrible.'

But in the midst of his grief, Albert had time to think of me.

I was deeply touched when he told me that he had written to Uncle Leopold, asking him if he would spare Aunt Louise to come and stay with me during his absence; and to my great pleasure this was agreed to.

So sadly I said *au revoir* to Albert, and warmly greeted Aunt Louise. It was wonderful to talk to her about the children.

I was a little annoyed because I was pregnant again and although, as I explained to Aunt Louise, it was wonderful to have children, and so many kings and queens suffered because they could not, I did feel that longer intervals between the bearing of them would have been more desirable.

Aunt Louise helped to lighten the days of separation. Albert and I wrote frequently. I treasured his letters; they mirrored the love we had for each other.

He wrote from Dover.

'Every step takes me farther from you—not a cheerful thought.'

There followed another letter immediately.

'My own darling, I have been here about an hour and regret the lost time I might have spent with you. You will, while I write, be getting ready for luncheon and you will find a place vacant where I sat yesterday. In your heart, however, I hope my place will not be vacant. You are even now half a day nearer to seeing me again. By the time you receive this letter you will be a whole one—thirteen more and I am again in your arms. Your most devoted Albert.'

But the one I liked best came from Cologne.

'Your picture has been hung everywhere so you look down on me from the walls . . .'

Of course they were delighted to see him there. They loved him dearly and that did not surprise me.

'Could you witness the happiness my return gave my family,' he wrote, 'you would have been amply repaid for the sacrifice of our separation. We have spoken so much of you . . .

'Farewell, my darling, and fortify yourself with the thought of my speedy return. God's blessing upon you and the dear children . . .'

There was no doubt in my mind that Albert realized how very much I missed him.

Aunt Louise returned home and Albert was due back at Windsor.

What a joyous reunion! We clung together. The absence was almost worth while for the pleasure of seeing each other again. He must go to the nursery; he must marvel over Vicky's charm and cleverness, sigh a little over Bertie's backwardness, and delight in Fatima's placid smile.

Afterwards, when we were alone, he told me of the visit; how sad it had been; how he had grieved, remembering his dear Papa who was now laid to rest.

'And how was Ernest?' I asked. 'He is, of course, the Duke now.'

'Oh, Ernest was much the same as usual.'

'I hope he is happy in his marriage and has given up his old ways.'

Albert was not sure of that. His stepmother—of whom he had been very fond—had been delighted to see him; and his grandmother had been overwhelmed with emotion.

'But it was sad for her,' said Albert, 'for she knew I should soon have to leave her.'

'They all wanted to know about the children, I suppose.'

'Oh yes, we talked of them a great deal, and I remembered some of Vicky's quaint sayings. They were much amused. You would have smiled to see them plying me with questions. My grandmother still calls me her little *Alberichen*.'

'She must love you dearly.'

'She does indeed. I saw Stockmar.'

'How delighted he must have been!'

'Oh, he was. I often think what we owe him. He has been of great help to us both.'

I agreed fervently.

'Of course he is with his family now and that is what he likes. I have hinted that we should like to see him here. I talked to him of Bertie. I am rather anxious about that boy.'

'Lady Lyttelton thinks highly of him.'

'She is rather a sentimental woman. She is fond of the child.'

'I am glad she is.'

'Yes, yes. But Bertie needs discipline. He will have great responsibilities.'

'Yes . . . in time.'

'He will have to be trained for them.'

Albert's lips tightened a little. 'It is amazing,' he said. '*I* have scarcely been treated with honour in this country.'

'All that is changing, Albert. I have tried so hard . . .'

'I know that, my love, but they still look on me as the outsider, the German.'

'People are like that.'

'I am the Queen's husband . . . that is all. It is amazing to contemplate that that stupid little boy can take precedence over me.'

'Oh . . . Bertie . . . I hadn't thought of it.'

'But he will, of course. The Prince of Wales is of greater importance than the Queen's husband.'

'Dear Albert, I wish I could make it otherwise.'

'Oh, it is of no importance. But it is just ironical . . . that is all.'

But it was important to him, I could see; and I was so sorry and wished I could have made him King. I would have done so immediately if that were possible.

'So,' he went on, 'Bertie must be disciplined. Stockmar would know exactly how to handle him.'

'We must try to persuade Stockmar to come,' I said.

It was my twenty-fifth birthday. I was getting old. Quite a matron. I would soon be the mother of four children.

Albert lovingly congratulated me and brought me his birthday present.

I cried out in joy for it was a portrait of himself. He looked so handsome—but of course not so handsome as he really was. I told him I could not have anything I liked more.

In the background of the picture the artist had painted a group of angels, their rosy fingers holding a medallion. The words on this were *'Heil und Segan.'*

'Health and blessing, my darling,' said Albert.

I kissed the portrait, at which he laughed, well contented.

That was a very happy birthday.

Almost immediately afterwards we heard that Nicholas the First of Russia was on his way to visit us. I was amazed and not a little disconcerted for my pregnancy had advanced to the seventh month, and at such a time I had neither the strength nor the inclination for such a visit.

Sir Robert said we owed this no doubt to my sojourn with Louis Philippe. The Emperor would not want to see too great a friendship between us and the French.

'I really do wish he had not invited himself,' I said. 'I hate to be seen like this . . . and what if he were shot?'

Sir Robert looked startled.

'There are so many anarchists in the world,' I went on, 'and the Russians go in for that sort of thing. I do believe he is a very strange man.'

'His visit will be good for relations between this country and Russia,' said Sir Robert.

And Albert agreed with him.

So I must perforce receive the Emperor. He arrived in his ship, the *Black Eagle*, and I took him to Windsor Castle, which seemed to me the most suitable place for the visit. He was most impressed by it, and said, in a rather courtly fashion, that it was worthy of me.

I was always delighted when people admired Windsor. After my initial dislike of it, it had become one of my favourite homes. Albert had made me appreciate it. He had loved it from his first sight of it; and the forest was an enchantment to him as it was becoming to me. I smiled to remember the old days when I had hated to leave London because it always seemed more alive than anywhere I knew. Now it seemed noisy, and I missed the wonderful country air which Albert had taught me to appreciate.

I found the Emperor a very strange man. His appearance was quite frightening; his eyelashes were white and his eyes had a stark staring look so that one could see the whites all round the pupils which made him look a little mad. I had heard that in his youth he had been a very handsome man. I could scarcely believe that.

He was a tough soldierly type but extremely courteous to me, though I must say that when he smiled he looked quite malevolent. He certainly had odd manners. In spite of the fact that I gave him a state bedroom in the castle, he sent his valet down to the stables to procure hay. He had brought with him a leather sack and the hay was stuffed into this; and this was his bed. He was most eccentric.

Sir Robert said we must not offend him and show him great honour during his visit as he was politically important. So I gave myself up to the task of entertaining him. He accompanied me on a review in Windsor Park; and I took him to the races and to the opera. I gave a concert in his honour in Buckingham Palace. Fortunately Joseph Joachim was in England at the time, so I engaged him to perform for the Emperor.

I found it all very tiring, due to my condition, and I went through one of those spells of resentment which descended on me during my pregnancies.

But in spite of his odd soldierly ways, I could not have had a more considerate companion than the Emperor; he was obviously impressed by Albert, and told me he had never seen a more handsome young man, who radiated not only nobility but goodness. Nothing pleased me more than when appreciation for Albert was expressed; and when Sir Robert discussed the uneasy state of Turkey with the Emperor, the latter said that he did not want an inch of Turkish soil for himself, but he would not allow anyone else to have any. Sir Robert thought the visit had been well worth while. And not only Sir Robert. In spite of the short notice and the inconvenient time it was universally proclaimed a success. It was yet another example of the fact that when one is a queen, one's royal duties must come before personal inclinations.

I was now getting to the unwieldy stages of pregnancy and not inclined to much activity. It was unfortunate that at this time a crisis should arise in the government.

The idea of losing Sir Robert Peel was now almost as alarming to me as, such a short while ago, it seemed, it had been of losing Lord Melbourne.

There was trouble everywhere. Indeed that seemed to be the usual state of parliaments. I had a notion that politicians were more concerned with their own advantage than they were for the country, for every time some trouble arose the opposition was always ready to put the entire blame for it on the government in power, instead of combining their energies with those of the government in an effort to put it right.

There was trouble in Ireland. When was there not? The French had imprisoned the British ambassador on the island of Tahiti, which they had recently occupied and this meant that our relations with France had deteriorated so considerably since I had enjoyed my visit to Louis Philippe that it was feared there might be war between our two countries. This was the last thing we wanted, and Sir Robert said we must do our best to improve relations.

The most significant of all was the defeat of the government in a proposal to reduce the tax on sugar. This was particularly disagreeable because the defeat had been brought about by rebels in the Tory party.

I was incensed. I was in no fit state to be worried; and if the government were defeated and had to go to the country, a Whig ministry might be formed and I should lose Sir Robert.

It seemed ironical that I should have once bemoaned the loss of the Whigs and was now alarmed that they should come back into power. But it was not the party which was of such importance to me; it was the leaders. I should never, of course, feel the same emotional attachment to Sir Robert as I had to Lord Melbourne. That would be impossible now that Albert was beside me. But Albert had opened my eyes and made me see what a wonderful man we had in Sir Robert; and the thought of losing him worried me considerably.

Sir Robert told us all about it. There was a group of rebels in the Tory party; and it was due to this that the crisis had arisen.

'Who are these rebels?' I asked.

'There is a certain Benjamin Disraeli,' Sir Robert told us. 'He is an odd fellow, and I believe one to be watched.'

'Most certainly he is, if he is going to attempt to bring about the fall of my government,' I retorted grimly.

'He is Jewish, and I would say very persistent. He was returned for Shrewsbury and he had the temerity to ask for a government post in the new ministry. I refused and he did not greatly care for that.'

'He was resentful, I daresay,' said Albert.

'He has a very high opinion of himself. A strange fellow. He has published a book. *Sybil.* The theme of this was that the rights of labour are as sacred as the rights of property. He is particularly articulate. He married Wyndham Lewis's widow, who brought him her fortune.'

'He sounds a most unsatisfactory type of person,' I said.

'She herself wrote to me extolling her husband,' said Sir Robert. 'She said how desirous he was of a place in the government.'

'She would appear to be fond of him,' I put in.

'It is hardly the way ministerial posts are given,' added Albert.

'I think, nevertheless,' went on Sir Robert, 'he is a man to be watched.'

'A trouble maker,' I said. 'I hope he gets what he deserves.'

There was great excitement everywhere because it was generally believed that the government would not survive the vote of no confidence. However, that little scare came to nothing. Men like that rebel Disraeli might want to oppose their leader, but the last thing they wanted was to see the Whigs in power; and at the critical moment the rebels supported the Prime Minister; and the government was saved.

I could now give myself up to preparations for my confinement.

August came—hot and stifling; and with it my fourth child. It was another boy. We called him Alfred and Ernest—after Albert's father and brother—and Albert after his father.

Two boys and two girls. Surely that was an adequate family.

Now I must have a rest from the wearisome business.

Before the month was out we had another royal visitor. This time it was the Prince of Prussia, brother to the King. I did not know then that he was to become the first Emperor of Germany.

We took a great liking to each other. Albert and he were immediately good friends, having so much in common. He was interested in the children and Vicky made a very good impression. Indeed everyone was amazed by her good looks and intelligence. Albert was growing more and more proud of her.

When the Prince left, Albert thought I needed a holiday. That year we had acquired Osborne House—a dear little place which had always fascinated me in the days when Mama and I stayed at Norris Castle on the Isle of Wight. Close to the castle was a copse called Money Copse. It was said that during the Civil War the owner of Osborne House had buried his money in the copse. It had been searched for innumerable times but never come to light. I doubted it ever would, but it added something to the place.

We had talked over the matter of having a little house to which we could retire when we were in need of a little solitude, and the Prime Minister had thought it an excellent idea to buy Osborne House. The only thing I had against it was that it had once belonged to Sir John Conroy. But I was ready to forget that because I had always liked it. Its one drawback was that the odious man had once lived there but as he had sold it some time before, that could no longer be held against it.

Albert was very interested and immediately started to make plans for improving it. He was very clever at that sort of thing; and he said that the position was so excellent that it was a pity it was so small and unworthy of me.

However, when a holiday was suggested—and I did feel I needed one after the ordeal through which I had just passed—I immediately thought of Osborne.

But Albert had another idea.

'You remember how much we enjoyed our visits to Scotland, my love? Why do we not take another tour of that delightful country. Moreover, you should become better acquainted with your subjects in the North.'

The outcome of that was our visit to Blair Athole.

When she heard we were going, Vicky declared she wanted to come too.

'Oh no, my darling,' I said. 'This is just to be Papa and Mama.'

'Vicky too,' said Vicky imperiously.

Albert took her onto his knee and explained to her that Mama needed a rest, and to have Papa to herself to look after her.

'I will look after Mama, too,' said Vicky adorably; and Albert was overcome by emotion.

She was not in the least afraid of him, as I believe poor Bertie was. He had never been very articulate and now his speech was marred by a stammer, which seemed worse in Albert's presence.

Vicky put her arms round Albert's neck and her lips to his ear. He smiled indulgently and stroked her hair.

'*Please*, Papa . . . please let me come,' I heard her say.

'I am sorry, *Liebchen* . . .'

Tears welled up in Vicky's eyes. She wept becomingly—quite differently from Bertie's bawling.

Albert looked at me and I thought he was going to burst into tears himself. How he loved his daughter.

Later he said to me: 'I do not see why we should not take Vicky.'

I burst out laughing. 'She is a witch,' I said, 'and you, my dear Albert, are under her spell.'

'She is the most adorable creature. She is so like you, my love.'

That was irresistible. We decided Vicky should come with us.

This threw her into transports of joy, and no doubt she went to the nursery to boast about it. Bertie demanded to come.

When he heard he could not he lay on the floor and kicked and screamed. Lady Lyttelton tried to comfort him; but Albert happened to hear of it.

I am sorry to say this resulted in a beating for Bertie. I was very upset because he was so young; but Albert said it was necessary to inflict punishment sometimes. It was wrong to do otherwise. One always had to do the right thing by children; and it was quite clear that Bertie was going to need special vigilance. This hurt him, he declared, more than it hurt the child.

Lady Lyttelton was so upset I thought she might resign her post.

As a matter of fact I think she would have done so had she not thought her presence there was necessary to protect Bertie.

'He is so young, M'am,' she kept saying to me. 'He is only a baby.'

'Dear Lady Lyttelton,' I replied, 'I know how fond you are of all the children, but Bertie's father knows what is best for him. Bertie will have a great position to uphold and he must be prepared for it.'

I had to admit that I hated to hear Bertie's sobs; but I had convinced myself that Albert was right and Bertie was in need of special correction.

We were up at a quarter to six on that morning in the month of September.

Vicky was in a state of great excitement and all ready to leave. Fatima and Baby Alfred were brought down to say goodbye and with them was a very subdued Bertie. By seven we were ready to get into the carriage and go to the railroad to take us to Paddington where our carriage was waiting for the journey to Woolwich.

As we left I saw Bertie grimace at Vicky in a most unpleasant way but I did not call Albert's attention to that. It seemed a pity to spoil the farewells, and all Albert could do was order some punishment which I was sure Lady Lyttelton would see was not carried out.

When we arrived at the port of Dundee two days later, a red carpet was laid down for us to step on as we came ashore and we walked out, I holding Albert's arm while he held Vicky's hand.

What a welcome we were given in Dundee! And it was a wonderful moment arriving at Lord Camperdown's place where we were met by Lady Camperdown and Lady Duncan, who had her little boy with her. The little boy looked splendid in his tartan Highland dress—like a little man. He carried a basket of fruit and flowers which he gave to Vicky. She received it with great dignity and I saw Albert's eyes shine with pride.

I told him afterwards that I was reminded of the visits I had made with Mama when I was a young Princess.

Oh, the beautiful Highlands! I have a special feeling for them. So indeed had Albert. I was so glad that he had taught me to appreciate the country. The journey was breath-takingly beautiful. We passed through Dunkeld, Cupar Angus, Pitlochrie to the magnificent Pass of Killiecrankie from which great height we could look down on wooded hills. Albert was absolutely enchanted.

Blair Athole, proved to be only four or five miles from Killiecrankie Pass. At the gates of Blair Castle Lord and Lady Glenlyon were waiting with their little boy to receive us.

What a glorious holiday that was! I would take walks with Albert and he would drive Vicky and me out in the pony phaeton. I had never seen such wild and beautiful country. Albert drew our attention to the points of interest. He was so anxious that we should miss nothing. I did a good deal of sketching and Albert went deer stalking. On one occasion I thought he was lost on the moors. However, all was well.

Vicky loved every minute. She was feeling very grown up to accompany Papa and Mama on one of their journeys. Her cheeks were rosy, her eyes bright, and when I said I was sure she was growing more plump, Albert delightedly agreed with me.

Albert said she must learn Gaelic and Vicky who was always so interested in everything about her—so different from sluggish Bertie—immediately began to do so. Albert thought she was wonderful and he laughed loudly at her efforts to pronounce the names of the mountains.

How he delighted in that child and how happy I was to have given her to him!

But all good things come to an end and very soon—too soon—we had to return to Buckingham Palace.

No sooner had we returned than Sir Robert told us we must receive Louis Philippe. Albert and I were taken aback as relations with France were very uneasy over the Tahiti affair. But Sir Robert explained that he was very eager to keep relations with the French on a cordial basis and this would be very much a political visit.

Albert saw the point at once and said we should do our part.

I was rather uneasy when I heard there was an outcry against the visit in the French Press; however the King had decided to come accompanied by his foreign minister Monsieur Guizot.

Albert went to Portsmouth, with the Duke of Wellington, to give the King an official welcome, and then they brought him to Windsor where we received him in the state apartments. He embraced me very warmly in a most paternal manner. He was determined to be friendly, and a very charming man he was. He said at once that he had not forgotten the many kindnesses he had had in England when he had lived among us in exile from his country; and how pained he was always when differences arose between our two countries.

That was a promising start, and I was sure that entertaining the King of France was not going to be as difficult as we had feared.

'You are the first King of France to come on a visit to a sovereign of this country,' I reminded him, as I led him up the grand staircase.

'I hope this visit will bring good fruits to us both,' he replied; then he commented on the grandeur of the castle.

We went to the white rooms where we had luncheon. Mama was present. She was always with us now. Albert said that was as it should be, and I agreed with him and was very happy to put the past behind me.

At dinner we told the King about our visit to Blair Athole, for we had only been returned a week.

'I should have delayed my visit perhaps,' said Louis Philippe.

'Indeed not,' I assured him. 'Being home after revelling in that Highland scenery did seem a little dull . . . but your visit has enlivened us a great deal.'

He was very grateful for these shows of affection, and said the most flattering things about the castle.

Albert commented on how many royal suites we had seen in the castle—that of the King of Prussia, the Emperor of Russia, the Duke of Saxony—and now the King of France.

Vicky was brought in and introduced to the King. She behaved impeccably and he thought her as delightful as the castle.

Later there were talks between Sir Robert Peel with Lord Aberdeen, our Foreign Secretary, and Louis Philippe and Guizot. Albert and I were present.

Louis Philippe was very frank. He talked about Tahiti and the trouble there and hinted that we English had become a little too excited about it. The French, he said, did not understand the principles of negotiations as the English did; but they liked to make a clatter.

'Like postilions,' he said with a smile. 'And they do not stop to consider the bad consequences this can have. They are less calm than you English. But war . . . no . . . no . . . no! France cannot make war on England, the Triton of the Seas . . . not on England who has the greatest empire in the world.'

I basked in such talk and thought how pleasant it was to be able to deal with matters of state in such a civilized manner.

So the King dismissed the Tahiti affair.

'I would fain see it at the bottom of the sea,' he said. 'All they want from it is the whalers. I hope to get rid of it altogether.'

We showed him the surrounding country and took him to Hampton Court; and the King had an understandable desire to see the house in which he had stayed during his exile. So we drove there and afterwards to Claremont.

When we returned to Windsor a crowd was waiting and they shouted loyal greetings. I was glad the people bore no animosity to Louis Philippe and cheered him generously.

I invested him with the Garter.

It was a really most successful visit. Sir Robert was delighted and I felt gratified that it had gone off so well. What really pleased me most was Louis Philippe's feelings for Albert whom it was clear he admired very much.

'He will do wonders,' he said to me. 'He is so wise. He does not push himself forward. He grows so much upon acquaintance and will always give you good advice.'

Fervently I agreed; and I told him that I had received a very similar comment from the Emperor of Russia.

I glowed with pleasure as I always did when people showed appreciation of my beloved Albert.

At last the visit was over and it was time for the King of France to leave us. Albert and I went with him to Portsmouth but when we arrived there the rain was teeming down and the gales blowing so hard that it would have been dangerous for the King to have embarked.

Albert thought it would have been better for him to have made the shorter crossing from Dover to Calais, and ascertaining that the weather was better there, in his usual efficient manner, he made all the arrangements for the switch; and considering the King's entourage and all that had to be done on the spur of the moment, this was no mean feat.

But then Albert was so wonderful at all organization.

There was great disappointment at Portsmouth naturally; but everyone realized that this was for the best.

'It is only in this admirable country that such a thing could be brought about with so little bustle,' said the King of France.

'Albert never makes difficulties,' I said proudly. 'He calmly does what others think is impossible.'

'He is the finest of young men. He deserves you and you deserve him.'

That was a charming thing to say and it sealed the success of the visit for me.

I went aboard the ship and delighted the French by proposing the King's health and the friendship between our two nations.

Then he sailed away.

There was no doubt about it—the people were pleased with me, far more than they had been since the unfortunate death of Flora Hastings. I did believe that they had taken me back completely into their favour.

Kind and flattering comments were made in the papers. They said no sovereign was more loved than I was. I was sure that was due to my happy domestic life.

I said to Albert: 'It is an example to them all.'

And he agreed.

This was the time of visits and there followed the most exciting of them all. I had rarely seen Albert so thrilled. He was taking me to see his homeland. Albert had so many happy memories of his childhood. I believed he would never think any trees as beautiful as those of the Thuringian Forest, no mountains to compare with those he had known in his youth.

We left the children at Osborne. They loved the sea and always seemed to benefit from the beautiful air. They were sad that we were going. Vicky had desperately pleaded to come with us and at one point I had thought that Albert was on the point of relenting; but he decided that she was too young for all the travelling there would have to be; and in spite of her entreaties we decided to leave her with the others.

Vicky and Alice were with me on that August morning as I dressed. Then we had breakfast with the four children, and Lady Lyttelton and I had a last talk about them. I knew I could leave them safely in her hands for she was so devoted to them; the only thing was that Albert feared she would spoil Bertie towards whom she had taken up a kind of protective attitude; sometimes almost as though she were sheltering him from us! Good woman that she was, Albert said she was over-sentimental, and did not entirely understand the need for discipline, especially in the case of a child by nature rebellious.

We went from Osborne to Buckingham Palace, which seemed quiet without the children. Sir Robert called to assure us that we need have no qualms about the state of the country. His measures with the Irish were proving effective; and there was nothing to worry about.

We had a rough passage and poor Albert suffered somewhat; but I was sure my presence was a comfort to him and the crossing was not really of long duration.

Unfortunately when we arrived at Antwerp the rain was teeming down but the people, who were determined to welcome us, had set up triangular illuminations on tall poles, which made a fine show.

We awoke next morning to driving rain, and even as we left the yacht for the royal carriage, which Uncle Leopold had sent for us, we were almost swept off our feet.

I was reminded of my visit two years before.

'It looks so different from home,' I said to Albert; and indeed it did. I watched the women in their hats and caps and cloaks with their brass jugs going to market; and I wished I had my sketch book handy. I should have liked to put them on paper.

What joy to find Uncle Leopold and Aunt Louise waiting for us at Malines! We embraced with emotion and there was so much to discuss. They were to accompany us to Verviers, and Uncle Leopold had arranged that a great welcome should be given us in all the towns through which we passed.

Uncle Leopold was proud of his country and it was wonderful to be with him and Aunt Louise. We talked endlessly and Uncle told us once more how delighted he was to see Albert and me living together in such obvious contentment.

'Never forget,' he said, 'that I worked for your union from the day both of you were born. I have seen a dream come true.'

I told him that Albert and I could never be grateful enough.

I felt sorry for those occasions when I had thought that Uncle Leopold was interfering and trying to make me act against the advice of my ministers. I could never have done that and he must know it; but he had been very persuasive and sometimes a little hurt. And although I was sorry I knew it had been inevitable; and I should be eternally grateful to him for bringing Albert and me together.

It was sad, as always, saying goodbye to them and after we had done so we were met at Aix-la-Chapelle by the King of Prussia and members of his family.

How I loved Germany! In some measure perhaps this was because of Albert's feeling for it. It was his homeland.

The King of Prussia was determined that we should be impressed by his country; and arrangements had been made for our entertainment.

From the Palace we watched the splendid *Zapfenstreich*, the tattoo in which five hundred military musicians took part, the scene being illuminated by torches and lamps of coloured glass. I was delighted when they played *God Save the Queen*.

We had to see the magnificent surrounding country, the view of

Kreuzberg, a convent high on a hill, and the seven mountains, the *Sieben Gebirge*. It gave me a wonderful feeling of exultation; and I saw that Albert was deeply moved by my reaction to his country.

One of the highlights was the banquet at which the King gave a most stirring and heartening speech.

'Fill your glasses,' he said. 'There is a word of inexpressible sweetness to British as well as to German hearts. Thirty years ago it echoed in the heights of Waterloo from British and German tongues, after days of hot and desperate fighting, to mark the glorious triumph of our brotherhood in arms. Now it resounds on the banks of our fair Rhine, amid the blessings of that peace which was the hallowed fruit of the great conflict. The word is Victoria. Gentlemen drink to the health of Her Majesty the Queen of the United Kingdom of Great Britain and Ireland and to that of her august Consort.'

I was so moved that I turned to the King and kissed him. It was an impulsive action but it resulted in ringing applause.

It was a truly great occasion.

Being in Germany there was a great deal of music to be enjoyed, which was acceptable both to me and to Albert; and when we arrived in Bonn the Beethoven Festival was being celebrated.

There was a concert—but alas not so much Beethoven as I should have liked. There was only a part of one of the symphonies brought into a cantata by Liszt, and the overture to Egmont. There were many students present, long-haired and bearded with dashing moustaches, many of them sporting the *Säbelhiebe*, the sword cut in their faces of which they were so proud as these were an insignia of their exploits in the art of duelling.

But what Albert was looking forward to with the greatest pleasure, and naturally I shared his feelings, was the arrival at Coburg. At the frontier there were flags and crowds of cheering people; and there was Ernest, now the Duke, looking splendid in full uniform waiting to greet us.

After an emotional reunion between the brothers, Albert and I got into an open carriage, drawn by six horses, to begin our drive.

The women were all dressed in costumes with pointed caps and numerous petticoats; and the men wore leather breeches. The girls carried wreaths of flowers. It was charming.

With Ernest we went to Ketschendorf which had been the residence of our dear dead grandmother, of whom Albert had been so fond. To our great joy Uncle Leopold and Aunt Louise were there.

We rode to the palace. There girls in white, wearing green scarves, were waiting for us with flowers and complimentary verses; I was introduced to someone who was of special interest to me—Ober-superintendent Genzler—because he had officiated at the marriage of my parents and had christened and confirmed Albert and Ernest.

To be in that beautiful country—Albert's country—to see his emotion, to listen to tales of his childhood, that seemed to bring us closer together. I did a great deal of sketching during those halcyon days; I felt I wanted to catch every important detail and hold it forever. The weather was perfect—long hot days merging into each other. Albert's birthday came and we were so happy to celebrate it, not only in his country, but in the actual place of his birth, Rosenau. Albert had talked of it so much that I felt I knew it before I saw it. It was twelve years since he had spent a birthday there. There was so much to show me: the forest where he had hunted; the room where he and Ernest had studied; the holes in the wall-paper where they had pricked it while fencing—relics of a child-hood of which I felt faintly jealous because I had not been there to share it.

It was a marvellous birthday. The band played in the morning to welcome the day. It was wonderful to listen to a Chorale and Reveil and *O Isis and Osirus* from *The Magic Flute*.

Helped by Ernest and Alexandrina I had arranged the table dressed with flowers on which I had placed the presents. Mama was there. She had been visiting relatives in Germany so she joined us. In the old days that would have thrown a damper over the proceedings. Not now. Albert was delighted to see her and so was I.

The birthday celebrations continued during the morning and both Albert and I were glad when they were over to leave us free to go for a walk alone.

How we talked! He told me that it was a dream of his that Vicky should marry into Germany.

I said: 'I believe you love Vicky more than me. You talk of her constantly.'

Albert was a little shocked. 'She is our daughter!' he said reproachfully.

'Of course. Of course. Stupid of me. But then you know how I am. I say the first thing that comes into my head.'

Albert smiled and patted my hand. 'As long as you know it, my dear, you can overcome it. I was saying I want Vicky to marry into Germany. I want her to be Queen of Prussia.'

I glowed with pleasure. What a wonderful man he was! His thoughts were always for his family.

'I sounded out the King,' he went on. 'He is interested.'

'She is young yet.'

'It is never too soon to think of these matters. There must be a meeting between her and young Frederick.'

'It is looking far ahead. I want to enjoy this moment. You and I alone, Albert . . . in your beloved forest.'

He smiled at me indulgently.

Oh, that was a perfect day, one I shall remember for the rest of my life—a perfect day, with perfect weather, in perfect surroundings, with the most perfect of men.

How sad I was to leave Rosenau and Germany! There were tears and pleadings that there should be more meetings. Poor Grandmama Saxe-Coburg was almost prostrate with grief.

On the way home we must visit the King of France. Sir Robert had impressed on us that that was of the utmost importance. France would be well aware of the trip to Germany, and as we had seen the Russians, there must be an even balance of these visits. I was not a young woman visiting her relatives; I was the State.

So at Treport we met Louis Philippe and we were joined there by Lord Aberdeen and Lord Liverpool; and the Prince de Joinville and Monsieur Guizot were with the King.

We were taken to the *château* and with a certain pride were shown into the Galerie Victoria which had been adorned with pictures including one depicting the King's visit to Windsor and two beautiful Winterhalter portraits of myself and Albert. For my special pleasure, knowing my love for music, he had brought the ninety-four members of the Opéra Comique from Paris to entertain us. They performed Boïeldieu's one-act opera *Le Nouveau Seigneur* and Grétry's *Le Roi Richard*, which were most amusing and entertaining.

The following day Lord Aberdeen and I had an important conversation about Spanish affairs which were giving some concern to England; and the King was most agreeable and friendly which Lord Aberdeen thought very satisfactory.

On the next day we sailed for home. It was a wonderful finale, for the sea was exquisitely blue and as calm as a lake.

It had been a most exhilarating experience: I had enjoyed every moment; but what a joy it was to embark on the dear familiar beach near Osborne!

Lady Lyttelton was at the door with all the children waiting to greet us.

Vicky ran straight into Albert's arms; and then we fondly embraced them all.

They looked so fat and well—and above all, happy to have us back.

Dear Osborne! What a joy it was to be there! I looked forward to lazy days with drives and alfresco meals with the children and talks with Albert. I told him that there were many times when I wished I was not a queen and that he was merely a country gentleman so that we could live a family life without onerous duties.

They were wonderful days which followed the visit. We talked to the children and Albert described to Vicky the beautiful mountains and forests and the dear kind German people; and how one day he was going to take her to Rosenau and show her his childhood home. He would take her to visit the Prussian royal family of whom he was very fond; and he was sure she was going to be fond of them too.

Such halcyon days could not remain so for long and we were soon plunged into trouble.

It had been a disastrous summer. The rain had spoiled the crops and particularly the potatoes in Ireland. There was great famine there.

Sir Robert Peel was in a dilemma. The Corn Laws had remained unaltered since 1842, but Sir Robert's mind was changing. He no longer believed in protection for agriculture and was convinced that the experiment had been a failure. Corn must be exported to Ireland, he said, to take the place of the potato crop; but unfortunately the English harvest had been poor. Sir Robert believed that the Corn Laws should be suspended and he would never be a party to their being reimposed.

He said firmly: 'The remedy is the removal of all impediments to the import of all kinds of human food—that is, the total and absolute repeal for ever of all duties on all articles of sustenance.'

There was much discussion. It was a quite extraordinary situation, for Peel stood against his own party. He wanted to introduce a measure involving the ultimate repeal of the Corn Laws.

I was very sad when Sir Robert came to me and said he must tender his resignation and once more I was reminded of that occasion when Lord Melbourne had come to me with the same story. I was older now, more in command of my feelings, thanks to Albert

who had made me so much more restrained; and in any case, much
as I admired Sir Robert as a very great statesman—greater I had to
admit than Lord Melbourne—I did not have the tender feelings for
him that I had had for my first Prime Minister.

Sir Robert told me that I should ask Lord John Russell to take
his place.

I was afraid the government would fall and the Whigs come
back. How strange that I had once thought of the Whigs as *my*
government!

I was pleased when Lord John Russell refused and Sir Robert
remained in office. But our troubles were by no means over. The
Tories were against their leader. He stood alone among them fighting for the Repeal of the Corn Laws—with the Opposition firmly
behind him.

Albert said there never could have been such a case before; and
Albert stood with Sir Robert, as I did.

I had now confirmed what I had suspected and I must say that
my mind was rather taken up with my own problems for I was
pregnant once more. The fact made me irritable and very quick-
tempered.

I complained bitterly to Albert, and although he was sympathetic, I fancied he was not at all displeased. He delighted in his
growing family which, I pointed out, was all very well for him. He
did not have to endure those wretched months of discomfort culminating in an excruciating ordeal.

He said that it was one of the duties which God had ordained
women should carry out. At which I said, most irreligiously, that
God was obviously of the male gender, which reminded me of Lord
Melbourne, for it was the kind of remark he would have made; and
then we should have laughed together. But Albert was deeply
shocked—and somehow he made me feel ashamed. So I grew
calmer and said that my temper was as bad as ever, to which Albert
replied that he did believe that, under his guidance, the outbursts
occurred less frequently.

I tried hard to be reconciled and thought of the joys children
brought.

'But this must be the last,' I said.

And Albert replied: 'It is in God's hands.'

There was a great deal of unrest in the country. Sir Robert looked
worn out as well he might be. Then Albert brought down a storm
of abuse on his head by going to the House of Commons when the
debate on the Corn Laws was in progress. He had had many dis-

cussions with Sir Robert and was vitally interested in the matter. His presence, of course, was noted and then the trouble started.

What right had foreigners in the House of Commons? The House of Commons was for elected Members. Was the Prince showing his approval of Peel, who was known to be a friend of his? The country would not tolerate such conduct. It must be made clear to Prince Albert that he must never again enter the House of Commons without invitation.

It was depressing that, after all he had done, after his interest in affairs, and the fact that he was the father of the heir to the throne, they called him a foreigner.

I felt disheartened. All this—and pregnancy too!

With the Whigs firmly behind him, Sir Robert brought about the Repeal of the Corn Laws. But the government was doomed to defeat. On the same day that the Bill was passed, the government was brought down over the Irish Bill. Peel was out of office and little John Russell came to Windsor. He had been able to form a government this time and the Whigs were back in power.

Bertie was giving us a great deal of concern. He was a difficult boy. He was not at all bright at his lessons; he was constantly in trouble in spite of the fact that Lady Lyttelton and Miss Hildyard, the governess, were always trying to shield him.

Of course Vicky's cleverness put him at a disadvantage. I once said to Albert that, but for Vicky, he would seem quite an ordinary boy.

Albert agreed that Vicky was exceptionally bright but in his opinion Bertie was exceptionally dull. There was that unfortunate stutter. The Prince of Wales stuttering! It was unheard of.

'Lady Lyttelton thinks it is due to nervousness,' I said. 'She insists that when she is alone with him he hardly ever does it.'

'Then he can stop it if he wishes.'

'I believe he tries, Albert.'

'The cane will make him try harder.'

I used to hate it when Bertie was beaten—a task which Albert nobly undertook himself. Bertie grew a little defiant; he said it wasn't fair.

I talked to him and told him what a good father he had, a father who suffered more than he did when punishment was necessary.

Bertie said: 'Papa only has to stop hurting me and then he won't have to suffer.'

I tried to explain that God sometimes had to inflict suffering or

people and it was always for their own good. All Bertie had to do
was be a better boy.

I talked to Lady Lyttelton. She pursed her lips and looked stubborn. I was very fond of her and in a way I was glad she was rather
soft. I knew that after one of the punishments, so necessarily in-
flicted by Albert, she went in and cuddled Bertie and comforted
him. She had some special ointment for the weals.

I should have told Albert, of course, but I knew he would have
stopped that comforting, and although I knew he was right, I am
afraid I was a little weak too; and after all Bertie was not so very
old.

Albert had entreated Stockmar to come to England as he wished
to consult him very earnestly about his eldest son; and to our joy
Stockmar came.

We went to Windsor with him and there we discussed Bertie's
conduct. Albert said sadly that he had been forced to administer the
cane, which was so very distressing for him, and moreover, so far,
it had had little effect on the boy.

Stockmar thought we had been too soft with him. 'You tell me
there are women in the nursery and the schoolroom. Women are
notoriously soft. There is no doubt that they pamper the boy. I
should like to see the schoolroom and speak to these ladies who are
in charge of it.'

We took him to the schoolroom.

Vicky was seated at the table writing. Bertie was beside her and
Alice was there too.

As we entered they all rose. Vicky and Alice curtsied and Bertie
bowed. They looked very sweet—except Bertie who had a smudge
on his blouse.

'Children,' I said, 'this is a great friend of Papa's and mine,
Baron Stockmar.'

The children looked at the Baron, and I could see they did not
greatly take to him.

'Vicky . . . Bertie . . .' said Albert, and they came forward.

'Our daughter,' said Albert proudly.

Vicky smiled.

'This is Bertie.'

'The backward one,' said the Baron, at which Bertie flinched.

'He does badly because he does not try,' said Albert.

I saw a defiant look creeping into Bertie's face. Oh dear, I
thought, he is going to be difficult.

Vicky who could not bear to have the attention turned from her said: 'I am not backward. I am very good . . . at everything.'

Albert smiled and laid a restraining hand on her shoulder. She smiled up at him charmingly, sure of his approval.

'You must not speak until the Baron addresses you, my child,' said Albert

'Why not?' asked Vicky.

Albert looked at me in tender exasperation.

'Because Papa says so,' I told her.

'Oh,' she said.

'The boy seems sullen,' said the Baron. 'Perhaps I should see his work.'

Miss Hildyard was rather flustered. She began talking of Bertie's qualities. She thought he had a good imagination. He was quite inventive. But the Baron thought that meant he had a tendency to lie.

'The younger children adore him,' said Miss Hildyard. 'It is good to see their little faces light up when he comes in. He makes up games for them and can amuse them for hours. They love him dearly as,' she looked at us defiantly—'we all do.'

'Yes, yes,' said Stockmar impatiently. 'I do not like overmuch what I hear.'

'I am sure,' Miss Hildyard went on, 'that Bertie will be good at his lessons . . . given time.'

The Baron said he had heard and seen enough and would like to talk in private with Albert and me.

When we were alone he said, 'How different he is from you, Prince Albert. I remember well how serious you were. I am afraid the boy takes after some of his Hanoverian ancestors. That must make us very watchful.'

'I want him to grow up exactly like his father,' I said.

'We shall have to work hard to bring about that miracle,' said Stockmar.

'We were hoping you might advise us,' I said

'In the first place he is surrounded by women, and saving Your Majesty's presence, women are too lenient where children are concerned. They spare the rod and spoil the child.'

'So I have always thought,' said Albert.

Stockmar went on: 'We shall take him from the care of that woman, Miss Hildyard.'

'She is a very clever woman,' I said.

'Maybe she is but she is no match for a slothful, wayward boy.

I propose that we engage a tutor. I will immediately look for the right man, and when I have found him, I will impress on him the need for sternest discipline.'

'Dear Baron,' I said, 'I knew you would find the solution.'

It was not long before Stockmar came to tell us that he had engaged Henry Birch, Rector of Prestwich, who had taught at Eton.

The fact of his calling made him appear to be eminently suitable and I was delighted.

In due course Henry Birch arrived and eagerly we awaited results.

He was clearly pleased by the appointment.

Albert and I, with the Baron, took him to the schoolroom.

'Here is the Prince of Wales,' I said. 'Come, Bertie, and greet your new tutor.'

Bertie came forward eyeing Mr. Birch with the utmost suspicion.

'You will find the Prince of Wales somewhat backward,' said Stockmar. 'He is not given to study. He needs to be prodded. I have worked out a curriculum with His Highness, the Prince, and I am sure that, if you will follow it, you cannot go wrong. You will need to be very firm and Her Majesty and the Prince give you the right to punish however severely you may deem necessary.'

'Oh,' said Mr. Birch, 'I hope that will not be necessary.'

I could see Bertie was growing a little fearful and I was not really surprised. In my heart I thought there was no need to give the child such a reputation before Mr. Birch had had a chance of finding out for himself.

Albert was saying: 'I have, on occasions, had to whip Bertie myself, which was most distressing to me.'

Bertie looked dismayed as though he was expecting the cane to be brought out immediately; and I must say I was rather glad when the meeting was over.

Mr. Birch remained behind with Bertie; and we all left him to discuss our impressions.

It had not been possible to assess Mr. Birch, but as the Baron said, his calling gave him a certain standing; and Albert said that as the Baron had chosen him, he was sure the choice would prove satisfactory.

And I believe it was. Mr. Birch reported that Bertie was by no means dull. His interest was easily aroused; he was improving in his lessons and was finding study quite absorbing.

I saw Bertie once or twice with his tutor. Bertie was smiling happily; he had lost his stutter; and it was clear to me that he was not in the least in awe of Mr. Birch.

I did not tell Albert this because I thought that he might be of the opinion that the boy *should* be afraid of his tutor if the tutor was doing his work properly; but in view of the progress he was making Albert did not raise this point.

As for Lady Lyttelton she seemed very happy about the arrangements. She could not say enough that was good about Mr. Birch.

I was very pleased. I hoped there would be no more trouble. It was so distressing for Albert to have to chastise Bertie.

Osborne was a great consolation during those difficult days.

We had decided that charming as it was, it was scarcely fit for a royal residence; and Albert was planning extensive alterations.

As everything Albert did was done with absolute thoroughness, he was completely absorbed in the project.

He was in consultation with Thomas Cubitt, that very modern builder, and they discussed the alterations at length before the plans were made.

The Solent reminded Albert of the Bay of Naples.

'So,' he said, 'we will have a Neapolitan villa—high towers, with perhaps a loggia on the first floor. There should be a pavilion wing and two eastern wings, with accommodation for servants and officials of the country who may have to come down from time to time.'

Albert had worked out how all this should be paid for. I had sold the Pavilion at Brighton to the Brighton Town Commissioners; and thanks to all the savings Albert had made on the household economies at Buckingham Palace, we had about a quarter of a million pounds to spend on this new Osborne.

Albert found great pleasure, not only in the rebuilding, but in the laying out of the gardens. He had tried to work on those of Buckingham Palace but the Commissioners had made such a fuss. Here it was different. We had our own house. I even had my own bathing-machine on the beach; it had a curtained veranda and was really charming. Albert had fir trees—Christmas trees, we called them now—imported from Germany; and we had a playroom sent over from Switzerland which we called the Swiss Cottage; and as he was anxious that the children should not be idle here, the girls learned to cook and do all sorts of domestic tasks, while the boys had tools and did woodwork. That was later on though.

We could see the ships sailing by and Albert said that perhaps the Prince of Wales would be impressed by them and want to join the Navy.

Osborne, the scene of many a delightful holiday, was precious to me because of Albert's creations.

While the work was progressing, he was constantly inspecting it. He would go out, even at night, because some little detail occurred to him.

There was an amusing incident which happened one night when he had thought of something he wanted to see in the grounds and had gone out in the dark to look at it.

A policeman, seeing him, arrested him.

Albert protested, but the policeman refused to listen to him; and as the servants' quarters were quite near, he took Albert to them.

The poor policeman was overcome with shame.

The next day Albert summoned him to appear before him. Albert was unsmiling and I am sure the poor man thought he was going to lose his job. Then Albert commended him on his prompt action and told him that he had recommended him for promotion.

The poor man went away bemused. Albert and I laughed a great deal over the incident.

'I should have been impulsive,' I said. 'I should have complimented him immediately. Just think what agonies he must have suffered during the night.'

'It would do him no harm,' said Albert. 'And it makes my approval even more appreciated.'

Dear Albert, he always thought of what was *good* for people.

To my horror, dismay and fury, I was once more pregnant. This would be my sixth child. It was too much. I hated the entire business. I had been enjoying life so much—and could have done so completely if there had not been so many unpleasant state matters which seemed to flare up every now and then.

I did not like the new Foreign Secretary, Lord Palmerston. How different from dear Lord Aberdeen! I was sure Lord Palmerston withheld information from us; and he and Albert were not on very good terms.

And now . . . another baby, which was due in April!

Then came terrible news.

There was revolution again in France. This was a repeat performance of what had happened at the end of last century. I had read of that in horror; I had wept for poor vain Marie Antoinette, whom I had seen as not unlike myself in my early days before I had learned so much from Albert, and poor Louis her husband who wanted to be good but was so weak. But this was different. This was people I knew.

The mob was marching on the Tuileries.

Poor Aunt Louise! She would be frantic. She was devoted to her family, and what would the mob do to her poor father? Not what they had done to his predecessor, I prayed.

News drifted in. How at midnight the tocsins had rung out, which was the sign of the people to revolt. Then the French King had abdicated.

I kept thinking of myself in similar circumstances. It is true that 'uneasy lies the head that wears a crown'.

Lord Palmerston came to see me. He was rather supercilious. Why had I ever thought I liked him? He used to pay me extravagant compliments and Lord Melbourne had told me stories about his amours which had seemed amusing then, but which would have shocked Albert and, therefore, now shocked me.

Albert was with me but Palmerston addressed himself to me as though counting Albert of no consequence.

He said: 'The King of France will doubtless attempt to leave his country. The Foreign Office would not object to a ship's being put at his disposal; but I must point out that, in my opinion, the country would object to harbouring members of the French Royal family on this soil.'

'I have family connections with the King of France,' I said.

'Most unfortunate, M'am. But you must remember how matters stand in this country at the moment. Your Majesty knows that there have been signs of unrest. It would not be wise to provoke them by taking sides in this foreign conflict.'

'You are advising me to desert my family,' I said.

Lord Palmerston lifted his shoulders, and began to speak slowly and clearly, as though to children. 'Unrest of this nature in our neighbours, who are so close to us, must make us pause to think. Revolution spreads like fire. We have to take precautions. We have to act with the utmost care.'

'In England . . .' I began.

He had the temerity to interrupt which was typical of Lord Palmerston. 'Even in England, M'am, and most certainly, I should say, in some of the smaller states of Europe.'

Alarm was in Albert's eyes. He murmured: 'This is true.'

'You say I may offer them a ship . . .'

How degrading to have to ask the permission of this man to help

my friends! I knew that he was right, of course; but that did not
make me like him any more.

Shortly afterwards he called on us again. Albert was with me when
I received him. He told me that the King and Queen of France were
in England.

'They landed at Newhaven,' he said, 'having been brought over
in the Steam Packet Express onto which they embarked at Le Havre
yesterday evening. When they heard that a Republic had been declared they thought it unsafe to stay in France. I understand that the
King's intentions are to remain in England in the strictest incognito;
and he and the Queen will assume the titles of the Count and Countess of Neuilly.'

I thought that the odious man was going to suggest that we send
them back, but he did not.

He went on: 'Perhaps Your Majesty could offer them Claremont.
It is, after all, almost a private residence.'

'We shall do that,' I said fervently, looking at Albert, who nodded, lowering his head, so great was his grief.

'They will leave Newhaven tomorrow,' added Lord Palmerston.

'At least,' I said to Albert when Lord Palmerston had left, 'we
can offer them shelter here.'

There were letters from Uncle Leopold and Aunt Louise; and I
was blinded by my tears as I read them. I was so desperately sorry
for Aunt Louise for I knew how fond she was of her parents.

As she was sealing her letter she heard that they had arrived in
England, and enclosed a letter for her mother which she begged me
to give to her.

Uncle Leopold wrote most pathetically, telling me how unwell
the news from Paris had made him. 'What will become of us, God
knows. Great efforts will be made to incite a revolution in this
country. We have a right to claim protection from England and
other powers. I can write no more. God bless you.'

Poor poor Uncle Leopold and even poorer Aunt Louise!

There was great uneasiness in the air. Life never seems to deal
one blow at a time. We heard that our dear Grandmother Coburg
had died. Albert who had been her special boy in his early days—
and always—was grief-stricken. There was no question of his going
to Coburg for the funeral. This was not a time to leave me and the
children.

There was more to follow.

Lord John Russell came to the Palace in a state of great perturbation. The Chartists were massing in Trafalgar Square and he feared they might decide to come to the Palace.

I was quite advanced in my pregnancy at this time and I felt utterly weary and very worried about the children.

I said they should be kept in the schoolroom and not told what was happening unless it was absolutely necessary. When Albert came in I clung to him, for if the mob broke into the Palace I feared he was the one they would attack. They had always hated him, jeered at him for being a German and refused to see all the good he had done; they shut their eyes to his fine character and called him smug.

In my imagination, I could hear the shouts of the people in the distance. I saw them surging up the Mall. I sat down, Albert beside me, holding my hand.

'If it comes,' I said, 'you will be beside me.'

'I shall protect you,' he replied.

'They will not harm me . . . in this condition.'

'I would not trust them.'

We sat there waiting as time passed. I listened. It seemed very quiet.

Lord John was shown in. He looked exhausted.

He said: 'I have come to tell Your Majesty that all is well. The crowds are dispersing. They had no real heart for revolution. Our people are not made of the same stuff as the French, M'am.'

'Thank God they are not,' I said with feeling.

Albert put his arm round me.

'They left Trafalgar Square shouting slogans,' said Lord John. 'Then they rushed into the Mall. There, some of them seemed to lose heart and drifted away. It was the signal for others to do so. I heard some of them say, "It is not the Queen's fault. It is her government and . . ."'

He did not finish and I knew he meant Albert.

I was indignant, but my relief was greater than all other emotions. I just leaned against Albert and gave myself up to the luxury of having him and the family safe.

Among all these emotional disturbances, I did not forget Lord Melbourne. I wrote to him regularly. I had heard that he hardly ever emerged from Brocket these days and that he had become a little absentminded at times, believing he was living in the past, remembering old glories, thinking of the days no doubt when he had been the confidant of the Queen. Dear Lord Melbourne, although I now looked back on my relationship with him with tender amusement, I still cherished many memories.

I wrote to him:

'The Queen cannot let this day pass without offering Lord Melbourne her and the Prince's best wishes for many happy returns in health and strength . . .'

A few days after I wrote that letter my child was born—another little girl: Louise Caroline Alberta. It had not been such a very difficult birth but it left me exhausted. I did not want to leave my bed but lay there listlessly, thinking of the terrible things which were happening in the world.

I felt so limp and ill; and I was growing quite fat which was distressing. Albert used to carry me from the bed to the sofa. I think he was very sorry for all I had to go through, bearing children. It must have seemed unfair—even to him—that women should have to bear the entire burden and when the child was born the husband had such delight in her as Albert had in Vicky. He was obviously her favourite, too, as she was his, yet I had been the one who had had to suffer for her.

Ignoble thoughts, no doubt. But then that was my nature. Albert would have been shocked if I spoke some of my thoughts aloud and would have pointed out the error of them. Well, I would indulge them while I pondered on the hateful process of giving birth. Something more dignified might have been devised.

It was April. Soon I should have another birthday. How quickly they seemed to come nowadays. I remembered how long I had waited for my eighteenth. Now the years sped by.

Albert was with me and about to read to me when Lord John arrived. I only had to look at his face to see his concern.

'Not fresh trouble, Lord John, I hope?' I said.

'I fear so, Your Majesty. The Chartists are to have a meeting on the tenth of this month and it will take place in London. It seems to your Cabinet that this time they may be bent on trouble.'

'Lord John,' I said, 'I am not yet recovered from the birth of the Princess. How can they do this?'

'They are concerned only with their rights, M'am. I have come to tell you that we shall take every precaution to protect you, your family and the Palace.'

'Do they say they are coming to me?'

'No, M'am. To the House of Commons. But mobs are unpredictable. One can never be sure what they will do. I thought you should be warned without delay. I shall return with Cabinet plans for the protection of you and the Palace.'

I felt horribly depressed. Oh, how hateful it all was! How different from the days when I had driven with Mama in my carriage and the people had shouted their good wishes for me.

Lord John called again.

'Your Majesty,' he said, 'the Cabinet have decided that you should leave as soon as possible for Osborne. There are a few days before the march is due to take place. Could you leave tomorrow?'

Albert said we could.

I was angry. To be turned out of my Palace by my subjects! It was inconceivable. I said I had a good mind to stay.

Albert looked at me with a sad shake of his head, reminding me that to lose my temper would be no use whatever.

On the eighth of April, two days before the Chartists' march was due to take place, we left for Osborne.

In any other circumstances I should have delighted in Osborne, but how could I when I did not know what was happening in London and when I contemplated the terrible situation in France!

Albert was very gloomy. He said that revolution was an evil weed which, once it had been allowed to take root, grew like wild fire and could appear anywhere . . . even in the most unexpected places. Europe trembled. Italy was in revolt; in Germany there were uprisings; and there was a great deal of uneasiness everywhere. This worried Albert very much and spoilt our wonderful Osborne for us both.

News came from London that the Chartists' march had come to nothing. Instead of the large numbers expected only a few arrived, and when they were warned by the police that the march was illegal, they immediately disbanded.

The leaders were taken to the House of Commons where they presented the petitions they had prepared, and that was the end of the matter.

We breathed more easily.

Albert said: 'The English are not of a revolutionary nature. Of course there will always be those who seek to arouse it. Some of these would come from abroad—or might even be natives. It is well known that the French Revolution owed its success to agitators. Thank God, this terrible thing has been averted.'

But a few days later one of the servants reported that Chartists had been seen on the Island.

The suspense was terrible. We herded the children into the schoolroom and Albert said we must prepare for the defence of the house, though how we could hold out against a gang of rioters I had no idea.

Happily this turned out to be a false alarm. The so-called Chartists were members of a club who had come to the island to enjoy a day's outing. Such was our state at that time that we were ready to believe our lives were in constant danger.

It was an uneasy summer. There was constant talk of revolution. Uncle Leopold stood firm in Belgium.

'The people must remember what he has done for them,' said Albert. 'I know that life has improved for them under his rule.'

'People are so stupid. They follow the mob, and if there is a fiery leader who can inspire them, they forget all that has been done for their good.'

Albert agreed with me.

Through the hot and hazy days the menace hung over us. The children played in the Swiss Cottage. They must have been aware of the tension. Vicky was too bright not to be. But they did their cooking, and Bertie and Affie—Alfred, of course—played with their woodwork tools. They had their lessons; and we tried to make everything seem normal.

Albert said: 'The Isle of Wight is very vulnerable . . . if there was trouble. I wonder if we might go farther afield. I should love to see Scotland again—a beautiful country.'

I thought that was an excellent idea.

Lord John came down to see us and when we mentioned our desire to see Scotland again he thought it would be a good plan for us to go. He told us that the tension had relaxed considerably. People remembered the terrible disaster the French had suffered last century. After all it was not so long ago. They had seen the effects of revolution and wanted none of it here.

He believed the English had too much good sense, and that we were coming through this scare as we had when the great revolution was raging in France.

'The English have not the mood for revolution,' he said. 'Europe is shaking, though. I think Russia will be safe. The Emperor has great control over his people; so much so that they would never be able to rise.'

He said he would make enquiries about a house in Scotland which we could rent.

'I should like it to be in the Highlands,' said Albert. 'I had only a brief glimpse of them, but I found the country magnificent.'

Shortly afterwards we heard of a house which could be rented from the Fife Trustees. It was Balmoral House.

Very soon we were preparing to go, and as soon as I saw Balmoral, I loved it . . . and so did Albert. It was small but very pretty; but it was the scenery around which was enchanting—it was wild, solitary and beautifully wooded.

'What a place I could make here!' said Albert; and I could see plans forming in his mind just as they had at Osborne.

I laughed at him; and it seemed that we were happy and at peace for the first time for months.

I had not been in Balmoral for a week before I knew that it was going to be important to us.

War and Mutiny

That had been a very disturbing year and I hoped never to pass through another like it.

In November, Lord Melbourne died. Although I knew that he had been ailing for some time, and life could not have been very good for him, I was deeply shocked.

I had often thought of him and his lonely life at Brocket—he who had sparkled in social gatherings, delivering that pithy wit, with its cynicism and unconventionality which had seemed so clever to me in those early days. How we had laughed together! How I had rejoiced in his friendship! How unhappy I had been when I feared to lose him! What he had meant to me I should never forget.

Albert had explained to me that he was not a statesman of the stature of Sir Robert Peel, and I had had to admit that Albert was right; but Lord Melbourne had been a very special person to me.

Albert could not understand the depth of my grief but it was there nonetheless.

It always saddened me when people died, even those whom I had not known very well; but when it was someone for whom I had cared as I had for Lord Melbourne, it was hard to bear—particularly in that alarming year of unrest.

I was glad when the New Year came.

I was spending more time with the children and finding them interesting now that they were growing up. It was just those frog-like babies who did not appeal to me; but as they began to assume human qualities I found them fascinating. I was pleased with my brood—even Bertie, who stuttered much less now that Mr. Birch had come. Mr. Birch gave us such good reports of him that Albert grew a little suspicious and said that he may have caught Lady Lyttelton's and Miss Hildyard's complaint—which was spoiling the boy.

However, Stockmar had chosen Mr. Birch, and that was in his favour. Although, said Albert, Bertie's attachment to the tutor must be watched.

Albert had been depressed about what was happening in France and Germany, and wanted a little peace for a while. He gave himself up to the pleasures of Osborne. There he spent hours in the Swiss Cottage with the children; he took them for walks and talked to them about the trees and plants.

I enjoyed it so much although there were times when I wished that Albert and I could be alone without the children. I had come to the conclusion that I was meant to be a wife rather than a mother. Much as I loved my children it was my husband who was all important to me.

I think I was a little jealous of Vicky for she claimed so much of his attention and sometimes he seemed to prefer to be with her rather than with me. Once I taxed him with it and we almost quarrelled—until he made me so ashamed. To be jealous of my own daughter!

I said that he was unfair to Bertie and that to talk about others spoiling him was amusing, considering how he spoilt Vicky.

The storm blew over, but a little resentment remained, though it did not spoil those happy days. And happy they were! For a short period I was not pregnant. A joy in itself! I could give myself up to the pleasures of Osborne—the sun, the sea breezes, the sight of the ships going up and down the Solent, my dear house which Albert had made, going down to the sea and from my bathing-machine experiencing the thrill of slipping into the water.

It was wonderful, and I was foolish to allow all that to be spoilt by petty jealousy of my own daughter on whom I doted as much as Albert did—or almost. I loved my children. It was just that I loved Albert more.

In the autumn we went back to Scotland and took Balmoral again. I think Scotland was even more wonderful than the Isle of Wight. Albert loved it more because it reminded him of the mountains and glens of his home.

He said: 'I should like Balmoral to be our very own. The house is small but I could turn it into a royal residence.'

Why not? I thought. He was so good. He should have been an architect; and it would give him and us all so much pleasure.

The dear people of Scotland took us to their hearts as we did them to ours. I was already learning the names of the tenants. There was old Mrs. Grant who was so tidy and clean; and none of them was in the least overawed by royalty, the dear simple folk! There was one woman of ninety—Kitty Kear—who sat near her open door spinning; as we passed and talked to her, she did not even stop her work but remarked about Vicky: 'Yon lassie has grown a wee bit since she were here last.' I learned about their families and characteristics; I dressed my children in kilts to show the people that we really felt ourselves to belong to their country.

I knew that Balmoral was going to be our favourite haven to which we could escape when affairs in London became too trying. There we felt far away . . . in a different world. It was just what we needed.

But alas, to my dismay and indignation, I was soon pregnant again.

There was terrible news from Ireland which was suffering acutely from the potato famine. People were dying in their thousands and being buried in communal graves. They had murdered some of the landlords. There was revolt there as in the European countries.

I was deeply shocked when, as we were driving down Constitution Hill, a man came up close to the carriage and fired at me. I should have been killed if the gun had been loaded.

He was an Irishman named William Hamilton who blamed me for the terrible state of affairs in his country.

I was sorry for the man. I understood his anger. It must be terrible to see one's family and friends suffering from starvation when others have plenty. I would have pardoned him—after all, he had only given me a fright. But Lord John pointed out that that sort of thing could not be allowed to go on. It was a mistake to show mercy when it could be counted as weakness.

William Hamilton was transported for seven years.

That May my child was born. A boy this time—Arthur William Patrick Albert. There were seven of them now—all strong and healthy. Even the people were finding my fertility a little monotonous and there were unpleasant murmurings about the cost of the royal family to the taxpayer.

I agreed with them that I had had enough. I was now thirty-one years old. Quite a mature age and a time when I thought I should have earned a respite from this onerous task. I had done my duty. Let it rest there.

Albert was full of ideas for an exhibition he was planning. It was to show the industrial products of the world. Under his direction a Royal Commission was set up. He was working very hard on the project and he thought Hyde Park would be the very place where it should be set up. It was to be like a big glass palace.

Of course he had to fight a great deal of opposition. There were those who could not agree to Hyde Park as the setting—when it was obviously the very best place. Albert was in despair.

'They are against me,' he said. 'They cannot forget that I am a German. I hear that on every side.'

'Only from the stupid,' I said. 'There are so many people who admire you and more and more are learning to do so.'

I shall never forget that July day when the tragic news was brought to me.

Sir Robert—whom I had begun by hating—was now a very dear friend and I could not believe this had happened to him. He was riding his horse up Constitution Hill when it became restive and threw him. He was carried to his home in Whitehall Gardens; and four days later he was dead.

It was a great blow to the country. We had lost one of our finest statesmen.

I was so distressed to think of poor Julia Peel. She had been such a good wife to him and they were such an exceptionally devoted couple that it had been a joy to see them together. She had made herself his companion and helpmeet throughout all his struggles and triumphs. They had five sons and two daughters—a devoted family, now plunged into mourning.

First my dear Lord Melbourne and now Sir Robert Peel. Life was very sad.

There had been so many deaths recently. Poor Aunt Sophia had gone. Aunt Gloucester was very feeble-minded and behaved oddly. It could not be long before she joined her sister. Uncle Cambridge was ill. Of course they were all getting old. Even I was thirty-one.

Then came terrible news from Uncle Leopold. Aunt Louise was very ill. The fate of her parents had upset her so much and she was so weakened that when illness came to her she was unable to fight it off. Uncle Leopold was very melancholy.

I took some of the children to visit Uncle Cambridge. He liked to see them and they cheered him considerably. Vicky was not with us; she was, as so often, with her father. Bertie seemed much brighter without her; and Alfred and Alice, who were with us on this occasion, were his devoted slaves.

We could not stay long at Kensington Palace because poor Uncle Cambridge was so very ill, and we were soon driving back to Buckingham Palace. The crowd pressed close to the carriage. The people were always interested to see the children. I had taught them to wave and Bertie did it with a special exuberance which always delighted the crowd.

Suddenly a man ran up to the carriage and lifting his cane he brought it down on my head. I was just aware of the children's bewildered faces as I fainted.

I was bruised and shaken and the doctors said that my bonnet had probably saved my life—or at least saved me from dreadful injuries.

These attempts on my life were becoming common occurrences. I supposed it was something which someone in my position should expect.

The doctors said I must rest, but I was due to go to the opera that evening, and as I felt well enough, I said I would go in spite of my bruises.

The reception I was given was tremendous. I think that incident did a great deal to bring out the loyalty of the people. It seemed incredible that a short time ago we were in fear of the Chartists who were planning to march on Buckingham Palace.

It was wonderful to have them applauding me again.

'Long live the Queen!' What glorious words! The incident was worth while to provoke such emotion. I must have looked grotesque. The skin round one eye was blue and yellow; but if my head was throbbing, I did not care. I just wanted to be there listening to their demonstrations of affection.

I was less pleased to discover the identity of the man who had attacked me. He was Robert Pate, whose father had been High Sheriff of Cambridge, so he came of a good family. It seemed incomprehensible that he could have behaved so. He was not insane, but he was sentenced to seven years transportation.

My bruises remained for several weeks and I felt very resentful that I should be exposed to insults and dangers of that kind, unable to go for a quiet drive without being in fear of my life.

It seemed extremely brutal to me, for a man to strike any woman, and far worse than attempting to shoot; and the fact that there seemed no real motive for this man's crime worried me considerably, particularly as he was of a good family.

There were two more deaths that year. Uncle Adolphus of Cambridge whom we had expected to die for he was very ill; but what was most tragic was that of Aunt Louise.

Poor Uncle Leopold. My grief for him was great. I thought of how he had lost his dear Charlotte all those years ago and found happiness with Louise. She had suffered so much in her fears for her family which must surely have hastened her end.

Oh, the wickedness of these violent people who seemed to find such pleasure in trying to wreck our lives.

It seemed that there must always be someone in the government who gave us trouble; and it was usually a person in a high place. The thorn in our flesh at this time was Lord Palmerston. Albert disliked him intensely. He had a rather amusing nickname for him. When we were alone Albert always called him *Pilgerstein* which came about by translating his name into German. *Pilger* palmer and *stein* stone.

I suppose there could not have been two men less alike than Albert and Lord Palmerston and this was probably responsible for Albert's antipathy. What Palmerston thought of Albert I was not entirely sure. I think he was one of those who regarded my husband as smug. He treated him with a modicum of respect but when we were together he would address himself to me as though to remind Albert that he was only the consort.

There was nothing more liable to wound Albert, for he did work very hard and was cognizant of affairs—in fact more so than I was and to be treated as though he were of no importance was very galling.

Palmerston's reputation was shady. He was known as a libertine and as a bachelor had had countless mistresses until he finally settled down at the age of fifty-five with the dowager Lady Cowper who was three years younger than he was.

Lady Cowper had been Emily Lamb, Lord Melbourne's sister, and she had married Earl Cowper when she was eighteen years old. She was a brilliant woman—as one would expect Lord Melbourne's sister to be—and the young and ambitious Palmerston was welcomed at the Cowpers' London residence as well as at Panshanger, their country seat. It was said that Emily and Palmerston had long been lovers and on the death of Earl Cowper they were married.

The marriage had turned out to be a great success. They were devoted to each other and she did everything possible to further his career. She was already a celebrated hostess and being deeply involved in politics she acted as his private secretary and adviser.

He was an individualist, determined to manage the Foreign Office as he thought best, going his own way and caring for no one. It was not surprising that he should incense us.

Albert and I discussed him continually, trying to think of ways of driving him from the Foreign Office, which, as I said to Albert, was just about the most dangerous post he could hold.

Albert thought he should be dismissed on moral grounds. There were all sorts of stories about him, one in which he had walked into a lady's bedchamber after the household had retired—in Windsor Castle of all places!—and attempted to make love to her. Sometimes I thought of what Lord Melbourne's comments would have been in these matters and I had to suppress a giggle, for they would certainly not have been Albert's.

Palmerston seemed to enjoy working against royalty and it was almost as though he placed himself on the side of the rebels. This was most disloyal. Some time before he had been accused of supplying Sicilian rebels with arms from the Royal Ordnance because he thought their fight against the tyrannical King was just. This had resulted in an apology being asked for from us to the King.

Lord John wanted to give Pam—as he was affectionately called by the people—an earldom and the Garter and send him to Ireland. I was against that. 'It would seem like rewarding him,' I said. In the end Palmerston apologized to the King and the affair was hushed up.

Lord John then asked me to receive him at Court, impressing on me that as he was my Foreign Minister, I could do nothing else; so Albert and I complied with icy politeness which only seemed to amuse Palmerston. He was incorrigible.

When the Austrian General Haynau was visiting England, Palmerston made his sympathy with rebels plain. Haynau had suppressed the people's rising in Hungary with great cruelty. We did hear in the Press that he had publicly flogged women, and there were many stories of his savagery.

When he was in London he visited a brewery where the draymen set upon him, handled him very roughly and might even have killed him if the police had not arrived in time.

General Haynau was furious at such treatment and demanded that the offenders be punished.

Lord Palmerston refused to allow this.

'General Haynau is regarded in this country as a criminal,' he said. 'He was treated by the draymen as people would treat a callous murderer if they caught him.'

Albert and I discussed the matter at great length.

'He was a visitor to England,' Albert pointed out. 'What was done was an insult to Austria, and an apology should be sent immediately.'

I wrote to Lord Palmerston and told him that I wanted him to write an apology and bring it to me for my approval before it was submitted.

When he arrived at the Palace I fancied there was a certain truculence about him, but there always was, as though he was reminding himself—and us—that the Foreign Office took orders from no one—not even the Queen.

I said how much I regretted what had happened.

'It is really a matter for rejoicing,' said Lord Palmerston blandly, 'for the police arrived in time. Otherwise the General might not be here to complain of his treatment.'

'Show me the apology,' I said.

He bowed and handed it to me.

It was cleverly worded and almost insolent, I thought. Palmerston had finished by saying that in view of the General's reputation, which had been freely commented upon here, it had been rather unwise of him to visit England.

'You cannot say that,' I said.

I held out the paper to Albert who read it and shook his head vigorously.

'That must be removed,' I said.

'It's too late, M'am,' said Palmerston with that impertinent grin of his. 'The apology has already been sent.'

'Then there must be another apology. We will say that this was a mistake. Please, Lord Palmerston, prepare a draft and I wish to see this one *before* it is sent.'

'It would not be possible, M'am, for your Foreign Secretary to do this.'

'But it is *my* wish. I shall insist.'

'Then if Your Majesty insists, I shall no longer be your Foreign Secretary. Have I Your Majesty's leave to retire?'

'Yes,' I said fiercely.

When he had gone my temper got the better of me. 'You must be calm,' said Albert. 'The Prime Minister is the only one who can dismiss the Foreign Secretary.'

'I shall insist that he dismisses Palmerston.'

Albert shook his head. 'Alas,' he repeated, 'it is for the Prime Minister to decide.'

'We must get rid of him.'

'One of these days he will go too far,' said Albert.

'I pray that day may be soon.'

* * *

I can only say that Palmerston was a most flamboyant man. He was always at the centre of some controversy. It was not long after the Haynau affair that he was involved in another crisis.

He was, in a manner of speaking, a public hero. The people applauded his actions. 'Good old Pam,' they said affectionately. If there was any trouble in any part of the world where he thought the prestige of Britain was threatened, he would send out gunboats to sail up and down the coast of the offending nation; and I have to say it usually had the desired effect. This show of strength was what people liked. Those who one day would be rioting would the next be waving flags and shouting 'Rule Britannia'. Gunboat Pam was a hero to them.

It was in the autumn when the Hungarian patriot, Kossuth, visited this country. I did wish these people would stay away. There was no reason why we should be involved in their quarrels.

Kossuth had tried to free Hungary from the Austrian yoke, and when he had failed, thousands of people had fled from Hungary and Poland seeking refuge in Turkey. Austria, with her ally Russia, had demanded that they be sent back.

Why Palmerston must involve us in the matter, I could not see— but Palmerston was a law unto himself. He advised the Sultan of Turkey to give the men refuge; and to show England's feelings in the matter, as was his practice, out came the gunboats to prowl through the Dardanelles. He was not threatening Russia, he explained, he was merely comforting the Turks. 'It is like holding a bottle of salts to a lady who has been frightened,' he said. 'I am the bottle holder.'

He had wonderful gifts of oratory and when he explained his outrageous actions in Parliament, he always seemed to be able to carry his listeners along with him, so that however hostile they had been at the beginning, he managed to win them over in the end.

As a result Kossuth visited England and the radicals gave him a tumultuous welcome.

'This is dangerous,' said Albert. 'No one disputes the fact that Kossuth is a brave man, but he was a rebel, and in the state of the world at the present time, however brave, rebels should not be encouraged.'

Palmerston then declared that not only would he receive Kossuth but he should be a guest in his house.

This was too much. As a private person Palmerston might invite whomsoever he pleased, but not as the British Foreign Secretary.

I sent for Lord John and told him that if Palmerston received

Kossuth in his house I would personally dismiss him from Court. On this occasion Lord John agreed with me.

I was delighted. Albert and I congratulated ourselves that we had at last got rid of our enemy.

But not so. When confronted with the ultimatum, Palmerston smilingly agreed that he would not invite Kossuth to his house.

'Opportunist!' I cried. 'Where are his finer feelings?'

One would have thought that that would have been a lesson to him; but Palmerston was not the sort to learn lessons. He went his own way; he was bold and could do so without harming his career; and when he saw danger, he just turned about. An odious man!

But this twisting and turning could not last.

News came that Louis Napoleon, Napoleon Bonaparte's nephew, who was now President of the French Republic, was proclaimed Napoleon III of France.

I was incensed. How dared these upstarts proclaim themselves royal!

I thought of poor Uncle Leopold and how infuriated this would make him; and how sad too. He must be almost glad that dear Aunt Louise had not lived to see this.

It was a dangerous precedent. Royalty all over Europe must tremble.

Lord John came to see me. His anxiety reflected my own.

'It is a very significant step,' he said; and I remembered what Lord Melbourne had said about governments making kings and queens—and realizing that they could as easily unmake them.

'We shall remain aloof,' said Lord John. 'We shall not question their right. It is not for us—a foreign power—to do so. But we can remain entirely passive . . . as though this has not happened.'

I agreed that this was the only thing we could do.

My astonishment was only overshadowed by my fury when I heard what had happened. The Foreign Secretary, without consulting his colleagues, had sent for the French ambassador and assured him of his cordial feelings for the new Emperor, and his friendly support.

'This time,' said Albert, 'I believe he has destroyed himself.'

It was not long before Lord John was with us. He deplored the Foreign Secretary's action, he said. It had put the ambassador, Lord Normanby, in a very embarrassing position. Palmerston was going to find it very difficult to explain to the House.

And to our great joy, he did. He might protest that his words were intended to convey his personal feelings; it would not do. He was the Foreign Secretary and he could not make public pronouncements and then explain them away as personal feelings.

I had written a carefully worded letter to Lord John in which I made it clear that he had been disrespectful to me. I said that he did not explain to me what he proposed to do in a given case, so that I was not sure to what I gave the royal assent. He would alter and modify certain matters, which I thought was a failure of sincerity. I must be informed fully before decisions were taken.

I asked that this letter be shown to Lord Palmerston.

Lord John did more than that. He read it to the House.

This turned the scale against Palmerston and in spite of his usual eloquent explanations of his conduct he was forced to resign.

Everyone was amazed at the decision Lord John had taken to read my letter to the House. It was considered ungentlemanly by some. Lady Palmerston called him 'that little blackguard' and Lord John was very unpopular in some quarters. Not so at Court. Nothing could have delighted us more.

I was pleased when Lord Granville was appointed Foreign Secretary.

Lady Palmerston, his 'Em' as Palmerston called her, was quite vitriolic in her comments. She gathered together the wits of the day and there they discussed the inadequacies of the new Foreign Secretary. 'A little lordling,' said Lady Em, 'who now and then whispers a speech about the Board of Trade, but he is very good at dancing attendance on Prince Albert.'

We did not care. We were rid of the enemy.

Between them, Albert and Stockmar had decided that Mr. Birch must go.

It was true that Bertie was doing a little better than he had been before Mr. Birch's arrival, but, as Stockmar pointed out, progress was not great.

'Bertie is not a scholar,' I said. 'But then, nor am I.'

'My dear,' said Albert, 'you were in the hands of Baroness Lehzen, and for that reason there is every excuse for you. When you think of the care we have given to Bertie, that is an entirely different case.'

'He seems so happy with Mr. Birch.'

'Happy!' said Albert. 'Of course he is happy. He is having a lazy, easy time.'

'I have studied the boy very closely,' said Stockmar.

Albert always listened attentively when Stockmar spoke.

'And,' went on the Baron, 'I do not like what I discover.'

My heart sank. I did hate to hear these complaints about Bertie and I had been so pleased to see him happy with Mr. Birch.

I said: 'The other children adore him. He is really very popular with them . . . far more so than Vicky is.'

That stung Albert. He could not bear any of them to be better at anything than Vicky.

'I have no doubt he is very good at childish games,' he said shortly.

'Affie just adores him. He follows him everywhere. I am told that when Affie had an earache, Bertie was the only one who could soothe him.'

'Unfortunately we do not have to train him to be a nurse,' said Albert.

There was nothing I could reply to that. I supposed he was right. Albert always was; and he was sure now that Mr. Birch was not the right tutor for Bertie.

'The Prince of Wales tries to win admiration,' said Stockmar, 'and it seems he is quite good at that . . . particularly among the women. He seems to have a fondness for them and they for him.'

Albert looked very shocked. 'A bad sign,' he said.

'Indeed yes,' agreed Stockmar.

'I ask myself what we can do to save him from himself,' went on Albert. 'When I think of what lies before . . . that stupid boy!'

'He is not really stupid, Albert,' I put in. 'Just a little lazy perhaps but many boys are like that.'

'My love, Bertie is not many boys.'

'I have been looking about,' said Stockmar, 'and I have found a very serious gentleman, a certain Mr. Frederick Gibbs. He is a barrister and would have no nonsense. I have made him aware that with a character such as that unfortunately possessed by the Prince of Wales, there must be no sparing of the rod.'

Albert thought that was a good plan and we should try Mr. Frederick Gibbs.

I shall never forget poor Bertie's face when he was summoned to us. I saw him look at his father and I could not quite understand the expression. Was it fear? I thought it was something more than that. Dislike? Impossible!

I spoke to him softly. 'Mr. Birch will be leaving us, and Mr. Gibbs will take his place.'

My heart smote me. I could not help it. I knew Albert was right, of course, but sometimes the good thing can hurt bitterly even though in the end it turns out to be right. But the misery in Bertie's face unnerved me a little. Had I been alone in this I should have said: 'Let us keep Mr. Birch, and make up our minds that Bertie is not going to be clever.'

'Well, Bertie,' I said gently.

'I . . . I . . . Mr. B . . . b . . .' stammered Bertie.

Albert looked exasperated.

'I thought we had rid ourselves of that stammer. Haven't you learned to speak yet?'

'Poor Bertie,' I said. 'It is a little shock. But it is all for the best.'

'You should be grateful to Baron Stockmar who has toiled so hard on your behalf,' said Albert. 'He and I have worked out a course of lessons. I can assure you we have given great care to this and you should be grateful.'

'Thank Papa, Bertie,' I prompted.

Bertie said: 'Is Mr. B—Birch going?'

Albert looked exasperated.

'That is what Papa has been telling you, Bertie,' I said.

'But . . . I—I love Mr. Birch.'

'Yes,' I said quickly, for I could see that Albert was getting irritated. 'He is a good man. Papa and the Baron chose him for you. They would not have chosen him otherwise.'

I knew Bertie was going to burst into tears so I told him to go to his room.

'He is quite childish,' said Albert in exasperation.

I could not get Bertie out of my mind. I kept seeing the misery on his little face.

I decided to see Mr. Birch alone. I felt that was necessary. When Albert was there I found myself thinking what he thought. I wanted to be by myself . . . absolutely . . . even if I was wrong.

Mr. Birch had accepted the termination of his engagement with dignity and I saw that he was thinking of Bertie rather than himself which made him bold and I sensed that he spoke out of the depth of his emotions, and, as an emotional person myself, I understood him.

He said: 'The Prince of Wales is misunderstood. He is not backward, though he is not brilliant. He will never be a scholar, but he has many good attributes. He has a charming nature for one thing. He is affectionate. He needs affection as we all do—especially children.'

I nodded, thinking of dear Lehzen in my childhood and Uncle

Leopold; and how fortunate I had been in spite of Albert's belief that I had been badly brought up by Lehzen. At least Lehzen had loved me.

'I have never believed that severe punishment brought out the best in children,' went on Mr. Birch. 'In the whole of my career I have never found it so.'

'I think that is where your methods have not entirely pleased the Prince and Baron Stockmar.'

'I have had results.'

'Yes . . . but Bertie is still not as advanced as his sister.'

'They are different children, Your Majesty. Their talents lie in different directions. The Prince of Wales is inventive; he is quick-witted.'

'The Prince and I have not noticed that.'

'No because . . .' Mr. Birch lifted his shoulders and went on: 'I am sorry to have failed Your Majesty. I shall be sorry to leave the Prince, but I hope he will be happy.'

'I am sure he will realize in time that everything we do is for his good.'

Mr. Birch made another attempt to speak for Bertie. 'He has great gifts. He is kind-hearted, fond of fun; he can make himself loved. Prince Alfred and Princess Alice adore him. He is so kind and gentle with them. Please, M'am, do not allow him to be treated with over-severity. It is not the way.'

I said: 'You are a good man, Mr. Birch, and I know you have tried to do everything you can for the Prince of Wales. I appreciate that. I could wish . . .'

I turned away. He was beginning to infect me with his emotion. He was even making me think that Albert and Stockmar might be wrong. I must not think that for it could not be true. Albert was always right. Bertie *was* lazy. Naturally he loved Mr. Birch, who had never applied the cane and had let him go his slothful way.

'May I show Your Majesty what I found on my pillow this morning?' asked Mr. Birch.

I nodded.

He showed me a crumpled piece of paper. In it lay a tin soldier dressed in the uniform of the pre-revolutionary French army. I took it from him.

'It is the best of his soldiers, his favourite,' said Mr. Birch. 'He sent it to me with this note.'

The note, written in Bertie's childish hand, said how much he loved Mr. Birch and how miserable he was because he was going away. He wanted him to have his best soldier as a keepsake.

Mr. Birch's lips quivered. I saw the tears in his eyes.

He bowed, took the paper and the soldier and begged leave to retire.

I was glad he had gone. A moment later and I should have been weeping with him. I must control my emotions, as Albert always said. My impulse was to rush to him and tell him that I was retaining Mr. Birch and that I did not care if Bertie never was a scholar.

Then I seemed to hear Albert's voice at my elbow. The note was badly written. A boy of Bertie's age should do better than that.

Albert was right. Of course he was right.

I had many a qualm about Bertie.

I knew that on the day Mr. Birch left he and Alfred stood at the window weeping bitterly—Bertie for Mr. Birch and Alfred mourned for Bertie. I noticed that even Alfred looked at Albert with something like hatred in his face. I hoped Albert did not notice. Fortunately Vicky was present and when she was there Albert never noticed any of the others.

Mr. Gibbs had been in the Palace for a few weeks taking over from Mr. Birch and I think that when Mr. Birch was there he restrained himself considerably. After Mr. Birch had left, lessons began in earnest and we heard that Bertie did not take at all kindly to them. He was sullen and refused to learn and was constantly being beaten, which did not appear to have the desired effect. Once he threw a stone at Mr. Gibbs. Alice and Alfred misbehaved too, siding with Bertie; even Helena and Louise set up a wail every time Mr. Gibbs appeared.

And it seemed that Bertie learned less under Mr. Gibbs than he had under Mr. Birch.

But Stockmar and Albert believed that Bertie had to be tamed and that the gentle hand of Mr. Birch would never have achieved anything.

Nothing Bertie did was right.

Sometimes when I was with him and the other children, without Albert, he would seem a little less sullen. We would laugh and sing together, and I would tell them about the past when I had lived in Kensington Palace, how I had saved for the doll, how I had had the typhoid fever and was so ill that my hair had come out. I told them about Lehzen and the uncles; and they listened avidly.

'Were you always the Queen?' asked Bertie.

'No,' I told him. 'It was only after Uncle William died. I was the next in line.'

I asked him if he knew what that meant; he did not, so I explained.

I finished: 'And after me you will be the Sovereign.'

Bertie shook his head. 'No, Mama,' he said, 'that will be Vicky. You and Papa don't love me. You love Vicky, so you will make her the Queen.'

I was shaken. I said indignantly: 'But of course we love you. You are our son.'

He was matter of fact. He said with conviction: 'It will be Vicky.'

'You think because Vicky is older than you she will be the Queen. But you are a boy and they come before girls.'

He looked unconvinced. 'But, you see, you and Papa don't love me. You do love Vicky . . . very much.'

I tried to explain to him that I loved them all equally. I saw a faraway look come into his eyes. He politely refrained from contradiction, but his expression implied that it was no use trying to convince him of something which he knew was simply not true.

I had many uneasy nights over Bertie and my feelings came to a head when Vicky was troublesome.

There was no doubt that Vicky had a high opinion of herself. It was natural, Albert would say. She was a pretty, very clever girl. It was more than that; she basked in an atmosphere of approval. Albert liked to talk to her. She could discuss most topics with intelligence. When he was making plans for Balmoral he showed them to her before he showed them to me. He would listen to her comments. 'Why, that is good,' he would say. 'An excellent idea.'

I felt a little irritated. She was only a child after all.

Then there was the incident which brought matters to a head. Albert had been unwell for some time. I believed he had been rather delicate in his boyhood and now he had a series of colds, one after the other, which was very worrying. I fussed over him a little and although he pretended to be impatient, I think he enjoyed it. There was a doctor in Windsor named Brown who was very highly regarded and I said why did we not ask his opinion instead of calling in Sir James Clark. I thought a fresh man might be able to put his finger on Albert's weakness. It might be something to do with the Windsor air and Brown knew Windsor.

Vicky heard Albert call the doctor Brown and when she spoke of him she referred to him in the same way.

'That is impolite,' I said. 'You must call him Dr. Brown.'

'Papa calls him Brown,' said Vicky, who always wanted to argue about everything.

'Papa is different. Papa may do as he wishes and he may be Brown to Papa but he is Dr. Brown to you.'

'I cannot see . . .' began Vicky.

'Never mind whether you see or not. Don't do it again.'

Vicky liked to show off in front of the others and again referred to Brown.

I saw Albert smile to himself; he thought it was amusing. I was angry that Vicky should be impolite to the doctor and ignore my orders.

I said that if I heard her call the doctor Brown again, she would go straight to bed.

The very next morning when Dr. Brown called she said: 'Good morning, Brown.' She was really a minx. She saw me looking at her and said: 'Good night, Brown. I am going to bed now.'

Then she left the room.

Albert could not contain his laughter—and he laughed rarely.

He explained to the doctor who joined in the mirth. Whether he thought it was funny I do not know. One is never sure with people. *I* was not amused.

I was even more annoyed when later Albert went to her room and came down smiling proudly.

'What a child!' he said. 'She is so amusing. Do you know, she told me that she did not mind spending the day in her bedroom. She had her books and she does enjoy them. So it is no punishment really, she said.'

I retorted: 'You encourage her in her naughtiness, Albert.'

'Such charming naughtiness,' he said.

'She defied me.'

'That was really witty at the end. Good morning . . . Good night, I am going to bed.'

'You can see no wrong in her, can you?' I said.

'My dear love, I see her as she is.'

'And how do you see Bertie?' I cried. Then it came out . . . all the thoughts that had been in my mind and which I had refused to consider. 'You can be cruel to Bertie your son while you pamper your daughter.'

Albert looked at me in amazement. 'I? Cruel to Bertie! What do you mean? Victoria, what are you saying?'

I had gone too far. I had said what I did not mean. Of course

Albert only wanted the best for Bertie. It was Bertie who was sloth-ful, who would not learn.

Albert went on: 'When I think of the trouble I have gone to for that boy . . . and you say . . .'

'Oh, it was nothing, I did not mean it. I have been worried about Bertie, and seeing how you are with Vicky . . .'

'Liebchen,' he began and he slipped into German. He had ne-glected me. I was jealous because he spent so much time with our daughter. She was growing up . . . she needed him. She was a dear, sweet, clever child and he had high hopes for her. He loved *all* our children. If he seemed cruel to Bertie it was only for Bertie's good. Did I want Bertie to grow into a criminal?

I began to feel wretched.

It was my impetuosity again.

'I'm sorry, Albert. I didn't mean it.'

He took my face in his hands.

'Little one,' he said, 'you are just a little jealous of Vicky. I have neglected my little wife . . . for my little daughter. It is because she is ours . . . yours and mine . . . that I love her so much.'

I was in tears. I lay against him.

He was so good. He was a saint. And it is sometimes not easy to live with saints.

I told him this and he stroked my hair and was very tender. He understood, he murmured. He understood . . . absolutely.

When death strikes it seems to do so in several directions all at once. Someone dies here, another there; and life seems changed somehow.

Dear Aunt Adelaide died and I was very sad remembering so many incidents from the past, her many kindnesses, the Big Doll she had given me, and how she had tried to get me to her children's balls because she had thought I was not having enough fun. Dear Aunt Adelaide! I hoped she was happy now with Uncle William, for they had truly loved each other.

Louis Philippe died at Claremont. How sad to die in exile! There was hardly any notice taken of his death. That old gossip, Greville, who was staying at Brighton at the time, said there was no more notice taken of the death of the King of France than there would have been of one of the old bathing women opposite his window.

But the death which was so tragic for Albert was that of George Anson, the secretary, whom he had been so reluctant to have in the beginning and whom he had grown to love. For weeks Albert was pale and sad. He had wept bitterly on the day of Anson's death and I with him.

We had lost a dear friend.

I think the death of Anson made him turn to planning feverishly for the exhibition; and because there was so much opposition in the beginning it helped Albert to overcome his grief. He became so angry and frustrated, and his mind was so filled with plans that he forgot to grieve.

The Great Exhibition was Albert's creation. How proud I was of him! This would show the people what a clever man he was. This exhibition was for them; it was for the whole world; it had been made to bring the nations together; it was to show how art and commerce could combine to make a better life for all people.

Joseph Paxton's crystal palace was superb; and, of course, Hyde Park was the best possible setting. While it was in progress I used to take the children to see it. I told them that this was all due to their Papa and how people from all over the world would come and marvel at it. We followed its progress with loving attention. It was going to astonish the world, I told Albert.

It seemed so long before the opening day. It was to be May the First. Little Arthur was just a year old so the day began with his birthday celebrations. He was quite a little man and was delighted by the presents which were brought to him. It was clear that Bertie was his favourite, and as he grasped his presents he handed them to Bertie as though for his approval. Bertie seemed to know just how to please the child. He certainly had a gift for that, even if mathematics was beyond him.

Opening the exhibition was the most wonderful experience of my life. Bertie walked beside me, and a few paces behind were Albert and Vicky. The peals of the organ rose to the crystal roof; the flowers were magnificent, the fountains splendid. There was an orchestra with two hundred instruments, and with it six hundred singers.

I laughed inwardly to think of all those who had tried to prevent this from being made. How stupid they would look now! Even Lord John Russell had made a nuisance of himself by raising an objection to the gun salutes being fired in the Park. He said they would shatter the glass; and he had wanted the guns to be fired in St. James's Park. That would not do, said Albert. It would not seem like part of the occasion if they were not fired in Hyde Park. Albert won the day. I must say I felt a little trepidation, lest Lord John might be right. But he was wrong, of course. The guns were fired in Hyde Park with no dire consequences.

When I heard people cheering Albert I was so moved. Nothing could have pleased me more.

Perhaps, I thought, they will appreciate him now.

There was no doubt of public approval. The glass palace was crammed with people of all kinds. I was touched to see the Duke of Wellington there. He was getting very old now and he came arm in arm with Lord Anglesey—such old men, both of them, but determined to be of the company. Lord Palmerston put in an appearance and on such a day I even felt kindly towards him.

'It is a very fine exhibition is it not, Lord Palmerston?' I said.

He gave me one of those mischievous looks and replied: 'Even I, M'am, can find no fault.'

I almost liked him then. He reminded me a little of my poor Lord M.

When we returned to the Palace I was so happy. The Duke of Wellington called to congratulate Albert; and little Arthur—who had been named after him and whose godfather he was—presented him with a little nosegay. Arthur did not know what it was all about but he did it perfectly.

The day was not over. In the evening we went to Covent Garden to see *The Huguenots*. On our way there, and in the theatre, we were cheered enthusiastically. I heard the cry in the streets: 'Good old Albert!' and my happiness was complete.

Happy days followed. There was no talk of anything but the glorious Exhibition. Mr. Thackeray wrote a beautiful May Day ode about it in which he said it:

> 'Leaps like a fountain from the grass
>   To meet the sun.'

The Prime Minister wrote to me:

'The grandeur of its conception, the zeal, invention and talent displayed in its execution, and the perfect order maintained from the first day to the last, have contributed together to give imperishable fame to Prince Albert.'

I wrote to Uncle Leopold:

'It was the happiest, proudest day in my life, and I can think of nothing else. Albert's dearest name is immortalized with this great conception, *his* own; and *my* own dear country showed she was worthy of it.'

Almost every day I was there. I would have everything explained to me—including the intricacies of the machinery which I could not understand at all.

Visitors came—royalty and the most humble. I had arranged for the head of the gillies at Balmoral to be brought to London to see the Exhibition. It was most amusing to watch his honest, open face. He was not exactly enthusiastic. I was sure he was wondering what use it was. They were so natural, so plain spoken, these dour Scotsmen. I liked them for their sincerity. They were such a contrast to so many people I met.

Among the visitors were the Crown Prince and Princess of Prussia; Albert and I were pleased that they had brought their son Prince Frederick William with them—Fritz, as he was called. He was twenty-two and although not exactly handsome had very attractive blue eyes. I was very interested in him because I knew Albert had plans for him and Vicky. His mother, the Princess Augusta, was a very amiable woman and I took to her at once. We talked together about Vicky and Fritz and she was very agreeable about the project; and it was comforting to see that Fritz and Vicky took quite a liking to each other.

At the end of July we went to Osborne. It was such a happy time because of the success of the Exhibition; we talked of it endlessly. It was to be closed on the 15th October—the twelfth anniversary of our engagement.

I said to Albert: 'It has taken all this time for people to get to know you, to understand you and appreciate your worth.'

In November that year Uncle Ernest died. It was quite a shock to me when I heard. I had never liked him; he had been a strange, mysterious man; but now that the bogey of my childhood was gone, oddly enough I felt a certain sadness. It was strange that he had been one of the most popular kings of Europe. He had taken a great interest in the affairs of his people, and when the rumble of revolution had spread through Europe, he had been able to suppress the beginnings of revolt in Hanover with ease. Now my poor blind cousin George had become King of Hanover

I was delighted with Lord Granville who was so different from Lord Palmerston. He was so charming and kept me informed regularly about everything; but where politics were concerned we could not be long without trouble.

There was worrying news from France because Louis Napoleon was changing the uniform of the army and having the imperial eagles restored to the flags. It seemed as though he had military ambitions. Lord John thought we should strengthen the local militia; Palmerston had other views. His foreign policy had always been aggressive; he had sent out his gunboats at the least provocation. Secretly, much as I disliked the man, I was inclined to agree with his policy, for I was convinced that there is nothing like a show of strength to intimidate troublemakers. Palmerston wanted a national militia and would agree to nothing else. So . . . he fought Lord John on this with the result that the government fell.

'I have had my tit-for-tat with Johnny,' was the irrepressible Pam's comment.

I sent for Lord Derby as leader of the Tories to form a government, which he did. It was weak and did not last long. What was significant was that Benjamin Disraeli was given the post of Chancellor of the Exchequer and Leader of the House.

I was very interested in this man. He was so unusual. At first I had recoiled from him with horror; he was so obviously Jewish with a dark complexion, very dark eyes and eyebrows, and black ringlets, which I heard afterwards he dyed. He had written several novels quite successfully and was a master of oratory, so I heard. I asked the Disraelis to the Palace to dine, which surprised many people for it was believed that Disraeli was the last person I should wish to have contact with unless it was inevitable.

But I was curious, for I had heard so much about him as he was talked of a good deal. It was said that he had married Mary Anne Wyndham for her money, but now there was not a more devoted couple in London—even Victoria and Albert. So naturally I wanted to see this pair.

I thought she was vulgar—not so much in her appearance as in her way of speaking. His speech was very flowery; but I found them interesting.

Then there was another death which affected me deeply—that of the Duke of Wellington. Of course he was very old; but he was agile. He had been a frequent visitor to the Exhibition and there had always been people to cheer him; he would never be forgotten as the hero of Waterloo. He had been in quite good health until a few days before his death. He had set out from Walmer Castle, where he had been living, for a drive to Dover, and when he returned ate a hearty dinner. That night he had a fit, and he died in the afternoon of the following day.

His funeral was a great occasion attended by much pomp. Tennyson wrote a magnificent ode on his death and even Lord Palmerston said that no man ever lived and died in the possession of more unanimous love, respect and esteem from his countrymen.

He lay in state at Walmer and was buried in St. Paul's in November after lying in state again in Chelsea Hospital. The funeral procession passed by Constitution Hill and Piccadilly and the Strand to St. Paul's followed by a million and a half sorrowing people.

I felt desolate. They were all going . . . all my dear old friends.

There was change everywhere. Lord Derby's ministry could not last, and I had to call on Lord Aberdeen to form a new government. It was an uneasy state of affairs. We needed a strong government. Nothing seemed the same . . . even names had to change. The Whigs were now calling themselves Liberals and the Tories were split between those in favour of Protection under Lord Derby and Benjamin Disraeli, and those who were still called Peelites and wanted Free Trade under Lord Aberdeen. They called themselves Conservatives.

It seemed impossible to do anything but form a coalition if there was to be a strong government; this Aberdeen tried to do; so he included Lord John Russell and Lord Palmerston from the Whigs— or Liberals—and Gladstone and himself from those who had been Tories and were now Peelites.

I was pleased with this for I was very fond of Lord Aberdeen; and it seemed a good idea to have the best men from the two parties. I did not like Palmerston, of course, but I knew he was a strong man; and the important thing was for the country to be firmly led, so I must stifle my prejudices.

In the midst of all this to my horror I became pregnant again. I had hoped that little Arthur would be the last; but it seemed that that was not to be.

I am afraid I was a little irritable, accusing Albert of indifference to my state, making wild condemnations against the powers who had designed women only for the horrors of childbirth, when it would only have been fair to make the men share a little of the burden.

Albert was kind, in that half indulgent, half exasperated, way of his, calling me 'dear child' as though I had never grown up and it needed all his patience to contend with me.

There was a grain of comfort. Sir James Clark who knew so much how I dreaded these births came to me and asked if I would like to try the new chloroform. I had heard of this. Albert was not very enthusiastic about it. He believed that God had meant women to suffer—presumably for being the one to offer Adam the apple—and that it was His will that suffering should be borne with fortitude.

But I was not in the mood to listen to Albert. Instead I wanted to hear more from Sir James who said that he thought there was no harm in it either to mother or child. It was true the Church railed against it. 'All men,' I said. There was a great deal of controversy in the Press. To use the painkiller or not?

I made a decision. I could endure no more. I would try the chloroform.

And I did.

I was amazed. How easy it all was! There I was in my bed and the pain was beginning to torment me . . . and the next moment I was lying there, not really exhausted coming out of what seemed like a peaceful sleep.

'Your Majesty has a son,' I heard, and I felt so joyous I could have burst into song. So it was over. Oh, blessed chloroform! And dear Sir James who had advised me to try it!

'This will make a good deal of difference,' said Sir James. 'There will be easy births all over the kingdom now. Your Majesty has blazed the trail. What you have done, everyone will want to do.'

I was so pleased and so very relieved.

We called the baby Leopold George Duncan Albert.

Alas, he was not as lusty as the others. We discovered later that he had a terrible disease. It was haemophilia, the bleeding disease. We were terrified that he would fall and cut himself in any way, for if he did, it would be difficult to stop the bleeding. He was the first of my children to be delicate.

I am afraid at this time there were storms in the household.

I was worried about the baby and still thought a great deal about Bertie's relations with his father. I tried to convince myself that the beatings and the general severity were right; but I could not get Bertie out of my mind. He himself seemed to have come to terms with them; but he really was far more mischievous than he had been under Mr. Birch. He still could not—or would not—learn. He was a great problem.

I would flare up at the slightest thing . . . against Albert. Something within me made me blame him. Mama always sided with him, and I felt I must be in the wrong; but that did not help.

Albert was always loving and tender, calling me his dear child until I wanted to scream at him that I was not a child. I was a queen. They should remember that. Then I would be regal and Albert would be withdrawn. After that he would be sorry. 'I should *help* you,' he would say, 'help you to overcome your nature which was not corrected in your youth.'

When I look back on that period which followed Leopold's birth I think that I was overwrought; I *had* to flare up; I wanted a quarrel and a quick making-up, and being happier than ever because we were reconciled.

We went to Balmoral in the autumn. It was not yet completed and I think Albert was rather glad of that. He did so love the work. When it was finished it would be magnificent with its one-hundred-foot tower, its gables and turrets. The views were splendid—mountains, forests and the River Dee. We had designed tartans to hang everywhere. My design was the Victoria Tartan, Albert's the Balmoral; and these were hung side by side with the Royal Stuart. I loved the fresh air and the dear simple honest people. I felt so much better there among those natural people like my special favourite, John Brown, who always held my pony when we went for mountain rides.

But I could not be free of my ministers even at Balmoral. Not that I wished to be far from Lord Aberdeen—that most charming man; he enjoyed Balmoral and threw himself whole-heartedly into the local customs. He wore a kilt and danced a reel with me—which was most amusing.

I could have done without the presence of Lord Palmerston. I noticed that his eyesight was not good and he was showing signs of age. He played billiards with Albert, who managed not to show his dislike of the man.

Lord Palmerston said there was trouble brewing in the East. We did not take much notice of it then.

What I had always feared more than anything had come to pass.

I knew that there was a certain uneasiness but I had hoped that with Lord Aberdeen's reasonable policies we should keep out of it.

Russia had invaded Turkey's principalities on the Danube, and Turkey was England's friend—a weak one, but nevertheless a friend.

I was at Balmoral when I heard that the British fleet had entered the Dardanelles. It was Palmerston's gunboat policy again; and Palmerston had persuaded Aberdeen to allow this action to be taken in my absence.

By October that year Turkey had declared war on Russia. Palmerston immediately demanded that we support the Turks with France as our ally. Lord Aberdeen was for peace; it was Palmerston who urged action. I was torn between the two of them. I did not believe that Aberdeen could bring the Emperor of Russia to see reason; and yet the idea of siding with Palmerston was obnoxious to me.

Aberdeen came to me one day in a state of anger against Palmerston who, unknown to him, had been in direct touch with our ambassador in Constantinople.

'Surely,' I said, 'that is treason.'

Aberdeen shrugged his shoulders. He was determined to keep us out of war, but his mild nature was no match for Palmerston. I swung over to Aberdeen's side.

'The Emperor must be victorious,' I said, 'and if the Russians are magnanimous and the Turks reasonable, perhaps that could be an end to this disagreeable matter.'

Then Lord Palmerston resigned.

That was the sign for the people to show their feelings. Mr. Gladstone was of the opinion that Palmerston should be called back to government. Lady Palmerston was working indefatigably to make everyone aware that the country needed her husband at this time and Lord Aberdeen was nervous. He thought the government would fall, which would be a disaster, and he did not see how he could survive unless Palmerston was recalled. Palmerston came back.

Then we heard that Russia had sunk the Turkish fleet.

Palmerston was the hero of the day. His prophecies had been correct. He had been warning the government of the impending trouble for months but they had preferred to shrug aside his warnings. The people thought we should be at war—as we should be now, they said, but for Palmerston's being pushed out.

With one accord the people named the scapegoat; and it was Albert.

Palmerston was the national hero; Albert the villain.

Articles about him appeared in the Press. Slogans were written on walls. People carried banners demanding that he go back to Germany where he belonged. Nothing was too bad to say about Albert. I could not believe that the Exhibition and all the good he had done could be so quickly forgotten.

Why had we not gone to the defence of poor little Turkey? Why indeed? Because Albert did not wish it. German Albert! The Queen had not wanted us to go because she was governed every time by Albert. Who ruled the country? German Albert. Who wanted England handed over to his German relations? He was related to the Russian royal family; he was a traitor to this country. He spoke

English like a German; he didn't even look like a man . . . not an Englishman. He was too pretty; he never laughed; he was cold, aloof, disdainful of the people. He was smug.

On the other hand was that gay debonair brilliant Pam. He had been something of a libertine in his youth. Of course he had. He was a man. A man who would laugh at life and enjoy it, and at the same time guide the affairs of the country in the way that they should go. He had always known how to subdue our enemies when he had been in power. Why? Because Lord Palmerston wanted to keep England for the English and not turn it over to a lot of goose-stepping, rapacious, smug Germans. Down with Albert!

Cartoons, caricatures and verses appeared everywhere. There was one of the latter which ended:

> 'You jolly old Turk now go to work
> And show the Bear your power
> It is rumoured over Britain's Isle
> That A is in the Tower.'

This gave rise to the rumour that Albert was being taken to the Tower and crowds assembled at the Traitor's Gate to jeer at him.

This was the state of hysteria to which the country was reduced.

I wept with rage and frustration and I railed against the stupid mob. 'How dare they?' I cried. 'Action must be taken.' I was not the only one who thought this.

Mr. Gladstone turned out to be a good friend to us. He wrote an article in the *Morning Post* which made a deep impression; the subject was brought up in the House and the accusations against Albert were laughed to scorn, and many spoke in a most complimentary fashion for the Prince—including Mr. Disraeli. Lord John Russell made a magnificent speech in which he said the hysteria must be stopped for it was utter nonsense.

This fortunately did have a calming effect on the people but there were fears in certain quarters that there might be an attempt on Albert's life. I was, after all, not a stranger to assassination attempts, and I was terrified for Albert.

When I opened Parliament, Albert was with me, and the Prime Minister insisted that every precaution should be taken and we rode through the streets heavily guarded. He was right; there were cheers for Lord Palmerston and hisses for Albert and me.

I was so wretched when the people showed their disapproval of me and at such times remembered how, as a little Princess, I had gone among them while they cheered me, shouting my name and their good wishes.

How sadly life changed!

Lord Aberdeen was loath to go to war but Palmerston threatened to resign unless a stronger line was taken; and the people were firmly behind Palmerston. War had a great appeal for them perhaps because it was so far away, and I could see that the country was inevitably drifting towards it.

In February an ultimatum was sent by our government to the Russians: unless they retired from the Danube Principalities before the end of April we should declare war. They did not reply and we were at war.

We could only attack Russia from the sea; our fleet sailed into the Baltic under Admiral Napier and in September landed in the Crimea. There were twenty-four thousand English, twenty-two thousand French and eight thousand Turks. Our object was to capture Sebastopol.

From the balcony of Buckingham Palace, I watched the troops march past on their way to war. I wanted them to see me and know that my heart was with them. Later I went to the wharf to see them. I remembered Lehzen's lessons about that queen, of whom I had never really been very fond during my childhood. *She* had gone to Tilbury to *her* troops; she had made a fine speech about being a weak woman and having the heart of an English king. I might not have been so gloriously articulate as she was—but I did want them to know how much I cared.

How I hated war! It dominated my thoughts. I hated the thought of all that death and destruction; and my subjects being at the heart of it.

Lord Palmerston was letting everyone know that had he been in power the war could have been avoided. It was the foolish policy of appeasement which was the cause of many a war. If Russia had not believed that England would stand aside, if we had not had a vacillating government, they would never have dared to take action.

I was beginning to think that Palmerston must be right.

I can hardly bear to think of that time and the terrible hardships endured by my people. The disaster of Balaclava, the empty triumphs of Alma and Inkerman, the terrible epidemics which raged through the armies and killed more men than the guns.

I was proud of Miss Florence Nightingale, who went out with her nurses to look after them. She was magnificent working under the most fearful conditions.

Albert was at his desk for hours; he was continually thinking up improvements for the army which were presented to the government; and almost all of them were adopted. He insisted that we needed more men; we needed a more efficient commissariat; we needed improvements everywhere. The government was weak; he was finding himself more and more in agreement with Palmerston. And in time the inevitable happened. Palmerston had to be there, at the head of affairs. The people believed he was the only man who could end this wretched war. I think we all knew it too.

In due course Palmerston came to the Palace; he kissed my hand in accordance with tradition and set about forming a government with himself as its Prime Minister.

There was fresh hope everywhere. People were dancing in the streets. 'Palmerston is back,' they cried. 'Soon we shall be victorious now.' And although there were no miracles, events did take a turn for the better. Palmerston, energetic, positive and constructive, had the people behind him. He and Albert were agreeing on many important matters and I felt my antipathy towards the man fading a little.

He was certain that he was right and determined not to sway for anything—not even his own position. I suppose that was an inherent honesty. The only people who were against Palmerston at that time were certain politicians. It has always amazed me how petty they can be; I suppose they are so ambitious for themselves, so eager not to miss the slightest chance of their advancement, that they cannot bear to see others leaping ahead. Mr. Disraeli was very disappointed. I believed he had set his heart on the premiership for himself; he resorted to personal abuse, calling Palmerston 'an old painted pantaloon, very deaf, very blind, with false teeth which were constantly threatening to fall out of his mouth'. Such items had nothing to do with winning the war and this was blatant envy. Palmerston *was* old; he was seventy, I believe; he may have touched up his cheeks; but I suspected Mr. Disraeli himself dyed his own hair. Mr. Disraeli had outstanding gifts, and it amazed me—as it has on many occasions—how men who are truly great can be so bemused by jealousy as to betray their baser side so childishly.

I received the news of the death of Tsar Nicholas with mixed feelings. There was great rejoicing. This was just retribution, it was said. The man who had been the cause of the deaths of thousands was now taken himself. I could only remember the man I had known, with his wild eyes and eccentric habits. He had really been rather charming.

But the war continued without him.

Albert crossed to France for a conference with the Emperor. He came back with copious notes and said he thought the Emperor was rather indolent. However, the visit improved relations with France and I was sure Albert had made a good impression.

We were now so friendly with the Emperor that he and his wife paid us a return visit. I was most interested to meet them. Louis Napoleon was a very charming man, but quite small in stature; and his wife was very tall and slender. We made a striking contrast, I being so short and, I have to admit, inclined to plumpness whereas Eugénie was so tall and willowy. On the other hand, Albert's tall figure called attention to the Emperor's lack of inches—so as far as appearances went we were an incongruous quartette.

I took them to Windsor which impressed them as it did all visitors.

I found them delightful which was a surprise because I had been expecting the Emperor to be something of an upstart. He was very complimentary to me and he had a soft gentle voice; he really knew how to charm women, and I noticed his eyes following some of our more spectacular beauties. Albert was inclined to suspect such men but I admit to a weakness in myself inasmuch as I did enjoy their company. And thus it was with the Emperor.

We took him to a review of the troops in the Park. He rode a magnificent chestnut and bowed so charmingly to the onlookers that he was loudly cheered. He told me that years ago when he had lived humbly in England he had once been among the crowd to watch me ride by. That had been fourteen years before. 'A sight so impressive, so touching in its dignity,' he said. 'I never forgot it . . . or you.' He was a very charming man. The Empress was delightful too.

When they were introduced to the children Vicky was overawed by her—not so much by her dignity as her beauty and the lovely clothes she so elegantly wore. The two of them were so natural with the children, which was rather delightful in persons of their position, and I was pleased to see that the Emperor took a special interest in Bertie. Bertie's response was immediate. He was so accustomed to being put in the shade by his brilliant sister that he responded to attention like a flower opening to a spell of rare sunshine.

He chattered away to the Emperor and I was glad Albert was not present or he would have restrained him, but I thought it would do Bertie no harm, and I could see that the Emperor was enjoying the boy's questions. Bertie wanted to know about the French army, the guns and the uniforms.

'I want to be a soldier when I grow up,' he confided to the Emperor.

'You'll be a good one,' replied the Emperor with a smile. 'I wish you would join my army.'

'Oh,' cried Bertie, 'so do I.' Then he said something which shocked me. 'I wish *you* were my father.'

I was about to protest but the Emperor was shrugging off the remark with great tact and I felt that the only way was to treat it lightly as a child's carelessly spoken word in a thoughtless moment.

But deep down in my heart I knew that Bertie meant what he said. In August we paid a return visit to France. The war was going moderately well and we received a great welcome there. There were processions through the streets with the people crying *'Vive la Reine d'Angleterre,'* and I was so glad that they did not forget to shout: *'Vive le Prince Albert.'*

I felt the Emperor and Empress really were our friends.

Albert's birthday occurred during that visit and we celebrated it at St. Cloud. It was a wonderful day. The Emperor had composed special music for the day and there was present-giving just as at home. Then we went out onto the palace balcony and three hundred French drummers paid tribute to Albert.

He was thirty-seven. I prayed God to bless him and protect him for many years to come.

My present to him was some beautiful studs. There was a blank space in them at the time and I told him that when Sebastopol fell, they should have that name on them, so that in years to come he would remember when I had given them to him.

Sebastopol! How we longed for it to fall! When it did that must signify the end of the war was in sight. But although the war was going well for us, Sebastopol continued to hold out.

I told Albert how enchanted I was by the Emperor.

He looked at me and smiled.

'My dear child, you do grow so enthusiastic so quickly.'

'I know.'

'It was only a little while ago that you were reviling him as an upstart, and now because he has whispered a few charming words in your ear . . .'

'It is nothing of the sort!' I protested. 'I know him now . . . personally. I didn't then.'

Albert was right, of course. He was so much more calm than I, so balanced, so less likely to be influenced by personal charm. But I had changed a great deal since my marriage. I was growing a little more like Albert. I wondered if when we were very old I should be exactly like him. That would be a great improvement, I knew; but I did wonder whether I should get so much fun out of life.

We were confident of victory now although the Russians still clung to Sebastopol, and it was suggested that I might take a holiday away from the cares of State—just for a few weeks. If my presence was needed in London I could be recalled.

So happily we set out for Scotland. It was particularly exciting this year because the new Balmoral had been completed, just as Albert had designed it; and we had been longing to see it for some time.

How I loved it! It was like a baronial castle. I loved the pitch pine and the tartan interior.

'Everything,' I cried, 'is perfection.' It was a delight to think that it was Albert's creation—his own building, his own laying out . . . as at Osborne. I could detect his wonderful good taste and his dear hand everywhere.

That was a never-to-be-forgotten stay at Balmoral, for we had not been there very long when the news came to us that Sebastopol had fallen. It was the news we had been waiting for. After three hundred and ninety-nine days, the city had capitulated.

Albert and I clasped hands and looked at each other. I think we were both near to tears. We went to the window and looked out. On a hill, well within sight of Balmoral, a pile of wood stood waiting; it had been there for a whole year.

Albert solemnly went out. I watched him climb the hill and set fire to the bonfire. It was the signal. Soon I saw a string of them blazing away, proclaiming the fall of Sebastopol.

There was something else which made that visit a memorable one.

Albert said to me: 'I have invited Fritz to Balmoral.'

I knew at once what he meant. His heart was set on a marriage between Vicky and Fritz; he wanted Vicky to be Queen of Prussia.

I said she was too young.

'The marriage could not take place until she is seventeen,' said Albert, 'but I want her to get to know Fritz. I do not want her to go straight to him. Let them be together . . . let them get to know each other . . . to like each other.'

I knew it was a good idea and I looked forward to welcoming Fritz to Balmoral.

I liked him very much. He was tall, broad-shouldered and pleasant-looking. He was greatly in awe of Albert and obviously had been told what a wonderful person he was. That made us both warm towards him.

Fritz fell into our ways with a charming ease. He was determined to make himself agreeable; and it was perfectly obvious that he greatly admired Vicky. It would have been surprising if any young man had not done so, for she was very pretty, and of course, so bright that she must be noticed.

Fritz went stalking with Albert, riding with us both and picnics with the family.

It was all very pleasant.

I was amused by my gillie, John Brown—such an honest, outspoken man! 'So he's to have yon lass,' he said to me.

I was rather taken aback and I said: 'Well, Brown, we hope it will turn out something like that.'

Albert thought they were too familiar, these gillies. My special favourites were Grant and Brown. I liked their honesty. 'They are not accustomed to royalty,' I said, 'and even if they were they could not pretend, even to us.'

Vicky, of course, enjoyed being the centre of the romance. She knew what it was all about and behaved in a rather coquettish manner, sometimes being quite affectionate to Fritz and at others indifferent.

I knew what was coming when Fritz asked if he could come to see me. I immediately granted the interview and he told me how happy he was to be with us and what a wonderful visit this had been. He admired Albert and me more than any people he knew, and he loved our daughter. Would we allow him to make a formal proposal for Vicky's hand?

I told him that it was what Albert and I had hoped for.

He was delighted. He was such a dear boy—though he was not such a boy really. He must have been about twenty-six then—so much older than Vicky, but not too old; and Vicky would never have lived happily with a very young man. She needed someone older, someone experienced; otherwise she would have been managing everything.

I told Albert what had happened.

I think he was a little upset. I could understand it was galling on occasions like this when people came to me, for in the ordinary way they would have gone to the father. But after all I was the Queen.

He was very emotional to think of his little Vicky . . . marrying. I always felt a faint irritation about his obsession with Vicky and much as I tried to suppress it, I could not always do so.

'It is what you wanted,' I said sharply. 'In fact it is what you arranged, and Fritz was your choice.'

'I know. I know. It has to happen. But how we shall miss her!'

'We have the others.'

He smiled sadly. 'They are not Vicky.'

'Oh, I know how you dote on her. She can do no wrong in your eyes. I hope she will have as lenient a husband as she has had a father.'

Albert wore that look of tender exasperation which meant he was trying to reason with a wayward child. It often irritated me and especially when the subject of contention was Vicky.

'Vicky,' I said, 'is talented and good-looking, but you do show that you care for her . . . more than for any of us.'

'*Liebchen!*'

'It is all very well to be shocked, to pretend . . . but it is obvious. Vicky this . . . and Vicky that . . . Vicky is always so good, so very good that Bertie has to be proved wrong to show how good Vicky is.'

'Victoria, what are you saying?'

I looked at him. My dear *dear* Albert. There were lines of pain on his beautiful face. He did work so hard, and all for the good of those about him . . . the country . . . the family . . . all of us. He suffered terribly from rheumatism. He was wearing a wig occasionally because his hair was thinning and his head became so cold. Its darkness made him look pale.

I was immediately contrite. I ran to him. 'Albert, you *must* take care of yourself.'

'My dear child, you flit from one subject to another.'

'The impulse comes and I say what I think. I have always been like that.'

He stroked my hair. 'It is not your fault. It is the way you were brought up . . . encouraged in tantrums . . . never corrected. My poor, poor child.'

I always hated those shafts at dear old Lehzen, but I was so worried about his frail looks that I let this one pass.

I had the fleeting thought that when Vicky was actually married, she would have to go to Prussia and that would leave the field clear for me.

It was an odd thought to have about one's own daughter. I suppose I was jealous of all the time Albert gave to her.

Albert arranged a ride to Craig-na-Ban. The entire family—apart from the very young ones—were to go.

We set out accompanied by two gillies, John Grant and John Brown, and we decided on the point where the carriage should pick up those who did not want to ride back.

The outing was a great success. Fritz had his chance. He and Vicky rode side by side and sat a little apart from the rest of us when we picnicked.

I could see by their faces that Fritz had proposed and that Vicky had accepted.

When we returned to the castle Vicky came to our room as I knew she would; she ran to Albert and threw her arms about him. 'Papa,' she said, 'I am going to marry Fritz.' Then she turned to me.

'We are not surprised,' I said kissing her. 'Your father thought it would be an excellent match.'

'But, Vicky, you would not have been forced or even pressed to take him . . . if it had not been your wish,' said Albert quickly.

'I know, dearest Papa,' said Vicky, smiling fondly at him.

'There will not be a wedding for some time,' said Albert.

'Oh no, Papa.' She looked at him in horror. 'How shall I bear to leave you . . .' Then looking at me: 'To leave you both.'

'It is in the nature of things,' I reminded her.

'And it will not be for three years,' comforted Albert; and they exchanged a loving look.

'I wonder how I can leave *you*,' said Vicky blankly.

'We shall see each other,' said Albert. 'We shall visit Prussia and you will come to England.'

'Oh yes, yes,' said Vicky. 'We shall meet . . . often, shan't we?'

Albert nodded. He put his arms round us both. 'I shall pray,' he said, 'that you, my dearest Vicky, will be as happy as your mother and I have been.'

There seemed to be spies everywhere. We had not wished the news of Vicky's engagement to be generally known for a while; she was so young and it would be some time before the marriage could take place. But almost immediately the Press were on to it.

'Who is this Frederick of Prussia?' asked the headlines. 'Another little German princeling.'

The old story of Albert's family taking over England was repeated.

The Prussians retaliated. Was it such a good match? What dowry was being offered? Frederick was the future King of Prussia. The English seemed to have forgotten that. The Princess would have to come to Germany to marry.

I was very angry when I heard this. These Germans were indeed arrogant. There was a little storm with Albert for he always made excuses for them. I accused him of agreeing with everything they said, of arranging a match which would be prestigious to Germany.

Albert tried to calm me.

'It is the usual outcry of the Press,' he said. 'They must have something controversial and sensational to sell their papers. Soon there will not be room enough in the same country for the Monarchy and *The Times*. The Monarchy wishes to do good; *The Times* wishes to make mischief. Do not let them irritate us, for that is their object. We can defeat it by ignoring it. In time everything must work out for the best—and, of course, Vicky will be married here.'

Of course he was right—as he always was.

The war in the Crimea was drawing to an end and I wanted to institute a medal which would be the highest order possible and which could be conferred on all those, military, naval and others, who had performed, in the presence of an enemy, some outstanding act of bravery and devotion to their country.

This was to be called the Victoria Cross and it was to take the form of a Maltese cross and to be made of bronze. The royal crown formed the centre, mounted by a lion; about the crown was a scroll on which were the words For Valour. We had at first thought that the words should be For the Brave, but that seemed to suggest that all of those who had not received the cross were not brave. For Valour seemed more to the point; the ribbon was blue for the navy and red for the army; and branches of laurel decorated the clasp, while the cross was supported from inside by the initial V.

If a man received the Victoria Cross and performed a further act of bravery worthy of it, he should have a bar across the ribbon; and in the case of non-commissioned officers and men there was to be a pension of ten pounds a year, and an extra five for a bar.

I had the pleasure of meeting that very wonderful woman Miss

Florence Nightingale who had done such excellent work by actually going out to the battlefields with her nurses.

When she was back in England I invited her to the Palace to dine with me. I was so surprised and so moved to meet her; she was quite attractive, gentle and ladylike . . . a delightful and amazing woman.

I told her how I envied her because she had done so much for our men; and that I had thought of her often during the darkest days, walking along the corridors of the hospital with her lamp—an inspiration to us all.

Over dinner she told me what life in the Crimea had been like and her stories were both heart-breaking and heart-warming.

I said to Albert afterwards that meeting people like Miss Nightingale and hearing of our brave soldiers and nurses restored my faith in the world and made me forget for a while all those horrible people who were trying to make trouble.

And finally the wretched war was over. How I rejoiced. Albert and I discussed the terms of peace; and Albert said he was quite satisfied with them. The Black Sea was secure for a while; Russia was humiliated and Turkey was safe.

At home there was great rejoicing. How happy I was, standing on the balcony of Buckingham Palace acknowledging the cheers of the people. I went down to Spithead to review the fleet; and in Aldershot I rode past the troops and the soldiers cheered me with enthusiasm, taking off their helmets and waving them above their heads; and the dragoons lifted their sabres and waved them while everyone shouted 'God Save the Queen.'

I was delighted to have Bertie with me. It was amazing how good he was on occasions like this. It was only book learning which defeated him. He looked very fine on his horse and the people shouted: 'Long Live the Prince of Wales,' which he acknowledged with a dignity which made me proud of him.

I told Albert about this afterwards and he smiled and said: 'Oh yes, Bertie is very good at receiving thanks for what he has not done.'

'They were applauding him because he is the heir to the throne.'

'Exactly,' said Albert. 'All he has to do is *be*. That he does nothing does not matter in the least.'

'He is rather young as yet to have done anything.'

'Except work hard and prepare himself.'

I did not pursue the matter. I was too happy to want to indulge in a storm.

It was wonderful that the people liked Bertie and he enjoyed parading before them; and most glorious of all: the wretched war was over.

I had been fortunate in escaping pregnancy for so long, but it could not continue. In the midst of all this excitement I discovered it had happened again!

Thanks to blessed chloroform, I did not regard the birth with such horror as I had done in the past; although of course there was the discomfort which could not be avoided.

And in due course I gave birth to my ninth child—a girl. I was very grateful for the blissful effects of the chloroform and I submitted to its administration with the utmost eagerness. Beatrice Mary Victoria Feodore was an April baby. Thank Heaven she was strong and healthy, unlike little Leopold who gave us such cause for anxiety. My conscience was eased by little Beatrice because I had had a nagging fear that my taking the chloroform might have had an effect on Leopold. The health of my little girl showed me clearly that this was not the case as I had enjoyed the same relief in giving birth to her . . . We had to choose with the utmost care those who would supply our baby's needs for we had had a terrible shock about a year after Leopold's birth to discover that his wet nurse Mary Brough had gone mad and murdered her six children. The idea of such a woman being in close contact with one of my children horrified me. I was thankful to Sir James Clark who had noticed that Mary Brough was a little strange after she had been with us for a while and had suggested a change. He had found a woman from Cowes so Mary Brough was not with Leopold for very long.

Such experiences made one very wary. However, Beatrice thrived and the whole family soon became devoted to Baby as we called her.

In June of that year I presented the first of the Victoria Crosses. There was a review in Hyde Park which was very splendid and moving and during it I pinned a medal onto the breasts of sixty-two men who were considered worthy to receive it.

Albert had suggested that now that Vicky was growing up and soon to be married, she might dine with us. I did not really wish this because these were the occasions when Albert and I were alone, and I cherished them. Now they were to be shared with Vicky.

Albert paid great attention to her and I would find myself often outside the conversation—which was rather galling.

Vicky was quick-witted, and as she was as devoted to Albert as he to her—or almost—she made a great effort to say what he wished her to say and I must admit she had the art of being controversial when that most amused him and acquiescent when that was the mood he sought. There was great rapport between them. They understood each other completely.

I loved my daughter; I was proud of her; but I did know that she was not the perfect being Albert believed her to be.

She was certainly vain; she loved admiration; she was wilful; she had enjoyed scoring over Bertie. Well, I suppose she was human. I could have accepted that if Albert had not believed she was such a little paragon. I was surprised that he, who should be so clear-sighted in everything else, should be so blind about Vicky.

Vicky was coquettish, inclined to be flirtatious; and Albert saw none of this. I remembered one occasion when we were driving she let her handkerchief fall over the side of the carriage. It was clear to me that she wanted the equerries to vie with each other for the favour of bringing it back to her. Realizing this, I stopped the carriage and I told her to get out and pick it up herself. She looked at me shrewdly, understanding that I saw into her mind. Perhaps being of the same sex I was more aware of those little foibles than Albert was.

Time was passing. I was in a state of uncertainty. There were times when I dreaded losing Vicky. Sometimes she seemed so young, so vulnerable; and I thought of my child going into a strange country. The Prussians were not exactly a merry people. Indeed, they were very serious, very rigid in their ideas; and I felt uneasy about her. And yet, on the other hand, when she had gone, I should have Albert more to myself.

At dinner, I used to long for ten o'clock when Vicky would leave us and I should have the rare happiness of being alone with Albert.

Once in one of our storms Albert accused me of wanting to get rid of Vicky. I was horrified; and yet there was a glimmer of truth in it.

The time had come when the wedding dominated our thoughts. With the prospect, there was the humiliating necessity of getting agreement in Parliament for Vicky's grant. I always hated this haggling over money and dreaded it, but I must say that Palmerston was magnificent. He knew how to handle these matters and—in spite of my feelings in the past—we could not have had a better man at the head of affairs at this time.

'The way to do it, M'am,' he said, with a twinkle in his eyes, 'is to sound out the Opposition before taking the matter into the House. We get agreement before we put it up to the vote.'

How right he was! And there were only eighteen dissensions, which was really infinitesimal. Vicky was given a dowry of £80,000 and £8,000 a year, which seemed quite satisfactory.

Owing to the opposition of the uncles Albert had never been given the title due to him. Every time the subject had been raised there had been howls of protest. Those uncles had all been afraid that Albert would take precedence over them. But now they were dead.

Albert was very concerned that one day, when he and Bertie were in the public eye, Bertie would take precedence over him. It would be very disconcerting for a father to have to take second place to his son. Of course Bertie was the Prince of Wales and if I should die, he would be King and stand above all. And without hope of any title Albert would be of little importance.

I discussed the matter with Lord Palmerston, who suggested that we should get Parliament to agree that Albert should be given the title of Prince Consort.

As he could not be King—and I saw this—I would be content with that title for Albert, and I left it in the capable hands of Lord Palmerston.

My horror was great when, just as I had thought the matter was to be settled, Palmerston came to tell me that the Lord Chancellor had discovered a legal impediment and that there would have to be an Act of Parliament to create Albert Prince Consort.

I was furious. They seemed to delight in humiliating Albert. Everything he did for their good was forgotten; they only remembered that he was a poor German who had become rich because he was the husband of the Queen. I was determined, though, that he should have some title. He should not go unrecognized any longer. I declared I would create him Prince Consort by letters patent.

Lord Palmerston smiled approvingly and said: 'Why not, M'am.'

And so, at last, after all these years, it was done.

A terrible disaster struck us. There was mutiny in India. I could not believe the horrific reports which kept coming in to me.

The Indians had arisen and were killing our people. Lord Palmerston came to see me. His calmness irritated me.

'Why? Why?' I demanded.

'It is difficult to say why, M'am. I would guess it has come about because of the rapid advances European civilization has been making, with the result that it is absorbing the national institutions of the country. Remember we have recently taken in the Punjab and Oude; and the Indians no doubt think that we intend to annex the whole of India, disregarding their old customs and faith. The Sepoys have been victorious under English command, and doubtless they think they can win battles on their own.'

'They must be subdued . . . at once.'

'As soon as possible, Your Majesty.'

I was haunted by the terrible things which were happening. Our people to be submitted to torture and death! It was unacceptable, I said to Palmerston. What was being done?

'Everything possible,' he replied.

'It is not enough,' I retorted. 'I want action.'

'It is fortunate for me that Your Majesty is not on the Opposition benches,' said Lord Palmerston.

He gave the impression of frivolity but I knew he was very seriously concerned. It was just his manner. He could never show panic. He must face every situation with a calmness and glint of humour—though where the humour was in this appalling tragedy I failed to see.

I think what shocked me more than anything were the atrocities committed on women and children. I was haunted by horrific visions; I found sleep impossible. Whatever I turned to there was this terrible mutiny in India hanging over me like a black shadow.

The cause of the uprising was said to be that the Sepoys believed that cartridges were greased with the fat of beef or pork and thus rendered unclean for both Hindu and Mohammedan; they thought it was a plot to destroy their caste.

I did not entirely believe this and thought they might be in revolt against the rules laid down by the East India Company.

Of course we were stronger than they were and they could not stand out against us for long. Sir John Lawrence was magnificent and with the help of Brigadier Napier and General Roberts, the mutiny was subdued. The Sepoys were handled with a firm but not severe hand, and the Sikhs were only too pleased to take advantage of British rule. What was most important of all was the transference of the administration of India from the East India Company to the Crown.

Lord Canning was the Governor-General, and I let it be known that the Indian people were my subjects, and there was no hatred for a brown skin. The colour of skin was immaterial to me. It was my greatest wish to see them happy, contented and flourishing.

Such a disaster had its effect. Oddly enough, Lord Palmerston slipped from his pedestal. How fickle was the mob! The hero of yesterday was the villain of today. Had not I myself seen that clearly enough. Disraeli had been somewhat vociferous about the mutiny and said he had seen trouble coming and had warned of it, only to be ignored. A new hero perhaps? In any case, poor Pam was out of favour.

I had to admire him. He simply did not care. He was after all about seventy-five years of age.

'It is incredible,' said Albert. 'A short time ago, he was said to be the great English statesman, the champion of liberty, and the man of the people. Now, without having changed in one respect, having the same virtues and faults which he always had and having succeeded in his policies, he is considered the head of a clique, the man of intrigue . . . past his work . . . In fact he is the target for hatred.'

It was true. But one could not hope for logic from the mob.

Palmerston shrugged his shoulders. He laughed at the people and went on just as before, a decrepit old dandy in his brightly coloured coat and trousers, his touched up complexion and dyed whiskers.

I had to admire him, because I had come to realize that he was a brilliant statesman.

The Great Disaster

Then something happened which took people's minds off mutiny. A man called Felice Orsini, in company with three others, had attempted to assassinate Napoleon III. We were horrified. Apparently the Emperor and Empress were in their carriage on the way to the opera when these men threw three bombs at the carriage. Although the Emperor and Empress were unhurt, ten people were killed and a hundred and fifty wounded. The men responsible were arrested; and the unfortunate fact was that Orsini had been living in England and the bombs had been made in our country, which drew us into it in a measure and I should have been more comfortable if they had been somewhere else, for the incident created a distinct coolness between us and the French, which was disappointing after all the efforts we had made to bring about friendly relations.

Orsini was a revolutionary and his great object was to bring Italy to revolt. In his opinion Napoleon was one of those who had helped to prevent it. Hence his desire to kill him.

It was a horrible incident to have taken place, just as we were about to celebrate the wedding. I was so relieved that the Emperor had survived this wicked attack, and sent despatches congratulating him on his escape.

We could not however let all this prevent our going ahead with the preparations for Vicky's wedding which was fixed for the 25th January; and a week or so before that, members of Albert's family began to arrive at Buckingham Palace. It was very touching to see dear Uncle Leopold again. He had aged considerably. Aunt Louise's death had been a great blow to him, and before that there had been all the trouble about her father's fall from power. It was sad what the years could do. Albert's brother, Ernest, was present, as debonair as ever and Albert was delighted to see him. The bridegroom's parents were naturally among the guests. What a large gathering it was! I must say that though I found the older German relations very pleasant, I did not greatly care for the younger men with their exaggerated moustaches and sabre cuts on their faces of which they were so proud because they had received them in duelling. Honourable scars, they called them. I called them evidence of folly!

Poor Albert was torn between the delight of seeing his family and the prospect of losing Vicky, which was making him more and more depressed every day.

There was a state dinner party which was a very grand affair; a gala performance of *Macbeth* was given at Her Majesty's Theatre in honour of the wedding; and there was a grand ball.

And then the great day had come. I could not but be reminded of my own wedding day. So much had happened since that glorious day when Albert and I were married. I had grown so far from that frivolous, pleasure-loving girl who thought the height of bliss was to stay up dancing into the early hours of morning. Albert had taught me so much. What a lot I owed him. What a lot the country owed him. However could I have lived through those years without him! And now here I was, Queen of this beloved country, mother of nine children. No wonder I was overcome with emotion; it was happy emotion. Not so Albert's. He could not bear the thought of parting with his daughter.

I wrote a note to Vicky as soon as I awoke. I found such relief in writing; it was always so much easier to say what I had in my mind if I put it on paper. I told her how important marriage was; it was a holy and intimate union, and that I believed it meant more to women than to men.

Vicky came in while I was dressing; she kissed me with emotion and thanked me for my note. She gave me a brooch containing a lock of her hair, and said she hoped she would be worthy of me, which touched me deeply.

She wanted to be dressed in my room so that I could tell her if all was well. How enchanting she looked in her white silk gown trimmed with Honiton lace. Albert came in and Vicky was daguerrotyped with us. It was very moving and I could not keep still, and so came out rather blurred. And then it was time to go.

When we left Buckingham Palace for St. James's, the streets were filled with cheering crowds. It was so like that other day eighteen years ago—and yet so different. Memories were certain to come on such a day. In Vicky's place I saw myself—a young and innocent girl, perhaps more innocent than Vicky. Young people were more advanced than they used to be, and I had led a very sheltered life. Oh yes, changes indeed. Lord Palmerston carried the Sword of State. I could not help being reminded of my poor dear Lord Melbourne who had been so proud of me on that day. I remembered how he had looked at me with tears in his eyes, and afterwards he had said: 'You did splendidly, M'am.' Such a wonderful comfort that had been to me.

And now it was Vicky's turn.

I was glad to see Mama there looking so splendid in violet-coloured velvet trimmed with ermine, and white and violet silk. Trust Mama to wear royal colours! I could not help recalling how, at the time of my wedding, we had not been good friends. How everything had changed! Albert had taught me—and perhaps Mama as well—to be more tolerant; and how much happier we were now that we were good friends! Mama's great delight was in the children; she loved them dearly and when they were naughty she used to beg that they should not be punished because their crying hurt her so. How different she had been with her own daughter! I shall never forget the sudden sharp jab of the holly I had been forced to wear under my chin.

I kept Arthur and Leopold beside me. I had impressed on them the solemnity of the occasion and the necessity for good behaviour. They were very impressed.

Then I saw Vicky come forward between Albert and Uncle Leopold; and Fritz looking pale and agitated but very tender.

It was moving to see those two dear young people now married, walking down the aisle to the strains of Mr. Mendelssohn's 'Wedding March'.

Then back to Buckingham Palace, and we stepped through the celebrated window while below the crowds cheered wildly.

It was a wonderful day of mixed emotions. Later the young couple drove off to Windsor for a few days' honeymoon.

The day for Vicky's departure was fast approaching. I was not looking forward to it because I knew how heart-breaking it was going to be to say goodbye to my daughter. I knew that at times I had wished she had not been a third party at those cosy dinners; but all the same she was my daughter; and the fact that she was now married seemed to bring her closer to me. I began to worry about the sort of life she would have in Prussia. She had been rather spoiled at home; I wondered whether her new family would be as doting as we—or rather Albert—had been.

The children wept bitterly and loudly when it was time to say goodbye and I tried to hold back my tears. Albert looked wan and ill and really heart-broken. He was going with them to Gravesend where they would embark. He must be with his daughter for as long as he possibly could.

As the carriage drove away it began to snow, and I watched the flakes through a blur of tears thinking how alarmingly quickly time passed, and that my little daughter was now a married woman.

When Albert came back from saying goodbye I could see he was really stricken.

I tried to comfort him, to tell him that I shared his sorrow; but he did not believe that. He would remember my petty jealousy of my daughter. He believed that the great sorrow was his. He would like to shut himself away to mourn, but I would not let him do that. He looked so ill I must share his sorrow.

I went to his room. He was at the table writing and I knew to whom. There were tears on his cheeks. I went to him and put my arms about him, and looking over his shoulder read:

'My heart was full when you laid your head on my breast and gave vent to your tears. I am not of a demonstrative nature and therefore you can hardly know how dear you have always been to me and what a void you have left behind in my heart; yet not on my heart for there assuredly you will abide henceforth as you have done till now, but in my daily life which is ever more reminding my heart of your absence.'

It was the letter a lover might have written, and Albert loved Vicky . . . deeply . . . perhaps more than he had ever loved anyone else.

I would not think of that. Vicky was gone; and Albert was *my* husband. I would comfort him. I would share his sorrow.

'Oh, Albert,' I said, 'let us comfort each other.'

And we clung together weeping.

I was writing to Vicky every day. I felt there was so much she ought to know. She wrote in return but not so frequently. She was romantic. No doubt she thought that marriage was all bliss; she would have to learn about the shadow side. I hoped she would not do that too soon.

I wanted confidences. I longed to help. I would have liked a detailed account of every day of her new life. How were they treating her, those Prussians? Did they appreciate the honour which had come to them through marriage with British royalty? Were they giving her the respect due to her?

Vicky wrote back a little guardedly. She loved Fritz and that made everything all right. She was not sure what the Prussians thought of her. They did think she was rather small.

'Small!' I cried in indignation. 'She is taller than I, and I am not a dwarf!'

I did feel she needed to be warned. I wrote to her telling her that even the noblest men could be self-centred when it came to marriage. Women were expected to be submissive to them and sometimes that could be humiliating.

I was disturbed when I heard that Vicky was pregnant.

'It is far too early,' I said.

Albert was so disturbed that he went to Prussia at the end of May to assure himself that she was all right.

He came back less worried. Vicky was well and looking forward to the birth of the child which was due in January.

In August, Albert and I visited her. It was five months before the child was due and Vicky appeared to be in good health. It was good to be with her again though I should have liked to be there with her alone so that we could have shared confidences. It must have been the one time in my life when I had not wished for Albert's company.

I told Vicky that I longed to be at her bedside when her child was born. I said: 'It is a right which the humblest mother can claim.'

'But you, dearest Mama, are not the humblest mother. You are the Queen.'

I sighed and contented myself with giving Vicky advice, warning her—without alarming her unduly—of the ordeal which lay ahead. When I looked back over my own experiences I thought how humiliating it was. Why hadn't nature thought of a different way of reproducing the race? Why should there be times in a woman's life when she must feel like an animal . . . a cow for instance.

When we returned I continued to write to Vicky daily; Albert told me that I should not do so.

'Do you not see that you are tiring Vicky with this perpetual correspondence?' he asked. 'She has enough to think of. She cannot answer your letters. She is being well cared for. She does not need your advice.'

'I suppose,' I retorted, '*you* want to be the only one who writes to Vicky.'

He sighed. 'I have heard from Stockmar that if you go on writing these letters to our daughter, she will be ill. You must stop meddling with these trivialities.'

'It is a very sad thing,' I replied, 'when one writes in spite of fatigue and trouble to be told that it bores the person to whom one writes.'

Albert assumed the patient manner and called me his dear child. 'Vicky is trying to adjust to life in a country which is not of her birth. She is going through a difficult time. Please, my love, do try to understand.'

'Do you think I don't understand? Do you think my thoughts are not with her every hour of the day?'

And so it went on.

But, of course, I did write less frequently to Vicky; but that did not stop my worrying about her.

It was strange but I was closer to her now that she was absent than I had been when she was with me.

In January, there was news from Prussia. Vicky had a son—Wilhelm—and hers had been a long and difficult labour.

I wrote to her at once:

'My precious darling, you suffered much more than I ever did. How I wish I could have lightened your burden.'

I felt moved and angry that women should have to suffer so much.

We were suddenly in the middle of a ministerial crisis due to the reverberations of the Orsini affair. This was because it was proved without doubt that the conspirators had actually hatched their plot in England. The French Foreign Minister, Walewski, sent a strongly worded note to Lord Palmerston demanding that foreigners rebelling against their own countries should not be given refuge in England. Palmerston's response was to introduce a rather weak Bill making conspiracy to murder an offence.

Palmerston was still an unpopular politician at this time and his enemies—those who sought his post—saw a good excuse for getting rid of him. I thought it was a good Bill but the verdict was that Palmerston was weakly giving way to his old friend Napoleon; and the Bill was defeated. Palmerston resigned, and I had no alternative but to summon Lord Derby, who was able to form a ministry.

It was all very disturbing. Moreover we were anxious about Bertie. He was not doing as well under Mr. Gibbs as he had under Mr. Birch. The Press was always eager for stories of him; he was a favourite with them and there were hints that Albert and I were cruel to him. Why was the Prince of Wales not seen more in public? was continually asked. On the rare occasions when he had appeared he had won the people's hearts. Let them see more of him.

Albert said that public approval would go to Bertie's head and make him more impossible than he already was.

We decided—or rather Albert did in consultation with Stockmar—that Bertie should have a governor instead of a tutor. The governor's rule was to be strict and Bertie would not be able to leave the house without reporting to him. Colonel Bruce had been chosen because he was a man who was firm and would enforce the laws.

Then it was thought that he should have a spell at Oxford or Cambridge. The Dean of Christ Church wanted Bertie to take up residence in the college but Albert would not hear of that. It would give him too much liberty. He should be in a private house with his governor watching every movement.

Bertie disliked learning. I had to have a little sympathy with him. After all, when I had been young I had made excuses to escape from my books. It was something Albert could not understand. I feared my son was not unlike me. Perhaps he had inherited his unsatisfactory traits from me—certainly they did not come from Albert.

There were other anxieties, too. We were constantly concerned that Leopold would fall and hurt himself and start to bleed. Alfred had expressed a wish to go into the Navy and then was heart-broken because it meant parting with Bertie.

Children were a mixed blessing.

Then I heard that Vicky was proposing to pay us a visit.

It was wonderful to see Albert's joy. He had been looking quite ill lately and I was really worried about his health. He suffered a lot of pain from rheumatism and that gave him a drawn look; he caught cold very easily and that was not good. I told him he worked too hard. We should take more holidays; he needed the sea breezes of Osborne or the clean mountain air of Balmoral.

But he looked almost his old self when he greeted Vicky. She was different, grown up, a wife and a mother. There was an air of worldliness about her; she had lost that beautiful innocence; she had already undergone the dreadful ordeal of childbirth and had suffered greatly because of it—more than I ever had. Poor Vicky!

Naturally I wanted to be alone with her, to have some of those little talks which can only take place between women; I wanted to know all the details of that terrible ordeal.

Vicky had something on her mind and it came out when she was with us both.

'Papa, Mama,' she said, 'there is something I have to tell you.'

'My darling . . .' began Albert alarmed.

'Tell us, Vicky dearest,' I said.

'It is about little Wilhelm.'

We waited in trepidation.

'Oh he is . . . very well. Otherwise . . . he is a perfect child . . . It is just . . .' She bit her lips and looked from one of us to the other. 'It is just that . . . well, it was a difficult birth. I don't know whether they told you how difficult. They thought I was going to die.'

A look of anguish crossed Albert's face. I felt as he did. But she was here, she was with us. So it had not happened.

'You see a difficult birth . . . a breech birth . . . His arm was dislocated when he was delivered.'

'You mean he has . . . a deformity?' I asked.

'It is just his arm,' she said.

'Can nothing be done?' asked Albert.

'We have had the best doctors and . . . nothing . . . But he is a perfect child in every other way.'

I went to her and put my arms round her. Albert was staring straight ahead. I knew he was not thinking of little Wilhelm's arm but of his adored Vicky, who might not have come through her ordeal.

How Albert enjoyed those *têtes-à-têtes* with Vicky. Sometimes I felt I was a little *de trop* and he would rather have had her entirely to himself. But that was nonsense of course. She was my daughter as well as his and I was the one who had suffered to bring her into the world. She was very sweet and loving to us both, more so with me than she had been at home. I thought: Being away has made her appreciate me more.

Albert loved to talk to her confidentially—as though she were adult, which of course she was now. We told her of our worries about Bertie.

'Dear Bertie,' she said, 'he is all right at heart, you know.'

'He is lazy,' said Albert. 'He does not realize his responsibilities.'

'He will manage when he has to bear them.' She gave me a loving look. 'It is not going to be for years and years.'

'Bertie is responsible *now* . . . as Prince of Wales,' said Albert. 'He will not study.'

'Some very good kings have been poor scholars,' Vicky reminded him.

It was pleasant to hear her putting in a good word for Bertie.

'You always overshadowed him, my dearest child,' said Albert. 'Compared with you . . .'

'He could do many things which I could not. He's at the university now and that must be quite a change for him. I must see him before I go. I shall go down and surprise him.'

'I am sure it will be the most pleasant surprise imaginable,' said Albert.

She did go and according to her it was a most enjoyable visit. According to Mrs. Bruce, the wife of the formidable Colonel, it brought out yet another deplorable trait in Bertie's character for with Vicky was one of the ladies she had brought with her from Prussia, one of her dearest friends, Lady Walburga Paget, who was a very attractive young woman.

Mrs. Bruce had seen something quite subversive in Bertie's behaviour towards Lady Walburga. He had been flirtatious and frivolous. Certain traits hitherto only suspected had been proved.

Bertie was too fond of the opposite sex. Bertie would have to be watched even more closely.

This led to further discussions on Bertie. 'He should be married,' said Albert.

'It would be the best thing possible,' I agreed.

'As a matter of fact,' said Albert, 'I have already given some thought to the matter.' Albert could always be trusted to see ahead of everyone. 'I have consulted with Uncle Leopold and Stockmar and have, as a matter of fact a list of princesses one of whom might be suitable for Bertie.'

'A list!' cried Vicky. 'Oh, do let me see it, Papa.'

'By all means,' said Albert, and he produced the list.

Vicky looked at it and smiled.

'You will know some of them,' said Albert.

'Yes, I have met a few.'

'You must watch for us, Vicky,' went on Albert. 'Report to us. See if you can select a bride for Bertie. If you approve I shall feel much happier.'

'I see,' said Vicky, 'that Alexandra of Denmark is on the list.'

'She is the last one—I imagine an afterthought of Uncle Leopold.'

'Well, of course,' said Vicky, 'she is Danish. The others are all German and in Uncle Leopold's and Stockmar's eyes, the fact that the others are Germans puts them ahead.'

We laughed with her.

'You sound as though you know this Alexandra.'

'I have met her. She is exceptionally beautiful. Very pleasant . . . unspoilt.'

'Well,' said Albert, 'let's keep her on the list.'

'Let me have it,' said Vicky. 'I will spy out the land.'

'You realize this is a very serious matter, my dearest,' Albert warned her.

'I do indeed. A marriage always is and the marriage of the Prince of Wales especially so.'

Albert was very sad when Vicky went back but there were repeated pledges to meet again very soon. Fortunately she was not so very far away from us and frequent visits were a possibility.

'That makes the situation just tolerable,' said Albert.

Meanwhile there were the usual crises. There was a general election with the result that Lord Palmerston was Prime Minister for a second time. The Whigs had now become the Liberals and his government consisted of various elements—people calling themselves Whigs, radicals, Peelites and followers of Palmerston—all united under the name of Liberal.

Mr. Gladstone joined their party and became Chancellor of the Exchequer in the government.

Palmerston was as energetic as ever. I heard he would sit listening to debates looking so serene that he might have been asleep; but when he spoke he would show that he had not missed a single relevant point.

He had quite a liking for Bertie and I was sure he was one of those who thought we were too severe with him. It was he who suggested that Bertie should visit Canada and America as representative of the country.

Albert was taken aback. The idea seemed incongruous.

'Not so,' said Palmerston with that slightly amused look he always seemed to bestow on Albert. 'I think they will like him.'

Disbelieving, we agreed. Albert said his governor, Colonel Bruce, should go with him so that he should continue with his studies.

'There will be no time for that with the programme I have pre-pared for him,' said the merry Pam. 'The Duke of Newcastle will accompany him and the Prince will be very busy. There is no point in making such a journey just to study. That could be done at home.'

Albert and I agreed at last, providing Colonel Bruce accompanied him.

That tour was a revelation. Bertie it seemed was a good ambassador. Lord Palmerston came to us rubbing his hands with glee. This visit has done diplomatic relations more good than a hundred conferences. They loved the Prince. Everyone wanted to talk to him. He had a smile for everyone. He has a flair for making speeches. The women adored him.

Of course we were delighted to hear of Bertie's success. Colonel Bruce reported that the Prince's fondness for the opposite sex appeared to have increased rather than diminished. He feared the worst. The Duke of Newcastle had other views. He said the Prince was charming and had delighted all who met him; he had done a great job for the country.

Albert said: 'There must have been an improvement as we are getting praise from every quarter. We owe all this to Colonel Bruce. I think he should be given some honour for the work he has done.'

'I will speak to Lord Palmerston,' I told him.

I was quite surprised at Lord Palmerston's reaction.

'Colonel Bruce, Your Majesty! This was not Colonel Bruce's doing. It was the Prince's. The success of the tour is entirely due to him.'

'The Prince Consort thinks it is due to the discipline which Colonel Bruce has imposed on him that he has improved sufficiently to behave as he did. We thought that the Order of the Bath . . .'

Lord Palmerston raised his eyebrows and slowly shook his head.

'I like people who do good work to be rewarded,' I said.

'As I do, M'am. It is the Prince who should be rewarded. This is his triumph. I do not think Your Majesty's government would consider giving rewards where they are not earned. No, M'am, I do not think it would bestow an order on the colonel.'

There were times when Lord Palmerston could be almost insolent, but in a light-hearted, amused sort of way, so that it was difficult to take offence.

'Your Majesty must be feeling very proud of the Prince,' he went on.

'I am glad he did well.'

'In spite of Bruce,' he said softly.

And I could see that look in his eyes. I knew he would be stubborn. There would be no order for Colonel Bruce. I could imagine his having the temerity to go to the country on such a matter.

I felt only mildly put out. Albert felt it more keenly. But I was glad that Bertie had achieved his success alone.

Bertie's triumph was short-lived. He was soon in trouble again. He had no doubt enjoyed too much freedom on his tour and did not relish settling down to work.

He was caught in an escapade which greatly disturbed Albert. He had actually escaped from the colonel and decided he would go to stay with some friends he had made when he was at Oxford.

This meant that first he would come to London and from there go to Oxford. Fortunately the plan was discovered. Colonel Bruce telegraphed to the Palace and when Bertie arrived in London a carriage was waiting to conduct him to the Palace.

Poor Albert was so distressed. Bertie was too old to be beaten now but Albert was determined that drastic measures should be adopted.

There were conferences and a great deal of thought was given to the matter. In due course we decided that he should not return to Cambridge.

He should have a spell of discipline with the army in Ireland.

He was sent to Curragh Camp.

Vicky paid us a second visit—this time with Fritz. We talked not only about a princess for Bertie but a husband for Alice. Dear placid Alice! I should hate to lose her but I knew I should have to do so. That was the way of the world. Vicky at least was happy with Fritz, although I believed she was not so much at ease with her Prussian relations.

I felt very well that autumn. Balmoral was a delight and it was always a great joy to escape to it. But I was worried about Albert's health. He would drive himself even when he was feeling ill. But he was better at Balmoral than anywhere else, I believed, and that made the place especially important to me.

I loved the Highland gatherings on Deeside, and that year I invited two hundred guests to join us. Uncle Leopold visited us and with him came Prince Louis of Hesse-Darmstadt and his brother. I was very interested to see that Prince Louis and Alice were quite interested in each other.

Vicky wrote that she was pregnant again. Mama and I were in agreement that it was too soon.

'Oh dear,' I sighed. 'I hope she is not going to follow my example. Nine times I underwent that ordeal!'

Albert was delighted although of course worried for Vicky.

'You will never understand what these ordeals are for women,' I told him irritably.

I was irritable because I was worried—about Vicky's pregnancy, Alice's prospects of marriage, Bertie's troubles, and most of all Albert's health.

It was a great relief to us when Vicky was safely delivered of a little girl. Charlotte, they called her. Albert said we must go to see her.

'I have a great desire to see Germany once more,' he said solemnly.

We took Alice with us. She was such a dear good girl, always so calm and helpful—an ideal daughter. I should miss her when she married.

Vicky was well and I thought the children were enchanting. Little Wilhelm's deformity was cleverly hidden and he was such a pretty child, sturdy and beautifully fair and very intelligent. The baby was delightful having passed out of the froggy stage.

Vicky seemed to be happy; and of course Albert was delighted to be in his homeland again. We visited Rosenau and he enjoyed telling Alice about his childhood. He was very sad though, because his stepmother—of whom he had been very fond—had died recently.

'Well,' said Albert philosophically, 'it is something we all come to in time.'

We met Duke Ernest and Alexandrina. Albert wanted to be alone quite a lot with Ernest. Sometimes, looking back, I feel that Albert had a premonition and wanted to relive every moment of his childhood.

A terrible incident happened which might have killed him. I was glad I did not hear of it until it was over. I was not with him at the time; he was driving in an open carriage drawn by four horses when they bolted. The coachman could do nothing and the horses went galloping off heading straight for a level crossing. Albert, always cool-headed, saw that action could not be delayed and he jumped out of the rapidly moving carriage just before it crashed into the barrier; the coachman was pinned down and unable to move and Albert lay unconscious on the ground. Fortunately two of the horses had released themselves and came back to the stables—so help reached the spot in time.

I had been out and when I came in was immediately told what had happened. In panic I rushed up to Albert's bedroom. His face was bruised and he was in bed looking very shocked.

Stockmar, with whom we had had a reunion in Saxe-Coburg, was by good luck, with us; he had immediately taken care of Albert and he told me that he was not as badly hurt as he had at first feared. The coachman was more seriously injured and one of the horses had to be shot.

I was horrified. How easy it was for disaster to overtake us! I thanked God that Albert was safe.

He made a quick recovery and we were able to go to Rosenau for his birthday, which was a great pleasure.

Albert and Stockmar spent a great deal of time together; I laughed at them and said they discussed their ailments as fervently as generals planned strategy in a major war.

Albert looked at me rather sadly. He said: 'Dearest child, I hope you will be happy.'

Which was odd, and later made me feel that he knew.

We had another visit from Louis of Hesse-Darmstadt. I had decided that I wanted him for Alice. She quite clearly liked him. I had noticed that she had had one or two intimate chats with Vicky who would give her a little initiation into the demands of married life; and still Alice seemed prepared to undertake it; she must have been really taken with Louis! I wondered if Vicky had shown her one of my letters to her which I had sent soon after the birth of William.

I had written:

'The despising of our poor degraded sex—for what else is it, as we poor creatures are born for man's pleasure and amusement—is a little in all clever men's natures. Dear Papa even is not quite exempt, though he would not admit it . . .'

Well, perhaps we know these things and still we go into them just as my dear Alice was preparing to do.

I prevailed on Albert to sound Louis out and it appeared that the young man was eager for the match.

'He is sensible and intelligent,' I said. 'He is very easy to get along with. He is almost like one of the family already. I rather like that weather-beaten face of his. I like handsome looks and I am glad if they are there, but I do not make them a condition.'

Albert gave me one of those tender exasperated looks and he said he supposed there would be no objections on either side to the match.

That evening there were several people present, but I saw Louis and Alice talking very seriously together.

I went over to them and Alice whispered: 'Mama, Louis has asked me to marry him. May I have your blessing?'

I smiled at her tenderly and murmured that this was hardly the place. We would meet later.

Albert was with me when I sent for Alice and Louis to come to us. We all embraced and we told the happy couple how delighted we were.

That was a very happy evening.

I shall never forget that March. Mama had not been well. She had had a very unpleasant abscess under her arm and Sir James thought she would not be better until it was removed.

This had been done and we thought she was recovering when we heard that she had a very bad cold. Sir James came to tell us that he was very worried about her.

Albert and I immediately went to Frogmore.

Mama was not in bed but lying on a sofa rather elaborately dressed in a beautiful *négligé*. I felt relieved because she looked so well; then I realized that I had thought this because the blinds were drawn.

'Albert and I came at once when we heard,' I said, and I knelt down, taking her hand and kissing it.

Mama looked at me vaguely. I glanced at Albert who laid his hand on my shoulder, and the appalling truth struck me that Mama did not know who I was.

Albert put his arm round me.

'We will stay here for the night,' he said.

Sleep was impossible. I knew that she was dying, and I felt a terrible sick remorse. Pictures from the past kept coming into my mind. I could not rest.

Very early the next morning—it was not yet four o'clock—I rose and went into her room.

She was lying very still. Her eyes were open but she did not see me.

In the morning I was at her bedside, but it was all over. She had gone.

Albert comforted me. 'These things must come to pass, my love,' he said.

I clung to him. He understood my remorse. I was very depressed. I read my Journals—all the hard things I had written about Mama. How tragic . . . that rift between us! All Mama had tried to do was protect me. Lehzen and I had said cruel things about her but all she wanted was the best for me. Albert had made me understand.

I wanted to explain to Mama, to tell her that I did not mean the cruel things I had written. I wanted her to know . . .

I would not go out. I would see no one. I was sunk in melancholy. Albert reasoned with me. People were talking. I was acting strangely. Because of my grandfather I must never act in a manner which could be called strange. People were only waiting to start rumours, to say wicked untruthful things about me.

I must stop grieving. I had been wrong, but I recognized my fault and was sorry for it. Those about me had been to blame. I had been only a child.

So he talked to me and he made me see everything in a reasonable light.

I must stop mourning for Mama.

I began to go out again. I was laughing once more. I was quite merry in fact. I began to see things differently. After all, Mama had not become perfect just because she was dead. She *had* endeavoured to bring herself into prominence; she *had* been rude to Uncle William and unkind to Aunt Adelaide.

I must be sensible. Whatever I had done wrong I was sorry for. I had been young and innocent. All the same I wished that I had been able to explain certain things to Mama.

Bertie had left Ireland and was back at Cambridge. Vicky's efforts to find a princess for him had not met with any success; and our thoughts were turning more and more to Princess Alexandra of Denmark. The Danish royal family was rather insignificant and very low down the list, but Vicky wrote that Alexandra herself was far the most beautiful of the princesses.

'In that case,' I said, 'we shall tell Bertie nothing about her. Let him remain in ignorance of her existence until we find someone more suitable.'

It was unfortunate that Albert's brother Ernest who was very much against an alliance between us and Denmark—as no doubt all the German relations were—wrote to Bertie advising him against the marriage. As it was the first Bertie had heard of it he was most intrigued.

Albert was very annoyed with Ernest and wrote reprimanding him.

We discussed it together. Bertie had met the Princess of Meiningen and the daughter of Prince Albrecht of Prussia and had not been in the least attracted by them. The daughter of Frederick of the Netherlands was too ugly. Louis of Hesse-Darmstadt had a sister, but Alice was to marry into that house and we did not want two connections with it.

It really did seem as though Alexandra of Denmark was the only one; and as there were reports of her dazzling beauty it was very likely that Bertie would have no objection to her.

Winter had come. Albert was suffering from a cold; his rheumatism was especially painful and he could not sleep at night.

Then on a gloomy November day the blow fell. I did not know at the time because Albert kept it from me. I should never have known if I had not gone through his papers afterwards and found the letter from Stockmar.

All I knew was that he had become withdrawn, deep in thought, very melancholy and uneasy.

I knew that he was brooding on something and I asked him what was wrong.

'Oh nothing . . . nothing that need concern you, my dear child.'

I presumed that he was merely not feeling well and I urged him to rest and above all not go out in the bad weather.

A few days later he said he must go to Cambridge. He wanted to see Bertie.

'Not in this weather,' I said. 'Bertie can wait.'

'I would rather go today,' he replied.

'No, Albert. Not in this weather, and you know you are not well.'

'I shall be there and back in a very short time.'

'I am going to forbid it,' I said.

'No, my love, this is something I must do. I am going to Cambridge.'

The firmness of his tone told me that I could not stop him, and against my wishes, he went.

When he returned he was cold and shivering. Then I did insist that he go to bed at once; and this time he did not protest.

I sat by his bed scolding him for disobeying my wishes. And just to see Bertie! It was senseless. How was Bertie?

Bertie was well. They had talked.

'As if that could not have waited!' I said.

He smiled at me and shook his head and I dropped the matter because I could see how tired he was.

Albert rallied a little the next day. I was delighted. He would throw off this cold; we would find something which would alleviate his rheumatism. He would be well again.

In the midst of this a crisis arose which threatened to be of international importance. A war had been raging in America between the north and the south; and the people of the south had sent two envoys to us to plead their cause. These two men, Mason and Slidell, were sailing in the *Trent*, which was an English ship. The ship was boarded by the enemies of the south and the envoys were taken off. This could not be allowed. No one must interfere with British ships on the high seas; any who did must be made aware of the might of Britain. It looked as though the Americans would be fighting us as well as each other.

There was a demand from the British government that the envoys must be released at once or our ambassador would be recalled from Washington. The government was ready to take firm action and I was behind them. Lord John Russell sent me a draft of the ultimatum he had decided to send.

I shall never forget the sight of Albert in his padded dressing-gown with the scarlet velvet collar and the fierce determination on his poor wan face.

'This will not do,' he said.

'Albert,' I chided, 'you will go back to bed at once. You are not well enough to concern yourself in these matters.'

'This is a very dangerous situation,' he replied. 'This cannot be sent . . . as it is.'

'But it is what we mean. We cannot allow these . . . ruffians . . . to board our ships.'

'These are special circumstances. We do not want war with America. We need peace . . . peace in this country.'

'Of course we need peace but we are not going to allow these people to dictate to us on land or sea.'

'It is a matter of wording the ultimatum. I am sure the Americans do not want war with us. They have enough to do fighting each other. But you must see that to receive a note like this would give them no alternative. It needs to be redrafted.'

'You had better tell Russell that. No . . . you had not. You had better get to bed and rest.'

'I cannot rest. I shall redraft this. I think we can avoid an ugly situation.'

'Dear Albert, you are ill.'

He lighted the little green lamp on his desk and sat down to work.

When he had finished writing he leaned his elbows on the desk and put his head in his hands.

'Victoria . . . my love,' he said, 'I feel so weak. It is an effort to hold a pen.'

'I told you you should not have done this. You will not listen to me.'

He smiled at me wanly.

I knew later that Albert's action then saved us from a very awkward situation which could have resulted in war. The affair of the *Trent* has consequently become one of those incidents which are hardly ever referred to in history books and Albert's part in it is forgotten by most; but it is just another example of the good Albert did for this country.

The next day he was very ill indeed and Sir James came to me and said he would like a second opinion.

Dr. Baly, who worked in conjunction with Sir James and of whom Albert had a high opinion, had recently been killed in a railway accident; and ever since the Flora Hastings affair I suspected that Sir James did not have a great deal of confidence in himself.

'Do you think the Prince is very ill then?' I demanded anxiously.

'I should like to call in a second opinion,' he replied.

'Well do so,' I told him.

He did, that day, and I was alarmed to see that the man he had called was Dr. William Jenner, a man who specialized in fevers—especially typhoid.

Dr. Jenner examined Albert and I waited fearfully for the verdict.

'The Prince does not have typhoid fever . . .' said Dr. Jenner.

'Thank God!' I cried.

'At the moment . . .' went on Dr. Jenner. 'But, M'am, I cannot hide from you the fact that there is a possibility he might be affected. We must be prepared.'

A terrible fear took possession of me. Typhoid! The dreaded disease! How many people had died of it. But not Albert . . . no! That must not be.

But Albert grew worse. It was no use hiding our eyes to the fact. He could not rest. He said he would sleep in a separate bed.

'No, no,' I cried. 'I do not mind your being restless. *I* do not want to sleep. I want to watch over you all the time.'

He smiled at me wanly. I believe Albert knew. He had known for some time.

I tried to weep but tears would not come. He saw that and did his best to comfort me.

'You will be all right, little one,' he said. 'You love life. I never did . . . as you did. It is only the thought of leaving those I love that hurts me.'

Albert rallied a little and after that our hopes soared. He said he wanted to hear some music and I sent Alice into the next room telling her to leave the door open and play. She played *Eine Feste Burg ist Unser Gott*; and he smiled.

'Dear Alice,' he murmured. 'Does Vicky know . . . about me?'

'I haven't told her you are ill. In her condition . . . she would be so upset.'

Vicky was expecting another child. I thought, if he does not recover, this will kill her. And even in that moment I felt the twinges of jealousy because he cared so much for her.

He was in such pain that I begged the doctors to do something for him. They gave him an opiate and he fell into a peaceful slumber. I sat by his bed watching his dear face. How he had changed since that day when we stood side by side at the altar!

He had a good night's sleep on account of the opiates, and the next day he seemed better. He asked Alice to read to him. She brought *Silas Marner* and sat there, but his attention strayed and he said he did not care for the book.

He was tossing and turning and I did not know what to do. For five nights I had scarcely slept. Albert was taking opiates; it was the only way he could rest. He was speaking mostly in German now and I believed that some of the time he thought he was a child again.

I felt as if my heart was breaking. I would look my fears in the face. I turned from Dr. Jenner to Sir James, because he wanted all the time to soothe me and to pretend that Albert would recover.

But at last Dr. Jenner told me. Albert was suffering from gastric fever . . . bowel fever. I knew what that meant, though he would not use the dreaded word 'Typhoid'.

I sat by Albert's bed. He knew I was there for he kept murmuring: '*Gutes Frauchen.*'

Jenner wanted to call in more opinions. There was Dr. Watson and Sir Henry Holland. I was afraid that so many doctors would alarm Albert and bring home to him the seriousness of his case.

Albert said: 'If Stockmar were here . . .'

I believed that, too. There was magic in the old man which perhaps we created, but what did that matter? It was there for us both.

I wanted to blame someone. So I blamed Stockmar for leaving us. If he were here Albert would recover.

I sat by the bed. Albert liked to lean his head on my shoulder. He said: 'It is comfortable like this, my dearest child.'

He was worrying about Vicky again. Does she know now?

'I have sent word to her that you are ill.'

'You should have told her I was dying.'

'No,' I said fiercely. 'No.'

That evening he asked me to come to his room after I had had dinner. Dinner! As if I cared for dinner!

I went to him. The doctor met me at the door.

'Your Majesty should not stay long. The Prince should rest.'

'Albert . . . my dearest Albert.'

He smiled at me.

'I must not stay.'

'It is the only time you can see me,' he said.

'It is the doctors. They tell me you must rest.'

I kissed his forehead and left him.

The next day Alice sent a message to Cambridge for Bertie to come.

She had not told him how ill his father was and Bertie seemed to think it was some minor indisposition. He was soon sobered.

Albert was passing into what they called the crisis.

All through the night we watched and waited. The doctors said there were grounds for hoping he would recover. That was six in the morning. I went to the Blue Room. In the light of the burned-out candles the doctor looked serious. Albert lay in bed, his beautiful eyes wide open but he did not seem to see what was there. He looked surprisingly young.

I went to his bedside and looked down at him.

All the children came in—except Beatrice—and kissed his hand. He was breathing heavily. He could not speak but his lips formed the words: 'Who is that?'

I cried: 'It is your little wife.'

I could not bear to stay there for I was facing the truth now. This dreadful tragedy was upon me. I hurried out of the room, the sobs shaking my body.

In a short while Alice was calling me back.

I knelt by his bed. Alice was on the other side; Bertie and Helena were at the foot of the bed. I was aware of others in the room.

His lips moved. *'Gutes Frauchen.'*

I felt I could bear no more. He had been holding my hand and I felt his grip slacken. I stood up and kissed his forehead.

'Oh my dear . . . my darling,' I whispered.

And it was all over. Albert was dead.

We were in mourning. The whole world should be mourning for the passing of Albert.

I was stunned. I could not believe this had happened. He was gone. How could I live without him? I had the children. They rallied round. Even Baby Beatrice tried to comfort me. Dear Alice was so gentle, so loving. What could she do for me? No one could do anything any more. He was gone. He had been my life and my life was now over.

I had no wish to see anyone, to go anywhere; I just wanted to be alone with my overwhelming grief.

Albert, the beloved, the saint, that most incomparable of men was gone forever.

Alexandra

When I made the discovery my anger was such that oddly enough, for a brief moment, it intruded in my grief and lessened it.

Bertie! My own son! Oh, it was so disgraceful. There was the letter from Stockmar. I remembered Albert's receiving it and how depressed he had been. A few days after he had said he would go to Cambridge and see Bertie. Now I knew why.

Bertie was in disgrace. Stockmar had written that while our son was at the Curragh Camp he had had a mistress. It had created scandal which had come to Stockmar's ears . . . and yet here we knew nothing of it! At least *I* did not know. I expect there was sniggering in certain circles at home.

I remembered that day well—the heavy rain, the cold wind. I had said to Albert, 'You cannot go to Cambridge in such weather,' and he had replied, 'I must.' So he had gone to see Bertie and he had come back with the fever . . . which had killed him.

Bertie had killed Albert!

My rage against my son was so great that I really did feel that for a time it overshadowed everything else. I kept saying to myself, If Albert had not gone to Cambridge he would be well today.

When Bertie came to me I could scarcely bear to look at him. He was now twenty years old, a man, I supposed. Bertie, who had always been such a disappointment to us. There could hardly be anyone in the world less like Albert; and yet he was Albert's son . . . the son who had killed his father!

No, that was not fair. But his wicked carelessness and his lustful conduct had helped to bring about Albert's death.

I could never keep things to myself. I had to let him know.

I said: 'It was Papa's visit to Cambridge which brought on his fever.'

'He was ill when he arrived, Mama.'

'I know he was ill. I begged him not to go.'

'He should never have come. It was bad weather, I remember.'

'He went because he believed he had to. You know why he went.'

A guilty flush spread itself across Bertie's face.

'He had heard what happened in the Curragh Camp,' I said.

'Oh that,' said Bertie. 'It was nothing really.'

'Nothing! A woman . . . a loose woman and the Prince of Wales! You call that nothing. Papa did not call it nothing. He risked his dear life . . .'

Bertie came to me and put his arms about me. Oddly enough I wanted the comfort his embrace could give me.

'He was ill before he came. He should not have come. There was no need for him to come. The affair was over. It was nothing. All of them . . . well, I was no different from the others . . . It was not my fault that he came. I did not ask it.'

I shook my head. 'You will never understand your father, Bertie,' I said. 'He was a saint.'

Then the tears began to flow and even my anger against Bertie could not assuage my grief.

I could find no comfort in anything—even those about me who loved me. I had lost the one being, the only one who could make my life happy.

For hours I sat remembering the past, every little detail. I suffered bitter remorse when I thought of all the storms I had created and how my angel had been so good, so tolerant, always right. That *he* should be taken, he, the one of whose wisdom we were all so much in need.

I wrote to Uncle Leopold:

'Though please God I am to see you soon, I must write these few lines to prepare you for the trying, sad existence you will find with your poor forlorn desolate child who drags on a weary pleasureless existence. I am so anxious to repeat one thing and that one is my firm resolve, my irrevocable decision that his wishes, his plans about everything are to be my law. And no human power will make me swerve from what he decided and wished . . . and I look to you to support and help me in this. I apply this particularly as regards our children—Bertie etc—for whose future he has traced everything so carefully . . .

'Though miserably weak and utterly shattered, my spirit rises when I think any wish or plan of his is to be touched . . . .

'I know you will help me in my utter darkness . . . He seems so near me, so quite my own, my precious darling. God bless and preserve you. Ever your wretched but devoted Child.'

Uncle Leopold thought that I should not remain at Windsor, but should go to Osborne. Everyone seemed to think this a good idea.

I had the room in which Albert had died photographed. My letter paper, my handkerchiefs were in black-edging for Mama. I had the edges widened to an inch. I had laurels hung over his portraits. I wanted a photograph taken with the children standing by a bust of him which was very lifelike. These little things gave comfort to me. They were something to do.

How dreary Osborne seemed without him! How could Uncle Leopold have thought I could find comfort anywhere! And at Osborne of all places, which he had changed so, which his brilliant talents had turned from a little house into a palace! How could I be happy there? Did it matter where I was? Nowhere could I ever be happy again.

I would sit at the window looking out at the sea. I put his portrait on the pillow beside me. I wept bitterly. I took his nightshirt and cradled it in my arms; in that I found a small grain of comfort.

Albert's brother came to Osborne. He arrived at midnight, cold and wet. It had been a dismal crossing, but nothing could be more dismal than our grief. We embraced and wept for the lost loved one.

On the 23rd December, Albert was laid to rest in St. George's Chapel, Windsor. He would lie there only temporarily for later he would be removed to the Mausoleum at Frogmore—the site of which I had chosen with Alice just after his death. One day—soon, I prayed—I should be lying there beside him.

It was a time to recall other Christmases when he had been with us. I thought of his sending for the Christmas trees from Coburg and how he had brought that fashion into the country so that it was universally followed. Dear Albert, how he had changed my life! And that of the English people!

He was too young to die. Forty years. It was tragic. Such a wonderful person, one who had done so much good in the world.

And so I went on.

I was not at his funeral in the flesh, but I was there in spirit.

Bertie was chief mourner. I wondered what he was thinking as he followed his father's coffin. What remorse he must be suffering. If only Albert had not gone to Cambridge . . .

I wanted to blame Bertie, although in my heart I knew it was not fair to do so. I really knew that Albert had been ill for a long time—so ill that he was unable to stand up to a major disease. But I wanted to blame someone. I blamed God for taking him, but it was easier to blame Bertie.

I sat there numb, staring out at the grey sea. Now the burial service would be beginning; the guns would be firing; the bells would be tolling.

They would be laying Albert's coffin at the entrance of the vault.

And when the mausoleum was completed it would be taken to Frogmore to await the day when I should be with Albert.

The children did their best to comfort me. My two girls, Alice and Beatrice, did help me, although there was very little they could do. Helena—whom Albert had called Lenchen—and Louise were wonderful, but Alice had a special tenderness. She always had since the days when as a fat little girl she had earned the name of Fatima. Alfred was seventeen. I used to be a little fearful for him because I believed he might resemble his elder brother; he had adored Bertie and made such a fuss when they were separated and I had feared he might follow in his footsteps. Arthur was sweet and especially endearing because he looked more like Albert than any of them. He was eleven at this time. Leopold, of course, had always been a source of anxiety because of his weakness.

But apart from Alice the one who did most for me at that time was little Beatrice. She was rather bewildered by the change in our household and clearly wished it to go on as before. Being the baby—she was only four years old—she had occupied a special place in our affections and her frank and amusing ways had endeared her to me and to Albert.

She used to come into my bed in the mornings and cuddle up to me. I believed Alice sent her. She was so charming in her innocence and did give me a little comfort. When I held her to me I thought of all I had endured in giving birth to these children and how I had dreaded those ordeals.

That would never happen again. But how willingly would I have endured it if it could bring Albert back.

Beatrice would sit solemnly watching me dress.

'Mama,' she said one morning, 'do not wear that sad cap.'

She was referring to the widow's cap which I wore now that I had lost my dear one.

'Mama must wear it now, Baby.'

'Baby does not like it. Baby does not want Mama to wear it.'

I was almost in tears. I held her to me. 'Mama does not like it either.'

Beatrice smiled. 'Then take it off.'

'Mama must wear it because Papa has gone.'

'When he comes back will you take off your sad cap?'

I could not answer. I shook my head.

'I wish Papa would come back.'

'You want him to be back, my darling. You miss him.'

Beatrice said firmly: 'I want Mama *not* to wear her sad cap.'

I could not help smiling. She was so single-minded, my little Beatrice. She could think of nothing but that I must not wear my sad cap—the symbol of widowhood.

I wished that Vicky was not so far away. I felt that she would understand my grief more than any of the others did. She had loved him as I had done. I should never forget their parting when she had left for Prussia. They had both been desolate; she had been almost as heart-broken to leave Albert as he had been to leave her. I remembered afresh those pangs of jealousy. I had not a very noble character I'm afraid; but then I compare myself with my saintly Albert. Perhaps compared with most people I was not so bad.

I re-read Vicky's letter which had come to me shortly after Albert's death:

'Today is a whole week since we began our new life of desolation. And when I look back upon it—dark, frightful and cruel—yet I have reason to be thankful. Papa shines like a bright star in our darkness . . .

'Papa read to me from the *Idylls of a King* at Osborne and wished me to draw something for him, and it has been my occupation for weeks—thinking of him, whether the drawings would please him, whether he would think them right. Do you wish to have them—shall I send them or bring them? They are the last I shall ever take pleasure in doing; as he ordered them I consider they belong to you . . . I know Papa's taste so well. As he was the most perfect model of all that was pure, good, virtuous and great—so was his judgement in all things concerning art—unerring.

'Oh how I tremble for you! How I pray that God may

support you through it as he has done through the rest. How
I shall bear it I do not know . . .

'Dear dear Mama, goodbye—and oh may God's everlast-
ing blessing rest on your beloved and precious head.'

What a wonderful letter! She understood as others could not.
Vicky's letters were wonderful. I used to read them again and weep
over them.

In a very short time she was writing again:

'How often Papa and I talked about death when I was sitting
with him of an evening in '56 and '57. He always said he
would not care if God took him at that moment . . . he always felt ready . . .

'Poor Bertie. How I pity him—but what sorrow he does
cause. Perhaps you do not know how much I grieve over his
'fall'. It was the first step to sin and whether it will be the
last no one knows. I fear not! The education of sons is an
awful responsibility and a great anxiety if they do not repay
one for one's care and trouble. It makes me tremble when I
think of my little Wilhelm and the future . . .'

Oh, what a comfort she was! Far more so than she had been
when she was at home with us. She alone understood the depth of
my grief.

I went over all the letters I had, my Journals, everything. I would
brood over the pictures of our wedding. Baby would sit on my lap
and look with me. She was a little put out because there were no
pictures of her in the early photographs.

'What a pity,' she said, 'that I was not old enough to go to your
wedding, Mama.'

Alice smiled fondly at her. Dear Baby! She did help so much.

Albert had made plans for Bertie to pay a visit to the Holy Land.
He thought the sight of so many relics and sanctified places might
have a sobering effect on his character.

I wrote to Vicky about it. She was so sound in her judgement
having spent so much time with Albert. She understood so well my
grief over Bertie's shortcomings; but she was inclined to be rather
lenient with him.

Bertie was weak. He would never be as clever as she was; but
he had some good points and he was popular with the people. Vicky

believed that if he were married to a suitable wife he would settle down.

Her favourite lady-in-waiting had been the Countess Walburga von Hohenthal who had married Augustus Paget, the ambassador to Denmark, which meant that Walburga had become very well acquainted with the Court of Denmark. She had given Vicky glowing reports of Alexandra, the daughter of Prince Christian. She was seventeen, beautiful and unaffected—for of course the family was very poor. They inhabited the Yellow Palace in Copenhagen through the bounty of King Christian. Alexandra would be so good for Bertie and although it was not exactly a brilliant match there were so few eligible princesses in Europe.

Vicky thought a meeting should be arranged between them. Albert had always said that Vicky was a shrewd diplomat, and I was very glad to take her advice. I felt it was almost like Albert speaking.

Bertie's visit to the Holy Land was planned but before he went Vicky invited him to Prussia. Vicky was a born match-maker and she arranged a visit to Speier Cathedral which Bertie could not have contemplated with any great enthusiasm for his interests were not for art and higher things. But when he was at the Cathedral he came face to face with Alexandra who Vicky knew would be there. They were introduced and, according to Vicky's reports, quite taken with each other.

'The first step,' commented Vicky.

After that he went to the Holy Land—as relieved to get away as I was for him to go. Whenever I saw him I was reminded of that visit to Cambridge, and I believed he could not forget it either.

Albert would have said that everything must go on as before. I dreamed of him and in my dreams he would sometimes remind me sternly of my duty.

I could not emerge from my mourning because I knew it was going on for the rest of my life.

Alice's wedding day had been fixed for July. It was only seven months since Albert's death—but I supposed it could not be postponed.

Alice was eager for it to take place. I could understand that. The poor child was in love. Perhaps she wanted to escape from this house of mourning. One could not expect the young to feel as I did.

Bertie was back. It would soon be his turn. Albert had said he needed marriage; and it seemed certain that Princess Alexandra, though not a great match, was very suitable in herself.

There could be no great celebrations, no rejoicing. When should we ever rejoice again? Alice should be married quietly at Osborne.

The dining-room was made into a chapel. Bertie was back and was with us, trying to look sad when he caught my eye but I could see that he was rather pleased with himself. The prospect of marriage was by no means repulsive to him.

The Archbishop of York, who was to perform the ceremony, was a most sympathetic man. I felt especially drawn to him because three years before he had lost his wife. We talked of the deaths of our dear ones and how one went on mourning for the rest of one's life. I was very glad that he was officiating.

I wore my heavy black and my widow's cap and I thought how different it would have been if Albert had been alive. I could picture his leading his daughter to the altar.

How sad it was! How sad my life was going to be right to the end!

So Alice was married.

She and her bridegroom were having a short honeymoon at Ryde before they left England.

So now my little Alice had become the Princess of Hesse-Darmstadt and she would no longer be there to give me that very special loving attention.

I turned to Lenchen and Louise.

In May I paid my first visit to Balmoral without Albert. I did not know how I should feel in that place which owed so much to him. There were too many memories. But I was given a warm welcome and sincere sympathy. Those good people accepted the fact that I was in mourning and some of them like Annie MacDonald, who acted as my personal maid there, and John Brown, the gillie who was taking on more and more important duties, rather hinted that I had to stop indulging in my grief and take an interest in life. The dear creatures, nothing on Earth would have made them say what they did not mean.

To my surprise I felt happier in Balmoral than I had anywhere else. I found Scotsmen and Scotswomen much less artificial than those people whom I met in the South. They were frank and spoke from the heart. I had long ago discovered this and made a point of choosing Scots for my servants at Balmoral—and they seemed to become my personal friends. They were much less courteous— indeed a little rough in their manners, but I liked that. John Brown especially appealed to me. He was the son of a farmer on the estate and had been an outdoor servant since '49, but I soon recognized his worth and he was in constant attendance. Albert had approved of him so I knew my trust was not misplaced. All his brothers had been found posts about the household and I was beginning to look upon John Brown as my personal friend.

I had been delighted to hear that the trouble about the *Trent* had been satisfactorily concluded. The Americans, after receiving the courteous note drafted by Albert, had acceded to the request by the British government, which they would almost certainly not have been able to do without humiliation if that first somewhat bellicose note had been sent.

When Lord Palmerston brought me the news, I reminded him that this peaceful issue of the American quarrel was due to Albert's work. I told him how ill he had been, so feeble that he could scarcely hold a pen, when he had sat up writing.

Palmerston nodded in agreement.

'Your Majesty,' he said, 'the tact and judgement and power of nice discrimination of the late Prince has always excited my constant and unbounded admiration.'

I smiled sadly. That was one of the occasions when I liked Lord Palmerston.

At Balmoral I laid the foundation stone of a cairn inscribed with the words:

'To the beloved memory of Albert the Great, Prince Consort, raised by his broken-hearted widow.'

The children were with me during the ceremony and their initials were carved on the stone.

I remembered so well Albert's delight when he had shown me his home and I felt a desire to go there once more, to walk through the woods where I had walked with him, to see Rosenau and listen to the birds, and see the room where he had learned his lessons and fenced with Ernest.

It was agreed that a visit would be an excellent idea. The children thought it would help me, and Palmerston had hinted that my period of mourning should be coming to an end and that I should be showing myself to my subjects. How insensitive people were! Did they think my mourning would ever come to an end? The people wanted to see my grief, no doubt, but that was my private affair.

I took Lenchen and Louise with me. They were taking over Alice's place. They were good girls, both of them, and eager to help me forget my grief—an impossible task!

I wanted to see Uncle Leopold so that we could mourn together.

Sombre in my widow's weeds I arrived at his Palace of Laeken. I threw my arms round him and burst into weeping; he wept with me.

I said to him: 'Here, Uncle, you see the most desolate creature in the world.'

'I suffer with you,' he told me. 'I share your grief.'

We talked for a long time about our sainted angel.

'At least,' said Uncle Leopold, 'you had twenty years of felicity with him. *I* lost my Charlotte very early and now Louise is gone.'

I knew he had suffered too; but nothing could really compare with the loss of Albert.

Uncle Leopold was very bent. I thought his wig was too luxuriant to match the rest of him. He told me he suffered greatly. His rheumatism plagued him, and he had so many ailments that when one subsided a little there was another to take its place.

He told me he had a surprise for me. Prince Christian of Denmark and his family were coming tomorrow and he trusted I would allow him to present them to me. 'They are such a simple, pleasant family,' he said. 'They are having a little holiday in Belgium. It would have been discourteous not to ask them.'

'I suppose they have their daughter with them?' I asked.

'Why yes, they have. I should like you to meet her. She is a beautiful, charming girl with exquisite manners and such good taste.'

I did understand, of course. Uncle Leopold had arranged this. A Danish marriage would be good for Belgium. Some of the European States were getting uneasy about the intentions of Prussia. A certain Bismarck-Schönhausen was making his presence felt throughout the continent. His plan was the aggrandizement of Prussia, which he wanted to see equal with Austria. He had visited London and talked to Lord Palmerston and Mr. Disraeli, who thought he was a man who would have to be watched.

When such situations arose it made an awkwardness for me because I was related to the heads of so many countries. There was Vicky who had become a Prussian and now Uncle Leopold was regarding Bismarck with suspicion.

There was no doubt that Uncle Leopold wanted the Danish alliance. He mentioned to me that Albert had been in favour of it for it had been brought forward before this calamitous event which had robbed the world of its greatest man and the only one who made life agreeable for me.

I was feeling overwrought. My talks with Uncle Leopold had

brought back my grief in full spate. I was living it all again, that day when he had looked at me with those dear haggard eyes and told me he must go to Cambridge; and I had tried to dissuade him. Oh, if only he had listened to me!

I wept and sat in my room thinking about it.

Lenchen came to me and said: 'Mama, they have arrived. Alexandra is lovely and they are all very nice.'

'My dear child, I cannot join them.'

'Oh, but, Mama, they are all waiting for you.'

'My dear, I cannot do it. You must understand that my loss is too recent. I cannot receive them. I do not want to eat. The thought of food nauseates me.'

'But, Mama, Uncle Leopold has arranged it so wonderfully.'

I shook my head.

I could not join them. I just sat in my room. The luncheon must proceed without me.

I sat there brooding and after an hour or so there was a gentle tap on my door. I did not answer it. I had no wish to see anyone. The door opened slightly and a face appeared. It was Walburga Paget—a girl I had always liked very much. She was very beautiful and I was susceptible to good looks.

'Your Majesty, may I come in?'

'Yes do, Wally.'

She ran to me and knelt beside me lifting her eyes to my face. I saw that they were full of tears. 'Dear child!' I murmured.

'Oh, Your Majesty, how you have suffered!'

I nodded.

'I thought of you so much, but there is nothing I can say. No one can say anything that is adequate. No one can understand your terrible suffering.'

I stroked her beautiful hair.

'He was the most wonderful of men,' she said.

'They don't appreciate him, Wally . . . none of them. They talk . . . but they forget.'

'Your Majesty will never forget.'

'Never!' I said vehemently. 'My dear child, it is good of you to come and see me.'

'I wanted to ever since I heard you were here.'

'You came with Prince Christian and his family?'

'Yes, they are very agreeable.'

'So I have heard.'

'Your Majesty, I believe it was *his* wish that there should be a match between the Prince of Wales and Alexandra.'

'He had it in mind. He had so much in mind.'

'He would wish you to be happy about this match. He would wish you to see the Princess.'

'Yes, I think he would wish that.'

'I think he would have approved of her. She has such exquisite taste . . . as he had. She is good and gentle . . . as he was . . .'

I nodded.

'Perhaps Your Majesty would wish to see the Princess now that you are both in this palace. It is such an opportunity. It seems as though it is God's will . . . as she is here . . . and you are here . . .'

God's will, I thought. And Uncle Leopold's.

I suppressed the thought. That was more the sort of thing Lord Melbourne would have said rather than Albert.

But I supposed Albert would have wished me to see her.

I said: 'Very well, I will see them. You may conduct me to them, Wally.'

She smiled radiantly. She seemed to be very fond of Princess Alexandra.

They were presented to me. The Prince was handsome in a Nordic way—not beautiful as Albert had been, but tall and fresh looking, rather like a sailor with blue, far-seeing eyes. Where would that family be but for the benevolence of King Christian who, Albert had told me when we were discussing the suitability of Alexandra, had given the man a commission in the army and the Yellow Palace for a home. Louise, his wife, was the daughter of the Landgrave of Hesse-Cassel; and the Landgravine was King Christian's sister. Hence the King's kindness to this rather impoverished family.

Alexandra, in view of all this, was hardly suitable to be the bride of the Prince of Wales. After all, Uncle Leopold had put her at the bottom of the list, but there was an urgent need to get Bertie married.

I did not greatly care for Christian's wife. She was a little hard of hearing and her complexion was not natural. Painted cheeks! I wondered what Albert would have thought of that! He did so hate any form of artificiality. But the girl was charming. She was all that Wally had said she was. How different from her mother!

I thought there was no point in pretending that the subject which was uppermost in our minds did not exist. I said to Christian and his wife: 'Everything will depend on the Prince of Wales. I do not know how affectionate he will feel towards your daughter.'

They looked taken aback, and so did Leopold; but he brought Alexandra forward. Such a pretty girl, and modest too. She raised her beautiful eyes to my face as she knelt and I could feel the sympathy in them.

Then I turned to Leopold. I think he was not very much at ease. I suppose the meeting had not gone as he had hoped.

I did not join them for dinner, I could not face that, but I went down afterwards. Alexandra was wearing a black dress, which was rather conspicuous among the others. She looked at me rather tremulously and I understood. What a delightful gesture! I was in mourning; she wished to respect that mourning and to share in it. I warmed to her from that moment.

They might be impoverished, they might be of little account but this girl was charming and I felt pleased that there was to be a match between her and Bertie.

I smiled at her and in that moment a bond was formed between us.

After leaving Uncle Leopold, I travelled to Coburg. There I visited the scenes of Albert's childhood. I recalled all that he had told me of them; it brought him back so vividly.

I was very disappointed in Ernest. He had been upset when Albert had died but I feared his feelings did not go very deep. When I thought that I might have married him, I thanked Fate for my lucky escape. But, of course, it had been my choice and I should never have chosen him.

I suspected him of all sorts of immorality. Who would not after the disgraceful affair which had so upset Albert. I guessed he was cured of that . . . physically . . . but nothing would stop his being the man he was. He was ambitious and very grasping.

He had no children and it had been Albert's wish that on Ernest's death Alfred should have the dukedom. It would go, of course, to Bertie, but Bertie would eventually be King of England and it was therefore suitable that the Dukedom of Saxe-Coburg should go to his brother.

Now a crisis had arisen in Greece. The popular assembly of that country had driven Otho, their King, from the throne and had offered the crown to Alfred.

At first I thought this was a very good proposition but I was finally convinced by Palmerston and Lord John that it was not practical. I was reminded that it had been Albert's wish that Alfred should have the Dukedom of Saxe-Coburg on Ernest's death.

When the offer was declined for Alfred, it was given to Ernest. I had thought this was a good idea for Ernest could go to Greece and Alfred could take over Saxe-Coburg without delay. But Ernest wanted the Greek crown *and* to retain his hold on Saxe-Coburg. He thought Alfred might go there as a kind of caretaker under his jurisdiction.

'That would not do,' said Palmerston. 'It would mean that Ernest would still control the Duchy and Alfred might well be held responsible for Ernest's misrule and the mountain of debts he has managed to pile up.'

There was a great deal of discussion between us on the matter and it spoilt my visit to Coburg which I had intended should be dedicated to the memory of Albert.

I was glad to leave.

I decided that Alexandra must come to Osborne. I must know more of this girl who might well become Bertie's wife. If she were, she would be Queen of England, and that meant she must be entirely suitable.

I already liked her. She had shown sensitivity when I had met her at Laeken, so the invitation was sent and Alexandra arrived at the Isle of Wight with her father. Christian was to stay with the Cambridges and leave Alexandra with me.

It was a cold and miserable day when she arrived. How I hated November! Albert had been very ill in November . . . and in December he had gone. And on the eve of Christmas! I should never celebrate that festivity again with any pleasure. Always there would be these memories.

I was pleased to see Alexandra. She looked very fresh and pretty. Christian was a little apprehensive and very eager for his daughter to make a good impression. What an advancement for the daughter of such a simple family!

But in spite of her somewhat homely upbringing Alexandra was by no means *gauche*. Her grace and beauty would always carry her through. They were very much in awe of me, I think. They all seemed so much taller than I, and I suppose because of my low stature I made up for it in regal dignity. But then I had been the Queen now for many years and that sort of thing grows on one.

I was glad when Christian left. His daughter seemed more at ease then. She was perfectly natural, and I had the impression that she was not trying to please because she was eager to make a brilliant marriage, but because she was generally good-hearted and understood my grief.

Baby thought her beautiful and in her frank way announced it to us all; Lenchen adored her; Louise, perhaps, was less impressed but she could find no fault with her. Alfred thought she was wonderful. In fact I was afraid he was going to complicate matters by falling in love with her himself. Alfred was very susceptible. He had so adored Bertie when they were boys and he imitated him slavishly in everything he did; and it seemed he had caught Bertie's interest in the opposite sex.

There was no doubt about it that Alexandra was an outstanding success. She asked me questions about Osborne and I described in detail how such a little house had been acquired and all that Albert had done to transform it. She was very impressed. She thought it was wonderful.

She understood my desolation; she gave me a sympathy which was heartfelt, I knew. She encouraged me to talk about Albert—not that I needed encouragement—but I felt that was a great help, for it was a comfort to talk of him to someone who could only know of his goodness by hearsay.

We went to Windsor which greatly impressed her. I told her how Albert had loved the place, how he had ridden in the forest and knew the names of all the trees and flowers. 'But I think Balmoral was his favourite place,' I told her. 'One day you will see that, dear child. I am sure you will love it as I do . . . as Albert did. The Scots are such good *honest* people. Albert built Balmoral. It is really magnificent, an example of his extraordinary talents.'

At the end of the month, Prince Christian left the Cambridges and came to take Alexandra home.

By that time we were the best of friends and I had no doubt that she was the right wife for Bertie.

There was no reason why the wedding should be delayed. I suggested January. There was opposition from Alexandra's mother. Her daughter could not possibly travel at that time of year. I had to concede that there was something in that.

Finally March was fixed. I was glad to have something to think of, but it brought the memory of Albert back all the more vividly because I kept thinking of how he would have arranged everything.

I decided that I would give Alexandra her wedding dress and that it should be trimmed with Honiton lace as mine had been. It was rather unfortunate that on her way to England she should stay for a few days at the Laeken Palace and when she was there Uncle Leopold—who was delighted with the match—gave her a wedding dress which was trimmed with Brussels lace.

Dear Uncle Leopold! He was wonderful, of course, but he *did* interfere. I could not have the wedding dress of the Princess of Wales trimmed with *foreign* lace. It must be Honiton.

I wrote to Uncle Leopold and explained. I knew he was very disappointed but I had long ago made him realize that as much as I loved him and no matter how poignant were memories of the past when he had meant so much to me, I could not allow him to interfere in the affairs of my country—and the marriage of the Prince of Wales was certainly that.

So Brussels lace it certainly was not. Alexandra was going to the altar in Honiton.

I sent my yacht, the *Victoria and Albert*, to meet Alexandra's party at Antwerp and it brought her to Gravesend where Bertie met her; from there they would drive to London and take the train to Windsor.

I was waiting with the girls to greet them on their arrival at the castle. How sweet the bride-to-be looked in her lavender cloak and gown. The dear girl had chosen lavender as a kind of half-mourning, I guessed. She could hardly have come in black, but she had made me see that Albert was in her thoughts.

What a sad contrast she made to me in my widow's black and what Baby persisted in calling 'my sad cap.'

I was so overcome with memories that I could not join them for dinner. I sat in my room thinking of the day Albert had come and how I had known at once that he was the one I should love for ever.

It was a great joy to see Vicky. She had brought four-year-old Wilhelm with her. It was a wonderful reunion and I looked forward to some intimate talks with her when we could remember Albert and mingle our tears.

On the day I reached the chapel, which was decorated in purple velvet, by a specially constructed path which had been covered so that I should not be seen for I did not wish to be stared at. I took my place in a box from which I could look down on the proceedings. I was in deep black with the ribbon of the Garter across my breast. I saw eyes turn to look at me, but my heart was too full for me to acknowledge these glances. My thoughts were back on that other day when Albert and I had been married.

I thought the girls looked lovely in their white dresses. Mary of

Cambridge led them, looking larger than ever, but quite splendid in lilac trimmed with lace—Honiton, of course. All the lace, I noted with satisfaction, was Honiton.

There was Beatrice, wide-eyed and looking round her with enthusiasm. She looked up and seeing me, waved. I smiled, in spite of everything, wondering what she was thinking and what odd remark she would come out with. She would be no respecter of places any more than she was of persons.

Little Wilhelm was there, standing between Arthur and Leopold. He looked very sweet—though somewhat mutinous, as though he were a little weary of the proceedings. How cleverly they disguised his arm with those special sleeves! Dear children! I wondered how much of this ceremony they would remember in the years to come.

Alexandra was beautiful and Bertie looked quite handsome too. What a pity he did not resemble his father more and that Arthur was the only one who bore a likeness. It was sad. I should have liked to see those divine features in some of them.

Of course we could not expect children to behave well. Such ceremonies must seem interminable to them. I saw Lenchen and Louis wipe their eyes and Baby watching them began to sob loudly.

Lenchen's hand on her shoulder tightened and Baby said in an audible voice: 'If *you* cry, why can't I? This is a wedding this is, where people have to cry.'

Dear Baby! How Albert would have smiled. I think he might have spoilt Baby as he had Vicky. He may have looked to Baby to take Vicky's place. I shall never be able to forget how heart-broken he was when Vicky went away.

There was more trouble from the children. Wilhelm was crawling on the floor. He had pulled the cairngorm out of his dirk, which was part of his costume and thrown it across the chapel floor. It happened during a silence and caused quite a noise.

Arthur bent down and whispered something to him and Wilhelm then bit Arthur's leg. Leopold tried to remonstrate and Wilhelm turned his attention to *his* leg.

Oh dear, I thought, I hope Leopold does not bleed.

Between them they managed to subdue Wilhelm and the service went on.

Everyone came back to the Castle for the wedding breakfast. I felt incapable of joining them. It had been a very emotional experience. There had been too many memories of that happy day when my own wedding had been celebrated.

Lenchen came to me afterwards. They told me that Wilhelm had thrown her muff out of the carriage and that Baby had said in a very loud voice, when they were driving through Windsor and she had seen the shops: 'I did not know before that they had stays in shops.'

We smiled. Baby could always amuse. She did produce some very funny comments.

After the wedding breakfast the bride and groom left for Osborne where they should spend their honeymoon.

I sighed with relief. Bertie was married.

Mr. Disraeli and Mr. Gladstone

Lord Palmerston came down to Windsor to see me. I sensed a certain reproach in his manner. He was thinking that the period of mourning should be coming to an end. He was really rather insensitive. As if my mourning would ever end!

He told me that he was delighted with the popularity of the Princess of Wales. She and the Prince were cheered everywhere they went; and the people were pleased with the marriage.

'Princess Alexandra is a dear girl,' I said.

'She and the Prince make an excellent combination, M'am,' replied Palmerston. 'It is a good thing that the Prince has no aversion to appearing in public.'

He gave me a sly look. I thought: I have never liked you, Lord Palmerston, but I know Albert thought you were a good politician and of course you are; but you are quite unlike Lord Melbourne. Oh, how I wished he were with me now—not the old man he had become but the Lord M I had known when I first came to the throne.

'The people like to see their Sovereign from time to time.'

'Lord Palmerston,' I retorted, 'I have suffered the greatest blow that life could have dealt me.'

'The world knows it, M'am.'

Again that irony as though they knew, not because of Albert's saintly reputation, but because I forced the knowledge on them.

My manner turned especially cold and regal.

'I hope, Lord Palmerston, that you have not brought bad news. Trouble never seems to be very far away.'

'It is life, M'am. But we have had this excellent wedding and we have the popularity of the young royal couple. That is something to rejoice in . . . particularly as Your Majesty has become such a recluse. The Prince is doing an excellent job. Let us be grateful for that. There is this matter of the throne of Greece.'

'Oh, is Duke Ernest being difficult again?'

'He is withdrawing from the contest. The next contender is a brother of the Princess of Wales.'

'Indeed!'

'It seems to me a good solution, M'am. Duke Ernest will remain in Saxe-Coburg and in due course it will be that duchy for Prince Alfred.'

'The eldest son of the Danish family will be the king of that country in due course.'

'Exactly, M'am. That is why it will not be the *eldest* son. It will be the next.'

'Is he not very young?'

'Royalty frequently has to shoulder burdens of state at an early age, as Your Majesty well knows.'

I sighed fleetingly thinking of that morning at Kensington Palace when I had awakened to find myself Queen.

'It seems that there is a universal agreement on this matter— which is a boon to us all,' said Lord Palmerston. 'But alas I see trouble ahead in that affair of Schleswig-Holstein. Bismarck is intent on one thing: aggrandizement of Prussia.'

'I do not like what I hear of that man. The Crown Prince and Princess of Prussia find him somewhat distasteful.'

'Alas, M'am, there are times when sovereigns are obliged to endure statesmen whom they do not like.'

He gave me that half-mocking look. He knew very well how much I had disliked him until Albert had discovered how good he could be dealing with the Crimean War and the Mutiny. He would have heard that I had abhorred Sir Robert Peel in the beginning, even though in time he had become my very good friend.

'Let us hope that does not grow into real trouble,' I said coolly.

'We can hope, M'am, but at the same time we must be prepared.'

I knew him well. He had come down for two main reasons: chiefly to warn me that I should show myself to the people who were getting a little irritated by my seclusion, and also to prepare me for trouble over those wretched Duchies of Schleswig and Holstein. Conflict between European states was always distressing, because I was related to so many heads of states and would find myself in the middle of warring relations, each trying to urge me to take their side. I did not relish that.

He left me with the wish that he would see me soon in London, to which I gave no definite reply, for I felt I could not face the people yet.

He said nothing about one other matter which was worrying me. Alfred, it seemed, was going the same way as Bertie. There was a scandal about his relations with a young woman whom he had met when stationed at Malta.

I wished to know more of this but I found it very hard to discover the facts. Bertie, of course, considered it a natural occurrence—commonplace, in fact. All young men had these affaires. They passed. They were not of any real consequence. I mentioned the matter later to Lord Palmerston who shrugged it aside with equal nonchalance.

'There will always be these rumours about royalty, M'am. Do not concern yourself with them. The people are indulgent. In fact, they like their princes to be human.'

How blasé they were, these men! How different from that incomparable being!

It was autumn—and Albert had always said that was the best time for Balmoral. At first I wondered whether I could endure to be there, but I liked to do exactly what we had done in the past. It seemed that Albert's spirit was close to me in that dear country.

Alice and her husband were with us. More than anyone Alice understood my grief. She had always been so gentle—I think the best loved of all my daughters. She was not clever, like Vicky, but Vicky had often irritated me by the way in which she monopolized Albert. Alice had always been *my* girl. I was sorry in a way that she had married and wished, selfishly, that I could have kept her with me; but I often had to remind myself of my poor mad grandfather who had ruined the lives of his daughters because he loved them so much that he could not bear to part with them—and most of them had lived frustrated lives. I would never be like that. However it was a comfort to have Alice with me.

They had decided, all of them, to come to Scotland for a holiday.

I had talked with Vicky and Fritz who were uneasy about the rise of Bismarck. King William, under the spell of Bismarck, had disagreed with his parliament and offered to abdicate. If he had done so Vicky and Fritz would have been Queen and King; but after a while the King decided against that, kept the throne and made Bismarck his chief minister. Vicky and Fritz were so openly opposed to Bismarck, whom the people supported, that they became very unpopular throughout Prussia. Bismarck's slogan was 'Blood and Iron', which meant that his aim was to see Prussia the dominant power in Europe.

I had known for some time that this was going on and asked myself what Albert would have done. Prussia was pitting itself against Austria who was the leader of the German states. What Bismarck really wanted was a unification of all the German states, presumably led by Prussia—which meant Bismarck.

It was pleasant to think that Vicky could have a brief respite here in Scotland, but what a tragedy that Albert was not here to solve Prussia's problems.

We had left Vicky and Fritz with their children at Abergeldie. They would join us later at Balmoral; and one morning Alice came to me and said: 'Let us go to Clova. You know how you love it, Mama.'

I smiled at her sadly. 'So many memories, my love.'

'I know. But they are everywhere. Do come. It will do you so much good.'

'Very well. If you wish it.'

'Just Lenchen, you and I, Mama.'

I nodded. 'Tell Brown to make some of that broth of his. Your father used to say that he had rarely tasted anything as good as Brown's broth in the Highlands.'

It was rather a hazy morning when we set out. Old Smith was driving the carriage. He was getting rather old and had been in our service for thirty years. Brown said he was getting unfit to drive the carriage, but Albert had said that he was a good man and I like to keep about me the old servants of whom Albert had approved.

By about half-past twelve we had reached Altnagiuthasach and Brown set out the picnic in his usual efficient way, warming the broth and cooking the potatoes. He chided me in his bluff way for not eating enough. 'You should eat something, woman. Ye've no more appetite than a wee birdie.' I took some more broth like an obedient child and I could not help smiling because of the way he spoke to me. He did not think of me as the Queen. Alice and Lenchen were a little shocked—although after all this time they should have been used to it. I could not explain that it comforted me to be bullied a little. Moreover it showed Brown's concern for me, which was genuine—far more so than all the gracefully worded sympathy I received in London.

After the picnic had been cleared away, we rode, as we used to, up and over Capel Month. It was snowing a little and the view was magnificent. We had always paused at this spot with Albert so that he could point out the beauties of the scenery. He taught us to appreciate so much. The weather made progress rather slow and the sun was beginning to set as we came to Loch Muick. I was very tired and sad and not at all sure whether it was good to revive so many memories of happier days.

Back at Altnagiuthasach we stopped and Brown made tea, which was warm and refreshing.

By this time it was dark and as we moved on it seemed to me that Smith was driving the carriage somewhat erratically. Brown was on the box behind and we had gone about two miles out of Altnagiuthasach when the carriage seemed to turn up on one side.

'What is happening?' I demanded.

'Oh, Mama,' cried Alice, 'I believe we are turning over.'

She was right. I am not sure what happened but the next moment, I found myself lying face downward on the ground. The carriage was lying on its side and the horses were down. It was frightening.

Then I heard Brown's voice: 'The Lord Almighty have mercy on us. Who ever did see the like of this before?'

He came to me and lifted me up.

'I thought ye were all killed,' he said. 'Are ye all right?'

I found I was not badly hurt though my face was scratched and my right thumb was throbbing painfully.

'Brown,' I said, 'help the others.'

Poor Smith stood by confused and helpless. Poor old man. Brown was right. He was past it.

Brown extricated Alice and Lenchen from the wreckage and though they were bruised and their clothes torn, they were not really hurt. Efficient Brown cut the traces and soon had the horses on their feet. I was greatly relieved to see that they were not harmed either.

'What do we do now?' I said. 'Here we are stranded on a lonely mountain.'

'I'll send Smith back with the horses,' said Brown. 'And they can send another carriage.'

'Do you think he'll be all right? He's very shaken. He is so . . . old.'

'He has to be all right. I'm not leaving ye here . . . you and the young women.'

I felt it was wonderful to have a strong man to take charge. Dear Brown! Albert had been right—as always—to see in him an excellent servant.

And so we waited. Brown found some claret, which was comforting; and Willem, Alice's black serving boy who had been on the box, held the lantern so that we were not completely in the dark.

So we waited and waited.

'Your father always said we must make the best of what cannot be altered,' I told the girls.

'How right he was!' said Alice.

'He was always right,' I said firmly. 'Oh dear, how I should love to tell him of this.'

'He knows it,' said Lenchen.

'Yes,' agreed Alice. 'I believe he was watching over us. We have all been so lucky.'

About half an hour later we heard the sound of horses' hoofs. It was Kennedy, a very favourite groom of Albert's. He had thought we were late and had come to see what had happened to us. He had brought ponies for us. Gratefully we mounted them, for we should have been waiting by the roadside until ten o'clock for the carriage to come. John Brown walked, holding my pony and Alice's. I protested because the poor man had hurt his knee when he jumped out of the carriage. He silenced me. He was in charge and had no intention of letting me ride on the rough road for fear there would be another accident.

Dear good faithful servant!

We progressed for some time in this way and in due course met Smith with the carriage to take us back.

What a fuss there was when we arrived! Fritz and Vicky had heard and came over. Louis was waiting anxiously. Brown said I must go to bed at once and ordered soup and fish to be sent to my room. I was shocked to see my bruised face and my thumb was swollen to twice its size. It was not broken though, which I felt it might be.

What a day that had been! But I was not sorry for in spite of my bruises and painful thumb, I had had yet another example of what a good and faithful servant I had in John Brown.

I knew, of course, that the trouble over Schleswig-Holstein had to erupt sooner or later.

A few weeks after the carriage accident, King Frederick of Denmark died and Alexandra's father became King. This was the signal for the trouble which had been threatening to break out. Both Germany and Denmark laid claims to the two Duchies, and with Bismarck at the head of affairs something was bound to happen.

There had been a conference in '52, under English guidance, when a compromise had been arranged and this was to preserve peace over this dangerous issue for eleven years, with the Danes holding the Duchies under German supervision.

Recently, as the time laid down at the conference was running out, Frederick of Denmark had laid claim to the Duchies and since his death, King Christian made it clear that he intended to carry on with Frederick's policy in this respect.

Now the Germans, with the help of Austria, were threatening to expel the Danes; the plan being that when the Danes were overcome, Germany and Austria should hold the territory until some plan was agreed on. There was another claimant. This was Duke Frederick of Schleswig-Holstein-Sonderburg-Augustenburg who was a German and claimed hereditary right to the Duchies. So there were three contestants—Prussia with Austria, Denmark and Duke Frederick.

I could see a very embarrassing situation emerging. Naturally my sympathies were with the Germans. Albert had been a German and I felt that that was where his heart would have been; but on the other hand, Bertie had married into Denmark and his wife's own father was right in the centre of the strife.

I was very upset when pleas for help came from Duke Frederick and Denmark. I was so deeply involved on all sides, for Duke Frederick was the husband of Feodore's daughter Adelaide and there was Bertie's wife—the daughter of the King of Denmark.

It was an impossible situation. If only Albert were here! He would be able to talk to them all, to make them see reason.

It was a war not only in Europe but within the family. They were all taking sides. There was Vicky hating Bismarck but certainly supporting Prussia; there was Feodore writing vehemently in support of her daughter's husband; and of course there was Alexandra who was fiercely for her father. She was expecting a baby and was very worried over the matter.

There were fierce arguments at the dinner table. I could see the family involved in such bitter quarrels that I forbade the subject of Schleswig-Holstein to be mentioned at the table.

There was great excitement throughout the country. People were naturally on the side of Denmark. 'Little Denmark' the Press called her; and an impression was given of a brave little country being threatened by bullies.

Moreover the Princess of Wales had won the hearts of the people and she and Bertie were appearing everywhere.

'We should be thankful to the Prince,' Palmerston had said slyly. 'He is keeping the people aware of the monarchy.'

A dig at me, of course. But I would not be dictated to by an old man who dyed his whiskers and coloured his cheeks and pranced about like a dandy at his time of life, even if he was Prime Minister.

Christmas came—a cheerless one, as all Christmases must now be, but this was an anxious one as well. The Schleswig-Holstein trouble hung over us all like a dark, dark cloud; and particularly over Alexandra, who was wan with anxiety. This was bad for her in her condition.

It was just after Christmas. Alexandra and Bertie were staying at Frogmore. I believed Bertie preferred it to Windsor and he was within reach of the castle. Bertie did not know the meaning of grief, and I was sure he had never appreciated his father. I knew that he lived a very merry existence and that he had taken a great fancy to the social side of his life. Lord Palmerston never failed to let me know this, and he applauded Bertie for it. There was a similarity between him and Bertie; they had both shrugged off Alfred's affair in Malta, and made light of it as though it was a cause for amusement rather than shame.

There were merry parties at Frogmore. I deplored this. How different the atmosphere there from that in the castle. Many of Bertie's friends were, in my opinion, raffish—the kind of whom Albert would never have approved.

Virginia Water was frozen over and I heard that Bertie and his friends organized skating parties. There were late nights, of course, and Alexandra should have been living quietly. The birth of the child was only two months away and the poor girl must be feeling exhausted, what with keeping up with Bertie and his exuberant friends, pregnancy, and all her anxieties about that wretched Schleswig-Holstein.

It happened during one of Bertie's skating parties. Alexandra had gone out with a few of her ladies to watch the skaters. I was glad to hear she was not so foolish as to try to skate. She had felt cold and had retired to the house. No sooner was she there than her pains started.

A messenger came over to the castle with the news, and I left for Frogmore immediately. I was glad to see that Dr. Brown was there for Albert had had a great regard for him.

Very soon after my arrival Dr. Brown came to me. I feared the worst, for Alexandra's child was not due for two months.

Dr. Brown said: 'Your Majesty, I am happy to tell you that the Princess is well. She is exhausted but that can be remedied. The child is fragile, but he will live.'

'A son! A seven months' child. But the Princess is well.'

'I am happy to say so, M'am. The birth was quick. It was all over in an hour.'

'Thank God she was spared much suffering!' I said with feeling, thinking that there had been many times when I had been less fortunate.

'Your Majesty would like to see the child?'

Most babies were repulsive with their frog-like faces—more like little old men about to leave the world than young things just born into it; and naturally this child, being premature, was even more ugly than most.

I went to see Alexandra. She looked frail but beautiful and she was very happy to have produced a son.

I kissed her tenderly. Poor child! She was learning something of the shadow side of marriage.

Later, when I saw Alexandra and Bertie together, I brought up what the child should be called.

Bertie said: 'I want him to be called Victor.'

'Victor!' I cried. 'There has never been a King Victor and don't forget this child is in line for the throne. He'll come immediately after you, Bertie.'

'Why should we go on in the same mould all the time,' said Bertie. 'Don't you think, Mama, that a change is sometimes refreshing.'

I said: 'I wish him to be called Albert.'

Bertie sighed.

'Albert Victor,' I went on. 'He should be named after his grandfather. It will remind people of all that he did for the country. People are so ungrateful . . . so forgetful . . .'

Bertie looked stubborn. I think he resented his father. I suppose one does when one has done a person a great wrong. Perhaps Bertie could not forget that his misconduct had taken Albert to Cambridge, and so hastened his death. To have that on one's conscience must be terrible. One would not want to be reminded. But then sometimes I thought Bertie had no conscience.

Alexandra, the peacemaker by nature, said: 'Albert Victor. I think that is rather good.'

I smiled warmly at her, the pretty creature.

'That,' I said firmly, 'seems an admirable choice.'

Bertie was not inclined to argue. I believe he was anxious to get back to his merry friends.

In spite of his premature birth the baby progressed. He was christened in St. George's Chapel, and I planted a tree at Frogmore to commemorate the occasion.

The Schleswig-Holstein matter was getting really acute, Alexandra was in despair. Her father wrote to her begging her to get help from her new country. Vicky was writing, blaming Bertie and Alexandra for playing for the sympathy of the British public and working to get the Press on their side. I reproved Vicky for daring to dictate to me and a coolness sprang up between us. Alexandra was reproachful because we did not help Palmerston and Lord John hinted that I was showing favour to Prussia and it would not do. The government favoured Denmark, and I said we must not become involved in war and if the cabinet decided on declaring it, I should feel impelled to dissolve Parliament.

I was amazed how strongly I could feel. I was trying to think all the time of what Albert would have done; and because Albert was not there, to act on my own initiative. I knew he would have been on the side of Prussia and would have fought hard against allowing England to go to war with Germany.

Meanwhile the Prussians had gone into action; they were invading Schleswig-Holstein and Fritz was with the army fighting against Alexandra's father.

Rarely had I felt so frustrated and miserable. The Crimean War had been much worse; we were fighting in that and our men were dying; but at least the family had been at one. There had not been this terrible disunity.

The Prussians with their allies, the Austrians, were having success after success. Palmerston pointed out that they were determined on conquest and, he thought, not only of the two Duchies in question. If some effort was not made, they would soon take Denmark itself. Since the rise of Bismarck, this had been their aim.

Lord John said it was what Bismarck meant by Blood and Iron. He wanted a Europe under German domination. He must be shown that Britain would not countenance that.

Lord Palmerston said: 'I have told the Austrian ambassador that if the Austrian fleet goes into the Baltic, they will find the British fleet meeting them there.'

'This is almost like an act of war,' I cried.

'Necessary, M'am,' said Palmerston. 'And in the name of the government I must ask Your Majesty not to show preference for the Prussians.'

I stared at him in dismay. How dared he tell me what I must or must not do—that gouty old man and Lord John with him! They should have retired long ago. They were two dreadful old men. And here they were, reproaching me, telling me what I ought to think, what I ought to do for the sake of the country!

'The Prince Consort was of the opinion that we should keep out of war unless it was of the absolute necessity to make it. He would never have agreed to make war on the Germans.'

'The Prince was a German, Your Majesty,' replied Palmerston. 'He was naturally devoted to his own country. But we, M'am, are English . . . and equally devoted to ours.'

The insolence! None but Palmerston would dare!

'War never did anyone any good.'

'It seems to be doing something for the Prussians. They will have Schleswig-Holstein—and Denmark, too, if they are allowed to. We cannot stop their taking the Duchies, M'am, and there are some who say they have a claim to them; but they must not be allowed to walk into Denmark.'

I was glad when they left. I had really felt very angry. But I had impressed on them that if they decided to declare war I should dissolve Parliament.

Palmerston did not want to go to war. He was wise enough to know the folly of that. But his sympathies were with Denmark.

'We want more than sympathy,' said Alexandra pathetically.

But we were not in a position to give more. Palmerston would send the fleet to the Baltic, much as he had sent out his gunboats, and that would prevent Prussia's invasion of Denmark, for no country would seek confrontation with the British fleet. Palmerston had hoped Napoleon would intervene. After all, geographically he was nearer to the area than we were. If Napoleon had gone in to help Denmark, we might have done so. I was glad he did not, for that would have meant our fighting against Vicky and Fritz.

What a dreadful state of affairs!

The matter was settled by April. The war was over. Prussia had taken Schleswig-Holstein. Alexandra was very unhappy and Bertie was sympathetic to her. Vicky and Fritz were triumphant; and once again I had to admit that Palmerston's methods had kept us out of war in spite of the exhortations of my family on all sides and the thoughtless urgings of the Press and people.

True, all along I had asked myself, What would Albert have done? But I had acted without his advice. I felt a certain gratification; and it was possible that my grief had lifted a little.

* * *

There were continual complaints about my seclusion. I could not bear to be in London. In the winter I was at Osborne and in summer in Scotland. Palmerston was constantly telling me of the people's discontent, and what great good luck it was that the Prince of Wales was so socially inclined.

I said I thought the Prince led rather a rackety life at which the Prime Minister smiled as though it was a very laudable thing to do.

He came down to Osborne with a piece of paper on one occasion. This, he said, had been attached to the gates of Buckingham Palace and he thought he ought to show it to me.

He smirked as he handed it to me.

'These Premises to be let or sold in consequence of the late Occupants declining business.'

'What impertinence!' I said.

'It shows what the people are thinking, M'am. We should always be grateful when they let us know what is in their minds.'

'Don't they understand?'

'Oh yes, M'am. They understand Your Majesty needs a period of mourning. What they are hinting is that it is of rather long duration. It is not wise for sovereigns to hide too long from the public. However, as I have said, we are fortunate in the Prince of Wales who is doing Your Majesty such a service.'

I could imagine them—Bertie and Alexandra—riding through the streets and all the gossip about Bertie's flamboyant life, which seemed to please the people. It was ironic when one thought how suspicious they had been of Albert who had done so much good for them with so little appreciation. But Bertie with his card parties and his fast friends . . . oh, he was a hero! And there was Alexandra, now sad and claiming their sympathy because we had failed to come to her family's aid and had allowed the Prussians—always hated—to take Schleswig-Holstein.

Uncle Leopold wrote. He seemed to know everything that was going on, and he had heard of the popularity of the Prince and Princess of Wales.

'It would seem that you have abdicated and handed over the crown to Bertie.'

That disturbed me. What would Albert have said? He had always believed that Bertie would be incapable of ruling unless he changed considerably. And had Bertie changed? He was still as unlike Albert as he had ever been, and he had more opportunity now of showing that dissimilarity. No. The last thing Albert would have wished was for Bertie to take my place.

I went to London. I rode through the streets in an open carriage. The people turned out in their multitudes to see the sad bereaved Queen who could not forget her husband.

The cheers were deafening.

Palmerston was delighted. 'Your subjects have had the chance to show their love and loyalty, M'am,' he said.

I was gratified. They had reminded me that I was the Queen. No one—not even Bertie and Alexandra—had had a welcome like that.

'Your Majesty must give your subjects further opportunities of expressing their love for you,' went on Palmerston.

Must I? Nobody said *must* to the Queen. I had no intention of coming out of my seclusion.

While I was at Osborne Dr. Jenner said I was not taking enough exercise. I told him that I had no heart for such things. Everywhere I went I was reminded of the Prince Consort. Of course, I was reminded of him in the house as well—but I just had no inclination to walk or ride.

Then one day Dr. Jenner came to me and told me he had taken a step of which he hoped I would approve. He had consulted with the Princess Alice who had begged him to go ahead as she thought it an excellent idea; he had also consulted Sir Charles Phipps.

I wondered what he was talking about. Sir Charles Phipps was the Keeper of the Privy Purse. It was all rather mysterious and he was so long in coming to the point.

'Your Majesty may not be pleased. If so, that can easily be rectified.'

'Do please tell me what this is all about.'

'We have taken the liberty of bringing one of your Scottish servants to Osborne, M'am. He looked after you so well in Scotland and Your Majesty was always so pleased with his service. We thought it could be to Your Majesty's benefit.'

'One of my servants from Scotland!'

'John Brown, Your Majesty. He was so pleased to come. If you do not wish him to be here, he can be sent back at once.'

I was smiling. John Brown . . . in Osborne! I laughed. 'I am pleased to have him here. Yes . . . very pleased. I was just wondering how John Brown would feel about being here.'

'John Brown is pleased to be where Your Majesty is, M'am.'

I felt very emotional. These dear good people were so concerned for my welfare.

* * *

I felt so much better now that John Brown was in attendance. He took care of me. He would lift me up and carry me if the occasion arose and without so much as a by your leave. He would put my cloak on for me and pin the brooch which held it. I was most amused one day when he pricked my chin. He said in a loud hectoring voice: 'Hoots! Can ye no hold up yer head?' If he did not like what I was wearing, he would say, 'What's that ye've got on?' It was so original, so outspoken. It was John Brown. But he was my good and faithful servant. If ever I was in danger he would be there to look after me.

I wrote to Uncle Leopold about him. 'He is *such* a comfort. He is devoted to me, so simple, so intelligent, so unlike an ordinary servant.'

He was no longer merely a gillie. I wanted him to be my personal servant. They did not know what to call him in the household and he became known as the Queen's Highland Servant.

I put up his wages and said I wished him to wait on me at all times. He used to come to me after breakfast and luncheon to get his orders and everything was always properly done; he was so quiet—taciturn almost—and had such a good memory. He was devoted, attached and clever; and I felt his only object in life was serving me; and indeed, at this time, feeling the lack of Albert, I wanted more than anything to be taken care of.

He was a very good-looking man and I had a weakness for good-looking men. They attracted me very much. Brown had a strong body, long legs, curly hair and the bluest of eyes. I noticed most of all that he had a firm chin. I always noticed people's chins. Perhaps because I had a very weak one myself. It used to bother me when I was quite young and I was constantly examining mine in a mirror. Lehzen used to say: 'You should not admire yourself so often, dearest. You are always peering into the looking-glass.' I explained that I was not admiring but deploring. 'You see, Lehzen,' I said, 'I have hardly *any* chin at all.' Lehzen retorted: 'Nonsense. You have as good a chin as anyone else.' But I knew that was not so. And one of the first things I noticed about John Brown was his chin.

I told him this one day. I said: 'People with strong chins have great determination.'

He looked at me then and said with that frank honest manner of his: 'Ye seem to manage very well, woman, without much of a one.' How very amusing! He made me laugh as I had not laughed since Albert died. So it had certainly done a great deal of good to bring John Brown south.

About this time Bertie and Alexandra went for a tour of the Continent. Naturally Alexandra wished to see her family. They had risen a great deal since we had first decided on Alexandra for Bertie. Alexandra's father had become King of Denmark and her brother King of Greece—and now her younger sister, Dagmar, was to marry the heir of Russia.

Well, they were a pleasant family—although I did not think much of the mother—and they were very fond of each other. The mother was too managing and it was disgraceful that she should paint her cheeks. However, I was glad for Alexandra's sake that they were no longer so poor and insignificant. She had suffered so much over that wretched Schleswig-Holstein affair.

But it was tricky visiting so soon after the war. I was against it but Alexandra was so eager to see her family. Bertie, who had been firmly for Denmark, I supposed because of his wife, made some very indiscreet remarks there about Prussia, which I was sure Vicky would hear of—and then there would be more of her vehement letters.

It was unthinkable that, at such a time, the Prince of Wales should visit Denmark and leave out Prussia. I sent orders that he was to leave at once for Stockholm, where he could take a short holiday incognito—as I did not want Vicky to know that he had gone to Denmark before going to her—and go from Stockholm to Prussia.

They acted most irresponsibly. Instead of passing through Sweden incognito, Bertie and Alexandra were entertained in the palace by the royal family; and worst of all, while they visited that Court, they had left the baby—whom we called Eddy—with King Christian and Queen Louise in Denmark.

I wrote furiously: Little Eddy was in line for the throne; he was his father's heir and his father was mine. If they did not return to Eddy at once, I should send someone to bring him to Windsor. Eddy's place, if not with his parents, was with me.

They returned immediately to Denmark and then the royal yacht took them into Kiel Harbour, where there was more trouble because Alexandra begged Bertie not to allow the Prussian flag to be flown.

I gathered that relations between Bertie and Vicky were cool. Their meeting was brief, which was diplomatic for Bertie and Alexandra had been so firmly against Prussia and had made their attitude known. They could not go to Berlin therefore and I knew they had only gone to Prussia because I had insisted that they should. The visit should never have been made at that time.

When they returned home, Alexandra was pregnant. Poor girl, I thought. It was not so long since she had given birth to Eddy. I wondered if she was going to prove as fertile as I had been. Children were all very well and one must have them—particularly if one was a queen—but the method! It made me quite nauseous to contemplate it. I was glad it was no longer possible for me to have children. But I could feel very sorry for Alexandra.

In due course the child was born. They called him George. Two sons! Alexandra was to be congratulated; and this time the little boy did not appear prematurely and he seemed healthier than his brother.

Alexandra was delighted with her children. She was a good mother, far more interested in them than I had been in mine. I often wondered about her life with Bertie. She seemed very fond of him, but I was sure that it was not in his nature to be a faithful husband. How sorry I was for that! It made me more than ever grateful for having had such a saintly man for my husband. Perhaps the children compensated her for having a really rather unreliable husband. I hoped so.

It was necessary for me to take a trip to Coburg for a statue of Albert was to be unveiled, and of course I must be the one to do it.

Travelling without Albert was a dreary business. It seemed that wherever I turned there was something to remind me.

All the children were with me. I had insisted on that.

'This is a memorial to your father,' I had said. 'You must all be there.'

We were welcomed by Ernest and Alexandra. How he had aged! I imagined he was still living an immoral life. Those sort of people do not change. I felt a resentment against fate for taking Albert and leaving him. He was older; he had suffered from a disgusting illness; he had led an irregular life—and he was the one to remain while Albert was taken!

He seemed fairly emotional when he talked of Albert, but I did not believe his grief went very deep.

Unveiling the statue was a very moving moment for me, revealing that dear face and remembering the time when he had been at this place with me. I showed the children all those spots which had been dear to him—his schoolroom, the sword marks on the wall, where he had fenced with Ernest, the forests he had loved, dear Rosenau.

Lenchen was very close to me at this time. She had taken Alice's place. She was a dear, good girl, with none of Vicky's cleverness, of course, and none of the arrogance which went with it.

It was while we were in Germany that we met Prince Christian of Schleswig-Holstein-Sonderburg-Augustenburg—a grand title for a man of very little means. He was young and handsome and managed to charm Lenchen, and she him. I liked to see young people happy together; they reminded me of Albert and myself. Before the visit was over it was obvious that my little Lenchen was going to be very unhappy if she said goodbye finally to her handsome Christian—and there was no doubt that he felt the same about her.

It would be said that he was not a very suitable match for a daughter of the Queen of England, for he was without hope of inheritance, being the younger brother of Duke Frederick, who had been one of the contestants in the struggle for Schleswig-Holstein; and his family had lost their estates when the Prussians were victorious.

However, they were touchingly in love and when Albert had married me he had very little. The Press had stressed that, Heaven knew, causing such anguish to my dear one. I should not stand in the way of love. If Lenchen and Christian could be happy together, then together they should be.

Nothing could be done about it immediately, of course; but when we left Germany, Lenchen was betrothed.

I could not leave the Continent without seeing Uncle Leopold. Poor Uncle Leopold! What a travesty of that handsome man I had known when a child. It was many years now since he had seemed to me the most wonderful being in the world; but I should never forget that he had been as a father to me. I had listened to him intently; I had believed that every word he uttered was divine wisdom. I should always love him. He was old and bent now. Worn out with physical pain and mental anguish, he said. He had lost so many loved ones. Charlotte, Louise and now Albert. We were able to talk of our grief and mingle our tears when we recalled Albert.

Uncle Leopold reminded me that when he had lost Charlotte he had devoted all his care and attention to me. He had planned for us, schemed for us, dreamed for us; and it was the greatest joy of his life when we were married.

He told me of his ailments in detail. He had always loved to talk of them and I did wonder how one who had suffered from so many could have lived for so long. Sometimes the thought came to me that he had enjoyed his ill health—as Stockmar had done. I believed that their ailments had, at the beginning, been the bond between them.

But he could not even now prevent himself from meddling. He talked a great deal about Bertie. I think he would have liked to advise Bertie; but Bertie was not the sort to listen to advice.

'I hear that he is very popular,' said Uncle Leopold. 'The people like Alexandra, too.'

'Oh yes, she is good-looking and they like that . . . and there was all that hysteria about little Denmark.'

'It was unfortunate for Christian that as soon as he came to the throne it should have happened. We shall have the Prussians sweeping across Europe. All the little kingdoms will go. That is what Bismarck is after.'

'He is an odious man. Vicky abhors him. I am afraid her lot is not an easy one. It should have been so different. Albert always wanted her to be Queen of Prussia. He would have been able to advise her and Fritz how to deal with that upstart Bismarck.'

'He certainly is making his mark on Europe,' said Uncle Leopold. 'Each day I wonder what he will do next.'

'He has accused Vicky of being pro-English,' I said indignantly. 'Did you ever hear such impertinence! Of course she remembers the country of her birth.'

'Men like that are a menace to the world. I wanted to talk to you about matters nearer at home for you. The English are a very *personal* people. To continue to love people they must see them.'

I sighed. It was the old complaint.

'Dear Uncle, I believe you do not understand my feelings.'

'I do. I do. I loved him myself. I have felt the deepest grief.'

'It is not the same,' I said sharply. 'He was my husband. We were hardly separated for twenty years . . . day and night . . .'

'I know, I know. But you are the Queen. Unless you want to hand over the crown to Bertie, you must show that you have some regard for your position.'

'Regard for my position! Do you think I ever forget?'

'I don't think so. But the people might. Bertie and Alexandra are constantly before the public in every imaginable way. The people must not forget that the Queen wears the crown.'

'I rode through the streets in my open carriage. You should have seen the people. I was greeted with far more enthusiasm than Bertie ever had.'

'I know it, and it bears out what I have said. You must try to emerge . . . gradually if you wish. But it is never wise to go against the wishes of the people.'

I looked at him fondly. Dear interfering Uncle Leopold; he was so pathetic with his built-up shoes to give him height, the colour in his cheeks, faintly but appreciably artificial, and that wig of luxuriant curls which was too young for his wrinkled face.

I kissed him tenderly.

I did not know then that that would be the last time I was to see him.

That October I suffered a shock. Lord Palmerston died. I had never liked him and I had always had the impression that he was laughing at me. Lord Melbourne had been a little like that, but he had smiled tenderly whereas Lord Palmerston had been amused in a ridiculing sort of way.

By a strange coincidence Lord Palmerston died at Brocket Hall, the same house in which Lord Melbourne had died. Of course Palmerston had married Lord Melbourne's sister and the house became hers, so that was understandable—but I still thought it odd.

When people die one remembers the good things about them. There could not have been two men less alike than Albert and Lord Palmerston; and that speaks for itself. Palmerston had had few of Albert's good qualities. He had been a rake and a dandy; but he had also been a good politician. Someone said of him that he had the great gift of judging the mood of the House and adjusting his utterances to it, which was one of the reasons why he had almost invariably carried opinion with him; he had been honest in politics and would not diverge from what he believed to be good for the country; he had the two most important assets for a politician: Courage and Confidence.

He was, therefore, a loss to the nation. I hated death; I hated a change of scene. Little things could change here and there almost unnoticed—and then suddenly the entire picture was different.

I thought of all the tussles we had had and I smiled at them now. He had been so outspoken and he had shown clearly that while he respected the crown, he saw those who wore it as frail human beings—which common sense told me was true. So when I heard of his death I was sad and I remembered not the irritation he had given me but his masterly conduct of the country in times of crisis.

We should miss Lord Palmerston.

It was only two months later when I was shattered by news of another death. This touched me more closely. It was hard to imagine a world which did not contain Uncle Leopold.

I had to shut myself away. I had to be alone to think back on all those happy times of my childhood. The visits to Claremont; the joy of seeing him. I remembered sitting on his knee and looking up into his beautiful face, for when he was young he was extremely handsome. I remembered how he had taught me to be good and prepare myself for a great destiny. It was he who had found Albert for me and brought us together.

He had been part of my life and now he was gone.

There had been little differences. After all I had had my storms even with Albert. But how much he had meant to me when I was a child . . . and after.

He had expressed a wish to be buried at Windsor. I knew how close he felt to this country and that it had been his great ambition to rule it . . . with Charlotte; and although that had been denied him, his love for England had not changed.

I set about planning the ceremonial funeral which we would give him at Windsor; but when I was in the midst of my plans, I heard that the Belgian government refused to send his body to England. He was the King of the Belgians, they said; and therefore he must be buried in Belgium.

I was very angry.

'Was there nothing we could do?' I demanded.

Nothing, said Lord John. Leopold *had* been King of the Belgians, and they would have him interred in Belgium.

So Uncle Leopold did not come to England.

Lenchen and Louise tried to comfort me. Brown was scornful, implying that it was no matter over which to lose any sleep.

'He's gone and that's an end of it,' he said.

'It is because they are Catholics,' I explained. 'I think that is the main objection.'

'Catholics are nasty beggars,' said John Brown.

'Oh, Brown,' I said with a little laugh, 'you are incorrigible.'

'I'm here to look after you, woman,' he said, 'and blubbering over a grave is nae good for ye health.'

What a man! My spirits were lifted just to listen to his quaint way of expressing himself and his good, honest, frank way of doing it.

On the death of Palmerston, I had called in Lord John, who had gone into the House of Lords as Earl Russell, and asked him to take Palmerston's place. My dear friend Lord Clarendon was given the post of Foreign Secretary which Russell had hitherto held; and the Chancellor of the Exchequer, William Gladstone, became leader of the House.

That year Alfred was coming of age and Lenchen's marriage was taking place. They would need grants and I was very eager that there should not be unpleasantness in Parliament about this.

Lord John urged me to come to London to open Parliament; and I felt that, in the circumstances, although it was five years since I had done so, I must give way on this occasion.

So I agreed to on condition that the ceremony should be performed without the usual fanfare of trumpets and gilded trappings which normally accompanied it. The state carriage was replaced by another of more modern style although it was drawn by eight cream-coloured horses. And I did not wish to wear the robes of state, but had them laid on a chair beside me. I was dressed in black with the type of cap which is always associated with Mary Stuart; my garments being brightened by the Ribbon of the Garter.

The people greeted me with warmth and it was clear that they were pleased to see me. I acknowledged their greetings rather solemnly because I wanted them to realize that I was still in mourning.

I was glad when there was no haggling about the allowances, and rather surprised that not a voice was raised in opposition. Helena was granted a dowry of £30,000 and an annuity of £6,000; d Alfred was to have a yearly sum of £15,000, which would be raised to £25,000 on his marriage.

This was very gratifying.

Later I went to Aldershot to review the troops.

I was pleased to hear that Mary of Cambridge had become engaged to the Duke of Teck. This gave me gratification because Mary was no longer young and she was too large to be really attractive. Moreover the Duke of Teck was connected with the Saxe-Coburg family, so I heartily approved of the match.

I attended Mary's wedding at Kew, dressed in deepest black in case anyone should think I had forgotten Albert; and a month later my dear Lenchen was married at Windsor.

I was very alarmed by the conflict which was growing between Prussia and Austria. Having taken Schleswig-Holstein, they were now quarrelling over the spoils. I understood what they wanted. It was the unification of German States, and the question was who should be at the head of them. Bismarck was determined that it should be Prussia; and he had not talked of Blood and Iron for nothing.

The struggle cut through the family. The Crown Prince naturally stood with Prussia; but Alice's Louis and my poor blind Cousin George of Hanover were for Austria. The idea of having two sons-in-law fighting against each other was abhorrent to me.

I knew that Albert would have wanted to see Prussia dominant; but the situation had changed since Albert's death, and I wondered what his feelings would be now. His hope had been that Vicky would one day be Queen of Prussia, and if Prussia succeeded it would mean that Vicky and Fritz would be two of the most powerful sovereigns in Europe. But what of Alice and Louis? What of poor blind George?

I begged Lord Russell to do everything possible to prevent war. I offered to act as mediator between the two states. Bismarck was almost contemptuous in his refusal. What an odious man! It was an unhappy day when he rose to power.

Not only was there all this trouble abroad, but domestic difficulties arose. Lord Russell told me that he thought the government might be defeated over the Bill which they had recently introduced. I knew that we needed this matter of the extended franchise settled, and that it had been going on for a long time.

Lord Russell said: 'Your Majesty's government thinks you should remain at Windsor instead of going to Balmoral this spring, for if a ministerial crisis arose, you should be on the spot.'

I refused and really I believed I was far more worried about what was happening on the Continent than at home.

The Reform Bill was in committee when the storm broke and war between Prussia and Austria broke out. Almost immediately Lord Russell sent his resignation to Balmoral.

I was very annoyed. I wrote to him that in the present state of Europe, I thought it was apathetic of the government to abandon their posts in consequence of a defeat on detail in a matter which demanded concessions on both sides. I asked him to reconsider their decision.

Lord Russell was adamant. I retorted that his withdrawal was betrayal; and I stayed on at Balmoral.

Lord Derby then accepted office and Benjamin Disraeli was the Chancellor of the Exchequer and Leader of the House. But it was the war in Europe which gave me sleepless nights. I wrote to Alice telling her to send her children to me because I had a terrible feeling that Hesse-Darmstadt was not going to stand out against the Prussians. I sent linen for the wounded. It was a dreadful feeling to be supporting Fritz's enemies, but his enemies were my beloved daughter and her husband. Strife in the family is like Civil War—the most heart-rending conflict of them all.

The Prussians overran Hanover, depriving poor George of his throne. He took refuge in Paris with his family. At least his life was saved.

Then . . . the war was over. In seven weeks. Prussia was victorious. Bismarck was getting his wish. Prussia's grasp of the Imperial Crown of Germany was in sight.

And the price: Hanover, part of the British Crown, was ours no longer. The First George had brought it to us and I should have been its Queen but for the Salic Law. Now that had passed out of our hands. Poor Louis had lost much of his territory and was greatly reduced in power—as were the smaller German States.

They would soon all be under one rule—that of the all-powerful Prussia. It had been a time of distress and I was glad to stay in Balmoral to discuss an account of Albert's early life which was to be published. I was helping to compile this with my secretary, General Grey; and although I wept bitterly over the letters—of which it mainly consisted—I could absorb myself completely and it was almost like having Albert with me.

When the book appeared it was a great success; and I decided that there should be a biography of Albert and for this I called in Sir Theodore Martin; and he set to work.

I was so engrossed in the work and the company of these men who seemed to have a special understanding of Albert that I decided to publish some writings of my own. I had always kept an account of day-to-day happenings and I went through some of them. It was amazing how those words brought back memories of the bygone days, so that I felt I was living them again.

Early in the following year my *Leaves from a Journal of Our Life in the Highlands from 1848 to 1861* appeared. It was a great success. Of course it was very simply written and from the heart, and I think people began to realize then my devotion to Albert, and to understand why I felt the need to shut myself away and mourn.

I was getting to know Benjamin Disraeli and I found him a very interesting man. Albert had not liked him very much. He was sure he dyed his hair. Perhaps he did but he was certainly most gracious in his manners, and what a respect he had for Albert! This made me warm to him and I found that I could talk to him easily. He was extremely clever; he was an author of some note and because I myself liked to write that was an added interest we had in each other.

He gave me a copy of his novel *Sybil* and I was very touched to see that it was dedicated to The Perfect Wife.

I said: 'You had the perfect wife, Mr. Disraeli. I had the perfect husband.'

He looked at me with great emotion and replied: 'It is the greatest good fortune, M'am, to find the perfect partner; and those to whom this falls are indeed to be envied.'

I could talk about Albert to him; he responded glowingly. He had always had the greatest respect for Albert, he told me. He had always seen him as the great statesman.

When *Leaves from a Journal* was published he came to congratulate me. 'I know how we authors feel when we see our work in print,' he said.

I laughed and replied that I was not an author in the sense that he was; but he thrust that aside and said that *Leaves* would live as long as literature lasted.

'I shall never forget the dedication. "To the dear memory of him who made the life of the writer bright and happy, these simple records are gratefully inscribed".'

'You remember it perfectly, Mr. Disraeli.'

'M'am, such words are not easily forgotten.'

I felt my spirits lifted; and my thoughts went back to those days when Lord Melbourne had made me so happy.

I believed I was going to find great comfort in Mr. Disraeli.

It was hardly to be expected that the people would allow me to rest in peace. It was difficult for them to understand how helpful John Brown was to me with his blunt manners and wonderful fidelity. They must besmirch everything that was good. I would never forget what they had said of Albert; now they turned their attention to John Brown, and it was their aim to hurt me through that excellent creature.

There was even a rumour that I had married him! But that was so absurd that I could only dismiss it as ridiculous. Memories of long ago came back to me. Ascot and that insidious and wicked murmur of 'Mrs. Melbourne', simply because a beautiful friendship had existed between us. Now they were turning their crude thoughts to John Brown . . . and me! They seemed to have forgotten that I was the Queen.

I tried to think what Lord Melbourne would have said if he could have heard these rumours. Or Lord Palmerston even. They were ridiculous, too absurd—and yet they persisted.

'Mrs. John Brown,' they were calling me. How dared they. And they were so blatant. *Punch* had published an imaginary Court Circular headed Balmoral.

'Mr. John Brown walked on the slopes. He partook of a haggis. In the evening Mr. John Brown was pleased to listen to a bagpipe.'

A scurrilous paper called the *Tomahawk* was publishing pieces which were all insolent and defamatory. There was one cartoon with a caption: 'Where is Britannia?' The robes of state were depicted draped over a throne with a crown perched precariously on the top of them, and obviously in a position soon to topple over, which I presumed was meant to be significant. 'It is so much more exhausting to entertain people of one's own rank than gillies and servants?' was printed below it.

How dared they! Had they no sympathy for bereavement; they were the victims of their own depraved minds.

It was amazing how little details seeped out to the Press. I had always known that John Brown liked what he called 'a wee dram', which meant that he was rather partial to Scotch whisky; and naturally there were occasions when he did not realize how much he had taken. Then he would be in a state which he described as 'a wee touch of the bashful', I rarely saw him when he was thus, for he would always keep away from me then and confess to me next day that he had been 'bashful' on the previous night.

I found this rather endearing and so honest.

There was another matter which caused a great deal of trouble. Prince Christian, who was staying with us, was apt to sit up late; he would sit smoking and talking until the early hours of the morning. John Brown mentioned to me that this kept him up late and I asked my equerry, Lord Charles Fitzroy, to drop a hint to Prince Christian that the smoking room should be closed at midnight.

This leaked out. Servants will talk. It caused a great deal of amusement. Royalty must bow to the wishes of Mr. John Brown. Why? Because Mrs. John Brown said it should be so.

There was one cartoon entitled 'The Brown Study', published in the obnoxious *Tomahawk*. It depicted John Brown, sprawling close to the throne with his back to it, a glass of whisky in his hand.

Bertie came to see me one evening. Brown barred his way and said: 'Ye canna see the Queen now. She's resting.'

Bertie hated Brown in any case, and he was furious.

'The Prince of Wales will see the Queen,' he said.

'It's your eldest,' called Brown. 'I've told him ye're too tired to see him the night.'

'Thank you, Brown,' I said.

I could imagine Bertie's fury, but I would not have him rude to Brown.

The following morning Bertie came to me waving a paper in his hand. I knew at once that it was 'The Brown Study'.

'This is disgraceful, Mama,' he said.

'I ignore such scurrilous nonsense.'

'It is an attack on you . . . on the crown. It should be considered. Mama, Brown must go. He was abominably rude to me. He was rude to Christian. He is quite impossible. It is all becoming a laughing stock.'

'He is my servant, Bertie. I will choose my own servants.'

'He is no ordinary servant.'

'You are right,' I retorted. 'Indeed he is not. He understands me as some of my family fail to, or perhaps do not take the trouble to.'

'We are all concerned.'

'I think, Bertie, that the family is more concerned about you than about me. I am sure Alexandra is quite sad about the manner in which you carry on. I know you have debts. I know of your fondness for gambling and fast women.'

'Oh, Mama!'

'You were always a trial to us, Bertie. Your beloved Papa had many an anxious hour worrying about you. Why, at the end of his life he went to Cambridge in that dreadful weather . . . I often think of what might have happened if he had not gone.'

It was the sure way to subdue Bertie. He lifted his shoulders and after a while took his leave.

I was annoyed with him and that wretched *Tomahawk*. How dared they print such libellous nonsense when all I wanted was the comfort of a good and faithful servant.

Alexandra was pregnant again. Really, it seemed as though she was going to have one child after another, as I had done. It would have been so much better for her not to have them so close. She was a very good mother—adored by her boys. She was very fond of her family and took their troubles to heart. I shall never forget how almost demented she was at the time of the Schleswig-Holstein affair. Now her sister, Dagmar, had had a disappointment. Her fiancé, Nicholas of Russia—a marriage which would have brought much glory to the Danish family—had died of tuberculosis; but

Nicholas had a brother Alexander and Dagmar was to have him instead. I shuddered and pictured myself losing Albert and having to take Ernest in his place. It was rather absurd to say that she found she loved Alexander after all; but it was what they always said in such cases.

Now Dagmar was to go to Russia and Bertie and Alexandra wanted to go to the wedding.

As Alexandra was pregnant and her first child had been born prematurely, the doctors said she was unfit to go. She was very upset but I forbade it. Bertie, however, was eager to go. I was very sad for Alexandra. How different Albert would have been! He had hated to be separated from me and would not have wanted the superficial glitter of such occasions. Not so Bertie. I told him that as Alexandra could not go he had a very good excuse for not going either. Bertie was sly. He went to the Prime Minister to ask his advice; and both Derby and Disraeli thought that Bertie should go since the Russians could believe that the absence of both Bertie and Alexandra could be construed as an insult.

So Bertie went, and I insisted that he call in at Prussia either on his way out or on his return. He was reluctant to do this. Vicky was so censorious, he said. She thought he was her little brother still.

He went to Paris as well. He was very fond of Paris and had always maintained a friendship with the Emperor with whom he was a great favourite since he had, so disloyally, told him that he wished he were his father. Vicky wrote that there were rumours throughout the Continent about his behaviour. He was very popular; there was not a doubt of that; but he was very much given to entertaining and being entertained by people of not the finest character—and particularly women.

I expected such letters from Vicky, but when I heard from Alice that there was scandal about Bertie I felt it was really grave.

If only Albert were here! I thought. I tried to imagine what he would have done. It was different now. Bertie was no longer a boy; he was in fact building up his own Court—men like himself, fond of gaiety and reckless living. Of course he was popular, far more than Albert had ever been—even at the time of the Great Exhibition. The government seemed to approve of him too. They called him a good ambassador; and if I raised any objections to his behaviour, I was met by oblique references to my own seclusion.

We were very anxious about Alexandra because she now began to suffer from pains in her limbs which mystified the doctors. She could scarcely walk. Eventually they diagnosed rheumatism. This was very worrying as she was about to have a child.

When her child was born she was very ill indeed. Bertie was away and the doctors, fearing she was going to die, sent for her parents. I hurried from Windsor to Marlborough House and when I arrived there, I found Alexandra's mother at her bedside and was told that her father would come as soon as he could.

I was rather annoyed. My permission had not been asked; but when I saw the tenderness between Queen Louise and her daughter, I softened. I was so fond of Alexandra and she told me it had done her so much good to see her mother and she was feeling better every instant since her arrival.

I then told Louise how glad I was that she had come, and how dearly I loved my daughter-in-law. And because she knew I was speaking the truth, we liked each other a little better.

Alexandra had given birth to a little girl—Louise Victoria Alexandra; I was so relieved that she had come through *that* ordeal; but she was still in pain.

The doctors said she had had rheumatic fever and that and the pregnancy had impaired her health considerably. She hobbled about on sticks, poor child, and still suffered a lot of pain. I told Bertie that it was due to the life they led and that Alexandra needed more peace. 'Your Papa and I liked nothing better than to be alone, to read to each other and play duets. That was so restful. Papa did not care for dancing . . . ever . . . and he would not have been so foolish as to gamble.'

'It is impossible for everyone to be like Papa,' he said.

'That is true,' I retorted. 'Least of all, it seems, you, Bertie. You are his son. You should be proud of that and try to be like him.'

Bertie had a way of appearing to listen when I guessed his thoughts were far away.

In time, Alexandra improved a little, but she walked with a limp. She was so pretty and dressed so charmingly and had such a natural air of elegance that nothing could deter from her attractiveness. Some of the ladies copied her walk. They thought it was very charming.

They called it the Alexandra Limp.

There was further trouble in Europe.

Although I was still on very friendly terms with Louis Napoleon, I did wonder what he was secretly planning. Napoleon's family were natural fighters; and he was hinting that owing to the new

Prussian supremacy in Europe his frontiers were threatened by the Duchy of Luxembourg, which the Prussians were fortifying right on his border. He was in conference with the King of Holland suggesting that the Duchy should now be part of France—or Belgium might have it if they gave him a strip of territory in exchange for it.

Prussia, flushed with victory, was not in the mood to agree.

We must keep the peace, I declared.

As a result there was a meeting in London and it was decided that the independence of Luxembourg should be guaranteed and the fortress dismantled.

Napoleon was then a little cool towards me. He wanted territory and he thought that, in my efforts to avert war by calling a conference, I had thwarted him.

I was appearing in public a little more at this time. I had laid the foundations of the Albert Hall which was to be built in honour of Albert; that ceremony had been very moving. But I had to do it for it would not have been seemly for anyone else to.

There were still scurrilous comments about my relationship with John Brown and I was not going to let myself be persuaded to send him back to Scotland, which I think some of them would have liked.

I had given way to pleadings for me to review the troops in Hyde Park. I would ride in my carriage and naturally John Brown would be on the box. In view of all the publicity John Brown had received, the crowd would, no doubt, turn out to see him and me together.

Lord Derby called on me and told me that it would be unwise for John Brown to be present.

'But why?' I demanded. 'His place is there. He is my Highland servant.'

'M'am, as you know there have been a number of scurrilous cartoons and articles in the papers.'

'Destined to destroy the character of a good and honest man . . . and their Queen. I know. I have no respect for such people. They should be punished severely.'

'There has to be freedom of the Press, Your Majesty, and sometimes that can be unfortunate. But I think it would be wise in the circumstances if John Brown did not appear at the review.'

But I was not going to give way. That would be weakness and I should despise myself if I did. My relationship with John Brown was that of a queen and her servant—a respected servant, it was true, but nevertheless a servant. And I would not give way to sen-sation-seeking scandalmongers.

I said firmly: 'John Brown shall go to the review.'

But it came about in a strange way that he did not.

A few years before, Napoleon had persuaded the Austrian Emperor's brother, the Archduke Maximilian, to accept the Imperial Crown of Mexico which the French were setting up in that republic. There was a close connection between the Archduke and myself because he had married Charlotte, Uncle Leopold's daughter, so it was another of those family affairs. The Mexicans, however, would not accept the Archduke as their Emperor and Napoleon was asked to withdraw his troops and the Archduke to resign his title. Charlotte came to Europe to rally help for her husband; but meanwhile the Mexicans restored the republic and the Archduke was shot by order of a court-martial.

I was very angry with Napoleon who had set up the Archduke and failed to support him. But the fact of the Archduke's assassination meant that the Court was in mourning, and there was no review in Hyde Park. I think Lord Derby was secretly relieved. He had been afraid that if John Brown had gone to the review the mob might have become dangerous.

While all this was happening, Napoleon was holding a great exhibition in Paris and heads of various states were invited there—Bertie among them.

Bertie was his usual gregarious self and his visit was considered to be a great success. When he was there he met the Sultan of Turkey and invited him to pay a visit to England sometime, to which invitation the Sultan responded with alacrity, and decided to come immediately.

I was not at all pleased because I could not remain in retirement while such visitors were in the country.

Alice and Louis were with me. Poor darlings, they were very sad, and still resentful over the Prussian War—such a disaster for them. However, I was glad to have Alice with me; she understood me better than any of the others did.

'The Prince of Wales invited the Sultan,' I said. 'He is Bertie's responsibility and he must do the honours.'

That would be an excellent idea, said Lord Derby; but there would be occasions when it would be necessary for me to be present. We did not want to offend the Sultan.

So Bertie did the entertaining and, knowing Bertie, I hoped it was not too disreputable.

I went to Osborne and received the visitors there. The Sultan was charming, and as I had been warned that I must be friendly towards him, I offered to bestow the Order of the Garter upon him.

He was delighted when Bertie explained what a great honour it was and told him that it was rarely bestowed. Bertie's sense of the theatrical prevailed and it was decided that the Sultan should receive the Order on board the royal yacht.

Alice and her husband naturally must be present on such an occasion. It was July but the sea was choppy and it soon became clear that the Sultan was not feeling very well. Bertie said that perhaps it had not been such a good idea to have the presentation at sea—even so close to land and in July—and it would be as well to proceed as quickly as possible with the ceremony.

I had John Brown with me. He stood close beside me as always with that amused expression on his rugged honest face which suggested that if anyone attacked me it would be the worse for them. I had often reproached him, told him I was in no danger, and that although I appreciated his care, on some occasions it was not necessary to show such bellicosity.

Bertie was right. We must get on with the ceremony as quickly as possible before the Sultan was ill.

I held out my hand for the ribbon—and then it became quite farcical. The first equerry turned to the second and said in a loud whisper: 'The ribbon.' The second equerry whispered back in agitation that he thought the first equerry had it. I could see that someone had forgotten to bring it.

Prince Louis was standing close to me and he was wearing the ribbon which I had bestowed on him. Then I heard John Brown: 'Stop mithering. Ye've nae brought the ribbon. This one will have to do.'

I saw his strong hand stretching out to take the ribbon which Louis was wearing.

'Give him this one,' said Brown to me. 'He'll nae ken the difference.'

I hesitated for half a second. Then I took it and gave it to the Sultan. Poor man, he was feeling too queasy to notice the little hitch.

I almost laughed aloud . . . something I rarely did then; and whenever I did it was usually due to something John Brown had said or done.

And so thanks to the ingenuity of my Highland servant that little matter was satisfactorily concluded.

Lord Derby was getting very old and I had noticed for some time that he was looking far from well, so I was not surprised when he came to me and told me he could no longer continue.

I understood perfectly, I said. The office of Prime Minister was scarcely a rest cure. He told me that he thought I should send for Benjamin Disraeli.

I did so with pleasure. So Mr. Disraeli came to Osborne to kiss my hand in the formal way and take on the Premiership. I felt an immediate response to him. There was something in his manner which appealed to me; he behaved as though he were spell-bound, enchanted, not only by my position but by me personally. He was so gracious that he made me feel young again.

I knew certain things about him because I had made it my business to find out. I could not help comparing him with Lord Melbourne. Lord Melbourne had been an exceptionally handsome man and that had made him immediately attractive to me. I am afraid that in those days I was rather frivolous and impressed by a little wickedness. That was before Albert had changed me.

Benjamin Disraeli was different. One could scarcely call *him* handsome. His skin was sallow, his eyes heavy-lidded, his nose prominent. I had always thought big noses were a sign of strength until Lord Melbourne had assured me that they were not. Disraeli had rather greasy hair which some said was dyed. What was so attractive about him was his manner, his way of expressing himself. He knew how to use words; he was gallant. Perhaps that was it. He made me feel that I was attractive, which I fear at that time of my life I was not. He knew just how to say the words which would make me feel that *I* was rather clever as well as attractive. It was a gift and Benjamin Disraeli certainly had it.

He was a good deal older than I. He had been born in '04—so that would make him some fifteen years my senior. He told me later that he was the second child of Isaac d'Israeli—Jewish, of course, and in comfortable circumstances—whose father had been an Italian Jew who had owned a prosperous business making straw bonnets. He said his family had been expelled from Spain by the Inquisition in 1492.

All this he told me as though he were unfolding a dramatic story; and I must confess I found it enthralling.

His father Isaac was, he told me, a Voltairean Freethinker, and he broke with Judaism, which meant that all his children were baptised into the Church of England.

'It was important to me, M'am,' he said, 'though I did not realize it at the time. If I had remained a Jew, I could not have become a Member of Parliament at the time when I took my seat. It was not until '58, when I had been a Member for more than twenty years, that Jews were permitted into the House.'

That was what made conversation with him so absorbing. He introduced facts like that in such a way that one remembered them.

'I have always been impatient, M'am. I did not want to wait for fortune to come to me. I wanted to reach out and snatch it. When I was twenty years old I was appalled by my lack of success. I constantly reminded myself that Pitt was Prime Minister at the age of twenty-four. "And where is Disraeli?" I would demand of myself. "Nowhere." '

'But your success was inevitable, Mr. Disraeli,' I said.

'Your Majesty is gracious. I tried to make a fortune on the Stock Exchange and all went well for a time. Then I tried publishing a newspaper. That was a disaster. Then I decided to be a novelist. *Vivian Grey*, my first, had a fair success. But I offended a lot of people with that book.'

'People are always ready to be offended. I think they were probably jealous of your success.'

That was how our conversation ran. It was so much more interesting than that of most of my Prime Ministers had been. It reminded me so much of the chats I had had with Lord Melbourne.

I knew Disraeli had had mistresses before his marriage; but, of course, we did not discuss that side of his life, though he did tell me about his friendship with Wyndham Lewis and how when he had been his protégé he had become friendly with Wyndham Lewis' wife.

'It was not love at first sight,' he said, 'but it grew to deep love. Mary Anne once said that although I married her for her money, now I would marry her for love.'

'And did you marry her for her money, Mr. Disraeli?'

'I confess I considered her fortune.'

'Oh, how mercenary!' I found myself laughing. Since Albert's death I laughed so rarely. John Brown could make me smile; but I was actually laughing with Mr. Disraeli.

He loved to talk of Mary Anne and I began to feel that I knew her well. He told me how devoted she was and how she sat up when he was late at the House and had a cold supper waiting for him, no matter what time he came in.

They were friends as well as lovers.

'I understand so well,' I said sadly.

'M'am, we have had something very rare in common—a happy marriage.'

How right he was!

He gave me a copy of *Sybil*, which I thought was very good indeed. I gave him a signed copy of *Leaves*.

He was constantly referring to me as a fellow author, which I had to admit I quite liked. I looked forward to his visits. It was like going back in time. I was remembering more and more of the days when I used to anticipate Lord Melbourne's visits with such pleasure. Now I looked forward to those of Benjamin Disraeli.

A certain savour had returned to life. I would not admit it but in my heart I knew it was there.

Such a happy state of affairs could not be expected to last. William Gladstone—whom I could not like—was making a great deal of fuss about the disestablishment of the Irish Church. The government was against the measure and was heavily defeated by a majority of sixty-five.

I was at Windsor and when Disraeli called on me I was delighted as ever to see him, not realizing what news he brought.

He quickly told me how things had gone in the Commons. 'And, M'am,' he added, 'I have no alternative but to offer Your Majesty my resignation.'

'Resignation!' I cried. 'Does that mean I shall have that dreadful man Gladstone here lecturing me?'

Disraeli lifted his shoulders and looked woeful.

'What is this nonsense about the Irish Church?' I demanded. 'The Church throughout the Kingdom is associated with the Crown.'

'Mr. Gladstone thinks otherwise, M'am. And so do others since we have been so heavily defeated.'

'If I accept your resignation,' I said, 'I shall be compelled to give your office to Mr. Gladstone and then the government would bring in the disestablishment. I think people should have plenty of time to think about such a step. No measure should be rushed through the House, which is what would happen if you resigned and I called in Gladstone.'

'Your Majesty could, of course, refuse to accept my resignation and dissolve Parliament.'

'That is what I will do. It will be some time before there can be an election and your government will remain in office until there is one.'

'That means, M'am, that I remain in office and we go to the country . . . say in six months' time.'

I had to be content with that. Six months is a long time in politics and one never knows what will happen to affect fickle public opinion; and there was a possibility that in six months' time the government might be returned.

Mr. Disraeli had somehow persuaded me that it might be a good idea to show myself a little. I had not held a Drawing-Room at Buckingham Palace since Albert died, but I decided to, and later I reviewed twenty thousand volunteers at Windsor Park and a few days later gave a party in the grounds of Buckingham Palace.

But I did not wish people to think that I was ready to undertake a round of engagements. In August I paid a visit to Switzerland, and to emphasize the fact that I wanted no fuss I travelled as the Duchess of Kent. Napoleon was most courteous and offered me his imperial train for my journey through France and in Paris I had a meeting with the Empress Eugénie. In Lucerne, however, I rented a villa near the lake, and there I enjoyed a very private holiday which was very pleasant.

All the same I was glad to return to Balmoral; and it was particularly interesting to go back because I had asked Brown to look out for a little house for me . . . a simple *homely* little house. Balmoral was really a castle, and what I wanted was a house where I could live with the utmost simplicity.

I could trust Brown to choose the right place. With great sensitivity he had selected a spot which had particularly impressed Albert. It was Glassalt Shiel which meant Darkness and Sorrow. How better interpret my mood! It was set among wildly beautiful scenery of almost forbidding grandeur where the Glassalt Burn tumbled down the mountainside into Loch Muick.

I called it my Widow's House for it was the only one which had not had the touch of Albert's hand. Osborne and Balmoral were his creations. Not so Glassalt Shiel.

Louise was with me and accompanied by one of the ladies—I think it was Jane Churchill—we set out for the place. The air was clear with a touch of frost—chilly for the first of October. We stopped for tea at Birkhill and John Grant joined us there with Arthur who had come from Geneva and had arrived in Ballater only a few hours before. Arthur got into the carriage with us and Grant joined Brown on the box.

I was so excited when we arrived at Glassalt Shiel. There were lights in the house as we were expected and the servants wanted to give us a good welcome.

It was such a compact little house and there seemed plenty of room in it for it was much bigger inside than it appeared from the outside. There was one staircase leading to the upper floor where there were several bedrooms—enough to accommodate the servants. On the ground floor were my sitting-room, bedroom and the maids' room; and on the other side of the hall the dining-room, a kitchen, steward's room, store closet and another room for the menservants to sleep in. There were good stables and keeper's cottage where the gillies slept.

After we had dined Brown came in unceremoniously and announced that everyone was ready for the house-warming, implying that I should join them, which I did.

Our meal had been cleared away and the dining-room was ready. There were nineteen of us altogether. Two of the men played the bagpipes and the rest began to dance reels. Brown said it would not be right if I did not dance with them. So I complied. How strange to dance again! I enjoyed it, remembering how excited I used to be about balls when I was very young—before Albert taught me that dancing was a useless and frivolous occupation.

So I danced the reels and these honest Scots saw nothing unusual in their Queen dancing with them.

When the first reel was over, Brown brought in what he called 'Whisky toddy'.

I declined but Brown was quite indignant. 'Come on, woman,' he said, 'you mun drink to the fire kindling.'

So I drank a little and Grant made a speech in which he called upon God to see that 'our royal mistress, our good Queen, should live long to reign over us.'

They cheered me and drank my health in whisky toddy and they all became very merry indeed.

I retired to my room soon after eleven o'clock but I believe they continued with the dancing and singing until the early morning.

I lay in bed thinking of the past and dear Albert who would have loved this place. I believed he was watching over me and that he would bless my little Widow's House.

And with that comforting thought I slept.

I was still in Scotland when the election took place. Disraeli's government was defeated and the Liberals came in with a majority of one hundred and twenty-eight.

And so, I thought, that odious Mr. Gladstone will now be my Prime Minister.

I received him coolly. The man irritated me. He talked in an authoritative way as though addressing a public meeting. His vehemence was overwhelming; it came out in a steady flow of forceful language. He was the sort of man who had no doubt that his ideas were the right ones, and one had the impression that he was determined to carry them out.

That he was a good man, I knew, for I made it my business to discover all I could about my Prime Ministers. I had so much to do with them that it was necessary for me to have a full acquaintance with their past as well as their present lives.

William Ewart Gladstone was the son of a Liverpool merchant who had immigrated to that city from Scotland. The father had been active in politics and besides being successful in business had sat in Parliament as a Tory for about ten years. Gladstone was sent to Eton and then Oxford where he had naturally soon distinguished himself in debate.

He was a man of conscience. At Eton his great friend had been Lord Lincoln, son of the Duke of Newcastle; and the Duke, impressed by Gladstone's amazing energy, eloquence and outstanding qualities generally, offered to help him win the seat of Lewark for the Tories. In the Gladstone home Canning had been a hero. He was now dead but the Duke of Newcastle had remarked in public that Canning had been the most profligate minister the country had ever had, and young Gladstone thought it would be disloyal to the memory of Canning to accept help from a man who had maligned him.

His father told him not to be a fool. He would never make much progress in life if he allowed opportunities to slip out of his hands. Eventually Gladstone saw the point and won the seat. Ever since he had been climbing up the political ladder, and it was inconceivable that a man of his talent and forceful dedication could remain unnoticed.

When he was a young man he had become very friendly with the Glynne family. Lady Glynne was a widow with two sons—one in Parliament—and two daughters, Catherine and Mary. He fell in love with Catherine, but it was apparently some time before she accepted his proposal of marriage. I could imagine his courtship. Did he address *her* as a public meeting? I thought that very likely. However she finally agreed and of course he had chosen very wise-

ly. He could not have found a better wife. She came from a political family, her grandfather was George Grenville, the Prime Minister who passed the Stamp Act and she was the niece of Lord
Grenville who was Prime Minister in '06; her great aunt was Chat-
ham's wife and William Pitt was her cousin. So she was related to
four Prime Ministers and it seemed only reasonable that she should
be married to one.

She was the opposite of her husband—bright, cheerful and popular; she was by no means approaching him in intellect—what a
formidable pair they would have been if she had!—but she was very
pleasant. I liked her as soon as I saw her, and I felt very sorry for
her because she was married to that man!

She had eight children—seven of whom survived. She clearly
humanized the household. I could imagine him—precise, neat in
life as he was in his mind. For him there would be a place for
everything. She was careless and had no time for method. But she
had charm and he was aware of it, having none himself. He was,
naturally, devoted to her as she was to him; and I had to applaud
that. She insisted that he take exercise, remove his wet things if he
was caught in a shower; she made sure that he was well wrapped
up against the cold. Like Mary Anne Disraeli, she always had a
supper for him when he came in from the House; she guarded him;
watched over him and even took an interest in politics—about
which, in spite of her relationship with all those Prime Ministers,
she was not really enthusiastic.

These items of news came to me through servants. I always had
my favourite maids who kept me informed. I knew that one of the
criticisms levelled against me—and Albert—was that we got on
better with the servants than the courtiers. There was an element of
truth in this and I was even more friendly with them than Albert
had been. I liked them to know that I was interested in their welfare.
They knew this and loved me for it; and it so happened that I did
glean all sorts of information of which I should otherwise have been
ignorant.

So that was the man who was now my Prime Minister. Admirable, no doubt, honest, stubborn on points which he believed to
be right, a man who would, in the old days, have gone to the stake
for his opinions.

I should have admired him. I should have welcomed him. But I
could not. I simply did not like him; and as my affections were
fierce so were my dislikes.

As soon as he was in power a large number of reforms were

undertaken, Gladstone was obsessed with reform. I had always firmly believed in religious toleration and the liberty of the subject; but Gladstone wanted to go farther than that. He was introducing Radicalism. It was absurd to attempt to abolish class distinction. Not that I believed that a person's birth was all important. What mattered was education, good behaviour and moral standards; and I had ample evidence to know that this existed in people who were not of high birth. Gladstone introduced measures with such rapidity that it was difficult to follow him. He would stand before me with that speaker's manner and expound at great length on his various projects and talk, talk, talk. He did not seem as if he could stop. He was eloquent. I had to admit that. I found my mind straying and wondering how poor Mrs. Gladstone put up with him.

I knew of course that, constitutionally, I could not oppose him. It was the elected government who made the decisions, not the Queen. But I did have a say in these matters and I determined to oppose him wherever possible.

His first measure was the disestablishment of the Irish Church. I knew that this was the question on which he had gone to the country, and the results of that election meant that the people were behind him. But the Lords threw out the Bill after it had been passed through the Commons. I knew this could cause a great deal of trouble, and in a case such as this the Upper House must bow to the Lower. I wanted the matter settled, for even though I did not agree with it, I did realize that the conflict was bad for the country. I asked the House of Lords to give way to the Commons. Let the principle be agreed on and the details thrashed out later.

The Bill was then passed, due to my intervention, but there was a good deal of quibbling about procedure. I was called in again and helped reconcile the two sides. I think I showed those people who thought that because I was mourning the loss of my husband I was neglecting my duties as Queen, that I was deeply involved in matters of state.

But the fact remained, I could not like Mr. Gladstone.

I wanted to show my appreciation of Disraeli and it seemed to me in order to offer him an earldom. I sent for him and told him what I had been thinking. He was overcome with gratitude; he kissed my hand and with tears in his eyes told me that he did not deserve such consideration from the most admirable of queens and the most delightful of women.

I laughed at his fulsomeness, but I must say I found it gratifying, and such a change from the lectures I received in the most stilted phrases from my Prime Minister.

Disraeli declined the earldom however. Perhaps he thought it would restrict him in the House of Commons.

But he said: 'Your Majesty has been so gracious to me that I will be so bold as to make a suggestion.'

'Please do,' I said.

He hesitated and I saw the look of pain cross his face. His features were always so expressive—as I suppose mine were.

'It is Mary Anne,' he said.

He always talked of his wife in a familiar way with me. I was glad he did. I felt I knew her already. He had made me see her as a wonderful woman. I remember how on one occasion he was going to make a very important speech in the Commons and she had driven there with him; as he alighted, she had caught her hand in the door. She had been in agony but did not mention it to him for fear it might worry him and take his mind off his speech.

I used to tell him of the virtues of Albert and he used to say, laughingly, that we vied with each other in telling of the virtues of our spouses.

Then we would sigh and say how lucky we were.

Now he said: 'Mary Anne is very ill. She thinks I do not know. She pretends that all is well. She has about a year to live.'

'Oh, how very sad! I am desperately sorry.'

'My dear, kind lady . . . how wonderful you are! Yes, I shall not long have my Mary Anne, and I know Your Majesty understands as few can the depth of my sorrow.'

I could scarcely bear to look at him.

After a brief silence he went on: 'My request is this. If Mary Anne could be created a peeress in her own right . . . before she dies . . .'

'Most certainly she shall,' I cried. 'I myself will make sure that this is done.'

He took my hand and raised it to his lips. His expression was one of more than gratitude; it was adoration.

So Mary Anne became the Countess of Beaconsfield.

He told me how happy she was and he thanked me for all I had done for him.

I told him it was nothing. He had done a great deal for me. He was my very good friend and always would be. And I trusted that, if a time should come when he was in need of comfort, he would turn to me.

Although I could not see him as often as I should have liked for there would have been protests from the government if I appeared too friendly with the Leader of the Opposition, nothing could prevent our writing to each other.

I looked forward to his letters. They were so amusingly written—racy, witty and full of gossip.

They cheered me considerably.

I sent him primroses from Osborne. He wrote me a most grateful letter. He said that from now on they would be his favourite flower.

The Fateful Fourteenth

The libellous comments about John Brown and myself were still being circulated. I had become so accustomed to them that I was ignoring them.

One which created a good deal of interest was my supposed interest in spiritualism. It was a cult which had swept through the country a little earlier and many people testified that they had been in touch with the dead. It was said that my friendship with John Brown could be explained by the fact that Brown was the medium who put me in touch with Albert.

If only I could have been in touch with my beloved one, how happy I should have been!

I knew that if it were possible for him to come to me he would have done so. Of course I was interested; I talked with some of my ladies; I listened to their stories of extraordinary experiences. I sat at a table in the dark with them. But Albert did not come.

And when I thought of frank, rather earthy John Brown having contact with the other world, it all seemed to be quite incongruous.

It was amazing how the stories were circulated; but I thought it was better for people to suspect John Brown as my medium rather than my lover.

I often thought how empty people's lives must be if they must pry and peep into those of others.

I always remembered how Albert had wanted writers to come to Court; he had thought they would be much more interesting than most of the people we met. I had stood out against that, fearing that the conversation might be so lofty that I should be shut out of it. I had been foolish and I believed I had deprived Albert of some pleasure.

I decided, therefore, that I would invite certain writers to Court. I was not very interested in books but I did admire the energy of people who produced them; and as Albert had been sure they would be interesting, I would do what I had been reluctant to in his lifetime.

I had always admired Tennyson, of course. His *In Memoriam* had comforted me a great deal and I had written to him to tell him so. He had been to visit me both at Osborne and Windsor. I found him charming and easy to talk to.

One of my ladies told me that Thomas Carlyle, who was apparently a highly respected writer, had lost his wife, so I sent him a note of condolence.

I read George Eliot's *Mill on the Floss* but the books I really found absorbing were those of Charles Dickens. I asked him to come to Buckingham Palace and I had a very interesting talk with him and afterwards reproached myself afresh for having turned away from Albert's suggestion to ask that sort of person to Court. They were different from the people I normally met. They had ideas. I was not sure that I should want to be with them for long, but to meet them after having read their books and in some measure had a glimpse into their minds, was interesting to see what they were like.

I could lose myself in Mr. Dickens' books, and it was exciting to be in a world which was so different from the one in which I had always lived.

I asked Mr. Dickens to present me with copies of his books which I should like him to sign for me. He expressed great pleasure in being asked to visit me; we talked about Little Nell and there were tears in our eyes. He was one of those warm, *feeling* men whom I liked instantly. So different from Mr. Gladstone.

I gave him a copy of *Leaves from a Journal* and he begged me to inscribe it for him.

'From the humblest writer to the greatest,' I wrote.

It was about this time that the Mordaunt case burst upon us.

Albert and I had always feared there would be trouble with Bertie. How right we had been!

I had always known that Bertie was living what is called 'a double life'. It was wicked of him. He had a wife who was good, loved by the people and said to be one of the most beautiful women in the country; he had four lovely children; it seemed to me that Bertie had everything. And yet he must involve himself in scandal. And what a scandal!

I had known that Bertie was riding for a fall. I knew there were late nights, actresses, gambling, including all those activities which are certain to end in disaster sooner or later; and I knew that Alexandra loved him—in spite of everything. Of course, Albert would never have approved of the way in which they brought up their children. There was no discipline in the nurseries. The children screamed and shouted and climbed all over Bertie while Alexandra looked on, applauding. It was not what Albert would have wished. Even to Vicky, with whom he had always been extraordinarily lenient, he had been a little remote, to be revered.

I said again and again that there would be trouble with those children.

'You should remember your own childhood, Bertie,' I told him. And he replied with a smile: 'Oh, I do, Mama. I do.' Which seemed somehow a criticism of Albert and me.

But this was terrible. I was stunned.

Bertie wrote to me: 'An unfortunate *contretemps* has arisen.' He had received an order to appear in court.

Appear in court! The Prince of Wales! I had never heard such a thing.

I sent for him at once. He explained to me that Sir Charles Mordaunt was bringing a divorce suit against his wife, and he had letters to her which had been written by Bertie, and Bertie's name had been mentioned with the result that he was summoned to appear in court.

'You had better tell me all about it,' I said.

He was clearly worried. Poor Alexandra! I thought, and tried to imagine myself in a similar position. Impossible with Albert!

'I am innocent,' said Bertie.

I think I was unable to hide my disbelief.

'It is unfortunate that you have made people of shady reputation your friends,' I said.

'I tell you, Mama. I am innocent.'

I suppose in a family when one member is threatened the rest rally round even though they are not convinced of the accused one's innocence. But Bertie was so firm in his protestations that I felt I must believe him.

'But you know the woman,' I said.

'Of course. I knew them both.'

'And Sir Charles Mordaunt is naming you as co-respondent.'

'No, no,' said Bertie quickly. 'He is naming Frederick Johnstone and Lord Cole.'

'And where do you come in?'

'She mentioned my name and there are letters.'

'Letters!' I cried. 'Do you remember how my Uncle George was in trouble over letters? You must have heard of that. Did you never think what harm letters can do?'

'I haven't your fondness for writing them, Mama, but occasionally I do find it necessary to take up my pen.'

'My letters,' I retorted, 'could be read in any court of law without bringing disgrace on anyone, Bertie. This is shocking. For the first time I am glad dear Papa is not here. This would distress him so much.'

'I am innocent,' Bertie repeated.

'And what does Alexandra think?'

'She is very unhappy about it.'

'Poor girl. *I* never had to suffer that sort of thing.'

'Papa was a saint, of course,' said Bertie with a lift of his lips. 'I fear, Mama, that I am not. But I am innocent in this case.'

'The heir to the throne summoned to a court of law!'

I showered him with questions and at length the story emerged. Lady Mordaunt had given birth to a child who was blind and she was very distressed. In fact, she was a hysterical woman at the best of times. She went into a frenzy and said it was her fault that the child was blind; she had sinned. She told Mordaunt that he was not the father of the child, but that Lord Cole was. She then burst out that she had been unfaithful with several men. She mentioned Frederick Johnstone and the Prince of Wales. Mordaunt searched her bureau and found bills which showed she had stayed at hotels with Cole and Johnstone . . . and there were letters from the Prince of Wales.

I was very upset. I wished Benjamin Disraeli would come to me. Etiquette forbade it. He was of the Opposition. I could have talked to him. How I should have been able to explain my feelings to Lord Melbourne! But all I had was Mr. Gladstone. How could one talk of such a matter to him? He would declaim and declaim and I should want to shout at him and order him out of my presence.

Albert foresaw something like this, I told myself. But there was no comfort in that. Albert was not here to advise me. And what could we do? There was nothing for it. Even royalty had to obey the courts of law and Bertie had been subpoenaed to appear in court.

I was very sorry for him. He was easy-going. That was the flaw in his character, but perhaps I was comparing him with the incomparable Albert, which was not fair. But Bertie was as he was, and he was my son. He had declared his innocence and I was sure he was speaking the truth. I thought of all the cruel things which had been said about Albert, all the calumnies which had been directed at Brown and myself.

I thought of Bertie as a little boy and how sometimes I had thought Albert too harsh with him; I remembered the tears when he had been beaten and how I had tried not to think of it. I remembered storms which had blown up between Albert and me because I thought Albert was too harsh with Bertie, too soft with Vicky.

I sat down and wrote to Bertie. I said I believed in him, but there were always people to attack us, but that he must stand up and come through this ordeal. He must know that his mother stood with him.

Bertie came to see me. He was so soft and gentle and grateful. He opened out and said that he was afraid at times he was a little indiscreet. He had written letters to Lady Mordaunt but they were quite innocuous. He had never been her lover; but he had known of her relationship with Cole and Johnstone. She was their affair, not his.

I said: 'If you are innocent, people will realize it. Innocence is the best defence a person can have.'

'Mordaunt has got Sergeant Ballantine to act for him. He is rather a terror.'

'Stand up and tell the truth, Bertie, and you will be a match for anyone.'

He embraced me. Oddly enough he seemed closer to me than he ever had.

Public interest was great. The papers were full of the case. I knew that this was a very serious matter for whatever the verdict Bertie would be thought guilty. People took a delight in condemning others—especially those in high places.

I heard an account of the proceedings. Bertie went into the box and answered the probing questions put to him by Sergeant Ballantine; he did it with calm and honesty, I believe; he admitted that he knew Lady Mordaunt and had been a friend of hers before marriage.

'Has there been any improper or criminal act between you and Lady Mordaunt?'

It was the vital question and Bertie answered with great firmness: 'There was not.'

Bertie was exonerated. Moreover it was proved that Lady Mordaunt was insane and the case was dismissed.

What a piece of luck for Bertie. I did hope it would be a lesson to him for the future.

I wondered what Vicky, Alice and Lenchen were hearing of it.

I felt compelled to write to Vicky for I felt sure that her opinion of Bertie was very low already, and that she was convinced of his guilt.

'I do not doubt his innocence,' I wrote, 'and his appearance in court did good, but it was painful and lowering. The heir to the throne should never have come into close contact with such people. I hope this will teach him a lesson. I shall use it as an example to remind him of what can happen, when the need arises. Believe me, children are a terrible anxiety and the sorrow they cause is far greater than the pleasure they give.'

How true that was!

But I was thankful that Bertie had emerged from a very delicate situation—not unscathed, for although his evidence had been accepted and Lady Mordaunt was proved to be mad, these matters always leave a smear.

Just as I was recovering from the shock of the Mordaunt case, trouble blew up in Europe. Lord Clarendon, on whose judgement I had relied so much, died, and Lord Granville took his place. Granville was a good man but I did not think he matched Lord Clarendon; and at this time we needed the very best of men at the Foreign Office. Conflict had been brewing for some time between France and Germany. I wrote to the rulers of both countries urging caution, but my entreaties were ignored and in July of that year Napoleon declared war. I thought that was unnecessary folly and when I heard that he wanted to destroy the independence of Belgium, I was firmly on the side of Germany.

Belgium was especially dear to me. How thankful I was that Uncle Leopold had not to suffer this threat to his kingdom. In spite of the fact that I did not like Bismarck my links with Germany were strong. It was almost a family affair. On the other hand I had friendship with Napoleon. Bertie was especially fond of him. So . . . we were about to be torn apart again. Oh, the stupidity of war and the men who insist on making it.

Vicky's husband and Alice's were both deeply involved and were actually fighting the French. I sent hospital stores to Alice at Darmstadt and I watched the progress of the war with great horror.

It was soon clear that the French were no match for the Germans who were overrunning France. I wrote to Vicky and Fritz, begging them to use their influence to stop the bombardment of Paris. To Bismarck's fury they asked for this not to be done and he complained bitterly of petticoat sentimentality which was hampering German progress.

I thought: A little more petticoat government and perhaps countries would not so easily become involved in wars which bring bereavement and tragedy to so many families.

The Emperor had surrendered at Sedan and Paris fell into the hands of the Germans. The war was over.

I was sorry for Napoleon and Eugénie and hated to see them so humbled. I had quite liked the Emperor; he had been a charming guest and Eugénie was very attractive.

Now they were outcasts with nowhere to go. Eugénie appealed to me and I offered her refuge in England. She came to Chichester. Napoleon was a prisoner of the Germans and they held him for some months, but when he was free he came to join Eugénie at Chichester.

Although I *did* disapprove of his policies and my sympathies were with the Germans—for most of my family were in that country and through Albert and my mother my ties with them were strong—I did not forget that Napoleon and Eugénie had been my friends.

Poor things! They were so grateful. How are the mighty fallen! I thought. A lesson to us all.

It was a very sad day for me when I heard that poor Lehzen had died. Memories came flooding back and I felt a twinge of conscience. We had been very close and in my young days she had been the most important person in my life. My dear Daisy! And I had called her Mother on some occasions. And then . . . she had gone and I hardly saw her again. Albert had made me see that he and she could not be under the same roof. I had had to make a choice and of course it must be Albert. I thought of us—dressing the dolls together, doing our reading; she had guarded me like a watchdog and would have given her life for me if necessary.

How sad that it had had to be as it was!

I mourned her and regretted that she had passed so completely out of my life; but I had never forgotten her. Dear Lehzen!

But she had been happy in her last years. She had loved her nieces and nephews and no doubt planned for them as she had once for me.

I hoped she had been happy and not thought too often and too sadly of the days at Kensington Palace.

Gladstone and his ministers were in a state of tension over what was happening on the Continent. The German States were united under one great Empire. This had been proclaimed to the world in the Hall of Mirrors at Versailles—stressing German supremacy over the French. It was a typical Bismarck gesture to hold the ceremony there. So now, instead of several small states, there was one Empire, a formidable power astride the Continent. Moreover, at the same time, France had become a republic.

Mr. Gladstone came to see me and standing before me—I would not invite him to sit down and he could not do so until I did—declaimed at length on the dangerous situation. A king had been deposed. All royalty must regard that with apprehension. It was very necessary for all sovereigns to have the people behind them.

The burden of this harangue was that the people's approval was not won by monarchs who shut themselves away. At the moment even the popularity of the Prince of Wales had foundered. The Mordaunt case had done him no good and whatever the verdict of the court there would be some mischief-makers who would try to make him seem guilty.

I told him to consult Dr. Jenner who had insisted that I needed quiet and rest.

'It was hard work which killed the Prince Consort,' I said. 'He never spared himself. If he had he would be here today.'

Mr. Gladstone went on with his speech about the dangers following the new state of affairs in Europe.

My mind wandered. *Poor* Mrs. Gladstone, I thought. How does she endure the man?

I think Alexandra was very sad at that time. She must have been very disillusioned about Bertie. I wondered what *she* thought of the Mordaunt case. But by this time she would have learned what he was like. Poor Alexandra. She had lost her baby, little Alexander. She consulted me about having a stained-glass window put into the church at Sandringham as a memorial. I thought it an excellent idea, and I think it cheered her considerably to talk about it with me.

Her rheumatic pains were troubling her again. When I thought of that bright and pretty girl I had first seen and how *feeling* she had been putting on a black dress to show she understood my mourning, I was saddened. She was beautiful—nothing could alter that; but she had lost her gaiety.

Perhaps I should speak to Bertie. Perhaps not. Speaking to Bertie had never done any good.

When we were at Balmoral, Louise had become very friendly with the Argylls and particularly with the Duke's son and heir, the Marquess of Lorne. I was rather taken aback when Louise told me that Lorne wanted to marry her.

A commoner! I thought. That was not really very suitable.

'My dear child,' I said, 'what do you *feel*?'

'I love him, Mama. I want to marry him. I hope you will give us your blessing.'

What could I do? The dear child was radiant.

'My dearest,' I said, 'I hope you will be happy.'

She threw her arms about me. 'Dear *good* Mama,' she said.

I was certainly happy to see her happy, but I did remind her that it was very rare for royal girls to marry commoners.

'I know, Mama. The last time was when Henry the Eighth's sister Mary married the Duke of Suffolk.'

'I believe,' I said, with an attempt at severity, 'she married him first and asked permission afterwards.'

'Well, Mama, that was the safest way with Henry the Eighth. You are not a tyrant but the dearest sweetest Mama in the world.'

I felt very emotional. I thought: They are all going . . . every one of them. There is only Beatrice left now. I could not bear to part with her.

I saw no reason why the marriage should be delayed, so it took place in March of the following year. I led the procession up the nave wearing rubies and diamonds and a dress of black satin covered in jet to remind everyone that I was still in mourning.

As on all such occasions I thought of Albert and pictured him standing beside me, and melancholy set in after the ceremony.

I was getting old; my children were growing up. Only Baby Beatrice left to me now!

I hoped she would never leave me.

Mr. Gladstone's words had had some effect on me and although I had no intention of coming entirely out of seclusion, I did open St. Thomas's Hospital and the Albert Hall.

I attended the Opening of Parliament wearing an ermine-trimmed dress which was in a way a sort of half-mourning; and I had a new crown which brightened up my appearance considerably.

Of course there was murmuring about that. Louise's dowry and Arthur's annuity would be discussed during this session and some of the papers pointed out that this may have been the explanation of my appearance and that I was preparing the way for when I came with my begging bowl. What with sly hints about the Mordaunt case and the dissatisfaction with my quiet life, the family prestige was very low at that time. Again and again Mr. Gladstone pointed out the dangers, particularly in view of what had happened in France; and when fifty-four votes were cast against Arthur's annuity that was a shock.

'The monarchy must be made visible and palpable to the people,' said Mr. Gladstone.

Arthur had his money, he went on, but the people expected some return for these sums.

Then I became ill. I awoke one morning to find my right elbow was very inflamed. At first I thought it was a sting but very soon I was developing a sore throat and other symptoms.

I was at Osborne and it was time for my visit to Balmoral and I was determined, ill as I was, to go.

Gladstone was all against my leaving. He thought I should not be so far away from Parliament. The trouble was that I had shut myself away for so long and had pleaded the state of my health so often that the people did not now believe me. This was galling as I had never been so ill since my attack of typhoid at Ramsgate.

I was receiving despatches from London. The papers were saying that I should abdicate and hand over the throne to the Prince of Wales. These articles were read in Scotland and I am glad to say that all the Scottish papers came out in my defence.

Dr. Jenner protected me magnificently. The sting in my arm was an abscess; it gave me a great deal of pain and I found it very difficult to rest at night. I was also suffering from gout and rheumatic pains. The gout prevented my walking and John Brown had to carry me from sofa to bed.

It was a most depressing time. Alfred came down to see me and immediately there was trouble between him and John Brown. Alfred gave me almost as much concern as Bertie. He had Bertie's tendency for flirtation—and worse. He was not so affable as Bertie and had a great sense of his own importance. He deliberately and pointedly ignored John Brown whom I liked to be treated not as a servant but as a friend; and when Alfred ordered some fiddlers to stop playing for the servants' reels, John Brown countermanded the order. Alfred was incensed but Brown was his imperturbable self.

Then there was another unpleasant scene which involved Vicky's daughter Charlotte who had come to stay with us at Balmoral.

Brown came into the room and I told Charlotte to say How do you do? to him and shake hands.

Charlotte said: 'How do you do? But I cannot shake hands with a servant. Mama says I must not.'

Vicky and I had a bitter disagreement about the behaviour of her children. She insisted that Charlotte had been right to refuse to shake hands with a servant. I said Brown was no ordinary servant and servants were human in any case. 'Indeed,' I added, 'I have had more consideration from them quite often than from people in high places.'

Vicky was firm and did not mince her words. She thought Brown had too important a place in the household. Did I forget that people had talked of him . . . and of me?

It was all very unpleasant.

But there was this trouble with Alfred and the fiddlers.

Brown did apologise—I think because he knew the affair was worrying me. I thanked him and said: 'Prince Alfred is now satisfied.' 'Well, I am satisfied too,' was his typical comment, which even in that state of discomfort and harassment made me smile.

Who would have children? I thought. Their entrance into the world reduced their unfortunate mothers to the state of an animal; they might be interesting and amusing as Baby had been in her early days—and then they grew up, some of them to be a continual source of anxiety.

A pamphlet was brought to my notice. It was the work of a Liberal Member of Parliament, and it was headed 'What does she do with it?'

The article was referring to the £385,000 a year from the Civil List and other legacies which the writer estimated to be somewhere in the region of another £200,000 a year. The impertinence of people was shocking!

At the end of September I was better, but still limp and suffering from vague rheumatic pains all over my body. I had lost two stones in weight and I felt rather gratified about this. It would show the people that I was not malingering.

Just as I felt I was improving, I heard that a certain Sir Charles Dilke had spoken at Newcastle and made a really vicious attack on me. He had told his audience that I had failed completely in my duty. Since the death of the Prince Consort I had rarely been seen in public. What was the use of the monarchy? It should be abolished and a republic set up. It would be cheaper than a queen in any case.

It was indeed dangerous talk.

I thought that Dilke should be repudiated by his party.

While all this was happening a blow was struck from another

direction. We were approaching the time of year which was always especially sombre to me. December! It was on the fourteenth of that dismal month that Albert had passed away.

Then came this message; Bertie was ill and the doctors had diagnosed typhoid. Typhoid! The dreaded disease which had killed Albert. And now it had stricken Bertie!

I took the train to Sandringham. Brown was with me—more brusque than ever. The dear man knew how anxious I was and he was anxious too . . . for me.

Sandringham was full of people. I was glad Alice was there. She was often with us. Poor Louis had not been a great catch when she married him and owing to that villain Bismarck she was in very poor circumstances now.

She was a great comfort to Alexandra who was a sad tragic figure. She told me that Bertie had been to Lord Londesborough's place in Scarborough. Lord Chesterfield had also been a guest and was now ill, so it seemed there must have been something wrong with the drains at the Londesboroughs.

It was like living it all over again. The weather was cold as it - had been then; there was snow at Sandringham. The news grew more and more alarming and I heard that one of the grooms who had accompanied Bertie to Scarborough was now ill with typhoid.

I went in to see Bertie. He did not look much like the jaunty Prince of Wales. His face was scarlet, his eyes over-bright; he was babbling something which I could not understand.

I thought: Very soon it will be the fourteenth of December.

Now the whole nation was waiting for news of Bertie. From a profligate rake, a seducer, cowering behind royal privilege he had now become a hero; the jaunty, jolly Prince was the People's Prince.

Strange how a virulent disease could transform a sinner into a saint!

He had the very best of doctors. My own Dr. Jenner was there, of course, and Alexandra had called in Doctors Gull, Clayton and Lowe to help him.

Bertie was delirious. He was calling out the names of people . . . women some of them. He clearly thought he was the King of England, so that could only mean that I was dead! He was quite exuberant, laughing a rattling horrible kind of laughter. It was quite distressing to listen to him.

The doctors insisted that there be a screen between me and the sick bed. It was a horrible and infectious disease.

He recovered and then grew worse.

The papers reported nothing else but the state of 'Good old Teddy's' health. He was known as Teddy for he was Edward not Albert to the people. They did not want an Albert for their King. He was to be another Edward—the Seventh.

There was an uncanny tension in the air. The papers reminded their readers that the Prince Consort had died on the fourteenth, and it seemed that everyone was waiting for the fourteenth to dawn.

There was a fatalistic notion that on that date Bertie was going to die. Special prayers were said all over the country, and Alexandra attended those in Sandringham Church. Alfred Austin, our poet laureate, wrote the banal lines which were quoted against him for long after:

> 'Flashed from his bed the electric message came
> He is not better; he is just the same.'

It was wonderful to have Alice with us. She moved about the sickroom with a quiet efficiency. She was a good nurse having had some practice during that terrible time which Bismarck had forced on Europe. Alexandra was indeed a devoted wife; and she loved Bertie in spite of the way he had treated her. I wondered whether I should have been so loving to a husband who had been notoriously unfaithful to me. I doubted it. But never in any circumstances could I imagine Albert unfaithful!

I remember vividly the thirteenth of December.

Bertie was worse.

We had heard that both Lord Chesterfield and the groom whose name was Blegge had died. Alexandra had made certain that Blegge had had the best attention—so we all feared the worst.

The fourteenth was close. That would be the day.

Sir Henry Ponsonby said that he must recover because it would be too much of a coincidence if he died on the same date as his father.

I clung to hope, but I greatly feared. I prayed incessantly that my son might be spared.

The dreaded fourteenth arrived. The whole country was waiting; and Bertie lay battling for life.

And then . . . the miracle happened. He came through the crisis. The fourteenth slipped into the fifteenth. The day of sorrow had passed.

The next day I saw him and he recognized me.

He smiled at me and kissed my hand. 'Dear Mama,' he said, 'I am so glad to see you. Have you been here all the time?'

'Oh, Bertie, Bertie,' I cried, and I could not restrain my tears.

All past differences were forgotten. He was alive.

I said there must be a thanksgiving service at which the whole country could rejoice.

I had a letter to the people published in which I thanked them for their concern. We were very popular. I wondered what that odious Charles Dilke was feeling now. His horrible schemes for destroying us had come to nothing—beaten by typhoid! We would show him and his kind that whatever he might think, the people still loved the monarchy. The concern that had been shown for Bertie proved that.

By the end of February, Bertie had recovered sufficiently to take part in the ceremony of rejoicing. I sat beside him in the carriage and it was heart-warming to see the people and hear their shouts.

'God bless the Queen! God bless the Prince of Wales.'

They were pleased with us because they had come near to losing Bertie.

It was a miracle, said the doctors. Few could have been so sorely smitten with the disease and come through. It had been God's will. He had listened to the people when they had cried: 'God save the Prince of Wales.'

At Temple Bar the crowd was most dense. It halted the carriages and I took Bertie's hand in mine and kissed it. There was a brief silence and then the cheers rang out.

As we went on to St. Paul's I thought of Gladstone's prophecies. This would show him that the monarchy had a deeper hold on the affections of the people than he was aware of. But it had taken a near-tragedy, such as this which had happened to the Prince of Wales, to show them how much a part of their lives we were.

But it was very gratifying all the same.

As Albert would have said: Often great joy comes out of suffering.

On the following day a very alarming incident took place.

I was riding in the carriage with Arthur. Brown was on the box, and I was thinking of how well the thanksgiving service had gone off and hoping that Bertie's terrible experience might have had some effect on his character. Alexandra had been so unswerving in her devotion to him. I hoped he would realize that he owed it to her to give up those fast women who had such attraction for him and to devote more time to his beautiful and virtuous wife.

It amazed me how fond Alexandra was of him; and his children were the same. I had seen them romping round him, not showing the least respect; and he was free and easy with them. In a way it was quite pleasant to watch, but I was not sure whether it was good for the children. Albert had been so different.

Then suddenly I saw a young man by the carriage . . . very close. He was looking straight at me and in his hand was a gun.

Everything seemed to stand still. It was not the first time I had looked death in the face—and in very similar circumstances.

In a flash Brown had leaped from the box; he was grappling with the young man and had thrown him to the ground. Arthur also had leaped from the carriage. He was grasping the man whom Brown had already overpowered.

I felt shaken. People were rushing up. The man who had wanted to shoot me was taken away.

Brown looked at me anxiously. 'You all right, woman?'

'Oh, Brown,' I said. 'You saved my life.'

Brown grunted and the carriage drove me back to the Palace.

I went to bed. They said I must. I was thinking that this was the sixth time someone had tried to kill me. Each time they had been foiled. Of course they had not all intended to kill me. But the shock was the same. I wondered about this latest young man. What was his motive?

It was not long before Mr. Gladstone arrived.

The man was Arthur O'Connor, an Irishman; and this had not been a serious attempt on my life as the pistol had not been loaded.

I said: 'That does not make the prompt action of John Brown any less commendable.'

Gladstone bowed his head.

'What loyalty!' I went on. 'What service!'

'O'Connor said he wished to frighten you into releasing Fenian prisoners. He was not going to shoot, he said. Only to frighten you.'

After Gladstone had gone I thought fondly of John Brown and I wondered how I could show my gratitude. I decided I would give him a medal to commemorate the occasion and an extra twenty-five pounds a year.

When this was known, Bertie—who like the rest of the family

did not care for John Brown—said that Arthur had also leaped from
the carriage and grappled with O'Connor.

'After John Brown had him in his grasp, yes.'

'Arthur acted bravely and he seems to be getting no recognition.
It all seems to be going to that fellow Brown.'

'Certainly it is not. I shall have a gold pin made for Arthur so
that he will know how much I appreciate his efforts to save me.'

'Well,' said Bertie, 'that is something. Not to be compared with
a gold medal and twenty-five pounds a year, but something.'

'What would Arthur want with a medal and twenty-five pounds
a year! I have worked hard to get him his annuity. You children are
a little ungrateful at times and I do not understand why you are all
so unkind to poor Brown. He gives me much more care and attention than I get from my family.'

Bertie raised his eyes to the ceiling and said: 'Good John Brown!
Not a word against him.'

Bertie was becoming quite unmanageable. All the care and attention he had had when he was ill, all that adulation afterwards
had gone to his head.

Gladstone came to tell me that O'Connor had been sentenced to
a year's imprisonment.

I was rather alarmed.

'One year!' I cried. 'What when he comes out? What if he tries
again? I should like to hear that he has been transported. It is not
that I want him more severely punished; I know that he is mad. But
I do not want to think of him here in this country.'

Gladstone made one of his speeches about the points of law and
how the court's sentence could not be changed. However, because
I felt so strongly and they understood my fears, O'Connor was
offered his fare to another country so that he could leave England
instead of serving his sentence.

This he accepted with alacrity. When he left I felt safer because
he was out of the country.

I received a very sad letter from Feodore. She begged me to come
and see her for she feared that if I did not come soon she would
never see me again.

'I am very ill,' she wrote, 'and something tells me that I have
not long to live. I want to see you before I go. I want to say goodbye.'

When I told Mr. Gladstone that I proposed visiting Baden-Baden
he shook his head and made one of his long speeches.

Recent events, he pointed out, such as the Prince's illness and the O'Connor attack had increased our popularity. We must hold on to it. We must see that we did not lose what we had gained. We must do nothing to diminish it.

I said: 'My sister is very ill. I am going to see her.'

And I went.

My dear Feodore! How she had changed from that bright and beautiful girl who used to sit in the garden while I watered the plants and she conducted her love affair with Cousin Augustus.

She had grown rather fat; she had lost her bright colour; and I saw at once that she was indeed very ill.

'I am so glad I came,' I said.

She became very sentimental talking of the past. She said: 'You were such a dear little child—so warm, so loving, so innocent. I was delighted with my little sister.'

It was a sad visit because we both knew we should not meet again. So we talked of the past which was the best way of not looking into the future.

'My Uncle George was very interested in you,' I reminded her. '*You* might have been Queen of England. I believe you could have been if Mama had wished it.'

'Mama wanted that rôle for you.'

'Yes,' I said. 'She wanted to rule through me, whereas she would never have been able to had you been Uncle George's Queen.'

'Does it ever strike you, little sister, what hundreds of possibilities there are in our lives? If you did this . . . if you did that at a certain time the whole course of your life could be changed.'

I admitted that I had thought of it.

The days sped past; we drove out in the carriage now and then. Feodore was not strong enough to walk or ride. She said I must not spend the whole time with her.

'Dear sister,' I replied, 'that is what I have come for. You have no idea what black looks I received from my Prime Minister when I told him I was coming. But I was determined to come all the same.'

'You are not happy with Mr. Gladstone. He is highly thought of here. They think he is a very strong man.'

'Strong he may be, but I find him most uncomfortable and difficult to talk to. How I wish people had had the sense not to send Mr. Disraeli away.'

Then I made her laugh with an imitation of Gladstone and his speaker's manner. 'I always feel like the audience at a meeting when he holds forth. His wife is quite a pleasant creature. I often pity her for having such a husband.'

'Perhaps she is fond of him.'

'Oddly enough, she seems to be.'

'People seem different to different people.'

Dreamy days they were. Sometimes I would forget how ill she was. She insisted that I do a little sightseeing and she arranged for me to see something of the place. I was shown the haunts of some of the worst characters of both sexes in Europe; but what I remember most was an instrument of torture which was used by the Inquisition. It was called the Iron Virgin—a case lined with knives into which those who were called heretics were thrust, and, as they said, embraced by the Virgin.

I had never seen anything like it—and I shall never forget it.

The time came for me to say goodbye to Feodore and I took leave of her with protestations of affection. We both knew it would be our last meeting and we tried to be brave about it. We embraced with great affection. We had always been such good friends. The only difference we had ever had had been at the time of that awful Schleswig-Holstein business when she had wanted my support for her daughter's husband and I had been unable to give it.

These beastly wars that made rifts in families!

But any rift between us was now healed; and with poignant tenderness we said our last farewells.

When I arrived back it was to find Mr. Gladstone in a tutorial mood. He came and talked, standing before me, rocking on his heels, expounding his views. He thought the Prince of Wales should be seen doing some work. It would please the people.

'What sort of work?' I asked.

Mr. Gladstone thought that as his father had been interested in art and science, they might be fields to explore. 'The Prince Consort had a knowledge of architecture,' he added.

'The Prince of Wales is not the Prince Consort,' I said. 'If only he resembled his father more I think we should have less cause for concern.'

'Perhaps philanthropy would be good for him,' Mr. Gladstone went on, rocking on his heels and discussing philanthropy as though I had never heard of it. He really was the most exhausting man I had ever met.

Finally, I said: 'I can see no point in planning for the Prince of Wales. I am told he is a good ambassador. Let him do what is asked of him, but the idea of forcing him into art, science or philanthropy, I think is hopeless. He would never give his mind to any of these.'

Mr. Gladstone seemed to be in agreement, only he could not say so simply. And it was decided that for the moment we should leave Bertie alone.

Death! It never seems to strike singly. Poor Feodore died, as I knew she must. Napoleon passed on at Chichester. How sad that he who had had such grandiose plans should have ended in exile.

One of the saddest deaths was that of the Countess of Beaconsfield. Poor Mr. Disraeli was heartbroken. He was such a *feeling* man. He wrote long letters to me and I wrote back expressing my sympathy. None knew better than I what the loss of one's partner meant. I could understand as few could, I sensed the depth of his feeling, his desolation.

He told me that she had been eighty-one. Well, it was a great age. He himself was sixty-eight. 'I knew she had to go before me,' he wrote. 'But that does not soften the blow.' Poor, *poor* Mr. Disraeli, my heart bled for him.

He wrote so beautifully, so poignantly. He brought back memories of my own loss. I wrote and told him of my feelings, how similar were our losses.

The death of his wife seemed to bring Mr. Disraeli closer to me.

But these were all expected deaths and there was one which was the most tragic of all.

How I suffered with the dearest of my daughters, my Alice. She had had seven children which I had always said was too many, but Alice loved them all dearly and did not mind so much as I had those months of pregnancy and the births. She accepted these pains and discomforts, thinking them worth while.

When I heard what had happened I could scarcely believe it. She had gone into the courtyard and her little Frederick William, who was about three years old, saw her and called out to her. He leaned out too far and fell onto the cobbles below.

A little later he died. Alice was heart-broken. How I suffered with her. I thank God that she had the others.

She had been dogged by ill luck since her marriage, poor girl. Louis had never been a great match—unlike Vicky's with the Crown Prince of Prussia—and Louis had lost a lot of what he had had at the time of his marriage—thanks to that arch-villain, Bismarck.

Alice and I had not been quite so close since her marriage. There had been one or two upsets. I had remonstrated with her because she would nurse the children herself. A wet nurse would have been so much more suitable. The business was distasteful reducing one to the level of a cow, I thought. A very crude joke of Nature's. But Alice insisted. She said she had saved the children from dysentery. Then I thought she had had too many too quickly, and it was quite clear that she resented my interference in this matter. She had more or less told me that it was entirely her affair.

Sometime before she had forgotten Vicky's birthday which upset Vicky very much and I had not invited Alice to England when Vicky was there because I feared a coldness between them.

I believed, too, that she and Alfred had put their heads together and made plans to draw me out of my seclusion. So although I never forgot that in the past Alice was the one who really came first in my affections, that had changed a little since her marriage.

Alfred, like Bertie, seemed destined to cause trouble. He must marry, of course, but he did seem to make the most unsuitable choices. Sometime previously he had contemplated marriage to Frederika, daughter of my blind cousin George, who had been driven from his throne of Hanover.

I had firmly quashed that. As her father was blind I said there was a possibility of that malady descending through his daughter; and as Alfred was not very determined that happily passed over. Then there was an involvement with a commoner. I feared that I was going to have even more trouble with Alfred than I had had with Bertie.

Now he was really serious. He wanted to marry a daughter of the Tsar.

I was not at all pleased about this. The Russians had been our enemies and I did not entirely trust them. I began to reconsider Frederika. I had been rather fond of my blind cousin at one time, and I believed she was quite a pleasant girl. But Alfred—fickle creature—had forgotten Frederika and was set on Marie of Russia.

The Tsar at first had not been eager for the match and then seemed to change his mind. I heard rumours which came through our ambassador in Russia that Marie had been involved with Prince Golitsyn—and not only him—and that the Russian royal family were now eager to see her settled. Hence the sudden acceptance of marriage with Alfred.

Naturally I did not want such a marriage, and as Alfred was so feckless I felt I must reason with him. His past would not bear too much scrutiny. I could think of several reasons why the marriage should not take place. The Russians were half oriental; they were self-indulgent; I did not have a great opinion of the Romanovs. There would be a marriage in the Greek Church. No. I was against the match.

It seemed that the Russians were not too keen now either. There was a great deal of shilly-shallying; and I wondered if Alfred's pride would allow him to accept that. But he seemed to be unaware of it and he was pursuing marriage to Marie with a tenacity which I wished he would give to more worthy matters.

At last to my dismay, the engagement was official. I asked that Marie should visit me at Balmoral at which I had a most impolite reply from the Tsar to the effect that he had no intention of sending his daughter for my approval. The Tsarina then suggested that I meet the Princess at Cologne.

'The impertinence!' I said. 'Do they expect *me* to run after *her*!'

I was furious when Alice wrote to me advising me—advising *me*!— to meet the Tsarina and her daughter at Cologne. 'The Tsarina feels the heat more than you do, Mama, and travelling is so tiresome for her. It is meeting half-way, and that seems reasonable.'

Reasonable! I thought. I picked up my pen and wrote to her:

'You have entirely taken the Russian side, and I do not think, dear child, that you should tell me—who have been nearly *twenty* years longer on the throne than the Emperor of Russia and am the Doyenne of Sovereigns and who am a reigning Sovereign which the Empress is not—what I ought to do. I do think I know *that*. How could I, who am not like any little Princess, be ready to run at the slightest call of the *mighty* Russians.'

Bertie and Alexander were, of course, in favour of the Russian marriage because Alexandra's sister Dagmar was married to the Tsarevitch. Bertie invited them to come to England, which they did. I found them very charming and I felt less animosity to the Russians after that. Alexandra's sister was a pleasant creature—not as beautiful as Alexandra, but the affection between them was strong, and I really became quite enchanted by them all.

And when I did meet Princess Marie I found her warm and loving, and I saw no reason why—if she would learn our English ways—she should not make Alfred a good wife. Heaven knew he needed a steadying influence.

I had a long talk with Alfred warning him of the duties and the responsibilities of marriage and expressed the fervent hope that he would change his life when he became a husband. But I did not believe he paid much attention.

At length they were married in St. Petersburg. I sent my dear friend Dean Stanley to perform the wedding ceremony after the Anglican rite. It was by all means a glittering occasion.

How fickle are the people! Those who had heralded Mr. Gladstone's ministry a few years before were now weary of him.

He had realized the signs of weakness in the Liberal party and that it no longer possessed the power to carry on in government.

He came to see me and delivered one of his harangues. I paid more attention this time because I realized he was thinking of relinquishing office. His Irish Universities Bill had been turned out and several Liberal candidates had been defeated in by-elections. Of course, he was a great reformer and although people clamour for this, when the reforms are brought in they see that they are not all they were made out to be.

I was reading the accounts of Alfred's grand wedding when I had a telegram from Mr. Gladstone telling me that the Cabinet had decided to dissolve Parliament.

There was an election. Mr. Gladstone retained his seat but it was a triumphant victory for the Tories.

I waited impatiently for my new Prime Minister to call.

He had aged a little. The sorrow he had suffered at the death of Mary Anne had affected him deeply. I saw this at once and when I held out my hand for him to kiss, I touched his head as he bent and said: 'Dear Mr. Disraeli, this is indeed a happy moment.'

'For me, M'am,' he replied, 'it is the start of life again.'

I knew what he meant. In his devotion to me, he could salve the grief he suffered at the death of Mary Anne.

Life was much happier for me now that I had my dear Mr. Disraeli as a constant visitor. Although we had kept in touch during his years in opposition, for we were both prolific letter writers, it was much more satisfying to see him in person.

I had to admit that Mr. Gladstone was a man of high principle and he had worked hard for his country; but then so did Mr. Disraeli and he did it gracefully, so that it was a pleasure to be with him. He made state affairs a matter of interest and amusement, as Lord Melbourne used to. That was a so much more effective way of dealing with them, for Mr. Gladstone's tedious speeches did have a tendency to send me to sleep.

Mr. Disraeli was a great talker and his descriptions were so vivid. I felt I knew so much about him, his ambitions, his determination to 'climb the greasy pole' as he expressed it, to the premiership. 'And,' he said, 'it is much harder, M'am, I do assure you, to stay at the top of it than climb it.' I was sure he was right.

It was from him that I learned of Mr. Gladstone's peregrinations after dark through the streets of London. 'His great desire, M'am, is to rescue ladies of easy virtue and bring them back to paths of righteousness.'

I was incredulous. 'Mr. Gladstone behaving so! I wonder what Mrs. Gladstone has to say.'

'She is a most devoted wife. She believes unshakably in the virtue of her husband.'

'Does she join him in this . . . er . . . work?'

'Indeed, M'am, I believe they have "rescued" one or two. It has been going on for years.'

'It seems to me an odd occupation for such a man.'

'It is a dangerous one.' He looked at me slyly. 'People are apt to misconstrue.'

'I cannot believe Mr. Gladstone would ever be anything but virtuous. Oh, dear, poor Mrs. Gladstone!'

Mr. Disraeli had a wonderful effect on me. I felt better than I had since Albert's death. I felt more alive. I felt younger, even attractive, not as a queen but as a woman.

I believe that in a way he was in love with me. People do not always understand these things. They think that love must be a physical thing. Far from it. I was never what is called 'physical' in that respect. I did not need that sort of contact; my emotions were of the spirit. I had heard that he had written of me that now that Mary Anne was dead, I was the only person in the world left to him to love. He was completely devoted to me; our meetings brought as much joy to him as they did to me. I knew that he called me 'The Faery Queen'. I thought that was rather charming and I was grateful to him.

People said rather crudely that 'he had got the length of my foot' and knew how to be sympathetic and that his sympathy might be expressed with his tongue in his cheek.

I knew these things were said, but I did not care. People always tried to spoil things which were beautiful and my relationship with him was beautiful. We were a joy and comfort to each other and what more could one ask of any relationship?

We agreed on so many things and when I was incensed by something and he did not agree with my views, he had such a comical way of raising his eyebrows and saying in a mock serious way

'*Dear* Madam,' which always amused me and made me reconsider my opinions.

We discussed Mr. Gladstone at great length. He was concerned about religion. He had defended Roman Catholicism and then published an *Expostulation* against the Catholic claims. He was a strange man—subversive, in a way. There was this obsession with religion and the nightly wanderings.

I would not say this to anyone else but Mr. Disraeli, but what if Mr. Gladstone were in secret a Catholic . . . and a libertine?

Mr. Disraeli just looked at me and said in his mock-severe voice: 'Dear Madam' which of course made me laugh.

The troubles between the family and John Brown continued. They were all against him. They could not understand that in his honest Highland way he was no respecter of persons. I had quickly realized this and so had Albert and we had told each other that loyalty and honesty came before lip service.

Two courtiers who held service in the household had threatened to resign because they could not accept the privileges accorded to Brown. Bertie said he would not go to Abergeldie because Brown was given shooting rights which ruined the sport for him. Someone said: 'Brown is a coarse animal.'

They were all trying to rid me of the very best servant I had, one whose loyalty to me was never in question.

The company Bertie was keeping was causing scandal everywhere. I had my anxieties over Alfred. Vicky was arrogant. I believe she thought the wife of the Crown Prince—one day to be Empress—was more important than the Queen of England; Alice—even Alice—had ceased to be the placid girl who had meant so much to me; Leopold frequently suffered from haemorrhages which were a constant anxiety; and I was terrified that Beatrice was going to fall in love and I found myself restricting her, keeping her from social activities, trying to arrange that she did not meet people outside the family. I thought often of my mad grandfather, George III, who had spoiled the lives of his daughters. I must remember that. Yet how could I bear to lose Beatrice!

There was always the danger of offending the public and it seemed that feelings against royalty were always simmering and ready to boil over.

Charles Greville's *Memoirs* were published and widely read. I thought them amusing at first but then I began to see how dangerous they were. He exposed too much and although he recorded actual events he did exaggerate them. His observations were quite cynical and no one was spared. This sort of thing did no good to the established State.

Mr. Disraeli was not very pleased at the publication. He said the book was a social outrage and that Greville was full of vanity. Someone else commented that it was like Judas writing the lives of the apostles—which I thought a rather witty and apt remark. I think it was Lord John Manners who said this.

But as I read on and saw how my poor uncles were pilloried, I realized how dangerous the book was.

Greville had been Clerk of the Council in Ordinary from '21 until '60 and had died in '65 and these Memoirs of the reigns of George IV and William IV were edited by a Henry Reeve; and when objection to their publication was raised, this man Reeve remarked that my behaviour would seem very good when set against that of my uncles. I had been fond of both Uncle George and Uncle William and I deplored this publication which, in any case, could do no good to the monarchy.

There was another unpleasant incident which had set the people against us—though I cannot think why we were to blame in any way, but people are quite illogical.

Our yacht the *Alberta* collided with another ship when we were crossing to Osborne. Three people were drowned and I was most distressed. The case was brought to court and the mob surrounded the court-house screaming threats against our captain. It was most unfortunate; and the case dragged on and on, and our enemies in the Press made the most of it. One would have thought that I had deliberately set out to collide with the other boat which was in our way and cared nothing that lives were lost as long as I could pursue my pleasure. Nothing could have been farther from the truth, and no one could have been more unhappy than I was that lives had been lost.

Then we had the dangerous Aylesford affair—another scandal involving Bertie. What a genius he had for getting himself into these scrapes. It was just as Albert had feared.

Disraeli had a great interest in India. 'One day I am going to make you Empress of India, M'am,' he said.

I smiled at him. He really did care for me so much.

He thought it would be a good idea if Bertie was sent to India.

'A very good background for his particular sort of mischief, I imagine,' I said.

'Dear Madam!'

I smiled at him. 'Well, you know Bertie has a habit of falling into mischief . . .'

'He is a good ambassador. The people like him.'

'He is too fond of fast women and gambling.'

'The people often like their heroes to have feet of clay. It makes them feel so much more like heroes themselves. I think the Prince will do very well.'

At length I decided that if the Prime Minister thought it advisable, it must be right.

Bertie was delighted; Alexandra less so, for she was not to go with him.

It was while he was in India that the trouble blew up. It was like the Mordaunt case all over again—with variations, of course. But Bertie being what he is, perhaps that was to be expected.

Dizzy, as he was universally called—and I found myself thinking of him thus for Mr. Disraeli was too remote an appellation for such a friend—came to see me.

'I'm afraid, M'am, that a little *contretemps* has blown up in the circle of the Prince of Wales.'

'Oh dear . . . not women again!'

'One woman, M'am.'

'Do please explain. I must hear the worst.'

'It is Lord Aylesford. His wife is threatening to divorce him.'

'Oh no . . . not Bertie!'

'Not exactly, M'am. I must give you the details as they have been given to me. Perhaps you did not know that Lord Aylesford is one of the Prince's greatest friends.'

'I know very well. I was against his going on tour with the Prince, but I was overruled. He is a gambling, sporty type.'

'Exactly so, M'am, and a member of the circle which is close to the Prince. I think he is considered to be a very amusing fellow.'

'And Aylesford's wife?'

'She was also on good terms with the Prince.'

'I feared that.'

'It is not on the Prince's account that Aylesford is threatening divorce. Lord Blandford is the man in the case. While Aylesford was in India Lady Aylesford set up house with Blandford. News of this reached Aylesford and he left for home—rather against the Prince's wishes for he liked Aylesford's company a good deal. The Prince despised Blandford and made some comments about him which were brought to the notice of Blandford's younger brother— Lord Randolph Churchill.'

'I never liked the man.'

'A fiery-tempered young fellow. He was furious that his brother should have been slandered, he said. Particularly . . .'

'Particularly?' I insisted.

'By the Prince. I believe he recalled the Mordaunt scandal and er . . .'

'Other scandals. You must tell me the truth you know, Mr. Disraeli.'

'Exactly, M'am. Your Majesty is too wise and the situation too delicate for us to mince our words. The fact is that Churchill says he wants the divorce stopped. He is a hot-headed idiot, as indiscreet as a man can be. He wants the Prince to stop the divorce. He says that he must use his influence with Aylesford and stop him proceeding further.'

'But why draw in the Prince?'

'Churchill resents what the Prince said about his brother. He says the Churchill family honour is at stake. He is a wild, impetuous young man, capable of any folly in the heat of anger; the sort who can do a great deal of harm. He has already sought an interview with the Princess of Wales.'

'Surely not! Oh, my poor Alexandra! It is bad enough for her to know of the Prince's . . . activities . . . but to be drawn into this!'

'It was a ridiculous thing to do, but then Churchill is ridiculous.'

'Why go to the Princess?'

'He wants her to impress on the Prince that he must forbid Aylesford to start divorce proceedings.'

'But what has the Prince to do with this?'

'M'am, according to Churchill, the Prince has written letters to Lady Aylesford. When Aylesford threatened divorce, she gave these letters to Blandford. They are now in Churchill's possession and if Aylesford goes through with the divorce, the letters written by the Prince will be handed to the Press.'

'This is terrible.'

'I fear it is a little unpleasant.'

'It reminds me of my Uncle George. He was always in difficulties with women and there were letters.'

'It may well be that the letters are quite innocent.'

I looked at him helplessly.

'Churchill says that if these letters are published the Prince will never be able to sit on the throne.'

I felt limp with exhaustion. If only Albert were here. He would know what to do. But if he were, how unhappy he would be! Perhaps I should be glad that he was not here . . . to suffer this.

What an unpleasant situation! Churchill was adamant. I had never liked him. I would never receive him at Court—not him nor his American wife.

I knew it was useless to rage against them and I knew, too, however innocent Bertie's part in all this—and I could hardly believe it was—the Press and public would make him appear guilty— and that was just as bad as though he were.

What fools young men were, writing letters to women! One would have thought that they would have learned from the example of others—but they never seemed to.

I was comforted to have Disraeli there. I felt that if anyone could bring us out of this unsavoury matter, he could.

'Will you leave this to me, M'am?' he asked.

'Most willingly, my dear friend,' I told him.

How clever he was! I know that he worked indefatigably for my good. He told me that he had approached Lord Hardwicke and impressed on him the danger of the situation and Lord Hardwicke had seen the point and promised to do what he could.

I am sure it was due to Disraeli's efforts that we came out of that as well as we did. Between them Lord Hardwicke and Mr. Disraeli managed to get Lord Aylesford to stop proceedings; and by the time Bertie came home, the matter was settled.

But as Disraeli said, there would have been rumours of the affair and it would be as well for Churchill to make an apology to the Prince.

At first Churchill refused to do this, but when his family and friends pointed out that he would be ruined at Court if he did not, he complied.

Bertie accepted the apology but Lord and Lady Randolph thought it necessary to travel abroad for a while and Bertie vowed that when he came back he would not receive him.

So another unsavoury matter was brought to an end.

Dear, clever Mr. Disraeli.

He was such a brilliant statesman. His Indian policy had brought about what he so ardently desired. I was created Empress of India. How proud he was! Of course the Opposition had done their best to prevent this; and Disraeli had to compromise to a certain extent by assuring them that the title would only be used for matters dealing with India.

I was worried about him for his health was not of the best and I insisted on bestowing a peerage on him and he became Lord Beaconsfield.

He had induced me to appear a little more in public and I had found the experience quite pleasurable. We had worked together over the Ashanti War and when it was over I had reviewed the soldiers, sailors and marines, distributing medals. I attended a concert at the Royal Albert Hall and inspected the wonderful Memorial—so beautifully elaborate with its large gilded figure of Albert in the centre.

There was trouble in Europe which made us very watchful. It was like the Crimean War all over again. Turkey and the Balkans were at loggerheads and Russia was threatening to come in.

Disraeli followed in Lord Palmerston's footsteps. He said that our interests in India and everywhere dictated that Turkey must not be violated. The Turks behaved with great ferocity in the Balkans and Mr. Gladstone who, a little while before, had announced his retirement came back to fulminate against the Turks because of the atrocities they had committed, and declared he was against any English support for Turkey.

I was furious with Gladstone. Self-righteous and moralizing, he was preventing Disraeli from acting as he thought best. Disraeli was a great enough politician to realize that personal feelings of repugnance must stand aside when the nation's interests were at stake.

Russia must be kept out. I wrote to Alice who was very concerned about the conflict; and she had a meeting with the Tsar at Darmstadt when he assured her that he had no desire to come into conflict with England.

So much for his promise. Russia almost immediately declared war on Turkey and in a short time was victorious.

I was very distressed when the Sultan made an appeal to me to beg the Russians to make lenient peace terms. As if Russia would do that! The terms were harsh and Disraeli suggested that we demand the settlement be agreed by a congress of European states.

This was an alarming situation and we were on the brink of war with Russia. I daresay Gladstone would have retreated; but not Lord Beaconsfield—and I stood firmly with him.

I shall never forget the day when Lord Beaconsfield came to me in a very serious frame of mind.

He said: 'We must at all costs prevent Russia from getting a foothold in the south of the Danube.'

I knew what those ominous words 'at all costs' meant.

I told him that I felt complete confidence in him and he must take the risk.

He left for Berlin where the conference was to be held and I was greatly disturbed when I heard that he and Prince Gortchakoff had reached deadlock, and Beaconsfield had remarked that if they could not come to an agreement the dispute would have to be settled 'by other means'.

I daresay Russia was not so eager to enter into conflict with us as she was with little Turkey; and a compromise was reached. Lord Beaconsfield returned home, bringing with him, as he said, 'Peace with honour.'

I was delighted to see him and welcomed him warmly. I was determined that all should know how I appreciated the good work he had done for the country; and I awarded him the Order of the Garter.

I suppose everyone knew of the happy relationship I enjoyed with my Prime Minister. I was certainly seeing more of people and they all knew that I had paid a visit to his country seat at Hughenden when I had planted a tree in honour of the occasion.

With the companionship of Lord Beaconsfield and the faithful attendance of John Brown, I felt I was very fortunate.

Leopold was a continual anxiety. He had just recovered from a very bad illness. I was always so worried even if he were only slightly ill. I dreaded that fearful bleeding. He was so reckless. He wanted to live as other people did—and I could understand that, but he assumed a certain indifference to danger which was very worrying for me.

I was slightly more reconciled to Bertie. Everybody liked him though none looked up to him; but it seemed that his character was the key to his popularity. Everyone had looked up to Albert—or should have done—but not many people really liked him.

Bertie was always considerate to the servants, and as I was the same, I liked that in him.

There are often troubles in families. I knew that Vicky was having trouble with young Wilhelm. He had always been an arrogant child, and I supposed that, to one of his temperament, having a deformed arm must be very frustrating. He always signed himself 'Prince Wilhelm of Prussia' even to me. He was so proud of being Prussian and made no secret of the fact that he despised his English blood, which enraged me. He actively disliked Vicky, it seemed—

his own mother! What infuriated him most, I believe, was that England was more important in the world than Germany, and Bismarck and his grandparents had instilled in him that this must not always be so. He never defended his mother when people spoke against her—which they did often because she was half-English. He laughed with them at her and her foreign ways. I knew Vicky was most distressed about this son of hers.

There was one thing which endeared Bertie to me. He might be unsatisfactory in many ways, but I was sure he would never listen to disparagement of me. He was a good son if one could forget those peccadilloes he fell into, mostly with regard to women.

Then there was Arthur. He was the most like Albert of all my children, and I never thought he would marry; but quite suddenly he fell in love and in an unexpected direction.

He chose Princess Louise Margaret, daughter of Prince Frederick Charles—a nephew of the German Emperor—and Princess Marianne of Prussia. It was rather an unfortunate choice because the Prince and Princess were separated. I wished he would not rush into this. If he had wanted to marry I could have found him a more suitable bride. But Arthur had made up his mind and I had never believed in forcing the children into a marriage which was distasteful to them.

However, when I met the girl I found her quite charming; and although she was not good-looking she had a very pleasant profile. I thought it was rather wonderful of Arthur to have rescued her from a broken home and I told myself that Louischen—which by this time she had become—was more likely to appreciate a man like Arthur and make a good marriage because she had had experience, through her parents, of the other kind.

I wrote to Vicky telling her how sorry I was about Wilhelm's behaviour. It made me realize that I was rather fortunate after all. Alfred and Leopold were often careless and wanting in consideration; Arthur had always been good and attentive; and I was beginning to think that those terrible scrapes through which Bertie had passed had been a lesson to him. And I did not think that any one of them would tolerate anyone's speaking ill of me.

But the child I was really worried about was Alice. She was not in good health. Bearing all those children had been too much for her. She was devoted to them all and had suffered tragically when little Frittie had died. He had been cursed with that terrible disease which it seemed passed through the family to the sons by the mothers. I had passed it on to Leopold and Alice had to Frittie. She had never really recovered from his death.

Almost immediately after, the Duke of Hesse-Darmstadt had died and Louis had succeeded him; and although it was a small state, much diminished by that odious Bismarck, official duties weighed heavily.

Alice was first and foremost a family person. She had been my devoted daughter—little Fatima, the placid one. When she married, of course, she had moved away from me, and we had had our little upsets; but she was still the best-loved child.

I was in a state of horror when I heard that her daughter Victoria had diphtheria and she was very ill indeed. Two days later her daughter Alix—called Alicky—caught it; then Baby May was the next victim. Then Ernest, her only son, and Ella.

It was November when the telegrams came. It was a time of year which I had dreaded since Albert's death. Memories always came back to me more vividly at that time. I had come to think of the fourteenth of December as a day of ill omen, when horrible catastrophes would overtake me. Bertie had come near to death on that date and by a miracle survived. But I did dread that time of year.

Alice had only six children left to her. They were the centre of her life. She was essentially the mother as I had never been. How she must have suffered when that little one had fallen from the window . . . and in a moment of delight at seeing her!

I waited eagerly for news. I could not sleep and the first thing I looked for in the mornings was news of Alice.

It came and it was very depressing. Louis had caught the terrible disease and Alice herself was the only one who was well.

I wrote pages to her. She must take care of herself. She must leave the care of her family to nurses. She must never go close to them for that was how the disease was passed on. She must not be tempted to embrace or kiss them. She *must* leave the entire care of them in the hands of servants, doctors and nurses.

Alice wrote back almost indignantly. I did not seem to understand. This was her beloved family. Did I imagine she would leave them in the hands of others? Indeed no. She was going to nurse them herself.

Lord Beaconsfield came and shared my grief.

'I wish that I could go there,' I cried. 'I would nurse them. I would send Alice away to safety. Dear Lord Beaconsfield, she is the most loved of all my children. She was always so different . . . so gentle. Albert loved her, although Vicky was his favourite . . .

but Alice was mine. She was such a good girl. She and Arthur are the only two in the least like their father. If I caught the disease, what would it matter? My life finished on that tragic fourteenth of December.'

He looked at me sorrowfully and said: 'Dear Madam.'

I smiled faintly. He was such a comfort to me.

There was further sad news. Little May—five years old, the baby and pet of the household—had died.

Alice's grief was terrible. The whole family was stricken.

The worst was to come. I heard afterwards what had happened. Her son, Ernest, who was also a victim, was so sorrowful when he heard of his little sister's death, and feeling that he himself would be the next, had turned to his mother in an access of grief, and she had embraced and kissed him.

The result of that embrace was that Alice herself was stricken.

This was what I had feared and I summoned as many of the family as I could and told them. They were in despair. Alice had been greatly loved and it was only two days to the fourteenth of December.

I was proud of them all as they gathered round to comfort me. Bertie was as charming as he knew how to be, and was especially so on occasions like this.

I prayed to God. I prayed to Albert. I tried to make terms with the Almighty. Save Alice and take me instead. Give me Alice and do anything You will. I had already, on that other fateful fourteenth, been dealt the cruellest blow which could possibly have befallen me and I was ready to face anything—just anything in return for Alice's life.

The thirteenth came. There was no news. I went through the day in a haze of apprehension; and I awoke to the fateful fourteenth.

Brown fussed over me, scolding me, telling me I was 'a foolish woman who could do nae good by fretting.'

I had almost known it would happen. I took the telegram in a state of numbed acceptance.

Alice was dead.

They stood round me, my dear family. Alice was the first child I had lost and the tragedy was almost more than I could bear.

Bertie put his arms round me and tried to comfort me. He had especially loved Alice. When they were young she had often tried to cover up his misdemeanours. I was sure she had saved him from many a beating.

We knew then how she had caught the infection. In expressing her love for her son, and trying to comfort him she had caught the disease herself. Beatrice wept bitterly and so did Alexandra. Dear girl, she was very much one of the family.

It was strange that it should have happened on the dreaded fourteenth.

Brown gave me some comfort with his silence and shocked looks; he urged me to drink a little. I could not eat. He said nothing but it is amazing what comfort there can be in silence.

Lord Beaconsfield called.

'I thought you would not wish for visitors at such a time,' he said. 'But I felt that if you could not bear to see me you would say so. Therefore I came. What can I say? I can only offer my deep sympathy.'

I was pleased to see him at any time, I told him. It was true that I should not have wished to see anyone else. I was able to talk to him about Alice, about Albert, the two whom I had loved best in the whole world—and I had lost them both.

'How well I understand, M'am,' he said, and I knew that he was thinking of Mary Anne.

'You had a wonderful wife,' I told him. 'I had a wonderful husband. You called her the perfect wife. Albert was, without doubt, the perfect husband. You have often said how fortunate we have been to have these wonderful beings even for a short time. But I have often wondered if we should have been happier if we had never known them. Then we should not have had to suffer their loss.'

He said he did not agree with me on that; and I was sure he was right.

Later he sent me a copy of the speech he had made in the House of Lords. I read it again and again and I could not stop the tears flowing as I did so.

'My Lords, there is something wonderfully piteous in the immediate cause of her death. The physician who permitted her to watch over her suffering family enjoined her under no circumstances to be tempted into an embrace. Her admirable self constraint guarded her, but it became her lot to break to her son the news of the death of his younger sister to whom he was devotedly attached. The boy was so overcome with misery that the agitated mother clasped him in her arms and thus she received the kiss of death.'

I was so touched, so deeply moved. How like Lord Beaconsfield to express it so beautifully!

When he came to see me we wept together.

'The kiss of death!' I said. 'It was so beautifully expressed. And that was what it was.'

He sat with me talking in his fluent way. He thought it was significant that Alice had died on the fourteenth of December.

'So you think Albert wanted her with him and he chose that day to take her?'

Lord Beaconsfield said he thought that might be the case.

'I should have thought he would have taken Vicky rather than Alice. Vicky was his favourite. She was the clever one. My dear sweet Alice was never that.'

It was all very mysterious, said Lord Beaconsfield; and we talked of death and the after-life and whether those who had passed on could come back to watch over those whom they had loved on earth.

And talking with Lord Beaconsfield assuaged my grief.

Farewell John Brown

How grateful I was to Lord Beaconsfield in every way. I thanked God for him. He was a solace in that time of trouble. I pictured what it would have been like if I had had to rely on Mr. Gladstone at that time. I knew Gladstone had his good points. He was very popular with the people. He was known in fact as 'The People's William'. But I could not like him. He saw me as a public institution whereas Lord Beaconsfield saw me as a woman.

The Zulu War had broken out. There was a great deal of unrest in South Africa. Sir Bartle Frere, the Governor of the Cape, was not the most diplomatic of men. Lord Beaconsfield did not approve of his actions, but, as he said to me, the government had to support its representatives. His great aim was to make us, and keep us, at the head of all states which, as he pointed out to me, meant an increase in our commitments.

There was a great deal of opposition from Gladstone who accused the government of Imperialism. Gladstone was one of those pacifists who will stand for peace at any price. I often thought that they with their timid approach are more responsible for wars than those who stand firm and strong. It is because our enemies suspect we are weak that they come to attack us.

Lord Beaconsfield agreed with me. It was the reason why, under his premiership, we were becoming mightier.

I had a terrible shock when I heard that the only son of the Empress of France, who was fighting the Zulus with us, had been captured and hacked to death by the savages. Poor Eugénie was heart-broken. I went to Chichester to comfort her. I, who had so recently lost my Alice, was in a position to understand.

It was heart-breaking. I determined to look after the poor sad creature and visit her often. Life was so cruel. It was hard to recognize in that poor woman, the dazzling Empress who had ruled over her court with Napoleon—so beautiful, so elegant—and now an exile, a sorrowing mother, who had lost her only child. I at least had eight left to me.

Meanwhile Gladstone was making virulent attacks on Lord Beaconsfield, deploring his Imperialism. What was the result of Mr. Gladstone's interference? War. I was furious.

Lord Beaconsfield smiled at my anger.

He said: 'It is true that I am ambitious. I want to secure for Your Majesty, greater powers than you already have. I believe it is the way for peace and prosperity, not only for us but for the whole world. I want you to dictate the affairs of Europe. For the sake of world peace I think it is necessary for Your Majesty to occupy the position I plan for you.'

I told him that I feared Prussia might be troublesome.

'Young Wilhelm has been brought up under Bismarck. It is not surprising that he is imbued with ideas for the aggrandizement of Prussia.'

'I am really beginning to dislike Wilhelm. It seems so strange that he should turn out like this. He was the first grandchild. Albert and I were so proud of him.'

'I only hope,' said Lord Beaconsfield, 'that I live long enough to see Your Majesty where you belong.'

'Please do not talk of your not being here. I have suffered so much lately. I could not bear any more.'

'Gladstone has a great following,' he said warningly. He smiled at me apologetically. 'Facts have to be faced, M'am.'

I was alarmed.

He nodded. 'Support is dropping away. It may be that before long we shall be obliged to go to the country and if we do . . .'

'Oh no. I could not bear that. Not that man again! I thought he had retired once. Why does he have to come back?'

'By public request, M'am. The people love their William.'

'Do they know he prowls the streets at night?'

'I think he has given that up. And it was said to be most virtuously done.'

'If one believes it!'

'Of Mr. Gladstone! Surely one must.'

'If I have to accept him . . . I . . . I shall abdicate!'

'Dear Madam!'

He left me very uneasy for I knew that unless he was almost sure that there would be a change of government he would not have suggested it to me at this time, for he would know how it disturbed me.

Of course he was right to prepare me and although I was deeply distressed when Parliament was dissolved and an election was called, it was not such a shock as it would have been if I had not been prepared.

The following day I went to Germany. I had to see Alice's stricken family who had now recovered from their illness and had to face their irreplaceable loss.

Two of the girls were going to be confirmed and I wanted to see the ceremony.

It was a very sad household. Alice had been greatly loved.

I visited Vicky in time to celebrate the betrothal of Wilhelm to Princess Victoria of Schleswig-Holstein-Sonderburg-Augustenburg, who was the daughter of that Duke Frederick who had laid claims to Schleswig-Holstein. Her mother was Feodore's daughter, so I had a special interest in the match; and I thought it excellent as Prussia had annexed Schleswig-Holstein. In a way it made reparations for their act.

So that was something of which I approved—though I had to say that Wilhelm's manners had not improved and I thought him quite an odious young man.

My great interest, of course, was in what was going on at home. I was in constant touch with Lord Beaconsfield and, alas, the news was gloomy.

Finally I had the result of the election. My Conservative Government had been defeated and the Liberals had a majority of one hundred and sixty.

It was indeed a tragedy.

I returned home distraught. Not Mr. Gladstone! I could not endure it; and it would be particularly hard to bear after the pleasant companionship I had enjoyed with dear Lord Beaconsfield.

Sir Henry Ponsonby, my secretary, who was always such a help, tried hard to comfort me.

'I would sooner abdicate,' I told him, 'than have anything to do with that half-mad firebrand who will ruin everything and try to dictate to me.'

Sir Henry soothed me. He said perhaps he would not be so bad as that. There were others. Mr. Gladstone was getting old. Perhaps he would be a little mellowed.

Mellowed! I could see no sign of that in his outbursts against Lord Beaconsfield, and his weak-kneed policy of peace at any price.

'Your Majesty could send for Lord Granville.'

'I don't want him.'

'Lord Hartington?'

'Hartington! Isn't he the one they call Harty Tarty.'

'Yes, Your Majesty.'

'A fine Prime Minister. Harty Tarty indeed! And wasn't he involved in that scandal with the Duchess of Manchester?'

'They were intimate friends, Your Majesty.'

'Until, I hear, he conceived a passion for some creature whom they called Skittles.'

'The lady was very much admired in several quarters.'

Sir Henry had the same sort of wit as Lord Melbourne had had. He liked to make sly little remarks. I believed Bertie had been involved with that shameless creature.

And these were the sort of men I was expected to have as my Prime Minister to take the place of Lord Beaconsfield!

They both declined to take on the premiership and most tactfully reminded me that there was one man whom the people wanted.

I had to wrestle with myself. Of course my threat to abdicate had not been serious. How could it be? I knew what was my duty. I tried to think what Albert would have done.

I knew, of course. There was only one thing I could do. I sent for Mr. Gladstone.

He came humbly enough, trying, I knew, to please me. He kissed my hand but I could not enforce any warmth into my manner.

So I had lost my dear friend and in his place was William Gladstone.

Gladstone's ministry directed its efforts to bringing an end to those wars which had been raging in Afghanistan and South Africa at the time of the election. Our troops were defeated at Maiwand and I was afraid that the new government would meekly accept the disaster and not try to regain our prestige as Lord Beaconsfield would have undoubtedly done. I was delighted therefore when Sir Frederick Roberts brought Afghanistan to submission by marching on Kandahar and installing a new emir who professed friendship for us.

When the Boer War broke out and General Colley died in the defeat of Majuba Hill, I was afraid that the government would take no action. I recommended Sir Frederick Roberts for the chief command of the Transvaal. But what was the use? The government pursued its peace at any price policy and in the negotiations gave way to the enemy.

I was deeply angry. If only Lord Beaconsfield had been at the head of affairs how different everything would be. When the soldiers came back I visited them and gave new colours to the Berkshire Regiment who had lost theirs at Maiwand. I wanted my soldiers to know how much I appreciated them and that I understood the sacrifices they made for their country.

I was horrified to learn that Sir Charles Dilke had been given the post of Under Secretary for Foreign Affairs in the government. I would never forget how he had fulminated against me and that he was in favour of abolishing the Monarchy. How could such a man be permitted to take part in the government?

If that were not bad enough I discovered that he had become a member of Bertie's circle. I thought that not only disloyal but foolish. When I remonstrated with Bertie he said that he mixed with all sorts of people and that it was the best way of discovering what was being said and thought. I supposed there was something in that but I should certainly not receive Dilke.

There was one sad fact which obsessed me at the time. Lord Beaconsfield became ill. He had been growing feebler since he took his place in the House of Lords and, indeed, I think he only accepted the peerage because he found the House of Commons demanded too much of him.

When I heard that he had taken to his bed at Hughenden, I wrote to him commanding him to send me word of his progress. He wrote back so charmingly that my letters did him so much good and that he immediately felt better on reading them. He said it was very cold at Hughenden and he found it difficult to keep his old bones warm.

In March he managed to come up to his place in Curzon Street. I was delighted because I thought that was a good sign.

I sent him primroses from Osborne and he wrote back to tell me that they cheered him.

It was April. He had not been out for three weeks and when I did not hear from him it occurred to me that he was too ill to write.

I would go to see this dear old friend. I would command him to get well. I could not lose any more of those I loved. But before I could go I heard that he had died.

His last words were: 'I am not afraid to die, but I would rather live.' Dear Lord Beaconsfield!

He had wanted to be buried in Hughenden church beside Mary Anne. I could not bear to be present—my grief was too intense—so I sent Bertie and Leopold to represent me. They took the primroses I wanted to be laid on the coffin. I wrote a card which was attached to them: 'His favourite flower.'

I knew, of course, that they were so because I had sent them to him.

I had lost a beloved friend whose one thought was the honour and glory of his country and unswerving devotion to the crown. His death was a national calamity and my sorrow was great and lasting.

Although it was his wish that he should be buried at Hughenden I ordered that a monument should be set up to him in Westminster Abbey.

Four days after the funeral, Beatrice and I went to Hughenden and I laid a wreath of white camellias on his coffin which lay in the open vault in the churchyard. I wanted everyone to know how much I had loved and honoured this man; and the following year I had a tablet set up in the church on which were the words:

'To the dear and honoured memory of Benjamin Disraeli, Earl of Beaconsfield, this memorial is placed by his grateful and affectionate Sovereign Victoria R.I.
"Kings love him that speakest right." Proverbs XVI 13.
    February 27th 1882.'

It seemed to me that death was in the air—a most depressing thought. I had recently heard of the assassination of Tsar Alexander, the father of Alfred's wife, and soon after that President Garfield of the United States met a similar end.

But before that there was trouble with Egypt when the Khedive's war minister Arabi Pasha brought about a successful coup and overthrew the Khedive. Egyptian finance was in chaos; France was involved with us but refused to reinstate the Khedive so we had to go ahead single-handed.

I was delighted when we had a decisive victory. I was at Balmoral at the time and ordered that a bonfire should be lighted at the top of Craig Gowan.

But of course I remembered the feeling of my 'peace at any price' government and once again I mourned Lord Beaconsfield and wished with all my heart that he was beside me so that we could enforce the strong policies in which we had both so fervently believed.

I was astonished when Leopold came to me and told me that he planned to marry. I had thought he never would. We had always been so watchful of him ever since we discovered he was cursed with that dreadful disease, haemophilia.

He was so careless of himself which I supposed was natural. He could not be expected to lead a completely sheltered life; after all he was a normal healthy young man in every other respect.

I had heard rumours of his attraction to a certain young woman who was making a stir in London. This was largely due to Bertie. But it was Leopold, so it was rumoured, who had seen her first.

She was a certain Mrs. Langtry, the daughter of the Dean of Jersey, who had married a Mr. Langtry. They would not have moved in very exalted circles but it seemed the woman was exceptionally beautiful, had been noticed by a nobleman and asked to his house.

There, Leopold had seen her and apparently fallen in love with her. Alas for Leopold, Bertie saw her picture, wanted to meet her, and then decided she was for him.

Such was Leopold's nature, and Bertie's too, that this did not result in any ill feeling between them. Bertie pursued Mrs. Langtry, was seen everywhere with her, and Leopold shrugged his shoulders and decided to take a trip on the Continent.

There he met Princess Helen Frederica Augusta, daughter of the Prince of Waldeck Pyrmont and decided he wished to marry her.

When I heard I was horrified—not by the thought of whom he had chosen, but because he was contemplating marriage. I feared he was not strong enough. I had lost my dear Alice and that had made my children who were left to me doubly precious; and because of Leopold's weakness I was afraid.

I discussed the matter with Bertie who thought that Leopold must marry if he wished to.

'Do you understand the nature of this terrible thing from which he is suffering?' I demanded.

'I know that if he bleeds he is in danger. But you have to let him live, Mama. He is just as well married as single.'

Of course he was right. I was being fatalistic. Whatever was coming I must be prepared for it.

So Leopold was betrothed and created Duke of Albany.

I was on my way to Windsor Castle and had left the train and taken my place in the carriage which was waiting for me at the station. The horses were just about to move forward when I heard a loud report, then a scuffle and Brown, white-faced and anxious, was at the window.

'A man has just fired at your carriage,' he said.

I felt quite ill. This was the seventh shock of this nature that I had had in my life. I should be used to it, but one never is.

'I'm taking ye on to the castle the noo,' said Brown. 'I'll soon have ye there.'

Later I learned exactly what had happened. Two boys from Eton School had been in the little group of people near the carriage. They had seen a man lift his hand with the pistol in it, directed straight at the carriage. One of them had knocked it out of the man's hand with his umbrella while the other had hit the assailant with his. Then they had seized him and clung to him until he was arrested.

This was a really serious attempt for the pistol had been loaded.

Mr. Gladstone came down to Windsor, all concern. I must say he did seem very sincere—and indeed, it was hard to imagine Mr. Gladstone ever anything else; but his manner irritated me even when he showed he was upset by the incident.

'The man is mad,' he said. 'All those who have made an attempt on Your Majesty's life have been mad. In other countries rulers are attacked for political reasons. It is gratifying that in this country all assassins are madmen.'

'The effect is the same on the victim, Mr. Gladstone,' I said coolly.

'Yes, M'am, that is so, but the motive is different; and madmen have not the same power to reason.'

Now I was going to get a lecture on the motives of madmen and the difference in assassins in England and other countries.

I cut him short.

'I shall be relieved to hear more of this matter,' I said.

He told me then about the bravery of the two boys from Eton who had without doubt averted a tragedy.

'I should like to let them know how much I appreciate their actions.'

That, he said, was an excellent idea.

It was arranged that I should receive the whole school—nine hundred boys—and very moving it was to see them assembled in the quadrangle. I spoke to them, commending the two of their

number who had so gallantly come to my rescue. Then the two
heroes themselves came forward and received my special thanks.

My would-be assailant turned out to be a certain Roderick
McLean who was brought to trial and found not guilty but insane.

I was incensed by the verdict. Not guilty when he had aimed a
loaded pistol at me which might have killed me but for the prompt
action of two schoolboys with their umbrellas! It seemed to me that
people who tried to kill my subjects were guilty of murder, but if
they tried to kill me, they were found to be insane.

'There is no doubt of the man's insanity,' said Mr. Gladstone.
'In this country it is always the insane who attempt to assassinate
the sovereigns.'

The man was detained 'during Her Majesty's pleasure'.

It would be my pleasure that he remained as long as I had any
say in the matter.

In his ponderous way Mr. Gladstone did see my point and said
that he would take up the matter of such cases and see if he could
bring about a change in the law.

My popularity soared after the attempt. That was always gratifying; and when one had come unscathed out of these incidents they
seemed almost worth while for the pleasure of enjoying the people's
acclaim.

About a month after the Roderick McLean affair, Leopold was
married. There had been the usual distasteful wrangle in Parliament
about his allowance. But at length it was agreed that it should be
raised to £25,000 a year. There was the expected outcry in the Press
about the money the royal family was receiving from the country,
the habitual murmuring about my seclusion, 'What does she do
with it and is she worth it to us?' was renewed, and forty-two
members voted against the allowance being raised. However the
majority which passed it was substantial enough.

I attended the ceremony in my black gown and over it I did wear
my white wedding lace and veil. I prayed fervently that Leopold
would not tax his strength. I greatly feared for him. The blood
losses he had suffered all his life had weakened him; and he must
realize that such a disease set him apart from normally healthy men.
Helen was a very capable young woman, not afraid of stating her
own mind—even to me. I had felt a little taken aback at first but
soon began to admire her spirit. I was beginning to think she was
just the wife for Leopold.

I was buying Claremont for them as a wedding present. It was a house of which I was particularly fond. Uncle Leopold had left it to me for the duration of my life, but I had thought I should like to own it so that I could give it to the newly married couple.

I soon began to worry less about Leopold for marriage seemed to suit him, and soon after the wedding Helen was pregnant. Her child was due to be born ten months after her wedding—which was really very prompt.

I had so many grandchildren that I had to concentrate to count them. But Leopold's would be rather special because I had never thought he would have children.

I was at Windsor. I had been down to Frogmore to be with Albert and when I came back I was very sad as I always was after these visits. I must have been deep in thought for as I was coming downstairs I slipped and fell.

There was consternation. Brown came rushing out, sweeping everyone aside. He picked me up looking very angry with me and said, 'What have ye done now, woman?' which made me smile in spite of the pain in my leg.

He carried me to my room. Everyone fussed round; but I said I should be all right in a day or two.

But the next morning I could not put my foot to the ground without pain. The upset had started my rheumaticky pains and they came on more virulently than ever.

The doctors came and said I must rest.

It was very tiresome. I hated to be inactive. But I certainly was bruised and my leg was painfully swollen.

Brown used to carry me from my bed to the sofa and then, because he thought I should get some fresh air, took what he called the wee pony chair and he would drive me round the park.

What should I do without Brown? I wondered.

Each morning he would come unceremoniously to my room with a 'What'll ye be wanting today?' as though I were a fractious child whose wish must be consulted to keep me quiet. It always amused me and the sight of him cheered me up.

Just over a week after my fall it was not Brown who came to my room for orders but one of the other servants.

'Where is Brown?' I asked.

'He is unable to wait on Your Majesty this morning.'

Oh, I thought, amused. I supposed he had been a little 'bashful' on the previous night.

'Very well,' I said.

I would tease him about it when he appeared.

But Brown did not appear. Later in the morning I sent for him. One of the others came instead.

'His face is swollen, Your Majesty,' I was told.

'Face swollen! What has happened? Has he had a fall or something?'

I had to find out for I could glean nothing from the servant.

'I want to see him,' I said. 'Send him to me.'

He came and the sight of him shocked me. His face was indeed red and swollen.

'What on earth has happened, Brown?' I asked.

'I dinna ken,' he said shortly. And I could see that he was ill. I told him to go back to bed at once. Then I sent for Dr. Jenner.

When Jenner had examined Brown he came to me and told me that he was suffering from erysipelas.

'Is that dangerous?' I asked.

Dr. Jenner shook his head.

'I want the best attention for him. You yourself, Dr. Jenner, and Dr. Reid.'

'That is hardly necessary, M'am . . .' began Dr. Jenner.

'It is my wish,' I said regally.

Dr. Jenner bowed. There would be gossip, I guessed, because I had ordered the royal physician to attend John Brown. But I did not care. He was of great importance to me.

Anxious as I was over John Brown, I was delighted to hear that Helen had been safely delivered of a little girl. So Leopold was a father!

I must visit the mother and child at once even though I had to be carried out to the carriage. Alas . . . not by John Brown.

I found Helen recovering from the birth looking fit and well, but lying on a sofa. Leopold had had one of his bleeding bouts and the doctors had warned him to take the utmost care for a while, so he was on another sofa. And because of my indisposition one had been put in for me.

The three of us reclining on sofas made quite an amusing scene.

The child was brought in and admired. Leopold was in the highest spirits; and as for Helen she was very proud of herself. It was a happy occasion but when I went back to Windsor I was greeted by alarming news. John Brown had taken a turn for the worse.

'For the worse!' I cried. 'But I thought that from which he was suffering was not very serious.'

'Your Majesty, he does not seem to be able to throw off the illness.'

'But he has twice the strength of an ordinary man!'

'That does not seem to help him, Your Majesty. John Brown is very ill indeed.'

I was deeply disturbed. I went to see him immediately. He looked quite different and he did not recognize me. He was muttering in delirium.

Oh no, I thought, this is too much!

But, alas, what I had begun to fear, happened.

The next morning they came to tell me that John Brown had died in the night.

I could not believe it. Not another death. People were dying all round me. Was that part of the pattern of getting old? It seemed only a short time before that I had lost my dear friend Lord Beaconsfield. John Brown had been a comfort to me then . . . and now he had gone.

It was such a blow that it stunned me. I could find no solace anywhere. None of the family mourned with me. They had never liked him and deplored my relationship with him. They did not understand, of course. They had called him one of the servants. He had not been a servant. He was something far closer than that.

I wanted to raise some memorial to him. Sir Henry Ponsonby was very uneasy. He dropped veiled warnings. We did not want to give the Press a field day. No doubt there would be damaging speculations as to my relationship with him if too much attention was paid to his passing.

I did not care. I was tired of the Press and trying to placate a fickle people. They listened to cruel libels and slander; and then when Bertie had nearly died and I might have been assassinated they found they loved us dearly. What was such shifting affection worth?

It was one's friends like Lord Beaconsfield and honest John Brown who mattered.

I had a statue of John Brown set up at Balmoral. I charged Lord Tennyson to write an inscription and he wrote:

> 'Friend more than servant, loyal, truthful, brave,
> Self less than duty, even to grave.'

I discovered that Brown had kept diaries and thinking what a magnificent job Sir Theodore Martin had made with his *Life of the Prince Consort*, I asked him to write a life of John Brown. I believe pressure must have been brought to bear on Sir Theodore for he declined on the grounds of his wife's ill health. I guessed that Sir Henry Ponsonby may have had something to do with this. Sir Henry was a dear friend but he had always been uneasy about the scandals concerning John Brown and he did not, I know, want these to be increased, which he believed would be the case if a life of Brown was brought out. But I wanted to show the world what a wonderful person he had been.

As Theodore Martin would not write the book I engaged a Miss Macgregor to edit the diaries with me.

To soothe myself I published an addition to *Leaves from a Journal* with *More Leaves from a Journal of Our Life in the Highland*.

With mingling sadness and pleasure I recalled those days with Albert when the children were young. It brought it all back so vividly. I could relive it all, but the sorrow of remembering what was past, was hard to bear.

I had many congratulations but the family was shocked.

I heard that the old Duchess of Cambridge had said that *Leaves* was vulgar, such bad English, trivial and boring.

I never liked the woman!

Even Bertie raised objections.

He thought it should not be generally circulated. 'It is all right for those of us in the family circle to read it,' he said, 'but not beyond that.' He added: 'It is rather private.'

'*I* think people are interested.'

'I think people are too interested in our doings.'

'There is nothing for me to be ashamed of in mine,' I said aiming a direct shaft at Bertie which went home. I added that Lord Beaconsfield had found *Leaves* enchanting. Perhaps because he was a writer himself and understood such things. He had often referred to us as fellow authors.

'He was always over eager to flatter. I heard he once said that he believed in flattery for all, but with royalty it had to be laid on with a trowel.'

I smiled. I could well believe the dear man had said that. But he really meant he had admired my book. He understood how one wanted to write as people like Bertie never would. But then when he was a boy he had shunned the pen—and had had many a beating for it. No, Bertie could not be expected to understand.

I believe there was a conspiracy to prevent Brown's Life being written and I suspected Sir Henry to be at the root of it; and of course he would have plenty of supporters, including the Prince of Wales.

Sir Henry then said he would consult the Bishop of Ripon, Dr. Cameron Lees of Edinburgh, about the Life of Brown.

'These are men who know about these things, Your Majesty,' he said.

He then brought in Lord Rowton. I wondered what Brown would have thought if he could have known about this. Important people were making such a to do over his simple writings.

Dr. Lees thought it would be desirable to postpone the Life for a while. They called in Randall Davison, the Dean of Windsor, who applauded the decision to postpone; and he ventured the opinion that it would be desirable if no more *Leaves* were published.

I was very angry with him. Was the wretched Dean implying that the publication was vulgar and unseemly in my position?

I could not prevent myself showing my anger; and the Dean, realizing how offended I was, sent in his resignation. He said that he had displeased me and was sorry for it; but there was not a word about changing his mind.

It was true that my anger rose quickly; but it did as speedily depart.

I began to think about the Dean. It was wrong that he should resign over such a matter. He had offended me and he knew it. Yet he had spoken what he believed to be the truth. I must bear no grudge for that and in my heart I knew that he was right.

In view of all the scandal attached to my relationship with John Brown, the publication of his Journals would only add to that. My life with Albert and the children was private too. I would read my Journals; I would recall it all. I must accept the truth, and honour those who gave their opinions to me at the risk of their careers.

I must be wise. No more *Leaves* then; and the memoirs of my beloved Highland servant must be indefinitely postponed.

It was a year since John Brown had died and I was still mourning. There were memories of him everywhere—especially at Balmoral.

Helen was pregnant again and her little Alexandra was still little more than a baby. It was obvious that Helen was going to be fruitful and it was a mercy to know that the dreadful haemophilia was only passed on through the female side to the sons, so Leopold's children would be safe.

Leopold had had one of his bouts of illness and the doctors had suggested he go off to the south of France. I heard from Helen that his health was greatly improved there.

On the very anniversary of John Brown's death, the 27th March, I received a telegram from Cannes to say that Leopold had fallen and injured his knees. Because on that day I had awoken to a cloud of depression thinking of my Highland servant whom I missed so much, I was filled with apprehension. I had a suspicious feeling about dates. My dearest Albert and Alice had actually both died on the 14th December. It was small wonder that I felt this significance. So strong was my premonition that I thought of leaving for Cannes, but before I could make plans to do so another telegram arrived. Leopold had had a fit which had resulted in haemorrhage of the brain. Leopold was dead.

Ever since we had known he was suffering from this fearsome malady we had been expecting this. Many weeks of anxiety I had suffered on Leopold's account. But later I had felt better about him and since his marriage and the birth of his first child I had begun to wonder whether I had been unduly anxious. I had reminded myself that he had had so many of those bouts of bleeding but had always recovered from them.

But Death was all round me. I felt there was no escaping from it. I wondered all the time at whom it would point its finger next.

They brought home Leopold's body and it was buried in St. George's Chapel at Windsor.

Two children lost to me as well as my beloved husband!

Three months after Leopold's death, Helen gave birth to a son.

The political situation was worrying; and each month it was brought home to me that Mr. Gladstone's methods were not those which had proved so successful in Lord Beaconsfield's day.

The trouble came from Egypt, which was at that time almost entirely administered by us. The inhabitants of the Sudan were led by a fanatical man called the Mahdi; and they were now menacing the Egyptian frontier. It was the task of the English government to decide whether to put down the rebellion or abandon the Sudan and cut it off from Egypt. The decision to abandon it was naturally taken by Gladstone and his supine supporters. How different it would have been if Lord Beaconsfield had been in command! Gladstone was terrified of what he called Imperialism. Had we been stronger in Egypt, as we should have been under Lord Beaconsfield, the Mahdi would never have risen against us. People like Gladstone with their weak so-called peace-loving policies, were the ones who were responsible for wars. We were drawn into these affrays through our weakness, never through our strength. Lord Palmerston had realized that and what was called his gun-boat policy had triumphed again and again. He believed in sending out a warning *before* hostilities commenced. Now the garrisons in Sudan must be rescued. The government was naturally dilatory in this; but the public demanded that General Gordon be sent out in order to negotiate with the Mahdi about the release of the beset garrisons.

I was very anxious particularly when Gordon was besieged by the Mahdi's forces in Khartoum. Again and again I warned the government that forces must be sent out to aid Gordon; but the government was afraid of war. I was glad to say that the public was with me; and finally Lord Wolseley was sent out to Gordon's aid. But he arrived too late. Khartoum was stormed and Gordon killed before Wolseley could get there.

I was horrified and so ashamed of my government. I told them I keenly felt the stain left on England. I had a bust made of Gordon and set up in one of the corridors of the castle.

I hoped the government would see the error of its ways. I hoped they would recall Lord Beaconsfield's energy and genius which they called Imperialism. They did not understand that having attained the territories we must support them and never, never show weakness.

I was deeply concerned about the garrisons in Sudan and bitterly ashamed of our performance there.

The entire mission was a failure and as a result, the Sudan which should never have been separated from Egypt, lapsed into barbarism.

Oh, dear Lord Beaconsfield! I wondered if he was looking down in dismay at what was happening to all the work which he had so zealously done.

Beatrice was the only one of the children who had not married. She had always been close to me since the days when she had enchanted us all with her quaint observations.

She had changed a great deal from that amusing little girl. She was not like her sisters, being shy and retiring. I knew she dreaded company and she confessed that she never knew what to say to people.

In a way I was glad of this. I am afraid it was rather selfish of me but I could not bear to face the possibility of Beatrice's leaving me.

I had gone to Darmstadt to attend the marriage of my grand-daughter Victoria of Hesse to her cousin Louis of Battenburg. Leopold's death was so recent and very much in my mind, and I had undertaken the journey in the hope that in the heart of my family I could forget.

It was a fateful occasion for at the wedding Beatrice met the bridegroom's brother, Henry of Battenburg; and Beatrice and Henry fell in love.

When Beatrice told me of her wish to marry I was overwhelmed with horror.

'Impossible!' I said. 'You have just been carried away.'

Beatrice said this was not the case. She and Henry were deeply in love; they had admitted this to each other and above everything else they wanted to marry.

I said she must forget it. I had suffered enough. Lord Beaconsfield had died; John Brown had died; and so had Leopold. Now I was expected to lose her—the last of my children to be with me!

Poor Beatrice, she was heart-broken; but being Beatrice she just bowed her head and looked resigned.

Of course I spent a miserable time. I could not eat; I could not sleep. To lose Beatrice! No, I could not face it. That would be the last straw. She would forget. She was not meant for marriage. After all, she was now twenty-seven—old enough for a girl to have put all that behind her. She had come so far without contemplating marriage. Why must she think of it now? It was ridiculous. It was absurd.

And yet I could not bear to see my poor Baby so sad.

This would not have happened, I said to myself, but for Leopold's death. Beatrice was so close to her brothers.

We returned to England, poor Beatrice looked wan and tragic.

I thought I cannot allow this to happen. I cannot be like my poor mad grandfather. I thought of the aunts who had always been of great interest to me when I was young. They had all seemed so strange—half mad some of them—and they had all had such sad lives. Their father had tried to keep them close to him, which was a very selfish thing to do.

I could endure it no more.

I said: 'Beatrice, you have changed so much.'

She did not deny it.

I sent for Henry of Battenburg.

I said to him: 'You know what Beatrice means to me. I find it impossible to do without her. I feel so lonely at times. I have lost so many who were dear to me. Suppose you were to make your home in England? Would that be possible? You could marry Beatrice and I could still have her with me.'

The joy in his face made me so happy.

I sent for Beatrice.

I said: 'Henry is going to live in England. I shall not lose you after all, dearest child . . .'

We embraced; we laughed; it was wonderful to see my dearest child so happy. It was a long time since I had felt so contented.

It was quite a simple wedding. I called it a 'village wedding'; but it was an extremely happy one; and I was delighted to see my child so happy with her Henry and he with her.

Political storms were rising at the time of Beatrice's wedding.

Gladstone's government was in difficulties—at which I was not surprised. I was not the only one who was disgusted by the weakness of his Egyptian policy. The country was ashamed, and the budget proposals were defeated, which meant Gladstone's resignation.

I offered him an earldom, hoping this would see the back of him as far as I was concerned; but he declined it.

I was delighted to invite Lord Salisbury, as leader of the Conservative Party, to come and see me, but he was not very eager to form a ministry since he was in the Lords and the task, he thought, should fall to Sir Stafford Northcote who was the leader of the party in the Commons. He really wanted to be in the Foreign Office, but he at last agreed that if he could combine the offices of Foreign Secretary and Prime Minister, and could get, in some measure the support of Gladstone during the few months which remained before Parliament was dissolved, he would do his best to form his ministry.

I must say that Gladstone was not very accommodating but at length Lord Salisbury agreed.

I was delighted. I liked him very much. Indeed, I believe I should have liked anyone after Gladstone. Lord Salisbury was the first of my Prime Ministers to be younger than I was. I supposed that was a reminder of how old I was getting.

That little respite did not last long. At the elections, the Liberals were back in power and I was once more faced with Mr. Gladstone.

What a trial that man was! He was now intent on bringing Home Rule to Ireland and had sprung his intentions of doing so on me and the country without giving anyone time for thought. I did not believe the country wanted it. As for myself it would mean I should break the oath I had taken at the coronation to maintain the union of the two kingdoms. I was unconvinced by his arguments.

I was delighted when quite a number of Liberals decided to vote against Gladstone's Home Rule Bill and it was rejected by the Commons.

It was a great relief when the government was once more defeated and Lord Salisbury called in.

I found Lord Salisbury a delight after Gladstone.

Salisbury was really an old friend. I had known him well as an associate of Lord Beaconsfield—and although it was not the same as having that dear man back again, it did in a measure give me some comfort. He was very knowledgeable in foreign affairs of which, in my opinion, Mr. Gladstone was totally ignorant.

I wanted him to sit for a portrait and when it was completed I had it placed in my own apartments which, I told Lord Salisbury, was the highest compliment I could pay anyone.

I was thankful that the bogey of Home Rule was set aside. Postponement was sometimes so helpful.

A very unsavoury scandal shook the political world at this time as well as filling the papers and having the whole country agog for more distasteful details.

I could not help being amused—disgraceful as it was—because it concerned my old enemy Sir Charles Dilke. It was extraordinary that those people who posed in public as being so concerned for the welfare of the people—wanted to abolish the monarchy and so on—were all the time behaving in their private lives in a manner which was far from exemplary.

It all blew up when a certain Mr. Crawford started divorce proceedings against his wife. Mr. Crawford was a member of Parliament and he had an attractive and somewhat frivolous wife. Dilke was connected with the Crawfords by marriage and was a frequent visitor to their home; and in view of the family relationship this caused no comment.

Mrs. Crawford had been having a flirtation with a certain Captain Forster and Mr. Crawford accused him of being her lover. The wife, when confronted, told her husband that not Forster but Sir Charles Dilke was the lover.

Then the unsavoury details about that defender of the rights of the underprivileged began to emerge. Apparently he had been Mrs.

Crawford's mother's lover; and Mrs. Crawford betrayed revelations about orgies concerning Dilke, herself and female servants.

The servants did not come forward, but as Mrs. Crawford had confessed to adultery, the divorce was granted.

I must confess to a certain satisfaction; and a great relief that Bertie was not involved in this one! Whenever I heard of a case of this nature in a certain circle—and Dilke was a friend of Bertie's—my immediate thoughts were: 'Please, God, don't let Bertie be discovered!'—which shows the fear which was in my mind; and that was natural after all the anxieties I had suffered on his account.

Of course Dilke's career was ruined.

I discussed it with Bertie and as was to be expected, he was on Dilke's side.

'It is disastrous for him,' he said. 'He was a great politician.'

'He was certainly skilled in living a double life,' I retorted.

'He might have been Prime Minister.'

'Then I am indeed glad this has happened. The idea of my being asked to receive such a man!'

'Mama, I believe that woman was exaggerating.'

'The court did not seem to think so.' I looked at him sadly. 'I am surprised, Bertie, that after all your father did for you, you do have some strange ideas. This man is a republican. He has clearly spoken against *us* . . . and you make him your friend!'

'Mama, he is clever, witty . . . He has ideas.'

'Ideas of destroying us! Very gratifying!'

That was not the end of the affair. Dilke, of course, could not be included in the government—it was Mr. Gladstone's government at this time because it had happened just before Salisbury came into power.

Joseph Chamberlain, who was a friend of Dilke and was eager for him to remain in the House, wanted the Queen's Proctor brought in to stop the divorce, pointing out that Dilke had not been proved guilty. He had not gone into the witness box—otherwise I was sure he would have been.

So the scandal flared up again. It proved to be the worst thing that could happen to Dilke. In the course of the enquiry which followed, it was discovered that the house which Mrs. Crawford had mentioned as the setting for the sexual orgies which had taken place between Dilke, Mrs. Crawford and two housemaids, was owned by a woman who had been housekeeper to Dilke. That appeared to explain a good deal.

There was another trial out of which Dilke came badly, for the jury decided that Mrs. Crawford had been telling the truth.

That was the end of Dilke.

I could not help experiencing a certain satisfaction. He had called himself a reformer. Let him begin by reforming his own life.

I thought about him a great deal and I began to feel a twinge of pity for him; and he had posed as such a virtuous man which made it all the worse for him. I wondered how an ambitious man felt to see his career in ruins.

I should rejoice. Another of my enemies brought to the dust. I did really feel a little suspicious after that of people who acclaimed so publicly their desire to do good.

That set me thinking of Mr. Gladstone and his nightly peregrinations. Was that one of the reasons why I disliked him so intensely?

At least it made him a little human.

No, I could not—much as I should like to—believe that Mr. Gladstone was such another as Sir Charles Dilke.

The Dilke affair added to the government's unpopularity over Egypt and the rejection over the budget proposals was certainly a factor in bringing it down.

In any case I was grateful to have Lord Salisbury as my Prime Minister.

Jubilee

The time was approaching when I should have been on the throne for fifty years. It was a fact which should be brought home to the people, said Lord Salisbury, for they must realize that it was an occasion for rejoicing.

I felt tired at the prospect, but, of course, he was right. Such anniversaries should not be allowed to pass unnoticed.

I had very worrying news from Vicky. Her husband, Fritz, was suffering from a terrible throat infection—which it was whispered was cancer. Vicky was very anxious because she lived uneasily at the Prussian Court. Her parents-in-law had been far from kind to her, and Bismarck was her enemy; her son treated her atrociously; and she had to endure reproaches for everything she did; she was condemned because of her English blood.

I knew all this and when the telegram came, in cypher, I guessed the position was very grave.

The deciphering of the message revealed that the German doctors wished to perform an operation, but she wanted, first of all, to consult one of our doctors, who was said to be a leading authority on such matters. This was Dr. Morell Mackenzie. Vicky begged me to send out Dr. Mackenzie at once. She was against the operation and she thought that Dr. Mackenzie might persuade the German doctors not to do it.

I immediately sent for my doctors to ask their opinion of Dr. Mackenzie. They said he was indeed skilful, but he was very eager to amass money, and for that reason should be watched.

I told this to Vicky.

The situation was very tense. The Emperor himself was in a low state of health and not expected to live long; if he died that would mean Fritz would be Emperor, and if *he* died, the mantle would fall on my grandson Wilhelm, who was no friend to his mother.

That was the state of affairs when the day of celebration arrived.

On the previous day I had awakened to a sunny morning and had my breakfast out of doors at Frogmore. One could not be private out of doors at the castle.

Crowds had gathered to see me drive to the station and there were loyal cheers which were gratifying. And when I alighted at Paddington, I drove through the Park to Buckingham Palace where I received more loyal acclaim.

How wonderful it was to be surrounded by my dear children! I thought how really remarkable it was that I had been for fifty years on the throne and been sustained through so many trials and sorrows.

The flowers were magnificent, for the growers had vied with each other to send their products to me. Among them was one bouquet four feet high, and on it were the letters V.R.I. picked out in scarlet blooms.

We had a dinner party with all the family that evening and what pleased me most was to have them all with me.

The next day, the 21st, the real celebrations began. I had refused to wear a crown and the state robes, for although this was a grand occasion I wanted it to be as simple as possible. The family was most put out. They thought it should be completely ceremonial. Alexandra was sent by the others to try to persuade me to wear my crown, but I told her it was not her affair and I would not be coerced. Lord Halifax was very irritated. He said the people wanted a gilding for their money, which I thought was rather a coarse way of expressing his views; and that interfering Joseph Chamberlain said a sovereign should be grand. I had decided to wear a bonnet. It should be very attractive—one made of white lace and diamonds—but still a bonnet.

Lord Rosebery said that an Empire should be ruled by sceptre and not bonnet. But I was adamant and commanded that all the ladies wore bonnets and long high dresses with mantel.

I thought as I always did on such occasions: If only Albert could have been there how proud he would have been!

I left the Palace in an open landau drawn by six cream horses with an escort of Indian cavalry. Next came the men of the family—three sons, five sons-in-law and nine grandsons.

Poor Fritz was suffering so much and yet putting on a bold appearance. His voice was almost non-existent and it really was very brave of him to have come. He drew perhaps the loudest of all cheers for he did look magnificent in white and silver with the

German eagle on his helmet. One could trust the Prussians to attract more attention than anyone else.

Following the family and myself were the processions in which Europe, India and the colonies were represented. There were four kings from Europe—Saxony, Belgium, the Hellenes and Denmark—with the Crown Princes of Prussia, Greece, Portugal, Sweden and Austria.

There could not have been a more glittering assembly; even the Pope sent someone to represent him. We passed through Constitution Hill, Piccadilly, Waterloo Place and Parliament Street to the Abbey for the thanksgiving service; and I walked into the Abbey to the sound of a Handel march.

I had insisted that Albert's *Te Deum* and his anthem *Gotha*—his own composition—should be part of the service, and when I heard it I was deeply moved, and it was almost as though he were there beside me.

We went back to the Palace via Whitehall and Pall Mall and I felt quite exhausted; but it was not the end of the day. There was luncheon at four and then I was on the balcony watching the bluejackets march past. In the evening there was a dinner party. I could hardly keep awake. But it had been wonderfully stimulating—a day to remember.

Lord Beaconsfield had aroused my interest in India and since I had become Empress I had wanted to know more about it. I should have liked to visit it but that seemed impracticable at this time.

With the party which had come to England to take its place in the Jubilee celebrations, were two Indians who attracted my attention. They were Abdul Karim who was about twenty-four years old and whose father was, I believed, a doctor, and Mahomet who was much older, rather fat and constantly smiling.

I engaged them to work in the royal household close to me so that I could learn more about them and their country. Karim was very intelligent but his grasp of English was not very good, so I engaged a tutor to teach him.

The tutor came eagerly, thinking he was going to teach one of the princes and when he realized his services were required for a servant—and a dark-skinned one at that—he was extremely put out.

I was irritated. I would not have people despised because their skin was a different colour from our English ones; and of course the foolish tutor dared not offend me.

I was most amused when Karim offered to teach *me* Hindustani and I agreed to the plan at once. I was fascinated and loved to be able to address Karim and Mahomet in their own language.

Karim cooked for me—hot Indian foods—which I thoroughly enjoyed. I felt much happier than I had since John Brown had died. My Indian servants soon became devoted to me.

It was good to have people like that about me.

While Fritz was in England he had had several sessions with Dr. Mackenzie and he was much better. He believed that Dr. Mackenzie could cure him and that lifted his spirits considerably. It was wonderful to see the change in him.

Vicky was delighted. Fritz was very important to her for he had stood beside her against all those who had been so unpleasant to her. I was well aware of what she had had to endure from Fritz's family and particularly from young Wilhelm who, she believed, was so hardhearted and ambitious that he was really longing for the deaths of his grandfather and father so that he could wear the Imperial crown.

He was a most unpleasant creature. He did nothing to stem the cruel rumours that his mother had a lover and that she had prevented her husband's operation because she wanted to keep him alive until after his father's death so that she might become Empress, after which Fritz could depart, leaving her with the Imperial pickings and her lover.

The wickedness of that young man infuriated me. I often thought of how proud Albert had been of her grand marriage. And what happiness had it brought her? Whereas Alice had been so happy with her Louis and Beatrice had been the same in her even more humble union with Henry of Battenburg.

Poor Vicky, so clever, so proud! And what must be the hardest to bear was the unloving attitude of her own son.

It was Bismarck and his grandparents who had ruined him; and perhaps that withered arm had embittered him.

In February of the next year, Fritz was operated on and a few weeks afterwards the Emperor died. Fritz was now Emperor of Germany and Vicky Empress.

It was wonderful to think of Vicky as an Empress. It was what Albert had wanted for her. He had loved her so much and been so proud of her. If only he had lived. Perhaps he could have guided Wilhelm.

I was worried about Vicky, because I knew, in my heart that Fritz was going to die. I wanted to see them both. I travelled abroad and spent a short time in Florence which I found most enjoyable. Albert had stayed in Italy at one time and it was very moving to visit the house in which he had stayed. I was greeted effusively everywhere and people were most gracious to Karim and Mahomet, thinking they were Indian princes. It was most amusing.

When Bismarck heard that I was going to see Fritz and Vicky he was most indignant; but in Berlin I had a meeting with this man who was feared throughout the whole of Europe. I must say that I could not dislike the man, in spite of everything he had done and all I had heard of him. He was strong and I liked strong men. I had an idea that he was rather impressed by me; so oddly enough, that meeting which might have been quite acrimonious went off very well indeed. I felt we were both agreeably surprised and in the future we should have more respect for each other.

I was grieved to see poor Fritz, for he was shrunken and looked so ill and was unable to speak. I knew he could not live long; but at least he had made Vicky Empress. I saw Wilhelm too—a very arrogant young man, but I did subdue him a little and I told him I was most displeased by his conduct and asked him to promise to mend his ways which—very much to my surprise—he did.

I left Vicky telling her that she must always call on me if she needed me. I would even come to Berlin if necessary.

When I returned home I summoned Dr. Mackenzie and asked for the truth about Fritz's condition. He told me he could not live more than three months.

It was June when that dreaded and not unexpected message came. Fritz was dead.

I sent a telegram to Wilhelm—now Emperor of Germany—telling him that I was heart-broken and commanded him to look after his mother. I signed myself Grandmama V.R.I.

Bertie went to Berlin for Fritz's funeral and came back in a state of smouldering fury. I had rarely seen him so enraged, because, although like me he could have sudden bouts of temper, he soon recovered from them. But Wilhelm had really upset him—more than that he had disturbed him.

He wanted me to understand the true nature of my grandson.

'I do not believe, Mama,' he said, 'that he is at all unhappy about the death of his father. In fact I would go so far as to say he rejoices in it, because it has given him the Imperial Crown.'

I replied that that did not surprise me for the envoy whom he had sent to me to announce his father's death had done it with an air of triumph which I had thought quite disgraceful.

'Germany is now a force to be reckoned with,' said Bertie. 'I believe that Wilhelm has big ideas for expansion. He was particularly disagreeable to me. I had an idea he was almost baiting me, implying that I was only heir to a throne while he was an Emperor. His manner to Vicky is really unforgivable. He is jealous of you. Even he knows that Germany is of less importance than Britain and he does not like that. I really believe he will seek to change it. I think he would like to turn you from your throne and take it himself.'

'Bertie, that's impossible!'

'Impossible for him to do such a ridiculous thing, yes. But to have such ideas, no. He has Bismarck behind him. Wilhelm's youthful vanity might give him foolhardy ideas, but Bismarck is a seasoned warrior, Mama. We ought to recognize that. He seeks to better me in every way. He is trying to point out all the time that he is a better man than I am. He called me Uncle in a way to suggest that I am ancient and he is on the threshold of life.'

'I can see we shall have to be watchful of our little Wilhelm.'

'Yes, indeed. He asked me to give him a kilt and everything that goes with it. It was to be in the Royal Stuart for a fancy-dress ball. I had this sent to him. I saw a picture of him, wearing it, and below he had written: "I bide my time." The picture was distributed throughout Germany.'

'This is outrageous.'

'Wilhelm is outrageous.'

I was so disturbed by that conversation that I took up the matter with Lord Salisbury who said that there was obviously an antipathy between the Prince of Wales and the Emperor of Germany; but the latter was very young to have come to such an exalted position and Salisbury believed that in time he would settle down.

It was a family quarrel and that must not be allowed to become discord between nations.

Vicky came to stay with us for a long visit. Both Bertie and Lord Salisbury thought it was unwise to invite her in view of the situation with Germany, but I upbraided them for their lack of feeling. Vicky was my daughter and she had just lost her husband; I was not going to allow her to be subjected to even more unhappiness than she was enduring through her son and Bismarck.

We had many long conversations during which I learned more

of the hard times through which she had passed during the whole
of her married life; and how it was only Fritz who had stood between her and even greater humiliation from her parents-in-law and
now her son who was dominated by Bismarck.

I said that Wilhelm should be made to understand that he could
not behave so to his mother. She begged me to invite him for a visit
so that I could discover for myself the way in which he was going.

Rather reluctantly I agreed that he should come for a short stay
in the summer.

To my surprise Wilhelm accepted the invitation with enthusiasm
and said how happy he was to be allowed to come to the dear old
home at Osborne. How should he come? Might he wear the uniform
of a British admiral? I said that he might and I had a delightful letter
from him which was almost humble. 'The same uniform as Lord
Nelson,' he wrote. 'It is enough to make one feel giddy.'

That was a good beginning.

I was amazed when he came. He was quite charming, calling
me 'dear Grandmama' and treating me with great respect and only
rarely showing glimpses of the great Emperor.

Was it after all just a natural antipathy to Bertie? Did he perhaps
think Bertie was a little frivolous—which in a way he was? Was
Vicky a little overbearing? She had always been a little too sure of
herself. Albert had spoiled her and refused to see it.

I remembered how thrilled Albert had been by his first grandchild. Wilhelm had always been his favourite.

I told Wilhelm this; he liked to hear stories of his babyhood and
listened attentively when I talked of Albert.

Strangely enough, the visit I had dreaded was a very pleasant
one; and when Wilhelm left I felt much happier than I had since
Fritz's death.

My Abdul Karim was most amusing. He was a dignified creature—
as some Indians are—and he had very graceful bearing. As a servant
he had to wait at table and he did not like that at all. He claimed
that in Agra he had been a clerk—what was called a Munshi; and
the tasks he was asked to perform here were not in keeping with
his dignity.

Those about me laughed at the arrogance of the young man but
I did not. I understood the meaning of dignity and whoever felt
theirs affronted must be treated with consideration. I said he was
not to wait at table but he should be known as the Munshi; and

when business arose appertaining to India, if a simple reply was needed, I gave it to him to deal with.

He was very happy after that—and devoted to me.

People were saying: 'Is he another John Brown?'

That was not so. There could never be another like him.

There was a certain amount of prejudice which had to be overcome. I forbade anyone to talk of Indians as blacks, for the term was used with a certain amount of contempt. I was getting on with my Hindustani lessons and could now address Indians in their native tongues, which was a great help.

I was Empress of India. Therefore I had a responsibility to that country.

My relations with Bertie had improved a good deal in the last years. He seemed to be so much more responsible—and so affectionate towards me. It was very gratifying. I thought he was learning to understand the tremendous tasks which lay ahead of him.

And then there was trouble again—with the scandal of Tranby Croft.

It was not women this time but almost equally as bad.

Bertie was the guest of honour at the house of a wealthy shipowner named Wilson who lived at Tranby Croft; and as Bertie was known to enjoy gambling, that was the feature of his visit.

One member of the company was Lieutenant-Colonel Sir William Gordon Cumming of the Scots Guards; and while they were playing baccarat Sir William was suspected of cheating.

After the company had retired there was a conference between the others to decide what action should be taken and the result was that they confronted Sir William who was naturally indignant. However, five members of the company said they had seen him in the act. He said he would leave the house and never speak to his accusers again.

Bertie was sympathetic as he always was to people in difficulties—no doubt having been in so many himself; and he was not sure whether to believe Sir William or those who said they had seen him cheat.

The evidence against Sir William seemed very strong; and Bertie, recklessly as it turned out, took charge of the investigation. True, he was a member of the party, and naturally they looked to him to do what was to be done; but he should have shown more discretion.

Between them they decided that Sir William could never be allowed to play baccarat again and that he should be made to sign a document agreeing to this.

Bertie said that naturally he would add his signature with the others. He had not, even at this time, learned the danger of putting anything in writing.

Sir William at first refused to sign and said that if he did so it would be tantamount to admitting his guilt. There was a great deal of argument and Bertie threw himself whole-heartedly into the dispute and eventually they did succeed in persuading Sir William to put his name to the paper.

That should have been the end of the matter; but these things have a habit of leaking out—through servants, I suspect; and there were the usual exaggerations. Great sums of money were mentioned as the stakes which had been played for at Tranby Croft. The papers took it and the extravagance of the Prince of Wales was the main topic. As for Sir William he was exposed as a man who cheated at cards and what had been a private matter was now a public cause.

Sir William decided that he had no alternative—if he were not going to be completely ruined—but to bring an action for slander against his accusers.

Bertie was horrified. He had had experience of a court before and he wanted no more; and the fact that he would almost certainly be called as a witness would give the case that publicity which they had all tried to avoid.

Sir William's military career was in jeopardy and he contemplated resigning from the army. Bertie wanted to prevent his doing this for if the case was tried in a military court it could be held in secret. Sir William's advisers wanted heavy damages which could only be won in a civil court.

When I heard how far matters had gone I was angry. Just as I had thought Bertie was becoming more aware of his responsibilities this had happened! He was no longer young enough to be excused for youthful follies.

It was most disturbing when he was subpoenaed to appear in court to give evidence. Whatever could have induced him to sign that paper! It was the utmost folly. And now here he was—for the second time—appearing in court to give evidence.

One would not have believed that the central figure in the case was William Gordon Cumming. It was the Prince of Wales who filled the papers. And even when the case was decided against

Gordon Cumming in such a manner that there could be little doubt of his guilt, it was Bertie whom the Press pilloried.

The future king, said the Press, is given to gambling, horse-racing and other activities . . . not concerned with matters of state. His income was clearly too large. There were other causes on which the money could be better spent. There had been a time when Mr. Gladstone had induced the Prince to take up some charitable work and he had become a member of the Royal Commission on the Housing of the Working Classes.

Bertie for all his faults had a kind heart and he had been horrified at some of the conditions in which the poor lived; he had made his views widely known. This gave the Press the opportunity of accusing him of hypocrisy. Here was the man who had been outraged by the misfortunes of others. He could do something about it. He could spend some of his vast income on helping the poor; but he preferred to play for large stakes at baccarat. Was this the man who would one day be King? He was given to pleasure. Of what use was he to the nation?

It was hard to believe that when he had been on the point of death they had mourned for him; and when there had been that triumphant journey to the cathedral to give thanks for his return to health they had cheered him so loudly. This was the mob.

One of the papers very alarmingly pointed out that it was conduct such as this which had brought about the French Revolution.

Wilhelm pretended to be infuriated. When Bertie had been in Prussia, Wilhelm had made him an honorary Colonel of the Prussian Guard. My grandson now wrote to me pompously stating that he was deeply put out that one of his colonels should behave in such a manner as to become involved in scandal.

I laughed contemptuously at the arrogant fellow and wished he was with me so that I could give him a piece of my mind. Bertie was outraged and the hatred between him and his nephew had become even greater than it was before.

We heard from Vicky that Wilhelm blew up the matter out of all proportion and that it took up a lot of space in the German Press.

One German paper—obviously inspired by Wilhelm—said that the Prince of Wales had a new motto: Ich Deal.

Poor Bertie! In spite of the fact that I deplored his way of life, I could feel almost sorry for him.

I think I had begun to change during my friendship with Lord Beaconsfield and from that time the Court was a little less sombre than it had been in the years following Albert's death. It was not that I mourned Albert any less; it was not that I did not think of him constantly, but I was taking an interest in certain recreations. I had always been fond of music; it was one of the pleasures which Albert and I had shared.

We were having private theatricals at Osborne in which guests took part. We had tableaux of various subjects, historical pastorals, scenes from operas and such things. I enjoyed preparing for these so much; they made me feel young again. For the first time since Albert's death I had players at the castle. They did a lovely performance of Gilbert and Sullivan's *The Gondoliers*. Later Eleonora Duse performed *La Locandiera*, and Mr. Tree brought his play *The Red Lamp* to Balmoral; and to celebrate my seventy-sixth birthday there was a performance of Verdi's *Il Trovatore*. I found such entertainments so stimulating and enjoyable; and I always thought: How Albert would have appreciated this.

Before this, however, my grandson Eddy—Albert Victor, Bertie's eldest son—had become engaged to Princess May of Teck.

Eddy had never been very bright; his brother George was his superior in learning; but Eddy had been a great favourite of his parents. I think Alexandra loved him especially not only because he was her first-born but because he was backward and he needed her more than the others. But of course all their children adored Alexandra and Bertie.

Eddy had not been very happy in his attachments. He had formed a great affection for his cousin Alicky and that had come to nothing; then he had fallen in love with Lady Sybil St. Clair Erskine—and she was not the only one. In fact poor Eddy had fallen in love frequently but with little success. Then there had been Princess Hèléne of Orléans, quite a suitable match that would have been, but we had to remember that as Bertie's eldest son he was destined for the throne, he could not marry a Catholic. There had been certain negotiations but the affair had lapsed.

So now it was such a pleasure to hear that he had become engaged to May. I was very fond of her mother and we had all been so surprised when she married for she was no longer in her first youth then; but it had worked out very well and she had given birth to her capable May. It was a very happy state of affairs.

He had 'spoken' to May at a ball at Luton Hoo and been accepted. She was such a nice girl—cheerful and capable—and quite pretty. She was just right for poor Eddy and he was delighted. He had for so long wanted to marry.

May's mother was pleased with the match. It meant that in time May would be Queen, and of course this was greatly approved of by the Cambridge side of the family.

The wedding was to take place on the 27th February.

Christmas had passed and we were in January when I received a telegram from Sandringham.

Eddy had influenza. Alexandra said he was going on quite well and there was no cause for alarm.

With Beatrice's help I was in the midst of planning eight tableaux which we were going to put on that evening. One which particularly interested me was that of the Empire; and Beatrice was to represent India. She was a little plump for an Indian. They all seemed to be rather thin. The Munshi was very happy directing us and putting us right as he loved to do. I thought Beatrice would be a great success. I was delighted that she was happily married and that I had her and Henry with me—almost always under the same roof. Their dear children were a delight to me. It was such a relief to know that I should keep Beatrice near me.

The tableaux were a great success and the following day there was another telegram from Sandringham. Eddy's influenza had turned to pneumonia. I noticed with dismay that it was the thirteenth of the month; I kept my superstitious dread of the fourteenth; but at least this was not December.

I wondered whether I should go to Sandringham, but there was always such a fuss when I visited and I guessed poor Alexandra would be too frantic to want me there.

On the next day—the fateful fourteenth—another telegram arrived. This one was from Bertie.

'Our darling Eddy has been taken from us.'

How heartbreakingly tragic! There was to have been a wedding and now there would be a funeral.

I was very sad when after a term of six years, Parliament was dissolved and I was horrified to hear that Gladstone was fighting an election with fire and enthusiasm.

I could not bear it if he were returned. I had had such a long rest from him. If he came back it would be intolerable.

'The idea,' I said to Ponsonby, 'of a deluded and excited man of eighty-two trying to govern England and her vast Empire with his miserable democrats is quite ridiculous. It is like a bad joke.'

And it turned out to be as bad as I feared. Although he failed to win the large majority which he apparently expected, I found myself with Gladstone as Prime Minister for the fourth time.

A few days after the election he came to Osborne to kiss my hand. He was very changed since I had last seen him; not only was he much older, but he walked in a bent way with a stick; his face appeared to have shrunk and he was deathly pale with a weird look in his eyes, a feeble expression about his lips; and even his voice had altered.

I said to him: 'You and I are much lamer than we used to be, Mr. Gladstone.' And that was as far as I could go. I could not show friendship for a man I could never like. He should know better than to cling to office. The people admired him for some reason; I supposed it was all that walking about at night which intrigued them. I doubted he did it now.

I wished I need not accept him, but of course I had to. He was the chosen of the people. But they did not show tremendous enthusiasm for him and I doubted that, with his small majority, he would get his will. He had an obsession about Ireland and was working hard to bring in Home Rule. I did not think he had a chance of getting through with it with his tiny majority.

He did, however, get it through the Commons, but it was thrown out of the Lords. I was delighted at that and I hoped it was the last we would hear of Home Rule for Ireland.

When one gets old the days seem to race by. One emerges from one into another and in no time a year has passed.

Poor Alexandra could not get over Eddy's death but I think when George became engaged to Princess May she felt a little happier. We all liked May so much, and it seemed right that, having lost one brother, she should take the other.

The wedding took place in the July of that year '93; the heat was great and poor Alexandra looked rather drawn. I think she could not stop herself thinking that it might have been Eddy who stood there with May instead of George.

But George was a good boy—so much more stable than Eddy had been. I felt sure that May would find a husband more to her liking in George than she would have done in Eddy.

I enjoyed the wedding very much, but it was marred by one incident. Mr. Gladstone actually had the temerity to come into my tent! I suppose he thought it was a Prime Minister's right. And not only did he enter but he sat down! I said: 'What does he think this is? A public tent?'

I was glad on that occasion to meet Nicholas the Tsarevitch who was an extremely charming young man and bore a striking resemblance to the bridegroom.

Soon after the wedding, Albert's brother Ernest died. This did not affect me very deeply because I had always been aware of his unworthiness and it had amazed me that two brothers could be so different. I had never ceased to thank the fates for giving me Albert instead of Ernest. I did take credit, of course, for my own judgement in choosing Albert for I could have had either. How fortunate I was to have chosen the saint instead of the sinner.

His death meant that Alfred inherited the Duchy of Saxe-Coburg, and almost immediately he was leaving to take up his position in his father's native land.

Dear Rosenau! I promised myself that I would visit Alfred there—but those visits were always such poignant mingling of pleasure in being in such perfect surroundings, and sorrow of having memories of Albert brought back to me more vividly than ever.

Sometimes life flows on evenly and peacefully, but there are periods when events of great importance follow fast on one another. '94 was one of those years.

In March Mr. Gladstone came to see me at Osborne and told me he thought he was too old to continue. I quite agreed with him and could not hide my pleasure. I knew that I must have betrayed it to him for I heard that in reporting the interview he said: 'She was at the height of her cheerfulness when I told her.'

Perhaps I should have been kinder to the old man; but I was never one to pretend to have, or not to have, affection for those about me.

His Cabinet was quite emotional when he told them of his intention to retire; he himself was unmoved; he made his last speech to the Commons in which he urged them to do battle with the House of Lords; he was still obsessed by the Home Rule Bill.

He came to me—I was at Windsor then—to tender his official resignation. He was eighty-four and almost blind, with cataracts in both eyes. I asked him to sit, which he did. We talked awhile but I had never had anything much to say to him. I was glad when he left and then I realized that I had not uttered the conventional thanks for his years of honourable service. I simply could not. I did not think he had done a great deal of good for the country. He was against all that Lord Beaconsfield—and I—had stood for. He would have liked to diminish the mighty Empire which it had so delighted Lord Beaconsfield to build. Good, one might think him, if one took a kindly view of all those wanderings in the night; but good men do not always make the best Prime Ministers.

When I sent for Lord Rosebery and invited him to become Prime Minister he came rather reluctantly. He turned out to be rather weak in the beginning and sent out appeals to his colleagues to support him—and, of course, after the manner of rival politicians, they did not.

It was really the end of Gladstone's Liberals. The country was not ripe for that sort of policy. The most wild proposals were put forth for the Home Rule for Ireland, 'mending or ending' the House of Lords, and the disestablishment of the Church in Wales, and even a veto on liquor sales.

Rosebery could not have continued in office without the support of the Irish members, and when he rashly declaimed that there would be no Home Rule for Ireland unless the majority of members for the English constituencies were in favour of it, support fell away from him. He had more or less let it be known that the Home Rule Bill was postponed indefinitely.

I despised him for his weakness. I did not think he was enjoying his role. After all, he had not exactly taken it with alacrity. He suffered from sleepless nights; he had influenza, and the by-elections were going against him. He had only been in office for about a year when he handed in his resignation.

Parliament was dissolved and to my great pleasure the Conservatives were returned and Lord Salisbury came to see me. I had a new Prime Minister and a dear friend.

Another event at that time was Alicky's engagement to the Tsarevitch Nicholas of Russia. Although I was suspicious of the Russians I did realize what a great match this was for Alicky—one of my very favourite grandchildren. She was a beautiful girl, clever and sensible . . . and my dear Alice's daughter, which in itself endeared her to me. In the space of three weeks the dear girl became a wife and Empress, for the Tsar died and Nicholas had stepped into his place taking my darling Alicky with him.

No one could deny it was a brilliant marriage.

Another matter for rejoicing was the birth of a son to George and May, which caused great excitement among the people who marvelled that I had a *great* grandchild. *I* did not think it was so wonderful. If Alicky had not refused Eddy in '89, I might have had one four years before.

Still, it was good to know that the people were pleased.

We must not expect life to go on too smoothly and I did not, but I was unprepared for the terrible tragedy which overtook us. Henry of Battenburg had left us to go with the expedition to Ashanti. I had not wanted him to go. One of my great comforts was to have him and Beatrice under my roof; they and their dear children had been a great solace to me during the last years and again and again it had been brought home to me what a wise decision it was to bring Henry to England and let him and Beatrice marry.

I believe Henry was looking for adventure. He probably thought that life spent between Osborne, Windsor and Buckingham Palace somewhat uneventful; however he had this urge to go and unselfish Beatrice had not stood in his way. I told him he would never be able to endure the climate but that had had no effect on him.

Just after he had left a very disturbing incident arose. There was trouble in South Africa where President Kruger was continually stirring up strife. He believed that the Boers should have control of the country. I did not trust the man and believed that we should have real trouble sooner or later.

The administrator of Rhodesia was a Dr. Jameson who had carried out a very daring plan to overthrow Kruger. It was a foolhardy thing to do but very brave. Stealing into the Transvaal at night, with a few hundred mounted police, he had tried to foster a revolt against ruger. His force was small; Kruger was powerful; and in a very short time Jameson and his men were overpowered. Unfortunately certain documents were taken which betrayed the fact that Cecil Rhodes and our Colonial Office, presided over by Joseph Chamberlain, were all involved in the scheme.

It was a disaster for us—and it did indeed lead to the Boer War which broke out some years later. But we did not know that then, and I felt a certain sympathy towards Dr. Jameson who seemed to me to have the right ideas and the courage to attempt to carry them out. The Boers were horrid people—cruel and overbearing.

What was so hard to bear was that Wilhelm had sent a telegram to Kruger, congratulating him on preserving his independence. This was unforgivable. We had suffered pinpricks from that arrogant young German Emperor before, but this was a direct blow. How dared he! Bertie was furious.

'He shall not be invited to Cowes this year,' he said.

I remembered that last year had been very difficult; he had been late for dinner when I was present; he had referred to us as colleagues, which irritated me as he was setting himself on a level with me, and not in a humorous way either. He had openly quarrelled with Lord Salisbury; he had referred to Bertie in the presence of people who had reported it, and lost no time in circulating it, that his uncle was an 'old popinjay'.

I wrote off a letter of reproval to him and told him that his action over the telegram would not be forgotten for a long time to come.

I do not think Wilhelm was greatly perturbed; he had such a high opinion of himself as a ruler as important as I was—and I am not sure that he did not think he was greater.

I believed then that Wilhelm was going to cause a great deal of aggravation in the years to come and this feeling did not lessen as time passed.

It was soon after this terrible raid that a telegram came to say that Henry was suffering from fever. For a week we awaited news. We heard that he was recovering. Alas, the recovery did not last; and on the twenty-second came the dreaded telegram. Henry was dead.

My poor Baby! She was distraught. It had been a true love match. Useless for me to say I had been through it all before. There was no comforting her.

She was very patient, very selfless—Beatrice always had been—and she bore her grief more secretly than I had borne mine.

I was desolate. Once again happiness had deserted the house.

The Approaching End

I was seventy-eight years of age and had been on the throne for sixty years which was longer than any monarch had been before—even my mad grandfather George III who had reigned for fifty-nine years and ninety-six days.

Everyone wanted a grand celebration. It was a rare occasion.

I agreed to the Diamond Jubilee. I said that I wanted it to show the Empire in all its glory. Its growth had been the outstanding feature of my reign, and I wanted all to know it. All the Prime Ministers of all the Colonies, representatives from India and the dependencies, must be present; and the armed forces should take a prominent part.

It was indeed a great occasion; and one I shall never forget in the years left to me. I wanted as many people to see me as possible and for it to be entirely memorable; I wanted the people to realize that I had worked for them—as well as I was able—for sixty long years; and that their welfare had always been my greatest concern.

It was wonderful to hear the guns in the Park booming to announce the great day. It seems that everyone was out in the streets. The crowds were intense; I hoped there would be no accidents.

I made a circular tour and was moved to tears by the loyal demonstrations of affection.

'She wrought her people lasting good,' said one banner.

'Our Hearts Thy Throne,' said another.

What beautiful sentiments!

I was so proud. If Albert could have been beside me my joy would have been complete. He had done so much, not only for me, but for these people; but they did not recognize it. They never would.

I rode with my family around me, with the troops and officials from India, Australia, South Africa, Canada, Cyprus, Hong Kong and Borneo. All the might of the Empire was displayed there. I hoped my people would realize the greatness of their country and that they would always work together to keep it great.

From Buckingham Palace to St. Paul's for the thanksgiving service; and then I drove over London Bridge to the poorer districts of the capital on the south side of the river. I came back over Westminster Bridge and St. James's Park.

The welcome I was given, the love which was expressed, was so moving. I could scarcely restrain my tears. I was exhausted, but so happy. I had always cared so much for the love of my people and had been most distressed when they had turned against me.

They were with me now.

I was deeply touched and amused when someone in one of the poorer streets cried out: 'Go it, old girl.'

I smiled and waved my hand in acknowledgement.

I was delighted at the reception Bertie received; there were cries of 'Good old Teddy!' I hoped the scandals of the Mordaunt case and Tranby Croft were all forgotten.

They must be on such a day.

When I returned to the Palace I sent off telegrams to all the people of the Colonies . . . everywhere . . . the length and breadth of the Empire.

From my heart I thanked my beloved people. May God bless them.

I was utterly exhausted and yet so happy.

Sixty years! It was indeed a great occasion.

Now I am old and tired, and the years are passing by with a speed which leave me bewildered.

A great deal has happened since the Jubilee.

Mr. Gladstone died the following year. His family were all round him at the end and his son Stephen read to him the prayers for the dying. He had been a good man, though I had always disliked him. Both Houses were adjourned immediately and there were tributes to his memory both in the Commons and the Lords.

There was a state funeral and at his lying in state great crowds paid their last respects to the man they had called the People's William. He was buried near the statues of Peel and Lord Beaconsfield.

Great sadness was clouding my days. Terrible events like the Boer War and the Boxer Rising in China against foreigners. And there was a tragedy which struck me more personally even than these wicked happenings.

My poor Alfred was suffering from an infection of the throat and I was reminded of Fritz and I greatly feared what this might mean in the end.

How right I was! My dear, dear son! To be robbed of another of my children at the age of eighty-one was cruel indeed.

But I am so old now, so tired, so ready to go.

Sometimes I sit and dream of the past. It is all written down for me to read. Sometimes I beguile myself by slipping back to the old days. How vivid they are! And I think that, looking back, I see myself and others more clearly than I did when those events were taking place. I can see myself as a young and eager girl, with Lehzen and Mama in those days of my youth. How impulsive I had been—how ready to give my warm affections and my hatred.

Albert had changed me. Before he came I had been frivolous, thinking it the height of pleasure to stay up late and dance. I sometimes wonder what I would have been like if Albert had not come into my life. Would I have gone on being that laughter-loving creature? No. My destiny was too serious for that. But Albert had moulded me, changed me, made me what I am. I always wanted to be good. That was what I had said when I had first discovered that I might inherit the crown. 'I will be good,' I said; and I had meant it. I think that one of my strongest characteristics has always been my honesty.

The people who had played the biggest part in my life and claimed my affection, have all been men: Uncle Leopold, Lord Melbourne, dear Albert, Lord Beaconsfield and John Brown . . . always men. That is surely significant. I think I am a woman who must be dominated by men. It put me in a somewhat incongruous position because I was higher than anyone else in the land: The Queen, the Sovereign, and they my subjects . . . every one of them . . . even Albert.

I have always been of a sentimental nature and perhaps always a little naive; and looking back I wondered whether that clouded my vision a little. Albert had moulded me and in my mind the conception of him was the perfect being, the incomparable one. But was he perfect, and had our union been quite that most happy of marriages? Suddenly I was remembering the storms—which always seemed to be my fault, or at least that was how I was sure Albert saw them . . . and made me see them. But was it always so? Had

Albert become the saint since his death—and with that our marriage become the perfect union?

These were disloyal thoughts.

Albert *had* been perfect. It was I . . . always I . . . who was at fault in those little skirmishes between us.

But they had existed. I had forgotten those over the years. I had been jealous because at times I had thought that he cared more for Vicky than for me. I had despised myself for that. But Albert had been jealous of Bertie, because he was the Prince of Wales and stood higher in the land than the Prince Consort could ever be.

Over the years came the sound of Bertie's crying when Albert had beaten him, and although he always said it hurt him more than it hurt Bertie, did it?

I am indeed old. I am getting foolish. How could I ever see Albert as anything but perfect?

If I did, all the years of mourning would lose their poignancy, their meaning.

No, I wanted to suppress those thoughts. Why did they come to me now that I am old and it is all over?

We have moved into a new century. What will it bring forth?

I shall never know.

And now it is time for me to lay down my pen.

Bibliography

V.R.I Queen Victoria, Her Life and Empire Argyle, Duke of
  National and Domestic History of England Aubrey, William
  Hickman Smith
Persons of Consequence, Queen Victoria and her Circle Auchin-
  closs, Louis
Queen Victoria Benson, E.F.
Queen Victoria's Daughters Benson, E.F.
Albert the Good Bolitho, Hector
The Reign of Queen Victoria Bolitho, Hector
The Prince Consort and his Brother Bolitho, Hector
Victoria, the Widow and her Son Bolitho, Hector
The Youthful Queen Victoria Creston, Dormer
Lord Melbourne Dunckley, Henry
Edward the Seventh Gavin, Catherine
The Greville Memoirs Greville, Charles C.H. (Edited by Henry
  Reeve)
The History of France Guizot, M. (Translated by Robert Black)
Life and Reign of William IV Huish, Robert
Queen Victoria, a Biography Lee, Sidney
Victoria, R.I. Longford, Elizabeth
The Early Court of Queen Victoria Jerrold, Clare
The Married Life of Queen Victoria Jerrold, Clare
Queen Victoria and her Ministers Marriott, Sir John A.R.
The Life of H.R.H. the Prince Consort Martin, Sir Theodore
The Creevy Papers Maxwell, Sir Herbert (Edited by)
Mr Gladstone Melrose, Andrew
The Life of Benjamin Disraeli, Earl of Beaconsfield Monypenny,
  W.F. and Buckle, G.E.
The Life of William Ewart Gladstone Morley, John
Queen Victoria, A Personal Sketch Mrs Oliphant

British Prime Ministers Pike, E. Royston

House of Hanover Redman, Alvin

The Life of Her Majesty, Queen Victoria Smith, G. Barnett

The Prime Ministers of Queen Victoria Smith, G. Barnett

Victoria of England Sitwell, Edith

Dictionary of National Biography Stephen, Sir Leslie and Lee, Sir Sidney (Edited by)

Queen Victoria Strachey, Lytton

The Personal Life of Queen Victoria Tooley, Sarah A.

The Life of Queen Alexandra Tooley, Sarah A.

Memoirs of William Lamb Second Viscount Melbourne Torrens W.M.

Letters of Queen Victoria First Series 1837–1861 Queen Victoria (edited by Benson, A.C. and Esher, Viscount)

Letters of Victoria Second Series 1862–1878 Queen Victoria (edited by Buckle, George Earle)

Letters of Victoria Third Series 1878–1891 Queen Victoria (edited by Buckle, George Earle)

Leaves from a Journal Queen Victoria

Victoria in the Highlands, A Personal Journal of Her Majesty Queen Victoria Queen Victoria

More Leaves from a Journal Queen Victoria

Dearest Mama. Letters between Queen Victoria and the Crown Princess of Prussia 1861–1864 Queen Victoria

Queen Victoria's Sketch Book Warner, Marina

British History Wade, John

About the Author

Jean Plaidy, who is Victoria Holt, resides in England. This is her twenty-fifth novel for Fawcett and the third in the Queens of England series.